Crown of Ashes

Celestra Forever After

Book 4

ADDISON MOORE

Edited by Paige Maroney Smith
Cover Design: Gaffey Media

Books by Addison Moore

Romance

Low Down and Dirty
Dirty Disaster (Low Down & Dirty 2)

Naughty by Nature

Beautiful Oblivion (Beautiful Oblivion 1)
Beautiful Illusions (Beautiful Oblivion 2)
Beautiful Elixir (Beautiful Oblivion 3)
Beautiful Submission (Beautiful Oblivion 4)

Someone to Love (Someone to Love 1)
Someone Like You (Someone to Love 2)
Someone For Me (Someone to Love 3)

3:AM Kisses (3:AM Kisses 1)
Winter Kisses (3:AM Kisses 2)
Sugar Kisses (3:AM Kisses 3)
Whiskey Kisses (3:AM Kisses 4)
Rock Candy Kisses (3:AM Kisses 5)
Velvet Kisses (3:AM Kisses 6)
Wild Kisses (3:AM Kisses 7)
Country Kisses (3:AM Kisses 8)

Forbidden Kisses (3:AM Kisses 9)
Dirty Kisses (3:AM Kisses 10)
Stolen Kisses (3:AM Kisses 11)
Lucky Kisses (3:AM Kisses 12)
Tender Kisses (A 3:AM Kisses Novella)
Revenge Kisses (3:AM Kisses 14)

Burning Through Gravity (Burning Through Gravity 1)
A Thousand Starry Nights (Burning Through Gravity 2) Fire in
an Amber Sky (Burning Through Gravity 3)

The Solitude of Passion

Celestra Forever After
The Dragon and the Rose (Celestra Forever After 2)
The Serpentine Butterfly (Celestra Forever After 3)
Crown of Ashes (Celestra Forever After 4)
Throne of Fire (Celestra Forever After 5) coming 2018

Perfect Love (A Celestra Novella)

Young Adult Romance

Melt With You (A Totally '80s Romance)
Tainted Love (A Totally '80s Romance 2)
Hold Me Now (A Totally '80s Romance 3)

Ethereal (Celestra Series Book 1)
Tremble (Celestra Series Book 2)
Burn (Celestra Series Book 3)
Wicked (Celestra Series Book 4)
Vex (Celestra Series Book 5)
Expel (Celestra Series Book 6)
Toxic Part One (Celestra Series Book 7)
Toxic Part Two (Celestra Series Book 8)
Elysian (Celestra Series Book 9)

Ethereal Knights (Celestra Knights)

Season of the Witch (A Celestra Novella)

Ephemeral (The Countenance Trilogy 1)
Evanescent (The Countenance Trilogy 2)
Entropy (The Countenance Trilogy 3)

Precious in the sight of the Lord is the death of His saints.

—Psalm 116:15

Prologue

Seasons come and go, each robed in its own rare majesty as decreed from the very hand of God. There is nothing more predictable in the seen, knowable world than their tiring revolution, fall to winter, winter to spring, spring to summer, repeating endlessly on a glorious loop. There is nothing more predictable in the seen, knowable world, perhaps other than death. Even our Savior was subjected to that infernal transformation all those thousands of years ago when he was known as the ringleader of the Nazarene sect. Death is no respecter of persons.

But a season of love had come into my life, a season of joy, a matrimonial union so vibrant and beautiful it brought on its heels the most tender of all blessings—two to be exact. Yes, first there was love—and then there was hatred. Love I found was fickle, untrustworthy, devoted to its own glorification. You pour yourself out for love, you feed it, you heed and ultimately, embarrassingly you need it. Love always holds the sharpest knife to threaten you with. Love doesn't disappoint to make good on its threats, slicing your heart in two—watching you bleed out is simply another of its attributes. Hatred is far simpler. It fuels itself. It adulates you in all your tarnished glory. It creates a membrane between you and the target of your ill affection. It nurses your wounds, whispers the lies you crave to hear. It sprinkles a crown of ashes over your head and declares you the king. But ultimately, hatred is the cheapest balm—an illusionary fix. When all is said and done, it covers you with the dust of shame before reminding you that what your heart desires still lingers just out of reach. It is what you truly crave—love—the indestructible crown fashioned from the hand of God Himself.

Lies spread before us like an open road, our feet embedded with the thorns of our indiscretion. The liars rule the earthen sphere and we are the liars, for even the angels are subject to reproach. While we distract ourselves with the minutia of everyday life, the enemy walks us deeper into the valley of the shadow of death—fashioning his scepter for ruling. While we looked lovingly into one another's eyes, the dragon's tail swept us up with its broom of destruction. Unknowingly, unwittingly, we have submitted to this ritual of darkness. Wickedness struggles to empty what we stand for and who we are under its submission. There is nothing new under the sun, even this treachery. And now, here we are, where the future meets the past, the agony of our new reality.

And then there is death—the curse that comes to all. It waits in patience for the time prescribed before striking with its sickle, reaping its harvest with a righteous bloodlust all its own. One moment you are here, and in less than that you are no more. Some say you go to the light. Some say you are enveloped in darkness. Both are correct in their estimations, for the believer goes one way, the infidel the next. Your time in the Transport is a wink, a microsecond—your destiny already sealed upon your departure. Not every soul lands on the emerald green lawn of the Elysian fields. Those who choose not to believe in the Son are chased from this planet by unspeakable terrors. Darkness waits eagerly for them, a horror of heat and destitution, only to land them in a realm where hope is a dream long out of reach. All is lost and they are not saved.

It seems that those in power always have a son they would very much like to venerate, that they believe should and by their might will be worshiped. Oh, what a treasure to be that shining son for all to see—the might, the power, all majesty and creation laid upon his feet. Those in power always seem to have that precious son, and in all of the ironies that life could afford, I had married one, the son of horrors, the son of the black-hearted chief of the Fems.

We were light and dark, good and evil, partaking of the fruit of one another so liberally we thought we could be unified as one. How naïve it is to believe that light could convert the darkness. How myopic to have thought my heart was the cure, my love the elixir to this tenacious disease. How sweet the boast would have been.

But the heart is where life truly lies. What you believe is as incriminating as it is liberating. It can hold you back. It can mold your destiny, sometimes in nefarious ways. God Himself understands how cheap the words that leave our mouths can be. He tests us. And once He doles out the exam, He is quiet. Like a good schoolmaster, He waits patiently while we navigate the briar patch set before us, the untamable wilderness. We feel so alone, so abandoned. We come to our end. How we crave our personal Egypt, the source of our once misery. How we look back with fondness upon that time of agony—never was there a greater sorrow than that moment. And yet we are never without Him. He waits, watches, inspects the depths of our heart. He searches the unknowable reaches and lays them bare, brushes His fingers over the nexus of our being. He never leaves us, never forsakes us, never lets us fall. He is the lover, the lifter of our souls. He strengthens us through familial bonds. Guides us by day like a cloud—lights up the darkness in pillars of fire. He is our comforter, and, if we are wise, we nestle in the shelter of His wings until disaster has passed.

For the things that are seen are temporary. Those that are unseen, eternal. Mortality will be swallowed up by life.

But ultimately, on occasion terribly, there is a time and season for everything. A time to be born—and a time to die. What happens in between is the gift. The seasons are stubbornly never-ending, but our lives are but a whisper in the grand scheme of things. Time is but a stranger in our lives—we only notice it upon reflection. But we bear the weight of its arrogance with each breath we take. We lumber forward in its shadow, numbering our days according to its whims. We are the victims of its callous design. Our faces etching a story across the arc of its measurements. We strive to stretch its fabric across the span of ten decades. But even the wise, the learned, the righteous cannot command it to heel. Your days are numbered, your steps determined by an Almighty hand with an Almighty design, outlined for you before you were ever knit in your mother's womb. The first day and the last each carefully orchestrated to help you achieve your purpose. But people waver. Destiny is malleable within the realm of free will. And with that a self-made disaster looms around every precious corner. But ultimately, sovereignly, fate will undeniably right itself. Try as you might, fail as you will, succeed if you can, burn under the fire of your own sun—fate will find you, chase you down, make you its own. In the end, as stubbornly as the seasons come and go, you too will fulfill your purpose. And finally, when the silver cord is broken, the spirit severed from the body, you will find that ultimately what was revealed ages ago was true—the end is truly the beginning. It will happen to us all—just you wait and see.

1

The Great Tribulation

Skyla

I have seen horrors before—lives snatched away too soon, destinies dismantled, an entire stream of chaos erupting around me. This season of my life had dissolved into turmoil, left me shattered in a single night—all alone to pick up the pieces. My life, my mind, my heart had become a hall of mirrors. Everywhere I turn there is Gage, laughing, then gone like smoke, Demetri and Wes—their faces all morph into one. There is no telling who is who anymore. It is up to me to rescue, redeem, revive what I can. I will do whatever needs to be done. I'll take an ax to the mirrors and break them all into shards, crushing them down into a pile of rubble until they somehow resemble my life once again. Demetri cannot win. I will not let him.

A dark spiral of stars leads out of the wicked Transfer as Chloe and I ride forward, each on our own prideful steeds. A spray of psychedelic lights, bursting in sunset colors, swirls all around us in a dizzying array of cosmic malfunction. Somehow, someway, I had harnessed all of my ripe anger into a clusterfuck of energy that tore a hole in Wesley's haunt. The Transfer and its midnight sky are no more. In its place is a gaping misfortune that resembles a toxic primordial stew, no more capable of gifting life than its nutrient deficient soil. No, this was no life-giving force my anger has sponsored. This is raw, unadulterated rage come to fruition—something tangible to impress all the right people. There are so many people I'd like to impress with my anger these days, and tonight Gage Oliver, my husband, has gleefully, woefully, added himself to the list. I don't know why his actions have shocked me. This is a world of fragile hearts. Where we don't know how to support one another, only tear one another down. I wish I could say I heard the music before the song ever began. But I didn't see this great deception coming. I was sidelined at best.

A tunnel forms ahead, comprised entirely of stars, liquid mercury waving us in with its solvent energy. Chloe calls to me from behind, but I let her voice whistle past me like dust in this nuclear breeze. Her voice grows more commanding, far more urgent, but I press on, unwilling, unable to stop myself from the task at hand.

This holy light of cosmic gases pulls us in with its powerful magnetic charge, but my drive to stomp out the fire that has erupted over the hillside of my life is far more potent than some invisible force—far more powerful than the destiny my mother has carved out for me. I spit on destiny. I spit on the thought of my mother, the puppet master, pulling my strings with her uncharitable heart. No. Gage Oliver is mine, and whatever the hell she thinks is going to happen, whatever the hell Demetri has bound and sealed with a wicked covenant shall be undone. I'll undo it with my own damn hands if I have to.

And lastly, I spit on Gage. I spit on the man who had no faith in me, in us, in our love, to overcome his greedy urge to slip away to the dark side. This is not the way we go down. This is not the end to our story. Fuck you, Gage Oliver, for ever thinking it was a good idea to bow to your evil father. And most of all, fuck you for doing so in secret.

Chloe and I enter the tunnel of light and a horrific roar explodes all around us. Gravity increases its grip, as my body weighs heavy on the stallion struggling to gallop beneath me. Time and place shift like a kaleidoscope, and I understand this on a primal level. Whatever this place is, whatever is happening all around us, one thing I know for certain, we are ebbing toward a new horizon in a new time and space—one that is very far from the Transfer and its adolescent level of brooding. I only know one thing for certain—I'm coming for you, Gage. And I'm bringing Chloe Bishop with me.

A flash of lightning blinds me. It rattles me right down to my weary bones and ignites me from the inside like a flash fire. The psychedelic stars, the tunnel of incomprehensible light grows increasingly brighter until it bursts under its own incandescence and in its place a sullen gray sky appears, a grassy knoll with tufts of weeds, the hillside we're on is steep enough to tax our horses until we end up on higher ground. Chloe and I pause on the open dirt road and scan the vicinity. Up in the distance lies an old-world village with structures made from stone, as dove gray as the sky. There's an unexplainable heaviness in the air, the weight of yesteryear, of simpler, yet equally dangerous, days gone by.

"Well, well, Messenger"—Chloe bleats as she fixes her sight on the dismal horizon—"it looks like we're not on Paragon anymore."

"We weren't on Paragon to begin with. You are quicker than that, aren't you? At least I'm hoping you are. Don't tell me I've just saddled myself with a nitwit," I say as we plod our way toward the shanty town in the distance. If we keep at this comfortable pace, it might take an hour at most before we arrive.

"You're the only nitwit around here, Skyla."

"Watch it." The words come from me so harsh and quick, I sound just like my mother. I glance up at the sky where the mother in question resides. She's a bit bitchy, that one. Lizbeth, my stepmother with whom I live, would have chortled right along with Chloe's rude quip and then most likely apologized for existing. She's just that nice. But thankfully, nice is not a requirement today, in this life in general for that matter. Nice is never required when dealing with the monster that gave the order to kill my father, and who killed my husband—first husband, Logan, by way of slicing off his head. No, nice is something I never need to be with Chloe Bishop. We have a long sordid history together, and not one moment of it was *nice*.

Chloe positions her horse alongside mine.

"What's this?" I smirk at the sight of her. "You never were good at coming in second." Chloe is a self-appointed leader in all areas of her mangled, mangy life.

"I don't come in second to anyone, Skyla. You of all people should know that." Her long dark hair blows back, full and thick in the breeze. Chloe has a cutthroat look about her, as beautiful on the outside as she is ugly on the inside. "I come out on top if I have anything to say about it. I was your superior at West, remember?"

"In cheerleading, Chloe. I think we've migrated past those pompom riddled days—hellish as they were. This is the new us, where you live in the Transfer with that lab rat brother-in-law of mine, and I live on Paragon with—" His name catches in my throat. I'm so livid with rage, I can't even speak my own husband's name.

"Wow," Chloe muses as we move through the countryside to our unknowable, yet drab, destination ahead. "One little foible and his very name makes you gag on the bile rising in your throat. Gage has turned into quite the four-letter word. You always were easy to trip up."

My blood boils in an instant. "Trust me, nobody has tripped me up." I'm not entirely sure that even I believe it. "I'm not anyone's bitch, Chloe. Most certainly not yours. Don't you forget it."

"Right." She scoffs at the thought. "You're the one in charge." Her foot extends to mine as she offers up a swift kick. "And you are, I suppose." She exhales hard while taking in the evergreens quickly coming up on our left. "But you and I both know your lady boner for the dark-haired Oliver will bring you to your knees once again, quite literally." Chloe moans to herself as if visualizing herself in a compromising position with my husband. I can almost guarantee it. Chloe has spent the last several years with a lady boner of her own to contend with for the dark-haired Oliver. "I bet Gage will make you get on all fours. You know, take you from behind. That will be his way of asserting dominance over you. He is the king."

"I'm not sleeping with him." Ever again if I can help it. That little stunt he pulled last night has left both me and my vagina recoiling.

"You *will*," Chloe snaps. "He's Gage Fucking Oliver—emphasis on the *fucking*. You always sleep with him. You're a fool in many ways, but when it comes to men, you are razor sharp and greedy as hell."

"Shut up, Chloe." It comes out far too quiet and morose because on an intrinsic level I know this is true.

"You'll sleep with Logan, too," she goes on, unwarranted. "He won't take you from behind like that. Too vulgar, not his style. Don't get me wrong. He is a dirty, *dirty* boy. He'll want you to ride him like that stallion you're on now. You should have seen the agony and the ecstasy on that boy's face as he gripped me, demanding I ride him harder, faster, stronger."

"He thought you were me." Just the idea of Chloe taking advantage of Logan that way makes me want to hurl. "And would you please stop sleeping with people under false pretenses? It's getting old. Stop using Laken's face, and for shit's sake, stop using mine." Laken happens to be the woman Chloe's husband, Wesley, is obsessed with. She also happens to share the title of my best friend along with Brielle.

"Back to Gage."

"Back to Gage." I scoff. "Anyone ever tell you, you're like a dog with a boner?"

"Gage can be my master anytime."

"He will be," I assure her. "If he has his way, he will be everyone's master." I can still see him there on that stone of sacrifice toasting to his new life, one with Demetri, as the leader of everything I oppose. "Wait a minute..." I squint ahead to the tiny ramshackle town coming upon us quickly. "Something tells me we're not on Yankee soil anymore."

"Took you long enough," Chloe huffs. "I'll give you another clue, oh fearless, *brainless* leader. We're not even in the same century anymore."

"Crap," I whimper as we plod closer to our temporal destiny. Music erupts from one of the establishments on the cobble-lined street. It's late in the day, evening ready to turn to an instant midnight, as bodies stream in and out of a raucous little saloon with enough candle power winking from inside to combust everyone stuffed in that carnal hall of desires in an infernal holocaust. Women in seedy dresses pour out of the entry with drunken men pawing at their cleavage, vomiting into the streets between their bouts of heartless groping.

"What are we doing here, Messenger? Aren't there enough men in the twenty-first century for you?"

"I don't know what we're doing here, or where *here* exactly is, but I have a feeling we're about to find out on both accounts. And I'm pretty sure we're not here for the men, Chloe. Put your ovaries on ice for a minute. Your brain might actually kick in and function."

Chloe and I park our exhausted horses alongside a few other majestic steeds tied and bound near the entry. It occurs to me as we stand outside of the open mouth of the establishment that I have no clue how to get us out of this dated, musty, dusty, rusty hovel for wayward women.

"It's a bar," Chloe muses.

"It's a whorehouse," I correct.

"Well then"—Chloe threads her arm through mine—"it looks like we've finally found that home away from home you've been looking for."

Inside, music belted out by a live band accosts our hearing, five overgrown men with missing teeth and lewd intentions stitched in their greasy smiles fog up the stage. It's loud as hell, the entire place is brimming with both boisterous activity and body odor—with wall-to-wall people—highly intoxicated as they might be—women in large bustling dresses, the backs longer than their short suggestive fronts, full and heavy breasts heave over their corseted tops, and suddenly the urge to nurse the twins hits me hard. I fed them just before I left. I nursed Tobie, too, Chloe's poor speck of a daughter who is only a month older than my twins. My heart tugs at the thought of the boys' perfect dark heads knit to my breasts. They're my two precious little olives, and I miss them with an indescribable ache.

"Maybe we should go?" I shout up over the roaring laughter, the howls of drunken men, the shrieking of cackling women. The entire place has a Halloween night appeal, something otherworldly, something out of an old silent movie, and right about now my exhausted eardrums crave a lull to the madness.

"Maybe we shouldn't."

A lone man sitting in the corner smoking a cigar catches my attention, and I recognize those blessed by God features, those whiskey-colored eyes, those lips that I've tasted while drinking down his kisses.

"*Logan*," I whisper and suddenly this entire new world feels like a dream. I take a step closer and the veil of smoke evaporates from around him, and just like that, his face morphs into someone else entirely as he speeds out of the room. "That was weird."

"You're weird." Chloe leans in as we absorb the scene together. "Looky there." She motions to the rear of the facility where a pianist tries to keep time with the band, invoking a disastrous sensory experience that I'm sure has long been declared illegal.

"What are we looking at? You want to dance on the stage? Introduce them all to a little Bishop twerking magic? I've got news for you. You're on your own." I take a few strides out in that direction and stop short. No, it wasn't the piano Chloe was pointing at. It was the girl in the red satin dress with a corset I've seen before—the exact one I sported on a ski trip once. "Oh my dear God." I walk numbly in that direction with Chloe on my heels. I see her, and not only do I know who she is, but her very presence puts in perspective where we are and the precise century to boot.

"1645." A dull laugh comes from me. I should have known. This harried, *whorish* scene has unfurled many a time in Marshall's living room. And a part of me very much wishes I were in Marshall's living room instead.

Marlena. I smirk at how much she looks like the witch by my side. Marlena is Chloe's long-lost something or other. For so long she's inserted herself into our narrative, our century, our world, and now here we are crashing hers. I suppose it's only fair. Although, I have no clue what good could come of this.

"I'm guessing she holds the key to this debauchery," I say as we fast approach her, and just as we're feet away, a man in a suit—dated as it might be—gropes her breast from behind. He buries his caramel-colored head into her neck and continues to squeeze the living shit out of her boob as if he were kneading dough. Normally I wouldn't think twice to interrupt, wouldn't care who the hairy scary man in the distinguished suit is, but I just so happen to recognize that head of hair, those strong hands that are currently exposing her left nipple as my very own spirit husband.

"Well, well, it looks as if we have a class A pervert on our hands," I say it loud enough for all involved to hear as a few stray women strut by and fan themselves with their feathered boas at the sight. Yes, Marshall Dudley has been cause for more than a heated moment or two in just about any century. He's a walking, talking erection, a human bottle of testosterone that attracts even the demurest of barflies.

"Oh, come on, Skyla." Chloe brazenly removes his hand from her great, great, a million times great-grandmother's tit, and Marshall opens a sleepy eye to get a better look at us.

His eye closes once again and his lips continue to move unabated by what he's just seen, and just like that, he freezes. His eyes spring open and he straightens rather lazily. Marshall moves Marlena to the side as if she were merely on the assembly line for the night, and knowing Dudley she most likely is. He squints into Chloe and me as if trying to place us before his eyes widen, hard and round, and his shoulders fly back as if at attention.

"Ms. Messenger—Ms. Bishop." He nods to the two of us before his crimson gaze narrows to mine with the slight look of disappointment. It's technically *Mrs. Oliver* and Mrs.

21

Edinger—Marshall knows that all too well. He's simply in the business of disparaging our marital status, thus reducing us to the monikers of yesteryear while we were still his charges at West Paragon High. Everything seemed so easy back then. But the nickname makes me feel nostalgic for all things past. That must be why I rarely fight him on it. "What in the world—let me rephrase this—who in the universe has brought you this far and why?" He glances over my shoulder. "Where is your nasty supervising spirit?"

I'm assuming he's talking to Chloe, considering her nasty supervising spirit is Demetri—*nasty* being the operative word.

"Skyla is the spirit who whisked us out to never-never land." Chloe offers a smug grin at the women who seem to be steadily amassing around us. "And quite successfully so. What the hell are we doing here, Messenger?" She slaps away the hand of an aggressive onlooker who's doing her best to fondle the fabric of Chloe's jeans.

"Ms. Messenger." Marshall takes me by the elbow and stalks us off toward a room in the back. "I'd like a word with you in private."

"By all means." I shoot Chloe a look as she continues her slapping spree with the grabby hands surrounding her. "God, wouldn't that be great if Chloe ended up in some seventeenth-century dungeon? To the tower with her!" I laugh while shouting over the lunatic-inspired piano music. I swear on all that is holy, it sounds just like that annoying player piano back at Marshall's estate.

"Whose ghost do you think haunts those keys, Skyla?" Marshall lands us in a dark corner, and oddly enough the scent of his cologne, the girth of his chest, that angry yet lewd smile twitching on his lips is every bit just the way I know him centuries later—cuttingly gorgeous to a fault.

"You can hear me." I sigh into the idea dreamily.

"Of course, I can hear you. I'm touching your flesh." He gifts my elbow a quick squeeze. "What's going on here? This isn't your time or your place. In fact, I'll go as far as saying this isn't any of your business. Where are Jock Strap and the Pretty One?" He grunts, craning his neck past me. "Is this some sort of interdimensional takeover? Of what use is any of this?"

"Trust me, I have no idea. Chloe and I were in the Transfer and we rode out on these majestic beasts. There was this tunnel of stars—"

"Tunnel of stars?" The cords in his neck jump. "Who gifted you these beasts?"

"They were just there." Marshall's familiar scent envelops me and I lean in if for nothing else but the comfort of home. "I instinctually understood they were for me."

"And Ms. Bishop?" His features harden as if I've purposefully unleashed a demon, and I might have. "What possessed you to schlep her along for the ride?"

"I have no one else, Marshall," I hiss so fast, it comes out like a threat.

"What about me?" He glides his finger over the curve of my cheek and a fire sizzles along with his touch. A strong vibration, like that of a tuning fork, rides through my bones, quivering down to that tender part of me that has secretly craved him from the beginning. Marshall has always held the ability to incite me without putting in much effort. And I frown at him because I happen to know he heard. "I have crossed oceans, continents, ethereal planes, and left the heavenlies for you, my dear—and still you give me no consideration?"

"Not true. I consider you just a notch above the enemy. It was you who showed me that dreadful sight tonight. You stood by my side while you-know-who drank Celestra blood—most likely mine by the way—before locking himself in a covenant with the dark side. Which means you could have easily revealed Demetri's nefarious plan earlier in the day, and I could have talked some sense into that stubborn ass I married." Still can't seem to bring myself to say his name.

"Skyla." He inches back a good foot. "I could no more deter what happened than you could. Don't embroil me in your anger. Be glad I'm not above revealing the intentions of others—timely as they are. I have no alliances other than you."

"You have the Sectors." Marshall is Sector of the highest order. The Sectors have outranked the Fems ever since—I suck in a breath. "Hey, isn't this the century where the Sectors and the Fems—"

He brings his finger to my lips and navigates us farther into the back where another little alcove reveals a tawdry looking stage and women flashing their granny panty fannies to an audience of inebriated, drooling men. It's then that I notice a large burly looking stick that rises from floor to ceiling in which each of the fanny bearing girls in question takes it for a spin.

"Dear God, is that a pole?"

"Yes, Ms. Messenger." He grunts while taking in the scene. "Of all the things human men can spend their time engineering, they build poles for naked women to spin on. *Poles*. Glorified sticks for topless dancing girls. Man hasn't moved all that far from his barbarous beginnings. A naked woman is still the greatest enchantress to the beasts in question."

I scan the vicinity at the room full of scantily clad women and frown. "My favorite Sector hasn't moved all that far from his barbarous beginnings either."

I wrap my arms around his waist and pull him in close as if we were a couple. Marshall would love for us to be one, and according to my candy apple mother in the sky, we eventually will be. "There is a spiritual battle brewing here." I raise an eyebrow in lieu of a wicked grin. "This is where you turned the tide, and now the Sectors rule over the Fems!"

"Hush," he says it so sweetly, so seductively, something in me trembles deep inside. "You have it backward. The Fems turn us over for a time—and then, of course, we come through victorious." He gives a little wink. "But there is another war brewing, Skyla. And it percolates around you."

A vision of me challenging Gage tonight at the christening comes to mind. I declared a new war, one between the Fems and my people—and I declared it would begin with him. My heart breaks at what's transpired between us.

"I don't want to talk about it." I shake my head while plucking Marshall off me. "If that's what this little visit is about, you can forget it!" I shout to the ceiling for my mother. God knows she's listening. I all but have a twenty-four seven homing device hardwired into my genes, and most likely she's the only way out of this seventeenth-century screw-up. "Yes, I declared war against the Fems, but if I'm being honest, we both know how that last war turned out. And for what? I'm not sure I should be stepping in that pile of dog shit once again."

The Logan lookalike with the cigar passes behind Marshall and offers me a smile curated from sorrow. His eyes lock with mine before he evaporates deeper into the smoky room.

"*Skyla*," Marshall balks. "You have no say in the matter. What Jock Strap has done is a well-placed chess move by the enemy. They are after you, my queen. They are looking to remove your knight from his sublime position." His lips curl up at the edges, proud of his own euphemisms.

"The Sectors must remain. If you disagree in any capacity, I bid you to imagine what a world under Fem rule would resemble. Humans would lose many vital freedoms. The Factions would lose all rights, all control. There would be one law, one sage—or should I say *Gage*, that should and will be obeyed."

"He would never do that. He would never commit to evil." The words garble as I struggle to evict them from my throat because Gage has already done it.

"Skyla." Marshall wipes a lone tear from my cheek that I hadn't even realized I shed. "This war"—he nods over his shoulder as if referencing the Sectors and the Fems—"it was never over. My victory is short-lived, relatively speaking. Your victory has the ability to last forever."

"A war." It comes out in less than a whisper, and the entire room seems to strum around me like a harp.

"A war," Marshall echoes back, and his voice reverberates right down to my marrow.

"Who is the enemy," I whisper as if it were a real question.

"You already know."

Chloe comes up with a man in tow. "Look who I found lurking in these parts?" She guffaws so obnoxiously loud, for a moment I wonder if Darla Johnson has possessed her. There's just something about Brielle's mother that lends itself easily to a cackling girl in a bar—especially with a man in tow.

I glance up, fully expecting to find the Logan lookalike, but am met with her brother, Brody Bishop, instead.

"Brody?" Personally, I welcome the sight—I welcome the sight of the both of them. I'd rather have a thousand Bishops flung in my face than continue with that demonic conversation regarding a war of all ludicrous things. For the life of me I can't believe I'm going down that thorny path again. Although this war will be different. I'm not letting the heavenlies, or my mother's destination station, decide when and where to thrust me into mortal combat. I'm not about to lose my mind to make it to some nebulous finish line only to have Logan Oliver's head hacked off. No thank you. My war. My rules.

I openly growl at Chloe since she was the one who hacked off Logan's head to begin with. Chloe is my personal hell. A tiny laugh huffs through me because I have plans for my own little personal demon that make me tingle all the way down my angelic little spine.

"*Mack* Bishop," Chloe corrects.

Brody's twin gives a jovial laugh before gesturing to Marshall. "Who are these sluts you've furnished us with this fine evening, Dudley?"

Sluts? I sneer at Chloe. Leave it to her to drag over the gutter trash—her long, long relation no doubt.

He lifts a brow toward Marshall. "The wench who resembles Marlena tells me she's from the New World—from a distant time. What malarkey is this? Women wearing pantaloons, no less?" He tips his head back and guffaws at the idea, and we get a toxic whiff of his eighty-proof breath. "God forbid this news travels to the throne. King Charles will have the entire lot of them dragged back by their ears." His hand circles around my waist and he gives my bottom a healthy pinch.

"*Ouch*!" I shout while slapping him reflexively.

He licks his greasy smile in approval to my less than enthused response. "I'll take the spirited one. I always appreciate a good rumble under the covers."

"The only thing *covering* you will be the lid of your casket if you try that again." I take a step forward and get in his face. "Try it again and see how fast you end up on the wrong side of British soil."

"I'm the spirited one." Chloe shoves me into Marshall's arms. "And neither of us is sleeping with you, Mack Daddy. Where did Marlena go, anyway?" She squints into the crowd.

"My sister?" He cocks his head. "Who the hell knows." He sucks from the wooden mug in his hand. "The little whore is rolling around on her back, I reckon."

Wow, he said *whore* like it was a term of endearment. It's nice to know we see eye to eye on some things because I happen to agree with his nutshell analysis of Marlena. And what the heck does Chloe want with the little whore, anyway?

"You hear that, Chloe?" I take a moment to rib her. "Your long-lost granny is off getting VD somewhere while lying on her back. The two of you have so much in common, and yet it's sort of a miracle you have relatives at all." Actually, if memory serves correct, Marlena tosses herself off a cliff soon after she discovers her lover was sent to the tower—wait, that's only partially correct. Marlena contracted the *Black Death*. The Black Death! THE PLAGUE! "Holy crap, I just remembered this entire time period is crawling with all things bubonic." I snatch Chloe by the arm. "We need to get the hell out of here before we're bubbling with boils. The afterlife sounds nice in theory, but I'm in no hurry to taste and see for myself."

Marshall keeps pace beside me as we navigate our way through the chortling can-can girls with their skirts to here and their tits to there, hanging out for the world to see. Dear Lord, this is a den of heathens if I ever saw one. The main saloon is filled with bodies so dense it's like swimming through a human wall just trying to hit the exit.

"There she is," Chloe growls and leads us to the left a bit until we're face-to-face with Marlena and a skanky looking girl with a tiny turned-up nose, red knotted hair that holds the promise of a rat's nest, pasty skin, and large round eyes that seem hungry to steal our souls. So odd. So unnatural, and honestly, so unnecessary.

"Come on, Chloe," I hiss. "I'm sure Marshall can summon that demon into his living room anytime you want. We have kids to think about. I'm pretty sure there's no routine vaccination for the diseases they're hosting. Hell, there probably aren't even proper names for them. This isn't head lice we're dealing with. This is life or black death!"

"Marlena." Chloe sizes her up as if claiming her prey before she pounces. "I believe we have unfinished business."

"Business?" I chirp. "Chloe, if you need to stay behind, I absolutely have no problem with that whatsoever." Forget the deal I worked out with her. Leaving her in these tampon, yeast infection cream deprived times might just be a special brand of torture. A dull smile comes to my lips, and the edgy redhead next to Marlena snaps her jaw at me as if she were rabid. Dear God, she probably is. Great. I can add rabies to the short list of things to be wary of.

Chloe scoffs as if a vacay in jolly old England wasn't even on the short list of hellscapes she's willing to burn time in. "I'm in the Transfer with Wesley." She keeps her eyes trained on Marlena. "He is my master, and I do as he says," she grits the words through her teeth as if a vision of Wes and his X-rated commands just whistled through her brain.

"What?" I try to shake Chloe from her bizarre need to confess her sins. "Nobody cares who you bow down to on the mattress, Chloe. And what's this master shit?"

Chloe's trance-like state remains unshakable as she continues to glare at her older, not all that wiser twin. "Traitors don't sit well with me. I suspect I'll be seeing you soon."

Marlena scoffs openly at Chloe's threat as if it were no more than a toddler throwing a tantrum. Little does she know that Chloe is far more lethal than any toddling babe. She's amassed quite the impressive body count—an attribute that had me leaning toward teaming up with her myself.

"I suspect you'll be seeing me when I'm good and ready." Marlena gives the flick of her wrist, exposing an exquisite black fan made of fine lace. If I didn't think it was laden with bionic super germs, I might have asked her to lend it to me before jettisoning off to a far more comfortable time and place. It's stifling in here, causing the thick, ripe body odor to roll to a boil. Can you say air conditioning and fire code? Two things I never thought I'd miss.

"Great." I slap my hands over Chloe's back in an effort to move her toward the exit. "Now that we've got all the fun details worked out, I'm sure you two will enjoy a rather hostile tête-à-tête sooner than later. But as for you and me, it's time to make Brexit."

"Not so fast." Chloe's feet seal to the floor like concrete, taking a step toward the snarling redhead. "Who's this little impish bitch?" She scowls at the—for lack of a better term, impish bitch that seems to be gloating next to Chloe's whore of a grandmother.

The redhead exposes a mouthful of unfortunate orthodontic events. "Cassandra Graham." She offers a hand to Chloe, and she wisely ignores it. Swear to God, the girl has gangrene setting in on three different nails. The sapphire ring on her finger snags my attention, but it's not the precious watery blue stone that has me ogling it—it's the thin slice of light running through it—a cat's eye. I've seen that before. I used to want one in the worst way back when my father was still alive. We had seen one on the finger of one of his coworkers, and I inquired about it. As soon as he said the words *cat's eye*, my young self was smitten with the idea of having a feline ocular vessel gracing my very own finger in the form of a blue stone. Blue as Gage Oliver's eyes, and I smirk at the thought.

Her smile expands, revealing the fact she's missing nearly every other tooth, the few she has seem a bit rusted looking, and I've gone from annoyed to feeling immensely sorry for her. Modern dentistry can be added to the list of things to be thankful for in the millennial age. "I know who you are." Her gaze drills straight into mine and a shiver rides up my back. There's something unnerving about her. Something very familiar yet haunting.

"Do I know you?" I back into Marshall, and that smooth vibration tingles along my spine. Everything about Marshall has the power to give me all the assurance I need.

"No." Her voice holds the slightest echo, and for a moment I wonder if my ears are responding to the raucous band pounding out a storm. "But you will, Skyla Oliver—nee Messenger. I'm not through with you." Her lips turn down on the sides and her face melts as if it were made of candle wax. "Not through with any of you."

Marshall places his hands over my shoulders and a powerful vibration wails through me—far more powerful than any of the vibratronics he's previously unleashed. If I didn't feel the need to ditch this tawdry tavern, I might opt for a nightcap and a nice long cuddle session with my favorite purring pervert. Instead, I do the only thing sanity will allow—I yank Chloe toward the exit.

"Swear to God, Messenger"—she pants as we struggle to thread our way through the boil of bodies—"if this morphs into a nightmare, I'm going to—"

"You're going to what, Chloe? Knife my head off? How very old school of you."

Focus, Skyla. Our paths must part. We shall reunite soon enough. Marshall strums the words right into my mind, and I can't help but give a private smile. It doesn't get more old school than Marshall drilling his

31

thoughts straight into my skull. It sort of reminds me of my time at West Paragon High where Marshall enjoyed tormenting me, exchanging kisses for visions. It reminds me of sweeter days gone by when Gage was ever so faithful and Logan—

A clearing opens in the crowd, and just as I'm about to make a break for it, a man steps in front of me and I bump right into his rock-hard chest.

Speak of the devil—or angel as it were. It's him again. That beautiful face, those citrine eyes. Can it be?

"*Logan?*" He sheds that wild smile of his that still makes my heart go pitter-patter. "I knew it was you." Which version I'm not so certain. There's the Treble-based version back on Paragon—and, of course, the holistic version in heaven. But this one wears a drab brown suit, and his bow tie is quite literally a string tied into a bow. He looks every bit as fashionably ritzy as the Transfer dwellers, and it occurs to me this is the century that those nefarious ghosts are most likely from.

His brows rise with amusement as he pulls a cigar to his lips and takes in a slow, smooth drag, but my heart is still melting over those gorgeous eyes, those lips I've kissed a thousand times.

"What are you doing, smoking a cigar?" I offer up an open-mouthed smile at this dapper, sexy, old-world reboot of the first boy who stole my heart.

His lips twitch a smile, but he's holding back, laughing ever so slightly.

"When in Rome." He blows a steady stream of smoke into my face, powder white, holding the scent of holiday spices, causing me to give a few hard, quick blinks. Along with the smoke, along with the power of seduction Logan holds in his voice, those heated nights of our short-lived honeymoon tread through my mind, achingly slow and heartbreakingly beautiful to witness even from afar—Logan and me openly lusting after one another, without a stitch of clothing between us. His face buried in my chest, between my legs, his lips pressed to mine for hours on end. Our time in the bath, warm as tears—Sector tears, he corrects—his teeth grazing over my flesh, his hot, lusty whispers, the steady lashing of his searing tongue. Logan is in me, fueling me with his love, thrusting himself high up into the deepest part of my being. Logan glides over me, stealing wet kisses, doing his best to pound his body into mine, and an aching moan escapes my throat. My body quivers at his command, and I'm right there. Logan dives down and offers one last frenetic kiss to the most tender part of me, and I let out a cry as my body shakes and quakes. My entire being cries out in pleasure, in pain, as I let out a vicious primal roar that lets the entire universe know I exist. That Logan and I once existed.

My lids flutter as if struggling to open, but in truth I wish they would remain sealed for far longer than this sliver of time. Reliving my honeymoon with Logan is the last thing I expected. It's the last thing I would have asked for, but in hindsight it's probably what I needed. Every part of me is aching over what Gage has done to me, to us, to our sweet little boys. Logan's distraction, though odd, was strangely welcome—reminding me of simpler times, happier times and gave my subconscious a bit of respite from the dark-haired prince who hacked my heart to pieces. It's as if the lights went out in my world and then the floor was taken from underneath me. Here I am falling, endlessly, painfully, into the deep abyss of grief.

But these aren't simpler times. Before my lids even

crack to welcome the dawn, I can feel the throb of pain filling me. Gage has crashed a sledgehammer over my life, over my physical body, and now I will never be the same. My heart has shattered. It has twisted itself into something unrecognizable. Thoughts of Chloe and those dark promises I whispered into her ear last night echo through my mind, and I break all over again. It is a horrible hell you've delved into when you need Chloe Bishop's help with anything.

My room forms around me, the sturdy furniture—purchased by Demetri, the carpeted walls—compliments of Tad. A strange glow emanates from the foot of my bed as my mother gives a slight wave from the chair. Not Lizbeth, not the mother one might suspect would be in my room holding one of the twins to her bosom, but Candace, the mother nobody would believe could be conned into a little babysitting while I jettisoned around metaphysical planes and, apparently, time continuums. As soon as she showed up in my room last night to offer up a bit of celestial comfort, I sat her iridescent bottom down and handed her a pacifier—two of them to be exact. It was late, and I had just fed the twins, but sleep was the last thing on my mind, which is ironic considering the fact I haven't slept in months.

"My dear, you truly need a rocking chair," she admonishes while struggling to adjust into a position of comfort in that old wooden seat I've only used a handful of times. She's holding Nathan, or perhaps it's Barron. As horrible as it sounds, I can't really tell. If my vision wasn't blurred with sleep, if they were in my arms, I might know the difference. *Might* being the operative word. But the only way I can be sure is by the fact I've painted Nathan's right toenail blue and Barron's red. As much as Gage cringes each time he's met with the cute little corn niblets that adorn their feet, I know he's appreciative of my determination to keep them straight. Even though the boys are fraternal, they look nearly identical. I'd feel terrible if there were a mix-up at this early stage in the game. I'm sure in a year we won't have a problem telling them apart. I hope.

"The horses last night—the ones from the Transfer—" I scoot to the edge of the bed. "Thank you." There—no pussyfooting around. The old me would have asked if she had anything to do with them, but the new me knows better. If you want to stay ahead of the game—correction, if you want to be *in* the game at all—you must come from a place of knowing with this unearthen being who bore me. Shoot straight from the hip and avoid circular conversation and logic like the plague—speaking of which...

"They're the finest stallions in my stalls." She brings a tiny dark-haired angel my way and drops a tender kiss to his forehead before completing the handoff. That one simple kiss brings a swell of relief. I didn't know how she would feel about the boys, considering who they sprang from. Gage isn't her first choice for me.

"Dear child." She scoffs and I can't help but feel as if I'm looking in a mirror—more so that I've somehow managed to multiply and now am able to move around the room in duplicate. "There are only three beings in the entire universe who can call me Your Grace. I dare not hold their father's sins against them. The Good Word overturned that ruling centuries and centuries ago. Heavens no. I'm not interested at all who spawned them, so long as they have your lifeblood in them. They are as good as mine. *Now*"— she flattens her airy white dress with her hands, and sparks fly around her in a fit of cosmic dust—"I've left Sage under the careful supervision of your father. We're taking her to the herd races. There's nothing quite as jolly as watching a plethora of species compete with such zeal. She'll be seated on one of the royal yaks." Her fingers land over her mouth as if holding back a prideful laugh. Sage is the daughter I lost. My twins were actually triplets until one was no more. "A beautiful beast of burden, if I don't say so myself." She lands a cool kiss to the top of my head. "Goodbye, my darling."

"Wait." I slip my hand over her wrist and those strumming vibrations filter from her. "I had a bit of a strange trip after Chloe and I left the Transfer. It was beyond weird. There were Marlena and her perverted brother, Mack, and a snarky looking skank named Cassandra. She said she knew me. Who is she?"

Her lips twist with a clear look of disdain. I know for a fact my mother is more than familiar with all of the aforementioned parties.

She retrieves Barron, offers him a kiss, and lands him in my arms as well. "How did you get back?"

"Logan—he blew cigar smoke in my face."

Her brows peak. "Logan! How lovely. Did he say anything to you?" She suddenly looks less than amused, and now I wonder if they're harboring some deep, dark secret.

"I asked him why he was smoking." I make a face because I suspect my mother knows exactly why and then some. "He said when in Rome, and then I woke up."

"When in Rome!" She laughs and claps her hands as if she not only understood the implications but was able to relive those heated nights right along with me. "Ah, yes"—she clutches her hand to her chest, her eyes closing for a moment—"Roma, my sweet, sweet, Roma. Forever you shall live in the recesses of my heart."

The sound of a car hitting the brakes screams from outside, followed by the horrible crashing sound of metal hitting metal.

"Oh dear." She scuttles to the window and cranes her neck toward the road. "That didn't take long," she snips under her breath.

"What didn't take long? God, that sounded terrible! It sounded like a freight train meeting with a wall. It wasn't a black truck, was it?" God forbid Gage get tangled and mangled before I can let into him properly. Not that I plan on anything other than the silent treatment—and that's just for starters.

She's quick to wave me off as she heads toward the closet. "You'll find out soon enough. Merry Christmas, Skyla. Remember, better to be the giver, always and forever." She turns and her entire being is swallowed up in light. "The giver holds the power—the receiver is only a little better than a beggar." She scowls over at me. "Don't beg, Skyla. It's most certainly not becoming. You spring from a royal lineage. You are a victor in every single capacity. My daughter is the head and not the tail." Her voice begins to evaporate right along with the rest of her. "This life is but a vapor, but eternity is yours and belongs to those you love. You are sealed—bought with a price. You are a—" and that's as far as I can possibly strain my ears to hear. But the silence in the room is short-lived as the wail of an ambulance tears through this little corner of Paragon, on this, the first Christmas Eve my children will experience.

I lounge in bed with the boys for the next few hours, feeding them, counting their perfect little toes, their tiny stubby little fingers, and I can't help but smile through the tears. I've shed a river, no thanks to Gage. What has happened? Why did it happen? Gage didn't trust me enough to get us through this. Deep down, I know he was right to do so. I'm not sure who I'm angrier with—him or me. But it's the resolution of how we might crawl away from this latest, greatest disaster to rock our world that breaks me. Chloe rings through my mind like a gong. If Gage thinks he will easily skip to the dark side, without so much of a mention of it, then I'm curious to see what he'll think of the hard medicine heading his way. I consider the irony for a moment. Chloe Bishop has been a lot of things to a lot of people—a savior isn't one of them. But there was no one else, and no matter what vomits from the situation at hand, I will be forced to stand by my decision.

That demonic stone my mother gifted me a while back—that demonic number that's etched over it comes to mind. There is a time, set and determined, that signifies the end of Gage Oliver's life—of my life as well. And together we're finding ourselves on the wrong end of the hourglass. I try to push all thoughts of him out of mind as I reach for my phone, half-expecting a spastic number of panicked texts left by the traitor himself, but instead, I find just one. **We need to talk.** Such brevity after a wild night of reckless abandon, on his part anyway.

Gage and I might need to have one serious sit-down, but not only am I in no mood to do so but I have a party to get ready for. If my earthly mother loves anything in this world, it's a good get-together where she's able to off her questionable cuisine to friends and family.

It's late by the time I get downstairs—ever so carefully carrying both boys in my arms as my mother greets me with a wild cry.

"Can you believe it's Christmas?" She claps up a storm before taking a startled Nathan from me. "What is this they're wearing?" She scoffs at their matching gray tracksuits. Oh no, no, *no!*" she trills as she scoops Barron up as well and traipses right back upstairs. "I picked up the cutest outfits for these two little elves! You'll just die when you see them!"

"I'm dying, all right." Please, God, don't let them come back dressed as elves. I smack my lips while looking at the jovial decorations. The banister is rung with garland, half-dead poinsettias are strewn about, the entire house drips Christmas in its every chaotic format. Dozens of candles sit calmly illuminating their peppermint-scented splendor into the vicinity. I could stare at the tiny red flames all day, so peaceful and quiet. That's the funny thing about candles. No matter how docile that flame looks, you still run the risk of getting burned. My marriage seemed docile for so long then—*bam*, I was left charred and smoking in a single night.

I walk down the hall only to be greeted by a miniature plastic Santa dressed as Elvis who shakes his hips as I walk on by. There's a fully decorated tree in both the living room and the family room. The one in the living room is winter white with matching lights and shiny red ornaments, a total rip-off of Emma's sanitized ode to the holidays. I happen to know for a fact the Olivers will be here tonight, so I suppose this is my mother's way of making her feel comfortable—or perhaps, it's my mother's way of giving her the finger for being so rude this entire last year. Rude has long since been Emma's MO with me in particular. But tonight, I'd happily deal with a thousand rude Emma's rather than a single Gage Oliver. Now there's irony for you.

My phone bleats in my back pocket, and it's a text from Laken. **At the mall! You need me to pick up any last-minute gifts?**

That witch I leashed myself to bounces through my mind. **Yes.** I text right back. **A bottle of perfume—*Chloe*. I'll pay you back.**

Laken doesn't waste a minute. **You don't have to pay me back. You've got boys in diapers. And are you sure about that perfume? I'll gladly pick up any other scent with a far less nefarious name. It's not actually for Chloe, is it?**

Laken and Coop left early last night so I doubt they witnessed the late, great demise of Gage and Skyla Oliver.

It's for Chloe.

A moment thumps by, and I can only imagine what she's thinking. **In that case, I'll let you pay me back. Kidding, sort of. Are you feeling well? You're not having some mental breakdown, are you?**

My mental health in general seems to be on a sliding scale as of late. **Well enough. Swing by when you're through. We're having a get-together. It's going to be real.**

I follow the red tongue of the shag rug my mother lined the hall with right into the family room and bypass my stepbrother Drake and his wife slash my bestie, Bree, on the way to the kitchen.

"Christmas," I mumble to no one in particular.

The thick scent of everything delicious lights up my senses, which can only mean Emily is at the culinary helm. Just seeing Em with her dark hair pinned to the top of her head, her dead-serious expression as she glares at me momentarily before getting back to the fine art of cooking, marks me with a sense of grief. Emily Morgan is a Viden, and Gage happens to be in charge of that slightly disenfranchised group. The Videns were formed through the union of Rothello of the Soullenium and a human host who gladly—or unwittingly offered up her uterus to him. Nevertheless, he sold his people to Demetri for a pittance, and thus Demetri gifted them to his most beloved son. I most likely wouldn't hate Demetri so much if he hadn't killed my father, pulled my husband to the dark side, and quite on purpose impregnated my mother with her youngest daughter, Mystery, aka Misty. Bastard. That about sums up Demetri Edinger in a nutshell.

"Merry Christmas to you, too, Skyla!" Brielle hops over, adorned with a festive sweater—a deer with a 3D ruby red nose that blinks on and off.

"May Kissmas!" Little Beau Geste mimics his mother, and little Misty and Ember sing something that closely resembles that in a choir of coos. Misty and Ember almost look like sisters with their dark hair and matching blue eyes. But Ember is Emily's lovechild with Drake. She's dating Ethan now, and well, in true Landon form, it's twisted.

"Same to you," I say, lackluster. I can't bring myself to use the proper, cheery wording a day like this commands.

"There's nothing happy about this day," Tad grumbles from behind his laptop and I roll my eyes at the sight of my ridiculous stepfather. "Your mother is infiltrating us with the enemy to my checking account. Do you know how many mouths she's saddled me to feed?" He lets out a robust *bah humbug* further cementing his status as the Scrooge in question. "Good thing ol' Demetri will be here with bells on. I can always count on my good buddy to donate toward the bottom line."

"As if." I scoff at the thought. Little does Tad know Demetri is the enemy that routinely helps himself to infiltrating my mother's bottom line. And dear God, I hope that's not true.

"What's gotten in your craw?" Drake barks and belches at the same time as he makes his way to the fridge.

"I'm tired," I offer in lieu of the truth. Come to think of it, that is the truth on a raw, I've-got-twins-hooked-to-my-udders-every-three-hours level.

"*Tired*?" Tad belts out a maniacal laugh as he clamps his laptop shut. "Welcome to the new normal! Bet you thought being a parent would be a breeze, didn't cha?" He leans forward with a renewed vigor as if my depleted state somehow enlivened him. "Bet you thought your mother would add those two little bugaboos to the family burial plot blooming in our bedroom, didn't cha?"

I'm not sure whether to be more offended over the fact

Tad just referred to my children as bugaboos or the entire conversation in general.

My mother waddles back in, hauling two adorable tiny Santas in tow, and my heart melts. Suddenly all is right with this twisted world again.

"Look at you!" I marvel at the two tiny faces with their olive-toned flesh, those midnight black caps of hair, and those eyes—large cobalt swimming pools I'd love to dive into, and yes, without even the hint of a smile, all four dimples dip in and out over and over. Dear God, my heart melts anew each time I lay eyes on these boys, and oddly each time I do just that, it feels as if it's all going by way too fast. Gone are their newborn frames with the frailty of brand new life, replaced with full cheeks, arms, and legs that show off yummy rolls of robust flesh. So sweet, so achingly small. I pick up Nathan and take in his powder fresh scent. "They look fantastic."

Mom touches a finger to each of their noses. "I hope you've been extra good! Mee-Maw and Tampa have a very special surprise for you!"

Just as I'm about to spew out some lame quip about expanding that child cemetery in their bedroom, I'm stopped cold still trying to digest that moniker I'm assuming she's relegated to Tad.

"Did you say *tampon*?" Dear God, if I have to educate my mother on the many reasons hygienic social etiquette dictates this is a very bad idea, I will slap the two of them silly for thinking it ingenious. Or perhaps myself so I can finally wake up out of this nightmare it seems I've drifted into.

She titters like a schoolgirl while leaning in. "It's Tad-Paw, you know, like Paw-Paw, but Tad insisted his name be a part of it. Anyway, the kids can't quite say it so, um, yes, he's been answering to a name shared with a feminine product. I'm just sort of going with it." She's quick to wave it off.

I hate to break it to her, but Tad has been the equivalent of a feminine product for several years now. In a way, it's the universe calling it as she sees it. The whole world is sort of going with it.

"What an unfortunate turn of events," I lament, and for the first time I mean it. Tad the tampon will never live this down. I might just make sure of it myself.

"Speaking of unfortunate events." She leans in. "Did you hear that horrible accident that happened this morning? It was right here on the corner. I heard some poor young girl didn't survive. Can you imagine? Losing your child on Christmas?" She thrusts Barron into my face as if forcing me to face that painful realization.

"God, no, that's just terrible. I feel for the poor girl, too." As cliché as it sounds, life is the most precious gift, and to lose it when you have an entire lifetime ahead of you is truly a heartbreak. And sadly, I can imagine how it feels to lose a child so young. I lost Sage. And just like that, my grief factor goes up exponentially.

I take a few steps closer to the kitchen and a horrible sour scent eats away at my nose, but I'd swear it has nothing to do with the meal Emily is whipping up.

I lean in and whisper, "Why does it smell like Drake tap-danced all over this house with his bare feet?" I wrinkle my nose as the scent drills in deeper.

Mom waves it off with a chuckle. "That's our new thing, right, Emily?" Crap. The last thing I wanted to do was insult the five-star chef that's been making all of our culinary dreams come true as of late. My mother is a nightmare in the kitchen, and Emily is a hallelujah choir at the foot of the living throne. And now that she thinks I've insulted her, I'll probably be relegated to eating crap cakes—

quite literally—for the rest of my stay at the Landon house of horrors.

Mom clears her throat as if a major announcement is afoot. "We no longer use commercial cleaning products in the house. It's all white vinegar, all the time! No chemicals. And it's green! Wait?" She looks to Em, confused. "White vinegar is technically considered green, isn't it?" She rolls her eyes. "You millennials and your lingo. I'll never keep it straight." Mom coos into Barron's tiny little face, "Yes, you will be smelling Uncle Drake's feet from here on out!"

"The Landon house." I blow gently into Nathan's little face, and he squirms happily. "The gift that keeps on giving," I tease and Mom gives me a wet kiss on the cheek.

"And you know you love it!"

"Because the alternative is living next door to Emma." I give a quick wink, and we share a laugh on behalf of my monster-in-law. Dear God, that was harsh even by my own standards. It's true. Gage somehow coerced me into using the payout that Ezrina and Nev gave me from the Gas Lab into buying a money pit smack next door to his mother. If that isn't a sign of fatigue induced psychosis I don't know what is.

The doorbell rings, and an influx of guests flood in. My heart picks up pace because I know Gage will be here. I'm not exactly looking forward to seeing Logan either after that scuffle that broke out between us, but still, Gage has garnered the majority of my ill will.

My mother-in-law, Emma, swoops in smelling as if someone dipped her in frankincense and myrrh, and I can hardly breathe. She snaps up one twin and passes him off to my angel of a father-in-law, Barron, then quickly plucks the other out of my arms as well.

"Merry Christmas to you, too," I say under my breath as she waltzes to the living room with nary a holiday greeting.

"She means well." Barron comes in and plants a kiss on my cheek while holding his namesake. He winces at me as if anticipating an outburst. "I'm sorry about what happened last night. I don't fully understand it. Gage won't say a word. But if it's strong enough to keep the two of you apart on the holiest night of the year, then this must be pretty serious."

"Serious, indeed." My voice quivers as I blink back tears. "Our boys will always come first." There it is, the battle cry of every couple that's on the rocks.

Mom claps her hands and stomps her feet as if she's at a hoedown. "This is a very casual buffet! Please take your plates, fill 'em to the brim, and find a seat wherever you like!" She speeds over to Emma and gives her a friendly tap over the shoulder, but judging by Emma's sourpuss, you'd think my mother just initiated a throwdown. "It's fair to say, last night went a little sideways. I'm sorry about that."

Sideways? I snort at the thought.

If by sideways she means death, murder, and betrayal, then she's got that right.

"Anyway, I'm toying with the idea of writing a cookbook. Casseroles are my specialty." Mom stoops farther into her insanity, and Emma shoots me a quick glance as if asking for backup. As if. I hope my mother torments her for a good long stretch of the evening. It's all her son's fault I had zero sleep last night. And it's all her son's fault I'll spend the rest of my days in bitter tears. Mom goes on and on. "Oh, and the broths! The broths I could do."

My stomach churns at the thought of that dirty sock juice she's been known to conjure, and I'm quick to lose myself in the crowd.

Bodies continue to flood in—Marshall, who I actually manage to smile at, and Demetri, sans his demented niece. Thank God for small miracles, but still, Demetri. I look past the two of them at the door gaping open, letting the fog seep in like an unwanted guest, and then finally Laken and her husband, Coop. Only Laken doesn't come in. She simply wags a bag at me from the entrance. Her caramel-colored hair is in perfect ringlets, and her lips are painted a cheery holiday red. Laken is a stunner on an average day, but putting in a little effort lands her to supermodel heights. And Coop, well, he reminds me so much of Logan my bones ache.

I speed over and pull them into a group hug.

"Come in." I step back, trying my best to coax them inside.

"We can't." Laken makes a face, but I manage to lead them deeper into the foyer. "Dr. Booth and my mother are having us over. I just wanted to make sure you had all you need." Dr. Booth was once my psychiatrist, but as fate would have it, we're just friends now and he's dating Laken's mother. She hands the gift bag to me between pinched fingers as if she were handing off a dirty diaper, and considering she knows it's for Chloe, it probably amounts to the same thing. "That was some christening last night." She glances to Coop. "We'll get together soon and figure out what to do about those rogue Videns. We can't have Spectators running around the planet. Mass hysteria is something we don't want. And for sure we don't want to piss off the government." Spectators is the official-unofficial name of those zombie-like creatures Demetri has transformed the Viden youth into. I'd give anything to reverse the effects on those poor people and turn Demetri into the one and only zombie coot.

"Yeah, well, it's too late for that. I'm betting the feds have sent in people by the droves. Two of their own are persona non grata, and I'm pretty sure we've managed to piss them off."

"Evening," a harrowing deep voice warbles from behind, and I turn to find Demetri shedding his Cheshire Cat grin as he makes his way to the stairwell where Darla Johnson, Bree's Mom, his blonde bombshell of an ex, stands. I crane my neck and spot Mom safely on the other end of the living room holding one of the boys. Figures. Emma probably shoved Nathan into her arms once she got into the coagulated meats portion of her cookbook. It's no wonder my mother is so obsessed with Demetri. He's basically a coagulated meathead.

"Don't let the fact it's an old coot kind of a night scare you from coming in." I say that out loud even though Laken and Coop didn't have the pleasure of hearing my internal tirade.

"Don't worry about it. We can't stay. We'll see you later!" Laken kisses my cheek. "We need to talk," she whispers before trotting past Demetri. If I were smart, I'd trot right along with her.

"Skyla, Mr. Flanders." Demetri nods to the two of us before waltzing into the Landon living room as if he were welcome, and sure enough, my mother tackles him like a three-hundred pound linebacker and douses his face. "Merry Christmas fancy European kisses!"

"Looks like all holy hell is breaking loose tonight," I murmur before giving Coop a brief hug goodbye.

"We have to talk, Skyla," he whispers ominously into my ear just the way Laken did a second ago, and I'm left to wonder if the left hand knows what the right hand is doing.

"What's this about?" I try to keep my voice low and even-keeled.

"It's about Wes." Coop's eyes darken. "I think he stole something very personal from Laken."

"Like what? A lock of her hair? A contact lens?" God, does Laken even wear contacts? Who the hell knows, but I do know one thing for sure, I wouldn't put it past Wes to steal an entire eyeball if given half a chance.

Coop's heavy eyes bear into mine, and I can feel the pain emanating off him like heat off a Transfer tin roof. "Her virginity."

"Her *what*?" I try to absorb this for a moment. I know for a fact that Laken and Coop have been the fornicating kind for quite some time because Gage and I once walked in on them doing the dirty deed—Coop does love Laken with an all-consuming passion. And secondly, they got hitched last summer, and they consummated that good time all over Whitehorse, the house that Logan built for me, that he also happened to penetrate Chloe Bishop in last spring. Ah, yes, good coital times. "But Laken said you were her first." I bear hard into Cooper Flander's desperate eyes, and for a moment it feels as if we're both stretching to believe it. "Or at least she implied it because she also happened to imply that she never slept with Wesley." Oh dear God, or did Wes and his constant desperation for the girl imply it? The good Lord knows Wesley's desperation has commanded him to have Chloe morph into Laken's likeness time and time again, so maybe that's what this is about? Wes has clearly confused reality and the chaos that goes on in his sex lab with Chloe.

Coop shakes his head, slow and dazed, his gaze still transfixed onto mine.

"The past is not always our friend, Skyla." The muscles in his jaw pop, and he looks vexingly like Logan, a hot twin, if I may, although I'm presently pissed at Coop's hot twin. Coop and Logan, it turns out, are long-lost relations of my dear and deviant spirit husband, Marshall Dudley himself.

"That *past*!" I close my eyes. "I will hang Wesley Edinger by his jingle bells if I find out he's manipulated his way back in time to steal Laken's V-card."

"Did I hear my name?" Wesley Edinger pops up behind Cooper and jolts us both to life.

There he is, looking every bit the Gage Oliver knockoff. That midnight hair, those eyes so bright, and the dimples that beg forgiveness. A horrible grief rinses through me, leaving me thick with its aching residue. But it's that cherub he's holding tight, dressed in her crimson velvet dress and arms that stretch to me, that makes me melt. It's safe to say, Tobie, *October* Edinger has stolen my heart.

"I'll take the baby. You deck him."

Wes pulls baby Tobie out of my range and dodges past the two of us on the way in.

"Merry Christmas, Coop!" he has the nerve to call out.

"I'm going to kill him." Cooper nods and leaves for the car, but there was something about the nonchalant way he said it, the complacent smile that ebbed at the edge of his lips that has me believing every word. I'm not convinced any of Demetri Edinger's children could ever really die, but if they could, Wesley would be a good start in cleansing the planet of all its ills. And horrifically, Gage might be a close second.

I close the door, and no sooner does the latch connect than a gentle knock emits from the other end. I pop it back open only to see Wesley again, and then my tired, newborn fried brain does the Edinger Oliver math and deduces that no, in fact, this isn't the least nefarious of Demetri's children. It's the most wicked of them all—Gage.

In that single moment, it feels as if an eternity slips by. I see our bumpy past, our heartbreaking future all in one swoop as I gaze deeply into his ocean blue eyes. I wonder what he sees when he looks at me. Does he see the heaven we once shared or the hell he thrust us in? Yes, everything I whispered to Chloe last night can be squarely pinned on Gage Oliver's Italian suited shoulders.

And it's only then I notice the scruff has been clipped from his face. He's clean-shaven. I almost want to laugh. He's let Emma groom him. Worse yet, he thinks I prefer this choirboy version of him. Mr. Clean Cut. Mr. Innocent. This version would no more take a walk on the wicked side than he would drive a digit over the speed limit. Clean-shaven, licked clean, spit-shined just for the occasion to placate my good senses. Like I would ever fall for that.

My thighs tremble at the sight of him, and my knees beg to fall to the ground in worship. Damn traitors.

"I like you better with the scruff," I muse and ironically mean it even though my body is about to have the big O simply from that lust-riddled look he's shooting my way. I bet that's one of his new superpowers. Big Daddy reissued him all of his oldie but goodie Femtastic powers last night. That was one part of his rambling dissertation I did understand. The rest of it was hocus-pocus, welcome to the dark side for the most part. Gage had both abandoned and betrayed me—that much I know is true.

Gage moves from the shadow and into the light, and then I see it and my heart thumps once with the requisite pride. A bright pink handprint stains his left cheek. The exact spot where I belted him last night in a fit of primal rage. Yes, I am damn proud of that token of my affection. My one and only Christmas gift to the boy I once would have died for. Dear God, a part of me wants to slap myself.

He frowns, sending his dimples digging for attention, and it's then I notice that his hair is crisply parted on the side—and no doubt licked back by his mother.

"*Skyla*," he whispers in that low, achingly desperate way only Gage knows how to do. He leans in, pleading with me before he ever says a word. "Do you trust me?"

"No. Not really." There. I didn't miss a beat because honest words are rarely hard to come by.

Gage closes his eyes a moment, the look of defeat marked over his features. "Merry Christmas, Skyla." He holds out two gold boxes between us, and I step aside to let him in. If this horror of an evening is bound to take place, I say let's get this holiday hoedown over with.

"Put them under the tree."

He steps in, full suit, cobalt tie the exact color of his eyes as if he had it dyed to match, and knowing Emma this is a very real possibility. He probably woke up and found it in his stocking with a note reading, *From Mommy Dearest! The one and only woman you will ever be honest with in your life and love and cherish forever and ever!*

"Skyla," he whispers, heated into my ear, and his cologne, a new and unfamiliar scent, assaults my senses with its violent seduction efforts. "There are things you need to know."

"I know enough." I make an attempt to step around him, and he blocks my path with the wall of his body, leaving me eye to eye with his dress shirt. The crisp white fabric is hypnotic. The way it creases with the tautness of his rock-hard chest is criminal. My fingers tremble to touch him. My lips part for just one simple kiss. I hate the way my hormones render me defenseless around him. I haven't always reacted this way to Gage. In the beginning, I was too sidelined by Logan. I'd do anything to have that mild indifference back if only for a while.

Gage latches his eyes over mine, and I'm forced to look at him. I spin my wedding ring with my thumb like an absentminded habit. For a moment, I toyed with taking it off last night, chucking it in his face, but nothing in me was able to pull off the feat.

"You and I will speak," he says it with a firmness unfamiliar to me, his demeanor unforgivably demanding. He bears in hard with his gaze, his anger percolating just below the surface. "You will hear what I have to say." And with that, he turns and walks into the party, to the triumphant cries of his mother and mine.

My heart gives one last wallop in his honor as if it needed to stabilize itself again after our brief exchange.

My eyes snag on Marshall's, and I head on over.

"Ms. Messenger." His lips twitch with that you-will-come-hither-and-we-both-know-it look of affection. He's so infernally arrogant it only adds to his charm. "You appear well-rested, considering your little side trip to the Mother Country just a few short hours ago."

"Yes, well, vengeance does become me." And, apparently, a little light drive doesn't hurt either.

"And who would it be that fills your pretty little head with such a diatribe?" His brows dip in that panty melting way that only Marshall's can, and for a brief moment, I'm ashamed that my raging hormones still succumb to his sexual superpowers. As much as I might have extreme displeasure with Gage, he is still my husband—still the one and only person who has the God-given right to melt my panties. A few fleeting thoughts of those perverse dreams I've had starring my favorite Sextor flit through my mind, and I don't bother to catch them.

Marshall growls low and aggressive like a rabid dog ready to attack.

"Down, boy," I whisper. "You know, you don't have to read every thought I'm having." I glance out at the motley crew my mother has amassed. "Where's Logan?"

"Recuperating. I'm sure he'll drag his carcass in shortly." He smacks his lips.

"What do you mean *recuperating*?" Come to think of it, I did dole out quite the beating last night, but mostly it was Gage who bore the brunt of my rage. I glance across the room and spot him holding one of the twins while speaking to my stepbrother Ethan, and Emily, and that handprint I gifted him calls out to me like a siren, waving back at me as he turns his head from side to side. My ghost hand it seems is congratulating me on marking him with humiliation. "Did he spend the night with you?" I'm sort of hoping Gage did choose Marshall's instead of his mother's. Although, either way I'm sure Emma helped lick his wounds.

"They both did." He gravels it out in annoyance. Both I assume includes Logan in the mix. "I disdain the way they insist in suckling off my teats as if I were their mother. It's time to wean them, Skyla."

I offer up a blank stare at my most treasured Sector. Though inappropriate almost ninety-nine percent of the time, he's as entertaining as all hell.

"Language." He gives a sly wink.

"I think there's a correction to be made. It's *my* teats they've been suckling off. I glance back and my gaze snags on his. Gage is watching me. Everywhere I go I can feel his eyes digging in like claws.

Brody and Brookelynn, Brielle's sister and Brody's one true love, file between us, and for once I'm relieved to see a Bishop. They're either back on again or they're making nice for the holiday. Either way, I'm glad to see them. Behind them streams Darla, or as I like to call her, the entertainment for the evening.

"Gimme those grandbabies!" she whoops, snatching one of the twins from Demetri's clutches, and I shiver. I hate how accessible my entire life has become to the man who killed my father. I'd give anything for my father to stroll through those doors next. After all, this is Paragon and stranger things have happened, like Ethan strolling in with Logan's soul embedded in his body, but that was high school and even that shit parade seems like a glory day memory in contrast to this new and unimproved shit parade I'm dealing with. I shoot Gage a curt look from across the room only to find him standing next to his nefarious twin—glaring at Marshall as if an ass beating were imminent.

I turn my body just enough to deny him the privilege of gaping at my countenance—now there's an ironic term.

"Where's Ezrina?" I ask, trying to sound chipper, begging to sound as if I care about this gathering at all. I did invite both her and Nevermore—*Heathcliff,* myself. I realize that Nev is going by his more formal name these days, but he'll always be Nevermore to me at heart. Once upon a time he was trapped in the body of a raven and gifted to me by Gage. And there I go perseverating on those dammed good old days once again—and I mean *dammed* as a literal term.

"Rina isn't feeling well." Marshall's brows furrow at the thought. "She's decided to convalesce at Whitehorse. I'll stop by in the morning and give them your love."

"Thank you. I would appreciate that. And what's up with not feeling well? If anyone should be feeling well twenty-four seven, it's Ezrina. She's got an entire state-of-the-art lab at her fingertips. If she can zap dead counts back to life, I'm sure a little head cold has nothing on her." Ezrina happens to occupy Chloe Bishop's old body and vice versa. Only, Chloe is now relegated to Ezrina's old servitude in the Transfer per post war orders. The war that I won. The war *Celestra* won, and apparently didn't have to because another war looms in the not-so distance, and this time it involves a much closer, much more clean-shaven enemy—my darling dimpled husband. "Don't tell me Chloe's body is defunct already." I smirk at the thought of the murderous wench I've chosen to lie in bed with. I may have made a proposition she couldn't refuse last night, but, in the end, it's a benefit to the Factions—more to the point, a benefit to me. Sometimes you need to offer a personal sacrifice for the greater good of all mankind.

I glance over my shoulder at Gage. I'm sure that's the exact logic he used to trot over to the malevolent side with Daddy Dearest.

"Skyla"—Marshall pins me with those molten lava eyes—"what kind of agreement have you worked out with Ms. Bishop?"

"A delicate one," I whisper. "And would you stop reading my mind like it's some gossip-worthy diary entry? I happen to value my personal space, and the fact you keep prying into my gray matter unnerves me."

It's a gray matter, all right. Nothing with Chloe is ever black and white.

The doorbell rings, and my heart thumps once because I'm fully expecting Logan to show up. But it's not the other Oliver I'm pissed at. It's the one I happen to like, Liam, and attached to his person is a very furry Michelle Miller. She's chinchilla from head to toe, and a part of me wants to be there when Emily spots her. Emily is as vegan, organic, nutty granola as one can get, and if you dare cross your eyes at an animal, she will knife you. No joke. And just as I'm about to head over, a pale ghost of a girl, pretty in an extra-ordinary, extra-bitchy way, if that's your thing, dark eyes, dark hair, dark soul—Chloe Bishop stains the entry. Chloe's skin usually holds a healthy bronzed glow, but since she's been a part of the underground brigade, she looks like a creature that just crawled from under a rock.

"Merry Christmas!" she chirps, sauntering inside as if she owns the place, strapped in a red bandage dress that looks as if it were soaked in blood. Come to think of it, this is Chloe. Of course, it's soaked in plasma. Chloe accessorizes with red blood cells the way others do earrings.

"Chloe Jessica Bishop! Welcome!" Mom is the first to throw herself at the daughter of darkness. And I'm a little disturbed that my own mother knows Chloe's middle name,

ADDISON MOORE

although it shouldn't surprise me. Last year while Chloe grumbled her way through nine long months as a human incubator, she and Mom bonded over all things vaginal. I wish my mother wouldn't bond with Chloe. I wish *I* wasn't bonding with Chloe.

"You look so beautiful!" Mom trills as the party rages on. "Didn't I tell you that nursing would get your uterus right back into shape?"

I smirk because I happen to know that Chloe isn't nursing. I'm the one nursing Tobie, or at least I was last night.

Chloe grins. "Why, thank you. I'm as happy as a cat with nine tails."

Marshall turns to me with a vexingly stern expression that lets me know I'm about to be admonished. "Who invited the beautiful pussy?"

I open my mouth, then close it. I can't tell if Marshall is simply enjoying his play on words or if there's an iota of a literal connotation behind it. Mr. Dudley—math teacher extraordinaire—made his sexual rounds when he first came to West, and for the life of me, I can't remember if Chloe was a victim of his one-man gang bang that seemed to span the entire female student population—sans me, of course. Oh hell, Chloe is never a victim.

"*Skyla*." Marshall closes his eyes, and my heart sinks because already I know how disappointed he is in me for befriending the viper—it mirrors the amount I am in myself.

Ellis and Giselle pour through the door with a man in tow that is so exceedingly tall he needs to duck just to enter the lowly Landon estate. He wears a cap of red hair and has a rather dull look about him. His eyes ping around the room as if someone in the vicinity owed him money—and seeing that he's at the Landon home they just might.

"Who invited the Nephilim?" Tad croaks and half the

56

room groans. Tad is such a *tampon* he forgets that *he*, in fact, is a descendant from that angelic spawned breed. Only Tad knows how to make a guest feel truly unwelcome.

Ellis, my favorite stoner, strides over with his larger than life friend.

"Meet Asbury Winters"—Ellis beams—"Host's newest acquisition to the basketball team."

"It's clear we're destined to win every game," I tease and give his behemoth hand a quick shake. I catch Gage stewing in his own jealous juices from across the room—still staunchly by Wesley's side, but this time he's cradling both boys, and my heart melts just a little. The twins look exactly like Gage. It's as if I had nothing to do with their DNA makeup, and considering the source of Gage's DNA, I pray that's not the case. Giselle pops up next to him and plucks a twin from his arms, effectively blocking me from his line of vision. Giselle is Gage's once deceased sister who died as a toddler but thanks to my celestial mother's mercy, and Emerson Kragger's body, Giselle officially lives to see another day. She's sort of never outgrown that toddler mentality though, but to her credit she is working on it.

"What brings you to Host?" Marshall lifts his chin. Marshall is tall by anybody's standards, but Asbury here dwarfs even him.

"My girl." Asbury nods into the heart-shaped admission. "She and I are pretty serious. Her father is going to sign her over to me when she's sixteen."

I glance to Ellis. Dear God, where is this going?

"How old is she now?" I'm afraid to ask, but it had to be done.

"Thirteen." The overgrown science experiment nods as if it were no big deal.

I scowl at Ellis for ushering this perv into our presence, and Ellis leans in close to my ear with a look that spells out something just this side of horror himself. "Hey, *dude*"—he whispers to me—"I took a shit last night and thought of you." My mouth falls open because, holy hell, I have no idea what craptastic sentiment could ever follow that. "*Damn*—I can't believe you had two kids the size of cinderblocks squeeze out of your bottom. I'm considering heading into the priesthood just to avoid putting poor G through that."

"Poor G? Make no mistake about it—it will be poor Ellis if you ever knock up G."

"*Hey*"—the cyclops Ellis hauled in barks—"where's the prime rib? I'm starved."

Ellis whoops. "That's what I'm talking about, man! Let's scour this place until we get all the food in our bellies."

"Good luck with that," I say under my breath. If prime rib is what they're after, they'll be scouring the house right into the next millennium. And food in their bellies? I suggest they watch *Soylent Green*. It amounts to the same principle around here with or without Em at the helm.

The door opens once again, and there he is—caramel-colored hair, classic good looks, eyes as citrine as a sunrise. Logan Oliver glows like an ethereal being. No, *really*—he's sort of literally glowing.

I shove an elbow into Marshall's ribs. "What's up with the Chernobyl tan? And should he be anywhere near the boys?" As in my precious angels that I can't wait to snuggle in bed with in the next few hours.

Marshall grunts. "It appears there was a bit of an issue last night. Taking a nap facedown in the rain after a good lightning strike can do a number of things to a person, living or dead."

"What is that supposed to mean? Does he have a lightning rod in his pants now?" Face it, Logan has always had a lightning rod in his pants. That boy is hung. So is Gage. I'd say it runs in the family, but it turns out they aren't even remotely related.

Marshall balks, "Skyla, must you always revert to the crass? And I'll have you know, yes, indeed, young Oliver has good genes. He acquired them from me, didn't he?" His lips curl in that proud way only a lightning rod owner can. I've no doubt Marshall is hung like a Clydesdale. If those seductive night wanderings I've experienced are even remotely true to life, Marshall's lower half should be considered a weapon of m-*ass* destruction.

"I may be crass, but I learn from the best, Professor Dudley." I give a quick wink as I head over to Logan. He looks a bit stunned as if he were still trying to get his bearings from that electric slap he received from above last night, and at any moment I expect to see him staggering around the foyer, but he doesn't. Logan walks up smoothly. His smile expands just for me, and he holds my gaze with those glowing amber eyes just before he offers a firm embrace.

"Merry Christmas, Skyla. I left the gifts for you and the boys at Barron's." He pulls back with that sad film over his features, the one he mastered not long after we met. "I'm hoping you'll stop by tomorrow."

"We won't be able to make it." *Ever again*, I want to add, but I know that's not true.

Skyla. His lids lower, and that eerie iridescent light emanating from him seems to dim with disappointment. His thoughts press on, but I'm only able to grasp every third word, *sorry, Gage, listen.*

I shake my head, trying hard to hang onto the powers that bearing the twins afforded me, but those seem to be fading like the many other things in my life.

"It's not working. I can't read your mind unless I touch you," I muse, perusing the room as my sisters pass around the eggnog on trays. Both Mia and Melissa have donned sexy elf costumes, complete with pointy green stilettos. Emma's obnoxious laughter lights up the room, and with the dizzying array of Christmas carols blasting from the boom box in the corner, I'm surprised the twins aren't screaming hara-kiri by now.

Logan presses out a cool smile. "Then we'll have to go back to touching." He wastes no time in threading our fingers together. His amber eyes bear hard into mine, and a spear of heat expands the length of my stomach. *Skyla Laurel Messenger—Oliver*. His smile stretches just enough, but that pained look takes over his features. *Talk to Gage. Don't drag this out. You and I both know you'll regret losing a single moment with him.*

I pull my hand free and smirk. "I should have known it was going to be an infomercial for the dark side. You shouldn't go so thick on the propaganda. It's not a becoming look on you. He's abandoned your people, too."

Before he can put in a rebuttal, Michelle Miller hops over in her sky-high FMs with Liam by her side, and we exchange the necessary holiday niceties. Michelle is a dark-haired beauty that has always reminded me a little of Chloe—deeply tanned skin—super model features, soul as black as night. Okay, so maybe that last descriptor is a little harsh. And Liam, well, he's just another Marshall knockoff along with Logan and Coop.

Michelle runs a finger along Logan's cheek, and that rage I've been brewing all night long demands to unleash all over her. "A thousand bucks says you and Lex are the next to tie the knot!" She tosses her long curls over her back and cackles up a storm.

"Not this shit again," I mutter under my breath. And just like that, Chloe pops up as if on cue.

"Skyla is right," she snarks while standing shoulder to shoulder with me in a shocking display of solidarity, and every eyebrow in the vicinity goes up, including mine. Crap. I should have gone over the short list of rules with Chloe. The first and most important of them being *act natural*. Declaring me right in any matter is a clear telltale sign that all is not *right* with the world.

Chloe drapes an arm around my shoulder, and I cringe as I glance to Logan. His eyes are the size of soccer balls, because for one, I haven't bothered to kick the Transfer troll back to the curb.

"Skyla and Logan were meant for one another." Chloe preens for my approval, but I can see the devil dancing in her eyes. "Have a little decorum, *Shelly*." Chloe glances over her shoulder at Dudley and bites down over her bottom lip seductively as if she were gunning for some of that Clydesdale action tonight. Her deep, black, bordering on auburn hair lies heavy over one eye as she turns back to face her old Bitch Squad recruit. Back in the day, Chloe was the leader of the mean girls at West Paragon High, which included Michelle, Lexy, and Emily. Not much has changed in that respect other than the fact I find Emily livable at best, considering we're held up under one roof. Plus, Em has mad skills when it comes to all things future. Emily is sort of a heavenly prognosticator, reciting visions from the Almighty Himself, and since most of her visions concerning me are, well, *concerning,* I tend to keep my distance.

"Damn right! Brielle pops up from behind and jumps on Chloe's back, causing her to let out an indelicate oomph. "God, it's nice to see my besties getting along! What the hell. It's Christmas, right?"

"Yes, what the hell?" Logan needles me with a private inquisition, but I refuse to go there with my glowing ex-husband. Logan and I were married for the short span of three days. It was bliss, and, as per usual, when I'm in any state of bliss, my mother up above puts the kibosh on that good time.

Chloe wraps an arm around me, and I can feel Logan stilling, reasoning whether or not I'll be in need of some serious help momentarily. I might be, but at this point I'm so wrapped up in rage I can most definitely take her.

"Skyla and I are working on rebuilding our relationship," she mewls, meek and innocent, but I can hear the dark laughter already brewing in her chest. "We'll be spending much more time together in the future, so you'd better get used to it." She gifts Logan a sly wink. "Aren't you lucky?"

Logan opens his mouth as if to say something just as my mother starts in on a howling spree. "*Attention!*" She claps and stomps her feet. Tad belts out one of his eardrum splitting whistles, and every baby in the room startles to life. I glance over to my own two cherubs, but they're both knotted up like turtles with their legs tucked underneath them, each fast asleep—one with their grandfather, Barron— one still safely tucked in his father's arms.

"It's present time!" Mom calls out. "Let the festivities begin!"

The entire house explodes in a fit of roars and laughter as gifts and wrapping paper alike go flying. I'm sure Emma is having a seizure at the scene. It takes twelve hours to open three gifts at the Olivers'.

I glance down at the small gift bag I'm still holding that Laken picked up for me and hand it to Chloe.

"This is for you." I force a dry smile. "It's just a little something to brighten your spirits."

Chloe wastes no time in dipping her fingers into it and plucking out the amber bottle.

"*Chloe*"—she plants a kiss over the glass—"my favorite perfume! How did you ever know?" She pulls me into a strong embrace, and it feels strange, traitorous to be touching her this way. Touching Chloe, embracing her in any physical or emotional way wasn't necessarily a part of our agreement, but for the sake of showmanship and rebuilding what we never really had, I go with it. "I have something for you, too." She fishes something out of her pocket and places it gingerly in my hand.

"It's a ring," I say, surprised as I study it a moment. It looks familiar—platinum or silver I can't tell. It's vintage, that's for sure, but there's something about that cat's eye sapphire that graces the top that clings to me like some distant memory long-forgotten—something about the way the precious metal is fashioned into two claws holding the blue heart together, and then it hits me and I gasp.

"Chloe!" I smack her on the arm before trying to stuff the haunted ring back into her hand, but she laughs and pulls away.

"Now—that's not how you say thank you, is it, Skyla?"

I pull her in and bury my lips in her ear. "You stole this from that hellion Cassandra? Are you insane? You of all people should know that manipulating the past is a piss-poor idea."

"Relax." She pulls back and fluffs my hair with her fingers. "You of all people know that you can't really change anything." My heart sinks when she says it because for a time I tried to save my father—the one *she* killed—or instructed Demetri to do so. They're both guilty in my eyes. "What's a little petty theft among friends and relations?" She scowls at me a moment, her jowls trembling as if she were rabid. "Relax, Messenger. It was gifted to me, and now I'm gifting it to you." She trots off toward Demetri, most likely to gloat over her latest acquisition—my assumed friendship. Neither Chloe nor I are in this to rebuild something we're not really interested in. We both came into our agreement with our own motivations, our own determined will to make it happen. And we will. If anything, Chloe and I share a ripe desperation, something animalistically charged and undeniably powerful.

I jab the sapphire ring on my right ring finger. It's not the ring's fault Chloe has committed an interdimensional robbery. It might as well be cared for and appreciated.

Logan wraps an arm around my waist and leads me into the deep end of the Oliver pool where Emma, Barron, and Gage huddle with the boys. Crap. I'll need a life preserver to survive this night, and Logan is proving to be more of a lead weight than a buoy.

"Skyla"—Barron dances his way over with his namesake in his arms—"dare I say you have the most well-behaved children here."

"I agree." I press a gentle kiss over the back of baby Barron's little warm head, and he nuzzles further into his grandfather's chest.

"You're welcome to join us tomorrow if you like." He extends the invitation with hopeful eyes, but I catch Emma twisting her lips.

"Of course, she'll be there," Gage offers and I force myself to look at him. It feels heavy and weighted just to meet with his gaze, and as ripe as my anger is, I can feel the tears just below the surface. There's a careful apprehension between the two of us. I'm still wearing my broken heart, and he's still wearing that slap I issued like a fresh tattoo.

Just as I'm about to think up a dozen reasons why I will not in fact be there, Mom and Demetri round out our circle.

"Well, look at this!" Mom bubbles. "It wouldn't be Christmas without all of our favorite people here!" She throws her arms around Demetri, pulling him into a sort of awkward side hug, and just the sight sends my stomach churning. It's one thing to have a secret lovechild with her favorite Fem, but to openly molest him for all to see—namely me, it makes the bile rise to the back of my throat.

Demetri's eyes glance to my waist, and it's only then I note that Logan is still securely attached. It's funny how Logan has become such a part of me, so integrally connected to my body and soul I no longer perseverate on the little details—platonic as they may be, and, in this case, they are every bit platonic.

Logan straightens and his hand slides back to his own side. "Wonderful party." He nods to my mother.

"Thank you!" Her entire face lights up to rival his own. "I'm thinking now that the twins are here we should get together far more often. I'd hate to wait for the holidays to roll around for us all to be in the same room. We're family now!" She waves a hand at Emma. "Besides, don't you think for a minute that these two lovebirds will let those sheets cool for too long." She giggles incessantly at the potential state of my uterus. It's clear someone has been hitting the eggnog a little too hard. "I'm expecting a basketball team from you two!"

"I think we're done," I spit the words out, looking right into those overgrown sapphires that belong to Gage Oliver. And I mean *done* in the most literal sense. A dull ache infiltrates me from the inside. Gage and I can never really be done, not with two precious souls between us—three counting our daughter who never made it out of the womb. My entire affect sags at the thought of Sage missing her first Christmas, every Christmas here on out.

Mom chortles at my response and smacks Demetri over the arm. "And we thought we were done, didn't we?"

The entire lot of us leers at the two of them with sober expressions.

Oh my shit. I swear on all that is holy if Demetri has knocked up my mother again I'll find a way to hack him to pieces.

"What's that supposed to mean?" I ask the obvious question.

Demetri chortles right alongside the loon still clutching him tight. "I think what Lizbeth is trying to say is that the best intentions sometimes go awry, Skyla." He bears those dark soulless eyes into mine as if he were stabbing each one out with a pitchfork. "We make plans and God laughs." The smug grin returns to his face. "God laughs when we try to manipulate our circumstances." He glances to Chloe in the not too far distance, and my stomach bubbles with the promise of an eruption. "Some things are simply meant to be. You cannot stop destiny—you cannot stop fate."

I step in close to him while Mom, Emma, and Barron busy themselves fussing over the twins. "Tad might annoy the ever-living hell out of me—and yes, I might wish I could light his head on fire a time or two, but he belongs with my mother. Keep your greasy claws to yourself, would you?"

Demetri's demented grin expands. "If wishes were horses, beggars would ride." He strums out a laugh. "Oh, what the heck, it's Christmas, Skyla." He gives a sly wink. "This one's for you."

Mom pulls me in and wraps her arms around me tight. "I mean we found our way back to one another after all of those years." Gross. "Never mind all of this deep thinking. It's Christmas! And in about five minutes I've got a surprise for the kids." She leans in and cups her hand around her lips. "We have a very special guest getting ready to make an appearance!"

Marshall leans in. "And *this* is my gift to you."

A series of choking sounds and choice expletives emit from the stairwell, and everyone stills and turns in that direction.

Down tumbles Tad, clad in a red Santa suit and a full

fuzzy white beard that looks as if he chopped up Mia's massive teddy bear collection to fashion it. He's donned a pair of large, rather ill-fitting boots that might actually be the cause of his forthcoming paralysis judging by the way he's taking the stairs four at a time, and I swear a leg just wrapped itself around his shoulders.

"Hock, hock, hock!" he barks it out like a threat—and dear God, he can't even get the terminology right. Mom chortles up a storm as does everyone else, and the room breaks out into a jovial mood.

Mom herds Misty, Beau, and Ember to the forefront of this madness. Thank God Almighty the boys are far too young to participate in the slaughtering of Santa. Tad Landon is a lot of things, a knockoff Santa he is not.

"Emma, get the boys!" Mom harps while waving wildly.

Emma snatches Nathan from Gage, and she and Barron are quick to comply with my mother's silly wishes.

I head over and, upon closer inspection, note Tad's Santa suit looks as if it was used to clean the inside of a deep fryer. Funny, I don't remember him ever donning the felt monstrosity before. Must be new, or more to the broke point, new to *him*. It's spotted and tattered with tiny holes sitting prominently on his shoulder.

Tad howls and whelps until he finally manages to stick the landing and stands proud at the base of the stairs.

"All right, round up the ankle biters!" He holds out his hands in an animated manner. "Who would like to be the first to sit on Santa's lap?"

His sleeve dips close to the candle on the end table next to him, and just as I'm about to move it out of the way, his entire arm erupts in flames.

"Jiminy Cricket! Bull hockey! Great Caesar's *ghost!*" Tad shrieks as loud as a schoolgirl as the flames lick ever so close to his head, and he begins on a wild spin. The room explodes in screams and shouts as Tad's entire suit erupts in a blaze with a loud roaring whoosh. Drake and Emily pull the kids to safety while Ethan throws a vase at Tad's head—and holy crap, that sounded like a skull cracker! I'm assuming he meant to douse him with its contents, but in a state of panic—and a burst of Landon brain cells—he's sent Tad staggering instead.

"Lizbeth!" Tad pauses—his entire body rife with an angry inferno, his eyes just as furious. "So help me God!" And just like that, his faux beard bursts into a wall of fire.

"My God, his head is on fire!" I scream, and at exactly that moment Demetri steps into my line of vision and offers a congratulatory nod.

An entire choir of *shit* circles around the room as the unbearable heat skyrockets, and someone swings the front door wide open—most likely in hopes Tad will fly right out. But he doesn't. Tad spasms around the foyer, shrieking for help that doesn't seem to come. Mom swats the crap out of him with a broom she's pulled from the closet, and just like that, his Santa hat ignites like a fiery cherry on top.

"Holy mother of God." I glance around in a panic for something, *anything* to put the damn fire out. So help me God, Tad Landon is not going to barbecue himself on my children's first Christmas.

Logan pulls the red runner off the floor, sending both Liam and Michelle flying straight into the bathroom as they go airborne.

"*Move*," he shouts to my mother as he beats Tad with the woven fabric. Marshall comes over and tosses an old quilt over him, and the heat along with the unnatural light all defuse in an instant, and yet my mother quickly plucks it right back off.

"Are you insane?" she balks. "That was my grandmother's!"

Every jaw in the room unhinges as my mother's need for nostalgia outweighs the fact her husband nearly burned alive before our very eyes. Come to think of it, maybe Tad's disco inferno was just as much for my mother as it was for me? I take a moment to glare at Demetri. If it was my wish to see his head burst into flames, maybe it was her wish to finish him off? Oh my God! I am very much fearing for Tad Landon's life.

Tad rolls around to douse the remaining flames while everyone disperses, and Logan ends up wrapping him in the rug like a giant red burrito.

The wail of an ambulance slices through the unexpected silence, and I spot Mia, Melissa, and that oversized beef-eating basketball star each on their phones recording the event to regale the Internet with no doubt.

The party disbands in less than thirty seconds and leaves a skeleton crew hovering around the charred moaning pile that was once my stepfather.

Marshall kisses each of the boys good night before nodding my way.

Did you enjoy your gift? He gives a sly wink before glancing to Tad who has seemingly recovered enough to belt out every curse known to man.

"*No*," I mouth in horror as poor Tad moans and groans his way through another choir of expletives.

Marshall pulls me into a quick embrace. "Do thank Demetri. It's poor form not to. Remember, it's the thought that counts." He pulls back and shakes his head ever so slightly as if something went wrong, and it sure as hell did. "That was my gift as well, Skyla." He picks up my hand, and his jaw redefines itself. Chloe's ring is already dazzling in the light. "Charming."

"Chloe gave it to me. It looks vintage." I bite down on my lip. I've never been able to hide a thing from Marshall.

"It is." And I'm pretty sure he knows why.

I hold it out for a moment and admire it in the light as the medical team hovers over Tad. "I have always wanted a cat's eye sapphire. How do you think she knew?"

"I believe you're looking for the term *star* sapphire. Ms. Bishop's bustling mind remains an utter mystery to me." He fondles the ring on my finger a moment, pulling it closer to him for inspection. "However this, my love, is neither a star sapphire nor a cat's eye." He pauses and takes a breath. "In the old days, this was referred to as lapis lazuli. They were baffled by its clear properties, but that was due to the fact precious sapphires were not readily available to them in their region. It's why the structure of the throne has an interchangeable term." A breath expels from him as if he were caught off-guard, and I inch back to get a better look at him. Nothing and no one has ever evoked that response in him. "This is chipped from the living throne of the Most High, Skyla. That slice of light you see is no iris."

I gasp at the thought. "What is it?" It takes everything in me not to shake the holy crap out of him.

"Temper." His lips curl at the edges as Gage pops up beside us holding both twins, and that sweet spot for him melts all over again. "It is the portal to a power only the creator Himself is privy to. We'll speak again soon enough. You might want to keep this around." He flicks the pendant floating at the base of my necklace. I've worn the protective hedge, The Eye of Refuge, off and on over the last two years, mostly along with the mirrored heart Logan gifted me for my birthday years ago, but I unceremoniously plucked that one off this morning before I donned the piece. I'm not feeling the love like I once did. I couldn't bring myself to wear that mirrored heart—not with its proclamation of his love written on the side of it. Not after what I witnessed last night.

"Why do I need this, Marshall?" I glare at him a moment. I'm so damned tired of being left in the dark.

Oh, Skyla. He closes his eyes a moment. "Good night." He bows to Gage a moment before ditching out into the icy night air.

Barron and Emma head over.

"Good night, you two." Barron offers the hint of a sad smile. "Skyla, we look forward to seeing you tomorrow."

Emma gives a curt lift of the hand as they head out the door, and Mia is quick to bolt after them. I'm sure it's to see her new boy toy who is not actually a boy. Rev is closer to my age than he ever is hers. He's Dr. Booth's renegade of a son—sort of a wannabe biker bad boy only I'm not so sure he's a wannabe.

"Good night," I say as I take the boys from Gage. "I'd better get them to bed."

"I'll help you," he says it more as a fact than a general offer, and something about his commanding demeanor all night sends my rage factor soaring one hundred Femtastic points.

"No." It comes out cold, unfeeling, and I don't like this new version of myself, of us.

"*Skyla.*" Gage leans in with that toxic cologne of his. I know the exact one, the blue water that sits in a bottle above his old desk in his old room. Gage's bedroom at his parents' house is untouched even though he's lived with me for the last year and a half. Last night was our first night apart, and tonight will mark the second. I hope he's ready to have the bed to himself for a good long while because I'm about to rain down a hailstorm of long and lonely nights. "It's Christmas." His brows plead as only they know how. "Let me stay. We can work this out later. I just want to be close to the boys." He cradles the back of Barron's head with his hand so tenderly my bones ache straight to the marrow.

Emily comes over with that dead expression she wears like a haunted mask. Her midnight hair sits in a tumble of curls knotted at the top of her head. Over the years, Emily and I have established a friendship of sorts. Kind of.

"I have a vision for you," she says, depleted of any enthusiasm.

"*No*," both Gage and I say in unison with the matching fervor required to reject whatever horror awaits us on the other side of that twisted prophecy. Em's visions never bode well for me in general.

She cracks the hint of a smile. "That was good." She starts back toward the living room. "Doesn't matter. It'll happen anyway."

The boys begin to squirm, and I start in on a slow bounce before heading for the stairs. The medics wheel a howling Tad out the door, and my mother runs screaming after them.

"*Skyla*"—Gage slices my name out sharp as a razor, and I catch both Logan and Liam glancing over from the living room—"you will be there tomorrow. I want a family picture next to the tree."

I will be there? I *will*? Who is this dominating man barking out orders as if I were actually inclined to follow them. An incredulous huff gets locked in my throat at this familial command that involves a half-dead evergreen.

"Is that so?" My eyes round out with fury. "I want things, too, Gage." I lean in, seething with a fury I can no longer contain. "I want a husband who would never dream of betraying me, who would never nail the coffin shut on our marriage without even telling me." A rush of adrenaline takes over as I struggle to catch my breath, and the boys suddenly feel heavy as iron. "Don't you tell me what to do and when to do it. That will never fly." A part of me feels victorious for getting all those venomous words out sans the use of a single expletive. Now that the boys are here, I'm changing all of my corrosive ways, sharpening my honor, spit-shining my soul just to be the best person I can for them—unlike some people. I glare openly at the man I love. "I took my beating heart and sewed it onto yours. You had me. You had all of me. And what did you do? You vomited us up at Demetri's feet. The very idea makes my head spin with rage. Don't you think you're getting away with this. Don't think for a minute you will ever be the victor. Try anything and I will cut the ground from underneath you."

The air stiffens between us. An uncomfortable fury snakes around us like a noose.

"You will be there tomorrow." His eyes widen with something just this side of anger. "We will take a family picture." His voice is stern, commanding. This is a new side of Gage that I have never seen before, expectant, demeaning, and as much as I hate it, that sweet spot between my thighs starts to quiver.

I speed my way up the stairs with the boys in tow as they writhe—their anxious whimpers turning into a full throttle cry as if they hated what's happened just as much as I do. No sooner do I get into my bedroom than I slam the door behind me and bolt each and every lock.

The boys wail away, on this, their very first Christmas Eve, and tears stream down my face right along with them.

No, there will be nothing silent about this holy night.

Gage

There have been two nights in my life that I have treasured equally above and beyond any other. The first, my wedding night with Skyla. I had dreamed of what it would be like, holding her, making her mine—body and soul, and that night surpassed every dream I knit in my imagination. The second was the birth of my boys, twins—one arrived on Skyla's birthday, and the other just a few minutes later on my own birthday. Skyla, Nathan, and Barron are my world, my universe, my life. So when it came down to brass tacks and I needed to either pass down a curse to one of my children—Barron I suspected for reasons that revolved around his birth in particular—or keep the curse for myself, I did the only thing a true father would do—I sacrificed my life so that my sons, my wife, could live in peace. But in doing so, I've unleashed a fresh hell that will ensure none of us will truly live in unity. The curse is harrowing any way you slice it, and right about now it's slicing my heart into a million irreparable slivers.

This would have been the third greatest night of my life, the first Christmas with my boys. Yes, I will see them in the morning, but what I wanted, what I needed deep down inside was to be in that bed with Skyla when the clock struck twelve. We would hold the boys between us, safe in our holy huddle. But Demetri had cast a pall on me—or rather I had cast it on myself. The curse in its entirety was made possible by my own decision to break faith with the Barricade—the very shit sandwich that I will root for, run, and enjoy posthumously. Yes, I have drunk the blood of a Celestra—my Celestra, Skyla—and entered into a covenant with my own demented lineage. I am a Fem. I am the sole—*soul*—proprietor of the curse I have brought upon myself. And in effect, I have become Skyla's enemy. Or at least that's Demetri's hopeful trajectory of things to come. I have plans of my own, and none of them involve hurting my wife or her people. I'm holding onto hope like the slippery string of a helium balloon. And God Almighty help me, I will fight this curse tooth and nail. I will buck against destiny and fate and claw my way through life to remain loyal and loving toward the woman I married. Her people are my people. Her cause is my cause. Celestra must remain in power. The Countenance and their vindictive ploys for domination are vile and wicked, and I could never succumb to those evil ideals. They are not mine. I do not hold them.

I watch the gaping hole at the top of the stairs, hoping that Skyla will have a change of heart—that she'll reappear and welcome me back to our bed, our life, but no such luck. Instead, I turn to find Demetri with his cool as a rotten to the core cucumber ever-passive grin.

"I'll be accompanying Lizbeth to the hospital. Should I message you with your father-in-law's prognosis regardless of the hour?"

"Yes." It comes out terse without meaning to. I have a feeling it will be that way for a very long time to come with this father of mine. I'm nothing more than a means to an end to him. It's Barron, the father who raised me, who shows me what true unconditional love is. Barron was just as pleased with me when I was a do-nothing Levatio without clout or standing in any of the Factions, let alone the Fems. And now that he knows I'm wrought from pure evil, he loves me just the same. "Text me regardless. Tell Lizbeth if she needs anything, I'm here." Lizbeth loves me. She adores me. And she might just be my way back into Skyla's heart.

Demetri leans in with those dark, empty eyes, and I can feel his mind taking ahold of my own like an iron hand. "You are loved, Gage Edinger. You are my prized creation, and you are most adored—and soon, you will be worshiped as well." He stalks off into the night and bursts into a vaporous fog before his feet ever hit the porch.

Logan nods to me from the living room, and I head over to say good night.

"I'm taking off." I give a quick glance around. "Where's Wes?"

"It's just me—unless they have a bed in the place everyone else is gone. Wes practically took Chloe by the ear. He's demanding to know what has Skyla acting so strange. She gave Chloe a *gift*." He cocks his head as if waiting for me to somehow quantify that.

"Dude, I do not know what the hell is going on." My heart thumps out an unnatural rhythm as if speaking to me in Morse code. "See if you can get close." I tick my head toward the charred stairs. "She loves you. She needs someone to lean on right now." A knot the size of that crooked Christmas tree builds in my throat, and it's painful as hell to get the next few words out. "Until she will hear me out—until she opens her heart back up to me, be a friend." There. I said friend. Logan has never been good at being just a friend to Skyla, and if he were to cross that line again— albeit the last time he crossed that line it was with Chloe pretending to be Skyla—I wouldn't interfere. In my mind and heart, I'm already as good as dead. What I did last night was throw dirt on my own coffin. Skyla knows it. I know it. And Logan knows it, too. It's his time to shine, and quite frankly, it doesn't matter where I point the damn finger anymore. It seems as if this train of destruction I'm on cannot and will not be stopped.

Logan pushes out a dry smile that dissipates faster than it stays. "I'm a friend to you both." His eyes darken as he presses into me with his gaze. "You are both more than my friends. You are both my family. I will and *have* died for you. I'm not some replacement of yours waiting in line, Gage. I don't want you weeping into your pillow, lamenting all that could have been with the woman you love—the woman who bore your children. She is your *wife*, Gage." He says *wife* so caustic and fast it sounds like *knife*. Right now, knife feels a bit more accurate—the blade protruding from my aching, bleeding, weeping heart is indeed Skyla. But I'm the one that planted her there. I take full responsibility for this fiasco. "Do not give up." He softens. "Do you hear me? Or does that thick head of hair prevent you from listening to the truth? Fight." He smacks me hard on the arm.

A ripe anger burns through me like a flash fire. "I *am* fighting." It takes everything in me to grit the words out. "I'm fucking fighting with more than I have to offer. Yes, I'm fighting for my wife. But I'm fighting for my boys, too. She has to understand that."

"And she will. You and I will work hard to make sure she hears the truth and understands that your arms were tied."

A dull huff of laughter pinches through the pain. "I sound like a pussy."

"A pussy would have let his own kid take the fall." He slaps me over the back as Mia and Melissa come screaming in with excitement, shouting something about it being midnight and that all presents from Santa are fair game. "Let's get out of here, dude."

Logan and I walk out into the navy velvet night. The sky is marbled with a mixture of boiling clouds and fog—not a star in the sky is able to make an appearance. A storm is brewing overhead, one that my mother swore earlier would be one for the ages. Just as we're about to part ways, the sky lights up with apocalyptic promise as lightning decorates the heavens in a show of electrifying brilliance. The sky growls and roars, but I'd swear on my quickly waning life that

Paragon just growled back with all the scathing anger that Skyla happens to hold.

"Holy shit." Logan laughs as he glances upward. "How about I head home with you? We'll hang out and watch a movie until Santa shows up." He gives a little wink. Logan knows this is destined to be a shit night for me.

Before I can answer, my phone buzzes in my hand, and I'm hopeful as an orphan on adoption day that Skyla is calling me back—back to our bed, back to our life. But it's not Skyla. It's a text from my father.

"Shit," I mutter under my breath, and the sky lights up in another show of glory. An uncharacteristically warm breeze wafts by, and both Logan and I glance at one another as if it might mean something. "I'll take a rain check on that movie. The refrigeration unit is out at the morgue. I'd better head over and wait for the repairman."

"You want company?"

"Nope. Go wait for Santa. Giselle's at the house tonight. That means Ellis will be pawing at her in the living room. Make sure they keep it G."

"Will do." Logan takes off, and I wait until his taillights disappear before climbing in my own truck. I lean forward and try to catch a glimpse of light coming from Skyla's bedroom window, but there's none. Not that there would be. Skyla and I have gotten used to operating under moonlight in hopes to keep the boys asleep, not that they believe in sleeping. Our own sleep cycles have become sort of a theory or fond memory at this point. "Come on, Skyla," I whisper, willing her to call me, but Skyla doesn't call. I glare at the road all the way to the morgue.

The Paragon Mortuary is the pride and joy of my

father, my proper father, Barron Oliver. Perhaps that's an exaggeration. My sister and I are his pride and joy, and I'm pretty sure Logan is included in that equation. My boys are his pride and joy as well, but, yes, the morgue is far more a family member than it ever is a business. He worked here right after completing his degree in mortuary sciences, then went on with school until he received his doctoral degree. Eventually, he was able to purchase this haunt filled with rotting bodies along with the surrounding land. My father is a brilliant man, and of all of the brilliant things he could be spending his time doing, he insists on hanging out with the dead.

The morgue is designed to look like a replica of the White House, miniaturized of course, and brimming with corpses. You wouldn't think we would get much business on the island, but even the neighboring islands have been burying their dead here for years. The cemetery in the back is owned and operated by my father as well, acres and acres of death and dying. It seems death has been my destiny all along, not only in the sense that it's a once in a lifetime opportunity for every living soul, but it's the way the souls in my family happen to make a living.

The sky crackles with brilliance, blinking on and off as if the light switch in the sky were broken. A lion-sized roar envelops the island, and the ground shakes with ferocity.

"*Shit*," I hiss, getting out of the truck just as the sky overturns those heavy tar-colored clouds like a bucket and the world is drenched in an instant. Paragon craves rain the way humans demand oxygen. Sickles fall from above as I make a run for the building, and the sky lights up again like a torch. I pause a moment, admiring the sheer elegance of this spider web of light descending from the heavens. A spiraling bolt touches down over the crematorium, and the entire building lights up like an x-ray. "Holy shit," I mutter as the sky blackens again, and I dive into the morgue for shelter.

"Hello?" I shout as I bolt the door locked behind me. It's what I always shout when I'm alone in this haunted hotel, because for one, it gives me the fucking creeps to be here sans another living being.

"What's up?" a friendly male voice calls from the back, followed by the clip clop of heavy footsteps in this general direction. I half-expect to find Wes here. He's been interning with my father, studying corpses as if he's about to write a thesis on the subject—if only Wesley would harness his wicked intentions toward a literary pursuit. The thought makes me want to laugh.

But it's not Wes. It's Rev, Dr. Booth's son who's been getting down and dirty with Skyla's little sister, Mia, as of late. I frown openly at him for that reason alone. Mia is like my own little sister, and I hate that this roughed-up wannabe biker is her new physical obsession.

"What's going on?" I'm only half-concerned to see him here. Rev, Revelyn, has taken a paying position as a morgue attendant, something a notch up from the intern he too used to be.

"I was about to leave when that damn fridge went on the fritz again. I called Al at The Big Chill. He'll be here in about twenty minutes." Rev is a bit on the beady-eyed side, with a face full of dark unshaven scruff and short fuzzy hair to match. He's cut and lean, so I kind of get Mia's budding obsession. He's the bad boy to her good girl. And as much as Skyla and I hate to see it happen, it's already happening whether or not we like it.

"Thanks. What were you doing here?" I'm only half-curious. Honestly, if this dude has some sick obsession with the freshly deceased, I'm not sure I want to know. On second thought...

"Hospital called and wanted to ship out a body, so your dad asked if I could cover. It should arrive any moment." He nods me toward the back, and we start making our way to the prep laboratory—otherwise known as the kitchen. "How'd Christmas go? Get everything your heart desires? I bet your daddy really comes through on checking that list, purchasing everything twice. Must be nice to be loaded." He belts out a caw of a laugh.

"What the hell are you talking about? Your father is the best psychiatrist on the island, and I'm betting he hauls twice as much as my father on a good day." I'm betting half of Rev's behaviors stem from the fact he's spoiled rotten.

"I'm not talking about Barron." He gives a dark chuckle as we enter the bowels of the prep station, and a red light blinks in a spasm, alerting us that we have a very dead visitor at the other end of that wall. I open the back—a glorified garage door that scrolls toward the celling with a yawn, and the EMTs waste no time wheeling in a body. Rev pulls back the sheet, revealing a girl, carly twenties maybe, long red hair, skin as pale blue as the western sky, lips black as coal.

Rev signs off on the paperwork, and as soon as the transport team takes off, I shut the door again, stopping the torrential downpour from making its way inside.

"Go ahead and take off, man," I say, helping Rev secure her to the gurney as we wheel her toward the defunct refrigeration unit. "I'll get her in a drawer. Wish your dad a Merry Christmas for me."

"Will do." Rev shoves his clipboard my way. "And tell your dad I said the same—Demetri, in the event you're wondering which one. He's the loaded one, remember?" He gives a slight wink before disappearing back through the kitchen, whistling an eerie tune that I happen to recognize—the theme to *M*A*S*H*, "Suicide is Painless". *M*A*S*H* is some old seventies TV show my father still tries to catch now and again. I've never cared much for the theme song.

A burst of lightning infiltrates the room, and an explosion shatters one of the windows facing the northern wall. The frenzied sound of glass crashing to the floor enlivens every one of my frayed nerves.

"*Shit.*" I jump back, sending the gurney over, right along with the body. "*Fuck.*" A peal of thunder so loud roars through the cavernous room, causing every single drawer behind me to rattle open a few good inches. I reach back and snap them all closed in an effort to keep the bodies as cool as possible. "Holy hell." I swing the gurney back to its upright position, and the poor girl's arms flail like dying fish.

Another round of lightning hits, and this time the lights in the kitchen dim down to pitch.

"Brown out. Just fucking great." I turn my phone into a flashlight just as the room trembles with another viral growl of thunder. "Sounds like a bag of cats on fire," I whisper, reaching for the clipboard that has sailed across the floor. It's time to tag and bag this poor girl. I need to get home— somehow get to Skyla so I can see my boys on Christmas morning the way I've been dreaming of.

A dull moan comes from behind, and I freeze. I glance out the window for a hint of lightning, but it's black as coal. It was probably just the rain. It's coming down like hammers out there.

Another dull moan comes from behind, and this time I pivot on my heels, my heart doing its best to leap from my chest.

"Hello?" I call out and my voice echoes. The lights flicker back on for a moment before dimming once again. "Anybody there?"

A sharp cry gurgles from the body in front of me.

"*Holy*—" I reach forward and snatch the thin sheet off

the corpse and do my best to unbuckle her from the metal bed as fast as I can. The girl lurches and vomits bile onto the floor in green soupy chunks. "Oh shit." I fumble with my phone. "I'll call for help." Only my fingers can't seem to navigate the numbers.

"No, don't!" she calls out with a strangled cry. "Call my mother." She tips her head as far off the gurney as possible and another waterfall of vomit splatters all over the place, wetting down the shins of my pants in the process.

I call 911 and shout an entire litany of obscenities into the phone while smacking the door open to the back of the facility for two very good reasons—one, it smells like the foulest puke I have ever had the displeasure to be around—and two, a fucking corpse just sprung back to life.

"It's okay." I try to soothe her while helping her sit up. Her face enlivens with color, that unearthly blue hue still lingers around her eyes. She's pretty in a Goth-I've-just-come-back-from-the-dead sort of way. Her dark reddish hair is matted in the back, and her eyes shine a kaleidoscope of green and brown. "What's your name?" I pull the clipboard forward to see if there are any outstanding details I can glean from it.

She grunts something unintelligible that sounds like *Audra* and spits onto the floor. "I need water."

I rush over and fill a cup from the tap before giving it to her.

The name on the clipboard reads Melody Winters. Not a match by a long shot. Shit. Looks as if the hospital fucked up big time.

"What happened?" She looks around at the facility with a dizzying grin springing to her lips as her legs swing over the side of the gurney. "I was dead, wasn't I?" The idea seems to have her elated. "My God, this is going to be great." Her affect sobers as she turns to me. "How old would you say I am?"

I check the clipboard. "It says here you're twenty-two."

"Ah!" She lets out an inebriated sort of a laugh. "What a magnificent age!" She jabs her finger into her mouth. "Good God! I've got all me teeth!"

Me teeth?

"What year is it?" she hisses it out markedly less friendly, far more like a command, and something about her in general is setting me on edge.

"What year do you think it is?"

"Don't you get fresh with me." She scowls a moment before winking as if she were suddenly in the mood to flirt. "And what the hell kind of a candle is that in your hand?"

"It's my phone." Everything about this chick is off by a cadaverous mile. The sharp wail of an ambulance cuts through the storm, and I've never been happier to hear that sound. I'm tired. It's Christmas. And for the love of God, this poor girl needs her head examined. She might have survived whatever tried to off her, but it's clear her brain is a bit scrambled at the moment.

Her head juts forward as she tries to sneak a glance at it. "What exactly is a phone?"

And there it is. Maybe I should have kept Rev here a little longer after all. At least with him there's an iota of a psychiatric connection, and this girl is in need of all things psychiatric. Poor girl—*lucky* girl all things considering.

"Don't worry about it, sweetie. You've had a rough night. I'm sure once they get your fluids back to normal, you'll be right as rain."

The EMTs rush in and transfer her to their own gurney, and she gives a wild wave, laughing and applauding as they wheel her back into the night.

"I'm sorry, kind sir!" she shouts over to me. "I don't believe I caught your name."

Ellis Harrison, I want to say. "Gage Oliver!" Integrity wins out every single time. Although Skyla might not agree with that one.

I hose off the vomit from the kitchen floor and take off once big Al shows up with his refrigeration crew. He lets me know there will be a special after hours charge for Christmas Eve, on top of the special after hours charge he usually fucks us with. And I assure him it's not a problem.

In truth, I'm getting used to being screwed on Christmas.

I head home, taking my clothes and shoes off on the side of the house before tossing them straight into the trash bin. For a moment, I let Paragon wash my naked body with her tears. I raise my hands to the sky, lean my head back, and drink down her fury, icy and harsh before teleporting to my bathroom into a waiting hot shower. This has been one hell of a long night, and once I get dressed, it's about to get longer.

In theory, I have always been a genetic mutation. A mash-up of human and angel lineage blended together to form a creature with powers that humans can only dream to have. I had about a third of these powers growing up, if that. When I was about seven, my parents, my mother and my only father at the time, sat both Logan and me down, explaining to each of us what made us so special. My blood had cemented me into the Levatio standing, or so we thought. And Logan, raised as my cousin, in truth my uncle, had a very peculiar strain of this celestial disease. He belongs to the Celestra Faction, a smidge of Countenance thrown in for good wicked measure. Celestra is a rare, quickly dying breed with far more power and status than the other five Factions. My mother holds strong blood ties to the Deorsum Faction. She has a way to make weak-minded individuals do her bidding. I'm guessing she wishes Skyla were weak-minded. Others might argue she is, but Skyla is stealth, strong-minded and strong-willed, case in point her insistence to have nothing to do with me at the moment. Normally I would accept this. Normally I would give her all of the time and space she needs, but this is no normal night, and I can feel both my time and space on this planet quickly drawing to a close.

That stone Candace gifted Skyla at the christening comes back to haunt me. Damn witch.

The sky electrifies in a show of prowess, and the entire house shakes as Skyla's mother growls over Paragon like a tiger with her tail on fire.

The stone boasts of my final countdown. That number has etched itself inside my eyelids. A round number that essentially is useless because it doesn't let us know if it were seconds, weeks, months, or years we were dealing with—but the options are whittling away rather quickly. Even if it were years, it still doesn't give me nearly enough time to spend with those I love.

I slap Skyla's favorite cologne over my neck, pull on my old sweats that Skyla claims she can't keep her hands off because they're soft as rain—her words, not mine—and check myself in the mirror while combing back my hair. I would do anything, alter myself in just about any manner to have Skyla accept me, keep me, beg me to stay. I'd morph my features to match Logan's if I knew it'd please her.

I sharpen my gaze in the mirror and will myself to do just that. A slow stretching, a warming of the flesh, and just like that, Logan Oliver is staring back at me.

"Son of a bitch," I whisper and close my eyes, demanding my own features fall back into place. No sooner do I open my eyes than there I am.

Yes. I am no longer a Levatio of humble, low standing. I am Demetri Edinger's son, a Fem through and through, my mother's own blood nearly insignificant to my cellular structure. I glare at myself a moment.

There is one solid truth I know for sure. Skyla could never hate me as much as I hate myself.

The room, my inglorious reflection, all dissipate in a powder blue fog. I'm deteriorating, evaporating, heading to Skyla's house old school—via teleportation. Ah, those old Levatio days. How I do miss them.

Skyla's room—our bedroom, materializes around me in blinks and seizures. Bed or closet, bed or closet, this far in the game I usually have my destination mapped out, but at the moment my head screams closet—do not blink to life next to her naked body. But my heart, my balls, they both scream for me to do exactly that.

The warmth of Skyla's body, the cushioned down of that all too soft mattress we've completely broken in—it seems my heart and my balls won out. They usually do.

Skyla rolls over and her eyes blink open like that of a doll, a quiet click. Those pale sky born eyes burn over my flesh and sear me with their wrath.

"Why are you here?" Her breath warms me with its minty scent, and my lips twitch to something just this side of a smile. She didn't claw my eyes out, so that right there has to be a pretty good sign.

"I belong here." It might be bold of me to say so, but it's true. It takes everything in me not to run my fingers through that blonde mane of hers. Skyla's hair is an entity all to itself.

Her mouth opens before compressing shut tight. The moon washes over her features, and Skyla glows like an emerging sunrise.

"You're so beautiful." My finger traces over her cheek, smooth as velvet. Skyla is perfection, quite literally, thanks to her mother. Candace Messenger ensured her daughter's beauty, her sparkle, that spitfire that loves to cork to the surface more often than not. I'm in love with her, with each and every facet of the jewel that lies beside me.

"Smooth." She reaches up and catches my finger as if insinuating that my words, my *thoughts*, were catering to her ability to read my mind.

"Every word is true as God."

She gives a slight nod, her lips bowing to the tip of my finger, and I close my eyes a moment with that simple kiss. I can't help but note the fact she's still wearing her wedding ring, and everything in me soars with hope.

The boys squirm and grunt at the same time and begin in on a choir of quiet brays. Skyla reaches over and picks up Barron, and I scoop Nathan into my arms. Her blouse falls open as she lays Barron to her breast, and I give her Nathan so he can latch on as well. Skyla doesn't prefer to feed them at the same time. She likes the one-on-one experience, but at night when she's bone-tired, she gives in and lets them take all they want so she can catch a decent wink before the sun cracks the horizon.

I scoot in close and brazenly wrap an arm around her, landing my palm over Barron's warm head of hair. My other hand lands over Nathan's back, and I soak in the rhythm of this beautiful family God has gifted me.

"I want to say my peace." The words swim around the room like a haunted whisper.

Skyla looks up, the whites of her eyes flashing with a refreshed level of rage.

Her hand shifts from Barron's side, landing her finger over my lips. Even in this repressed light, Skyla is an undeniable work of art. I can't drink her in fast enough, her perfect bow tie lips, the full curves of her body.

"I love you," I say before playfully biting down on her finger. "I promise, I will never be your enemy." My eyes linger over hers as a morbid sorrow blankets the room. "I will love you forever."

Tears moisten her eyes, cutting through the moonlight like shards of glass. "Get out."

And there it is. I knew those words were coming. With Skyla, you either feel the love or not—and tonight she's decided to unceremoniously give me the boot. I lean over and place a kiss to each of the boys in turn.

"Merry Christmas." I lean in to kiss her goodbye, and she turns away, landing my lips to the edge of her jawline. "I'll see you at my parents' house." I flick her ear gently with my finger, and she flinches with a frown already pointed my way. "We're taking a picture as a family."

And I leave.

"A reanimation?" My sister's eyes bulge with delight at the idea.

It's ten after three, the time my mother deemed a perfect hour for Christmas dinner, and she's already scowling at me from across the living room because Skyla is holding up her party. I don't really see the problem. There's not much of a party—just Liam, his main squeeze, Michelle Miller, Ellis and Giselle, me and nobody. I asked Logan to head over to the Landon house and help bring Skyla and the boys over, but that was over an hour ago.

"Dude." Ellis shudders. "If a corpse puked on me, I'd effing puke right back."

"I came close." There's the truth.

Dad clears his throat, obviously not as riveted by my

tales of the crypt as G and Ellis. "I've dealt with the authorities twice this morning. One would hope they're grilling the staff at the emergency room far more efficiently than they are me." He glides his glasses back up his nose absentmindedly. It's a habit of his that has always endeared me to him, and now that Demetri has put a dent in our special bond, I appreciate Barron, my true father, all that much more. "It's as if they're blaming me for bringing the dead back to life."

Mom huffs, adjusting the Battenberg lace apron tied to her waist. She's emulating a 1950s housewife to a T tonight—long wool dress, a string of iridescent pearls floating around her neck, bright holiday red lipstick, and her hair pinched in a neat bun. My mother is a powerhouse of a businesswoman with the most successful and largest daycare center on the island. She's a master cook, master baker, and runs a household like a boss. The only thing she can't seem to do is find a soft spot in her heart for the woman I love.

"They should be so lucky we could resurrect a soul or two." Mom scowls at the thought. "The next thing you know, they'll be slapping us with fines for housing sick individuals against their will! And just you wait—those feds that are crawling all around the island like a small army will be knocking on your door soon enough. I've got a good mind to put a sign out there, *do not knock lest ye wake the dead*."

Giselle chortles at my mother's attempt at humor, and a brisk knock erupts over the front door on cue.

I half-expect it to be the feds. My mother is right. Paragon is infested with government workers forced to take a break from their own holiday festivities in search of Moser and Killion. Those two aforementioned feds were slaughtered by a hungry Spectator in the woods behind Demetri's estate the night of the christening. As much as

Coop promised to clean up the place, you have to figure it's laced with enough DNA to rouse the suspicion of any government agency.

I follow my father to the door as Christmas carols dance lightly through the air. Not the raucous old-school cheerful carols of last night at the Landons', but a far more demure instrumental version that only the discerning ear could tag as a familiar holiday tune. Everything about this house is demure in contrast to last night's fiasco. Not that Lizbeth's decorating skills are a fiasco. They're bright and happy, and that's the exact environment I'd like my sons to grow up in. My mother's décor leans toward Christmas art deco, more of the idea of the holiday in hues of white and silver than actually any hard evidence of the jolly elf himself. There isn't anything here that screams Christmas sans the crystal white tree in the living room. That plastic wonder is carefully festooned with enough bright red ribbons and bulbs to make up for the rest of the monochromatic holiday theme.

Mom swings the door open with a frown, but quickly bounces a smile on her lips.

"Kresley, one of my favorite girls!" She leans in and offers a hearty embrace to the tall brunette at the door. I have never heard her reference Skyla as her favorite anything. "You do look lovely. Merry Christmas, sweetheart. *Gage*—help Kresley in. I need to tend to the kitchen."

"Gage Oliver!" Kresley presses that lustful gaze of hers my way before lunging in for a hug and latching on for dear life. Kres is Wesley's old girlfriend. She's pretty in an aggressive pile on too much war paint kind of way. But it's her personality that's a solid turn-off for me. She's a take them by the balls, hold no prisoners kind of a girl. And unfortunately for me, it's my balls she's after these days.

"Merry Christmas. Can't breathe." I choke out that last

word exaggeratingly so, but I'd lie, cheat, and steal just to get Kresley the hell off me.

The minivan pulls up in the driveway with Logan behind the wheel, and I catch Skyla already glaring at me from over Kresley's shoulder.

Shit. I pull away and manage to pluck myself free while scooping up the packages on the porch beside Kres.

"You are a hero!" She beams. "Mellie Winters is Grayson's roommate's sister." She gives a curt nod as if I should understand any of the lunacy she spouted. "And boy are you ever the talk of the island right now."

Skyla comes up quickly with a car seat in her arms before I can ask what the hell that was about, and I land the packages in the foyer so I can assist her.

Kresley tags along down the porch as Paragon kisses us with an urgent peppering of light rain. "She says you gave her mouth-to-mouth, held her hand until authorities arrived, and then gave her your number. She said you gave her *life* again. That's incredible! Is it because, you *know*, you have Demetri's blood in you?"

Skyla grunts as she dodges past the two of us. "I don't even want to know."

"I didn't give her my number," I shout after Skyla and take Barron still nestled in his car seat from Logan. "Thanks, man." I pull him in quickly. Logan smells thick with cologne, and something about that simple act of hygiene makes my stomach churn. Logan smells good, looks great, and is dressed to the nines. Skyla and I are out of bounds, so that leaves—

"I chatted you up all the way here, man." He slaps me over the back, and I give a wry smile as we head into the warmth of the house. It takes minimal skin-on-skin contact for Logan to read my thoughts, and yet it never seems to be on my mind. It's a gift both Skyla and he share, along with their Celestra lineage. Skyla and Logan have always had it all in common, and the Treble Candace gifted him only seems to have brought them closer together. Skyla and I only seem to drift farther apart.

Mom quickly excavates baby Barron from his restraint and raises him in the air, his legs still curled under him from the nap on the ride over.

I speed into the living room to find everyone on their feet, greeting the boys first and foremost. Skyla's hair looks a bit wild the way it does when she first wakes up in the morning, and my bones ache to witness that firsthand once again. Her eyes are bloodshot, and she has bags underneath them large enough to stuff both Nathan and Barron inside. I'd do anything to lighten her load, help her out when she needs it most all night long.

"I didn't give anyone my phone number," I reiterate while attempting to pull her into a hug, but she lunges at Ellis instead. "Certainly not a girl."

The room quiets down, and it's all eyes on me.

"Just clarifying." I nod toward Skyla, and my father gives an iffy thumbs-up.

Kresley clutches onto my arm, her tits trembling out of her all too exposed cleavage, and I take a full step back because I refuse to fall into the titty trap Kresley has set out for me.

"You're talking about Mellie, right?" Kresley is still enthralled with this, I can tell. Her arms latch over mine once again as if it were simply a magnetic response.

"Yes." I carefully pluck myself free, my eyes still sealed over Skyla. "There was a corpse at the morgue, only she wasn't a corpse. I knocked the gurney over, and she started to puke. The next thing I know, the paramedics are taking her back to the hospital. End of story."

"That's quite the whale of a tale." Skyla smacks her

lips, not looking the slightest bit amused.

"She was in a car wreck, Skyla." Kresley is quick to admonish the love of my life. "Her family thought they lost her—on Christmas Eve of all nights. Can you imagine?"

"I refuse to," Mom chimes in, still happily rocking Barron. "I'm just glad there was a Christmas miracle after all. There's nothing more painful than losing a child." She offers a stern look to Giselle as if it were her fault she was run over by a car—and it might have been. "But I also know the blessing of getting her back. I'll have to send the Winters family a muffin basket."

"Muffins, huh?" Skyla muses while glancing to Michelle. "I'll have to remember that for the next reanimation."

Giselle clicks her tongue. "I *knew* it was a reanimation. Santa wouldn't let anyone die on Christmas Eve. He practically has to do a Christmas miracle. It's in the Bible."

"And on that note!" Mom hands Barron back to me. "It's time to say grace. Dinner is getting cold."

Skyla and I place the babies back into their car seats and set them a few feet from the table where we can keep an eye on them. They're both fast asleep. Two miniature versions of myself sleeping and passing gas as they please. It looks like heaven, really. As nice as it is to have a peaceful meal, I'd prefer they scream their vocal cords right out of their throats now rather than at what Skyla and I have dubbed the witching hour. As much as I hated not sleeping with my family last night, as soon as I popped back into my old room, I drank down every glorious moment of shut-eye as if it were the finest wine, exotic, expensive, far too precious to guzzle all at once. And that's exactly why I feel so bad for Skyla. The lack of sleep we've undergone is criminal, inhumane. It holds the power to make you insane. And if you wanted to get down to some psychological basics, it's certainly played a factor in the madness that's taken over our lives as of late. I'm not blaming my new covenant with my father on sleeplessness, but certainly how I've handled just about every situation has been skewed by having my better judgment rendered useless.

Dinner drags on with incremental conversation regarding the refrigeration unit at the morgue and my mother's own Christmas memories.

Mom points to me with a cube of steak on the edge of her fork. "Now that you're a parent, you'll have to steep the boys full of your own Christmas traditions."

"Now that *you're* a parent?" Skyla whispers mostly to herself as if she's still trying to process the slight. It would have been nice if my mother pluralized the noun.

"Of course"—Mom wags her bloody square of bovine toward the fireplace—"I've started you off in the right direction. I stayed up hand stitching those stockings for the boys last night. I used the exact felt and thread I used on yours all those years ago. I saved it for just this occasion."

I glance back at the fireplace housing a happy row of stockings. Mom, Dad, Giselle, Logan, and Liam are off to the right, and to the far left, Nathan and Barron sit next to my own stocking. I glance to Skyla and catch the heavy look of hurt weighing down her features.

"I'm sure you're still working on Skyla's." I give a tight smile to my mother.

But Skyla scoffs and waves the idea off before she can answer. "Save it, Gage. You and I both know that will never happen."

"Then I'll take them all down." My words come out a little louder, a little harsher than I meant for them, and Logan shakes his head as if begging me to make a U-turn.

Liam grunts. "What's going on at that end of the table? Quit your clamoring. Hold it together for the kids, would you?" He moans through a mouthful of food, and I take a moment to glare at him. Liam has been lucky with the ladies ever since he stepped foot on Paragon, and now he seems to be lucky in love with Michelle Miller, an odd combination considering her infatuation with Logan, not to mention Liam's facial proximity to his. They could be twins. But I'll let it ride. What I won't let ride is someone who hasn't even experienced a hiccup when it comes to matters of the heart sit there and tell me to hold it together when he has no clue regarding half the shit Skyla and I have gone through.

"I'll quit my clamoring." Skyla picks up her glass as if toasting him, but her eyes settle on mine with sharp intent. "I'm quitting a lot of things."

"Well"—Mom balks as if it's her place to do so—"we'll be discussing my son's right to those children with a prized attorney. Ellis, put your mother on standby. I won't let a little hus—"

"*Enough*," I roar so loud the cutlery trembles, and the boys both let out a sharp gasp and start in on a hacking cry. Skyla and I dive over them and scoop them into our arms without thinking twice. We may not see eye to eye at the moment, but we are a united front when it comes to our children.

Giselle taps a knife to her wine glass, and the room quiets down with the steady chiming. Even the boys seem to fall back to sleep as Skyla and I rock them.

"I know exactly what would make everyone feel better." She giggles through each word. Giselle might be in her late teens, in her senior year of high school—no thanks to Emerson Kragger's body, but her mind and spirit are still very much her preschool self. "*Presents!*" she shrieks so loud the boys are right back to crying again. Dinner is quickly abandoned as we retreat to the living room—mostly I think people are trying to escape the noise. Who knew two tiny beings could house such dynamic pipes?

Logan dons the Santa hat along with my dad, and before we know it, everyone has a small pile of gifts at their feet. Skyla and I have the bulk—which judging by the cartoon-inspired wrapping paper, I'm guessing they're all for the boys.

Mom insists we do the traditional rounds—one each, oldest to youngest, so it takes forever to get to Nathan and Barron.

"Go ahead." I nudge Skyla to tear one open, but she's quick to shake her head, that pinched frown of hers never leaving her face.

"I'll do it!" Giselle volunteers and dives right in. "It's a toy!" she squeals. "It's an aquarium that plays music! And when the lights go off, the fish swim *and* glow." She clutches it to her chest, her elations quickly replaced with distress. "I must have this," she pleads to Skyla with large watery eyes. Giselle is a stunner, a sweetheart with a strong will who seems to be faring well enough in the world. Although, at this moment I'm a bit afraid to see her so attached to a toy designed for a newborn. "I love fish! And I'm afraid of the dark. Oh please, oh please, let me keep it!"

"Sure." Skyla doesn't seem to mind at all. It has always warmed me how much Skyla cares for my sister.

"That's actually from me." Mom raises her brows as if this were of concern. "Giselle, all gifts for the boys that are from your father and me will remain at this house. God knows they have enough mishmash at the Landons'. I'll see about getting you a replacement." She offers G a quick wink, therefore staving off the inevitable tantrum.

"All the boys' gifts from Emma stay here?" Skyla looks to Ellis, amused. It's clear Skyla has deemed both Ellis and Michelle a safe place during this visit. I'm guessing that doesn't bode well for Logan. "Giselle, why don't you tear through the rest of the gifts right away. I have to get the babies to bed soon."

"Oh goodie!" My sister is quick to comply, sending wrapping paper flying, and my mother scoops it into a trash bag right behind her. Soon Giselle is surrounded by every whirling, twirling gadget and gizmo a newborn, and perhaps teenager, could lust after. It's a mountain of plastic, dare I say crap, and a part of me is glad all of it will be stashed far away from that tiny room Skyla and I share. Did share.

Skyla pulls up a box of felt blocks with animals and shapes depicted on all sides.

"I've really wanted these for the boys. Looks like I'll have to get a set of my own." She glances at my mother, and my heart sinks. Skyla should have the final say in what stays where as far as the boys' belongings go. It's becoming clear that Skyla would very much want every last box to do with as she wishes. My heart turns to stone toward my mother and her ridiculous demands. Who the hell cares where everything is stashed? Skyla and I should decide those things, not anybody else—certainly not my mother.

"We'll take them home," I say it loud and clear to avoid any confusion. "In fact, we'll take all of it home." I look over to my mother with her slap-shocked expression, her mouth gaping open in protest. "Skyla and I will bring over a few things to entertain the boys each time we visit. I promise, they will never be bored."

"Those things stay here, Gage Oliver," Mom snaps with a look of venom shooting my way, and now it's me with my mouth open with surprise.

Skyla chuckles. "Those things stay here, Gage Oliver." Her eyes meet mine with a sting. "And so do *you*." She rises and gathers the diaper bag, readying to leave.

Giselle shouts for everyone to open the rest of their gifts at once, and much to my mother's protest an unwrapping-fest ensues.

"Skyla, wait." I'm about to impart my best plea when Mom pops up with a small bag and hands it to Skyla.

"This too is for the boys." Mom offers Skyla her best smile. And even though her lips are hiked in the right direction, there's something sinister in her tone and my gut twists. Who the hell knows where this is headed. "And *this* you may take with you." She tips her head to Skyla as if to trump her.

"Oh, the suspense." Skyla glances from my mother to me without the right amount of enthusiasm. "I can hardly wait." She reaches into the tiny red bag and pulls out a small brown bottle. "Syrup of ipecac?" Skyla shakes her head at the two of us as if to ask the question.

"That's right." Mom beams. "Now that's something they can really use." Her eyes grow wide the way they do when she's sure she's bested someone. "It's to be administered in the event they've accidentally been poisoned. Now if you'll excuse me." She traipses off toward Giselle and coos at whatever it is Santa has gifted my sister.

Skyla shoves the bottle back into the bag with a marked aggression. "I'd say thank you if I could, but I really don't think I can. I'd better go before I accidently poison someone"—she glares hard at me—"and it won't be either of the boys."

"Don't go," I plead when I know I shouldn't. In all honesty, it's a bad idea that either of us stays. Skyla is right about my mother. She's always been right, and it took almost losing her to see this. God, I haven't lost her, have I? "Things are just about to kick into high gear. I have a gift for Giselle from the two of us. A walking talking robot that will follow her around that big mansion—and it even says her name. I got it half off. I couldn't resist."

"Oh? I think things have already kicked into high

gear." Her voice swings heavily toward sarcasm. "What with talk of custody delineation, the rousing discussion on how I no longer have access to my own children's gifts, and let's not forget the Christmas traditions you'll be starting on your own. That stocking debacle is quite the ode to your new family—one without *me*."

"I would never cut you out. You are my family." I block her from bolting. "You are the reason I live and breathe. You and these boys are my life," I grit the words in an effort to keep it together. "I will protect you until the day I die, and then I'll protect you from beyond the grave. There is no power in this universe that can stop me."

Her chest expands the way it does just before we get intimate. And what I wouldn't do to get intimate with my wife one more time. Tonight preferably.

"Except Demetri," she says as she scoops up the car seat and sets it on the sofa.

"Don't put the baby down," I bark it out like an order without meaning to. "We're taking a family picture. I navigate her to the tree, surprisingly without protest, and hand my phone to Logan. "Just a few quick ones." I cradle Barron in my right arm as Skyla holds Nathan closest to me. I glance to Skyla, my beautiful wife, the mother of my children, and my heart breaks because her rage toward me is so alive, so palpable on her face. This isn't quite the moment I was hoping to encapsulate. "Smile, Skyla," I whisper. "Smile for the damn picture."

Her eyes round out, and her lips twitch in the right direction. Skyla has always loved it when I talk dirty. I'm guessing my alpha commands are having the same effect on her, and I'm glad because I'm fine with being stern if I have to. I'd growl and bark at her all day and all night if it landed me in our bed again.

We stand next to the tree, each with a sleeping boy in

our arms, and smile for the damn camera.
And just like that, it's a merry Christmas after all.

Logan

The sky covers Paragon with a cloak of darkness, thick as midnight, and at two in the afternoon it's an amazing feat to witness. If Paragon had fallen into the sea, the rest of the world would simply carry on without us. Those endless L.A. commutes would continue without batting a false eyelash. Hunger and war would rage on to see another day. It seems that Paragon has to battle for her very existence. Despite the fog, she demands to be seen. I realize there are places in this world where night swallows down the day, hour after hour, but technically, Paragon isn't one of them. But this afternoon the island has lost her will to fight and has succumb to the dark winter and his dark charm. There isn't an inch of promise on the horizon. Instead, the storm batters Paragon with an incessant beating. This is a lashing from the heavens, corporal punishment for all of Paragon's blatant sins. After all, this is the nexus of the battle of the spiritual forces that rule our universe. Perhaps we deserve the biggest beating, the most devastating blows that Mother Nature has to offer. Celestra and all of its formidable power has taken a back seat to Wesley's Steel Barricade. Wesley and his wicked father, Demetri, are in fact proving to be made of something far stronger than steel—they had become the sun, and the rest of the Factions are simply spinning in their orbit. Celestra is slowly being swallowed by the night, and Wesley is at the helm of the darkness.

The Paragon Bowling Alley sits like a stone anchored in an angry sea. I can see Whitehorse, my home, the home I built for Skyla, across the street from the doors leading into the arcade. The bowling alley itself is original, save for the kitchen, which caught fire, followed by a renovation a few years back. The blaze was set by Fems trying to kill Skyla—

or me—a second time around. I suppose you can never be too sure. The one thing I am certain of is that the Fems are far more demonic than they ever are angelic. Yes, they love the Master, and the Master's Son, but they can't seem to fathom the fact the Sectors, their spiritual equals, are in fact *superior* to them in the earthen realm, and thus in the heavenlies as well. It's all about saving face—a power grab. Who gets the head seat at the dinner table. Who rides shotgun. Nothing more than a juvenile battle of the wills. But when you get down to brass tacks, the Sectors—picture a million Marshall Dudleys—are for Celestra and the ethics and morals we stand for. The Fems have aligned themselves with the Countenance Faction, which superstitiously is out for themselves. As much as the Fems want control of the spiritual realm, the Counts have lusted after control of the Factions. The only thing the Fems and the Counts really have in common is their shared hatred for Celestra.

I head into my office and pull out an old file marked *pricing*. Inside, I have all of Wesley's latest and greatest moves mapped out in a series of symbols, a shorthand that only I can understand, and half the time it's too far gone for even me to remember what I was trying to say. I fall into my seat, the cheap office chair with its chipping faux leather raining black confetti all over the floor, and start pouring over my notes.

Wesley has reanimated the Viden youth as Spectators. In other words, he's turned them into a roving band of people hungry zombies. Skyla and I had them roped and tied in the Tenebrous Woods, the old tunnels the Counts once used as a blood harvesting station for Celestra. Brute assholes. But nevertheless, every last Celestra is free, and as of the christening, Wesley—correction, *Demetri* freed the Viden Spectators as well.

I thump my pencil over my desk trying to drink this in.

Wes has thousands of people ready and willing to wreak havoc on our unsuspecting world. Demetri finally has Gage where he wants him—sworn to lead the rat pack of destruction as the head Fem in charge. Gage had no choice. When he left the Barricade, he was cursed—the heart of one he loved would turn against him. Once his sons were born, it was clear the curse would be passed to them, and in an effort to save his children from a lifetime of wickedness—thus breaking their mother's heart—he assumed the curse on himself. He did what any good father and husband would have done. Gage is a hero.

And that's where we are today. So, what is Wesley Edinger's next move?

I hold the paper up as if that might actually shed light on the disaster. Demetri has already caused a significant rift between Skyla and Gage. That was easy enough. Now that Wes has his right-hand man back on his side, he'll move as quick as greased lightning to achieve his overall goal—but what exactly is that? World domination? Too broad. Nope. I'm pretty sure once he kicks Celestra to the curb he'll let the rest of us in on his little nefarious plot. No time to wait for that bullshit. The thing with someone as crooked as Wes and Demetri is that you'd better stay ten steps ahead of them or they'll eat your lunch. Hell, they'll eat your breakfast and dinner, too.

"Logan?" Lexy Bakova pops her head in. Despite the many other things going on in Lexy's life, she still makes time to help out at the bowling alley. Of my original crew from West Paragon High, only she and Ellis remain. She's vamped up from head to toe in black—low-cut on top, high-cut on bottom, spiked heels, bright red lipstick. I used to not think too much of the fact that Lex looks as if she's headed clubbing after a shift until Liam pointed out that the show was just for me. Liam has leashed himself to Michelle

Miller—who in effect is Lexy's best friend. Michelle made it clear to my brother that if she couldn't have me, she's rooting for Lex. And believe me, the two of them are campaigning hard. "There's someone out here who wants you." She runs her tongue slowly over her lips as if she were letting me know she wants me, too.

"On my way." I tuck the file back and head inside, fully expecting to find the place filled with government drones, each in a matching suit, those same dull expressions that Moser and Killion wore like a mask—that is, right up until they were eaten alive. I didn't have the displeasure of seeing Moser torn to pieces, but I witnessed poor Killion with her body in a Spectator's mouth. That horrified look on her face—the one that realized death was imminent—has been staining my nightmares ever since. But there's only one suit in the entire place, and it doesn't belong to the feds—or thankfully, Marshall Dudley. It belongs to Heathcliff O'Hare. But it's not the suit he's wearing that surprises me. It's the somber look on his face. Ever since Candace freed him from the body of a raven, he's worn a perennial smile. Mostly that has to do with the fact he's married to the love of his life, Ezrina, so the frown is new and I'm not loving it.

"What's up my, old friend?" I slap him over the shoulder as we navigate to the nearest table. It's empty inside, not even a ghost is willing to spend its precious time haunting the place.

"I'm afraid Rina is up—or should I say down." Nev rests his elbows onto the table and lands his head in his hands. "I don't know what's gotten into her as of late. She's ornery, and rigid, and runs hot and cold from moment to moment."

"Sounds like a woman." My shit-eating grin melts away just as fast as I shed it while I do a quick sweep for any females in the vicinity. I'm not afraid of Lexy Bakova, but my heart would break if Skyla heard the disparaging remark, especially since she's markedly pissed at the moment. "Look, I don't mean that. Something is obviously eating at her. Maybe it's hormones. Maybe it's that time of the month?" Wow, now I'm really glad there's not a female around to witness my chauvinistic side shining through. "Okay, I don't mean that either. Women have every right to get upset. Did you piss her off? Are you leaving the toilet seat up again? That drives them fucking nuts. Pardon my language."

"Heavens no." Nev perks back to life. "It only takes once for me to learn a sharp lesson, and Rina does like to dole them out sharply. I would never dishonor my ladylove in that way—in any way for that matter. The water closet rules are strict, and mind you I happily abide by them. Which is why I'm truly stumped. I spoke with Master Dudley this morning. He suggested I demand she snap out of it."

"Don't listen to him."

"That's what I informed him, so he suggested I speak with you. He assured me you have vast experience with disappointing women and losing them." He frowns.

I groan at how swift and deeply Dudley hit the disappointing nail on the head. "He is a charmer, isn't he?"

"So, it's true?" Nevermore seems intrigued by my unique abilities.

"Only to an extent. Look, every woman is different. Every relationship is different. What works with Skyla won't necessarily work with Ezrina."

"So it's still Skyla you pine for." He gives a gentle nod as if apologizing for my useless endeavor. "I'm sorry, my friend. In no way have I come to highlight your defeat—excuse the term, disappointment."

"You had it right the first time."

He rises to leave, and it feels as if our short-lived

conversation had turned into a freight train that bumped over my body. I do love Skyla. I very much still pine for her. But she's not my wife anymore. She belongs to Gage. Heck, she's had his children and has cemented their familial standing now and forever. A thought comes to me. "Has Ezrina been eating strange things?"

Nev pauses to consider this. "Only if you consider cheeseburgers by the dozens strange. Rina doesn't think twice about what she consumes these days." He lifts his finger. "I'll see you at the house, my friend." He takes off, and my mouth falls open.

Ezrina is acting erratic and eating a record number of cheeseburgers? She's emulating Skyla's behavior to a T for the entire last year—at least while she was with child, children to be exact. If Ezrina and Nev are about to become parents, I think I'll let them stumble upon that sure-to-be-adorable nugget on their own.

Ellis comes my way with a giant grin floating on his stoned face. Ellis Harrison truly does believe a joint before noon is the breakfast of champions.

"Guess who you are looking at, man?" He tips his head back and lets out a howl that echoes through this cavernous dump on a loop.

"I'm afraid to guess." True as God. Ellis only ever smiles because he's chemically altered to do so. If that silly grin on his face is due to the fact he thinks he has a capital idea, then I'd better run for cover. I want nothing to do with it.

"Dude, you are looking at the next Paragon Island millionaire." He blows on his fingernails. "Not that a few lousy million bucks is what it used to be, but it's seed money, dude. With my daddy's money burning a hole in my back pocket, I'm ready to tackle the world, man!"

"Your trust fund finally kicked in." I stand up and slap

him five. "Congratulations, man. I'll buy you a drink. Soda okay?"

"Okay for now. But I'm thinking you might want to beef up the menu, add some of the hard stuff, and draw in a crowd that really knows how to spend its money."

I think on it as I swipe a cup from the dispenser and fill it to the brim with ice and soda before handing it off to Ellis. "I don't know. When my father opened this place, he didn't exactly have a liquor store in mind." My father ran the bowling alley up until he and my mother moved to Oregon to be near her elderly parents. They hadn't planned on staying long but made the most of their time there by working the farmland. They raised enough pumpkins three years in a row to sell to the public, and that was their final swan song. There was a fire, then—my mother, my father— they were gone. I was burned beyond recognition. Decades of surgeries deemed me functional yet imprisoned in a painfully contractured body. All hopes of a normal life were off the table until a sweet soul with an angel's face came into my life and fell in love with me and wanted me—for her daughter. Candace Messenger and I do share quite the checkered past. There are details I have yet to share with Skyla about those clandestine visits. Skyla is right. I never tell her the entire truth. There are just some things I don't want to know myself.

"No liquor." I glance out at the bowling alley with its depressed dim lighting, its empty lanes, the silence that permeates like a cancer eating up any remnants of joy my parents might have envisioned for the place. "Okay, maybe liquor, but what this place really needs is a bulldozer." I'm only partially teasing.

"That's what I was thinking, man." Ellis drapes his arm over my shoulder. "I did a little research. You own the land, dude. You're an effing land baron."

"True in theory only."

A shadow darkens the entry, and Liam comes bustling over looking as forlorn and down as Nev did. God forbid he knocked up Miller. I doubt it would end as well for them.

"What's stinging your crotch?" I slap my brother over the back in an attempt to shake the sour mood out of him.

"I'm useless." He takes a seat on the edge of the table and slumps. "The seed money Barron gifted me to get my life back on track has done a disappearing act. I'm busted. I'm broke. I need a job."

Why do I get the feeling *seed money* is the term of the day?

"A *career*," Ellis corrects with an alarming amount of enthusiasm. "Logan and I were just discussing our plans to raze this place and resurrect it bigger and better than before."

"We were?" I'm only half-amused because it sounds like something I might actually be interested in.

"That's right," Ellis booms. "This place will rain booze and chicks. But don't you worry"— he slings an arm over my shoulder—"we'll still have a kiddie section, a better kiddie section where your kids can play."

"What kids?"

"The ones with Skyla."

"Ellis, those kids belong to Gage."

"Gage, *you*—what's the difference? You and I both know you've got a ménage situation going with the two of them. Those kids are as good as yours."

I hate it when Ellis is right about anything. Not the ménage part—that's twisted. But those boys feel every bit mine as they do to Gage.

"Get on with your point." I've always had a very hard limit of how much Harrison I can handle in one day, and we just skidded across that line at ménage.

The thought of Skyla and me going at it while Gage supervises thumps through my mind, and I squeeze my eyes shut. Damn Ellis.

"The point is"—Ellis barrels on with it—"we get a bulldozer over here and level the shit out of this place. I'm thinking a total rebuild is in order."

"What's this?" Liam slaps his hand over my shoulder and pulls me in. "Dude, who did you fuck, and how fast can I get her number?" He offers a congratulatory pat to my arm. "You're glowing." The greasy grin of his fades. "Do I want to know why?"

I am glowing—literally, and have been ever since that lightning bolt kissed my forehead.

I'm about to tell Liam all about that peep show I was privy to that involved our nephew and his nefarious future, but Ellis holds up a hand.

"He's glowing because we're about to reduce this place to matchsticks. I'm talking bring on the gasoline. This bowling alley is about to turn into the biggest bonfire the island has ever seen."

Liam scours me with his concern. Staring at my brother is like looking in a mirror, usually one that scowls and drools after girls, so for once it warms me to see him pouring out his worry for me.

"What the hell's gotten into you, kid?" He smacks the back of my head with his palm. Liam was always more of a big brother to me in the head-thumping sense than Barron was—that's because I still see Barron as my adoptive uncle—father. He is in many ways just that.

"I've gotten into him." Ellis thumps the back of Liam's head as if eager to get in on the brotherly action. "We're turning this place into something people actually want to patronize. We're revamping the kiddie zone and thinking bigger and better. We're getting a liquor license and dumping the pizza oven for a five-star chef. What do you think?"

Liam will be the first to protest. He spent his youth haunting this place.

"I'm sold." He slaps Ellis five, and I'm dumbfounded.

"You're sold? He's not talking a renovation, Liam. He wants to raze the entire structure. The bones that our father built—that he designed with our mother—will be for not."

Liam glances around as if assessing the gravity of my words. "Don't be such a dramatic pussy."

"Yeah, Logan." Ellis smacks me over the arm. "Stop being such a damn pussy."

Liam winces. "I think change would be good. We can make it modern, make it our own. Whether we like it or not, change is something that's good for us. And in this case, it might actually breathe a little financial life into the place."

Ellis has already implemented his fair share of ideas into the bowling alley, and as much as I hate to admit it, all of them were winners. But it still wasn't enough to push us over that magical black line—not for long at least.

"And there's a ton of land here." Ellis shakes his head at me as if this were somehow my fault. "You're swimming in prime Paragon real estate. I say we pull the bowling alley to the street and put the parking out back. Or hell, let's build a whole other structure next door."

Liam gives Ellis a shove in the chest, and personally I'm relieved he's finally come to his senses. "A gym!"

Shit.

Ellis lets out an ear-piercing whoop that echoes throughout the empty facility like dynamite. "That's what I'm effing talking about! Finally, an Oliver who speaks my language." They head over to the table, brimming with erratic thoughts and irrational ideas—all of which spell out the Paragon Bowling Alley's doom—and all of which happen to be pretty damn good ideas even if I don't want to admit it.

My heart sinks as I cast a mournful look around the place. The bowling alley as I know it is sitting on the wrong end of the hourglass. I can feel it. Liam is right. Whether or not we like it, sometimes, change is good for us. The word *sometimes* is my own addition to his newest catchphrase—and Liam is full of them as of late. But Skyla embracing Chloe back into her life is anything but good. Skyla and Gage at odds over anything at all isn't a good thing, let alone warring over which angelic being will rule the ethereal roost. I'd say let the Fems and Sectors duke it out, but it's too late for that.

A jag of lightning brightens the world outside our windows as if the sun itself came down to kiss us, and both Ellis and Liam howl like a couple of wolves. Then the thunder starts in, a low demonic growl with the volume set to high, and it mellows them right back down again.

A familiar face stains the entry, tall and brooding, eyes the color of a new dawn that we may never be privy to see again.

"Gage." I head over and pull him into a partial embrace. It's been a week since Christmas, and I've steered clear of both him and Skyla.

"How's she doing?" he whispers it low like a secret, but the disruption taking place between Skyla and Gage has been anything but a secret on Paragon. Once Lexy got wind of their marital discord, she ran with it like the wind. And just like the wind, there's not a damn place on this island that it hasn't touched. Not that too many people are concerned with Skyla's love life—outside of the Factions and a few classmates from West. In short, I think Lexy just seems to enjoy annoying the hell out of Skyla.

"I have no clue, man. Give her a call." I sock him hard on the arm. I want it to hurt. I want to wake him the hell up so he can see what's happened and then figure out how to fix this pile of shit Demetri landed us in. "I have no intention of becoming the middleman." There. I said it.

Gage blinks to life with a smile, and those dimples of his dig in deep. Haven't seen them in a while, and it feels good to know his joy is still within reach. "Dude, I'm the middleman, and we both know it. I've always been caught in the middle between you two. Don't fight me on it." He rubs his arm before his affect softens. "Look, I mean it. I need you. She's off the rails, and I need her to be whole. I broke her. I didn't mean to, but I did. You need to go in and dig deep. Get to the bottom of this Bishop mystery. Skyla knows better than to mess with Chloe."

"That's what's scary. She's voluntarily messing with Chloe." A shiver runs through me. "She's playing with fire— and she will get burned in the end. I can't fathom what's going through her mind."

"Yeah, well, like I said, I'm the reason she's derailing. She has every right to hate me. But I need in again. I crave those boys as much as I do her. I'd do anything to have my old life back."

Gage will never have his old life back. There isn't a chance in hell, and we both know it. But instead of stating the obvious, I offer up a falsely encouraging nod.

"What's with all the enthusiasm?" He nods to Ellis and Liam who have busted out the legal pad and are jotting down every bad idea that comes to mind.

"They're deconstructing my life. Nothing new, my friend." I've already swum in the deep end of the insanity pool with Ellis and Liam. And I'm not eager to abandon the conversation. "So, what's next with Skyla? When was the last time you spoke with her? When did you see the boys?"

"I just left the house. As soon as I showed up, Skyla took a shower so I had a chance to spend some time with them." He winces. "I can't live apart from my boys, Logan. Skyla has to hear me out. She has to know I would die to protect my family."

Ellis and Liam abandon their brainstorming efforts and head on over.

"New Year's Eve—my house." Ellis points to the two of us. "I'd have it here, but dude, this place is deader than the effing morgue. Get it? Deader than the morgue?" He offers himself a robust round of applause. "It's going to be *huge*. This is bigger and better than anything I've ever done before. I've got an all-star lineup. Live bands imported from Host will be rocking us all night long. Get someone to sit on those kids, would you?" he shouts to Gage while walking backward toward the door. "I want Messenger's fine ass over there, too!"

Gage growls at Ellis for his inability to keep it clean. That's exactly why I love Gage with Skyla. Contrary to what she believes, he is protective—right down to Ellis' foul mouth.

"So, you good with the teardown?" Liam gives me a shove as if my opinion didn't really matter. It probably doesn't, or shouldn't at this point, considering I've been administering CPR to the place for as long as I can remember and I can't get it off go.

"I'm rooting for the bonfire."

Gage shakes his head ever so slightly. "You're not tearing down this place."

"Yes, we are." It's nice to see Liam doesn't give much credence to Gage's opinion either. "We're rebuilding and putting in a gym next door. Ellis Harrison is brilliant."

Gage and I groan at the thought of Ellis' brilliance. It's heresy at its finest.

"Maybe so." Gage pumps a small laugh from his chest. "For my sister's sake, he'd better be. Anyway, I'm up for some construction myself, so maybe I can use whoever you hire to help out with the old Walsh place."

Skyla and Gage just purchased their very first home a few months back. Skyla's not crazy about it. And it's not the fact it's virtually a haunted fixer-upper that's making her skittish. It's the fact it's planted smack next door to Barron and Emma that has her spooked. Can't say I blame her. Emma has proven to be every bit the nightmare when it comes to my ex-wife.

Ex-wife. A dull laugh rides through me. That sounds bitter and cold, and that's not at all how Skyla and I are—with the exception of this very moment. I narrow my gaze at my nephew for getting me into this bitter cold pickle to begin with.

"Back to Skyla."

"And I'm out of here." Liam throws his hands in the air. "I'll see you clowns tomorrow night at Harrison's. Leave the drama behind and let's start the new year fresh. There's a lot to be said about forgiveness." His voice trembles through the walls as he ducks out into the dark armpit of the storm.

"Skyla isn't going to forgive me anytime soon," Gage muses. "Maybe not you either."

That dry smile materializes on my face once again. Deep down, it's me Skyla should resent, *hate*—not Gage. Never Gage. I'm the one who singlehandedly turned her life upside down and tossed her to the celestial wolves. But life doesn't have a rewind button, and time travel doesn't work that way either. This is the shit hole we're in, and both Gage and Skyla Oliver are going to work this damn thing out. I'll make sure of it if it's the last thing my dead body accomplishes on this planet.

"I know what you're thinking, dude." He smacks me over the arm before giving my shoulder one of those bionic squeezes. Same ones he used to dole out in high school before a big game. Gage always gave the best pep talks. In fact, the coach gave him the floor more often than not. "You'll get your time with her." He looks past me, his eyes wide and vacant as if drifting into some invisible horizon that erases his existence altogether. "It will happen much sooner than you think."

I kick his foot out from under him, and he stumbles a moment before righting himself. "Snap out of it." I sling an arm around his shoulder. "You are, and always will be, the love of that woman's life. You have given her a gift—*two* gifts—for which she is eternally grateful. The two of you have bonded your souls, through love, in ways that most people wish they could experience for just a moment in this life. This heartache, this heartbreak sponsored by the Fems—it too shall pass. Mark my words, Gage. By this time next year, this will all just be a blip on the radar."

"Blip on the radar, huh? Sounds like something—or someone is about to bite the big one."

"Are you saying I'm not a good cheerleader?"

Gage scuffs my hair up and rubs his knuckles hard over my head. "I'm saying you're a good prognosticator. Trouble is coming, Logan. I can feel it in my creaky bones. My days are numbered, and I don't know what the hell to do about it." He heads for the exit, and I follow him to the door.

"Don't get your panties in a twist, sweetheart," I tease at a weak attempt to add levity to the situation. "My days are over, and I'm still parading around this planet like I mean it."

"So, you're saying it's not over even when it's over?" A dry laugh pumps through him. "In that case, you might be a better cheerleader than you think."

"I'm also a bit delusional." I turn back and look at the empty bowling alley with its tired paint job and well-worn floors—the shoes lining the counter in bad need of repair themselves. Hell, even the ratted-out loafers look poised to run the hell out of here. "It's over for this place, isn't it?"

"It is, but you and I both know what lies ahead. A fresh beginning is the only real cure."

"So, I cut my losses?"

"You have no more losses—only victories from here on out." He pulls me into a tight embrace. "You always were the winner between the two of us."

Gage ducks out into the storm, the downpour flattening his hair, bouncing off his jacket as if he were bulletproof. In a lot of ways, Gage Oliver is just that—bulletproof. His demented father will make sure Gage emerges the winner, but it's not Skyla's heart he's concerned about. I just pray Gage can rise above the wickedness bubbling in his veins, stay strong enough to fight, to *resist* the evil he was wrought from. Gage cannot lose Skyla. That is something he would very much not survive.

That chilling vision I had the night of the christening comes back to me. Gage on a throne. His body morphing into a demonic creature, a living, breathing dragon.

Yes, much like the mascot with its ironic moniker on Host, it was an omen. A horrible, horrible truth that must be stopped before it ever comes to fruition.

Skyla and Gage could survive a lot of things, but his reign of wickedness would not be one of them.

Gage is right. His days are very much numbered. The only thing he doesn't realize is that he holds the key to life and death—to Skyla's heart, to her love and her hatred for him.

Skyla and Gage will survive.

I hope.

2

Fear No Evil

Skyla

New Year's Eve has always been one of my favorite holidays. No gifts, no expectations, no gluttony, no greed, no need to do hard time with the family. That's not necessarily true. Back when my father was alive, we held fast to our New Year's Eve traditions. My mother—Lizbeth—cooked up a boatload of crab and lobsters. I'm not sure why crustaceans were on the menu at the close of each year, but nonetheless, it was a feast we didn't partake in for the next twelve months. We watched television, and as soon as Dick Clark announced it was midnight, we banged pots and pans loud enough to wake the living and the dead. Back when my father was alive, the promise of a bright new year seemed plausible, possible, and wholly immanent. And after he passed away, each new year felt dim, a regretful waste, unyielding in the horrible ache he left in his wake.

I scoop Nathan and Barron into my arms. Two tiny perfect beings who I would die for, sacrifice anything for—and just like that, Gage weighs heavy on me like granite. In his mind, I'm sure he thinks he's done this for us. I can only imagine his reasoning, but I'm quick to push it away. My concern is the welfare and happiness of these twin angels, these dark-haired mini studs that will soon break hearts all over Paragon just like their daddy. Will they love Gage as deeply and spiritually as I love my own father? They must. Deep down, I love Gage that way—the old version, the one I thought I knew. This new version feels more like a disruption than a reality, but the truth is, he is still their father. I want that special bond to form quickly and permanently. If I can't save Gage from himself—Chloe lights up my mind, and I blow her out like a birthday candle—then these boys will reach him. They will keep him grounded, keep his compass honed to true north, to good and not evil. They must, and they will. With Gage under the cloak of the Steel Barricade, there is no more immediacy to save him than there is now. Demetri's words come back to haunt me. *The hour of the Dragon is upon us. The age of the Serpent has arrived.* Gage is a lot of things, but he is no monster. Please, dear God, don't let it be so.

The boys begin to fuss in turn, and I head downstairs with my tiny crew. I've already fed and changed them, but it's noon and Emma hounded me within an inch of my sanity that she and Gage needed to see the boys today for a visit. I know for a fact she's already sniffing around Ellis' legal eagle of a mother because she informed me of this custody drama herself. God, *custody.* It sounds awful. It sounds like something just south of prison, and if Gage and I can't make this work, then I'm up for a lifetime of regular separations from my boys. My heart bleeds just thinking of it. There is no way in hell I will ever share custody of my babies—not with their father, not with anyone. I can't go an hour without missing them. I can't imagine them being carted off for an entire day—worse yet, an entire weekend. I can see it now. I slave away all week, and Gage and Emma swoop in and take all the fun days. No way. Hell no. *Fuck* no. Not happening on my partial human, Celestra-blooded, overseer of the Factions celestial watch.

I clutch the boys extra tight as I descend the stairs and

hear a bevy of voices rising in a panic coming from the kitchen—Mom and Tad specifically, but it sounds like a riot even if it is just the two of them.

Just as I'm about to break out into a full sprint with the boys in hand, I spot Gage and Emma sitting in the tranquility of the living room—if you can call it that with a week's worth of old wrapping paper still strewn around the room, a pile of unwanted gifts rotting in the corner, and dear God, has that bowl of eggnog really been sitting out for seven solid days? Emma's OCD must be silently killing her on the inside.

"Hello," I say, trying to sound amicable, but as soon as she spots the boys, her face brightens and she's quick to snatch one from me and hand him off to Gage and then take the other for herself.

"Why hello, little mister! How are you today?" She wiggles her brows into poor Barron's face until he starts to fidget and cry. "Oh no, you don't, Mister Fussy Pants! Your grandmother is here to save the day—that's right. I am saving the *day*."

From what pray tell, I want to ask but don't.

Gage steps in front of me, and it takes herculean strength to lift my eyes to his, but once I do, my stomach drops straight through the floorboards.

"I just saw Tad." He leans in with that hopeful look on his face, and my heart wants to break all over again, but I refuse it the right. "He looks better. You look beautiful." He tracks my eyes with his, just trying to get a lock on me. Tad spent a few nights in the burn unit but has come right back home with his body bandaged up and his left arm in a straight splint to allow the skin to heal properly. For the most part, he looks as if he kissed the sun and things went horribly wrong.

Gage dips in with a sad smile, and my heart grows

heavy as the ocean as I brush back Nathan's hair in lieu of a thank you. The commotion in the kitchen hits riotous levels, and I nod in that direction before taking off. My heart pounds all the way to the family room as if my own head were on fire. I've never felt so vulnerable, so heartbroken around Gage before. A part of me wants to shake some sense into him, but another very real part of me knows that once I touch him I won't want to let go.

The family room is flooded with the usual suspects, Bree and Drake tossing marshmallows into one another's mouths as if it were their latest party trick. Ethan with his bare feet on top of D-O-G, Mia's dog, aka *Bullet* the oversized living rug, while the equally oversized TV features a bevy of talking heads before they flash to scenes of dark woods from all over the country, New York, Maine, Colorado, New Mexico.

"What's this?" I lean in, trying to hear what has the news and just about half the country in a tizzy. Normally I would dive straight into that argument, still ripe in the kitchen, but something about those Paragon-esque settings has my nerves jumping.

"Clowns." Ethan grunts and belches at the very same time.

"Clowns?" I step in further, and both little Beau Geste and Misty wrap themselves around my legs.

"Kyla!" Beau gives my shirt a tug. "I went—I went poo poo under the Kissmas *tee!*"

"That's nice," I say catatonically as Ethan turns up the volume.

"*Clowns have been spotted all over the country, terrorizing adults and children alike. Authorities are looking to question these individuals, one of which was seen brandishing a gun.*" The camera zooms in on one of the demonic creatures with its misshapen head, that pale skin, a blood stroke of a wicked grin. I've seen that haunted face before. This is no Halloween mask. That's a Fem. *"If you spot anyone suspicious, the authorities caution you to stay away and call the police."*

Long svelte fingers pick up the remote and turn the channel to a bunch of people sitting around on a group date naked, and I look to find those long svelte fingers connected to none other than the demon herself.

"Chloe?" I take a step back, still dazed from the trance of that clown's face. "What are you doing here?" I glance behind her to find Mom and Tad both red-faced—Tad with petroleum jelly smeared all over his skin, his left arm extended in its splint to keep the skin from contracting. To say the least, his burns were serious. Demetri is most certainly not off the hook. There are plenty of other gifts he could have given me, and lighting Tad on fire wasn't anywhere near my list. Ditto for Marshall. I expect more from my favorite Sector, and I don't mean more burns. That was a barbaric act I'd expect from the Fems, certainly not from him. Just the thought of Demetri and Marshall teaming up to gift me a well-roasted Tad sets my teeth on edge.

"I'm here for *you*." Chloe offers up a friendly shoulder bump. "Sleeping until noon, Skyla? Really? The Olivers showed up an entire hour ago. How could you keep your man waiting like that?" Her lips curve into a sinister smile when she says *your man*, and I groan. I'd give anything to be back in bed with my boys curled around me like puppies. My favorite part of the day is feeling their naked flesh warming mine while I nurse. There is nothing more bonding than flesh against flesh. Speaking of which...

"Where's Tobie?" I can feel my milk coming in again just thinking about that pink little cherub. God knows I've nursed Chloe's child more than she has.

Chloe scoffs. "With Ezrina? Wesley maybe? Who the hell gives a shit."

"Watch your language." I study the dark-haired devil before me who has brought so much heartbreak into my world. Dear God, what have I gotten myself into? "We don't do that anymore at this house." I clamp my hands over little Misty's ears before carefully removing her from my leg.

Tad lets out a yelp, and I turn to find my mother detangling him from his arm brace.

"Of all the shit, shitty shit *shit* things to happen!" he rages as the two of them spin into a tornado of howls.

"*Enough!*" Chloe barks over at them as the room falls strangely silent. "Watch your language." Her voice hacks through the air like a throwing star. "We don't do that anymore in this house."

Slowly the melee of the Landon home grinds to life again as Chloe turns to me with a sinister smile.

"Your wish is my command, master." She gives a sly wink. This is precisely why teaming up with Chloe is a piss-poor idea. She's a loose cannon.

"For one, I did not command you to holler like a drill sergeant. And secondly—"

"She's right!" Mom hacks over Tad's incessant verbal tirade. "This is a house of proper manners, and we will *not* tolerate such verbal outbursts."

"Mee-Maw!" Beau shouts from the hall. "I made poo poo on the stairs!"

"All of them?" My mother's voice warbles in horror.

"I was *sliding!*"

Drake and Brielle slap one another five as if their son just managed to cross something major off their bucket list, and, knowing the two of them, gliding down a feces-covered stairwell just might be on it.

Mom dashes out of the room with a roll of paper towels

and manages to snatch Drake on her way out.

Good move. It's about time at least one of Beau's parents is held responsible for his potty shenanigans. Lord knows I've found brown mounds on *top* of the toilet seat, in the bathroom sink, in the kitchen sink, on the doorstep, and in the pantry—and all of that was just last week.

Chloe leans in. "I'm sure Gage and Emma are quite entertained." She lifts a sharp angled brow. "Especially since shitty shenanigans are their specialty."

"Right." I scoff at the idea. "I'm sure they'll have an entire swat team of social services crawling all over this feces-infested place within an hour." I glare at her a moment. "Why am I talking to you?" I grit through my teeth. "Why am I *looking* at you? This is not your home, Chloe. Don't get too comfortable. I'm not looking for a bestie. That position is filled."

"By *me*." Brielle wraps me in a hug from behind. "Big party at Ellis' tonight, and I expect to see both you bitches there." She leans over and pinches Chloe's cheek as if she were a three-year-old, but Chloe growls.

"No using the *B* word, Bree." She gives a sly wink my way.

Brielle is quick to brush her off. "God, it's so nice to see you both in the same room and not clawing one another's eyes out. Isn't this crazy? Back at West I could never have predicted this. I thought for sure one of you would have ended up dead by now."

A small laugh trembles through me. Chloe is all but dead. Ezrina's body is well over three hundred years old. But apparently well-preserved, considering she looks twenty and was able to birth a child a few months back. I'm guessing every valve and chamber is in good working condition. Just my luck.

"Of course, we'll be there." Chloe blinks over to me

with those dark bat caves she calls eyes. "Skyla and I will be at all of the important parties that Paragon has to offer— together. But make no mistake about it. We are the important ones."

We. I shudder as she says it. As much as I hate the thought of being so intricately connected to Chloe, we've become just that. Oh hell, we've always been intricately connected, long before I killed her and long before she killed my father. In the celestial mother of all ironies, the only thing we really have in common is the fact we're both killers—that and our Celestra lineage.

"Dear God." Mom stalks back in, retching with her hand over her mouth. "Brielle, help Drake call out a carpet cleaning service."

Tad groans so loud you would think he were ready to blow to bits.

"Oh"—Mom throws her hands in the air, exasperated— "the kids are paying for it for shit's sake!"

Chloe's about to say something, and I hold up a finger. She frowns my way, but it is nice to know she's willing to comply—for now. Her eyes widen as she looks over my shoulder, and I turn to find Gage strolling in with Nathan in his arms, or at least from here I think it's Nathan. The boys might be fraternal, but there is not one noticeable difference at this point.

"Hello, Gage." Chloe's entire face opens up for him— much like her legs would gladly do, I'm sure.

"Down, girl," I whisper. It's nice to be holding the whip and the chair for once in this bedraggled relationship.

Chloe's chest pumps with a silent laugh, her eyes still very much pegged to my betrothed. "Don't you ever liken me to a dog again, Skyla."

"If the bitch shoe fits."

Gage steps in close, examining the two of us as if trying

to see which one is easier to read. I'll give him a hint. It is most definitely not me. I bet it's killing him to see me with this demon by my side, killing him to know what I might be thinking, staging, preparing, all in the name of our twisted love. Whatever becomes of us, of Chloe and me, Gage and me, I can squarely peg the outcome on Gage Oliver's shoulders.

You did this, I want to say. You have unraveled us, and now I've come undone.

He leans in and takes in a breath with his eyes closed, his face seemingly relaxed for the first time. "You smell nice."

"It's me," Chloe volunteers. "It's my new perfume— *Chloe*. Skyla gave it to me for Christmas." God, she's such an attention whore around him I'm almost embarrassed for her.

His eyes widen with fright before looking to me. "Skyla." My name comes out in a depressed whisper. "I need to talk to you."

Nathan fidgets in his arms, and if I didn't know better, I'd think he was wiggling in my direction so I scoop him on over.

"Not now." There. I've given him a modicum of hope. He can run with it all the way back to the Olivers' for all I care.

Chloe takes a step into him, and I note how creepy it is the way her eyes remain trained on his, wide and full of expectation. All Gage has ever given her is rejection, but Chloe is resilient in her pursuit of him. Apparently to some people, delusions are nothing but a springboard of hope.

"We'll be at the party tonight." Chloe nods slowly as if trying to hypnotize him. "We expect to see you there."

"I won't be there. I'll be with the boys."

Mom pokes her head into our tiny circle. "I'll be with

the boys. Actually, Emma just informed me she will, too."
She wrinkles her nose and waves to Chloe with one finger.
"It's so nice to see you around the house again." She coos for
a moment while fondling the blob of paper towels in her
hands. "Anyway, I'm having a get-together here tonight and
the Olivers are coming." She nods my way. "So you, young
lady, go out and have a little fun." She hitches her head
toward Gage and makes all sorts of crazy eyes before
zooming past us once again on route to the slip and slide
disaster on the stairs. Little Beau is singlehandedly turning
this entire house into a hygienic nightmare.

"Then it's set." Chloe slings an arm around me as
Nathan arches his back and starts in on a cry that sounds
very much like the bleating of a lamb. "We're partying like
it's our last night on earth." She never takes her eyes off
Gage. "Last chance for love and all that other good stuff."
She struts over to Em and Bree in the kitchen, and for once
I'm sorry that Chloe Bishop has left my presence. Who knew
Chloe would turn out to be a life preserver in my darkest
hour? A lead-lined life preserver, but still.

"Then it's set." Gage washes those cobalt eyes over
mine, no smile. "Yes, I have things I need to explain"—he
shoots a quick glance to Chloe—"but apparently, so do you."
His arm comes in low around my waist as he attempts to
pull me in, but I flinch and he retracts. "Let's go upstairs."

"The stairs are indisposed if you haven't been paying
attention. And no, this isn't the time or place."

His eyes narrow in over mine, angry and brooding. "I
don't want to start the new year off this way with you."

I lean in, my blood, my temper, and my growing
discontent for him coming to a roiling boil. "Then you
should have considered that before pledging to darkness," I
hiss so fast it's Gage who flinches this time.

Emma blinks into the room with Barron, and Mia

swoops in behind her only to take the baby from her arms.

Gage takes a step back. His dimples invert with dissatisfaction. That's the magic of those beautiful divots. They don't need a smile to perform at maximum capacity. The boys are the same way. I've watched for hours as those deep wells of cuteness go off in their sleep.

"We'd better take off. We were on our way to the daycare center. I offered to take a look at the plumbing, but I wanted to stop by." He leans in and offers a kiss to Nathan. His hand grazes over my swollen chest, and our eyes meet. No apology from him, but then, I didn't expect one. "I'll see you tonight. Know this, Skyla"—his gaze weighs heavy on me like the sea pressing over the ocean floor, letting me know I will never emerge the victor, he will lay over my heart forever—"I love you. It's you I'm fighting for. Always you, Skyla."

He escorts his mother out of the room, and the air around me feels thick with loneliness. Even in our anger Gage seems to make it a little easier to breathe. I'm sure that's what Demetri wanted when he manipulated this designer union. Gage and I were never pieced together by my mother and her destination station—we were forged by wickedness and now the light has shown through the broken pieces of who we've become and is exposing us for the sham we really are.

Mia swoops in with a wiggly little Barron, and my heart melts as his hand reaches for his brother. They're practically conjoined all night in their tiny bassinet. I don't know how much longer they'll be able to sleep together, but I don't have the heart to separate them just yet.

"Too bad you're saddled with kids at such a young age." Mia snorts while bouncing Barron in her arms, and my mouth falls open. "Don't worry, Skyla. I won't screw up my life like you did." Her eyes meet mine with a renewed enthusiasm. "I'm going out tonight! Melissa and I are heading to the *it* party on Paragon." She holds a finger to her lips. "Don't tell Mom and Tad." She passes Barron to me, and now my arms are full of love, and yet my mind is still mildly pissed at the slight my sister just gave me. "I'm going to *party*, Skyla. I'm going to live life for the both of us." Her face opens with such sincerity I almost want to laugh.

"Please, Mia, I'm not dead."

"But you're basically an old lady. You're like *Mom.*" She makes our mother sound like an infectious disease. "Face it, you can't have fun anymore. And you're uneducated. This is all you'll ever be now—a mom." Her face falls despondent before she livens up once again. Mia has fully grown into a mirrored version of myself, unlike Melissa, our stepsister who looks every bit the dark-haired, dark-eyed Landon with a questionable dark soul to boot. Although, at the moment, I would very much like to give this mirrored version in front of me a swift kick in the ass. She leans in and whispers, "I've got a hot date tonight, but don't think for a minute I won't make him use protection."

"*Mia!*" I bounce the boys between us. "You keep your legs shut, young lady. You hear me?"

"Ha!" She yelps out a laugh all the way down the hall. "You're such a mom!"

Chloe seeps in like a dark fog with Emily by her side. "*My*—isn't she going to be surprised to see you, an old lady, show up at Ellis' party."

"She's going to Ellis' party?" I straighten at the thought.

"That's right. He's not only the hottest party on Paragon, he's the only show in town."

"Then that's where I'll be." I dot a kiss to each of the boys' foreheads, soft as peaches.

"Good thing," Em huffs while gliding forward as if she

were floating. Emily is stone-faced with dead eyes, very much her day-to-day self. "I have a vision, Skyla." She shakes her head, and I'm afraid to guess why. "I need you there. I can't get this out fast enough."

"Do it now." Chloe taps her shoulder into Em's as if cajoling her along. She's such a snake. Of course, Chloe would love to start my new year off with a message from the Master concerning the bleakness of my future.

"No, thanks. Not now, not tonight." No way, no how. If I never hear another vision from Emily Morgan, I'll be a happy little bird.

"I have to." Em's eyes bug out, and my insides tremble. That's more emotion she's shown than in the last five years combined. "I'll blow if I don't get this one out, and I don't think your mother wants me defacing her dining room again. We'll do it at the Harrisons'. Gage needs to be there, too. This is a big one."

"The last one was a big one," I correct as I display the boys before her. Emily accurately foretold the birth of my children, including the third triplet, my daughter Sage who never made it to this madhouse known as earth. Emily isn't a fortuneteller or a psychic per se. She's akin to an Old Testament prophet who receives her visions straight from the throne of God—or in the least my celestial mother. The Master strictly forbids witches, warlocks, fortunetellers and the like, so Emily really does have a pipeline to both heaven and the future. She's a Viden, and that's their gift. Only lately, and come to think of it *always*, the visions are enough to make me rethink the idea of a future altogether. Her visions are dark, ominous, and most definitely nothing to be giddy over, unlike the troll to my left.

"Wipe that smile from your face," I tell Chloe, and she slowly complies.

"Messenger's right." Emily huffs in the wicked witch's

direction, "You'd better wipe that smirk off your face, Bishop. I've got one for you, too."

My eyes round out just as wide as Chloe's.

"*Me,*" Chloe says it like fact more than a question. "I haven't had one since—"

"Since word was sent you were about to be hacked to death in the forest." Emily Morgan bleeds a silent smile. "That's right, Chloe. There is something urgent inside of me that I'm just dying to divulge. I'll see the two of you later." She starts to take off, then backtracks. "And don't think you can avoid it. Whether or not you bitches show up makes no difference." Em looks right at me with those dark unknowable eyes. "Your fate is sealed." She snaps up Ember and takes off down the hall.

Chloe fans herself a moment. "Well, she's a breath of fresh air. I think I'll go find Ethan and see if he'd like to play a round of hide-and-go-seek-the-penis like we did in the old days." She offers a seductive wink my way, and I'm sick straight to my stomach.

"Don't you dare. You know Em and Ethan are practically married. They're raising Ember together. Ethan loves that baby as if it were his own. Don't go screwing up someone else's life just because you don't have one."

Chloe's gaze hardens over mine. "I can and I will." She steps in close. "Don't think just because you tell me to jump I'm going to ask how high. Yes, I am in line with our agreement. But it was just that, *ours.*"

I lean in until we're nose to nose, clutching the boys to my chest with a vise grip. "Yes—Chloe, we very much have an agreement. Don't you forget it."

"You don't hold all the cards, Skyla," she seethes and her chest palpitates dramatically. Here she is, the living, breathing bitch I always knew her to be. Gone is the Pollyanna routine. *Yes, Skyla—no, Skyla* will soon be replaced with death threats and very real follow-ups. I knew I was playing with fire, but it's her fire I'm after. "You *never* hold all the cards," she spits the words right over my mouth, and I half-expect a kiss in the process. "Don't *you* forget *that*."

Chloe takes off, and I hear the door to Ethan and Emily's room open and close. There's that. Give Chloe a solid piece of advice, and the first thing she does is go out of her way not to listen to it. I hope Tobie grows up to be a firecracker of a teenager so Chloe can get a taste of her own poisonous medicine. On second thought, I'd rather Tobie grow up to be a respectable, sweet, young woman, not another thorn in my side. I doubt Chloe would care either way. She's a python of a mother. I'm shocked she hasn't eaten the poor thing by now.

Brielle, my oldest and sweetest bestie, pops up and her features harden with concern—a look I've virtually never seen on her before. She plucks a sleeping Barron out of my arms and cradles him.

"Why is Chloe here?" Her voice is low and tempered, and for the first time in a long while, it feels as if I have my best friend back from a long bubble-headed hiatus. "You need her for something, don't you?"

"The Savior needed Judas to accomplish his goals, and I need Chloe to accomplish mine."

Bree tosses back her strawberry blonde hair as if I've struck her. "Who do you think you're going to save?"

"Gage."

New Year's Eve has always represented more than just the touchdown of a new year. It's the promise of a better tomorrow, a better year, and an overall better you. I nurse the boys for over an hour just sitting in the comfortable glider my mother—the one who makes her home in the heavenlies—squeezed in here while I wasn't looking, loving on my boys, counting their delicate fingers and adorable toes over and over. Wondering all the while what these little angels will do in life. Where will these precious feet take them? These beautiful hands, what will they build? What will they destroy?

I settle them both in Nathan's bassinet and yank outfit after outfit from my closet wondering how the hell my waist was ever the size that my ankle is now. I finally settle on the white dress I squeezed myself into for that demonic renewing of the vows in the Transfer—a maternity dress no less. It hangs baggy and sickly, making me look all together dumpy, so I cinch it in the back with a safety pin I dig out of my jewelry box. The protective hedge winks at me, so over my neck it goes, but Logan's mirrored heart—I run my finger over it. Not tonight. I feel just as betrayed by Logan as I do Gage. But that ring Chloe gifted me—that little bit of heaven—I pop it right onto my finger. Lapis Lazuli—or sapphire as it were, from the very throne of God? I kiss it for good luck, and a current travels from my lips all the way to my toes. I marvel at the tiny wonder for a moment. Yes, this ring is special, and I cannot wait to find out all of the amazing things it's capable of.

I peer in on the boys with their eyes sealed shut, their dark lashes so long and lovely. Two miniature versions of Gage. My boys are so beautiful it makes my heart weep. I turn on the nanny cam Logan gifted me for Christmas and make sure the app is synced to my phone. Enabling me to see and hear almost the entirety of my bedroom while anywhere on this planet is a stroke of genius. I might be angry with Logan, but this gift makes me very, *very* happy. I press a barely there kiss to each of their warm heads and leave the room with a silent click of the door.

Downstairs the house is lit up bright. Drake painted a hasty coat of whitewash over the blackened wall where Tad ignited like a Roman candle so it looks mostly presentable again. Mom has the tree lit, sans a single candle in the vicinity, and to my surprise there are a handful of guests already milling around, laughing, swinging their hips to the music Mom has pumping from the speakers in the family room. Mom and Tad don't have many friends, so I don't expect things to get out of control, but it's nice seeing them expanding their social wings a bit.

"*Skyla.* You look fantastic!" Mom beams while fluffing my hair with her fingers. "Gage is going to drop dead when he sees you!"

Oddly I feel rather ambivalent at the thought of Gage dropping dead, and a dull smile comes to me. Of course, I myself would die if he died. It would be a parental disaster for the boys, but in theory I wouldn't mind stopping Gage Oliver's heart for once. Honestly, I think it's in need of a reboot.

"Now"—she adjusts my dress around the hips, her affect growing quickly serious—"it's time to let go of the past and dive into a brand new future—together. Emma and I both agree this cold shoulder nonsense needs to end right this minute. You hear me, young lady?" Her eyes needle into mine as if a ripe punishment waited for me at the other end of this threat.

"Well, if you and Emma insist." I glance down at my phone and check on the boys. "Where is the wicked witch, anyway?"

"*Skyla!*"

Tad waltzes in with his arm extended because obviously Dr. Frankenstein isn't quite through with him just yet.

"How are you feeling?" I ask, hopeful that his fleshly torment is over. "I don't know what the hell Marshall was thinking," I say under my breath. God knows I understand completely where Demetri's evil head was.

"Don't be too hard on Mr. Dudley." Mom waves off the quite literal gas lighting of her husband. "His heart was in the right place."

"What are you talking about? He lit him up like a birthday candle."

Mom inches back as if I just backhanded her. "What are *you* talking about? He donated the suit. It was his idea we have Santa show up for the boys. He said it was his gift to you."

"Oh." Now I'm the one inching back. So, Marshall's gift wasn't the Tad-based bonfire? Oh! It was the suit! Of course, it was. Marshall would never set a human ablaze in front of their family on Christmas of all days. What kind of monster would ever do that?

"Demetri's here." Tad gruffs, and just like that, I have my answer. "And he's brought a date." Tad jumps as if this somehow pleases him. It should totally please him because we both know damn well my mother has the hots for the flame-wielding demon.

"A date?" Mom forces a laugh. "You mean his niece. He mentioned something about her traveling to Greece soon." She narrows in on Tad with a look of smug satisfaction. "Unfortunately, you won't see the likes of her for a while now. Althorpe is shipping her off to help with its European branch."

"Oh dear God." I suck in a quick breath and look to Tad in horror. "You don't think they're going to ship you off to the European branch, do you?" Please, God, anything but that. Demetri and my mother will be coiled around one another before Tad's ferry ever gets to Seattle.

Tad staggers forward with his arm swinging wildly. "You bet your sweet patootie they won't! It looks like Mee-Maw here didn't give you the memo. I've been *canned*! I'm done. I'm toast. Stick a fork in me. I'm deader than a Thanksgiving Day turkey basted in formaldehyde. I'm eating gravel. Sucking up exhaust. Taking a dirt nap. Becoming a root inspector. Living challenged—"

"Enough already." Mom tosses both hands in the air as the demon of darkness enters the room with a lady friend by his side who is neither his breasty niece, Isis, nor is it Brielle's mother, Darla Johnson. Nope, this new and slightly improved slut-alicious skank is six feet of redheaded glory with a face that can set sail to a thousand European ships, high cheekbones cut in marble, perfectly pouty blood red lips, and a distinguished, sexy as all hell mole between her lip and left cheek—and hair, oh dear God, that glorious hair, how even I crave to touch it. My mother had better hope this is a new relation of his or else some serious competition just swooped into town.

And an unemployed Tad? *Gah!* Althorpe has clearly gone off the government watch-list rails. Who else are they going to pin all their otherworldly shenanigans on?

Come to think of it—most likely me.

"Why, who is this?" Mom walks past Tad, clipping his limb extension and sending him moaning with agony. I'd offer to soothe him, but I can't seem to look away from this redheaded train wreck about to crash right through my mother's rockin' New Year's Eve.

Demetri sheds his signature hellish grin and nods with a slight bow. Dear God, it's as if he's constantly performing. Figures. Demetri's entire existence is one, long, wicked performance piece.

"Let me introduce to you the lovely, most beautiful Mrs. Dominique Winters." Most beautiful? My mother is seeing red—and most likely black and blue from the offensive she's ready to divvy up. "Dom and I are old acquaintances. Dominique, this is my first true love, Lizbeth." He set the record straight pretty quick. Figures. "And her darling daughter, Skyla." He preens my way with that demonic grin. "Skyla is married to my most treasured son." Wow, I bet Wes would love to have heard that. "They've just gifted me two of the world's best grandchildren a man could ever ask for. Twins." Poor Tobie.

"*Children?*" She smacks her crimson stained lips when she says it. Either she likens them to a late-night snack or she's truly repulsed by the idea. Her gaze sharpens over me, revealing pools of lavender, an eye color not anywhere in nature, and already I'm doubting her human standing. And back up the train. There were so many things wrong with Demetri's intro. For one, he has more than one son, but per usual, Wesley gets the shaft. And secondly, I didn't pump out two beautiful babies just to give Demetri a gift, and third—hello, hot mama. What grave did he dig this stunner out of? And what kind of a spell did he cast to make her pretend to like him?

My mother's jaw roots to the floor as she examines her potential replacement.

"*Lizbeth.*" Demetri nods to her with a smug smile of satisfaction, but before he has a chance to rub in his redheaded hussy, Tad grunts and hops his way over. He maneuvers his extended splint wide to the left and whacks my mother on the side of the head with an audible thump.

"*Shit!*" I hiss under my breath as Mom blinks back the stars in her eyes.

"Tad Landon." My bumbling stepfather offers an awkward handshake to Demetri's *femme* fetale, and this time nearly takes out the king of pain himself, but Demetri wisely ducks. Darn. Tad will just have to try harder next time. "Welcome to my estate! *Me* casa *you* casa. I've got a butt roast heating just for you and enough beer over at the refreshment table to make this a night to remember. Please feel free to help yourself to whatever I might have to offer. Anything for a beautiful woman."

As if the thought of Tad offering up the questionable hindquarters of a pig's behind and warm beer weren't appetizing enough, I think he's just thrown himself into the unappetizing mix.

Tad offers up an awkward bow and manages to poke her in the chest with his petrified arm. Oh my dear God. Tad just stole second base in front of God and Demetri—not that my mother cares. But, wow. Copping a feel of Demetri's date? I'm guessing that butt roast isn't the only thing that will be burning tonight. If Tad and his wandering fingers aren't careful Demetri will finish him off before midnight.

I glance to my poor mother who is presently nursing both a bruised heart and a shattered skull—from two different men.

"So, what are you doing in town, Dom?" I offer my own smug smile at the use of the flirty little nickname Demetri gifted her.

Her hair flickers like a flame as she ticks her head slightly my way. It's as if she's a wind-up doll and swift staccato movements are all she's capable of, and knowing Demetri, this might actually be the case. Her skin is smoother than porcelain, and her face has a mannequin-esque quality that I can't quite put my finger on. Something about her—I've seen that look before—but not on a mannequin.

A gasp gets locked in my throat. A corpse! *Gah!* Yes, that's it! She's got that whole I've just been embalmed by the best, half-past deceased glow about her. (The best being Barron Senior. Nobody wields embalming fluid like my father-in-law.) My heart sinks because it doesn't quite feel like he's my anything anymore.

"What am I *doing*?" Dominique squares her gaze over me as if I were a spider than needing to be dealt with by the wrong end of her stiletto. I can tell by her tone I've managed to vex her. I'm not too sorry about it either. "I've lived on this island longer than you've roamed the planet." Her voice cuts through the air like razor wire, and an odd tension springs up in its wake.

Demetri clears his throat my way as if he were attempting to manage me, and I almost want to laugh. If anything, he's the one who needs to be managed. Who does he think he is hauling this hussy over and flaunting her in front of my mother? Not to mention the fact she's flat out rude.

"Impressive. I haven't seen you around. I guess Paragon does like to keep her secrets." I glance down at my phone to find Mia and Melissa in my bedroom stealing kisses from the boys. And before I can say a single rotten thing about Emma, she pops up on the screen as well and my sisters scatter like birds. Figures. Even they can't stand her. "I'd better run. My sitter is here and, apparently, there's a new year to be ushered in." Truthfully, I'm a little bummed I'll be missing the rest of The Dominatrix Show. Judging by that clearly pissed expression on my mother's face, there will be fireworks at the Landons' first social bash after all.

"Lizbeth"—Dominique ignores my trivial excuse to ditch the senior center this place is quickly morphing into and steps in toward my mother—"Demetri has told me *all* about you." A dull laugh rattles through her chest as she razes my mother with a scathing sweep of the eyes. Dear God, what did that vile villain say? "You are every bit the fragile little bird, aren't you?"

My mouth opens, and just as I'm about to tell this

redheaded heathen off, a body swoops in behind me—Bree.

"It's time to get our groove on, little mama!" Brielle's hair is a freshly dyed darker version of red tonight. She's been blonde for so long I'm half-convinced Dom here has duplicated herself for a moment and is doing her best to get rid of me. But it's clear Bree is determined to start the new year off with a redheaded bang, and I can't blame her. It's a good look on her.

"Just one second." I stutter on my heels as Tad yanks on his tie, his eyes still very much plastered on the new object of his affection.

Tad squints into the queen of evil hearts. "Come to think of it, I've seen you around a time or two."

"I run the apothecary." She smirks at him as if he were a rat that just crawled from muddy waters. "But perhaps you know me from the picture the paper ran of my family this morning."

"*Aha*! That's where I've seen you!" Tad slaps his thigh, and a cracking sound echoes throughout the room. Dear God, don't break a leg over this apothecary dominating demon. And who the hell runs an apothecary? It's obvious Demetri's hauled a witch into our midst. If my mother is wise, she'll tie her to a stake and burn her at midnight. She should hogtie Demetri while she's at it. Cleansing the island of all its evil sounds like a great way to start the new year.

I break out of Bree's grip for a moment and step in close to the wicked witch. "Tad is the only person on the planet who reads the paper. What were *you* doing in it?" It comes out far more accusatory than I meant it, but hell, I meant it. Besides, I have a feeling the only good that can come from that paper is if this rotten fish was wrapped in it.

"Skyla!" my mother balks as if it took my brazenness to breathe her back to life. "Excuse my daughter. She suffers from a severe lack of sleep." She wraps an arm around my shoulders and gives me a rattle. "The things that come out of this girl's mouth"—she chortles—"it's sleep deprivation at its finest!"

Dominique grunts at this measly sleep deprived excuse. "My daughter was killed by a sleep deprived motorist on Christmas Eve, right here on the corner of your very street." She bares her sharp, glistening fangs at my mother for a moment as if it were her fault this horrible tragedy happened. "But she's better now."

Better? Sounds like Dom isn't the only reanimated corpse in the family.

"That's nice," Bree interrupts.

Misty and Beau saunter in with their hair covered in something brown and greasy that smells like shit and—

Everyone in a square mile sucks in a breath at once.

"Mee-Maw!" Beau sings with pride. "Misty made poo poo in my hay!" *Hay* is as close to *hair* as little Beau gets these days, and after this craptastic fiasco, he'll be lucky if every inch of *hay* isn't shaved off before midnight.

"We'll catch you later!" Bree sails me out the door faster than I can protest. "We've got a party to hit, and we need to leave now if we plan on waking the dead ourselves!"

"*Wait!*" I try to stop Bree's stronghold on me, but it's too late. We're down the porch and in the minivan where an irritated Drake cusses up a storm over the fact we're missing all the fat blunts. Freaking Ellis has infiltrated the Landon frontlines. Drake is a certified card-carrying midnight toker.

My mind drifts back to my poor mother. Although, I can't help but think that Misty and Beau's crap-infested heads are a metaphor for my mother's obsession with Demetri.

"That woman's daughter," I say mostly to myself since Bree is cussing right back at Drake at top volume. "She's the one that Gage saved at the morgue." I'm not quite sure *save* is the correct terminology, but still, she's back from the dead. Melody Winters—Dominique Winters.

I text Marshall and tell him to meet me at the party. There are two no-good reasons I need to speak with him.

The fog billows over the island in large vats of white powder. It's cold enough to snow, but Paragon is too stubborn to give such a spectacular show. She likes it dark and damp. She likes turning the roads into wet, slick tongues that inspire cars to spin out—wet enough to send a girl straight through the windshield and into the afterlife.

Yes, winter has arrived on Paragon and dragged its wicked namesake right along with it.

Something rotten this way comes.

In fact, I have a feeling it's already arrived.

The Harrison estate—unlike the Landon estate, per Tad's pretentious pipe dream—stands proud over on the ritzy side of town that is gated and guarded and happens to hoard the most expensive chunks of real estate this haunted island has to offer. Some of its residents include the dominating demon himself, Demetri, the Havers' home where our Faction meetings have been routinely held until I kicked the Factions and their useless meetings on their angelic ears, the Kraggers—the family that has spawned a thousand forms of evil, Marshall, my rough around the sexy edges, refined around the crooked heart spirit husband, the Olivers, Gage and his new home—I refuse to have anything to do with him or the house he tricked me into buying. Good God, do not—I repeat, *do not* make huge life decisions when every one of your hormones is out of whack. How I ever thought owning a home next door to Emma was a good idea I will never know.

The minivan comes to an abrupt stop as Drake uses his good judgment to block the entry to the enormous circular driveway, thus penning in the dozen or so vehicles already resting rubber on the Italian imported cobblestone. I have no clue whether or not the Harrisons are old money or new money—at this financially draining point in my life, I'd be honored to be either or both—but their taste for all things pricey is made clear by the almost disturbing visual of their not-so humble home. Ellis' mother, Olivia, has undertaken an ongoing renovation, and each time I pop into their home, something newer and flashier than before assaults my attention.

"Time to get ripped!" Brielle whoops so loud she manages to saw each of my nerves in half before I ever get out of the car.

The night air is crisp, but it feels good to my overheated body that stubbornly refuses to shed an ounce of the weight I packed on while incubating my two little olives. I thought for sure after I had them, and drained the swimming pool that formed inside me, I would have magically lost the seventy pounds I decided to pad myself with, but nope. I'm still as robust as can be and damn pissed about it, too. Chloe mentioned she gained twelve pounds— twelve fucking pounds—and got right back into her skinny jeans the night she booted Tobie from her vajayjay. I sneer at the thought as I stagger toward the Harrisons' home like the zombie my sleep deprived self is slowly morphing into. Speaking of vajayjays, I force myself to do a quick rep of Kegels. My mother has convinced me that the vag-inspired move will stave off unwanted bladder malfunctions—which I'm embarrassed to say have occurred on the odd occasion— the odd occasion being a laugh or a sneeze. There's no way I'm going to stock up on diapers right alongside the boys, so I've been doubling up on the Kegel routine instead.

"Hey, chica." Bree hooks her arm through mine in a seemingly friendly gesture, but I can tell by the way she's pulling me she just wants to hustle to the open bar Ellis inevitably has flowing with all things lethal. "Do you think you and Logan will kiss and make up tonight?"

"You mean Gage." I hate that she made me say his name. It sounds so normal coming from my lips, so vaguely benign. I'm afraid she might be trying to delude my outrage toward him, and that's something I just can't afford to let happen.

"I mean Logan." She struts us right past the gargantuan fountain lit up that eerie Countenance blue with its dozen or so life-sized stone lions roaming around the waterworks. Truthfully, that fountain has always jolted me a bit. At night, when the moon hits it just right, you would swear those lions were the real breathing, moving, hungry as hell deal. "Isn't it about time you switched? I mean, Gage isn't going to be up at bat forever, right? You told me so yourself. He gets booted off home plate by Logan, and then you hit the sheets with Dudley." Brielle groans and quivers as if she just hit the big O thinking about her once wild romp with our ex-math teacher. God, he was such a perv, but then, Bree was no angel. Not in the sexual sense anyway.

"I don't want to talk about it." I certainly don't want to entertain Candace Messenger's supposed brilliant plan for my life or my vagina. Brielle isn't entirely off. In fact, she's spot-on, and it makes my stomach turn just thinking about it.

We head into the dark home, with a pulsating red light coming from the cavernous living room that can double as an airplane hangar, and the scent of weed is already thick in the air.

"Messenger!" Ellis beams as he comes my way, his eyes heavy and glossy, that goofy baked smile on his face. Ellis is handsome in a millionaire surfer-slash-derelict kind of way, and Giselle, Gage's sweet baby sis, is completely smitten with Paragon's resident stoner much to Emma's chagrin—and that only makes me appreciate him that much more. "You left the STDs at home for once. Nice to see you out and about again."

"My children are not sexually transmitted diseases, Ellis." Although, technically, they were sexually transmitted.

"What? No way." His chest bucks with laughter. "What I meant was *studley twin dudes.*" He slaps me five, and I unaesthetically slap him back.

"Nice save." Not. I tread deeper into the foyer until I have a bird's eye view of the entire room in front of me. The music is so loud the backbeat pulsates from my chest, and my brain begins to rattle to the rhythm. Ellis remains dutifully by my side as we watch Bree hop up on a marble table and start shaking what her mama gave her. I can't help but notice a brand new sparkling chandelier the size of an SUV floating from the expansive ceiling above.

"Impressive," I hiss as I continue to ogle at its sparkling glory.

"Eh." Ellis shrugs off its magnificence. "It's just a little antique the 'rents picked up from the Mother Country. My ma's been hitting the back alleys of London, hard, scouring for shit to clutter this place up with. My dad's cool with it, though."

Ellis' dad is cool with a lot of things, like wearing the crown as resident slumlord, no thanks to those crappy apartments he rents out to innocent college students on Host. Also, he openly sleeps around. I've met one or two of his adolescent—and I mean that in the literal sense—girlfriends. I could never keep it straight if his parents are exes, or simply spouses with side benefits.

"And that"—Ellis points to the corner of the room at a

giant work of questionable art that looks like a stick drawing of a person come to life—"is a bronze statue she had shipped from France. It's called *The Walking Man*."

"Awesome," I muse. Dear God, if my mother shoved that in any part of our home I'd have nightmares for weeks. I still might, and I've only laid eyes on it for the last thirty seconds. Although, I'd actually have to fall asleep in order to have those blessed events.

"Anyway"—Ellis slings an arm over my shoulder— "Bishop's looking for you." He cranes his neck for a moment before leaning in and squinting into the crowd. "Don't get goofy on me, but I see something that might piss you off, straight ahead at twelve o'clock."

My eyes snap to high noon, and I fully expect to find Bishop herself sucking off my future ex-husband like the tall drink of water he is, but it's not Chloe siphoning off Gage. It's a gyrating, turbo twerking, engaged in a demonic level of calisthenics looking redhead using Gage as a stripper pole. Granted he's not joining in on the fun. He is still very much in the center of her skanky affection.

"Nice," I muse. "What's Super Freak's stage name? Let me guess—C U Next Tuesday?"

A familiar scent comes from behind. *Chloe.* That perfume I gifted her works like a calling card alerting my senses to her demonic presence before that sourpuss ever hits.

"What's the matter, Skyla?" she shouts up over the seizure of a song. "Seeing your man engaging in a little cunt-punting getting you down?" She narrows her gaze in their direction. "She looks familiar. I'd know that booty shaking skank anywhere."

Laken pops up and pulls me into a quick embrace. "It's Melody Winters." She beats Chloe to the punch. "She was dead, and now she's alive."

"Well, hello"—I lean back and watch the freak show as it continues to dazzle the crowd—"is she ever thankful to my husband." First time I've claimed him as such in over a week.

"That's our Mellie." Chloe frowns over at the scene, clearly not enthused to have her obsession being accosted by yet another vagina to the face. "Mellie Winters." Chloe ticks her head to the side as if curious of the cadaverous turn of events and wastes no time in heading over. Figures. Chloe isn't about to stand for this shit—and normally neither would I.

Laken threads her arm through mine. "Come on, Skyla. We're not missing the grand finale."

Mellie, or Melody, or Werkin' Twerkin Winters springs into a handstand and lands her bare feet over Gage Oliver's shoulders. His hands grip her ankles as if it were a reflex, and he takes a half-step back in an attempt not to fall over. But Mellie is relentless in her pursuit of him as her hips grind into his chest offering up a pussy platter for the evening.

"*Wow*—he's free for a week, and it's freaking rumspringa," I growl to Laken, and she laughs.

"He's not free. Believe me. Coop says he's downright miserable. Mellie's just chosen the wrong boy. I'm sure she doesn't mean her little hop on pop. Odd, though. She seemed so shy in all of my classes."

"You mean she's acting out of character?" A thought comes to me, lingering vaguely in the back of my mind, and I refuse to acknowledge it.

"Completely." Laken scoffs as if it were the honest truth. "But it is New Year's Eve. Finals were a bitch. She's probably just cutting loose. You know, knocking one too many back."

Chloe jostles her way through the crowd and knocks

Mellie and her smelly snatch right off my husband. It's sort of funny how he's "my husband" once things go carnally south.

"Skyla." Gage devours the distance between us with fierceness and rage as he pulls me into an embrace without hesitating. Lucky for him, he doesn't reek even slightly of dead girl's feet or her pink parts. Instead, he holds that familiar spiced scent that I love so much, and I can't help but take it in deeply. I memorize how solid he feels, the granite of his chest up against my body. My fingers glide over the cool slick hair around his neck before I pull away and pretend that moment wasn't everything my bleeding heart needed to fix it.

"That wasn't what it looked like," he's quick to contest, but I keep my gaze set straight ahead as the music pumps violently through the speakers. There are so many people, so many bodies here. Chloe and Laken are off talking to Mellie. Hopefully drilling her a brand new smelly crotch. God, Mia might even be here, and I really wouldn't know it. "Can I see your phone?" he asks as his shoulders press over my back. Everything about his body is familiar to mine, and my natural instinct insists I wrap my arms around him, but I'm quick to tell my natural instincts to go to hell.

Gage didn't get a chance to install the baby cam app onto his phone yet, so I hand it over and wait while he chuckles to himself a moment.

"It looks like the boys are giving my parents a run for their money. Hopefully, they'll sleep when we get home."

"We? My—aren't you presumptuous?"

Before he can defend his mattress standing, Laken, Chloe, and the bouncing beast make their way over. The first thing I notice about her is those eyes, a mix of colors that are clearly toxic even in this low lighting. Kaleidoscope eyes. I've seen them somewhere before. Something about this demon seems so gnawingly familiar.

Melody Winters is scrawny, living under a rock pale—but God, aren't we all? Paragon doesn't really give you a choice in the matter. Her hair is draped in gorgeous red tresses just like her dominatrix of a mother. She's got a heart-shaped face, but that wicked gleam in her eyes, that never-ending I've got an edge over you smile, suggests she's not all hearts and roses after all.

"So you're the wife." She scowls as she holds her hand out and I shake it. That ring Chloe gifted me for Christmas winks like a beacon, and I'm quick to hide it behind my back. Melody leans in and runs her finger along the protective hedge dangling over my chest and draws it to her.

"Spectacular." She glances back at Chloe, and something in that one suspicious action lifts the veil ever so slightly in this entire smelly Mellie farce. "Per chance we can get to know one another better?" Mellie returns her gaze to Gage and runs her finger over his cheek, letting us know exactly who she would like to get to know better and how.

I slap her down by the wrist without hesitation. "Whatever action it is you're used to getting on Host, we're far more conservative on this island. Keep your hands and your hips to yourself." I don't need to look at Gage to know that he's gloating. As angry as I am with him, the last thing we need worming into our lives and our bed is another woman.

Mellie glances over at me, her body language still very much begging my husband to take her. "Very well. I'm sure we'll all be fast friends." She cackles and snaps her fingers high up over her head in rhythm to the drumming of the music. "This night, this *life* isn't through by a long shot!" She looks to Gage, and those eyes of hers light up as if she were looking into the face of God Himself. "So many years I've waited." She lets out a strangled cry before jumping up onto the coffee table and knocking Bree off while gyrating like a chimp on fire.

Gage huffs at the sight of her. "I can't believe she can move like that—move in general after that accident. You'd think she would be in bed after what she went through."

"She does want to be in bed." Chloe slithers up on the other side of Gage, her arm rubbing over his, and he flinches. "With *you*." Chloe looks to me and bleeds her signature black smile. "We don't want that, now, do we, Skyla?"

"It's not happening," I say it to Gage like a threat. The pussy patrol isn't infiltrating my hubby, future ex or not, tonight or any other night while we're still legally bound and gagged.

"What's not happening?" a deep voice strums from behind as Logan wraps his arms around me for a moment. His hand covers mine. *And why the hell is Chloe here?*

I turn to glare at him as he steps into our circle. *Hello, my Elysian. The one who stands in line to fuck me.*

Logan's eyes round out in horror, but I can't help it. I'm still royally pissed at all Olivers at the moment—with the exception of those who dropped out of my womb and perhaps Dr. O. Liam is iffy.

I shake my head at him because it's clear I've befuddled him. "The corpse bride showed up and got jiggy with your nephew. It looks like she's chosen a groom for herself, but he's leashed to me at the moment."

Gage flinches as if I struck him. "I'm not leaving you, Skyla."

Chloe runs her fingers through his hair, and he takes a step over to me.

"The devotion is charming," I muse as I take a step in the opposite direction.

Logan leans in, his features hardened to stone as he

examines the only other woman he's slept with, sans me, of course. Logan and Chloe have a sordid history of sleeping together—mostly accidentally, no thanks to Chloe's ability to morph into whomever she pleases when it suits her—and the fact she decapitated him in the final round of the Faction war doesn't faze her in the least from trying to wrap her legs around him time and time again. Chloe likes her rage with a side of homicide on the regular. My poor dead father can attest to that.

Logan smirks openly at the queen of mean. "What's with your devotion to this monster, Skyla?"

Chloe clicks her tongue at the slight. "Testy, are we? Whatever happened to forgive and forget? Or don't you pay attention to your Sunday morning sermons?"

"You're the devil, Chloe," Logan is quick to remind her. "You are well past redemption, and everyone here knows it." He looks to me with an accusatory glare. "*Skyla.*" His voice hisses low like a tire expiring air.

"Don't you *Skyla* me." Rage brews in my veins, and right now it's all for this judgmental ass Logan Oliver has transformed himself into. "Don't you judge me for who I choose to forgive or who I choose to spend my time with. I'm all grown up now, Logan.

I've cut the strings off my body so you don't have to bounce me around like a puppet anymore, pulling me into your schemes, your useless dreams that landed me in this predicament to begin with."

"Whoa." Gage attempts to step between us in an effort to break up the real party and I push him away.

"Chloe, deal with this." My voice quivers with anger as each of my muscles bundles into its own knot.

"Your wish is my command." Chloe pulls Gage back a few steps, and Laken and Coop surround the two of them as if a war were about to break out. Ellis and Giselle fill in their circle, and Gage looks resigned to watching me from afar.

"Look"—Logan pinches his eyes shut a moment—"I don't want to pick a fight with you."

"You don't have to pick one. We're in it. And I'm not relenting. Gone is the pussy of a girl who would bow to your greatness. I'm not looking for an earthly god to worship anymore. Certainly, I'm not swimming to the Oliver end of the pool to do so. *You*"—I stab my finger in his chest—"are a walking, talking megalomaniac who is only out for himself. You let Gage deconstruct without consulting me, and you expected fully to keep yet another secret from me without regard to the fact I've threatened you within an inch of your dead life from doing so!" I rage the words so loud and proud into his face my throat rubs raw.

Logan towers over me, backing me into the refreshment table, hovering over me with those amber eyes filled with a mixture of rage and hurt. "Collect yourself, Skyla," he grits the words from his teeth, and I'm almost amused.

"Did you just tell me to collect myself?" A laugh gets caught in my throat. To think I once believed Logan was fully on my side, and all this time I was just something fully on the side for him.

"Yes," he whispers it pained. "Deep down, you know both Gage and I love you. We love you *deeply*, more than we could have imagined love for any woman, any human being. You taught us to love, Skyla."

"And did I teach you to lie? Did I teach you deception? What other things are you going to heap on me because of that four-letter word?" A small crowd amasses around us, and I really don't care. I hope they settle in and enjoy the show because this feels good. It feels like much-needed medicine going down, healing me right to my weary bones.

"Let us speak to you!" His voice vibrates over the

music. Logan's frustration with me is so thick you can sink your teeth into it. It tastes like desperation. And in a sick way, I find it satisfyingly delicious.

"I don't give a shit what you have to say."

A small gasp circles the crowd.

Logan's eyes round out with fury. "Well, maybe you should give a shit. Maybe that's the problem here. Maybe the *real* problem is the fact you're not willing to listen!" He swipes the refreshment table clean of all its contents, sending a piñata's worth of red Solo cups flying through the air, and a group of girls howl as if the party were really getting started. It is. "Maybe he's not the problem, Skyla," Logan seethes over at me as his chest pumps with rage. "Maybe it's you."

I straighten for a moment, staring out at the stubbornly blank faces in the crowd, trying to digest the idea of me being the problem. Logan and I have grown so close over the years it's almost like arguing with a brother. You just look past all the bullshit and know that forgiveness is inevitable. Or at least it used to be. The fair-haired Oliver has really managed to piss me off this time.

I look up and meet with those root beer-colored eyes, and in one pornographic microsecond, I can feel him in me, his naked body raking over mine, back in that bed we shared in Rome.

"Remember when I cut you?" My words come out almost inaudible as the music switches to some skull thumping techno beat you can feel deep in your chest. Once long ago, I sliced Logan Oliver's face open wide with a broken bottle. It was done in a fit of rage much like this one, and for a long time afterward I regretted it—but if there were a silver lining, it would be the fact I managed to gift the side of his face with the world's most endearing dimple.

Every time he smiles I'm reminded of that day, that moment.

"Yes, Skyla, I do remember." His voice is cool and even, meeting me right where I am. Logan and I had worn each other out like children.

"The night of the christening, both Gage and you cut me." My hand covers my chest. "I feel it here, every moment of every day."

Before Logan can put together a rebuttal, some useless apology, Ethan gets in my face, and I'm startled to see him.

"Dude, you need to talk to Emily. She's about to blow. She's been looking for you for like an hour."

"Not now," Logan thunders, shoving Ethan out of our midst as effortlessly as tossing a paper plane across the room.

Chloe pops up and latches onto me with an awkward side hug. "Skyla? There seems to be a problem."

A light winks from my hand, and I look down to find that ring she gifted me going off again like some Halloween fun toy. Only it's not a Halloween fun toy. It's about as far away from that as you can get.

"What's this?" Logan pulls my hand close, and I'm quick to retract it.

Chloe leans in. "Come now, the fun is about to begin." She threads us through the dense crowd with the enthusiasm only danger can bring. "Emily is about to volcano shit a prophecy out of her ass, and she demands the two of us are present together. Isn't that exciting?"

An arm pulls me away from Chloe, and I turn to find Gage as he flexes his fingers around my hand.

"You're not going anywhere with her." His tone is gruff and his body language coarse as he stops us cold in the great room. Something about his obnoxious level of insistence makes that secret spot between my thighs quiver for him.

Damn him and his sudden need to pull rank. And damn me and my sudden need to be dominated.

"*Ooh*," Chloe moans, stroking her torso over his. It's clear Alpha Gage has her just as worked up as he does me. "Demanding, *commanding*. I bet you'd like to dole out a spanking right about now, wouldn't you, Oliver? Something hard and fast that leaves a bright red impression right over Messenger's shiny white—"

"As for you"—Emily comes from out of nowhere and grips my shoulders as if she were holding onto the handrail of a rollercoaster—"there shall be a time of great sorrow. A grief so piercing, a deception so wide—"

"That's old news, Em. Tell me something I don't already know or else you're just wasting both our time." I fling her off my body without so much of a flick of the arm, and she flies into the wall with a thud.

Emily's entire body jolts as if I had electrocuted her, and for a moment I'm horrified that I might have landed her on exposed wiring. God knows the remodeling around here never really ends. That oversized chandelier newly installed overhead gives this room more of a ballroom appeal. It's not just dripping with your average clear crystals, but sprinkled throughout are smoky tones of blues and gray. It's an expensive sight to behold as it sparkles even in this dull light. Ellis' mother's redecorating prowess knows no financial bounds. And crushed gold flakes in your new flooring, Olivia? Really? It's as if the Harrisons have nothing better to do with their wealth than embed it in the mausoleum they'll spend the rest of their lives crafting and redrafting. I bet Olivia thinks she's under some curse if she ever stops building, and soon there will be an entire slew of doors that lead to nowhere—a metaphor representative of my life if ever there was one.

"*Skyla.*" Emily groans as if she's about to be sick. Her hand stretches in my direction as she staggers over zombie-like and sedated. Another hard groan comes from her, and her eyes ignite a brilliant shock of red. Her hair stands on end, her face has grown increasingly pale, and those audible groans assure the blooming throngs around us of vomitus things to come.

The crowd gasps. A few girls let out a wild cry of terror. For as many angelic half breeds that might be running around this island, there are more than that many natural humans who will be forever haunted by Emily's little *Rocky Horror Picture Show* routine.

I glance around as if searching for help, for an *escape* route in the event things get wild. Oh hell, they're far past wild.

Emily bucks and lets out the roar of a lioness that rattles the chandelier up above. The rest of the light fixtures around the room pop one by one, and the speakers let out a high-pitched squeak.

"*Hey!*" Ellis barks as he barrels forward, good and pissed. This is Ellis' hoedown, and nobody in their right mind messes with one of his epic end-of-the-year parties. However, it's becoming evident Em here isn't at all in her right mind.

Emily jumps in Ellis' face and lets out a scream that sounds like a thousand swords striking up against one another. Then as quick as a flash, Em hops up on his shoulders, and in a bizarre gymnast-inspired move, she leaps to the chandelier overhead as if it were a waiting trapeze. Olivia's prized antique she had imported from the Mother Country, that survived wars and rumors of wars and an entire era of times gone by, sways back and forth while Emily Morgan does her best Tarzan impersonation for all to see. That dark heavily coiled mass of hair she wears thick like a carpet blows back as she howls and screams in such distress you would think Demetri himself had just peeled off her skin and dipped her in lemon juice.

The room lights up with cell phones all pointed and poised to record every lunatic-inspired moment of Emily's performance piece. But Em is undeterred. She rattles the chandelier as if she were shaking it, strangling it, and soon enough, jewels rain down over the crowd like falling stars.

"*Shit*." Logan hops up on the sofa table and tries his best to catch her feet as she swings on by, but he only manages to clip her and sends Em into a wild spin instead.

"*Ellis!*" Gage barks. "Get a ladder!"

"Dude." Ellis' mouth hangs open. He doesn't dare take his eyes off Emily and her violent spinning top routine. "This is like the effin' circus or some shit. Who the hell taught her these moves?"

"This isn't choreographed, Ellis." Seriously? I'm fearing for Emily's cranium and he's amazed by her acrobatics. It is damn impressive, though, if I do say so myself. "We have to stop her before she tears the house apart." And if a single gold flake happens to get chipped from the floor, I'm pocketing the sucker and setting it aside for the boys' college fund.

Laken gives my arm a tug. "Skyla, what the hell is happening?"

"Emily was just about to give me a prophecy, and as usual things went to shit. She typically whips it out on paper. But the performance piece is a refreshing change of pace." I'm only half-kidding.

The chandelier gyrates heavily from side to side. The crowd breaks out into a collective scream and overall chaos as the room bleeds dry of people. Emily yanks and tugs, flexing her feet to the ceiling as she hoists her body in that direction as if readying for a dramatic dismount.

ADDISON MOORE

A strangulating sound evicts from her throat. Dear God, if I didn't know better, I'd think Emily were engaging in some primitive form of yodeling—reckless and terrible as it might be.

"*Shit!*" Ellis grips his hair at the temples. "She's coming down!"

A horrible snapping sound comes from the ceiling as a fissure blooms overhead in a large jagged line. An entire series of awful cracks emerge on the ceiling, all stemming from the epicenter, as they race to the periphery of the room.

Emily goes silent for five solid seconds before screaming at the top of her lungs, and both she and the chandelier come crashing down in slow motion. The sound of glass exploding fills the room, crushing our eardrums with the detonation. Emily lies silent while buried under the rubble, her entire body glistening as the crystal teardrops cover her body like a glass canopy.

In this moment of utter tragedy, there is an underlying beauty about it. Emily is the sleeping princess clothed in candescent glory.

Emily's eyes spring open wide before a single soul can get to her. Her body snaps and bucks. She jumps to her feet, sending those crystal teardrops shooting for miles.

"*Shit*," Laken whispers as she pulls me back a few feet.

A strange humming sound comes from Em as her head vibrates.

Laken leans in. "I'm starting to believe she's malfunctioning. Should we have the boys tackle her from behind?"

"No. This is big." As much as I've grown to detest Emily's visions, whatever is bubbling out of her seems critical.

Emily snatches up the bronze statue of the walking man in the corner and lifts it over her head with superhuman strength. I've never thought too much about the Videns' powers, but it's becoming clear as the crystal she destroyed that strength is one of them. I don't see why not. Strength and speed are commonalities of the other five Factions as well.

Em tips her head back and starts in on a wail that vaguely resembles a sad, sad song. She wields the statue over her head from side to side, causing the crowd to sway along with her while erupting in screams of terror. Emily takes that bronze statue and crashes it into a glass-covered hutch filled with tiny little crystal sculptures that I can only guess Ellis' poor mother picked up on one of her many travels.

"Holy shit!" Ellis heads over in a rage just as Em swings that weighted statue his way and he ducks, missing a decapitation by a millisecond.

Emily's voice carries on with its odd swansong at top volume as she hoists her bronze companion right out the front door, and the mob of stragglers we've become follows along.

"She's lost her mind," Laken huffs as we push our way to the front of the crowd to keep an eye on our possessed little friend.

"She's in a *Godly* state of mind," Chloe corrects, huffing and puffing right along with us.

Emily swings the magnificent sculpture by its feet in a dangerous circle, quickening her pace until she's nothing but a blur, and a couple runs out from the bushes behind her, adjusting their clothes—the girl screaming herself senseless. But it's the girl's familiar frame, her familiar face I recognize as my own.

"*Mia*?" I say mostly to myself as I gasp at the fact my baby sis just strutted her slutty stuff in front of every single onlooker planted on the Harrisons' driveway. I struggle to make out the boy she was with, but he's long gone, dissolved efficiently by Paragon's signature fog. I'll deal with her later. Him, too. The fog may not give him up, but someone will, and when I find out who he is, I'll make sure he gives up the ghost. He's a dead man walking. Of course, deep down, I know it's Rev, and secretly I look forward to administering the beating.

Gage takes a few staggering steps forward before thinking better of it and turns to the crowd. "Get the hell out!" he roars. "That thing's about to launch like a missile!" He stops to take in the unmoved crowd. "I said *now!*"

Bodies scramble in a fury like ants, but there are several of us that act as if our feet had taken root. I can't take my eyes off the whirling, twirling tornado Emily Morgan has become. Laken is right. She's lost her mind. And I'm terrified that Chloe might be right, too. That this barbaric display might just be attributed to some Godly message—one that directly affects me.

Marshall walks up from across the street, measured and calm, completely his unmoved self, and takes his place by my side. "It looks to me Mr. Harrison has spiked the punch with bath salts. I'd steer clear of the refreshment table if I were you."

"That's Emily. She has a vision for me." The words swim from my lips numbly.

And just like that, Em's twister of fun gravitates toward the center of the driveway. The sky up above quivers with the light of noonday as a crack of thunder so loud roars over the island it starts a whole new choir of screams from the people who were once Ellis' party guests. Emily comes to a staggering finish, the statue resting at her side with the walking man seated on his bronze head.

"And then they will make a request unto the Lord!" Her voice booms in a deep, unnatural manner. Gone is any trace of femininity, and in its place the sound of a thousand rushing rivers. "They shall beg for peace—beg to have their enemy broken—for their enemy to relent. They will say take my life in exchange for the one you seek, but I will remind them of the covenant they had made with me, and they shall be forced to drink the bitter cup of their father."

"That must be Gage," I whisper.

Lightning blinks in the western sky, flickering manically as if God Himself were playing with the switch. Emily screams, low at first then rising to the crescendo of a horrific tiger with its tail ablaze. She hoists up that bronzed statue once again, and the crowd gasps. Lightning strobes up above like a police siren, like a warning.

Emily Morgan takes that statue and hurls it at one of those prized lions sitting peacefully by the fountain. My heart aches as the lion's head explodes, sending pieces of marble flying like shrapnel. Then one after another, with each scream far more violent than the last, she goes on a hacking spree, tearing each helpless lion's head right off its menacing body.

"SHIT!" Ellis howls while doing his best to yank out his hair. "You are going to fucking pay for this, Morgan!" Every vein in his head bounces. For as long as I've known Ellis, he has been twice as calm and mellow as Marshall, and here he looks as if his head is about to pop right off in keeping with the theme.

In a fit of shouts and fury, Emily pitches the bronzed statue high into the sky. It launches toward the heavens like a cannon and sends the remainder of us ducking for cover. Marshall pulls me behind a Range Rover sitting at the base of the driveway, but it's Gage and Logan who all but throw themselves over my body. Then with a heavy thud, not unlike an earthquake, it's over and we emerge with the rest of the curious onlookers to find a smoking hole in the Harrisons' roof.

Emily falls face-first into the pool of shimmering water at the base of the fountain she singlehandedly destroyed. Twelve headless lions and one seemingly dead as a doornail Emily Morgan.

"And there she goes," Logan says before bolting in her direction.

Logan and Gage pluck Emily out as a siren saws its music through this unsettled night, making its way over. Emily sits up on her own, looking mildly dazed but thankfully alive.

Laken pulls me into a quick embrace. "I'm so glad it's finally over." Her mouth touches over my ear. "Don't you dare overanalyze any of that psychotic crap." She pulls back and forces a smile, patting my arms as if she just offered a pep talk. In a way, she has, but it's altogether too late.

"No," I whisper as I take a catatonic step toward the destruction.

Marshall wraps an arm around me, weighted and uncomfortable. "Yes, Ms. Messenger, I'm afraid it's so. Don't fret. There is a method to this madness. No matter what the circumstances life throws your way—you are the victor. There is a Son seated to the right of the Master who ensured just that."

Chloe snorts at Marshall's cryptic words. "So, you're saying if it isn't ending well, it isn't the end?"

Marshall snaps his neck in her direction so quick and curt a natural human would have severed their spinal cord. "Precisely, Ms. Bishop." But there is something in his tone, a harshness he has never invoked with her before that sets my teeth on edge. Everything about tonight, about the last few weeks, has eaten at my sanity. What is this new world Demetri and his cursed goblet filled with my own blood has ushered us into?

How is it that life and all of its offerings are suddenly so bitter, so randomly grievous and destructive?

I glance over and spot Melody Winters clinging to Gage.

Why have the dead forgotten their boundaries? Why has the universe unleashed her fury and forgotten to keep the natural order of things in check?

The smoke finally settles at the base of the decimated fountain and Ethan helps Emily down the driveway.

"Good show!" Chloe claps as Em passes us by. "Bravissimo! Bravissimo! Tell us, Em!" Chloe's voice echoes into the night like a haunted refrain. "Who was the statue? Was it Gage or Skyla? Let me guess! It was *me*!" That's one thing about this demon by my side. Chloe owns her wickedness. She understands the full impact of her destruction and doesn't apologize for its aftermath. Of course, heavy as lead, dumb as a stick—or statue as it were, is Chloe. Chloe has destroyed and decapitated more people than I care to count.

Emily turns our way, her weary eyes a muted shade of red, glowing like embers lit in a jack-o-lantern. "It's all of you. Destruction has come to devour you, to have you devour each other. This is the beginning of the end."

A stunted silence strangulates the crowd.

"Good night!" Chloe trills to Em as if they just had a friendly powwow regarding something cheer related, the only real topic, outside of Gage, that could excite Chloe.

I glance over my shoulder where Gage and Logan stand, pale-faced and stunned. The slight look of anger rings my husband's eyes as he locks his gaze with mine.

The beginning of the end. I nod his way.
It sounds incredibly fitting.

Gage

There have been many battles I've fought in my short, spirited tenure on this planet, and I've fought every single one of those for Skyla. In her name, for her people, for our love, and now for our children. There have been victories, and there have been losses. I'm not entirely sure how to quantify the latest war I've landed myself in, but I guarantee I will emerge the victor. Skyla and her people will prosper, and my boys will be safe, secure, and most of all, well on the side of good and not evil. I'm not entirely sure how Demetri Edinger, my genetic supplier, the designer of my being, passes himself off as an angel of light, but this war he's waging, these lunatic ideals he's hell-bent on passing along to the rest of humanity, has me eroding on the inside. His words have become my affliction, his ideals the necrotic growth that's eroding me from the inside.

Logan and I survey the disaster that was once Ellis' greatest feat. His New Year's bash has turned to a pile of shit, and the clock is nowhere near midnight. A few of the partygoers have staggered inside only to emerge back out after being chased into the night by Ellis himself.

"Let's get her home." Logan pats my back, and we head over to Skyla. When she walked into the room tonight, she illuminated the darkness like the brightest star. Skyla chose to wear the exact dress she wore to our vow renewal last September. I'd like to think that was a peace offering, a beacon of hope of things to come. The potential symbolism wasn't lost on me. But then, I'm desperate and refusing to believe the fact she didn't have anything else to wear. With all of my heart I want to believe that Skyla is on the cusp of forgiveness, that a sit-down between the two of us, an honest to God heart-to-heart is just on the horizon. I can't stand the idea of the clock striking midnight and her anger still percolating against me. I need Skyla and her love. I need all of her approval just to navigate the rocky bottom that I've landed on. Skyla needs me, too, doesn't she?

"I'll give you a ride." I land an arm over her shoulder, soft as cotton. It made my stomach turn to see Dudley doing this exact same thing just a few minutes prior. He's chomping at the bit to have her, and I know damn well a desperate Sector is a dangerous one.

"Laken is taking me." Skyla zips into Cooper Flander's waiting car like she was fleeing a poltergeist, and they take off before I can refute the idea. I don't mind her taking off with Laken and Coop. It's Chloe and Dudley I'd have issues with.

I pat Logan on the shoulder. "You okay?" He's still holding the back of his neck while staring at the carnage. I know him. He's ten steps ahead, trying to piece together how this madness fits into the grand scheme of our lives. The prophecy might not have affected Logan directly, but anything that touches Skyla and me affects him directly. Most likely the same goes for Chloe.

He breaks free from his trance. "I'm fine. I'm going to head in and help Ellis out. Something tells me he can use a clear head right about now." His brows pinch at the center. Logan has that pained look in his eyes that he gets so often these days when he looks at me as if I've caused the pain to begin with. I know I have. And I also know that he loves me. I'm so sick of bringing pain to those I love the most. Just the thought sends a toxic level of grief right into the pit of my gut. "Why don't you head home and kiss your boys good night?"

"Now that's a great idea." If my parents weren't there, I would have given that great idea pause. As much as I miss the boys, as badly as I want to hold them and land a kiss to each of their tender foreheads, I want Skyla to know that I'm still working with her. I'm giving her time, but I think we both know I'm on the losing end of the hourglass. That ridiculous rock with my personal number monogramed on the back of it comes to mind. That number. I shake it out of my head. "I'll see you soon." I pull him in and give a tight squeeze. "Happy New Year, buddy. I hope it's everything you want it to be."

"It will be," he assures. Logan pulls back and catches my gaze. "You have the power to control your own destiny, Gage. Do not buy into the bullshit anyone tries to feed you."

Anyone is a long list of complicated people and entities—my father, Candace herself, my crooked-minded brother, and now Emily has joined that long and wicked roster.

"I am who I am." A part of me knows there are no truer words. "I will accomplish all that I set out to do for those that I love and no one else. I promise you this. No one and nothing will ever take my heart away from those that I love and all that I believe to be true."

And with those words, I let the night eat away at my shadow as I evaporate into nothing.

For a moment, I pause from my journey. The closet in the bedroom I share with Skyla is where I'm all but programed to go, but I hesitate and opt for the front door. Yes, my parents are up there with the boys, but a part of me demanded I go formal and I can't figure out why.

The Landon house is lit up like a pumpkin at Halloween. Laughter and music seep from inside as the entire wooden structure vibrates from the party going on. My blood boils a minute. Who in their right mind is having a party? Drake and Ethan were both at Ellis', weren't they? Wait—this can't be the little get-together Lizbeth mentioned, could it?

I ring the doorbell, but the raucous music inside swallows up any hope of someone answering. I didn't drive tonight so I don't have a key. I've been teleporting freely ever since Skyla put me in the doghouse. But I'd much rather travel at a snail's pace, bogged down with car seats and diaper bags, making two and three trips to and from the house. It might be an ordeal to go anywhere with the twins, but it's our ordeal. A beautiful ordeal.

I give a stiff knock, and when no one bothers to open, I do a brief glance around and teleport myself right into the foyer.

"Son." Demetri appears before me with a mildly stunned redheaded woman by his side. Come to think of it, she looks more amused than she ever does shocked at what she's just witnessed. "Do practice discretion. There are a myriad of far more discreet locales to materialize. Our people are in peril these days, you know." He brings a glass to his lips and wraps a smile around the edge before taking a sip of the bubbling liquid. I glance past him at the sea of people at or above the age of my parents, and I'll admit I'm a bit impressed with the way they have the house rocking.

"I'll consider that." He's right. Discretion is the name of the game. And every last part of me hates it when he's right, but I'm suddenly understanding the urge to teleport in this exact location rather than the closet upstairs. I'd bet every dirty dollar I don't have that it was Demetri who was prompting me to do just that. He smelled me outside that door like the hellhound he is and all but summoned me. That will teach me to respond to any geographical urges again.

"Who's the friend?" I glance to the older redhead in a tight black dress, tits hanging out like twin pale moons. I'm surprised to see how beautiful she is. She's about his age, which puts her in the running, I suppose, and oddly this makes me feel bad for Lizbeth. Her longtime crush on my father spans back to the time they were both living in L.A. Of course, Demetri was simply stalking her then—waiting for the right to claim her. It's a wonder why he ever let Tad marry her to begin with. And now my interest into their bizarre love triangle is piqued.

"Dominique Winters." She extends a delicate hand, and I shake it. Cold, *bony*, yet firm. Her features are textbook villain, sharp, dark brows that peak without warrant. Hard features and a blood red smile that looks more like a curse than anything born of kindness. "You must be the prince that rescued my daughter from a certain death in the freezer." Her lips turn down at the corners as if she might be sick.

"Yes." I straighten at the memory. So that's who she is. "In fact, I saw your daughter tonight." More of her daughter than necessary. "She seems quite healthy, and in a great mood. It's good to see she's moving on." And God, those moves. I'm still traumatized from the private lap dance she thrust upon me.

"We'll be suing the hospital, of course." Her tone is matter-of-fact, and a chill runs up my spine at what she might say next. The morgue isn't doing that great. One swift lawsuit to the ass and Mom and Dad will have to bury their finances in one of those empty plots in the back. They own the cemetery, too, which has always proven to be the big winner as far as businesses in their repertoire, but it's as dead as a corpse as far as profits stand. It's amazing what people are willing to pay to send their loved one off in style, but my father has never believed in price-gouging the grieving, so even in that they are not wealthy—not by anybody's means. "For you though, I have a reward." Her lips expand, revealing an entire mouthful of knife-sharp teeth, each one a pointed canine, and I glance to my father for explanation, but he's as unmoved as that ridiculous grin on his face he can't seem to shake. And back the hell up. Did I just seamlessly consider him my father? That has to end.

"A reward won't be necessary," I quickly assure her. A part of me wonders, though, what's the going rate for a daughter brought back to life. Not that I had anything to do with her miraculous rousing from the dead. I doubt the poor thing wasn't dead to begin with. She's right to sue the living shit out of the hospital. I almost shoved her in the fridge and called it a night. Come to think of it, if the refrigeration unit weren't busted, I wouldn't have been there at all.

Demetri's brows peak and he offers a slight nod as if letting me know I'm onto something.

Bastard. **Do not read my mind. You are not welcome here.**

His brows dip as if disappointed, and I put up a missile defense shield around my thoughts.

"Nonsense." Dominique takes up my hand and lays her thumb against my palm. She leans in and bears her gaze into mine. Her eyes are made up of one too many colors for me to keep track of, and if I didn't know better, I'd say she's doing something nefarious with this feel-you-up, stare-you-down routine so I pull my hand back and stuff them both into my pockets. Holy shit, is she reading my mind, too?

"Your father tells me you have an account with the Bank of Paragon. I'll be making a rather large deposit into your name come Monday. There's not a thing you can do about it. When I set out to do something, no one and nothing can stop me." She laughs a large, hacking laugh, full of power and loud as hell. She manages to compose herself just as quick as she erupted and glares from Demetri to me. "I'd best thank the hostess for a pleasant evening."

"So soon?" Demetri's eyes squint out a laugh all their own. "We've only minutes until the new year. Do stay. Whoever shall I kiss at the stroke of midnight?"

She grunts as if ready to vomit. "If you insist." She stalks off in the direction of the chaos, and I take a moment to inspect this devil before me.

"What is she?" I'm not entirely sure I know who she is either—I don't have a lot of faith in the things my *father's* friends tell me. "Let me guess, a demon like you."

"Hush." His eyes widen as he hisses out the word. In all the years I have known Demetri, this moment, right here, is perhaps the most animated he's ever been. "Never again equate me with those sons of perdition. I chose to side with the Son. I am no more a devil than you are." His eyes twirl a toxic hue of molasses and blood. "We are God's. I am created to serve, and you are born as an heir to the throne. I won't have you dragging our good names through the celestial mud." His brows hike a moment before that greasy grin reappears once again. "You are my heir as well. I have no doubt you will serve your people well."

"The Videns don't really need—"

"I'm not talking about the Videns," he doesn't hesitate to cut me off. "I'm talking about your Fem lineage, your alliance with the Countenance—a superb organization that's already agreed to meet with you, though you've yet to officially take the throne."

His whip, sharp tone, his demanding demeanor, it all sets my blood to lava.

"I have a throne in the event you have conveniently forgotten. One in which I find no use of. As I was saying before you so rudely cut me off, the Videns are Skyla's people, not mine. *She* is their leader, just as *she* is the leader of the rest of the Factions. I may have swallowed that curse you force-fed me, but let me be clear about one thing—I will never turn my back on her or what she believes in." There. Those words purged something deep down inside of me, and my entire body feels lighter, healthier, albeit not much wiser. Words are just that. But that curse has already proven to be a millstone.

"You are correct." He leans in just enough. Demetri's heavy pine-scented cologne weighs down my senses. Doesn't he know that scent alone is associated with urinal cakes and sparkling kitchen floors? "You will never be forced to go against your love, her beliefs, or yours. That is the beauty, Gage. I can no more force your hand than press a crown over your unwilling head. But you are willing," he muses as he bears in hard over me with that menacing gaze. "You are more than willing to yield to what is right for your people, my son. In this, the eleventh hour of humanity, it is more important than ever that our kind take command of the spiritual reins. What is proclaimed on earth is sealed in heaven, and our victory over the Sectors will be an everlasting one. Eternal implications lie in the balance."

I try to take in his words, but they speed by like cars on a highway. "Wait—are you saying that the last one standing as a ruling authority once the planet wraps up is left in a power position for all eternity? Why would that make sense? Once the planet project is through, there isn't a lot to take command of." The planet project. Why the hell did that just come out of my mouth? I've never called the end times anything so cold-hearted before. A shiver rips through me at the thought I might be acquiescing to Demetri's wickedness so soon.

His brows flicker like twin black flames. "Once again you are correct. Eternal implications are in the balance. So you see how very important the part you play is on behalf of the Fems. You alone are capable to usher in this new era—the final era that will yield much for both our kind and humanity."

The door behind me bursts open and in tumbles Bree, Em, Drake, and Ethan. Skyla comes up, and the mere sight of her takes my breath away. Skyla is stunning on any night, but tonight, in that wedding dress, she shines like the star from heaven she is.

She pauses and looks up, stunned with her crystal-clear eyes darting from my demon of a father to me. Skyla's eyes are the clearest blue, but you really have to scour to see the color. I have never seen that shade, that level of transparency on any other human. Mia might be her lookalike in every way, but her eyes hold a darker hue. Skyla is one of a kind in every respect. Candace, her biological mother, might be far more of a twin to her than Mia, but the truth is, Skyla's heart is made of pure gold.

"Discussing your descent into hell?" Skyla cracks a dull smile before disappearing up the stairs.

"I'd better go. I've got far more important work to do than assuring your people rule the celestial roost well past kingdom come." I start up the steps then backtrack, shooting a quick glance into the family room where Bree and Em shake their hips to the music. "Emily Morgan shared some kind of a twisted prophecy tonight."

He steps in, that greasy grin of his slips right off his face. "Whatever did it say?"

"She didn't draw it out. This wasn't some old-school Viden vision. It was more of a performance piece. She went nuts and singlehandedly destroyed the Harrison estate. She swung from the chandelier. She knocked the heads off that giant lion fountain they have out front. She treated a bronze sculpture twice her size as if it were a football, and now there's a crater in their living room large enough to drive a car through." My breathing ticks up a notch as a newfound fury rides through me. There's not a part of me that believes Demetri doesn't hold the answer to what that bizarre act might have meant tonight.

He looks past my shoulder at the door with such earnest intent, I half-expect it to blow off its hinges. "Who specifically was the vision for?"

"Skyla, myself—and get this, your wicked pet, Chloe Bishop." Demetri has been Chloe's spirit guide for years.

"The three of you?" His attention snaps back to me with amusement before his expression darkens. "It was no accident Ms. Morgan chose to forgo the proper medium in which the vision was to be given." The cold as steel gaze of his hardens over me once again. "It can only mean one thing—a rebellion is at hand." That painful smile curls on his lips. "Rebel as you might, it will most certainly lead to destruction. Know this, son. No good comes of it." He turns to leave, then pauses. "And did you suggest my cologne is reminiscent of urinal cakes?" He ticks his head to the side as if shocked by this. "I'll be sure to find something far more pleasing to the senses to grace your presence with." He gives a slight bow. "Your highness." He stalks off into the heart of the party without so much as a good tiding for the new year at hand. Figures. Demetri was practically giddy at the thought of a good destruction sitting on the horizon.

A thought comes to me. I never said that remark about urinal cakes out loud. He's in my head, in my veins, in my blood and marrow. Escaping Demetri will prove impossible.

But I've got news for the monster that is my father. The only thing I plan on destroying is him.

The chaos from the party slowly fades as I head upstairs. The door to our room is slightly ajar, and I step in just in time to witness my mother christening one of the twins with a sneeze.

"Emma!" Skyla howls so sharp the baby in her arm jerks to life.

Crap. My mother of all people knows better than to sneeze in the face of an infant, *my* infant for that matter.

"Here." I take the baby from her and inspect his brightly colored toenail affirming that it's Nathan.

"Excuse me." Mom fans her watery red eyes. "My allergies really hit hard as soon as I entered this tiny hole you cage yourselves up in."

"Hole?" I ask, looking to my father as if to ask what the hell has gotten into her, and he simply shrugs as if powerless to control her mouth—which happens to be entirely true. Although I probably shouldn't have repeated the slight, judging by the way Skyla's chest is pumping with fury.

"Yes, it's a hole, Gage," Skyla snaps. "Don't pretend you haven't noticed. And you"—she jabs her heated gaze toward my mother, who at the moment I don't feel sorry for in the least—"I'm not buying your *allergies*. You have a full-blown cold. I could tell the minute I walked in that it sounded as if someone was pinching your nose shut when you said hello. If you weren't feeling well, I'm sure my mother would have gladly come up to relieve you."

Mom is quick to wave her off while gathering her things. "That wasn't necessary. Happy New Year to you both." She pecks my cheek with a kiss. "I'd lay low if I were you," she whispers.

"I heard that," Skyla sneers as she and my father exchange a polite embrace.

"If you need anything, call." My father winks as they disappear and click the door shut behind them.

A welcome silence fills in the air around us as the boys both indulge in thick sleep that will hopefully last the duration of the night. If the boys enjoy one thing, it's staying awake and crying out to let the whole world know about it.

The room vibrates for a moment as the crowd below shouts in unison, "Three-two-one—*Happy New Year!*"

"Happy New Year, Skyla." I lean in and steal a sweet kiss off her velvet soft cheek and savor it as if it were our last. I hope to God it's not anywhere near our final goodbye.

She bats her lashes at me a moment. "You said goodbye the night you chose your father over me," she says it low, each word measured with grief.

"It was me or the boys, Skyla. I made a sacrifice that any father would make."

"Every other father would have consulted with their wife—if they were smart." She holds up a hand as if to end it and places Barron down in his bassinet. I do the same with Nathan, and they both start in on a hacking cry. "I think tomorrow I'm going to have the swings brought up. I swear it's the only way they sleep—even if it is for ten minutes at a time." She picks up Nathan and hands him right back to me and does the same with Barron.

"Why wait until tomorrow? I'll do it now. It will be a serious game of *Tetris* getting them to fit, but at this point I'd rather chuck the bassinets altogether."

"Knock, knock," a voice calls out softly from the doorway, and I don't need to turn around to know it's Lizbeth. I'd be lying if I didn't say I was irritated. This conversation regarding bassinets and baby swings was the longest Skyla and I have had since the incident, and I was enjoying the hell out of how normal it all felt.

"*Aww,*" she coos as she makes her way over and kisses both the boys in turn and somehow miraculously they seem calmer for it. "Happy New Year, kids." She roughs up my hair and gives a little wink. "I'm so glad to see you working it out. I'm headed to bed. Enjoy the rest of the night."

"What about your party?" Skyla's eyes widen with mild panic as if she might be expected to tend to the melee herself.

"Demetri and his guest just left. Bree and Drake are down there having a good time. I'm sure they'll handle it."

Skyla's lips twist in that adorable way that lets me know she's irritated herself. "Is that what has you down—Demetri?" she asks sweetly just above a whisper as if trying to coax the answer from her.

"He *kissed* her at midnight," she hisses as if suddenly they were alone in the room and ready to gossip. Lizbeth is incensed, and a part of me wonders if this were the sole purpose of Demetri's redheaded guest.

Skyla's chest rumbles with a dark chuckle. "He kissed her? I bet that was hard for you to witness. Him gnawing on the face of his lady friend while you were forced to kiss Tad."

"*Skyla.*" Lizbeth rolls her eyes. The two of them have gone around the block when it comes to Lizbeth's mostly inappropriate obsession with my DNA donor. "Good night, you two." The boys ratchet up their cries as if detecting the fact she's about to vacate the premises. They do seem to love their Mee-Maw. My mother almost stroked out when she heard what Lizbeth insisted her grandchildren call her. And to her credit, she only referenced Tad and Lizbeth as the Paragon Hillbillies just once after that. My father put down his seldom-used iron fist and refused her the right to use that verbiage ever again.

"Be good, boys," she sings as she makes her way to the door. "And you two be nice to one another, too. The boys are cranky because they can feel your tension. Once the two of you kiss and make up, they'll sleep like the little princes they are. You'll see. Try me on this!" She gives a sly wink my way, and I mouth *thank you* before the door seals shut once again.

I turn to Skyla, each of us bouncing a baby in our arms, and my soul melts at how precious this moment is. "Let's be nice." I take a step in and take in her soft vanilla scent. My guts cinches at how easily aroused I am around her. Skyla and I haven't been together for two solid weeks and my balls are aching, about to malfunction without her. "How about we head up to the butterfly room?"

"How about you go and get the swings, Gage?" She puts the baby down and takes Nathan from me. "And then go home and take care of your sick mother." Her head ticks to the side. "How was that for nice?"

"Perfect." It may not be equal to some alone time in the butterfly room, but I'll take it. I head down and Ethan helps me hoist the swings upstairs. Somewhere we've got another set, most likely in the garage with a pile of unopened boxes we had no room for after the baby shower.

No sooner do we get the swings situated in the last patch of free space in the bedroom than the boys miraculously fall asleep in them. Skyla shoos both Ethan and me out of the room and bolts the door behind us. I can't blame her. She's eager to get a single moment of shut-eye. Between nursing and no sleep, I don't know how she's surviving. Most likely she's fueled off her hatred for me. And that alone brings a wry smile to my face.

"Still in the doghouse huh, dude?" Ethan gives my arm a swift sock and I grunt.

"Yes," I say incredulously, rubbing the shit out of the bruise quickly forming. Ethan is a darker, meaner looking version of his brother Drake. Sort of a Landon add-on, since he didn't move here with the original crew. "How are things with Em?"

He winces as if I just sucker punched him right back. "She's a freaking mess, dude. Half her relatives are missing." He spears me with a look as if I'm the one who turned the Videns into a thing of horror. "You fucking take care of that shit. You got it?"

"Her relatives volunteered for this shit," I correct. My blood courses with rage at the thought of anyone pinning the blame on me. "Emily of all people should know that."

"Signed up for it?" He glances toward the bottom of the stairs. "I doubt it. Em mentioned something about it being mandatory, something about compensation." He smacks me over the arm. "Do what you can, dude. She's really losing her mind." He takes off, and I can't stop thinking about it.

The Videns are *my* people. The thought they signed up for anything so sinister is enough to piss me off, but the thought of them being forced into something so wicked makes me want to snap my biological father's head right off. And knowing that demon—another, far more sinister head would grow back right in its place.

I take a step back and take in the sweet sound of silence coming from the bedroom. My hand touches over the door, and I say a short prayer over my family, for the new year, for the distant future, and everything in between. Something tells me there aren't enough prayers that will ever make a difference with this fine mess I'm in.

The next day, *both* of my parents are knocked out in bed. It turns out my mother's "allergies" have morphed into an all-out flu. Giselle got wind of it and swung by with enough groceries to feed half the island.

"I'm going to cook and clean, and make sure they both feel their very best by this time next year!"

I take in poor innocent G with the face of Emerson Kragger and the mind of a kindergartner and shake my head. "They should be back in shape by the weekend. But who knows, with all that pampering you're about to do, they might be well by nightfall. Do us both a favor and wash your hands up to your elbows every time you leave their room. Don't touch your nose, eyes, or mouth, and whatever you do, don't kiss Ellis. That could prove deadly for everyone involved." Him especially if I catch them in the act. I caught them in a far more nefarious act a few months back and nearly bashed his skull in. I still don't feel too bad about that. At any given time, Ellis Harrison is higher than ten hippies. For the life of me I can't wrap my head around the fact my sister has chosen him of all people to fall in love with.

Her eyes expand the size of dinner plates. "Oh, I won't. I've been dead myself, and I don't think Ellis would like that very much." She leans in with her hand to her mouth. "They don't light it up nearly as much as Ellis would care for."

"Nice." I think. "I'll see you later. I'd better check on Skyla and the kids, make sure they didn't catch anything." I take off and head for the Landon house. There's no way in hell I'm even mentioning the fact my parents are all but on their deathbeds. Skyla will have my head on a platter. I'm sure at this point it would take very little to land me there.

All I can think about on the drive over is how in the hell to get our marriage back on track. An unfamiliar car is pulled high in the driveway as if it belongs here. A small blue Corolla with a clown's head in the rearview window and I almost want to laugh. Skyla used to detest the sight of those haunted looking phantasms, but not anymore thanks to my father, Barron, the proper one.

But who would be visiting with that ode to Skyla's old fear? I suppose it could be coincidental, but I've learned long ago that not many things around here are.

"Knock, knock," I say as I let myself in with a key this time, old school. The scents of onions and celery and something thicker collide in an appetizing crescendo, and if I didn't know better, it smells a lot like the chicken soup Giselle was starting on.

Melissa whizzes by me with a smirk. "You have guts to show your face around here." She jogs up the stairs, taking them two by two.

"Happy New Year to you, too!" I call after her.

Mia bops down the hall and takes a bouncing step back when she spots me. "You're here!" she squeals. "Skyla, he's here! You can cut his balls off just like you promised!" She races into the family room ahead of me, and I groan at the thought of having yet another body part theoretically on the chopping block.

"Happy New Year," I call out but am met with a few meager grunts.

Both Lizbeth and Tad are at the table. Lizbeth is feeding Misty while Tad ignores the entire population by burying his head in a newspaper. Brielle is huddled with Skyla, each with a baby on their lap, and a dark-haired girl keeps her head bowed while looking at her laptop.

Skyla glances back, and her eyes light up the room. Skyla's eyes have a way of making the reality around you feel like a lie. I would have sworn there was enough light in this room until she looked this way and flooded the house with the brightness of two suns. "Your mother did this." She glances at the dark-haired girl. "Make sure you get two. I don't want the boys sharing any more germs than they have to."

The boys are red-faced and squirming, choking as they struggle to cry, and my heart shreds to pieces knowing they're not feeling well. Tiny mucus bubbles ooze from their nostrils, and Bree periodically suctions it out with a blue nasal aspirator.

"Come here." I scoop Barron from her and hold him close as he swipes at my face a few good times as if trying to slap me. He just might be. I wouldn't blame him if he were. I've been thinking of doing the same thing to myself lately.

The dark-haired girl looks up, and it's Chloe. For a moment I'm stunned into submission—not sure why. Chloe is suddenly Skyla's new shadow. I don't see why I shouldn't expect to see her at the Landon house.

"Stellar start to the new year, Oliver." She shakes her head as if she were just as pissed at me as Skyla. "I'll order three since it's on the Oliver dime. Nothing but the best for your boys, Skyla."

Skyla looks up and nods as if answering every errant question misfiring in my mind. "I always thought I had the best."

Bree takes Nathan from her and starts in on a manic rocking session. "Make sure to get the Snotty Totty. It's the only sure-fire way you'll ever get some sleep again."

"He's sleeping just fine," Skyla quips as she glances my way.

Lizbeth swoops over. "She means you, Skyla." She leans in toward Chloe's laptop. "Believe me, those are the best tools of the trade. And they're so easy to use!" She turns to me and shakes her head. "You just plug the tip into the boys' nostrils and gently suction all of the mucus right on out!" She snaps her fingers as if to exemplify its ease of use.

"Isn't that what Bree was just doing?" I want nothing but the best for my boys just as much as—apparently *Chloe* does, but I'm also far more wary of falling into the consumer trap set out by the baby industry. Half that stuff we've got just seems like an overpriced rip-off. I lean in to get a look at the price tag on one of those fancy nose pumps. $49.99.

Shit. I hope this isn't Skyla trying to stick it to me by way of my credit card. And, judging by the boys, somehow, I doubt that.

"Oh, heavens no!" Lizbeth snatches the nasal aspirator right out of Brielle's hand as if she were taking a loaded gun from her. "This is garbage is what it is. The Snotty Totty comes with a hose that you plug into their nostrils. You plug the other end right into your mouth, young man." She taps her finger over my lips, and I'm suddenly uncomfortable on many levels.

"So you physically suction the—junk out." I'm afraid I know where my services will be needed in just a few hours.

Skyla gives an annoyed blink my way. "I'm sure you'll have fun. You seem to have a habit of imbibing questionable fluids at midnight."

Lizbeth swats her over the shoulder. "We won't dare wait that long. These boys need relief now. Chloe, make sure you opt for one-hour shipping."

Mia takes a seat on the coffee table. "When are you cutting his head off, Skyla?"

"He needs his head for now." Skyla manufactures a sweet smile my way. "But soon."

Mia gets up to leave but not before outright gifting me the finger. Shit. I can't help but avert my eyes at that one.

"Skyla, I need to speak with you."

Lizbeth nods over to Bree. "Why don't we get the boys in their swings. They've been up all night. They can use some sleep."

I wait until they're out of earshot before sitting on the coffee table across from Skyla and Chloe. I can't help but look from my sweet angel of a wife to the witch by her side and think she's in way over her head.

"What the hell is going on?" I growl it out far more aggressive than I meant to, but with Chloe around I can't seem to help it.

Skyla sharpens her gaze over mine as if she were ready to ax my skull in two. "The Tenebrous Woods are empty. Your father and brother swiped every petrified Viden soul right out of there and planted them worldwide to cause a mass panic, or don't you pay attention to the news?"

Chloe gives a solemn nod. "It's in every paper. Every talking head is flapping their frantic jaw about it. You can't open the Internet without reading another story of a scary clown sighting, a monster chasing children in the woods. The world has gone to hell in a handbasket, Gage Oliver, and—" She looks to Skyla a moment. "And what?"

"Precisely." I swallow down a laugh. "Skyla—Chloe doesn't see a problem with any of this. Whatever it is you're doing with her has to stop. You're dancing in the flames." I pick up her cool fingers and cradle them in my palm. "I promise you, things are going to end badly. She killed your father," I whisper the horrible reminder. "Logan, too." It hurts just to say it.

She retracts her hand. "I know." Skyla closes her eyes a moment and takes a deep breath as if trying to keep from getting sick. And then just as easily, her eyes snap open like a ventriloquist doll and she gives an eerie blink. "But we've moved on." She reaches over and takes up Chloe's hand, and now it's me who's going to be sick. For a moment, I try to recall which arm of hers once belonged to Chloe, and if she's holding her own hand by proxy—but then, Chloe is no longer in her own body. She's in Ezrina's.

Chloe bleeds that desolate smile, the smile of death, the smile that says I am ten steps ahead of you both—and you will most certainly be sorry you ever fucked with me.

And trust me, I'm already sorry.

"Skyla and I have mended fences." She bounces my wife's hand on her lap, and I want to free her. Every last part of Chloe is nothing more than a bear trap. "We've moved on from our childish ways and become a united front." She looks to Skyla and gives a somber nod as if encouraging her to go along with the farce.

"United," Skyla says with her eyes locked over on the girl who has been her enemy as far back as I can remember. "Chloe and I are going to change things, Gage." Skyla doesn't take her eyes off the sinister devil next to her. If I were to suggest one thing with this strange demonic friendship brewing, it would be just that—keep your eyes wide open. "We are going to start with you."

"With me," I say more to myself than anyone else in the room.

Chloe lets out a bubbling laugh. "She's traded you in for me, Gage. Isn't that something?" She loses herself in a stream of laughter she can't seem to contain just as Lizbeth breezes back into the room, forcing her to pause and appraise the three of us.

"What's this?" Tad balks. "She's traded in Greg for a woman?" He staggers over with his arm swinging wide, still locked up in that baseball bat of a splint. His face is red and glossed with petroleum jelly to keep his skin from crusting over. "Is that what's going on here?" he huffs as he struggles to get the words out. "Lizbeth!" he barks at his poor, emotionally neglected wife. I've no doubt that right there is the reason she seems so attracted to Demetri in the first place. He has a way of shining the spotlight on her whenever he's in the room. And Tad has a way of ripping her to pieces with his caustic tongue. The math is pretty easy to do. "Your daughter here has given Greg the boot so she can entertain her lady friend." His eyes bug out so far, I'm half-expecting them to shoot across the room. I want to say I feel the same way, Tad. My own head demands to explode over this bizarre union.

"It's not like that." Lizbeth digs her fists into her hips, ready to go ten rounds if she had to. "Skyla and Chloe do not have an intimate relationship. For God's sake, use your head. She's got Gage Oliver to fulfill her needs. Why in the heck would she look in any other direction?"

A sheepish grin comes to me as I look to my wife. But Skyla rolls her eyes at the idea. I know what she's thinking. Lizbeth has had a bizarre infatuation with me since the beginning. She's as much on my team as Candace is on Logan's. Too bad for me, Lizbeth has no say in just about anything that has to do with my destiny. Demetri pops to mind, and I glance up at her as if seeing Skyla's stepmother for the very first time.

"*Shit,*" I hiss, stunned. Lizbeth might just be my saving grace after all. Nobody has pull with my father like she does.

"I *know*!" Tad does an odd little tap dance. "I'm just as shocked as you are." His head juts out over and over in his wife's direction like a chicken. "Like it or not, Lizbeth, I heard the whole thing with my own two ears! She's traded him in for a new model, and that new model is missing a few boy parts!" He blinks back as if he's just slapped himself. "Wait a minute. This might be the only form of birth control that will work. On second thought, congratulations, girls. I'll have Lizbeth bake a cake to celebrate. If we gather all the loose socks in the house, we might be able to fashion together a rainbow flag."

"Chloe's got a kid," I whip the words out before Tad decides to throw my wife and her fictional lesbian lover a party. "And a husband." That should nail the coffin on that rainbow-colored conversation.

"Jumping Jehoshaphat, Lizbeth!" Tad bucks as if the thought of another mouth to feed has him gripped with pain. "No way, no how are we taking in boarders. This nonsense has got to stop. *Greg"*—he grunts as he turns my way, and I narrowly duck in time, avoiding a splint to the eye—"you get that house of horrors of yours whipped into shape, you hear me? As soon as princess here has a castle of her own to fill with all the screaming babies she wants—I'm sure she'll hightail it right back to you."

"Tad Landon!" Lizbeth barks so loud the boys start in on a bleating cry from the living room. "Now look what you've done," she seethes through her teeth. "Don't you ever try to kick my daughter out of *our* home. Skyla and whomever she loves is more than welcome here." She ticks her head my way. "You, too, Gage."

I blink over at Chloe a moment who isn't missing the opportunity to gloat.

Holy crap. What alternate universe am I living in?

"Come on, Tad." Lizbeth leads him back to the table. "We've got mountains of unemployment paperwork to fill out. I want to be on the first ferry to the mainland in the morning. Those unemployment lines are just about as fun as the DMV."

"I've got nothing but time on my hands, Lizbeth. In fact, I might even take up gardening, or golfing. The leisure activities I'll have time for now are endless!"

Two tiny bodies run past me, naked—covered in what looks like chocolate—but holy hell that smell gives it away. That ain't chocolate.

Lizbeth screams at the sight. "Misty and Beau Landon! I have had it up to here with your potty shenanigans!"

Misty dives in and wraps herself around Tad's legs, and he lets out a yelp while hobbling toward the back. "Open the door, Lizbeth! We'll clean the little shits off with the hose!"

Shit, indeed. I lean in to Skyla. "Tad lost his job?"

"That's right." Her nose wrinkles with her growing irritation—and perhaps the stench. "That three-headed, zero-hearted father of yours swiped it right from under him. Tad is persona non grata at Althorpe. Maybe you can put in a good word for him, now that you and Daddy Dearest are playing on the same team."

There's a strange sexual connotation there that I'm not touching. "I'm pretty sure your mother has more pull with him than I do." Especially in that arena.

"*What?*" both Skyla and Chloe shout in unison. Skyla and Chloe doing anything in unison is unnerving on just about every level.

"It's true." I'm pained to think that she's taken it as a slight. I lean in and whisper, "In a single conversation, your mother could sweet talk my father into just about anything."

"Holy hell." Skyla tosses up her arms. "Just when I thought you couldn't sink any lower, Gage Oliver. Okay, playtime is over. Go and head back to the cave you crawled out of." Her finger darts to the door. She might as well have socked me in the gut—I couldn't feel worse if I tried.

"That's not what I meant." My eyes never stray from hers. "I love you, Skyla. I will always love you."

I take off for the living room where the boys finally look to be resting, sleeping peacefully in the swings. They've either been hauled back downstairs or someone yanked out the new set from the garage. No sooner do I get out the door than Chloe appears by my side.

"Whatever it is, you can save it," I toss it out there before she segues into her head games. Chloe is a master at just that.

"Aren't you in the least bit interested?" She blinks those spider lashes at me.

"No."

"Know this. I'm always on your side, Gage. I'm a lot of things, and one of them is loyal to a fault—to *you*." Her finger curls under my chin, and I turn my head.

"Don't think for a minute that Skyla doesn't know that." I head to my truck, jumping down the stairs two at a time. "And I don't need you on my side, Chloe."

Every damn side she's on is the wrong one.

Other than Skyla and the boys, there is just one more person I'm anxious to see today—my brother. I park the truck back at the house and don't even bother leaving the driver's seat before teleporting to the Transfer. I land on solid ground in this dark, hellish nightmare of a pit. The Transfer is a plane that belongs to the Counts. With little to no light, a perennial darkness seeps over the landscape in tones of violet and navy blue. There's a jagged line in the sky that looks as if it were ripped open then stitched back together again, and I marvel at it because I've never noticed it before. A battered and bruised countryside appears with cobbled roadways, weed-riddled hillsides. Everywhere you look dozens of long dead spirits tread transparent yet not forgotten with their old-fashioned dress codes, men in dapper suits, women in full hoop skirts, ghostly pale tits out to there. A group of them scuttle by without bothering to go around me. And a mean shiver runs up my spine as a robust woman walks right through my chest.

"Nice," I muse. "Happy New Year to you, too!" I call after them, annoyed as I iron my shirt with my palms, and the entire group breaks out into a cackle. They're a jovial bunch, I'll give them that.

I glance back and spot a dull blue light emanating from the cave-like entrance that leads to Ezrina's old stomping grounds. Ezrina was once bound to the Counts for hundreds of years, no thanks to Candace and her linear march for justice. Too bad for Ezrina, Candace sees justice through an unforgiving lens, but Skyla managed to talk her mother into giving both Ezrina and Nevermore another chance, and that's precisely why Nev is wearing Pierce Kragger's dead body like a sports coat, and Ezrina is tooling around in Chloe's old haunted shell.

Chloe.

Just the thought of her makes my stomach boil in its own acids. I stalk down the road past the old—original—mansion with its haunted White House appeal. It's cavernous inside, dark as crap, illuminated with the dim light of a thousand dusty candles. There's a piano set in the formal living room that some old coot is constantly bouncing on, and for whatever reason, the entire phantasmic estate holds the scent of fresh apples. Skyla and I exchanged our wedding vows there last September. September thirteenth to be exact. It was a day to remember, with both the living and the dead present, and I would do anything if we could rewind time and go right back to that magical moment. I wouldn't have missed the birth of my firstborn son—Logan cut Nathan's cord. I would have had a minute to think on how I might have escaped the covenant I had entered into, but, in reality, deep down inside, I realize there was no escaping my true destiny. Demetri had sown the seeds to my destruction the moment he ejaculated me into existence.

I grimace at my raw and rather disgusting analogy as I enter through the gates of my brother's estate, an exact replica of the one down the road but bigger, newer, and all around better. Not that living in the Transfer is anything to boast about. Surely the fact he's raising my niece in this haunted hovel is something we will most certainly have to address. The child needs sunlight for God's sake. She'll wither down here physically, and with Chloe Bishop as her mother, who the hell knows what she's up against emotionally.

"Wesley?" I bark as I enter the massive foyer. The entire mansion has a medieval appeal. It's clear he's taken the décor into a whole different era. The OG mansion down the road is Victorian through and through. "*Wes.*" My voice roars in duplicate before my brother comes bounding from the hall. A tiny pink bundle in his arms screws her tiny fists into her eyes as if struggling to rouse herself.

"There she is." I give her foot a soft pinch as Wesley lays her down in a playpen and tosses a blanket over her waist. Tobie is a dark-haired, bright-eyed beauty, plump and happy despite the fact her mother neither cares to feed her nor cares for her in general. Chloe has left all the work to my brother, which he in turn has relegated all the work to Ezrina. "The boys have colds."

"So, you've come to share your germs?" His dark brows arch with something just this side of fury, and a dull smile twitches on my lips. Wesley Edinger is my exact representation. It's odd because he was only vaguely that in the beginning, and as Demetri's sinister scheme laid out, it became painfully clear he was a Johnny one-note when it came to propagating his genetics. I'd say I was the mold, but Wesley is slightly older by a year, I believe. I don't really care at this point. As far as I'm concerned, we're both equally impotent when it comes to defying our wicked father.

"Don't worry. I won't kiss her. I won't kiss you either, sweetheart. Where's Rina?"

"She's not feeling well." He kick-starts a dying fire until the room lights up with the inferno-like blaze.

"I guess there's a first time for everything." I consider this a moment. Ezrina is the great physician, just one notch below the Almighty. It almost doesn't make sense. "Skyla and Chloe have teamed up. What the hell is up, Wes?" I twist my fist into his T-shirt and pull him in close. "We're on the same team now—remember, *brother*?" I force a smile to come and go as I glower at this demented version of myself. "Tell me what you know."

"I know nothing." He offers me a firm shove off his person. "Why would Skyla of all people even get near Chloe? Skyla is dangerous if she thinks that's a good idea." He takes a few steps over to the bar and fixes himself a shot of whiskey, neat, and offers it to me.

I wave it off. I have enough poison coursing through my veins these days. "Your wife is the dangerous one, Wes. Find out whatever you can and report back to me. We need to stick together. We need each other. This can be damning to both sides." Appealing to his ego *and* his people is the only way to approach things with my knockoff brother.

"So that's where she's been." Wes sways on his feet a moment, his drink swilling in his hand as he considers this. "That means Chloe has an all access pass to Paragon. She hasn't been around the house but twice in the last two weeks." His gaze remains fixed on the flames licking free from the fireplace. "Chloe and Skyla." He shakes his head. "Nothing good is going to come of this."

"But logic dictates something very much will come of this. Any news on the warfront? Skyla mentioned the Videns are back in the wild. Back to haunting the masses? So you're setting up the rogue Factions for a fall." That's about as much as I can figure. Wesley isn't all that much into secret motives. He operates in your face for the most part, and that's the most frightening enemy of them all. "You are moving in a singular direction. Panic the public, point the finger at the Factions unwilling to bow at your feet, and then play the part of the false savior you are."

That dark grin of his widens, his brows twitching with amusement at the fact I've reduced his menacing plans to a nutshell. "You, my brother, are the savior. Make no bones about it. I am simply your humble servant." He offers a mock bow. "Do you like the clowns? I thought it was a nice touch myself. Sort of an ode to Skyla if you will. The world is in near hysterics. Some of the moronic humans are getting in on it, too. Their copycat tactics have only added to the chaos." He toasts their efforts, and the amber liquid in his glass glows in the light of the flames. "They need us, Gage. They're already begging for someone to step in and end the madness."

"Somebody let me in on the fact that the Videns didn't go in willingly. Demetri is outright using my people." I swallow hard at the idea of having people in general. When the Videns were gifted to me—*me* as their fearless leader—I wanted to laugh. I've never taken a gift Demetri has tried to shove in my direction seriously, and now it's becoming clear I should have done just that. I don't know them the way a leader should know their people. I had no idea what they were up against, and yet here I'm up against the very same thing—my father.

Wes ticks his head to the side as if he's genuinely surprised to hear it. "Who said that?"

I'm leaving Ethan out of it. "That's not the point. The point is, I need to make a concerted effort to speak with the Videns and find out what's going on." I'll start with Em's family and work my way out. "If this is true, you and I will both work to rectify the situation. You don't need them, Wes. You have enough minions, enough defectors from the rest of the Factions to set the world on fire."

"Now *that* is true." He toasts me once again before knocking back the rest of his drink. He sucks in a quick breath through his teeth before setting his glass onto the counter. "I'll work with you if that's the case. But not before launching a full-scale investigation of my own."

A dull smile comes to my face. "You don't trust me."

"The river runs both ways."

The clicking of heels comes from the entry, and we turn to find the queen demon herself haunting the doorway—Chloe.

"Here you are." Chloe breezes into the room and smirks over at Tobie before settling in our midst. "I was so confident I'd find you here. This is the first place I looked." She hikes up on her tiptoes and offers an unwarranted embrace. "What I'm doing is for your benefit and mine," she whispers hot into my ear, and I pull her off me. "Skyla needs you asap, so do not pass go, do not stop by home to check on your poor sick mother. Head straight to Landon jail. The boys are waiting to have the snot sucked out of their noses by yours truly. I bet you're thrilled you fathered an entire liter of snotty little pups, aren't you?"

Wes shoots me a questioning look, and I shake my head at him.

Instead, I focus my earnest efforts on being nice and reasonable with the witch at hand. "What's going on with you and Skyla?"

Chloe has always held her mean beauty, her mean heart close to the vest like a very sharp knife. In the beginning, I played along. I wanted to know her secrets, be her friend, but in the end, I couldn't give her what she really wanted—myself. It was Chloe and I that fashioned together that butterfly room above Skyla's closet. It was Chloe's intense obsession for me that fueled so much heartbreak, so much loss and devastation. Perhaps it is truly the nexus of what caused Chloe's death to begin with. Yes, Skyla played a part, but I was the kernel that grew into a strangulating vine and wrapped myself around her neck whether I like to admit it or not. But I don't blame myself. Chloe's incessant need to have me far outweighs the borders of sanity.

Chloe blinks to life as if she were tuned into my internal conversation and shakes her head as if to rebuff my theory.

"I'm just being her friend, Gage. Skyla and I haven't always seen eye to eye, but we've found something we can bond over, agree on, and we're moving in the right direction for the right reason. That's all you need to know." She pins my brother with a crooked smile. "That's all either of you need to know." Chloe takes off into the bowels of this megastructure, and I head for the door myself.

"Gage"—Wes calls out, and I turn around—"I'll keep an ear out." He nods toward his raging lunatic of a wife. "We'll get to the bottom of both this and the Videns, together."

Together. I offer a peaceable smile as I head out the door and dissolve to nothing.

For so long it was Logan who stood staunchly by my side, and Wesley was nothing more than an interloper in our midst.

But for the first time in a long while, Wes feels less like an interloper and a lot more like a brother.

Logan

Weeks whip by with Paragon locked in a windy fury, blowing the fog banks across the island in angry volatile jags. It's almost offensive in nature to watch. The fog has been here for us for as long as I can remember, and the bitter wind is something new, novel, that most residents of the island want nothing to do with. Watching the fog get bumped around saddens me, like watching an elderly relative get shoved by some menacing bully, and yet there's not a thing you can do about it. But Paragon doesn't relinquish the fog. She refuses to dismiss the thick layer of dark clouds that lurk overhead, either. But she is relentless in shooing away this wind-born stranger, rebuffing his incessant need to claim her. No, Paragon is stubborn, and, for this arrogant pride alone, I find her endearing. Paragon wins again and again. She reminds me a lot of Skyla.

The Landon house is dark inside, mostly because, according to Gage, they are in serious conservation mode. Rumor has it, Tad is officially on the outs with Althorpe and is trying desperately to manufacture a plan that might keep his bustling inn up and running. In fact, that, in part, is what's prompted my visit. As much as I didn't appreciate the shakedown Tad and Lizbeth elicited on the bowling alley last year during that well-thought-out slip and fall routine, I would do anything to help this family out. But I can't save the world. Hell, I can't even save myself. I'm simply here to pay a visit to my favorite people on the planet. Gage and his tiny beautiful family.

Mia lets me in with a huff and grunts something about Rev under her breath. I know for a fact she's seeing him, sleeping with him, according to Skyla, but if the disgruntled look on Mia's face suggests anything, it's that things are not going well in paradise. They seldom do. I know this firsthand, considering I'm there at the moment and simultaneously here. I'm still a bit puzzled why Candace chose to gift me a Treble, a permanent yet not official placement on planet earth, where I'm free to roam and stalk Skyla as I wish. And dear God Almighty, how I wish.

I head upstairs, give a gentle knock over their bedroom door, and Gage moans for me to come in. Even though he's still very much in the dog house, Skyla has relented enough to have him over to help out with the boys. Gage has become the official snot sucker of the family, an act and title I could have never imagined, still don't want to. But, if anything, that alone should prove to Skyla that Gage Oliver is devoted to his little clan, through and snotty nose through.

"Logan." Skyla gives a limp wristed wave that looks suspiciously like the white flag of surrender as the babies lie slumped in her arms. "They were up all night. They really do hate me."

The boys both raise their fists in tandem and writhe with their eyes closed as if they were about to fall into a heavy afternoon nap. My heart melts at the sight of those dark-haired angels with their twitching dimples, their pudgy little arms and legs that I can't get enough of. Deep down, I suspected that both Skyla and Gage would have adorable children one day. I just never imagined they would be having them together.

"Nobody hates you." I thread my way through the cramped space, trying not to look at the clutter that abounds—diapers and clothes on every surface, a pile of towels and blankets amassing against the window. A part of me wonders if this is a fire hazard. The entire room looks like a tinderbox. I lean in and offer my beautiful princess a kiss to the cheek and her flesh feels hot and clammy. The room smells thick with sickness and sweat intermingled with the slight hint of baby powder, but I'll be the last to point out they should put a crack in the window.

"Put a crack in the window," Skyla belts the command out to Gage faster than I can process the fact she's just read my mind.

"My abilities are fading." Her legs curl under herself on the mattress as she pats a spot next to her. "You can leave, Gage." She dismisses her husband as if he were a mere servant, a paid employee, and at this point Gage would be honored to be both.

Gage puts a crack in the window just like he's told but takes a seat at the edge of the bed next to me in an outright act of defiance. I shake my head at him. Gage and I have gone around the block regarding how to fix this mess. Skyla simply isn't ready to hear anything that transpired that night with Demetri. And I get it. She's not opposed to what Gage has done—or at least I'm hoping she won't be—but she's opposed to us making another move behind her back. And that's exactly what we did—what we seem to keep doing.

"Emily isn't talking." Gage looks to the two of us. "I'm trying to figure out if the Videns went in against their will. Ethan swears it's the truth. The Faction isn't willing to come to the meetings anymore, so I'm basically thinking of heading door to door."

"I'll go with you." I tap my knee over his. Gage and Skyla have both been knocked out by the flu—or as Skyla calls it, The Great Emma Plague of the Millennium. Emma and Barron have yet to fully recover themselves. And believe me, Emma has made herself that much more miserable knowing her grandchildren had to suffer for it.

"And I won't go with you," Skyla quips. "Again, you can leave now." Her voice wobbles as she blinks back the moisture in her eyes.

"Did I walk in on something?" I rise to leave, and Skyla lands her leg over my thighs, pinning me down once again.

"You know, on second thought, I think I can use some air." She scoots past me and lays the boys down in a single bassinet and neither of them makes a sound. "I'll get dressed"—she heads to the closet—"maybe you can supervise me as I try to run around the block?" Her hair billows over her head, an entire foot like a blonde halo, and she looks comical in a breathtaking way. Skyla's kinky curls have always delighted me. Her hair, those velum clear eyes, everything about her has a personality of its own.

"I can be your trainer," I whisper as loud as I can as she entombs herself inside the walk-in. Gage shoots me a look, and a twinge of guilt eats at me. "Sorry, man." I slap a hand over my nephew's knee.

"No, it's fine." He rubs his eyes in a lethargic move. Gage looks as if he hasn't slept in months, and he hasn't.

"Just thought of something." I offer a congratulatory pat to his back. "The boys are two months old to the day."

"Nathan." His head bobs with the admission. "Barron is holding out until tomorrow."

We share a quiet laugh. The boys were born minutes apart on two different days, just like Skyla and Gage themselves, and on exactly their birthdays. Nathan on Skyla's and Barron on Gage's big day.

"Hey"—he whispers as he cuts a quick glance to the closet—"I want to talk to you about something real quick."

"What's up, man?" It hurts my heart to see Skyla and Gage not getting along. Hell, it hurts my heart that she's still pretty pissed at me as well, but the fact she wants to go anywhere with me is a huge step in the right direction. "You want me to talk to her?"

"No—yes, *maybe*." He grinds his palm into his hand. "I don't know. Actually, I wanted to let you know that I went to the bank this morning." He frowns at the closet door a moment. "A few weeks back, Demetri brought this woman to the New Year's party Lizbeth threw, and I met her. Her name was Dominique. It turns out she's Melody Winters' mother, the chick from the morgue."

I shoot a quick glance out the window, trying to absorb this. "I take it her mother was grateful."

"Too grateful. She said she wanted to give me a reward. She mentioned something about making a straight deposit to my account. I didn't think too much of it at the time, and then the boys got sick and I got slammed. So this morning when I went in to deposit a few checks, I about dropped dead when I saw the balance."

"She was generous." I nod, trying to put the pieces together. The fact this is Demetri's friend we're talking about sends off all sorts of bells and whistles. "What are we talking? A hundred bucks? A thousand? Ten thousand?"

He shakes his head and hitches his thumb in the air. "One hundred thousand dollars."

"Holy shit." My body heat spikes just hearing the number. "Did you tell Skyla?"

"Nope." His brows hike a notch. "I called Mrs. Winters to let her know I couldn't accept it, but she said I could donate it to any charity I wished. She's not taking it back."

"What are you going to do?" A part of me wonders if I'm the charity in question. I wouldn't take a dime even if Gage offered it.

"I'm keeping it." His dimples dig in deep. "I'm setting some aside for the boys' education, and I'm using the rest to fix that damn house."

That Damn House is just about the official name of the haunted shack Skyla and Gage purchased a few months back. It just so happens to sit on the property next to Barron and Emma's. Skyla will be her mother-in-law's next-door neighbor one day, that is, if she and Gage survive this current crisis, and I have no doubt they will. And when they do, Skyla will have a whole new crisis to deal with. I wish I could have stopped them from making the purchase, but That Damn House is behind the *damn* gates, which means it has the potential to be worth a lot of damn money one day.

I reach over and slap him a quick five. "I'm damn glad for you, man. Just let me know what I can do to help."

"You really want to break your back with me?"

"All day long, dude. All the *damn* day long."

"Thanks, man." He reaches over and pulls me in for a quick pat to the back. "And another thing, something isn't sitting right with me about the Winters. I asked Brody about them, and he didn't seem to know too much. He said he'd look into it for me."

"It'll be interesting to see what comes of that."

"Maybe a little too interesting."

Skyla emerges in a pair of black leggings and Gage's old practice sweatshirt from our football days at West. Just looking at Cerberus' ugly three-headed mug on her chest brings a crooked smile to my face. She whips her hair into a ponytail and nods for me to follow her out the door. I give Gage a quick wave, and he falls back on the bed, his eyes close before he ever hits the pillow.

Skyla and I are off—let's hope my balls survive the effort.

Skyla leads us straight downstairs, past the heavy argument Tad and Lizbeth are engaged in, past Mia and Melissa's squabble over a hairbrush—that one of them is threatening to shove up the other's ass, past a giant beast of a dog that I only vaguely recognize, and out into a fresh burst of powder white Paragon fog.

Skyla throws her arms back and turns her face to the sky, a wide smile spreading across her face as if her freedom were newly issued, and in a way it has been, temporarily at least.

"I love the way Paragon kisses me. First kiss of the new year. First day outside in weeks."

My own smile quickly fades as I try to wrap my head around the idea. "You mean you haven't left the house in a month?"

Her expression sours as she leads us down to the street. "It hasn't quite been a month. But it's crazy, right? I mean, people literally lose their minds staying cooped up like that, and believe me, in that house in particular, the odds of being sane are never in your favor."

After the melee I just witnessed in that one small thirty-second microcosm, I'd have to agree. But seeing that I'm walking a fine line, the last thing I'm going to do is insult her family.

"Ha." She gives a tiny laugh, half-hearted at best. "I heard you. My powers are fading, though." I look down and marvel at the fact we're not touching. She takes a moment to rework her ponytail until her hair is in a bun. *I love Skyla with a bun. Hell, I'd love her bald. Did you hear that? I love you, Skyla Oliver.* I pump a smile and wait for a response, but she bends over and tightens the strings on her tennis shoes, and I can't tell if she didn't hear or if I'm still in the doghouse.

"Doghouse." She stands up straight and gives a quick wink. "I know you love me, Logan." A cloudbank of fog bursts between us as if Paragon herself has something she'd like to insert regarding our love. She can save it. This island doesn't have a right to something so sacred. "I know you love me in a lot of ways, but not in the way I would hope. Even if you won't admit it, I know you love Gage just a little bit more." Her crystal eyes sharpen over mine when she says it.

There it is, the slap in the face. Her bitter words penetrate to my marrow and poison my blood—toxic enough to kill me, that is, if I were living.

"No." I can hardly get the word out. I take a step in, closing the distance between us. "A thousand times, *no*. I love you *more* than him." It's true. I'm not sure how it's possible because my love for Gage is infinite, but I know this to be true. "I wanted to protect you. I was a fool not to tell you, but if I did, it would have hurt you more in the end."

"*Ugh!*" She tosses a hand in the air and walks away, fading into the mist. "Stop being so obstinate."

"Stop being so stubborn," I bark as I run up ahead of her, jogging backward just to keep pace.

Skyla lets out a grunt, shaking her head at just how obstinate I can be. "You've got nerve."

"And you've got to listen." It comes out with far more fury than it ever does pleading. "If you knew the facts, we could work with them—make them our bitch."

"Why would you need the facts to be your bitch, Logan? *I'm* your bitch, remember?" She hits her stride with a light jog, and I take up the position beside her.

"Don't talk like that. You're the love of my life. My *wife*." There. I said it. "I still see you that way, Skyla. I would bend over backward for you, crawl through blood, kill or be killed. I would die for you, my queen, and I did." The words come out sharp as knives. A poem dipped in ashes and soot. I never was good at sweet talk.

She flits her irritated gaze my way and stops short, already panting out of breath, and we haven't even cleared the next driveway. "You're a *liar,* Logan. You always have been—always feeding me half-truths just to appease me. If that's any indication of your undying love for me, then you must love me about as much as you love Chloe."

"I'm too tired to fight with you. Whatever you're doing with Chloe, it's going to backfire spectacularly in your face. Shit. I fully expect it to. I've been watching you long enough to know there's no other way." My stomach clenches when I cast that barb without meaning to. If I could only take it back. There are so many things that I've allowed to happen to the two of us that I would gladly take back.

She stops cold. Those steely eyes of hers pierce into mine with sorrow and pain and outrage all at once. "I think I'm going to run." Her cheeks pinch bright pink when she says it. "I think running might be better. How about I run to the end of the block and you time me?" she pants the words through an open mouth, her face straining as if begging for mercy before she ever begins.

She's closing me off, putting our argument on the shelf for the time being. Skyla has a gift of carrying her grudges and her arguments and dividing them, compartmentalizing them for later, and for whatever reason, I'm okay with it. I don't think I could take her anger all at once. It's too hot under the white light of her fury. I can't take the heat.

"All right, as your coach, I say move it." I clap my hands as she takes off, legs already kicking wild, her arms jamming down like hammers as she takes a few gyrating steps forward. She hits the middle of the block and stops cold, bends her head over her knees like she might vomit. A dry laugh pumps from me as I catch up to her.

"You okay?"

"No, I'm not okay. I'm never getting my body back." She squeezes her eyes shut tight as she straightens. "At this point I'm not too sure I care. I need sleep, Logan." She latches onto me without warning, and my body adheres to hers. Skyla lays her full weight onto me. Her warm breath heats my chest, and it feels like heaven. "I'm taking us to Whitehorse." She wheezes into my chest. "I think I can." Her head writhes from side to side. Skyla is delirious with fatigue. "We're just going to lie in bed a minute. I'm gonna try to get some sleep."

The world around us fades in and out like a bad dream as we land on a soft mattress. The walls around us form, and the room is suddenly familiar. Skyla hasn't landed us at Whitehorse, far from it. We're in my old bedroom at Barron's. Skyla has been in my room hundreds of times. It makes sense. This is where her mind equates my bed.

"Did I do good?" Her body curls into mine, but she doesn't bother opening her eyes to inspect the surroundings.

"You did good." I don't have the heart to tell her otherwise. Instead, I lean over and land a gentle kiss to the top of her head.

A light knock comes over the door. "Logan, is that you?" Emma calls from the other side.

"It's me." I try to sound casual, not at all as if I'm in bed with my nephew's wife.

The door swings open, and Emma leans in with a smile that quickly fades to a scowl.

"Oh, for shit's sake." She steps back out and shuts the door with a slam. In all my life, I think that's the one expletive she's ever spoken in my presence, at least toward me—or more to the point, toward the woman lying in bed with me wrapped lovingly in my arms the way I thought it would be from the beginning. The way fate decided that it wouldn't be, at least *not* in the beginning, and everything about that sad scenario breaks my heart.

Skyla jolts to attention and gives a sleepy-eyed glance around. "Oops! Wrong house." A sheepish giggle strums from her. "I'll try again."

"No, it's fine." I try to assure her, but the words come out too late, leaving my voice behind in a room that our bodies have already vacated.

Another room forms around us—dark paneling, darker furniture, a ridiculous amount of Victorian décor, and this time we're not alone on the oversized mattress. Lying down with nothing but a sheet precariously covering home plate, Marshall Dudley relaxes on his elbows with the remote in hand while some psychotic screams her head off on the IMAX-sized television blaring in front of us, and he's quick to mute it.

"I didn't realize I should have prepared for guests." He offers a bored glance my way as if I were nothing more significant than a gnat in his presence, but his fingers find their way into Skyla's hair as if they belonged there. "My love—you've finally come to your senses."

A deep-welled groan evicts from her simply from his touch, and she does her best to burrow into his mattress before offering a groggy look around.

"Am I dreaming?" She looks from him to me. "Oh no." She buries her face into the pillow for a moment before coming up for air and locking those red, tired eyes my way. "Is this going to turn into one of those flesh-fests where you suck my nipples?" She turns to Dudley. "And you lick my—"

"All right." I pull Skyla toward me before she initiates anything she might regret. "You're tired. Get some rest. When you wake up, I'll get you home." Her eyes seal shut before I can finish.

I glare over at the wily Sector who's trying to hide his boner under that sheet snaking around his body. "Party's over, sweetheart. Get dressed. We're going downstairs. There are a few things we need to discuss."

His fingers dance over Skyla's bare arm, and she takes in a soothing breath as if she hasn't felt that level of comfort in years.

"I'll meet you down there," he grumbles, his sexed-up gaze is still very much fixed on the sleeping beauty between us.

"I'm not leaving." I lean back and focus in on the screen. I'm not interested in inspecting his junk. I'm interested in protecting Skyla from it. My body melts into the butter soft sheets, the mattress that seems to be made from angel feathers. Damn, this bed is comfortable.

"Very well." Dudley rises, suddenly fully clothed in a suit minus the jacket. His fingers work over the buttons around his wrists as if he actually put in the effort rather than materialized the clothing onto his body. "I'll meet you downstairs." His body evaporates quicker than the fog, and just like that, he's gone.

Skyla nestles against me, and my urge to vacate the premises goes out the door right along with Dudley. I lean over and brush my lips against the soft velvet of her cheek.

"Sleep tight, princess." I press in another quick peck, and this time I savor the feel.

Downstairs, Dudley's home is still festooned with Christmas décor, an impeccable Victorian motif that Lexy mentioned she helped him with. His tree is lit in the living room with thousands of tiny white lights, and a large raging fire fills the room with a homey glow, but believe me, there is not a single homey thing about this mausoleum. It's stale, as welcoming as a museum, a morgue for that matter.

"What have you been up to these days, young Oliver?" Dudley takes a seat on the couch and kicks his Italian

ADDISON MOORE

leather shoes up onto the coffee table. He flicks on the television right back to that raging, talking head he was glued to upstairs. FNX News. It's the same station that's kept Barron and Emma riveted for years. "Are you keeping up with the humor these days?" He raises the volume on the one-eyed monster, and a panel of angry men and women rage about the recent clown sightings that have half the country in a state of panic.

"It's just Wes up to his old games. I don't need a road map to draw that conclusion."

"That it is. But the Videns aren't doing this for Wesley. Aren't you in the least bit interested as to who exactly has taken an interest in joining forces with him?" He mutes the cacophony of sound once again, and the fire crackles, soothing the room with its flickering rhythm.

"Fems." I close my eyes a moment. "So it begins."

"Not yet." Dudley tosses the remote onto the table and misses by a mile, but that remote floats right back into the air and lands softly on the marbled top table as if Dudley scored the first time. Only on rare occasions have I seen Dudley do anything so blatantly unhuman around me. Not that there is anything remotely human about Dudley. He's the only created being outside of Demetri that I know of roaming this planet. "They're waiting for their leader."

"Gage doesn't take the position until he's good and dead," I say the words lower than a whisper, because let's face it, there is nothing good about Gage's impending death. "And I plan on keeping him around for a long time to come."

"I'm afraid his father doesn't share your sentiment. In fact, he's worth more to him without his heart pumping away in that useless body. He's procured his heirs—heralded one magnificent commitment from his favorite offspring. That was some covenant ceremony. Skyla was quite pleased to witness the event."

"You wish. She's still pissed as hell."

"She should be."

I pick up a small pillow and beam it at his head, but Dudley catches it like a pro at the last game of the World Series and launches it back, nearly decapitating me in the process.

"Do refrain from physical violence. I'd loathe rearranging that pretty face I've gifted you. And you're welcome."

It's true. It was revealed not that long ago that Dudley here is an Oliver gene generator, and that somewhere back in time our lineage meets up with Coop's as well. That explains the good-looking family dynamics, although there's not enough left to gift me any Sector glory. I scowl over at this created being that somehow managed to infiltrate my DNA.

"Why is Skyla suddenly friendly with Bishop?" I growl as if it were somehow his fault. A thought comes to me. "You know what? It is your damn fault, too."

"Language." Dudley's eyes boil like rusty cauldrons as he glowers my way. "I know not what you speak of. Ms. Messenger and Ms. Bishop haven't seen eye to evil eye in years."

"Until this year." I lean in, ready to pounce and strangle this menace I'm facing. "If you didn't invite Skyla to that hell Gage put himself through at the christening, then she never would have turned to Chloe. It's clear she's trying to get back at him—hell, she's pissed at me, too. But what I don't get is how she could ever think it's a good idea."

"That's funny. She said the same about you and Tweedledum the night he grafted himself to darkness." He offers a shit-eating grin that melts off his face just as quick as it came. "The Fems, though not a fallen brotherhood, are just as damning to mankind as the nefarious ones, much like Bishop herself."

"That's where you're wrong. Chloe is fallen. She is evil through and through. I know for a fact she's feeding Skyla whatever bullshit it is she wants to hear. And right now, I'd prefer bullshit to the truth myself. The truth is pretty bad." I think that's where Skyla is at with Chloe. She's a bandage covering up the real wound, which is Gage. But why Chloe? To piss us off? She's achieved that.

"Were you present at the hour when Jock Strap laid himself on the altar to his new master?"

The thought of Demetri being Gage's anything makes my stomach turn.

"Are you senile? Yes, I was there. Or were you too busy getting a boner watching Skyla lose her mind?"

"Must you always either invoke an expletive or a sexual analogy? Does your mind offer any other avenue of expression other than one that leads to the gutter? Please keep the grime of your thoughts to yourself, young man. You are in desperate need of my supervising services. You've informed me of this yourself just this afternoon, or perhaps you've forgotten and it's you who's going senile."

"Wait." I can only catch so many of Dudley's verbal throwing stars at a time. "Back up. Yes, I was present at the altar call for darkness." I tick my head in his direction. "And?"

"You seemed to have been paying attention to what was being said—you tell me."

That night comes back to me in jags—Gage and I following Demetri into the woods like lost children to the slaughter, Demetri's dissertation on wickedness, Gage stretching out his hands to heaven, begging forgiveness. Then it comes back to me. "Demetri—there was something he said that stood out to me. He mentioned something about the Steel Barricade, about the Fems, but he never mentioned that Gage was bound to the Counts."

"Relay it to me word-for-word." A smug grin twitches up his lips.

"I can't do that. I can hardly remember what I had for breakfast."

"Who's the senile one now?" Dudley closes his eyes for a moment and takes in a quick breath. "He said—may the Lord of Glory find favor upon my son, Gage Edinger, who is willing to war against the enemy in the name of the Steel Barricade, in the name of the glorious Fems, upon the dissolution of his soul from the flesh that is mortal. And that, my friend, is word-for-word."

I drink down his words a moment, examining them as they swim by. "Okay, you're better than me. You are not senile. I'm senile in comparison. But I was right. The Counts are left out of the equation. Yes, the Steel Barricade is a reboot, but it's not a Faction. It's a rebellion. If the Barricade is dismantled, then Gage is—"

"Still the king. He's a Fem. Demetri is gifting Gage his right as leader of the pack." He forces a tight smile. "Gage Oliver is a Fem, and he is their future king. There is no changing the facts."

"No changing the facts." I scan the carpet while trying to decipher his words as if they were a riddle. "What if the Fems suddenly sided with Skyla and her people? What would it really matter if Gage was the king of the Fems? There would be no discourse."

"Young Oliver." He sighs with that perennial look of boredom returning to his face. "The Fems are insistent on removing the Sectors from their high place. We side with the light. We side with Celestra. We side with Skyla. Our beings entered into a bonding covenant with Celestra long ago, as did the Fems with the Counts. The ramifications during the church age are significant yes, but the real struggle holds eternity in the bounds. Time is running out. The Sectors must hold secure their standing."

"Gage will gladly give it to you. For the life of me, I can't figure out why Demetri didn't just slap a crown on Wesley's head and call it a wicked day. He's far more enthused with the idea of ruining our people and running over whoever the hell he needs to on the way to ruling the world."

"Wesley is greedy, yes. An attribute one would think valuable, considering the circumstances. But Skyla doesn't care for Wesley, nor is she willing to bear his children."

"So Demetri wants Gage *and* the twins." Shit. Shit. Shit.

"That is the prize package. I'm sure he has fantastic plans for them all." He glowers at the fire, and it rages ten times in ferocity, igniting the room in a flash of nuclear light.

"You're right. I'm going to need your help." A thought comes to me as abrupt as a slap to the face. "But *I* didn't visit you this afternoon." I'm not even going to bother suggesting Dudley is losing his mind after his word-for-word play-by-play. If Dudley says it happened, then it did. "Which version of me was it?" I already know the answer. It's the same version that met me in the woods that horrible night Gage committed his soul to all of Demetri's no-good intentions.

"The one that counts. You saw a vision that night after Skyla let you have it. He mentioned you saw Gage on his throne, his body transfiguring into the serpent he is destined to become."

"The dragon." It's true. I saw Gage on a throne with fire and rage shooting from him as he rose up and morphed into a hideous beast with wings—breath born of fire.

"You will need me, indeed, but not in any way that you imagine."

"I can't lose him. I can't lose Gage. We have to save him. He cannot die."

"You of all people understand there is only life after life."

"The longer Gage lives in his body, the less time he has to get his hands dirty with the Fems. And in the event you were being literal—because death sucks if you haven't noticed—it hurts to be separated. It hurts that nothing is the same—even if we do get to see him again. Nothing ever gets to be normal again." I fall into the seat next to him as I try to envision that dismal version of the future.

His brows hike into his forehead as if I've amused him on some level. "Which version of normal is it that you're looking to preserve?"

Skyla blinks onto my lap, naked as the day she was born and moaning, "Are we done with our run?" She looks up at me with sleepy eyes as my arms swoop over her body to cradle her, my fingers drinking in the feel of her bare, heated flesh.

"Yes, we're done."

"Oh, that's right." She glances over to Dudley and offers a weak wave. "I took a nap. It was heaven."

My gaze dips down to her oversized nipples, her tits heavy and weighted with milk, and my heat index spikes without meaning to.

"I'd better get you home." I glare at Dudley a moment. "Dressed and in bed, please."

He glares right back before offering the hint of a crooked grin. "As you wish."

The room disperses as Skyla and I float through time and space. A thick darkness envelops me. The air is heavy and moist as something settles over my head, and I'm quick to snap it off—Skyla's sweatpants.

Both Skyla and I have landed back in her bed, Skyla stark naked and me with her sweatshirt twisted around my legs.

"You're not funny, Dudley," I whisper as Gage sits up next to me and frowns over at his deliriously exhausted, yet decidedly naked wife.

He offers up a grunt. "A good time was had by all, I assume."

"Something like that." I roll Skyla onto the mattress and blow a kiss to each of the boys before turning back to Gage. "I just want you to know that I have your back."

He lifts a brow as he sweeps his gaze over his wife's luscious curves. "I can see you have something going on behind my back too."

It's not worth getting into. Not with both Gage and Skyla running on empty. "We'll talk."

"Whatever, dude." Gage presses his head against the pillow and closes those sleepy lids of his.

No sooner do I get on the other side of the door than I hear the boys roaring back to life with their hacking cries. Both Skyla and Gage moan in unison.

And that's when I realize I'm powerless to help Gage with his life in any real capacity.

January drags its tired feet through Paragon's muddy waters and ends with as much lackluster enthusiasm as it began—at least when it comes to the customer base at the bowling alley. So I've summoned together what little employees I have and filled them in on the fact I'll be letting them go in the next few weeks for a remodel that just might span the length of Nathan's and Barron's childhood. Nobody seems too surprised by the news. In fact, the girls who work the kitchen head back to their post as if I've just filled them in on a new menu item that they couldn't care less about.

"Cool beans." Brielle winks as she takes a sip of her soda. Bree hasn't taken a formal check from me in months, but still shows up to work the odd shift when I need her. In fact, I called in several people—Gage and Skyla, who in turn brought the boys out to the bowling alley for the very first time. Ellis and Giselle, Drake and Ethan, Emily, Liam, Natalie Coleman, Michelle, and Lexy all stare back at me, flabbergasted, as if I've just announced the fact I'm taking a jackhammer to the entire damn island. Laken and Coop walk in late, but Gage leans over and whispers my plans of deconstruction and then hopefully construction. The only person who isn't shocked as hell is Ellis. Ellis Harrison, my new partner in corporate crime, stands staunchly by my side with an ear-to-ear grin.

"Dude, we are going to kill it." He slaps the back of his hand into his right palm. "Tell them about the gym. Tell them about the hookah parlor."

"No hookah parlor," I say under my breath.

Skyla gags for a moment, the first person even remotely interested in speaking out. "Why haven't you discussed this with any of us? And by any of us, I mean me." She holds her hands over the ears of the twin in her arms as if attempting to shelter him from my stupidity. *Good luck with that*, I want to tell her. I'm teaming up with Ellis. That alone speaks volumes about a lot of things going on in my life right now.

Lexy glares over at Skyla as if she could deck her. "He's discussing things right now in the event your blonde highness hasn't noticed." Lex turns her full attention back to me, batting her lashes in yet another fruitless, flirtatious endeavor.

But as much as Lexy wants to impress me, she's just taken my affections down a very dark corridor. "You may *never* disparage my ex-wife in my establishment again."

The room clots up with an uncomfortable silence. I'm not sure anyone knows what to do with the fact I've just scolded Lexy as if she were a child, and I'm too busy trying to assess if I'm actually sorry to apologize. I'm not so sure it ends there.

"Yes, sir, Logan Oliver." Lexy's eyes grow wild with what looks to be admiration. If telling her off was meant to send her packing, it backfired. Lexy swoons toward me as if I've just cemented myself in her tiny demented heart. Just another thing that exemplifies the fact I can't get a thing right if I try. "What can we do to help? You need a demo crew? We're there. You need emotional support sitting by a nice warm fire? I'm there. Anything and everything. Our time, our bodies, our worlds are at your feet."

Another round of stunted silence crops up, only this time it's attributed to Lexy's bizarre outburst.

"I *know*." Lexy's arm spikes into the air as if we were back in school. Although, I can't recall a single class in which Lexy was so eager to participate. "We'll throw a party!"

Bree gasps as if it were the best idea. "A goodbye to the bowling alley bash!" Brielle is always quick to board any crazy train that has the remote possibility of a good time. "We practically grew up in this place. We need to give it a proper sendoff."

The room fills with a light buzz before Lexy clears her throat. "We'll do a theme party, something retro."

"Great Gatsby!" Michelle is suddenly onboard. "All the guys can sport zoot suits and submachine guns."

"No guns." I grimace at the thought. With all the feds crawling up my ass, I'm pretty sure high-powered assault replicas aren't the best idea.

"Logan hates that idea," Lex is quick to reprimand.

Skyla bites down on her lip as if she's about to cry. "I'm going to miss this place."

"It will be back. And it will be better. It's only leaving temporarily." I swallow hard because a part of me feels as if we just took a sideline and we were suddenly talking about ourselves. It's selfish of me to think so, considering the fact I love her husband just as much as she does, sans the sexual nature.

Laken raises her hand to her chin briefly, and I nod to her. "How about an '80s dance? That was sort of a wild decade, and the music will be fun. Not that I should have any say in it but—"

Bree huffs so loud I half-expect her to lunge across the room and deck her. "Darn right you shouldn't have a say in it. This is for the true people of Paragon, not some outsider who's been around for like five minutes."

"*Bree*," I bark so loud my voice manages to echo on a loop. "Laken and Coop are family. Get along or get out." There. I've asserted my bullish authority twice in one day— making me feel *and* look like twice the asshole I was five minutes ago. I glance to Skyla, and she gives a furtive nod.

Bree's face slaps pink. "For your information, *we* are family, Logan Oliver. We may not be blood, but this island and all of its milkshake muddy waters are running through your veins just like they are mine."

A part of me wants to correct her. There is not a damn thing running through my veins these days other than the dangerous affection of Candace Messenger. But I offer a kind smile to my old friend instead.

"Yes, Bree. We are family, indeed."

"So, why isn't Chloe here?" Brielle demands. "She's family, too, you know. I can't stand the way everyone's ostracized her for the last five years—and for what? For getting herself kidnapped? No one has ever treated her the same since she's come back."

Half the room turns to stare at Brielle Landon, nee Johnson. It's as if nothing that's happened in the timeframe she's allotted has truly penetrated her mind. Bree has her own truths, and she sticks by them. She never had to exonerate Chloe of a damn thing because she never believed in anything other than some fantasy version of her.

Lexy growls at Brielle for me. "Chloe isn't here because Logan hates her guts. Everyone basically hates her, and if you need a bullet point reminder on why—catch me when I have a free twenty-four hours because that's how long the list is. Logan Oliver can't stand the witch. That's enough for me, and that should be enough for you. And for the record, I hate her, too."

A dull smile rides on my lips. Lexy doesn't hate Chloe. She's merely saying it to impress me, and in truth it might be working. Letting the bowling alley go has left my ego severely bruised, and anyone who wishes to stroke it is welcome.

"For the record"—Skyla raises her hand a moment before wrapping it back around that beautiful baby in her arms—"I don't mind Chloe so much." Her mouth contorts unnaturally as she says it because it's a bald-face lie, and we all know it.

Brielle slaps her hands together. "About damn time my besties pull it together!"

Shit. "An '80s party it is." I take a deep breath. "Any of you are welcome to commandeer it."

"I'll be in charge." Lexy demands more than she asks. "How's a few weeks sound? Maybe middle of March?"

"How about the Ides of March?" I say it with a nod. "It sounds appropriate."

Lex gives a deafening clap. "Set your calendars, bitches. This is going to be one party you will never forget."

The baby in Gage's arms starts to fuss, and one by one the small crowd settles into conversations amongst themselves.

Liam comes over and clasps his hand over my shoulder. "You know I'm in. This is our endeavor." He winces. "I'm not stepping on your toes, though. I'm still one hundred percent behind this decision. The bowling alley is your baby. I'll settle for the title of silent partner. Just keep me in the loop." He frowns out at the bodies before us. "Maybe ahead of everyone else next time. Besides, I'm starting to line things up for myself."

"Such as?" I hope to God Ellis hasn't hit him up to run his impending hookah parlor.

"Construction. *Oliver* Construction. I've been taking night courses ever since I came back. Hopefully by the end of spring I'll have my contractor's license."

A part of me breathes a sigh of relief that he is in no way certified to help me out at the moment. I'm counting on an entire host of certified professionals to piece this place back together—and quickly at that.

"And I've already got my first job." He holds out his arms expectantly, and I can't find it in me to break my brother's heart. He laid down his life so I could have mine. His sacrifice was something far nobler than anything I could ever comprehend.

"You bet, man. I'm sure you'll turn this place into a sight to behold." I'm not sure I meant that as a compliment.

"Not this place. *Dude*"—he winces as if I've lost my ever-loving mind, and relief pools in me—"Gage wants me to help renovate his house. It'll be a good hands-on learning experience for me, and I'll get a chance to bond with our little nephew."

I glance over at our *little* nephew with his refrigerator-like build, that babe in his arms. Our little nephew is all grown up and has turned into one upright man. My stomach sours because I pray to God he stays that way.

"Sounds like an adventure. Hey, everything going good with Miller?" Liam and Michelle Miller have had a tumultuous on-again, off-again relationship ever since he's come back to Paragon just about two years ago.

"She's good." He frowns over at her as if she's not. "She's a little wild. She's not one of us. I always thought I'd marry a Faction girl. I think that's the missing link in our relationship. I want to talk to her about things, but every time I try, she says it's just fables and folklore. She thinks her friends are in some weird cult. She doesn't get it."

"I'm sorry, man. Maybe over time. And if it makes you feel better, there are some of us who still feel the same way she does." Tad Landon comes to mind. I've never met anyone so full of disbelief in all my life. I know for a fact when a Nephilim offspring is that disbelieving, they water down their powers due to a lack of faith.

Michelle purrs to Liam with the curl of her finger, and he heads over to her with his tongue wagging. He might be unsure of her as a whole, but he sure is pussy-whipped.

Brody and Brookelynn stride in, shaking the rain off their bodies like a couple of huskies. Bree squeals and screams at the sight of her sister.

"Just in time! We're making plans!" She bounces over to them as if we were in the throes of a party—one that celebrates the demise of my business career.

I glance over to Gage because I know that he's patiently waited to find out what Brody has to say about the Winters, and they both tread over to where I'm standing.

"How's it going?" Gage looks nervous as if Brody Bishop were about to deliver a grim diagnosis.

"I'll take this one." I pluck the baby out of his arms, and instantly I know it's Barron. Skyla mentioned that the boys now have distinct personalities, and I agree. Barron is far fussier, far more agitated and alert. But when he pins those cobalt blue eyes of his onto yours, it makes it feel as if there isn't a care in the world. Barron has the ability to soothe me as if he's silently letting me know everything is going to be okay. It's ironic, though, when Gage touched Barron for the very first time, he had a strange vision, a flashback to when Demetri threatened him—that if he left the Barricade, the one that he loves would turn against him. Gage was terrified it was Barron who would pledge to Demetri one day. That the curse Gage himself brought onto his family would fall on his precious son, and now he's taken that curse upon himself. And as far as I know, Skyla and Gage still haven't spoken about it. Her anger has been set to simmer for all of these weeks, two months and counting. They hardly speak, and Gage has spent every single night since the christening back in his old bedroom at Barron and Emma's. Enough is enough I say. This beautiful family is begging for restoration whether or not Skyla realizes it. That is the direction in which they are headed.

I nod Coop over, and he slaps me on the back. "Sorry about the tough day, buddy. What's going on?"

"Brody is about to fill us in on this woman who's been hanging around with Demetri."

Coop gives a knowing nod. "The one whose daughter came back to life at the morgue." He glances to Gage.

"So, Dominique Winters—" Brody shakes his head. Those dark brows of his lay over his eyes like a hedge. The same way Chloe's do when she's too deep inside her wicked head. "I did a little digging—talked to Luke Jenson. I grew up with the guy. He's the Winters' next-door neighbor. He says the old lady is batshit. He said she had a major heart attack about seven years ago." Brody does a quick visual sweep of the three of us before leaning in. "They wheeled her out of there as good as dead, but some nurse kept pumping oxygen into her—CPR. Forty-six minutes later, they covered her with a sheet." He snaps his fingers, and both Gage and I jerk back. "She woke up. Came home like nothing happened. That's when she started to act erratic."

Gage glances to me. "How so?"

"Building shit. She's been tacking on rooms to her house ever since she came home."

"What do you mean tacking rooms onto her house?" For the life of me, I can't figure out why I haven't heard of this woman. Paragon isn't all that big. "You mean, like Winchester mystery mansion action?"

"Exactly." Brody looks from Gage to me. "Except it all makes sense. No doorways or stairways to nowhere. She lives in that mega-hovel with her daughter and two sons. Melody, Asbury, and *Cash*. I've seen Mel over at Host a few times. Cash"—Brody glances past the two of us, boring a hole through the wall with a ripe hatred for the guy. Brody starts to stalk off, and I catch him by the arm. I can hardy pull him back. Brody is built like a wall.

"What about Cash?" I hiss so fast it sounds like a threat.

Brody wipes down his face as if this entire endeavor both exhausted and pissed him off. "It's stupid. I found out this afternoon he's dating Carly. I went over, and she was there. It just brought back some memories. Made me think of someone I hadn't seen in a while."

"Carly Foster?" Gage tips his head back, trying to keep track of where Brody is leading the conversation.

"Yes." Brody cuts a quick look to Brookelynn from across the room. "We had a son, years ago—Carly and me. He's about six now. I wasn't ready to step up to the plate back then. He was taken to New York and raised by her dad, as her brother. His name is Lucas." His entire body sags, and my heart breaks for the guy. "I gotta go." He makes a beeline for Bree and her sister, and we don't stop him.

"What was that about?" Skyla breezes right into the empty spot he left between us, but neither Gage nor I are eager to fill her in on the details. "*Ah*"—her eyes light up like stars—"more secrets to keep from the blonde ditz. I get it." She shrugs, rocking Nathan in her arms.

"Not true." I swallow hard. I can't do it. I can't keep another thing from the woman I love.

"You mind if I talk to you alone for a minute?" She nods toward the kitchen, and Gage takes off without saying a word. It feels awful—gut-wrenching to witness as this fissure in their relationship gets wider and wider.

"Don't tell me that wasn't awkward." I pull Barron to my shoulder as I lead her back toward the pizza oven, farther still until we hit the opened door with a view of the fog eating away at the forest that lies behind the bowling alley. "I can shut it if you want."

"No, it's fine. The boys are bundled." Nathan spikes his arms up one by one, punching thin air, and Skyla pulls up her sweater without thinking twice. Her full breast drops out the bottom of her bra, and Nathan twists his head into her until he hits home. But that large pale moon of a nipple is still visible, so I force my gaze to stray anywhere but there.

"I can't believe I'm still nursing." She huffs a dull laugh. "I mean, I love it. God, I'd have twenty babies right now if I could. It leashes me down a bit—the nursing. But it doesn't hurt as much now. Thank God I'm not cracked and bleeding anymore."

"Bleeding?" As horrified and concerned as I am for her, a part of me demands to run to another subject. But I don't. This is Skyla. My ex-wife. Hell, my *wife*. And if she wants to discuss bleeding nipples, then so be it. "I'm sorry you went through that."

"It's fine now. My mother and her maternal superpowers really did come in handy. But I'm thinking about quitting." She blinks back tears as she looks to Nathan's anxious suckling. "I feel terrible, Logan." Her voice cracks. "I'm a failure. But I'm desperate to get my body back. It's selfish. I want to nurse, but I miss things. It sounds stupid, I know."

"Not stupid at all. Like what kinds of things?" I'm sure her freedom is one. It has to be tough feeding the boys for a majority of the day.

"Like...beer."

"*Beer*?" I hike a brow at the idea. "You don't drink beer, Skyla."

"I know"—her voice pitches to a wail, and the waterworks start full force—"and now I can't even start if I wanted to."

A quiet laugh rumbles from me. Barron stirs to life and grabs ahold of my ear with all his little might. "Come here, Skyla." I pull her in with Nathan carefully sandwiched between us as Barron turns and reaches for his mother. I lean in and steal a sweet kiss off her cheek, catching a tear with my lips.

"Damn hormones." She wipes her face clean just as Gage and Ellis head over.

I take a step back and hand Barron to his father.

"Everything okay?" Gage offers a mournful smile to Skyla, but all she offers is a quiet nod.

Ellis and Giselle come up, and we all take a step out under the awning as Paragon's wintery breath puffs by. "So, what are you going to do with the rest of it?" Ellis wraps his arm around Giselle as they take in the forest haunting the landscape. Fog billows off the top of the evergreens like smoke.

"Rest of what?" I'm only mildly curious about anything Ellis has to say. Most of the time I'm mildly alarmed.

"The land." He nods out toward the forest. "I went to the city, and you own these woods, dude."

I glance to Gage. "I'm pretty sure my land ends where my feet stand."

Ellis shakes his head at the idea. "That might have been true once upon a time, but about ten years ago the city granted you the next thirty acres."

"*Thirty* acres?" Skyla, Gage, and I say in unison, and the sound of our collective voices sound sweet, downright lovely.

"That's right." Ellis sniffs the air. "The city map says that it butts up right against the gates. All these woods are yours to do as you wish."

"To do as I wish?" My mind swirls with the possibilities. My father, my mother. They would have loved this. Land. Soil. Something they could get their hands dirty with. "What do you mean the city granted me the acreage? I'm pretty sure the people at the planning department aren't allowed to gift land as they see fit."

"Dude"—he gives me a light sock to the arm—"I found out they were rectifying an error. When your dad bought this place, he got more than he bargained for. He just didn't know it. Some damn clerical error that they cleared up for you."

Clerical error? I glance to the sky, and a quiver of lightning illuminates through the fog. Yes, I suspect Candace Messenger is at the bottom of this thirty-acre clerical error.

"So, what's it going to be?" Ellis slaps his arm over my shoulder. "Apartment buildings? Condos? A high-rise? Dude, you can parcel off the units for millions."

I can't stop staring at those evergreens, at that forest of possibilities. "No apartments, condos, or high-rises." I shake my head, still dazed at the thought that all this might actually be mine. "I'm thinking a farm."

"A farm?" Skyla, Gage, and Ellis don't miss a beat.

"A pumpkin patch." I fold my arms over my chest. "Maybe some fresh vegetables and fruit trees. We'll have an entire section dedicated to Christmas trees, too. Paragon needs this."

"A pumpkin patch!" Giselle shrieks with glee so loud that a dozen birds fly from the branches overhead.

"An effing *pumpkin* patch?" Ellis is less than dazzled by my line of thinking.

"That's right." I glance down at Nathan and Barron. "I want to be their favorite uncle—so a pumpkin patch it is."

Gage and Skyla share a quiet smile, and that alone was worth the effort.

"Ellis"—Gage nods to him—"Logan's parents, my grandparents, ran a pumpkin farm back in Oregon. It's in his blood."

Skyla looks toward the woods as the fog plays hide-and-seek between its old sturdy trunks. "And now it's in his destiny."

Destiny. I almost want to laugh, and I do.

Skyla has her destiny as the leader of the Factions.

Gage will be king.

And I—I will be a pumpkin farmer.

Yes.

This is destiny at her finest.

3

Schemers, and Dreamers, and Liars, Oh My...

Skyla

In an irony that only the universe can provide, the longer you go without sleep, the more life itself feels like a dream, an uncomfortable waking nightmare. That alone can explain why lying in bed next to me in this late February morning is Chloe Bishop instead of my beautiful husband who has been relegated to his childhood bed at his childhood home miles away from the boys and me. Yes, Gage is here almost all of the time. I would never deny him access to our precious babes, but our marital bed is simply for quick naps—not that I'm getting anything but that these days. The long, thick drag of the night, I spend alone. He has never fought me on that. Never challenged me. And a part of me believes that he enjoys taking a regular hit off the drug that sleep has become, and at the moment the only supplier is the Oliver house. But he stays late with the boys and me and comes back early—sometimes so early he's only gone an hour as a symbol of our discord. Not this morning, though. This morning Gage is away. He texted—mentioned something to do with the morgue. He could be lying in it for all I know, I'm so dizzy with fatigue. And now that his classes at Host have started up once again, I suppose I'll see even less of him. He suggested that I sign up again in the fall, and I plan to, but only so I can crawl into some unsuspecting coed's dorm and fall into a sleep deprived coma just the way I fantasize.

Chloe kicks my foot with her own.

"Don't touch me with your bare feet." I groan. I loathe feet. The only feet I appreciate are those of the people I love, and even that list is extremely narrowed. Of course, I love the adorable, miniature feet of my children. I spend the livelong day meditating over them with kisses while the boys suckle off my breasts. I love my husband's feet. God, I love every inch of my husband, and with that thought, a horrid grief envelops me.

The boys fuss and fidget, and slowly one by one turn a brutish electric shade of blue.

"No, no, no!" I chastise softly, and the ethereal hue dissipates on command. It's an odd thing that they've been doing ever since they were tucked deep in my belly, but I've found with slight reprimanding they return to normal within minutes. God knows they can't go through life the color of a blueberry.

My temples explode with a headache to end all headaches, and I can directly place the blame on my serious lack of shut-eye. I never knew how delicious sleep could be. How I would savor the memory of it. How I could be so jealous of my friends who bask in its glory each and every night on the regular. It's true. I think of Laken, imagining what her thick, lazy nights must feel like, uninterrupted, so perfectly docile and happy in her dreams. Her limbs tangled with Cooper's the way I used to with Gage once upon a childless time.

"I want to start having fun," Chloe mewls as if this long-drawn-out, bored extraction she's living is entirely my fault. She picks up my hand, begins twirling the ring she gifted me for Christmas between her fingers, and I swear I feel a sizzle of heat from her touch. Figures. Not even the throne of God wants any part of Chloe.

The brilliant blue stone winks at me as if it were gospel.

"Ask Wes to do something with you." I give her arm a light shove. "Scoot over, would you? And why don't you ever bring Tobie with you? The boys need to spend more time with their cousin." Tobie is absolutely precious. She's essentially the female version of the boys, and every time I look at her I think of Sage, the daughter I lost. Sage didn't survive the pregnancy, but I think of her every single day. I think of how precious her feet, her entire miniature body would have been. What it would have felt like to be a mother to a daughter as well.

Chloe grunts at the thought of her husband. "Wesley can go jerk off. And, trust me, he does so on the regular. He only summons me when he wants a toothless blowjob."

"A what?" I'm not quite sure why I asked, but fatigue, and well, Chloe herself are grinding my resolve to nothing.

"My vagina, you idiot." She scoffs. "I hate the bastard. I couldn't care less if either me or my vagina ever saw him again."

"Wow, I knew things weren't perfect between you two, but of all the people in the world, one would think that a Gage Oliver knockoff would have the best chance to capture your heart."

Barron lets out a sharp cry at the mention of his father's name, and my own heart breaks as I bring him to where he wants to be. His mouth roots for milk until I unbutton my nightshirt, and he happily finds it.

"What side does he sleep on?" Chloe hums while molesting the sheets as if they were Gage himself. Chloe has one singular thought ever on her mind, and that is my husband. If anyone can keep me laser-focused on Gage, it's Chloe. As twisted as that sounds, it is the God's honest truth.

"The side you're on. Don't get too excited. That's just a technicality. His favorite side is on top of me."

She shimmies her body over the sheets as if soaking him in, then frowns. "I hate that he's with you, Skyla. Gage Oliver's favorite place in the world should be on top of *me*." Chloe expels an explosive sigh at the thought.

But I let her words run over my head like water. That's not news to me or anyone else on the aforementioned planet. "So, what's Wes got planned next? He has the world in a tizzy with those clowns. Nice touch, but logic only persists that he's going to follow through with these empty terrors."

"Oh, Skyla," Chloe moans as she sits up and hugs her smooth brown legs. "Don't you ever think ahead? He has this island crawling with G-men. Two of which he fed to those beasts your husband governs. Rumor has it, you had front row seats. It must have been quite the *Spectator* sport." She gives a little wink at her play on words. The memory of Killian and Moser being eaten alive razes through me. I'll never forget the way her eyes bulged to the point of launching at me like missiles. I tried to save her. I tried my damn hardest to free her from that hideous creature. That's where Chloe has the story wrong. They weren't Spectators per se. They were Videns. Wesley has created a monster of the Viden youth, quite literally.

The boys both squirm on cue, and Nathan begins to articulate what sounds like his vowels.

"Such a smart boy," I coo as I give the swing he's lying in a tiny kick with my foot. "I bet Tobie is ready to say her first word." I bite down over my lip while I look to Chloe. "Wesley is going to die the first time she says daddy."

"Don't you wish." Chloe rides a finger over her bare arm. She didn't spend the night, but as soon as she popped into the room, she practically disrobed to nothing before crawling into bed next to me. And trust me, there was nothing even remotely sexual about that gesture. There simply isn't a comfortable place to sit or stand in this crowded, little overheated hole. Chloe is the last person I want to be bedmates with, but we are just that, both literally and metaphorically at the moment.

"God, how I can't wait for Wes to die," she moans with delight. "I'll celebrate that day each year. It'll be the greatest holiday ever." Leave it to Chloe to take my words at face value. "But Wesley's death is miles away. It's Gage we need to be concerned with. Demetri has plans for your man, Skyla, and it has nothing to do with pumping blood through that beating heart of his. If anything, that beating heart is an obstacle he'd very much like to extinguish. Gage's life stands in the way of everything he wants to and *will* accomplish. Some people stop at nothing to make sure all of their dreams come true, and Demetri Edinger has always gotten what he wants."

"He doesn't have my mother." It comes out quiet, catatonic, as I silently wonder if he does and if he's had her all along.

"Please. Have you seen that kid of theirs? She's got Demetri's soulless eyes."

"Watch it. That's my little sister you're talking about." God, she's right. I can't even look at Misty anymore without seeing Demetri's miniature face. It's shocking to me the way she's brazenly morphing into him. Soon enough even Tad will be forced to face the DNA, and this entire family will go to hell in a Fem-gifted handbasket.

"Demetri Edinger gets who and what he wants. If he wants Gage Oliver dead"—Chloe touches the tip of Barron's

231

foot, and he donkey kicks her until she withdraws her claw—
"then dead is exactly what he'll be."

My heart ratchets up into my throat. "We have to do something."

"*We*? Don't look at me. I signed up for Faction detail."

I glower at her a moment. "Liar, liar. I would love to set your pants and the rest of you on fire." Chloe signed up for so much more. Chloe and I are both Celestra—thankfully, her host body was, too. Speaking of my favorite ax wielding mad scientist. "I think maybe we should pay Ezrina and Nev a visit."

Her brows rise at the thought. "That old hag has been foaming at the mouth with revenge for years against the idiots who cost her freedom."

"And killed her family. They thwarted her love with Heathcliff for centuries. Ezrina is the perfect weapon."

"*We* are the perfect weapon, Skyla. Once you relegate the victory to someone else, you may as well give up. What we should really do is snuff our own husbands. I'll kill Wesley, and you smother the last living breath out of Gage." She scowls a moment as if she were sorry she didn't assign that task to herself.

"And then what? Demetri finds a way to resurrect his sons, and we're still in a shit position."

"Demetri isn't God, Skyla. Who holds the key to life? The Creator or Demetri? If Demetri had that power, don't you think he would have resurrected the dead to haunt this world? What the hell is a zombie—or a Fem dressed as a ridiculous clown—when compared to a reanimated corpse? If he had that power, Dr. Oliver would have been out of business long ago. Demetri wouldn't waste any time in bringing back the entire cemetery."

"Ezrina can bring back the dead—Counts. And Dr. Oliver did bring you back."

"You brought me back," she says it so fast it feels like a slap in the face. And believe me, I want to slap my own face for the endeavor.

"My blood, Chloe, never me. I'm the one that put you in the ground to begin with, remember?" That was the only concerted effort I put into this fiasco.

"Yes, Skyla." Chloe tosses her arms in the air with exasperation. "You killed me. You slaughtered me in the woods like a boss. You're the *greatest*. I'm just a peon that lives in a dark cave in some physical plane that mankind has no clue about. I'm at your mercy. I'm the—"

"Oh, would you stop. Get it together or you can leave," I hiss. Nathan shouts something that sounds like an agreement, and I can't help but give a little smile. "Okay, we'll both get it together, Chloe. Now that Nathan and Barron have finally gotten over their Emma plague, I can refocus on the task at hand. I think we need to roll into action."

"About damn time. And I know just where to start."

"Speak." More often than not, I resort to Ezrina's style of verbal brevity around Chloe. Just because we're joined at the hip as of late doesn't mean I have to like it.

"Maybe we should kill the Kraggers first?" She strums her fingertips over one another.

"That would be a great place to start. Killing the Kraggers is like delousing society. But I think I killed them all."

Chloe straightens. "I killed Emerson."

"Correction, Chloe, *I* killed Emerson by not stopping you."

She blinks with dismay. "My, aren't you the blonde martyr. What about Arson? Shall we kill him next?"

A smile pulls on my lips, but I refuse to give it. "I suppose we shall." Leading Chloe by the nose is far easier than expected. "On second thought, killing Big Daddy K might lead to more problems than it would solve. We need solid ideas."

"We need that witch of a mother of yours." She glances at the ceiling. "Or are you more of a warlock, Candace? I've always suspected you've been hiding a pair of very large, hairy balls under that white toga you run around in."

My eyes close involuntarily, and I groan. "Stop it, Chloe. My mother doesn't respond to belittling. I should know. I tried it all through high school. In fact, my mother doesn't respond to almost anything. She's impossible to get ahold of unless she's in the mood to play." It's true. But as of late, it does seem she's been a bit easier to connect with. Having the boys—and, of course, Sage, has bonded us on a level I didn't think was possible. Who knew it would be the children I'd have with Gage that would bring us closer? My mother may not be Gage Oliver's biggest fan, but she does love his children.

"She's not going to answer us. I'd take us to her if I could, but any extra powers these babies have gifted me are quickly fading." I've had the ability to head to Ahava on my own, but with the boys and Chloe, I don't think I can make the trip.

"She'll respond, Skyla. You're forgetting, I'm a lot like Demetri. When I want something or someone, I most certainly move heaven and hell, life and death, to get my way." Her words sizzle around the room like eggs on a hot skillet. "Candace fucking Messenger, get down here right this minute! I'm in bed with your precious child, and I'm thinking about humping her for the hell of it. I'm within biting distance of those babes you hold dear but never near. And I'm about to touch one and lay claim to his soul," Chloe moans as if she's conducting a séance, and both boys fuss and kick.

"You're such a circus, Chloe. Would you knock it off? In fact, I think you should go."

But Chloe doesn't leave. Instead, she gets on all fours, and her face contorts into a holy menace as she bears her teeth toward Barron.

"I am going to *eat* you!" she chides as I roll my eyes and kick her in the shin. "Then I'm going to *eat* your little brother, too!"

"Would you stop? There's no way my mother is falling for that. She's way too—"

An explosion of blinding light goes off in the closet, forcing us to close our eyes. A rumble of thunder growls around the room before the door slowly opens, revealing not only my mother in all her incandescent glory but a button-nosed little girl with her daddy's dark hair, deep-welled dimples, and a smile that makes my heart melt.

"*Sage!*" I can't contain my excitement. My heart bursts open with joy like a piñata as I extend my arms toward her. Sage didn't make the duration of my pregnancy. I lost her early on, but my mother has taken her under her feathery wing. And since my mother wants nothing whatsoever to do with infants, she's aged Sage to about the ripe old age of five. "Come to Mommy." I don't hesitate with the moniker. It feels natural.

"Mommy?" She tries it out on her perfect bow tie lips as she hops on over. She was so painfully shy the last time I saw her—still wrapping herself around my mother's legs like a tree post. She looks up at Candace, the smile quelling on her face. "May I, Your Grace Candace?"

"Yes, you may." My mother chortles. It seems Sage has even managed to bring my mother's sour countenance a sprinkle of joy. And if anything, my mother does appreciate a good game of Mother May I. It seems to be our go-to shenanigan each time we're together. Only in my case my mother repeatedly disallows my next move.

I wrap my arm around Sage and bury my face in her dark, glossy hair. She holds the scent of lemons and peppermint. Just holding her like this is heaven. I can't bear to let go. Gage should be here. He needs to see what he's lost, too. She's so much like him in every way it breaks my heart all over.

"This is your brother, Barron." I hold him out for her to see, and he dislodges from my nipple.

"And this is Nathan." My mother scoops the baby out of the swing. "Skyla, why do you insist on keeping them in that dizzying contraption?"

"Because they insist on not sleeping. Can't you cast a spell or something and make this happen? I'm knee-deep in delirium."

"Skyla!" my mother barks. "I do not *cast spells*." She coos into Nathan's face as she holds him over her head, "No, Your Grace does not partake in such abominations."

Sage touches the tip of Barron's big toe, and he gives a husky giggle of delight.

"He's laughing." I marvel as his tiny dimples go off. It's a bona fide Gage Oliver dimple explosion in the room, and the only living person I'm able to share this special moment with is Chloe. A thick sadness spreads over me at the thought. In the least I should have Logan here, but I'm currently still pissed at him as well.

Sage settles her eyes on the dark-haired demon to my left. "And who is this, Mommy?"

My heart warms when she says my name once again. "This is Chloe Bishop. She's sort of a friend." Dear God, did I just spout off a blatant lie to my own child? In all honesty, though, at the moment, Chloe and I have called an official truce. That whole friendship thing is true in effect.

"Chloe?" Her tiny dark brows furrow with worry before her entire face lights up. "Oh, yes! Uncle Logan has told me all about you!" Her mouth grows wide with surprise, but my heart tugs at the fact *Uncle Logan* has spent precious time with my little angel. I know which Logan she's referring to, the one already on the other side of the great cosmic divide. The one that just so happened to land there right after Chloe chopped his head off. "You're wicked!"

Chloe grunts and growls before a slim smile tugs at her lips. "Why, yes. Yes, I am *wicked*. Your Uncle Logan is correct." She matches her fingertips together while perfectly impersonating a villain. "You may look like your daddy, but you are your mother's child through and through—speaking before thinking. Actions, then consideration or lack thereof." She smacks her lips with disdain at my precious little girl. "I wouldn't get too close. I happen to think little children taste like candy, and my appetite is churning for a treat."

"*Chloe*," I bite her name out like a reprimand.

"Oh, Mommy, you're so brave!" Sage leans in toward the wicked wart taking up precious real estate on my mattress. "She's so close to you, and to the babies! I bet she really is going to eat them. Aren't you?" Sage's fascination with the nefarious witch only seems to grow.

"Yes, I am, little Sage Oliver." Chloe's dark, hollow eyes fixate on my precious baby girl. "I'm going to eat your mommy and your *daddy*, too!" Chloe wiggles her fingers at my beautiful princess, and I lift my foot to her until she relents.

"*Behave.*"

My mother belts out a bubbling laugh. "Oh, Skyla. Chloe doesn't know the meaning of the word. But I'll take care of the nuisance for you." She heads over to the casement window and scrolls it open. "Where is that dingbat and his betrothed that I gifted you?"

"Holden," I whisper like a secret to Sage, and she wrinkles her tiny little nose as if she's already been apprised of who he is as well. I bet my father and Logan are having a ball with her in paradise. I would. And just like that, I'm terminally jealous of the fact my father and Logan are dead. Go figure.

"No! Not Holden, *please.*" Chloe gags and writhes, which can only mean my raven and his lady bird friend are quickly drawing near. Holden is essentially Chloe repellent, which is why I appreciate him so damn much. "I have to go." Chloe claws against the walls as if she were about to fashion a brand new exit.

"What?" my mother balks. "And miss the party?" She gives another bubbling laugh. "But you're my daughter's closest confidant." Her words are cutting, dripping with sarcasm. "You're working together now, aren't you? We were just about to strategize her next move. Aren't you in the least bit curious what that might be? Please, do stay."

A guttural groan evicts from Chloe's throat. "Can't breathe—*so sick.*" She holds a hand out to Sage who wisely backs away. Her tiny face fills with horror. Both Nathan and Barron pick up on the agitation in the room and begin to grunt and kick.

"Chloe, you're scaring the kids. Mother, get rid of her."

Chloe claws at my leg as if begging for mercy.

Skyla, help me. Her eyes bulge as though they were about to burst from her skull.

I glare at Chloe, doing my best to use my mental abilities to ship her back to the hell she came from, but it's no use. Either my new powers have evaporated to nothing or my mother has a binding hedge over the girl who's quickly turning green in my bed.

"Dear God! She's going to puke!" I curl up in a ball toward Sage, trying my best to protect little Barron from the inevitable splatter.

"No puking on my watch." My mother waves a finger over to Chloe. "Lips be sewn, nostrils for breathing." She glares at Chloe as she writhes and gags.

Thankfully, she's been incapacitated from streaming her bile all over my tiny room, but just watching her muscles jump, her limbs pop in the air every other second is a thing of holy terror that I'm not interested in witnessing—nor am I interested in scarring Sage for all eternity.

"Be gone, Chloe," I growl while landing my hand over hers in an effort to will her the hell away from me. Chloe latches on with a death grip while I harden my gaze upon her, doing my best to send her back to the Transfer.

Holden and his pale plus one show up at the window. His paper white bride, Serena Kragger nee Taylor, a mid-century Deorsum who got on my mother's bad side once upon a century ago, pecks her way over.

Chloe detaches from me with a violent jolt. Her entire body defies gravity as it rises into the air, levitating a moment before it flattens against the wall, spread eagle with her face wild with surprise.

"Good show, Your Grace!" Sage giggles and claps. And dear God, I now have every right to be alarmed at how much interaction my celestial mother has with my child. Sage may be formally deceased, but that doesn't mean I don't have her best interests at heart. "Make her spin!"

Chloe shakes her head wildly, moaning something inaudible and yet clearly a protest.

"No," I'm quick to object to my daughter's twisted wishes. "She's hurting," I say softly to Sage while getting lost in those epic blue eyes and I'm mesmerized. God, I miss her father just as much as I miss her. "We shouldn't want to see people hurt."

Gage is hurting. I'm hurting, too.

"Mother—I've put in a request." Sage's tiny features squint with confusion. "*Your Grace*"—she spits it out curt, her features hardening to a staunch look of irritation—"I said make her *spin*." Sage never takes her eyes off me, and there's something in them that lets me know I've disappointed her on some level—and pissed her the hell off, too.

My mother scoffs as she steps in close and pets Sage as if she were her favorite kitten. "My dear, I can't deny you anything, now can I?" She solidifies a vengeful look to Chloe. "Spin, my little darling plaything. Spin like a top and fly far, far away."

Chloe moves clockwise, slow at first then building with speed, ratcheting up with velocity until her hair, her elongated limbs are nothing but a blur. Chloe Bishop emits a horrible howl, the groaning of an injured animal, as she turns into a dark rainbow that looks almost hollow as if you can stick your hand right through her. Then slowly, painfully slowly, Chloe and the wheel of misfortune she's become evaporates to nothing. As soon as the last molecule blinks out of the room, I hear the sound of her violent puking all the way from the Transfer.

"Nice show!" Sage jumps up while showering my mother with praise and joy.

"Not a nice show." I'm careful to reprimand as I pull Sage over with my free hand. Her flesh is so butter soft I want to kiss it. "Come sit with me." I hoist her up until she's nestled on the bed. I'm half-tempted to text Gage and tell him to get the hell over here, but I'm all out of hands at the moment and a bit flustered from the *show* I've just witnessed. "It's never a nice thing to make someone else feel bad." I try to say it as lovingly as possible. The last thing on earth I want is for my mother to turn my sweet baby girl into an asshole.

"But, Mommy"—Sage's eyes pull down as if she might cry—"Chloe is wicked. Your Grace says you must never trust the wicked. They don't have pure intentions toward you. As soon as you turn around, they'll have your head on the chopping block!"

"God, that's so Chloe." I close my eyes a moment.

"Your Grace?" Sage looks to my mother as if she were her universe. "What is an *asshole*?" Oh shit. Sage says *asshole* so slowly and purely it makes even that putrid word sound wholesome.

"*Skyla!*" my mother roars so loud both Holden and his bride enter into a flapping spree that sends black and white feathers floating to the ceiling. "You realize she can hear you when you're touching. You do remember the rules of the game, don't you?"

"I do now." I shrink in horror at the thought. Of course, she can hear me. She's my daughter. "She's one of us. She's a Celestra." Tears come, and I can hardly blink them away. "My people are so heavily outnumbered, and she could have been here. Why did you take her, Mother?"

"Because she's not the one."

"The *one*?" It doesn't take long for me to do the Logan Oliver math. "Then take away her powers. Give her back to me, fully human."

"*No!*" Sage's little face contours with horror as she leaps from the bed. "Oh, please, Your Grace, don't listen to her. She's demented! Her mind is all twisted up in knots because my bratty little brothers won't give her a wink of sleep. Can't you see? That's why she's cavorting with the wicked one! Oh, please, Your Grace, I'll be anything but human. Make me a cat or a *rat*! But I can't live without my powers!" She scowls over at me with venom in her beautiful little eyes, and I'm more than slightly alarmed.

My eyes widen with a slight horror of my own. "But, Sage, if you give them up, you'll be able to live with your *brothers." Who are not even remotely close to bratty, unlike some people,* I want to add but don't. "You'll grow up together. And think of all the fun you'll have with Mommy— we can paint our nails and bake cookies! I'll teach you the ins and outs of the Factions, and you can even head up the meetings one day." I'm pleading through tears, both my voice and lips quivering.

"Your Grace," her tone is tight and angry, "I bid you to take me away from this woman right this minute. She wants to steal my powers, and I'm frightened!"

"Not true." I shake my head manically, trying to calm her down.

My mother frowns at the incessant plea, and truthfully, it's my only relief in this panic Sage has incited in me. "I can't leave yet. My business is unfinished."

But Sage tries to bolt from the room anyway.

"No, Sage, don't go." I tighten my grip over her hand, but she wiggles free and makes her way to my mother. "Please, I won't say that again. Just stay." Barron lets out a sharp cry, and I rock him urgently, trying to get him to settle. I don't think Sage can handle an ounce more of agitation.

"I'm leaving now, *Skyla,* and I won't be back," Sage seethes, those stormy eyes of hers as unknowable as the ocean. "Let this be a lesson to you. Never threaten me again." Her voice spikes with anger before she turns to my mother. "If you're unable to take me, I'll leave on my own!"

"And travel through the heavens all by your lonesome?" Mother frowns at her mini me. "Angels have been deposed by wrestling with dark powers. I'd shudder to think what they might do to you, my love."

What in the hell? Aren't dead people supposed to be safe?

"*Fine!*" Sage's anger surges as her face screws up into a tight knot of anger. "Have Grandpa pick me up. Or send Uncle Logan. They'll both do anything for me!" Her tiny eyes squint with a newfound rage. "I'm leaving now, regardless of what you say—and neither of you can stop me." She stomps her feet, and I shake my head in dismay at my mother because honestly? This is what happens when you let a child spend copious amounts of time with her.

My mother lifts a hand, and a powerful light bursts into the room. Standing beside her, fully formed, is my father and my open-mouthed surprise quickly transforms into a smile.

"Daddy!" I sob out his name, so very tired of everything in this world. I'm ready for his embrace. I thirst for it like water.

"Skyla." He leans in and kisses both Barron and me before scooping Nathan from my mother's arms. "I love you all. Don't you ever forget that," he says it directly into his namesake's eyes.

"Put that thing *down*, Grandpa!" Sage commands. "You're to take me home at once. I'm not welcome here." She cuts me a lethal look with that last sentence. "That mean person wants to take away my powers, and she's called me a *very* bad word."

"Skyla?" My father looks befuddled as my mother extracts the baby from his arms.

"You may not speak with her!" Sage barks. "We're leaving now."

"I love you so much." The words strangle from my throat as I look to my irate little daughter. My beautiful dark angel with those sapphire eyes and dimpled cheeks. I love her so much my bones ache right down to my miserable soul.

She jumps up into my father's arms and gives his chest a hard shove. "I said now, Grandpa! Don't you pay attention to her! You may not choose her over me." And just like that, they're reduced to a quivering shadow before the room clears up once again.

"*Goodbye!*" I shout into the nothingness they've left behind, and it feels as if they've taken my heart right along with them. "Never in a million years would I have wanted to upset her." My chest heaves with a dry sob at the thought.

"Well, now—it didn't take you a million years, did it?" Candace takes a seat at the edge of the bed with that I-knew-it smug look on her face—my face as it were.

"You're raising her to be just like you." I pin her with a look to alert her to the fact this is not necessarily a good thing—because everyone in the universe can attest to the fact it's a piss-poor idea.

"Then I'm raising her *right*." She indulges in a prideful smile. "I just love seeing that flame of independence flicker alive in her. You really should have named her Feisty."

"*Feisty?*" It comes out with defeat because whether or not I gifted her that name—or cursed her with it, take your pick—it doesn't make a difference. That's exactly what she is. "You said she wasn't the one. What makes you so sure I'm having a child with Logan? It's Celestra's spring. I'm yawning awake to my own rebellion. I promise you I can be just as feisty as the next girl."

"Come now, you can't manipulate me into handing her back." She lays Nathan over my chest and sighs dreamily into him. "And as much as I admire the loving care and devotion you've given these two, I think it's time to meet with the Factions. You have very serious business to take care of, my dear."

"You're right. I've yet to oversee the Factions or the Retribution League properly. And don't even get me started on that government bullshit that Wesley is pulling. But I'm still nursing." Nathan begins to root around my chest as he searches for food, and I give it to him. "Case in point." He latches on, and I suck in a breath. That needle in the nipple sensation still gets me each time they get started.

"And you're still able to speak with me. Case in point." She forces a quick smile to come and go. "You can and will do both."

"There isn't any real business to conduct. Besides, the island is crawling with feds. I'm sure they have the Haver estate on lockdown. The government wants answers. They're going door-to-door. There's a rumor going around that they're giving out cash and gift incentives. I hate the thought of being ratted out because someone desperately wanted a twenty-five-dollar gift card to the Burger Shack."

"Would anyone you know do such a thing?" She's egging me on. I can tell by the tone in her voice that she's leading me down a fiery stepfather-ish path.

"Tad."

"Only Tad?"

"Okay, fine. Half the island would sell me out for a free burger." My chest bucks at the thought, and both boys bounce over me, inciting one of them to offer up a husky giggle.

"Then we need to stay ahead of the curve. You and your people will be ratted out as you so eloquently put it. What do you propose we do?"

"You have the solution mother. Spit it out." I'm not in the mood for her head games. My heart is still aching from that bizarre quasi-argument I had with Sage.

"No, Skyla. If I recall, it is your springtime. Knowledge is your sharpest weapon. I suggest you arm yourself with it. You are the rebel. I suggest you put on your rebellious thinking cap." She picks up my hand, and the stone on my throne ring electrifies a brilliant shade of cobalt—the exact representation of my husband's eyes, and I sigh dreamily to myself for a moment. "Who are they going to bring in for questioning?"

"Forget questioning. That would be merciful compared to what they have planned for my people. They'll cage us up if they feel we're a big enough threat—and we are most definitely a big enough threat."

"Cage those precious babes in your arms?" Her voice drips with concern, but there's something unrelenting in her eyes I can't quite determine. "Really, Skyla? Would a good mother like you ever let that happen?"

"Hell no—pardon my French. I'd offer up just about anyone else before I let them lay one finger on my children— on my *people* for that matter. But I'm not Wesley. I'm not about to ask which of my people are willing to sacrifice themselves for the greater good. Besides, once they capture a single one of us, they'll want every last Nephilim contained. There just isn't an easy way out."

"No, there isn't, is there?" She bops Holden over his feathered head, and he lets out a screeching yelp.

"Mother." I lift my foot with an empty threat. "You can't be cruel to small animals. God forbid Sage ask you to make some poor creature spin until they vomit their guts up. That wasn't appropriate by the way." Not that I'm necessarily defending Chloe. No, some might argue she deserves far worse, but Sage should never want to see a person suffer.

"Sage isn't here, Skyla. You are." She bops poor, *poor* Holden over the head again, this time far more pronounced, and he hops the hell away from her. Can't say I blame him.

"Wait a minute..." I scoot up a bit and draw the boys close to me. "You're not intentionally being cruel to Holden." I think on this for a minute. "You're telling me something." My gaze shifts from one bird to the next. "Holden and Serena. You think I should use these two as a diversion." I can't take my eyes off the fidgeting creatures. If I had to guess, I'd say they'll be the next to vomit. "You think they can provide a solution. The feds are looking to put us in cages. Birds belong in cages..."

She gives a quick shake of the head. "Think harder, Skyla. Think outside of the cage. This is your springtime." She doesn't bother to hide her sarcasm anymore. I get it. I've inadvertently pissed her off with my promise not to listen to her advice.

"Well, if they're not in a cage, they're free and God knows the feds aren't about to offer burger incentives to a flock of birds...they'd have to be"—dear God, she's a genius—"*human.*"

She tips her head back a moment and glares down at me with those lucent blue eyes. "Are the feds interested in humans, Skyla? Dear heavens, not even your own daughter is interested in that."

I place the boys back in their shared bassinet and head over to where Holden and Serena jump nervously from desk to desk.

"They can't be human or Nephilim—unless..." I land my hand gently over Serena's back. "They'll have to be reverted back to their original Nephilim state."

"And then what?"

"They'll get arrested," I flatline as the pure genius of it all hits home. "I really like where this is headed." Holden lets out a riotous scream as if protesting the idea. "But I'm afraid Wesley has the feds believing there's an entire infantry out there. I'm not sure the government would be satisfied with just two poor souls." I thump Holden over the head myself.

"Too bad there's not a way to give them more." She picks up my hand and fondles the ring Chloe gave me.

"I guess there's Emerson, but that could realistically only be the start. I'd need to resurrect half the cemetery to appease the government." The cemetery... "The cemetery?" I look to my mother as the epiphany hits.

"The cemetery would provide a healthy supply of specialty forces." She shakes her head as if this were both wonderful and unfortunate.

Of course, it's unfortunate. Death isn't exactly a sought-after attribute in this scenario. My mind flexes in a sea of possibilities—all of them ironically impossible at the moment.

"Specialty forces... This is a time of war. Just about all things are permissible during wartime." I think on this a moment. "But if I could resurrect the dead, I'd want Sage brought back first."

"I see where your daughter gets her demanding demeanor." She scoffs and flicks her finger in the air just the way I do. It's funny how you think something is your own—an inflection, a mannerism—then you see your parents do it, and you realize that not only are you a physical carbon copy, but your mannerisms, perhaps even your nefarious thought process is not truly your own. "No. The specialty forces will be subject to government testing, and I can't have that done to my special little angel."

Holden and Serena start in on a squawking spree and do their best to squeeze themselves right out the window.

"Oh no, you don't." I close that tiny air gap before they can squeeze through it. "Go ahead, Mother. Work that holy and right magic on the two of them." I hold up a finger in thought. "Only—they can't stay here. And what's to stop them from running?"

"They'll be bound." She cups her palm over Serena's back, and the delicate bird shudders. "They'll also be willing." She twists both birds around by the tail, jackknifing them until they face her. "Do you, Serena Taylor and Holden Kragger, accept the task of becoming human for a time to do a good work for the Celestra people?"

"Sounds like a wedding ceremony," I whisper.

"It is a covenant." My mother raises her brows. I've always marveled at her sharp hook-shaped brows. Honestly, they're the stuff that Disney villains are made of.

My mother chuckles as Holden and Serena take a moment to coo between themselves. Really? What's there to consider? Burgers or worms. It's not a hard decision.

"What are you laughing at?" I nudge my mother in the arm.

"*You*. Admiring my Disney villain brows." She arches one my way with all of the drama she can afford. "Have you looked in the mirror lately—oh Skyla the Springtime Villainess?"

"Right." I glance back at my reflection, and sure enough, there she is, my very own villain staring back at me. "Never mind. The cemetery it is. When can we wake the dead? I'm sure the Olivers are going to love this. As in *not*. If I've ever given Emma a reason to hate me, I have a feeling digging up the graveyard that keeps her financial gravy train running is really going to piss her off."

"I'm not concerned with Emma, and you shouldn't be either. What you should concern yourself with is her son—your husband. You do realize the fact freezing him out isn't going to make things better any time soon. It's only going to cast a divide amongst you."

"Are you aware of what he's done?"

"Yes. And are *you* aware of the fact that marriages are built on compromises?"

"A compromise of this magnitude does not a happy marriage make. It makes life a living hell." Perhaps quite literally.

Holden and Serena's squawking hits an all-time high and both my mother and I hiss at them to keep it down. The boys are happily cooing away, and I'd like to keep it that way.

"Happy marriage?" My mother looks stumped by the concept. "Skyla, there hasn't been one of those in all of human history. Every union bears its strife. If anything, an unhappy marriage is a common lot in life. Show me a couple who espouses a happy façade and I will show you a couple of bald-faced liars."

"Oh, come on. Gage and I were plenty happy before things went to shit. Pardon my French once again." My mother loathes my salty sailor talk just as much as Marshall seems to.

Her hair glows a bright iridescent pink before defusing as if the expletive had the power to initiate a celestial riot in her.

"Were you happy?" She gives a few rapid blinks my way as if I were trying her patience, and I have no doubt I am. "Or were you striving to be so? When have you had a moment's peace, Skyla?"

"Before Dad died." I didn't even have to think about that one. "Ever since I set foot on Paragon—not to get literary on you, but it's been the best of times and the worst of times."

"That's the burden of life, my love. Everyone has their cross to bear. It just so happens that yours consists of the wings of a thousand Nephilim. Do rectify things with Gage. It hurts the Father to see such strife. He is a proponent of maintaining earthly covenants." A wicked grin curves her lips. "But try as you might, that matrimonial good time isn't allowed anywhere near the afterlife. Resurrection will be bliss, I tell you. Not a single leash to bind you." She gives a wistful shake of the head. "As for upturning the cemetery, don't worry about ruffling Emma's celestial feathers. And as for your husband, I may be advocating your reunion, but I am far from pleased with him."

"Was this—wasn't this—um—could this have been—" No matter how hard I try, I can't formulate the words to ask the question. Most likely because I hate the question.

"Was it his destiny?" Her brows arch clear up to her forehead, an Olympian-worthy feat if you ask me.

A slow nod is all I can offer.

"Skyla." She closes her eyes as she draws me close. I cannot remember too many times that my mother has held me this way, at least not post those three months on earth where she was my primary caretaker, and I recall nothing of those. But this moment, her warmth, that vibration she exudes, which is something far sweeter than what Marshall is capable of, I could sleep well in my mother's arms. "Destiny is a finicky thing. It's only as stable as the obedience of its recipient."

"Obedience." My personal rebellion comes to mind. "I'm veering from fate." I pull back to get a better look at what amounts to my reflection. "Gage can veer, too."

Holden and Serena squawk up a storm before she can answer.

"It's that time." She smacks them both over the head in turn. "Feathers to feathers, no sins to atone—rise to your feet in flesh and in bone."

A billowing fog permeates the room, bitter and blue that dissipates as quick as it came, and in its place, is a fully formed Holden and Serena.

A heavy breath escapes me as Holden and Serena marvel at their fleshly appendages. He looks every bit as lanky, and mind you *Kraggery*, with that squared jaw, that dirty blond hair, and those mean-spirited eyes—although, at the moment those eyes look pleasantly impressed with his new form. And Serena looks every bit the Nordic goddess her pale feathers would have you believe she was. She's a beautiful sight to behold. I just hope she's still enamored with the cranky Kragger next to her.

"You did it!" I pant as the boys begin to cry. I pick up Nathan, and my mother takes Barron.

"Of course, I did it."

"Thank you, Candace." Holden falls to his knees. He looks every bit as familiar as the day he was banished into Nevermore's form. "I beg of you to free my sister, if only for a time."

"Only for a time is correct." She sneers toward Mia and Melissa's room. "She's willing." She lifts a finger, and the faint sound of my sisters' screaming permeates through the wall.

"Emerson's here?" I clutch onto Nathan a little tighter. "Good God! This had better end well."

"It does end." My mother hands off Barron to Serena.

A horrible thought comes to mind. "What about Giselle? My God, Emma is going to kill me if she discovers I've traded her precious daughter in for a Kragger." I glance to Holden. "No offense."

"None taken," he offers a cheesy wink.

My mother balks at the idea. "I've a temporal home for Emerson. She's merely a visitor. Precious Giselle is alive and well."

Thank goodness. Not that I really fear Emma—but G truly is precious and I'd hate to blink her out of existence on a whim.

"Now"—my mother clasps her hands while looking to Holden and Serena—"once you're taken captive by those nasty federal agents, I'll look into a reversal of your newfound fortune. The three of you are bound to this mission. Enjoy each and every breath through human nostrils while it lasts—it won't last. And, Skyla, take care of that husband situation." She addresses my marriage as if it were an oil spill, and she wants me to take care of it? "And mind, Ezrina." She expels a heavy sigh. "For goodness' sake, the entire lot of you belongs on leashes." And just like that, she's gone.

"Wait! How do I go about resurrecting the dead?"

Holden stands and narrows that familiar sinister gaze my way. "Now what, Messenger?"

"Now what, *indeed*."

Marshall isn't at home, and, per his usual secretive Sector ways, he isn't answering his texts. He thinks technology is *cute* and more of a pest than a reliable source of communication. But, thankfully, Ezrina and Nev don't feel the same. When I ask Nevermore about Marshall's whereabouts, not only is the wily Sector at the Gas Lab but so is Ezrina—another hard-to-find extraordinary creature. Technically, she's Nephilim, always has been, but since she's taking up occupancy in Chloe's old body, *creature* sounds about right.

So off to the Gas Lab I go with my newfound trio of friends. There's Emerson—the OG version, which looks more like she can be Giselle's sister than she can twin. I keep forgetting my mother added the dimples, and Giselle's bright and cheery affect really does do wonders for a face. But I digress. Not only is a sulking Emerson with me—for God's sake you'd think she'd be thrilled to be rid of the feathers, but Holden—he's both seemingly cheery and *nice*! In his case the feathers really did him a world of good. I'm finally ready to put that whole quasi-sexual assault behind us. And lest not we forget the stunningly beautiful Serena— blonde hair, blue-eyed, pale as winter snow—okay, we're talking deathly pale on a scary level, but in her dermal defense, she has been stark white raven mad for the last few hundred years. Okay, so it wasn't that funny. But in addition to that motley crew, I've also dragged my precious babies out of the house for this little celestial field trip. The same baby boys who suffered unconscionably for a month, no thanks to Emma and her *allergies*. Damn lies I tell you, and that woman can spew them. Allergy alibi, my ass.

I pause a moment and take a rather benign head count of the Kraggers in their newly issued bodies with those old familiar faces, sans Serena, of course, who is so stunning I'm half-afraid someone will haul her off this oversized rock and offer her a modeling contract before she explodes right back into a ball of feathers.

"Stick close to me." I search my mind as to what I can possibly do with these former plumes, considering the fact I'll soon have an entire army of graveyard soldiers at my disposal. "You know, unless something changes, I want the three of you to enjoy your stay on Paragon."

Holden shoots up a brow.

"I mean it," I'm quick to make it clear. "I kind of feel bad about that whole feathered nightmare. And, honestly, you'll only be here for a few minutes in the grand scheme of things. Go ahead and have some fun. On me." I give a crooked smile. The truth is, I don't want to utilize a single Kragger unless I absolutely have to. The only thing I can rely on them to do is rattle off my secrets to Big Daddy K, and I'm pretty sure no matter how well I threaten them not to, the big blab session is inevitable.

We head into the Gas Lab like the unruly mob we are, me with a double stroller that Holden actually helped figure out how to get into a locked position—total gentleman! Serena can't stop cooing over the boys. And really? Who can blame her? My mini Gages are basically a hit with women wherever we go. Wait until she sees the real deal. Just because Gage and I are on the outs doesn't mean I don't appreciate his seismic beauty. And obviously and thankfully, when God made him, he didn't break the mold. He elected to use it at least two more times with our precious boys.

I spot the sexy Sector near the back, staring into his laptop as if he were just another human sipping the java and checking out cat porn. God, cat porn had better be the only lewd content that extraterrestrial being scopes out on the Internet. I stroll on over, and just as I'm about to do the resurrected intros, I see the crew I was leading has already gone astray.

"*Gah*! Marshall, watch the boys for a minute." I practically dive back to the front where Holden is carrying on a conversation with Nevermore.

"He's not Pierce!" I shout so loud half the customers turn to gawk my way. His nametag might read *Pierce*, but he's Nevermore, Heathcliff O'Hare through and through.

Holden sheds a rather relaxed smile. I'm still far from used to this subdued version of the Kragger in question. "I realize that, Skyla. I was just introducing myself and my wife. It's pretty cool that even though Pierce is gone he sort of lives on. Don't get me wrong. I'd rather be a bird than dead."

Serena giggles at the thought. "I'm sure dead is great, too. But Holden and I sort of consider the feathered life a liberating one. And after seeing the price of a cup of coffee, I'm happier than ever before to roam the earth freely."

"Nice." I think. Honestly, dead probably trumps feathers, but then, she and Holden did have hatchlings last spring. Feathered sex must be amazing. I look to Nev. "Where's Ezrina?"

Nev glances back to the kitchen. "It appears she's entertaining a guest. Here she comes now."

Ezrina and Emerson emerge from the back. Double *gah*!

Holy shit. I'm going to go gray or bald trying to keep track of Kraggers 2.0.

"Emerson, this isn't really—"

"I got it. She's not Chloe." She grunts, looking out at the place. "Who I really want to see is my dad."

"*No!*" I shout so loud I hear Barron choke with a cry. It's funny how distinctly different their cries are. I'm so thrilled I can finally tell them apart to the point I'm no longer paranoid I'll mix them up for good and each will grow up as the other. "Your dad thinks—"

"I know." She's quick to wave me off. "My dad loves me, Skyla. Haven't you ever missed anyone so bad that you need to see them no matter what?"

Deep down, I knew this was a bad idea. "Once your father gets wind of what you're doing and for who, it will kill the purpose of the operation." Would it, though? How could the Counts possibly stop me?

Ezrina and Nev exchange a glance.

"I won't tell." She shrugs as if it's as easy as that. "Come on, Holden. We'll walk over."

"It's six miles from here," he balks at the ambulatory idea.

"You haven't used your legs in years." She's quick to point out. "You should be glad you have them."

Holden frowns as he looks to me. "What say you, Messenger?"

For one, I'm floored that Holden is actually somewhat tame and obedient. I mull over the catastrophic possibilities—like for instance Wesley piecing together the brilliance of this plan and putting a stop to it. Not to mention the dilemma of the two Emersons. But I can only hope this provides a way to keep Arson on a leash.

"I say you can visit." A smile blinks on and off from my lips. "But if your father wants details—swear him to secrecy because if Wesley hears of this, and believe me, I will be appraised of this—it's back to the feathered pound for the three of you." It will be regardless. A thought comes to me. "And keep it brief. I'm not sure I want you living with Daddy Dearest. I'll try to find someplace for you to stay." I glance to Nev, knowing full well they'll be shacking up in Arson's mega hovel in less than five minutes. "Would you mind giving Holden your phone?" Nev is quick to comply. "I'll text you in a few hours. You'll be residents elsewhere for the duration of your stay. Remember—you don't spill a single secret."

"No worries, Messenger." Holden shakes my hand, and the three of them are quick to begin their journey.

Nev steps in front of me, his eyes dark and menacing. "What are they doing in the flesh, and why have you practically sent them into enemy territory?"

"They're here to take one for the team so to speak. The government wants bodies, and we're about to give them just that."

His eyes enlarge. "But how did you do this?" Nev was a bird for so long I'm sure he tried a thousand ways till Sunday to free himself of the feathered binding.

"My mother."

"Skyla." Ezrina closes her eyes. "The Kraggers will sideline everything. And Arson? He is the worst of them all."

Nev gives a solemn nod. "You're about to see your plan unravel before the dead get to pay their dues." It's clear Holden has already spilled the resurrected beans.

"That may be." A sly smile plays on my lips as I watch the fog absorb the three of them from the window. "But, trust me, I've got this. There is no way this is backfiring. It's a done deal no matter how hard Arson or Wesley tries to foil this endeavor. Besides—the three of them? That's just the tip of the Paragon cemetery iceberg. Maybe it's time Wes and his deconstruction crew were in on my plan for a change— one in which they are impotent to do anything about." How's that for a role reversal?

The boys begin to make their verbal presence known, and Marshall calls my name as if his voice box had magically transformed into a megaphone.

"The babes!" Ezrina makes a beeline for the back, and Nev and I join her. Before I can inquire about anything that might help solve the mystery surrounding my hatchet-wielding friend, she lifts Barron into Nevermore's arms and takes Nathan for herself. The boys coo and gaze up at the new friendly faces, their eyes mesmerized, tiny giggles breaking out at random.

"They're laughing." It fills me with joy to have two tiny dimpled bundles who love to chat and smile. It's a simple world I've quickly gotten used to. Yes, there is no sleep in this world, but I've discovered that with every good thing there is a little hell to pay. And sadly, that perfectly describes my marriage to Gage.

Ezrina and Nev step away while rocking and amusing the boys with silly faces and sounds.

"*Skyla.*" Marshall glowers over at me as if I've wrung out a dirty diaper in his coffee.

"Oh, stop. You know I had to do something. Besides, it was my insane mother who—" The entire building trembles with thunder. "Okay, so it was my idea, but she totally egged me on until I came up with every last dead and dirty detail. But trust me, it's a good thing. The government needs bodies. *Supernatural* bodies," I whisper so low it's hardly audible, but I'd swear on my life ten people just turned around to gawk. "And my boys will never play the part of guinea pig as long as I have breath in my body."

He grunts as he looks up at the angelic beings. "And your stepfather is looking forward to this, I imagine? Three guests? I suppose you'll cram them in your bedroom as well." He takes a sip of his coffee with the satisfied self-righteous grin blooming on his face.

"Heavens no." I shake my head as I slip into the seat across from him. "There will be far more than three." I reach over and pick up his hand in an effort to appeal to the most primal part of him, and that vibrating goodness strums through my bones, appealing to the most primal part of me. "There will be many—there will be legions. And I'll need them all to stay with you."

"No," he says it so fast, without a hint of hesitation, it fills me with an indignant rage.

"What do you mean, *no*? What am I going to do with all of these reanimated corpses?" Hopefully, there will be hundreds, thousands even.

"I mean no, Skyla. Find somewhere else to play your graveyard games. My estate is off-limits."

"But you love to entertain the dead. Think of Marlena and her call girl friends. How is this any different?" Marshall seems to host a hoedown whoredown just about every other day with those seventeenth-century hussies.

"It just is."

He pulls his laptop forward and begins nonchalantly inputting something.

"What are you doing?" I try to peer over at the screen, but he inches it away.

"Calculating how long it will take you to figure out what to do with the dead."

"No, you're not." I lean in farther. It's a list of some sort.

"Fine." He snaps the laptop closed just inches from clipping my nose. "Your mother and I are planning an extravagant first birthday party for the little goats."

"The little goats? Marshall, they're not even three months old!"

"Your mother—"

"Never mind. I know my mother." A moment bounces by where it's just Marshall and me, this heavenly handsome as all hell being with those cutting maroon eyes and a sly smile that screams *the better to eat you with*. Marshall was there for the birth of the boys, and now he's planning their first birthday party. For some reason, the fact he was embroiled in the event that involves the two pieces of my heart floating around on the planet makes him vexingly sexy on a dangerous level. "So"—I clear my throat—"can I use your home? Just one room. Trust me, they're used to tight confined spaces. A whole room will feel like the Taj."

"You have a home, Skyla. House them there."

"The Landon estate?" A laugh gets caught in my throat. "If I do that, you can add Tad to the number of corpses."

Marshall frowns and nods west.

Wait—what's west? West, *west*? As in West Paragon High? No, they have enough zombified bodies wandering around campus. The only thing past that is the estates where—

I suck in a quick breath. "The old Walsh home?"

He forces his lips to curl in a nefarious grin. "I believe it is the new Oliver home. Yes, Skyla. You yourself have referred to the hovel as a haunted house. And now you can have all the ghosts you wish to fill it."

"Very funny." The old Walsh home, my home, is a death trap at the moment. I'm pretty sure it's not safe to house corpses in—resurrected or not.

I think on this for a minute. God, what do I say? I've never needed Marshall's full support on this level before. That horrid *surprise* spirit wedding that took place years ago crosses my mind.

"Lest I remind you that I let you marry me." I blink up at him in a weak attempt to seduce him toward my line of thinking.

He glances up, almost bored with the fact—not the slightest bemusement on his part. It wasn't so much that I let him marry me than the fact I was sort of ambushed and it *happened* to me.

"Okay, so I didn't really let you marry me, but I totally would have if I had my better judgment about me. Good thing you stepped in when you did. Shall we have Demetri throw us a vow renewal in the Transfer? There's nothing like a bunch of disembodied spirits to make it feel official." I should know. I did the very same thing last September with Gage.

He folds his arms, his affect unflinching. "A party for the ages—at the devil's house no less. My, Skyla, you do dream big, don't you?"

"I dream of you." It comes out wistful and for good reason. Marshall has been haunting my dreams—or more accurately, my subconscious has been haunting my dreams with Marshall. And, mind you, these are not your average nocturnal wanderings. These are sultry, erotic, panty-melting, grip-the-sheets sex-rated dreams. Nothing at all the stuff that should be filling the head of a very married woman. But, honest to God, there's no getting off this sexual merry-go-round. The more I try to fight them, the *harder*—pun intended—they seem to come.

My lips purse for a moment as I reflect on Gage and how hurtful it must be knowing this goes on each and every night. He figured it out a long time ago and has never held it against me. If Gage were having nonstop porn dreams about Kresley, I would have hung him by his oversized balls by now.

"My"—a dark laugh strums from Marshall—"that took you away to a special place."

A light tap falls on my shoulder, and I look up to find Laken hovering above me. "Speaking of special places. Fancy seeing you here."

"Laken!" I jump up and give her a strong hug. "God, I've missed you."

"I've missed you. And my God! Look how big these boys are! It's only been a few weeks since we saw you at the bowling alley and they've already doubled in size." She holds her arms out as Nev hands Barron over.

"What's up?" Cooper comes from behind. "You ready for another Retribution League sit-down?"

"You read my mind. I'll schedule it soon. You won't believe the ace that just crawled up our sleeve."

Laken and Coop exchange a quick look.

"Don't worry. This is going to be brilliant." Nathan starts to fuss and I try to take him from Ezrina, but she spins on her heels.

"Mine." She presses a kiss to the top of his head and evokes a bubbling laugh from him.

"*Ezrina*," I cry in awe at my happy baby boy.

Laken bounces Barron a few feet away over to where Ezrina is holding Nathan hostage, and I steal the opportunity to have a quick one-on-one with Coop.

I lean in and whisper, "Have you kicked Wesley's ass yet for stealing your wife's virginity?" I give a single nod because I'd love for it to be true more than anything.

Coop gives a quick shake of the head as Laken and Ezrina bounce back in this direction.

Laken rubs her cheek over Barron's feather soft hair. "You're so lucky you get to love on these two little cuddle bunnies all day and all night."

"Don't I know it. But soon enough, you'll have an entire fleet of mini-Coopers to love and cuddle all day and night. And I do mean all night. It turns out cuddle bunnies are in extreme opposition to getting any sleep."

Laken and Coop share a laugh—Coop's being the loudest and longest.

"We'll see what happens in the future. We both applied to grad school." He shoots a look to Ezrina and Nev. "How about you two? Any kids in your future? I know you're both busy, but, like my mother says, don't wait for the perfect time."

Sounds like Coop's mama is gunning for a mini-Cooper just as much as I am. I'd love for Laken to have kids close in age with the boys.

Ezrina and Nev grow quiet with Nev suddenly craning his neck toward the kitchen and Ezrina tossing up a hand in defeat.

"It's happened." Her voice cracks. "I'm with child."

A collective gasp comes from our little group. Marshall jumps to his feet before I can congratulate either of them and bows toward the mother-to-be.

"Well done, Rina." He picks up her hand and lands a gentle kiss to the back. "How ardent, how ruddy your cheeks. I should dare say you look resplendent with child."

My jaw goes slack a moment. I don't remember a single ardent, ruby, or resplendent compliment while I was expecting. But, truthfully, I looked like a pile of diarrhea on fire, so I can't really blame him. Marshall does staunchly believe in telling the truth.

"*Ezrina!*" Laken and I lunge over her at the same time. "This is amazing," I pant. "You and Nev will be parents. How beautiful is that?"

"Yes." She pulls back with her hand on her stomach, and I can't help but think she looks forlorn. "Chloe's child, too."

"Oh no." I try to pull her out of that Bishop stupor. "This will be yours through and through."

"I've come to peace with it." She lifts a hand. "Just like I came to peace with it when Tobie was born."

I never thought of it that way. Chloe had Tobie while in Ezrina's body. So, yes, that child is genetically Ezrina's. No wonder she went running with bells on the minute Wesley hired her as a nanny. It was her own baby she was looking after. I'll make it a point to bring Tobie around more often. I think Ezrina would appreciate that.

"Ezrina." Laken pulls her in for a quick hug, but Ezrina yanks free with a wild look in her eyes that I haven't seen since she and I were on opposite ends of the fighting arena.

"I have to go." She lands the baby back in my arms and takes off for the kitchen.

A strangulating awkwardness permeates our small group.

I look to Nev. "What was that about?" My heart thumps wild because Ezrina isn't known for acting erratic—at least not anymore.

Nev glances to Laken, his cheeks flushing with color. "I'm afraid her temperament as of late has yet to adjust to the needs of creating new life." He nods toward the floor as if he had just spilled an honest truth. "If you'll excuse me." He gives a slight bow and starts toward the kitchen, but I cut him off and pull him to the side.

"Nev, you know something. I can see it in your eyes." Nevermore may have only been mine in raven form for a short while, but I'd like to think we've gotten to know one another beyond the borders of the flesh. "Tell me what it is. Shed light on this mystery for me." My mother said that something was up with Ezrina, and I highly doubt it had to do with that baby brewing in her belly.

"Skyla—" He cranes his neck past me trying to get a better look at Ezrina who has long since disappeared into the bowels of the kitchen. "I'm afraid this isn't my matter." He closes his eyes a moment. You can see the fear, the disappointment pulsating through his surface veins. "Now let me comfort my wife."

"I'm here for you, Nev. I know that something is afoot with Ezrina. My mother warned me."

"Your mother!" Nevermore blanches with fear at the mention of her. She's the one who put him in the raven's body and the same one who took him right back out again. Needless to say, she can produce quite the reversal of feathered fortune if need be.

"Wait, Nev!" I call after him, but he's long gone. Nathan pulls at my hair and bubbles with a laugh as he looks lovingly into my eyes. "Oh my God," I whisper, the panic quickly draining from me. "You make everything better." I gift him a little kiss to the forehead.

Laken steps forward, a stern look on her face. "What was that about?"

Marshall and Cooper close in our circle as the three of them await an answer.

"Ezrina is up to something." I glance back at the kitchen. "And it's not that bun she's got in the oven."

"Knew it." Coop digs his hands into his pockets as he gazes past me. "I went down last week to speak with her, and she ushered me out of the lab so fast you would think it were on fire."

Ezrina comes out once again and gets straight to helping a customer out. Marshall pins her with a look, and I can tell by the way his eyes do that sexy little squint that he's engaging with her somehow.

"What is it?" I'm breathless at the prospect. Ezrina is a wild card. There is so much good she can do for our people, but one misstep could cost us everything.

Marshall lets out a hard breath as he continues to glower at her. "*Rina.*" Her name bleeds from his lips with the utmost disappointment. Whatever it is, Marshall has just been apprised, and judging by his response, he's not that thrilled with her either. Both my mother and Marshall are disappointed in her? Strikes one and two. I'm betting strike three will be me as soon as I get wind of whatever it is she's cooking up.

Before I can shake the answer out of him, the door to the Gas Lab bursts open and a rather odd entourage steps in. Melody Winters and a young man around her age are both decked out as if they were headed to a Halloween party. She's dressed like one of Marshall's old-world hussies with a long frilly black and pink dress, low-cut in the front—on both top and bottom—and a bustle in the back that makes her ass look as if it's better suited for a donkey. And he's wearing—God, he's dressed like those long-deceased souls in the Transfer. An old-world suit with a string for a tie. So odd.

The ring on my finger begins to glow like a moonbeam, and I clamp my hand over it in the event it decides to cause a neon scene. But it's too late. Melody and her old-world cohort speed on over.

"What's this?" She flicks her finger over my hand—over the glowing morsel of the King's throne itself, and her jaw goes slack. "Well, well, Sector Marshall. It looks as if we have a time traveling thief on our hands."

Gage

Whitehorse wafts in and out of the fog like a dream, like a nightmare. Logan purchased this plot of land in Silent Cove a few years back and built this—some might say monstrosity, some might say tender gesture for his future wife—*my* wife.

The wind picks up, bites its way through my jacket as I make my way up the clean white porch. I can't help but note the verse arched above the doorway, *I love you more than the heavens love the sun and the moon.* He does. Logan loves Skyla exactly that much and more, and even though it sets off an inner rage in me, I understand it. Skyla is the kind of woman that leaves you breathless and wanting more. And as much as I want to, I can't forget the fact it was Logan she wanted first. The love we share might have blossomed from our friendship, but there's not a thing in me that believes what we share today isn't real.

A dry laugh strums through me. Skyla hasn't spoken more than a few words to me in months. The only reason we still share a bed on occasion is because we're both exhausted from taking care of the boys. Our lips, our bodies have been virtual strangers to one another ever since I pledged allegiance to the dark side.

The doorknob gives in my hand, and I step in without bothering to knock. "*Yo!*" I bark and a tiny female frame startles on the sofa—dark copper hair cut above her shoulders, that permanent scowl on her face. It's Lex.

"Is that what you do in your spare time, Gage Oliver? Barge into other people's homes without knocking?" Lexy Bakova spikes up on the sofa, pulling a blanket up to her chin and turning the volume down on the television.

"*Logan!*" she shouts, clearly annoyed by my presence. "Gage is here!"

"What brings you here?" I'll admit, I'm slightly amused at the size of Lexy's balls. Logan has made it known to her more times than I can count that he's not interested, and she relentlessly continues to knit herself into his life. A shallow part of me is cheering her on, but I know Logan better than I know myself—lately that sentiment is true to a fault—Logan doesn't want Lexy—not in that way. He's not interested in some close second to Skyla, not that there is one. He wants Skyla and only Skyla. Can't blame him. I feel the same.

"What brings *you* here?" She cranes her neck past me as if she needed me to move so she can see that goliath screen. Logan's television takes up the wall, something that one might think screams *my financial dick is bigger than yours*, but in Logan's case, he just wants to feel like he's at the game. We spent our lives in worship of college football up until Skyla showed up, and ever since we've spent the remainder of our time worshiping her.

Logan pops in before I can answer.

"Glad you're here, man." He slaps me five and pulls me into a partial embrace. Logan called and said I needed to get my sorry ass down to Whitehorse as soon as possible.

"I came right over. What's up?"

His forehead wrinkles with concern, and I can tell he's holding back. I can only assume it's because Lex is in the room. "There's some stuff I wanted to go over with you downstairs."

Technically, there is no downstairs at this particular Oliver estate. The only thing down there is the subterranean lab he built for Ezrina to emulate the one she had in the Transfer—but in typical Logan fashion, it's infinitely larger than the facility the Counts furnished her with. It's been a godsend, but something tells me that's up for debate at the moment. I follow Logan into the kitchen and through the pantry, which leads to the stairwell that spirals down to the lab. To say it's enormous down here doesn't do it justice. A football field might be dwarfed. I've never walked the periphery, but from what I can tell it spans a great deal past his lot lines.

"What's up with Bakova?" I ask, jogging to keep up with him. "She still trying to heat the sheets?"

"That would be it." He shakes his head at the thought. "She's company, though."

"For who?" Logan has been at the house we grew up in as much as I have these last few months.

"I pop in every now and again, and it's nice to have someone to carry on a conversation with." He cuts me a quick look, and his cheek twitches. "Relax. I'm shitting with you. Trying to stave off her hormones is like holding up a wall. She's relentless as they come." He frowns as we head down the corridor that leads to Ezrina's shiny new chop shop. "But she's with the Barricade—she's one of you."

I pull him back by the shirt like a reflex and shove him against the wall. "Don't say that, dude."

Those lucent yellow eyes of his meet up with mine, and a sober moment bounces between us. "Own it, Gage. You went in with a purpose. You and I both know you went in to save your children—and now that you're in, we can use this."

"Is that what you dragged me down here for?" I give him a hard shove, and the back of his head hits the wall with a thud.

"No." He squeezes his eyes shut tight as if that knock to the skull actually hurt. "But you asked what Lex was doing here. I'm telling you there's a need to infiltrate."

"So you infiltrate with Lexy, and Skyla infiltrates with Chloe." And I infiltrate on my own, but I leave that dismal bit of obvious news out. I bypass him and head into the stainless lab with its white-on-white décor that messes with your head. "Tell me, Logan. Has Skyla given you the slightest hint of what she's up to, or is that something the two of you have decided to keep from me?" I run my hand along the stainless sink, so squeaky clean you could eat right out of it.

"I don't have any clue. But if I did, I wouldn't keep it from you. Just like I'm not keeping this from you." He motions for me to follow him farther down the hall to the room where Ezrina has a legion of oversized glass tubes on display, each filled with blue keeping solution, each one void of one quasi-human body. She built this resurrection wing in hopes to bring back the Videns from their impending doom. A third of the Videns have gone MIA, gifting their life to Wesley's cause. There's no real way to know if they went in knowing they'd convert into Spectators—something Wes is busy spooking the world with. The hope is to capture them and return them to their pre-Spectator state. But how do you convince a dead man that he should want to live if he prefers the alternative in order to progress a demonic movement? This room tells life and all of its hard questions to go to hell. Ezrina is determined to help me save them.

"I know all about this room, Logan." I touch one of the tanks with my hand and let the icy current enliven my anger once again. The Videns were gifted to me as a people, and the fact that a significant number of its youth is now all but dead speaks volumes to my leadership skills. I don't give a shit if they wanted to go in—they made the wrong decision. I should have been the one to guide them, not Wes with his deadly intentions.

"Did you know about *this*?" He heads to the corner, where a white curtain surrounds one of the glass coffins, the blue solution glows from behind, and near the top it looks as if the fluid is percolating. Logan pulls the partition away with an easy flick of the wrist.

"Shit." I take a quick step back, my heart leaping into my throat at the sight. "Is that—"

"Laken." He gives the side of the tank a quick knock, but the girl inside doesn't flinch.

Laken Flanders floats submerged with her eyes closed, her mouth sealed shut, her long brown hair floating around her like tendrils. She's neatly tucked in a skintight wetsuit of some sort that Ezrina used to dress the Counts in.

"Shit. Does Coop know about this?" My head beats erratic, echoing through my skull at the insane amount of grief my friend must be feeling, or will feel. Hell, I care about Laken myself, and seeing her lifeless body spinning silently in that bubbling brew pains me.

"I don't know. But that's not Laken—at least not the version we know. As soon as I saw it, I ran like hell to tell him, and lo and behold he was having dinner with his wife. Whoever this is—whatever Ezrina has done, has something to do with—"

"*Wes*." My eyes close a moment at the thought of my brother having anything to do with this at all. "Who is she? Laken never mentioned a twin. I met her sisters at the wedding, and this isn't one of them."

Logan and I look up at the girl silently bobbing in the bright blue watery grave. Her uncanny resemblance to Laken is impossibly perfect.

"It's not a twin." He glares at the girl a moment. "She might not be one of us. Hell, she might not even be human."

The sound of heels clicking down the hall behind us echoes into the room. "Logan?"

"It's Skyla." Logan looks to the curtain, and I can tell that for a brief moment he considers covering up this latest, perhaps not greatest, dirty little secret of ours. But he doesn't do it. I think the days of keeping things from Skyla—even if it had fallen under the banner of her safety—are long gone.

"Gage?" Her face lights up for a moment when she sees me, and just as quickly her expression dims when she sees the horror in the room. "What in the hell?" Skyla staggers forward, her wool coat cinches her waist, emphasizing the fact she's all but bounced back into shape. Skyla is beautiful in any shape or size, but I've heard her lament more times than not how much she craves to have her old body back. God, how I've missed her body in any state.

Logan smacks me in the gut and pulls me out of my stupor.

"*Skyla.*" I lunge forward and wrap my arms around her. "It's not Laken."

"No." Her voice comes out small. Her gaze never leaves that liquid casket. "I just left her. But—"

"We don't know what's going on." My arms tighten around her waist, and every cell in my body relaxes for the first time in months. I haven't held Skyla like this since December. Not holding your wife for months should be criminal. My heart thumps back to life as if it were waiting for her touch all along. And it has.

Logan steps over, and the three of us stare up at the girl, the *thing* together. "I stumbled upon her this afternoon."

"And you called Gage." Skyla gently breaks free from my arms and walks over to the tank, running her hand along the glass as I did moments before. "Of course, you did. He's the one you trust," she says it so low it's as if she's speaking to herself.

Logan and I exchange a quick glance. It pains us both to have lost Skyla's trust. Logan and I have spent years breaking Skyla's heart in just that fashion.

"So, this is what Marshall and Nev were talking about." A deep sigh expels from her as she sags at the sight of the girl above. "This must be Ezrina's secret project." She turns toward the two of us, the look of indifference on her face. "And that's all I know." She blinks a sarcastic smile. "Gage." Her expression darkens. "Just the person I wanted to talk to."

I can feel Logan flinch by my side. "I think I'll head upstairs. I was thinking about making dinner. How about I make enough for the three of us?" He takes off without bothering to wait for an answer.

"*Four,*" Skyla calls after him as he takes off. "Don't forget your precious little Lexy Poo! Sluts have to eat, too, you know!" She turns to me and growls as if I were somehow harboring a slut of my own. But as irritated as she is, I'm that happy. In fact, I'm bursting with joy inside because my beautiful wife and I are alone, not another living soul in the room with us—and God knows that Laken lookalike isn't able to take her next breath.

"Why are you dimpling at me?" She scowls at my cheeks as if the God-given divots I sport have somehow harnessed the ability to piss her off. It wouldn't surprise me. Everything about me pisses Skyla off lately. And I'm not sure it shouldn't.

"Because you're beautiful—and you're still my wife." That last part comes out unnaturally aggressive. "And because it was me you wanted to speak with. I'd be lying if I didn't say it stroked my ego a bit." There—a single truth rolls around between us, hard and cold as a marble.

Her brows rise a notch as anger dissipates, replaced with amusement. "I bet there's something far more tangible than your ego you'd like me to stroke."

I don't hesitate to run with it. "Can I put in a request for your tongue to do the stroking?" She drew first euphemism. Skyla and I have always enjoyed a healthy dose of sexual banter. It feels normal, necessary, and yes, desperate on my part just a bit. But then, I think the world knows I've always been desperate for Skyla on some level.

"I'd laugh, but that bulge forming in your jeans lets me know you're not joking." Her demeanor flattens once again. "Control that dragon in your pants, Oliver. He's not taking flight in my vagina anytime soon." She steps in front of the glass vial, and the glow from the keeping solution washes her skin an electric shade of blue. "Nevertheless." Her voice grows breathy in a way that I haven't heard in months, and my dick grows ten times harder. It takes far more willpower than I have to get myself off that sexual ledge. I should have mastered this skill by now. In high school, for as much as we were messing around, we weren't *fucking* around, and thus my inhuman ability to get my hard-on to go the hell away.

"Nevertheless." I step in behind her and tuck my lips just shy of her neck. I can't help it. That word sounded like a promise. At this point I'll take an insult from the woman I love, let alone a vow.

"That's what Ezrina is calling her, *Nevertheless*." She runs her fingers across a small bronze strip adhered near the bottom of the tank. "Ezrina always gives them a proper name—their given name. But not this one. She's opted for an idea rather than a truth." Skyla tips her head toward me and doesn't bother hiding the smile tugging at her lips. "I guess the two of you have something in common after all."

A tired laugh dies within my chest. Skyla thinks I've opted for an idea rather than the truth. What she won't let me tell her is that the truth is darker, far more frightening than she ever wants to know. A part of me doesn't want to tell her. It's morbid and hellish, and without a ray of light. What's the point? Although, I need for her to understand—and so there it is, the double-edged sword.

"You were looking for me?" I sweep the hair off her shoulder and soak in the heat from her body as I take a bold step closer.

Skyla looks up with those heaven-sent eyes, those barely there lenses that look clear as glass—a color impossible in nature. Those eyes alone should tip people off that she's not quite human.

"Yes," she whispers, glancing to the ground as her cheeks heat with color. "Tell me everything you know about Melody Winters."

And just like that, my heart plummets because this isn't the topic at all I was hoping for.

"Why? What's up?" I look back up at the girl with Laken's face. She's about as much a mystery as Melody is to me at the moment.

"She says I stole this ring from her." Skyla holds up her hand, and the large blue stone on her finger glows like a fallen star. I glance to her other hand and she's still miraculously wearing her wedding ring, and that sight alone makes my heart soar.

"Where'd you get the ring?" I pick up her hand, pretending to be morbidly interested in her newfound jewelry, but the truth is, I'm thirsty to hold her, so very thirsty for her touch.

"Chloe gave it to me for Christmas." She carefully pulls her hand away and fondles the ring with her thumb.

"*Chloe?*" I try to hold back my judgment of their new bond, but for the life of me I can't. "Skyla, what are you doing with Chloe of all people? You know you can't trust her."

"I can't trust anybody." She shrugs it off like a fact. "And don't worry about what I'm doing with Chloe. I'm guessing you have bigger things to burden you these days." Her eyes darken as she stares me down with something just this side of hatred. Skyla sinks to her knees next to the floating casket by our side and releases a nozzle near the bottom that sends both the fluid draining and the entire glass capsule tipping to its side.

"What are you doing?"

"I'm freeing this poor thing. What does it look like I'm doing?" She glides a metal gurney from the corner and rolls it over. "You can help if you want, but trust me—I don't need you."

Those last few words cut like a knife. "I need you," I say as I help her hoist the glass the vial on its ear. Skyla meets up with my gaze a brief moment before twisting open the top of the contraption, and the smell of something a little more pleasant than formaldehyde hits my nostrils.

"Shit." I tuck my face into my arm a moment to catch my breath.

"You think that's bad. Imagine a world of servitude with this stench. I smelled this in my sleep for months—tasted it in my food."

Skyla was taken captive and worked with Ezrina for a time. It was a dark season in our lives. It seems as if our lives are continually peppered with dark seasons.

"I'm sorry about that."

"You don't have to be sorry about that." She grunts as she pulls the girl free from her confinement and lands her onto the glorified metal bathtub before her.

"I'm sorry about everything, Skyla." As difficult as this conversation is, I'm relentlessly pursuing it. "Let's take a moment and talk things through."

"No." Her eyes flicker to mine like flames. "Right now, I want to talk about Melody Winters—not to mention the fact—figuring out what in the hell Ezrina is doing with Laken 2.0. And before you say it, *yes*, I smell Wes at the other end of this disaster."

"So we're on the same page regarding that." I watch as Skyla runs her hand over the girl's face, examining her with the precision of a surgeon. "Melody is Dominique Winters' daughter. She has two brothers, Asbury and Cash. They live on the other end of town in some weird mega house that has some never-ending construction project going on. The mother, Dominique, had a major heart attack about seven years ago. She was DOA when she got to the hospital and then miraculously woke up about an hour later as if nothing happened."

Skyla stops all movement and glances up at me. "Sounds like a familiar story, doesn't it?"

"It's close to what happened to Melody, only she woke up at the morgue."

She gives a wistful shake of the head as she rolls the girl on her side. "I always suspected you could wake the dead." She does a finger sweep of the girl's mouth. "Especially the estrogen card carrying variety." Skyla shoves her finger down the girl's throat, and a burst of blue liquid vomits from her. "There we go," she says it softly as if speaking to the girl. "If only I could figure out how to resurrect the dead myself."

A burst of blue light shines through the Laken lookalike as she coughs and sputters to life.

"*Skyla.*" I hold an arm over the girl in the event she's about to attack.

Ezrina and Nev hurry into the room along with Logan and Lexy.

"What have you done?" Ezrina shrieks and sends us both jumping back. "*Skyla!*" she growls so loud it sounds like a cat with its tail on fire.

Skyla takes a careful step in toward Ezrina. "Who is she and what does Wesley think he's about to do with her?"

The room grows strangely silent as Ezrina and Skyla have a momentary standoff. But the girl groans and vomits another vat full of keeping solution and brings everyone's attention right back to her regurgitating self.

Nevermore clears his throat. "I do believe we have a life on our hands. Rina, please tend to the girl so she doesn't suffer."

"I'll deal with you later," Ezrina growls at Skyla before barking commands at Nev for her tools.

Skyla backs up slowly, her face washed white with shock as she stares down at that ring Chloe gifted her. "I have to go."

Logan grips her by the shoulders. "What happened? Did you pull her out?"

Skyla glances up at me a moment. "The boys are at your mother's house. Bring them home for me." She darts down the corridor before anyone can stop her.

"Skyla!" I run after her, but she's out the front door and I'm chasing taillights into the night. "Where the hell are you going?" I pant as I try to catch my breath.

Logan and Lexy run out the door, and I join them on the porch.

"Skyla's friends with that girl." Lexy shudders. "I bet she's off to tell Coop."

"That's not Laken." Logan takes a seat on the porch, and I join him. "Would you mind giving me a minute with Gage?"

Lexy clicks her tongue and huffs toward the door. "Fine, but remember I came over to discuss the dance. It'll be here before you know it, and there are still a ton of details we need to cover." She slams the door behind her as if to annunciate the point.

"Yes, the dance." Logan bounces his knee to mine a moment. "Lexy just put it all in perspective. Who gives a crap about a mysterious girl wearing someone else's face or the fact you and Skyla had a moment alone—when we've got an '80s dance on the horizon?"

"Yup. How I wish that was my greatest worry."

"Can I ask what happened between you and Skyla?"

"She wanted to know about Melody Winters."

"What about her?"

"I don't know." I wipe my face down with my hands. "Something about Chloe gifting Skyla a ring that Melody says she stole. I told her everything I knew about that chick. Anyway, nothing too earth-shattering happened between Skyla and me. I'm still in the doghouse, barking at the moon like a fucking loon. Dude, it's days like this that have me believing I've screwed things up for good."

"My dad—your grandpa had a saying"—Logan claps his hand over my shoulder—"all's well that ends well, and if it isn't ending well, it isn't the end."

"That sounds ominous."

"It sounds good to me, and I'm dead."

A dull laugh rumbles from me. "I'm a dead man, too. It's just a matter of time, dude. This is nothing but a long farewell for me."

"But those boys—" His voice trails off. "They can sure use you around for the next six decades or so. I know what it's like to lose a parent—both parents. It sucks. No offense to Barron and Emma. God knows I appreciate them, but there's something about having your own mother and father around that's a special blessing."

"And that's why I'm fighting." I stare out at the unmapped darkness that bleeds into the ocean. "What exactly I'm fighting against, I am not sure."

Logan slaps me over the knee. "Then it's time to find out. You up for a drive?"

"Depends on where we're headed."

"We're going on a hunt." He jumps up, and I'm slow to follow. "Lex"—he shouts through the screen—"I'll be back in a little while."

"Okay, hon! Take your time. I'll be right here waiting."

Logan jogs down to his truck, and a quiet laugh strums from him. "That's what I'm afraid of," he says for my ears only.

I hop in next to him as he revs the engine. "So, what are we hunting for?" I slip on my seat belt as the truck jackknifes out of the driveway with a jolt.

"Answers."

Paragon is known for many things, but answers are not on the list.

The highway stretches out before us, hardly visible beneath the white plumes of fog cropping up like ghosts. We drive deeper into the night as the terrain gives way to large stretches of shadowed land without the hint of a streetlight to guide our way. I've walked along this stretch of road before, so unknowably black in the night with a darkness so enveloping it convinces you to surrender. It tempts you to lie down between the evergreens and fall into a deep slumber with eternity curling its fingers for you to follow along for the ride.

I know where we're headed, and the closer we get, the less I want to be here.

Logan pulls in high up on the driveway as Demetri's house sprouts up like an overgrown haunted jack-o-lantern.

"He's not going to tell us anything new. Why bother?"

"Dude." Logan winces as we hop out of the car and into the damp Paragon night. "You need to loosen up. You're already in deep shit. What the hell do you have to lose?"

We head on up, and I give a brisk knock to the door before letting myself inside. "The damn thing is never locked."

"Of course, it's not"—Logan smirks—"the most dangerous person on the island is in the house. He probably craves the challenge."

We step through the foyer and into the cavernous living room with its wall-to-wall marble flooring, the enormous fireplace blazing with flames, and not too far from that, Demetri laughs it up with some dude dressed in a trench coat.

"Dudley?" Logan and I say in unison.

"Gentlemen!" Demetri holds out his arms, welcoming us, an amber-colored drink cradled in one hand and a cigar in the other. Dudley is sporting the same toxic duet.

I pause a moment, taking in the strange sight. First, I don't know Demetri and Dudley to be scotch toting, cigar smoking friends. Second—"What the hell is up with the celebration?" My blood boils at the thought of the two of them saluting my efforts to take a walk on the wicked side.

"Young Olivers." Dudley frowns at the sight of us before taking a puff of that stogie in his hand.

"Son!" Demetri takes a few steps forward as Logan and I head over. "Please—you and your uncle must partake." He points to the bar behind him. "Whiskey aged seven hundred years in an oak barrel."

Dudley grunts. "How many times do I have to inform you it's scotch? It's from Scotland. It must be referred to as scotch."

I called it.

"I suppose the whiskey is in the details." Demetri winks my way.

"It's the devil," Logan says, heading over and pouring himself a finger length and one for myself. Neither Logan nor I are big drinkers, but something this rare should probably wet our tongues if for nothing else but the novelty of it.

"Cuban cigars." Demetri tips his head to the humidor resting next to the whiskey—scotch whatever.

"Interesting." I take up two and hand one to Logan.

Logan looks to Dudley. "When in Rome."

Buried in that phrase is a barb about his honeymoon with Skyla. I'm not sure how Dudley fits into the equation, but I know for a fact he does. Dudley always seems to factor into the equation.

Demetri lights us up, and before you know it, the four of us are smoking cigars and swilling scotch like old friends. I wish I could say there was tension in the room. I wish I could say that Logan and I were about to go postal and toss both of their celestial asses into the fire, but the truth is, we're too busy amusing ourselves with the flavor of smoke on our tongues. I take a sip of the scotch, and a fire burns straight down through my esophagus. Tastes bitter and sweet at the same time—like life and death all rolled into one. It tastes like my own tears the night I gifted my destiny to the devil standing before me.

"What brings you this way?" Dudley blows a plume of smoke in our direction. "Let me guess. Skyla has you lathered in a tizzy, and now you've come to claw your way out of the havoc you've ensnared yourself in." He and Demetri share a laugh, and it stuns me.

"Is this what you do in your spare time?" I'm talking to Dudley more than I am Demetri. "Laugh at the state of Skyla's world? I am a part of her world whether or not you've bothered to notice."

Dudley's affect falls hard and flat. "I am Skyla's world. The two of you are simply stepping stones that destiny has laid out to ease her path to me."

Logan scoffs at the arrogant Sector. "The boys are her world, Dudley. Check your ego. I'm no stepping-stone, and neither is Gage. We are boulders, *partitions* to a love that you will never feel. You'll never have her heart. Not the way we have it."

A silent laugh bounces through me, but I can't help it. Logan is right. Skyla loves us both. I'm not up for sharing, though. Honest to God, half the time I think I'm the boulder, the partition to his love with Skyla. But I'm greedy as hell when it comes to that girl. She's mine, and I'm not sharing with anyone.

"Interesting." Dudley pegs me with a look that assures me he's heard every word. I don't know all of the details concerning his powers, and I'm not interested. Instead, I take another puff of the cigar and blow my own billow of smoke his way. I take another swig of the scotch and enjoy the burn all the way down.

"What men you've turned into." Dudley scoffs, that dead look in his eyes is targeted right at me. "It must make you feel quite grown up with a drink in your hand, a Cuban at the ready."

"Now, now, *Dudley*." Demetri gives a sarcastic smile to the Sector. It's clear he's playing off the name Logan and I choose to use with him. "This is a rite of passage. And a privilege, considering the aged libation, the aged Cuban in our hands as well."

"What are you boys celebrating, anyway?" Logan puffs away on his cigar as if all of the angst and tension he just ushered into the room a few moments ago were simply for show.

"Ezrina." Dudley tips his head toward him. "She's with child. She and Heathcliff will be parents come fall."

"Whoa." Logan and I exchange a quick glance.

"That's great news." I take a step back, trying to ingest it. "We were just with her, and she didn't say a word. We'll have to congratulate her the next time we see her." We were just with her, and she didn't say a word because she was livid with Skyla for waking the dead.

I glance to Dudley. If he heard me earlier, he heard me now.

His demeanor hardens over mine. Knew it. The bastard has been reading my thoughts all along. "Great news, indeed." He knocks back the rest of his drink. "I'm hoping for a boy. Marshall is a splendid name."

Demetri is quick to elbow him. "I'm vying for my own name. Nothing says male virility like Demetri."

"I see that's why you named your son Gage." Dudley lifts his drink, and I'm about a second from knocking it out of his hand.

"All right—enough shooting the shit." I set my drink down hard onto the coffee table. It's probably fashioned out of some poor soul's casket once Demetri ate the body for breakfast. He's a monster. I can't lose sight of that.

"I'm no monster. I'm your father, Gage." Demetri lifts his glass.

So he heard. The house must work in the same way Ahava does, linking thoughts or some shit.

"DNA donor." I offer a tight smile. "What's the real powwow about?" I glare at Dudley a moment. "I don't buy for a minute that you've stopped your wicked day to toast Ezrina's maternal milestone."

"Ah, yes, the truth. Perhaps it was the scotch itself." Demetri tips his head toward me. "I had forgotten all about that barrel my grandfather had stored in the basement until I stumbled upon it this afternoon. Do feel free to help yourself whenever you please." He glances to Logan. "I extend the invitation to you as well. Bring your brothers if you'd like. I might even break it out for the twins' first birthday party. Nothing but the best for my grandchildren."

Logan scoffs at the thought. "That won't be necessary, and I highly doubt you'll make the invite list. Skyla is their mother, and I respect her wishes."

Logan shoots me a curt look. I know what he wants—for me to let Demetri know he doesn't meet my standards for the invite list either. But I can't do it. I don't want to or plan on rejecting him in any way. The truth is, I need Demetri as much as I need Skyla at this point. He holds the curse, or at least the reins to it.

"The curse." Demetri nods, and I hold back a satisfied smile at how easy that was for me. "I'll tell you this, son—one day, fairly soon, you will refer to it as a blessing."

"Doubtful." I take a deep breath and glare at Dudley a moment. "But according to Wesley, very much possible. So, what's next? I'm here. You're here. Fill me in on what's to come. Maybe you don't know this about your long-lost son, but I hate suspense."

Dudley's chest bounces with a silent laugh. "You are the personification of suspense, Gage. As much as the universe is holding its breath to see what becomes of your wife, it's equally invested in your next move. Don't discount who you are or what you're destined for. This road before you doesn't lie in your father's bounds. This is your journey. You will dictate where the road leads. So, if you're asking him what comes next, you are asking the wrong person. Find a mirror and repeat the question."

The room clogs up with a stunned silence.

According to Dudley, I'm in charge. I fashion my next step. I choose the road. I choose who I love, who I hate, who I kill, and who I let live. Then it's easy. I choose Skyla. I choose home. I choose my boys. I choose life and not death. I choose Celestra and not the Counts or whatever the heck they're calling themselves these days. I choose the Sectors over the Fems because God knows they will not plunge the world into darkness. And I most certainly choose to liberate the Viden youth out of their current state of Spectator bondage. There. Done. Simple. I hope to hell everyone in the room heard it.

I glower at Demetri and Dudley in turn, but their peaceable smiles, those content looks on their faces don't offer me a clue as to what they're thinking.

"Well intended." Dudley gives an approving nod my way, but there's something about that veiled sadness on his face that lets me know it was most likely for not. Dudley doesn't shit around.

Demetri puts out his cigar on the marble stand next to the fire. "You'll do well by yourself if you follow your heart." He glances to me with that strange penetrative look that spells out my defeat before I ever get there. "You will, indeed, follow your heart. That is the beauty of your destiny, Gage. Not even you will be able to deny it."

"He can, and he will." Logan slaps a hand over my shoulder. "He's got his heart in the right place. A heart of gold. There's not an ounce of wickedness in him. I know him better than I know myself."

"That may be so." Dudley breezes by the two of us, dropping his cigar into his scotch before abandoning his drink. "But this isn't about wickedness. It's about control. I assure you those are two very different things. The Sectors are immovable, Jock Strap. You remember that."

"Sector Marshall," Demetri calls after him, and Dudley turns one last time. "You've been removed before. It will happen again."

Dudley frowns over to me before reverting his gaze back to Demetri. "If you're counting on him to get you where you need to be, then you have a tougher road ahead of you than one can imagine."

"And you're counting on the girl?" Demetri hollers after him, that perennial smile still tight on his face.

The girl being Skyla. Logan and I exchange glances because neither of us appreciates him framing her as a simple girl.

Dudley takes a few steps back into the room. "That girl is my spirit wife. Don't underestimate her. Each time I've done so myself, I've lived to regret it." He takes off, and I spring after him.

"Dudley, wait." I chase him down the stairs into the damp fog.

"What is it, Jock Strap?" His body turns vaporous, see-through like smoke right before my eyes, and it's like talking to a ghost. Something in me enrages when he calls me by that locker room riddled moniker. I've hated it for years. I'm sick of it, and I'm sick of all of the bullshit surrounding my life at the moment.

"My name is *Gage*—a perfectly fine name for a man. It'd be good for you to learn it—to use it—if you want to see me on your side."

Those fiery red eyes of his illuminate the night as he presses all of his own rage into me. I can feel it, scalding me from the inside like a boiling kettle. "And so it begins."

He evaporates into the night, and a calm fills the surrounding area.

And so it begins. My heart thumps hard in my chest as Logan and Demetri make their way out onto the porch. Is Dudley right? Am I already teaming up with Demetri simply because of my disdain toward that particular Sector? Shit. I can't let that happen. I'll need to find a way to make peace with him somehow. There's no way I should be caving in so easily. Dudley is one of the good guys whether I want to admit it or not. This isn't the time for me to be an asshole and hold past grievances against him.

"Everything okay?" Logan pulls out his keys, and his truck burps to life.

"Yeah, it's fine. Why don't you head back to Whitehorse and take care of whatever it is you have to do with Lex? I'm gonna hang out for a sec. I'll teleport home. Better yet, I might just walk. I think I need to clear my head a bit."

"No worries." He slaps me five and takes off into the night.

"Come." Demetri tries to lure me back into the house, but I make my way up to the porch, and that's about as far as I'm willing to move.

"What's going on?" I call out into the night as if he were on the other side of the island. "I need you to be truthful with me at all times if this thing between us is going to work." There. Those are words I could never have said around Logan. For as much as Logan wants me to burn this area of my life to the ground, a part of me understands that I had better own it before it owns me.

Demetri lands his right hand over my shoulder, his dark eyes bearing into mine. "I solemnly swear on all that is holy that I will always be truthful with you, my prized son. You are my child, born of my own flesh and blood. You are my heir, the light of my eyes, the life-force that makes my heart beat."

"I see two problems with this, *Pops*. Your eyes shine like coal, and I'm pretty certain you don't have a heart. I'm a pawn. I get it. You need me. You are confident in my lack of understanding of the situation, and you believe with all of the heart you don't really have that I will inadvertently, all on my own, fuck things up for my wife and her people."

ADDISON MOORE

He winces with the expletive. "In truth, yes and no. I do believe that your lack of understanding is your own, but like anyone in life, you'll ask the questions and seek out the answers. The answers stem from you as much as the questions. And as for foiling the efforts of your precious beloved, I cannot foresee that the things you will do to hamper her efforts—perhaps they will be accidental on your part. *Dudley* may have underestimated your wife on occasion, but I never have. You see, I understand the principle that once someone is filled with a holy desire to do right by their people, there is nothing in heaven or on earth that can stop them. Skyla is her father's daughter. Far more dangerous than that, she is her mother's daughter. Both of those aforementioned *deceased* in-laws of yours were never ones to follow the rules to get what they wanted. They both paid with their lives, Gage. Let that be a lesson to you." His eyes flare like heated coals, an irony within an irony. "You will pay with your life if you decided to forge a path that bristles destiny's desire."

"By destiny's desire, you mean the curse I've cloaked myself with."

"It is a blessing, son." He steps down and pulls me into a partial embrace. "And one day you will see it that way, too." He heads inside, and the door seals itself shut with a hiss.

The fog moves in quick, covering the porch in a dense billow of clouds, and it's hard to tell which way is up in this whitewashed world anymore.

My phone buzzes in my pocket— it's a text from my dad. The only father I'll ever have in my eyes.

Rev says the refrigeration unit is on the fritz again. Are you able to run by the morgue?

I text right back. **I'm on it.**

I'd walk around the proverbial block for my father, but for Demetri I wouldn't cross the street.

That stone Skyla handed me all those weeks ago at the boys' christening party comes back to mind. Everything Demetri just said was bullshit because I happen to know that no matter what I do, my days are numbered.

I'm about to bristle destiny's desire.

That's for damn sure.

I don't bother with the late night walk I had hoped would clear my head. Instead, I use my old tried and true Levatio transportation system and teleport over to the morgue.

The Paragon Cemetery bears the family name, albeit subtly on a wall plaque as you head into the foyer. My father, the one who I count as such, is a humble, decent man who would move the heavens to make sure I had my true heart's desire, a simple life with Skyla and my children by my side. I'm pretty certain that whoever is in charge of doling out destinies up there—and yes, Candace, I'm looking at you and your cohorts—that they royally effed up because I'm no king, no prince of the Countenance underworld. I'm not even remotely interested in helping the Fems or the Sectors if you get right down to it. I'll go kicking and screaming all the way down to the armpit where they store that rusted out throne they think I'll call home one day. Nope. *Bristling* just so happens to be my new favorite word. I am bristling destiny, out loud, in the open, for everyone seated in that destination station to see.

There's a light in the room indelicately called the kitchen—the prep area for corpses. My dad has a smidge of

Ezrina in him, and that's one of the things I like about him among many.

"Rev?" I spot him kneeling over an electrical panel in the back. His hair is growing back from its recent shorn state, and he looks halfway like a law-abiding citizen—halfway. His beat-up leather jacket rides up his back, exposing a mean looking tat scrawled over his torso. Rev, or Revelyn, is Dr. Booth's son. I'm not sure how many kids Dr. B has, but if they're all like Rev here, I don't care to meet too many.

He falls back on his ass before bouncing to his feet. Rev is tall and wide as a linebacker. He's a little older than me, but looks hardened by life with a nasty looking ridge outlining his cheek that looks as if it was gifted to him by way of a knife and currently three steady lines that dig into his forehead.

"Dude, this whole system is shit, but I think I fixed it." He kicks the grill shut and slides his tools toward the wall. "I called the service, but the fastest they can get out here is Monday. It should hold until then." He wipes the sweat off his brow.

"Thanks, man. I appreciate it. I know my dad does, too." Suddenly, I'm feeling for the guy. He's a part-time employee running a little more than an internship as he works toward his mortuary science degree. He's been a good guy to have around the place, and I'm glad my dad is finally getting some trustworthy help. "Why don't you take off? I'll lock up around here."

"Cool." He slaps me five, and the grease from his hand gets transferred to mine. "I've got Mia crawling all over my ass. I guess I'll give her a call and let her know I'm free."

"What are you doing with her, anyway?" I try to hide the fact that I want to punch him for it. Mia is just as much my little sister as she is Skyla's. There's no way I want this guy sniffing around her—as if that's the only thing he'll be doing. "You can get any girl you want at Host. *Legal* girls—emphasis on the legal." There. Feed his ego and see how far that gets you.

"You don't think I know that?" He winces, and those bushy brows frame his face just the way Dr. Booth's do. "But chicks like Mia, dude, they're clingers. They get one taste of the goods"—he clutches onto his dick and shakes it—"and they can't get enough."

"Shit," I hiss under my breath as I try to maintain my composure. "You'd better get going before I shove you into one of these drawers. You're not to touch her. You got that?"

"You got it, chief." He tips his head back as he ducks out of the kitchen. "Don't bother venturing out back. Heard some noises earlier. I think we got a pack of coyotes. I've already scared them off once tonight." The slam of the front door echoes around the room like a gunshot.

For a second, I consider giving Skyla the heads-up about Rev, but the boys pop into my head. Crap. I should probably shoot her a quick text and let her know where I am. I know she wanted me to pick up the boys for her, and I feel bad. She's probably already home with them, nursing or begging them to go to sleep. I know two things about our boys for sure—they're boob men, and they like to burn the candle at both ends. Those kids do not understand the concept of a solid eight. I know it's making Skyla insane. I've tried to help out, stay over, but for the most part, she gives me the boot each and every time.

I head to the refrigeration unit and check out the temps. A chilly thirty-eight degrees should keep all of the guests at the Oliver Inn crisp for the night. Just as I'm about to kill the lights, a pronounced thump comes from somewhere deep inside the walls.

A mean shiver runs through me. That was no coyote. I head out through the back door, and the fog welcomes me with an icy embrace. The cemetery is covered in a blanket of white as the fog lifts her skirt and dances over the gravestones.

"Anybody out here?" That was no animal. It was a solid wallop against the side of the building. I follow the walkway around the structure until I come upon the mausoleum. The moon hangs low, barely visible through the dense plumes bursting through the air like powder. It's a magical kind of night, and if I wasn't standing in a glorified body farm, it might even be beautiful—hell, it is beautiful. This is exactly the kind of night I wish I could share with Skyla.

A muted bang comes from the left, and my heart stops on command.

"Holy shit." My muscles freeze as a paralyzing fear grips me.

I'm not afraid of the dark. I'm not afraid of the cemetery—at least not under normal conditions. But I'll admit that being here on my own, well after hours, is beginning to edge on my nerves.

Those Spectators of Wesley's come to mind, and I usher them right back out. I can take them if I have to. But the idea of wrestling with a brain hungry corpse ties my stomach up in knots.

"Anybody out there?" My voice thunders through the mist and comes back to me as a haunting echo. "Shit." I head over to the mausoleum and stand still at the mouth of that cavernous marble entry. There are bodies interred on the outside in what is aptly named the Hall of Heavens. And, of course, there is the oversized structure itself, a two-story building that contains thousands of bodies of yesteryear that have been lounging here far longer than my family has owned the place. The Hallowed Hall. No offense to my father, but I've always thought it smells like rot in here.

Rump, thump!

"Hello?" My heart detonates time and time again, deafening me from the inside. My blood runs cold at what that sound might be. Definitely coming from the Hall of Heavens. I head over and stagger my way slowly down the first row with its dull metal plaques gleaming under the stage lights we installed a few years back in hopes to deter any freaks that might want to confiscate a body for the hell of it.

A sonic boom goes off from the left, shaking the metal vases hanging loosely in their couplets.

Crap. Exploding body perhaps? Dad filled me in on the phenomenon one year after he came back from a casket convention. He assured me it would never get hot enough on Paragon to insight such a messy spectacle, but then, humans are comprised of enough gases to cause even the most caustic explosion whether they're dead or alive. Case in point, both Drake and Ethan Landon.

Nevertheless, my father, being the precautionary gentleman he is, made sure all crypts were connected with a meager ventilation and drainage system. Yes, drainage. Corpses have a way of leaking even after being embalmed to the hilt. The air vents help the gases escape, thus sidestepping the exploding casket scenario, and the drainage system helps with seepage and leakage. Barron Oliver—Senior—has all of his cryptic bases covered.

Of all the bodies buried in this mausoleum, I personally have only known one. I come across Kate Winston's marker and place my hand over her name. Kate and I grew up together. I'll always remember her as the sweet little blonde who told bad jokes and would go out of her way to make you smile. Back in high school, Kate was accidentally beheaded during a school-sponsored ski trip. It just so happened that it was Skyla's ski that brought on that tragedy. Hell, it was probably Demetri working on Chloe's command. Demetri is her supervising spirit bitch, and it wouldn't surprise me if she had him hacking the heads off anyone she deemed fit. And by deemed fit, I mean pissed her off. Chloe is so easy to piss off, it's shocking half the island still has their heads attached.

About a year after Kate was killed, Chloe thought best to pull the poor girl's corpse from the morgue and took her detached head to homecoming where Kate's main apex was hurled over the field like a football. It was a thing of horror as only Chloe could produce. Chloe is a thing of horror, which is exactly why I'm so damn alarmed that Skyla has anything to do with her.

Thump! Thump! Thump!

Kate's marker jumps beneath me, and I retract my hand as if from a fire.

"*Fuck!*" I roar as I jump back ten feet. I stalk over to the crypt once again that's housing my old friend, her beheaded body, albeit her head set in its traditional location.

I pull out my phone and text Logan. **Morgue. Now!** That meager phrase will have to do. I shove the phone back where it came from and head to the marker that's bowed from the pressure.

"Oh shit." I grunt as my hand runs over the deformed metal. It's at least an eighth of an inch thick.

Thump! Thump! Thump! Thump! Thump! Thump!

The walls, the ground shakes with the racket as the sound gets louder, far more severe, and the façade of the structure begins to crumble. I waste no time. Instead, I run like hell back into the kitchen and reach for the tool bag underneath the sink until I come up with a crowbar.

"Holy hell." I run back toward the thundering clatter that has the entire cemetery under siege with its persistent banging, it's jackhammer-like aggression.

"*Enough!*" I roar to no one in particular as I attempt to flick the marker off Kate's grave. The ground rattles beneath my feet. The loud continual booming deafens me as I struggle to ease the pressure of whatever the hell is going on.

"Gage!" Logan calls my name from somewhere on the other side of the cemetery, but I'm expending all my energy prying off the plaque. It's not until my Levatio strength, or something far more sinister than that in me initiates does the marker go flying like a Frisbee. The metal sheet beneath it bucks in and out like a heartbeat, and I shove the crowbar in as far as it will go until it too goes airborne like a flying saucer.

Logan gets closer. His shouting rises above the rabid thumping from inside of Kate's grave.

I reach into the dark mouth of the crypt to grab ahold of the casket, but it's bucking like a bronco in that small concrete space.

"Shit!" I growl as I reach in with both hands and pull the trembling coffin out of the enclosure, and it flies right past me like a mahogany missile, falling to the ground with a thud and bringing with it an unsurpassed silence I thought I'd never hear again.

The casket has landed on its side, splitting open as it rests over the marble floor like a tent.

"Shit. Shit. Shit." I kick the casket over onto its back to reveal her corpse in two pieces lying on the floor. Kate lies still in her formal gown. The scarf that was wrapped around her neck blows past me with the wind, but her head lies crooked to the side, face up, those eyes that were once sealed shut with my father's eyelash glue fidget as if blinking to life. Her hands twitch, once then twice before tapping over the floor before snagging a finger around a single blonde curl. "*Kate*," I whisper as I witness the atrocity.

She pulls at her head, tugs it over, rolling and bumping her face over the cold hard tile before grasping it with both hands and situating it on the base of her neck—her face is set a little too far over her shoulder, offering her an unnatural disposition. Not that anything about this is fucking natural.

"Kate?" There she is, blonde and petite as ever with pale doll-like features, a pert nose, and tiny little lips you can hardly tell are there.

She slaps her hand over the floor as if begging for assistance before pointing to her skull.

"Your head." I fall to my knees and do my best to twist her head in the right direction. "Hang on." I leap over and gather the white silk scarf that's wrapped itself around a fallen vase. In all of the earthquake-like melee, the mausoleum looks as if it's been ransacked of all its flowers, leaving all of its plastic floral displays scattered like debris.

I wrap the scarf around her neck and do my best to secure her head to the rest of her before pulling her up and cradling her stiff, cold body in my arms. I'm going to have to shower for a week before I touch the boys again.

She pries her lips open with her fingers, then her eyes—two milky blue orbs stare back at me. There is nothing more disconcerting than having an eye or a mouth pop open during a viewing, so we like to glue them closed along with the mouth. But in Kate's case, she was glued shut twice. My father is meticulous about the state of his corpses. And I'm sure he won't appreciate the fact that I've been present during two reanimations in such a short span of time.

"*Gage*," she mouths my name as she settles her eyes over me. An eerie grimace takes over her face as she struggles to smile.

Footsteps speed this way and stop abruptly.

"Oh fuck." Logan staggers and sways on his feet as he gets in close. "What in the hell have you done now?"

"I don't know, dude. But something tells me we're going to need Ezrina."

No sooner do the words leave my mouth than the cemetery rumbles and grumbles as if experiencing a seizure of its own.

"Forget Ezrina"—Logan gives a suspicious glance around—"we're going to need Dudley."

A shadow elongates over the cold stone floor and then another.

"No need to call Dudley." Skyla appears with Chloe by her side, both bleached white with terror, their eyes set over the rolling earth as the gravestones disjoint, undoing the symmetrical, *linear* as hell pattern my father has worked so hard to perfect over the last few decades. "I already did."

"Skyla." I gently lay Kate over the floor, and her body bucks as she crawls spastically sideways much like a spider.

"For shit's sake!" Chloe screeches. "Kill it with fire!"

"Oh hush." Skyla bolts to her old friend and lays her hand over her forehead as if checking for a fever. "She's warming up." Skyla looks over to Logan and me, panting through a smile. "She was the first I tried to wake, and here she is."

"Only she's not one of us," Chloe snaps. "You let that stupid beating heart of yours get in the way, and, as usual, you've fucked things up before they've ever began."

"Shut the hell up, Chloe." Skyla struggles to help Kate to her feet, and I jump over to assist. Kate wobbles before toppling backward, stiff as a board, and I help Skyla lay her back on the ground. "It's going to be fine." A single tear streams down Skyla's face, falling over Kate's forehead like an afterthought. And just like that, the color pours back into her flesh. Her lips turn a ruddy shade of pink as she manages to sit up and pant as if she actually had a working set of lungs.

Logan leans in to get a better look. "What the hell is going on, Skyla? Why is Kate sitting here? Why is the entire cemetery doing the graveyard hop?"

Skyla glances up at him with a vengeance in her eyes. "Stop asking so many questions, Logan, and get a damn shovel."

There is a moment of pause as both Logan and I exchange a brief glance.

Skyla has done this? How has Skyla done this? More to the point, how has Chloe done this?

"Shit." I take a few steps back and nearly land on my ass until the ground stops quaking beneath my feet. "We can't dig up the cemetery, Skyla."

"We don't have a choice." She pulls out her phone, and before she can touch her thumb to the screen, Dudley strides on over as if this were the norm—as if the ground jumping, the jackhammering of a thousand corpses begging to escape their casket prisons were an everyday occurrence—and apparently on Paragon, it's not far from reality.

"Silence!" His voice roars over the dark expanse, and in a show of bravado on his part, a miracle on nature's part, the fog rolls back like a scroll, receding from the graveyard as if it were chased by a demon, or in this case a Sector—and for a good five solid seconds the graveyard returns to its unanimated state. "*Skyla*," he barks, looking back at her with his face screwed up in anger. "What in heaven's name have you done?"

That tone he's invoked with her sets a fresh rage percolating in me. "Don't talk to my wife that way."

Skyla bursts past me as she gets in his face. "Don't you act surprised. I was kind enough to *brief* you!"

"When it was nothing more than a fantasy." His voice hits its upper register, his chest is puffed out like a gorilla, his nostrils flaring. He doesn't take those heated eyes off her. He is pissed as hell and doesn't mind showing it. I've yet to see Dudley agitated. For sure I've yet to see him reach that level with Skyla.

I don't hesitate pulling her in and wrapping my arms around her. Skyla is trembling, her breathing hitting an erratic pace the way it used to in the bedroom.

"What's happening?" I whisper just above her ear and steal the moment to take in her warm vanilla scent.

"It's this ring." She rubs her thumb over a blue heart-shaped stone sitting on her forefinger. "Chloe gave it to me." She pauses long enough to scowl over at the demon. "It has powers. Marshall said something a while back about it being a portal of power only the creator Himself is privy to. I wasn't aware of the power it held until I woke that girl up in Ezrina's lab."

"You woke the girl." Dudley closes his eyes with a worrisome look of boredom. Dudley only invokes that placid expression when things have truly gone to shit.

"Not me. The ring," she insists.

"This ring." Logan comes over and picks up her hand, forcing the ring to sparkle in the dull light. Kate coughs and sputters behind us, but we take a moment to focus in on that ring with its eerie blue glow. "Where did it come from, Chloe?"

Chloe giggles out a dark laugh as she heads to Kate and helps her stagger to her feet, unsteady as a toddler. "Wouldn't you like to know."

"I think I do know." Skyla hitches a brow over to the girl she's pretending to favor. "Melody Winters said I stole it from her." She tilts her head toward Bishop as Kate writhes unsteadily in her arms. "More to the point, she called me a time traveling thief."

Dudley offers up a slow clap, more of an insult than an encouragement, but I'm pretty sure he knows that. He seems to be up on his put-downs. "Now you're warm, Ms. Messenger." He cuts a look to the cemetery with its markers and stones in disarray. "And how in heaven's name do the four of you think you're going to excavate this bone yard of its bodies? Each person in his or her own crypt six feet under? In a concrete encapsulated tomb at that? Even with your shared strength and impressive powers, be they meager in comparison to my own, this will take you a year."

"Nice." Skyla scoffs openly at him. "It's good to see you offering your encouragement and support. Do you have any other brilliant, yet discouraging, line items you feel the need to point out? Because if you're done, I suggest you find a tractor, or, better yet, use your most impressive supernatural powers to excavate the place for us."

"Whoa, whoa, whoa." I pull her in tight. "We're not digging this place up."

"That's exactly what we're doing." She abruptly removes my arms from her waist. She looks to Logan and me with something just this side of pleading. "It's a part of the plan."

"The plan." Chloe nods almost sarcastically. Why the hell can't Skyla see that she's pretending to befriend her for kicks? This is nothing but a game to Chloe.

"I can't help you, Skyla." Dudley takes a few steps toward the graveyard. "Heaven will have my wings. This is something I'm afraid I'm unable to concern myself with." He tips his head toward her as if he were about to take off.

"Oh no, you don't." She latches onto his arm. "I forbid you from leaving. I forbid any of you from leaving," she growls at Logan and me but offers a deadly glare to Chloe. "I need you. Celestra needs you. We need these bodies."

"Who did these bodies once belong to?" Logan is stern with his former wife. It seems waking the dead has the ability to piss off her ex-husband and her delusional spirit husband as well. Oddly, I'm not pissed. I'm just very fucking concerned.

"Celestra." She glances to Chloe as if to silence her. "Among other Factions. I took the cemetery map book from your father's office." She looks right at me. "It was the only way I'd know who was who. I needed to resurrect those I thought might be willing."

"Willing to do what?" My heart plummets to my feet because I can feel my brother's name bubbling up her throat.

"To thwart Wesley." She sharpens her eyes over mine when she says it. "To thwart those millions of feds he has sniffing around the island."

"Shit." I close my eyes at how far down both Demetri and Wes have sent us spiraling. "What are you going to do with them?"

Chloe steps up next to me as if we were suddenly on the same team. If you ever find yourself on the same team as Chloe Bishop, just know you're on the wrong side.

"I know"—Chloe slings a hand over my shoulder casually—"we could put them in Tenebrous. The tunnels belong to you now, Skyla. So that shouldn't be an issue."

"Tenebrous." Skyla shakes her head. "Too far and too much work to transport them all. Besides, we need them handy, and we need them plausibly human. They'll need to be present if they're ever going to get caught."

"So they'll be taken." The words strum from me numbly. People who have already crossed that great divide are coming back for more hell on earth because my own brother has sentenced the Nephilim to a fate, ironically, worse than death—government experimentation.

"Marshall"—Skyla struts toward him, tits out as if she were trying to seduce him—"you have to help. I need these bodies freed before morning."

"Impossible," he shoots back, his chin up as if he enjoyed defying her on some level.

"Oh, come on"—she gives his tie a firm tug—"nothing is impossible with *you*."

"All right." I stride forward and carefully remove her hand from Dudley's tie before I decide I need to knock him into eternity where he belongs. "I'll do it. Show me what bodies you need excavated, and I'll power through it."

Chloe huffs a laugh. "I'll help. Skyla, you go home and let the little ones swing off your boobs or whatever it is you do with them." She scuttles up to me with her hair and tits bouncing, and I'm quick to look away. "I highlighted all of the areas we hit in that journal your dad keeps." She wags one of his composition notebooks at me. "You can use that as a road map. And don't worry, Gage. A shovel fits in my hand, too. I'll be right by your side as we power through it together." Her hand glides over my shoulder. "It's going to be a long, hard, sweaty night."

"There, you see?" Dudley sheds a shit-eating grin. "You've a hero or two to keep you on your morbid *deadline*." He scowls toward the east. "I'd best check on Ezrina and see what's become of her latest pet project."

"Marshall"—Skyla pulls him back as he starts to take off—"that girl looks exactly like Laken. You tell Ezrina she better have a damn good explanation for it. And for the love of all things holy, do not let me catch that girl down in the Transfer."

"I'll pass the word along." He tips his imaginary hat as he walks into the open arms of the fog. "Good night, all."

And with that, his body evaporates into a watery state before dissipating altogether.

Chloe leans in toward Skyla. "What's this about a Laken clone that Ezrina is housing?"

"I'm sure Wes will fill you in soon enough." Skyla takes the book out of Chloe's hand. "I'm not leaving." She locks her eyes over mine, and for a moment I could swear something real just bounced between us. "Ask your mom if she can watch the boys for a few more hours. She never picks up when I call." She opens the book, and Logan leans in to peer over her shoulder.

A slapping sound from behind gets our attention, and we find Kate pounding her foot against the ground as if she's having a seizure.

"Kate!" Skyla rushes over as Logan and I help the poor girl to a sitting position.

Her lips contort as if she's desperately trying to tell us something.

Chloe scoffs. "It doesn't work so well without the vocal cords, does it, Kate?"

"Be quiet, Chloe." Skyla pulls out her phone and hands it to the girl we were once close friends with. I know this is technically Kate, but seeing her like this, her limbs looking slightly mangled, her hair badly tangled from a few restless years in a casket makes her unrecognizable.

Kate does her best to punch in the tiny letters popping up on Skyla's screen, but she's choppy at best. I doubt we'll get a clear message out of her this way.

"Emksa?" Skyla shakes her head. "Kate, I don't know what you're trying to say. I'll get a pen and some paper for you when we get settled back at the house."

"You're taking her home?" Normally, I wouldn't question Skyla taking a friend to the house. Hell, Chloe has slept in my bed more than I have lately. But Kate is dead—

was dead. Her body is putrefied and most likely crawling with microbes that no antibiotic could hope to cure. "Not with the boys," I say it lower than a whisper as not to insult our newly reanimated friend.

"She'll stay with me." Logan gives her a light tap over the knee, and her leg goes slack as if it's just slipped right out of joint.

Chloe takes the phone from Skyla. "Wait a minute. Are you trying to say *Emma*?"

Kate gives a spastic clap of the hands and touches her finger to her nose, an old charades' trick to let someone know they're right.

"Emma?" I lean in and look into Kate Winston's jaundice-colored eyes as she nods frantic into me. "As in my mother?"

Her hand slaps against the ground, and her forefinger touches her nose over and over, bending the cartilage off to the side.

The cemetery starts to rumble at top volume again as the thundering of a thousand corpses rises as they beg to be set free.

Chloe sits down next to Kate and picks up her hand. "I'll keep Kate company while the three of you tend to that unruly herd of the undead just clamoring to join us." She gives a little wink my way. "Don't get too tired. I have plans for you later."

Skyla groans. "It never gets old, does it, Chloe?"

"How could it? Only someone as foolish as you would cut a man like Gage Oliver loose."

"Did you just call me foolish?" Skyla leans in, and Chloe shakes her head frantically as if she were a three-year-old about to be punished by her mother. "That's not what I meant. I'm strictly speaking from the heart—or between the legs as it were. Gage isn't a toy you toss to the side when you're bored with him."

"I was far from bored with him." Her voice grows curt, her expression tight. "I was *betrayed*, Chloe. A word you often confuse with greed. Your gain always equals someone else's pain." Skyla stalks off toward the thumping and rumbling out in the field. "Keep it down! I'm coming!"

"We're still friends, though, right?" Chloe calls after her and gifts her the middle finger once she turns her back.

"Nice." Logan shakes his head as he follows Skyla out to the chaos brewing in the cemetery.

"I don't think it's nice, Chloe. I think whatever this thing you and Skyla have going on is downright bizarre."

"She'll get over it. We've been arguing like an old married couple all week. It's cabin fever, and believe you me, I'm sick of her shit, too. Kate and the rest of the dead-on-arrival gang should liven things up a bit." She leans back and attempts to comb her fingers through Kate's hair. The tiara Kate's mother planted over her skull clings for dear life. But Kate stares off straight ahead, her lips mouthing the same thing over and over again at a frenetic pace. If I didn't know better, I'd think it was my mother's name.

It does beg the question. What have you done now, Mother?

Logan

The fog shrouds itself around the cemetery like a faithful witness as body after body is slowly exhumed from the ground, and from the mausoleum as well. In the future, I might suggest my brother bury anyone with a drop of Nephilim blood inside that den of easily accessible corpses in the event Skyla feels the need to summon the dead once again. Skyla has made it abundantly clear that this is her baby. Chloe didn't play into the decision making one bit. In fact, Chloe isn't exactly helping with any part of the process, and it makes me wonder if she wants to absolve herself of malfeasance altogether. Instead, she sits back with our old— newly resurrected friend, Kate, watching her mime out a conversation and laughing her ass off. Poor Kate has signaled that she wanted paper and a pen, but Chloe couldn't be bothered. Why put someone out of their misery when you can torment them for hours? I would have helped Kate out hours ago myself, but, as it is, I'm covered with dirt, sweat, and blood. The blood is my own from a cut I incurred while prying open a crypt. Who knew I could bleed? I guess I'm a real boy after all.

"*Logan.*" Skyla waves me over to the precipice where she's standing. "Look at that." She marvels at the small mounds Gage is tapping down with a shovel to minimize the damage we've done. "It's not that bad. I can't believe he's gone back over every single hole we've dug and smoothed it over."

"You sound proud of him."

"I'm"—her lips screw up in a fit of confusion—"I'm just saying he's going the extra mile." She slaps her hands over her jeans. Whether or not Skyla wants to acknowledge it, she's getting her figure back to her pre-pregnancy state. She looks great, and she's a great mother like I always knew she'd be. "Can you believe this?" She looks over at the crowd of the walking dead, each in their formal prom-like attire. They all look pretty damn good as a whole, which is a testament to Barron's embalming skills. "They didn't all choose to come." She wraps an arm around my waist. "Once I tapped their gravestone, I suppose they had a decision to make. And to be honest, I didn't think this many would show. Not on this grand scale."

"One hundred ninety-two bodies. The oldest of which was born in 1805." I should know, I'm keeping track and keeping them from straying as Drake and Ethan help transport them all in our trucks over to the house that Gage and Skyla purchased last fall. Yes, it will be crowded as hell, and *feel* like hell since they've all been privy to paradise, but, as Skyla pointed out, it's far more spacious than a casket. Collectively they look stiff, but as the early hours of the morning fast approach, they've been testing out their old bodies, stretching and jogging in place as if readying for a marathon. Their voices, however, aren't louder than a whisper, which is something that I'm hoping will clear up once those vocal cords get lubed up once again. The whispering phenomenon could be enough to trip up the feds long before we're ready.

"Amazing." She offers a firm squeeze to my ribs. "And they understand completely that they'll be ushered right back to eternity once their calling is through. The only thing I'm unsure about is"—she lowers her voice to a whisper—"God, Logan, what if they feel pain? I don't see why they wouldn't, but I hadn't really considered it. That would be just as bad as putting the living through it."

"That may be so, but for them it's a mission. They've got one task to complete, and they're doing it for the good of the living. I think your biggest problem is sitting right over there." I nod back to where Chloe is doing her best to remove that scarf poor Kate scrambled to retrieve. A rotten thing to do, considering it's what's securing Kate's head to the rest of her.

"Chloe won't tell." Skyla wraps her arm around mine like a vine. "I own her. I own Chloe Bishop." Her voice drops into its lower octave, dark and seductive, as if the prospect of owning Chloe left her sexually charged. "She is my bitch just the way God intended."

"Things are going to end badly." The words weren't even necessary. At this point, anyone can surmise it.

"They would have anyway."

Just as I'm about to beg Skyla for a hint on the dirt she has on Chloe, or perhaps more to the point the kinds of promises she might have made to her—and either has to be big in order for Chloe to do her bidding—one of the older gentlemen near me coughs explosively into his hand. You have to give it to them, still considering others when it comes to germs. There are some hygienic practices not even death can beat out of you.

He leans in toward Skyla and me. "I was just saying it used to snow on Paragon—big giant heaps of"—he gags and bucks forward as a stream of neon green vomit spews from his mouth.

"*Shit.*" I pull Skyla back as a chunky waterfall of putrid barf splatters through the air.

A collective groan works its way through the crowd as body after body doubles over and pukes right where they're standing.

"Oh no." Skyla covers her mouth with her hand as throngs of those long-deceased bathe the ground in a sea of vomit. "*Shit, shit, shit!*" She jumps back, and just as I'm about to grab a hose from the side of the mausoleum, Barron pops up—about as unwanted as a puking corpse in a cemetery.

Crap. "Hey, Barron." I give a quick nod his way as if our little corner of the world weren't falling to shit. "What brings you out tonight?"

"It's morning in the event you haven't noticed." That mean glare he's casting my way says it all. My brother has always been a man of few words, studious to a fault, and a peaceful, amicable soul. But, at the moment, he's raging-bull mad, ready to fire off his anger at the first familiar face he comes across, and as fate would have it, that would be me.

"What in the world is going on, Logan?" His voice shakes with fury. His glasses steam up, and it has nothing to do with the fog. "Why are you having a party in the middle of the cemetery, and why in God's name are they all regurgitating their dinner at the very same time?"

Skyla buries her face in her hands a moment. "We're not having a party, Dr. Oliver." I've always thought it was sweet the way she continues to call him by his proper name. She's his daughter-in-law now. She could easily call him Barron, or *Dad* if she liked. "And they're not regurgitating their dinner. I'm pretty sure it's those embalming fluids you filled them up with. These people are actually at *home*. You see—Logan and Gage dug them up from their respective graves."

I blink her way, stunned at how easily she threw both Gage and me under the bus—and I also find it cute as hell.

Technically, she's right. It was Gage and I that did all the heavy lifting, but I can't help but chuckle at the thought of Skyla omitting herself from the tragedy unfolding.

"Fine." She smacks me over the arm. "It was my idea."

Barron's eyes bug out like a pair of golf balls. "Holy shit." He does a quick spin into the crowd as the bodies fall to the ground and pant for water.

I've heard Barron shed an expletive or two in my day, but they are rare and few between, and usually signify a shitload of trouble—case in point.

He leans in to inspect the moaning crowd. "My God, these are people I've buried! The legal ramifications of unearthing the dead are innumerous. Are you insane?" He stops short as he spots his son nestled among the gravestones. "Gage Oliver! Get back here right this minute!"

Gage does a double take before tossing down his equipment and doing as he's told.

"I have a very good explanation," Skyla starts, but Barron holds up a hand, unable to look her way. The brunt of his rage is very much pinned on Gage at the moment.

"Did you give the green light to this circus?" His voice pitches as white plumes burst from his mouth.

"*Shit*," Gage says it under his breath as he makes his way over. His face is covered in a thin layer of dirt, and it makes his eyes siren out ten times brighter than before. "Look, I've got everything under control."

"You must be kidding me," Barron barks so loud half the newly awakened dead stagger on over. "Do you see the unfortunate state of these people? They belong in caskets. They belong *under* Paragon soil, not on it! If word gets out that I've dug up half the bodies in my possession, I'll lose my license, my house, and never mind my sanity." He growls over toward Skyla, "I've already lost that." Barron stalks over to the side of the morgue and starts the hose running.

"Great minds," I muse. "I was just about to do the same thing. I'd better go help out."

"No, wait." Gage stops me. "I'd better do it." He looks to Skyla with that forlorn expression he wears whenever she's around. "A few more trips and everyone will be settled at the house. As soon as I clean this place up, I'll help you get the boys."

She offers a silent nod, and Gage jogs off to clean up the mess.

"He's good at that," I muse.

"At what?" Skyla doesn't take her eyes off him. I know this separation is killing her just the same.

"At cleaning up messes. That's all he was doing, Skyla—cleaning up a mess."

"I know," she says it quiet, with a touch of defeat in her voice.

"So, are you ready to hear him out?" Here it is, the moment Gage has been waiting months for. All Skyla needs to do is understand his motives and she'll see he never betrayed her—not in the way she thinks he did.

"Not tonight." She heads over to Drake and Ethan, and they cuss up a storm at the prospect of vomit-covered passengers. They're still knee-deep in transports, and it looks as if they're ready to throw in the vomit-covered towel.

"*Dude.*" Drake gets in my face. "I don't see you offering these assholes a ride. Do you know the last few trips they puked their guts up in the back of the van? Brielle is going to shit a brick when she sees I need to recarpet the ceiling."

"Tell you what." I fish the keys to my truck out and hand them over. "Pile as many as you like in the back. No pukers in the cab. And why don't you buy Brielle a new car for the hell of it? Trust me, you'll be thanking me when you see how happy it makes her." If I know one thing about Bree, it's that she loves new things. And if I know one thing about Drake, it's that he likes to get laid by his wife. It sounds like a win-win to me. Besides, Drake and Bree are rolling in it. Drake has amassed more wealth in the last year alone to qualify him for the Forbes 500. Bree isn't doing so bad either with that nail polish line Ezrina helped her hone. If someone would have told me that two people who I graduated high school with would strike it rich right off the bat, I would never have pegged it to be this particular dynamic duo.

"Good thinking." He stalks off, and I help him and Ethan load up the last of the formerly dead.

Ethan nods over to Skyla, and she heads on over. "What's the deal?" He waves a hand at the truck full of dead men and women anxious to get this next, most likely disastrous, part of their new lives underway. "You throw a party and don't bother inviting Em and me?" He shakes his head in disgust.

"Be thankful." Skyla averts her eyes with measured drama. "It looks like a bad case of food poisoning."

I'm almost amused that Ethan bought the excuse. Gage told both Drake and Ethan we were having a graveyard bash and needed help transporting the guests. He said our valet took off. If by *valet* he meant hearse, then yes, those took off years ago.

"Did you cook?" Ethan looks affronted at the idea, and Skyla gives a sorrowful nod. "Damn straight they got sick. You need to get this shit catered. This is too many people to be slaving over a stove for. You got kids now. You're not Wonder Woman." He takes off, and we watch as their taillights wash the cemetery in a bloodbath of red.

"You are Wonder Woman." I wrap an arm around her shoulders as Barron and Gage come up.

"I want you all off the property." Barron's eyes widen as he observers something from over my shoulder. "Good God and take it with you!"

We turn to find Kate staggering over, her head dangling by her waist as she grips it by the hair. Her mouth is moving, her eyes blinking frenetically—it's enough to make a grown man vomit, and Barron heads over to the bushes and does just that.

Chloe comes up from behind and tosses Kate's scarf over her disembodied head. "I'm taking off. Don't worry about a thing. This reanimation-fest will be our little secret." She offers a dark smile to Skyla that reeks of wickedness. Skyla has to see through this bullshit. "Wes is too busy with that little brat to notice anything anyway. He says he's hired some hot little nanny to replace Ezrina, now that she's down for the count." She glances at her fingernails as if the thought of her own child reminded her of the fact she's in need of a manicure. And what's with calling your own kid a brat? I'm pretty sure that moniker is reserved for non-relations, or at least it should be. "I'll catch you losers later," she says it with a wink and a smile before looking to me. "Can't wait to don my legwarmers and neon heels for that party you're throwing." She spots Gage, and her arms stretch wide as if gunning for a hug. "I'll be sure to save the sexiest dance for you."

Skyla reaches over and knocks her in the forehead with the palm of her hand. "Good night, Chloe."

And just like that, Chloe Bishop blinks out of this plane and into the Transfer.

"I wondered how you did that." Gage smiles down at her, and they share a quick laugh, but Skyla stops short as if startling back to reality—a reality where laughing with Gage simply isn't permitted.

Barron offers us a curt nod. "I'll be staying the remainder of the day." He looks out at the cemetery as the sun comes up over the hillside. "Fielding phone calls, undoubtedly. I'll be closing the grounds for repairs for the rest of the week." He stalks off inside.

Ethan brings my truck back and takes off in his own car before I can thank him.

"That's my ride." I help navigate Kate over to the passenger's side.

ADDISON MOORE

"I'll help get her head on," Skyla offers and I get out of the way.

Gage comes over with those tired bloodshot eyes. "Thanks, man. I couldn't have done it without you."

"Same." I give him a quick fist to the shoulder. I glance over to find that Skyla has Kate's head in the right spot and that scarf of hers tight as a noose. She's scouring the glove compartment for what I'm assuming is a pen, and she holds one up to the light victoriously before handing it to Kate.

Gage leans in. "What do you think Kate has to say about my mom?" He folds his arms over his chest and offers a disappointed look in the direction of the family home as if he senses the news isn't favorable.

"I don't know. Did she even know your mom? Maybe she went to the preschool? Emma runs the largest preschool on the island. I think at some point everyone under twenty-five passed through those doors. I bet that's what it is. She probably has some long suppressed memory of how wonderful she is and she wants to thank her. Don't underestimate your mother." I hate that I'm essentially echoing Dudley's words. "She leaves a damn good impression." I offer a mock sock to his shoulder.

"That's probably it." He offers a quick pat to my back. "I'll catch you later." We head over to Skyla, and she quickly crumbles the note in her hand and buries it in her pocket. Her face looks unreasonably pale, despite the fact she's dusted with fresh Paragon soil like the rest of us. Whatever Kate jotted down, Skyla isn't up for show and tell.

"Go ahead and get the boys, get a shower, and some sleep." I offer her a quick embrace. "I'll make sure Kate is comfortable." As comfortable as you can be without your head formally attached. "I'll have Ezrina look at her come morning."

She gives a frantic nod. "That's great." She looks to Gage. "Why don't you call your mom and ask her to get the boys ready? I'll meet you in the truck. I just want to say good night to Kate."

Gage gives a quick wave and heads to his truck.

"What did the note say, Skyla?" I glance to Kate who looks morbidly exhausted and, in truth, I'm paranoid she might keel over again on the ride back to the house.

"It said"—the words pull from Skyla's lips in slow motion as she looks to our old undead friend—"Emma is trouble."

"Trouble? How?" I glance to Kate. Her eyes are glazed over, fatigued beyond reason. That just goes to show, some dirt naps are never long enough.

Skyla shakes her head just barely. "She wouldn't say. She clammed up and just kept mumbling Emma's name over and over again as if it were some chant." Skyla gently combs Kate's hair to the side of her face. "Good night. Sleep tight," she whispers before taking a step back, and I shut the door for her. "*Logan*." Skyla closes her eyes a moment too long as if her body were begging for respite any way it can get it. "What could she have meant? Is there something about Emma that you're keeping from me?" Her voice is soft, but that accusatory look in her eyes is sharp as a lion's claw. Skyla is lacerating me with a simple glance.

"No. I swear it."

Gage revs up the engine before pulling alongside of us. He teleported back to Whitehorse before Ethan and Drake came over and retrieved it but refused to teleport the masses—not with the feds lying in wait for some paranormal phenomenon, and it would have been just that.

"There's my ride." Skyla's brows pitch as if offering me one last chance to pony up the confession, but there isn't one. A deafening silence fills the void instead.

I watch as they take off. Skyla and Gage, together again if only for a moment. *That's the way it should be*, I try to tell myself, but that knot in the pit of my stomach rejects it every single time.

I hop in and drive Kate home in silence. Lexy is there when we arrive to gift her the enthusiastic greeting she deserves. It sounds like a party in the house, and that's just Lex bubbling with excitement. But I'm quick to ditch the reunion and get to bed.

I dream of Skyla all night long, of the two of us swimming through corpses, blood rising over us in waves, washing us red as a reminder of the new catastrophe I'm afraid we've pulled ourselves into.

Oh, Skyla. What have we done?

How do we always manage to slip in the shit of our own making?

The next few days are spent cataloging the formerly dead, manically emptying all the thrift stores on the island of their casual ware and shoes, and turning the bowling alley kitchen into a bona fide pizza delivery service. It turns out newly reanimated bodies like to eat. Scratch that—they are ravenous to put things other than earthworms into their pie holes. In light of the fact, I've been syphoning food from the bowling alley and sending a steady stream of pizza delivery to Skyla's home behind the gates—the old Walsh residence where we stand now with the dilapidated kitchen serving as crisis central.

Dudley steps up beside me as we watch Skyla and Ellis try to work out a plan of attack on paper as far as how to best utilize our newfound army of volunteers.

"Nothing like the stench of death in the afternoon to enliven the senses." His crimson eyes glance my way before nodding to the disheveled masses.

"That, my friend, is the scent of pepperoni and sausage. It turns out that death can really enliven your carnivore tendencies." I glance to Skyla hard at work trying to figure out where the undead puzzle pieces fit best. "What do you think we should do?"

Dudley leans in and redirects my line of vision back to his ugly mug. "As your supervising spirit, I'd suggest you back away slowly from the puddle of blood seeping your way, but it's too late for that. You're covered in it, sealed with its iniquity—its stench branded upon your very soul." The look of discontent crosses his face. It's an expression I've grown familiar with coming from him. Unfortunately, Dudley is right more than he is ever wrong, and once again, unfortunately, he is never, ever wrong.

"So, you're staying out of it." I figured as much. Dudley has made it clear that the graveyard grovel was something he'd rather keep his sooted wings far away from.

He frowns over at me—a look I've grown accustomed to. "Have you ever heard the saying *measure twice cut once?*"

"Yes." My insides tense because I can feel the barb before he ever lets it fly from his mouth.

"Formulating a plan and executing it should be two distinct actions, preferably the former followed by the latter. Do you see something contradictory with this picture?" He glares over at Skyla for a moment.

"I get it." I hold up a hand to cut him off. "We jumped in. But in her defense, it's a brilliant plan and one approved by the leader of the Decision Council herself."

His finger bounces off his lips as if deep in thought, an action I've been prone to do myself, and the idea amuses me.

Somewhere down the lineage line, our ancestry has crossed wires. Dudley here is my not-so-great gramps thanks to his less than stellar, albeit frequents, romps throughout history. His celestial seedlings escaped the one-eyed snake, and here I am, all but a carbon copy of the Sector himself.

"Has Candace approved this?" His voice curls toward the incredulous. "Have you thought through the repercussions, young Oliver? Has it ever occurred to you this might be a master manipulation? A setup as it were?" The lights dim, and Dudley stands at attention, his gaze dialed in straight ahead as if he were half-expecting his superior to strut in front of him.

Chloe strides up before I can answer him. Her cruel dark eyes narrow in over mine as her face curves into a snarl. "What's this I hear about Logan Oliver becoming a *bumpkin* farmer?" She spits the words out with a nauseous look.

"Do my future plans offend you?" I'm not amused. And God knows I'm not in the mood to entertain this wench today or any other day.

Her full lips twist in a knot, and a brief memory of the two of us fucking freely back in her old bedroom—Skyla's new bedroom, before I ever knew Skyla existed, runs through my mind. "Hell yes, they offend me. They—"

"Good," I cut her off at the pass. "I hope everything about me offends you, Chloe. I hope the sight of me makes your stomach turn the way mine does when I see you. All you have ever done to me or anyone else is caused outrageous levels of misery. I can't imagine what I would have done if you had only approved. Thanks for solidifying my actions with your discontent. It's how I know I'm moving in the right direction."

Ellis scoffs from the end of the table. "Dude, she's right. This idea sucks big hairy balls. You need to rethink the squash-fest. You and I need to pool our funds and open up a chain of breasteraunts on the island."

"Breasteraunts?" Chloe chokes on the word as if she were equally offended by his idea, as she was mine. In truth, I happen to agree with her on that one. "Skyla—evict every idea that stoner offers. We can't trust his judgment."

"And we can trust yours?" Dudley smiles as he delivers the quip.

Chloe straightens, her eyes dim to a disheartening shade of soot. "My, *my*, isn't this the pot calling the kettle black? You are quite the charmer, aren't you, Sector Dudley—flaunting your manhood through the ages as if you were some starry host B list celebrity that has a dick ax to grind with the female population at large. I'll have you know—"

"Enough." The words come from him calm as he lifts a finger with ease, and Chloe levitates into the air with her back adhering to the ceiling.

Skyla and I exchange a brief glance before we scan the room for onlookers, as if the dead should find this the least bit bazaar. Truth be told, every last detail of our world has turned into a mindfuck as of late. Not sure why Chloe on the ceiling should jar me in any way.

"Shit!" Chloe squeals. "Please, dear God, don't spin me! Skyla, don't you let him spin me!" she screams as a round of oohs and ahhs erupt amongst the crowd gathering at the spectacle.

I'll give Dudley credit. It is an amusing party trick—one he played on me not too many years ago. Although, I don't recall any spinning.

Dudley growls up at her as if threatening her with a quick spin before he glowers over at me. "Bring Skyla to my home this evening. I've a dead man's bone to pick with the two of you."

"What about Gage?" It only seems natural. It's always been the three of us against the world even if the two of them are at odds at the moment.

"I forbid that menace to cross my property line." He seethes over at Skyla, "Don't be tardy, Ms. Messenger." He butts shoulders with the dearly departed and disintegrates long before he hits the exit, which spurs a spontaneous round of applause from the easily impressed crowd.

"Sectors are the best." A bubbly blonde shoulders up next to me. She's tiny and cute, and startlingly young, a pre-teen perhaps. She holds the air of innocence about her with the exception of a gaping wound that glides across her cheek. I can tell it's been filled in with the mortuary's finest cosmetics—dried and cracking with age. "I'm Casey." She offers me a svelte hand, and I shake it, surprised to see how warm it is.

"I'm Logan."

"Logan Oliver." Her eyes brighten a peculiar shade of lavender. "Once dead and now you're alive in a Treble gifted from your highness Candace Messenger—mother of Skyla, our great warrior princess who is destined to secure a rightful place of leadership with Celestra through her marital bond with Sector Marshall. I'm all up on my Warring Angels 101."

Skyla looks up from the spastic notes eating up the table and offers a quiet laugh. Her eyes connect with mine, and we share an intimate moment right here in the madness, the eye of the hurricane we've seated ourselves in once again.

"Nice to meet you, Casey." I offer her a quick shake. "And yes, Skyla is our great warrior princess."

That wide-eyed stare of hers never dissipates. "You're sexy." Her fingers cover her mouth as she giggles.

"I second that," Skyla calls out, and Chloe grunts from above as if she's been supernaturally muted. And judging by the fact she's no longer cursing up a storm, I'd say that might very well be the case. "Giselle says it's okay to use that word." She nods into the idea as if she's been eager to use that word for centuries. "You are sexy. We all think so." She motions back to a small crowd of girls gathered in a bunch near the sofa leering at me with perky little grins. I give a quick wave, and the entire lot of them breaks out into titters. Casey glides her hand up over my shoulder, taking a step in with a look in her eye that suddenly screams anything but innocence. "It's so lonely in here. How about you give a girl a ride in that *big* white truck of yours?" She gives a little wink.

Skyla clears her throat as if to say something, but her mouth opens and she's suddenly as mute as Chloe and she shrugs up at me instead.

"Pardon me." A tall dapper man, the oldest of the bunch as far as time goes, steps up. "I'm afraid young Casey is needed in the next room." He shakes his head at her ever so slightly as if it were a reprimand and escorts her quickly in that direction. I know the dude, David Copeland. He looks like an Abe Lincoln caricature if you ask me. He died in his late thirties—in 1898. I know Casey, too. Casey Fields was just fifteen the day she met her demise in 1948 by way of a tractor plow. It's safe to say, I've made it a point to commit each newly reanimated corpse and the nature of their demise to memory. I shake my head at the thought of being hit on by a girl who is technically slightly older than my mother. And speaking of my mother—and my father. I'll admit, I was holding out hope that they, too, would have been a part of this heroic assignment. But, as it stands, they were cremated by the Counts far before they ever were by the morgue, and it appears Candace is only allowing us to utilize those with bodies available to reanimate. Barron had their ashes scattered partially throughout the farm back in Oregon and here on the island—the bowling alley, the beach, they both loved Pike's Reef where I spend my birthday each year. And each year I celebrate at that locale, I feel close to my mother and father.

"Wow, Logan"—Skyla marvels with that sarcastic look in her beautiful blue eyes that I've grown to love—"you really know how to bring the dead girls to the yard—*graveyard.*" She gives a little wink. "Oh, who am I kidding? There's not a girl, dead or alive, who doesn't want a piece of you."

Chloe grunts from above and struggles to move her limbs.

"Yes, Chloe"—Skyla glares at the demon who's found an unwanted home on the ceiling—"everybody knows how you feel about Logan Oliver. Now, get the hell off the ceiling. You're causing a scene."

Chloe falls face-first into the table below, and Skyla rolls her off and gets back to work without giving it another thought.

"I hate this old house," Chloe grumbles as she scrambles to her feet and dusts herself off. "And what are you staring at?" she hisses my way. "Get that deconstruction crew you hired to build that Shangri-la-la land you gifted your ex-wife and fix up this haunted hovel or bulldoze the damn thing. It's a wreck, and the décor leaves a hell of a lot to be desired." She scowls at the table as if it personally offended her. And judging by that bloodied nose of hers, it did. "You'll have to get Lex out here." She snarls over at Skyla. "Just pray she can wield her magic."

"I don't need Lexy Bakova or her magic arts." Skyla lifts her gaze to me a moment and scoffs. It's clear Skyla thinks there's something going on between Lex and me. There's not. There never will be, but I'd be lying if I didn't admit that having her around didn't kill the sting of silence in the air. Ezrina and Nev are mostly subterranean at this point.

Skyla taps her pencil in front of the resident stoner in order to garner his attention. "*Ellis*—why don't you take Chloe to the restroom and help her clean up?"

"I'm fine." Chloe cradles her nose in her hand for a few seconds, and the mess disappears right along with the swelling. She struts over to Skyla and peers over her shoulder at the plans she's working on. "What do we have here—more bullshit to sidestep Wesley?" She lets out a huge sigh as if sidestepping that idiot husband of hers were impossible. And it might be. For starters, Wesley Edinger is unfortunately no idiot.

"Ellis thinks we need bona fide employment for them all." Skyla shakes her head at the thought. "But the unemployment rate on the island stands at thirty percent. I say they can work for Logan and Dr. Oliver."

"You need to mix it up." Ellis jabs his finger at the paper in front of Skyla. "You need a few entrepreneurs in the mix. I've got a handful of recruits willing to break their back at the weed farm."

"No reefer farmers." I take a seat next to Skyla just as Giselle comes bubbling in with excitement.

"This is so fantastic, Skyla!" She beams as she hugs Ellis from behind. "It's like old home week. I never thought I'd see these people again—at least not until I bite the big one again. Speaking of which, can you put in a good word for me with your mother? I'd rather not land under a tire again. I was thinking of having a house fall on me this time. That's terribly romantic."

"Giselle!" Skyla's eyes expand with a flash of fire. Skyla has the most beautiful eyes known to man. If there were a color to describe them, it would be stardust. "Having a house fall on you is about as far away from romantic as you can get."

"Oh, *Skyla*." Giselle brushes her off with a flick of her wrist. "I saw it in a movie. It's totally romantic. A cyclone will hit the island, and it'll pick up all sorts of things, men in boats and cute little dogs—and Chloe, you can be the mean old crotchety woman on her bicycle!" Chloe growls over at her, and Giselle cowers behind Ellis a moment. "And finally, the wind will pick up the rattiest old house on the island— most likely this one—and it'll fall right on top of me! Then some nice soul will come along and steal my shiny red slippers and have a grand adventure of her own!"

Ellis nods into this ludicrous theory. "G loves *The Wizard of Oz*. We watch it every night before we get to bed." His mouth falls open as he catches himself, and I shake my head at him.

The urge to kick some Harrison ass sets in strong. "Get out of here, Ellis, before I throw you out."

"Cool." He jumps to his feet and stretches his arms to the ceiling. "Dudley wanted to see me about something anyway. I'll go hang out where I'm wanted."

"I'm not going with you!" Giselle is quick to protest as he heads for the door. "Darnell Woodley was just about to tell us what happened when a steam engine was coming his way and his shoe caught on the track!"

Chloe burps a short-lived laugh. "Spoiler alert! He *dies*!"

"*Chloe*," Giselle whines as the crowd swallows both Ellis and her.

"You are a killjoy," Skyla muses, still keeping her eyes peeled to the map of resurrected humanity before her.

I wrap my hands over her shoulders and offer up an impromptu massage. "She's a *killer*, Skyla," I say as Chloe takes Ellis' seat, and I fall in next to Skyla. "Chloe, why don't

326

you go ahead and play in Dudley's supernatural sandbox, too? I'm sure there's another dimension he'd be happy to shove you in." That ring on Skyla's finger catches my attention. Its deep blue stone set in that old-world filigree reminds me a lot of the protective hedge. Speaking of which, Skyla has the Eye of Refuge tucked safely around her neck. She had taken it off for a time, but I'm glad to see it where it rightfully belongs. But that ring—something about it—the way it catches the light. It seems more of a magical treasure, something far more superior than a simple piece of jewelry. I hate to say it, but it makes the protective hedge look like something out of a cheap coin machine. I run my finger over the peacock blue ring just to quell the urge to fondle it, and the stone lights up bright as lightning.

"Whoa." Skyla holds her hand out. "Did you see that?" she asks Chloe without missing a beat.

I tap my knuckles in front of her. "Yes, *I* saw that." It frustrates me that she just put Chloe before me. I'm not sure what the hell is going on between the two of them, but I want answers, dammit. "Skyla"—I give a quick glance around—"this is Chloe Bishop you've befriended. She's a fucking nut in the event you need reminding."

Chloe offers up a swift kick to my shin from underneath the table. "A fucking nut that's sitting *right here.*"

"See? She's not afraid to admit it." I shake my head pleadingly to Skyla as I latch onto her hand. "Come to your senses. I promise you, this will not end well."

"That's because it won't end." She extracts her fingers from mine. "Chloe belongs to me. She's *mine*. What I choose to do with her is *my* business. How many times do we need to go over this? Honestly, it's getting old."

A moment of silence thumps by, and I cast a quick glance to Chloe to size up how much she might appreciate being touted as one of Skyla's possessions, and oddly enough, she doesn't seem fazed by this. Amusing.

"Skyla owns you, Chloe?" I tip my head to the living demon.

Skyla slaps her hand down over her notebook and tips her head back with a reserved level of boredom only Dudley seemed to have mastered until now. "That's right, Logan." Her gaze digs into mine as her budding annoyance with me shines right through. "Do you have a problem with this? Because if you do, I suggest you keep it to yourself. Neither Chloe nor I owe *you* or anyone else an explanation of our true intentions." She leans in with those eyes of hers glowing like ice. "Do you hear me, Logan Oliver?" Pure wrath exudes from her—spelling out the fact it's none of my damn business.

Like a reflex, my own hand slams over the table just a hair away from hers. "It *is* my damn business, Skyla. *You* are my damn business. Everything concerning *you* concerns *me*." Our eyes hook into one another, and I can feel her anger, her ripe discontent roaring like an invisible fire between us. For a moment, it feels as if she might pull a knife to my throat. "So, pardon me if I don't apologize for scrutinizing this false friendship the two of you are touting. Which by the way, not a soul alive or dead is buying. The only two lost in this delusion would be her and you—and sadly, I'm afraid it's just really you."

Her pretty pink lips part as her anger gives way to hurt. But deep in her eyes, that rage she has for me still simmers. I don't need for her to outline the reasons why. I get it. I betrayed her by keeping Gage's secrets safe. She thinks I chose Gage over her, and in a sad reality I think I did, too. Protecting her is how I love her. Shielding her from the truth is ironically how I've disrespected her most. It's how Skyla believes I may have even hated her.

"You're right, Logan." Her words are lower than a whisper. "I am delusional and have been in a lot of ways, and not one of them concerns Chloe Backstabbing Bishop." She sighs down at those feverish lists she's been compiling the greater part of the afternoon.

"Forget the list." Chloe lands her claws over Skyla's arm before raking her nails across her flesh, leaving a trail of white lines that quickly turn pink. "You look great. Have you finally cut the burgers from your diet? I hear those saturated fat Frisbees are murder on your arteries."

As if Chloe cares about the hardening of Skyla's heart. I'm sure she's much more interested in knifing open her flesh like she's currently doing.

"Not really. I just had to get out of the habit of eating for three, and, of course, trying not to snack around the clock or eat anything after dinner. But it's really tough, so most of the time I'm munching on pickles between meals. You know, the ones I like."

"The sweet bread and butter ones with a kick of heat." Chloe doesn't miss a beat. And why the hell don't I know what kind of pickles Skyla likes? "Wesley loves those, too. Speaking of which, he made me promise I'd do a grocery run before I go home. He's picking me up in a few minutes at his dad's. I'd better head over. I've got fuck detail tonight."

"Oh, come on." Skyla laughs at Chloe's sexual quip. "You know it's the highlight of your week. He does look just like your favorite Oliver."

Chloe reaches over and slaps Skyla five. "You know what they say, fake it till you make it."

They share a disconcerting laugh, and I'm suddenly sick to my stomach just watching the exchange.

Chloe stands and leans toward Skyla. "I'll keep an ear out and see if he makes that noise when he hits a homer. Maybe they *are* more alike than we think."

That noise? Is Skyla actually dishing out private details of her love life to this witch? On second thought, I don't want to know. It feels strange sitting here listening to them gab about having sex with their lookalike husbands—and whatever the hell that noise might be.

"Oh, hey, you want a ride?" Skyla offers. "I'm sure Logan won't mind."

Chloe smears a greasy grin my way because I'm pretty sure the two of them realize I very much mind. "No, thanks. I prefer the fresh air."

"Watch out for falling houses." I cross my arms over my chest as she makes her way past me. "Word on the golden streets is we've really pissed off the grim reaper."

"I'm not worried." She gives a sly wink, those dark lashes of hers collapsing as if a moth were dying right there on her lid. "Word in the Transfer is it's Oliver blood he's thirsty for."

"I'm not worried either." Chloe can follow her empty threats straight to hell where she came from.

"Do the math. You're already dead, Logan."

Chloe dissipates right along with that signature perfume she's been bathing in ever since Skyla bopped her over the head with a great big bottle for Christmas.

"Did she just threaten Gage?"

Skyla's cheek rises on one side as if she were threatening her husband right along with her, and it sends chills down to my core. "I'd tell that nephew of yours to watch out for falling houses." She gathers her paperwork and starts to rise.

"Skyla, wait"—I gently grab ahold of her wrist and pull her toward me—"Dudley wants to see us tonight."

Those lucent eyes of hers skirt the room. "Let me finish up here. I'll need to feed the boys, and then I'll see if I can squeeze you in." She takes off for the living room, and the crowd surges toward her like a magnet.

Squeeze me in. Those words alone make me feel as if I'm nothing more than a bump in the road. That's about all I've become to her, an afterthought, an irritant at best.

Skyla and I once had something special. We still do. She just can't see it at the moment.

And, at the moment, my vision isn't so great either. I've hurt her. Scarred her heart. Maybe it's time I stopped acting as if I have an all access pass to the girl I love. Maybe there are hard lines—there always have been, and I've crossed every single one of them.

Skyla clears her throat before calling the room to order. "I'd like to appoint each of you with an employment post, and then we'll go over the rules and regulations on what to do once you've been captured by the government." Groans and cheers break out amongst those ready and willing to lay down their temporary lives for the sake of others.

But it's not the dead that have my attention. My eyes, my heart can't seem to stray from that celestial being that glows with love from within for each and every soul in this room. Casey had it right. Skyla is a warrior princess. She is our strong leader, and if she's proving anything, it's that she doesn't need Gage or me by her side to accomplish her goals. We are ephemeral, two dark shadows passing in the night, haphazard objects in her path, unnecessary, and in the end, not needed. Skyla has this handled. I always knew she could do it.

That sinister smile she shed at the thought of Gage's untimely demise comes to mind. Gage Oliver is the polarizing figure that has drawn Skyla and Chloe together. There is no doubt in my mind about that. But for what? Their shared loved for him? Doubtful. Their hatred? Nope.

Discontent would be more like it. But his death? Now that would be downright alarming. There is no way in hell Skyla would be a cheerleader to her husband's demise.

Would she?

Paragon wraps me in a coat of fog as I walk down the cool lonely street without a single resurrected body from the cemetery to keep me company. After the pomp and circumstance of inputting the information Skyla managed to pull together into a rather ambitious database, I'm heading over to Dudley's. Skyla went next door to Barron's to nurse the twins. In that respect, her new home is in the perfect location. Although, I'm not too sure Skyla is thrilled with the idea of being Emma's new neighbor. I'll be honest, it alarms me more than a little.

Kate and her ominous assessment of my sister-in-law come to mind. What in the world would make her think that Emma is trouble? When I left this morning, Lexy was busy showing Kate all of the new social media apps she's missed out on since the time of her demise. She even sent me a picture of the two of them with overlays of cartooned puppy faces and, of course, Lexy's exaggeratingly long tongue swooping out at me for a quick lick. It's strange seeing Kate in pictures taken just minutes prior. It's odd seeing her anywhere. She's dead. And considering the fact she doesn't have a drop of angelic blood in her, she probably should have stayed that way. There's no way in hell I'm letting Kate leave the house. She's not one to be taken by the feds. And for damn sure, I don't want to sponsor some post mortuary family reunion. We cannot tip off her family or else God forbid this blows up and the media gets involved. Things will fall to shit for the people of Paragon faster than you can say Marshall Dudley.

I give a brisk knock over the slimy Sector's door before letting myself in. I take that back. Dudley isn't slimy. His intentions toward Skyla may not be chaste, but his deformed heart seems to be in the right place.

The spacious interior to his home is dimly lit. The fireplace lets out a muted roar as the flames fill the room with their glow. A murmur of voices stems from the dining room, and I head over to find Laken and Coop, Ezrina and Nev staunchly seated with Dudley at the helm.

"I guess I'm late to the party." I head in with a smile and slap Cooper five, but the expressions of just about everyone else remain cold as stone.

The entire lot of them rises to their feet at once.

"We'll discuss this in length at another time." Dudley gives a slight bow like a stage actor coming to the end of this performance. "Mr. Flanders, I assume you understand what is expected of you."

"Expected of you?" I look to Coop for a clue, but he merely grunts at Dudley as he heads to the exit. "What's going on?" I try to slow both him and Laken down, but they seem determined to get to the other side of that door—can't say I blame them.

"Nothing." He takes a deep breath and pats me on the back. "Looking forward to the big party you're throwing this weekend." His forced grin melts into a pained look of pity. "Are you really okay with this?"

"Decimating my youth?" I grimace at the thought. The bowling alley will be destroyed soon after the big bash I'm hosting, and a part of me is dying all over again. "I'm petrified. But hey, do something that scares you every day, right? Isn't that how the saying goes?"

Laken offers a sorrowful laugh. "I'm pretty sure Eleanor Roosevelt's esoteric quote was suggesting something a little more positive." She leans in and gives my cheek a pinch as if I were a child. "You really do look like Coop. You should bring your girlfriend around sometime and the four of us can double date." Her entire countenance brightens at the idea.

"My what?" I'm momentarily perplexed, and before I can piece it together Coop laughs it off.

"Logan and Lexy aren't really together."

"What?" she squawks so loud Ezrina shouts *bless you* from the next room. "But I thought—she said—"

"No, it's my fault." I grind my fist into my eye, trying to get both the fatigue and the regret out. "Lexy has this thing for me, and I can't seem to get rid of her. I'm a one-woman man, and that woman happens to be Skyla." The words grind down to a whisper, but I think they get the gist.

"I'm sorry." Laken clutches at her chest. "I just thought—oh, never mind what I thought. How is she, anyway?" Her lips curl into a scowl. "We haven't exactly been on speaking terms. I mean—outside of bumping into her, I'm not really calling or heading over to see her."

"Why not?" My heart thumps so loud it rattles me. I'm not sure why it kick-starts on occasion, but I'm always up for anything that makes me feel genuinely alive again, and usually I can trace that rare thump right back to Skyla.

"Because she eschewed my advice and insists on latching onto that rat with angel wings. Chloe is a menace, and as long as Skyla is buddying up with her, I can't see our friendship moving forward."

"*Ouch.*" Coop wraps an arm around his wife's waist. "On that note, I think we'll head out."

"I'll catch you later." I don't stop them as they head out the door, but Coop has to know I'll be grilling him on whatever the hell was happening here tonight.

Nev passes me by with a wave while Ezrina lays her hand tenderly over her swollen belly. A few weeks back Dudley let me know the cat was out of the bag—or the baby as it were. I've always suspected Ezrina had a nurturing bone in her body, and now here she is making it come to fruition.

"Whoa." I step in front of them blocking their path. "What's going on?" They're pretty loyal to Dudley, but hey, I let them live rent-free and eat all the pizza from the bowling alley they want, so it's worth a shot.

"Frightful." Ezrina shudders.

Nev leans in, towering over her from behind. "She means what you've done. How you think dragging the dead into this will play out in your favor is beyond me," he says it sternly like a father to a child, and I can't help but shed a tiny smile. Nevermore is going to make a damn good father. "We'll see you back at the house."

I take it that's a hard no as far as letting me in on their little powwow. "Will do."

"Logan"—Ezrina pauses before they hit the door—"the girl's head has been stitched on proper." Her jowls harden as she glares my way. I know she's talking about Kate. I asked her to help out with that entire headless mess.

"And the corpse you resurrected, Ezrina? How is she doing?"

The two of them suck in a fresh lungful of air, shocked as shit that I went there.

Nev ushers his bride out the door in haste as if I had threatened them. "We'll see you at the house."

"What's chasing them out the door?" Dudley springs up from behind just as the two of them rocket through the fog.

"None of your business."

"It's all my business. There isn't a move you make that doesn't concern me."

"It's not my moves you need to worry about."

"I beg to differ."

Skyla appears through the mist as if she had materialized right here on the porch, her face glowing, her cheeks piqued with color. "I just nursed the boys and put them to bed." She flashes a megawatt smile as she strides through the door. Skyla is fierce and beautiful, and the thought of her nurturing those precious boys with her own body melts me to the core. If I were Gage, I'd grovel on my knees day in and day out until I wore her down and she forgave me, if for nothing else but to shut me the hell up. "I'm exhausted. Can we make this quick?"

Dudley jets past me and takes up her hand. "Anything for you, my love. Let's get down to business." He ushers us into his dining room, the seats still warm from his previous questionable meeting. "Are the two of you aware of the ramifications of what you've done?"

"It's wartime," Skyla says it soft, her eyes quickly glossing over with fatigue. "It may not be official, but when you sic the feds on the asses of my people, you can bet that's an act of vitriolic aggression."

"Agreed." Dudley's brows rise slowly as if he were waiting for the last second to spring this bit of news on us.

"Good." Skyla straightens in her seat, but I can tell by that deep sigh that just expelled from her she's as relieved as I am. Dudley is a good barometer as far as how the Decision Council will weigh. "I've got this under control, Marshall. I don't want to drag you into this."

"Nor will you." He slices those disapproving lenses from Skyla to me. "The time of the dragon is near."

"Gage is the dragon?" Skyla groans at the idea, which in my opinion is a good sign. It means she still sees the good in him. She should. He's still good right down to the marrow. "I don't want to discuss him."

Dudley's gaze lingers over hers. "Then perhaps we should start with his father. Demetri is all too aware that his time is short."

"Demetri is indestructible," I counter. "His time is far too long if you ask me."

Dudley blinks a smile. "His earthly time to secure an eternal post for the Fems. The Sectors have staked their rightful claim ages ago. He's been anxious ever since the Fems lost their footing. The great and dreadful day of the Lord is at hand, and once it arrives, our destinies are forever carved in stone, if you will."

"The great and dreadful day of the Lord," I whisper. "And when will this be?"

His eyes dart to mine, sharp as knives. "Not even the Son is apprised of the hour. And besides, that's neither here nor there. It is imminent. The Fems are desperate. Demetri is quickly becoming a joke in all the important celestial circles. This does not bode well with him or his troops. His people loathe humiliation above just about anything else. It's a culture of pride they foster—one which brought their demise to begin with. It's not a matter of *if* but of when he decides to strike back. He's simply building his forces, working the enemy into a fervor—rolling out the smoke, holding up the mirrors." He looks at the two of us as if we should be filling in the blanks.

Skyla clicks her tongue. "You think the feds are a ruse? For what?"

"A double-edged sword." I lean in. "Our people are hauled off, and in the meantime, whatever he and Wes are cooking up, front burner, we won't know about until it blows up in our face."

"Precisely." Dudley folds his hands together and knocks them over the table like a gavel. "Have you delved into Revelation?"

"Yes," Skyla and I answer simultaneously. We share a brief look before returning our gaze to Dudley because we seem to have stumped ourselves at our sudden thirst for Biblical revelation as it were.

"The time is at hand to leave your mark, your legacy, to lead the way to freedom for your people." Marshall's voice rolls like thunder. "Never before have they faced such an enemy, never before has the enemy felt the blade against his neck as painfully as he does this hour. It is pertinent we walk the line together." His eyes skirt to mine before returning to Skyla's. "There was once a man in the early fourteen hundreds who engineered the slaughter of hundreds of thousands of your Nephilim brothers and sisters. It was ethnic cleansing at its best, and it was commandeered in the short span of a year by the temperament of a beguiling character, someone so charismatic, comely, and magnetic. Every word he spoke was twisted, and yet do you know who he had carry out the atrocities?"

"His son?" Skyla tilts her head with a touch of sarcasm.

"His enemy." Dudley grins as if this were the best news. And just as easily as that grin came, his wicked scowls returns to its rightful post. "He masterminded a play of action that in context was indeed brilliant. What better way to slaughter your adversary than by their own hand?"

"My people"—Skyla stumbles over the words—"the Nephilim were manipulated into near eradication."

"That they were." His eyes sear over hers. "Let me ask you this. Would it have been moral for someone with that foreknowledge to travel back in time, locate him as a babe in a pram, and snuff the life out of his infant nostrils?"

Skyla's chest hiccups at the thought. Her eyes bounce to mine a moment before she closes them in consideration. "Yes," she whispers so low it comes out a hiss.

My heart seizes with pain at the thought of Skyla processing that horrific what-if scenario.

"Dudley"—I bark—"in light of the fact that Skyla is a new mother, I think it's particularly tasteless of you to play this twisted game with her. You and I both know it's impossible to go back and change someone's destiny."

Dudley leans against his seat, the muscles in his jaw jumping as he sets that look of near-hatred upon me. "You and I both know this—do we? Tell me this, young Oliver. Was it time for those poor souls to perish in what is now referred to as the Celestra killing season? Do you recall a little trial that involved the two of you? I believe it resulted in a war and a beheading—yours to be exact."

"He's got you there," Skyla muses.

"To answer your question, I don't know. Perhaps it was their time to die." By way of the spirit sword—by my hand. The war and the damn beheading bounce through my mind. I lean in and rest my chin on my fist. "We had power—we just wielded it poorly."

"We reversed the death of Ichabod Travers, so technically we disjointed destiny a bit—although briefly." Skyla shudders. "That was a disaster that thankfully got mopped up quickly."

"Because of your mother," Dudley notes. "The trial was thrown out because of your mother." He looks to me with those bloodlets he calls eyes. "You sit among us because of her mother."

Skyla reaches over and takes up my hand. It feels like a peace offering, and I'll take it. "I may not always show it, but I'm so thankful for that Treble."

"Not the Treble." Dudley gives a disparaging sigh as if disappointed we're not able to follow him down the dimly lit—crooked as hell path he's leading us down. "The time before that."

"My first reentry?" It's true. Candace sponsored that little visit as well.

"Precisely." He leans in. "How old were you when Gage was born?"

The first alarming detail is the fact that he just used Gage's proper name, a loaded gun of a moment if you ask me. The second fucking alarming detail is the fact he wants me to cannonball into the numbers end of the swimming pool—details I myself have spent my new lifetime trying to forget. For whatever reason, placing the microscope over the past makes me feel less real, less than genuine in this new reality. I hate this, and suddenly I want to be anywhere but here.

"Logan?" Skyla gives my hand a squeeze. "I guess you were alive, weren't you?"

"I was. I don't remember exactly. I might have been twelve."

"Twelve?" Dudley plays the part of being amused, poorly at that. He's no thespian, but then he's bent on turning my life into a circus so I give him the floor. "You were about eighteen years younger than Barron. Is that correct?" I give a slight nod. "Jock Strap came bumbling into the world when Barron was in his thirties. And when did Your Grace come to the facility to visit your twisted, deformed body?" His head tilts with curiosity. I was disfigured from the burns. My body never healed from the fire that took my parents' life.

"In my thirties? I can't remember." It comes out low, like a threat, and I'm pretty sure it is one. I don't know where Dudley is going with this, but I'm one hundred percent sure I don't like it.

"How old was Gage at that time?" Skyla asks it for him.

Dudley grins on cue. "Early twenties—that would bring us to date, wouldn't it?" He turns to Skyla. "Gage and you alone on Paragon. Can you imagine that? You and Jock Strap running around on the island with no one else to muck up the love-struck waters."

Skyla leans in with her lips curving at the corners. "Did that reality ever exist?"

"Of course, it did." Dudley glances back at me. "For a time."

"Then"—Skyla looks right through the wall as she pieces it all together—"my mother changed our destinies. All of them."

"Why would she do such a thing, Skyla?" He's probing her, jabbing her in a corner with his imaginary blade of truth until she comes to the conclusion herself.

"This is old news." I give Skyla's hand a quick rattle, trying my hardest to pull her out from his spell.

"Old news in a new light." She leans back in her seat, her eyes unable to focus on any one object in the room as she tries to force the puzzle pieces together. "My mother changed our destinies at this juncture." Skyla fastens her eyes on me once again. "She could have done it when you were a baby, but she didn't. Was there something there she was trying to salvage in that alternate reality—something she needed before you could move on?"

"What could it be?" Dudley is clearly goading her along, that sarcastic infraction in his voice says it all.

"I guess that's for me to find out." The words leave her lips breathlessly.

"You look exhausted, dear." Dudley helps her rise to her feet, and I follow suit.

Dudley rocks his knuckles over the table. "I'm about to take the two of you on a little field trip." He scowls my way as if I were the uninvited third wheel. He nods me over, and I land a hand over his arm, with the other wrapped around Skyla's waist. "Shall we start at the beginning?"

"Always." Skyla's voice vibrates and warbles as the molecules around us shatter and break and a new alien structure surrounds us. "A hospital?" Skyla looks down and gasps. An entire row of infants sits in clear bassinets in the spacious room we've landed ourselves. "The newborn nursery!" Her voice is locked in an excited whisper.

Here we are in what looks to be the exact place where Skyla gave birth, the words *Paragon Hospital* are printed on the adjacent wall with a list of nurses on call. Something is different. The mustard-colored walls, the cheap linoleum squares lining the floor, the flimsy looking acrylic bassinets that each stores their own bundle of joy—all of it seems just a little bit off.

"God, they're all so adorable!" Skyla muses as she peruses the aisles of infants as if they were puppies. "My God"—she leans in toward a dark-haired boy and extracts him gently from his plastic confinement—"this one looks like my sweet baby Barron!"

"Skyla." I glance behind her as a group of nurses share a laugh over something. They might be momentarily distracted, but I'm guessing we'll have a security issue on our hands before long—the issue being us.

"We're undetectable," Dudley is quick to inform. "Although, I'm sure a floating infant might be cause for alarm."

"This is *Paragon*." Skyla rubs her cheek against the tiny being.

Dudley towers over her shoulder as they inspect the precious infant together. "What if I told you this seemingly innocent babe would one day be responsible for the destruction of your people? Should we snuff the life out of his tiny little nostrils? Snuff out the fire, Skyla. You're living in revisionist history."

"*Marshall!*" She spins the baby away from him before nuzzling into his miniature face. "Maybe he's more like Nathan? I would swear he was one of mine. You're not going to tell me I have another son, are you?"

"Heavens no." Dudley scoffs at the idea. "But I will tell you they have a father."

Both Skyla and I open our mouths with surprise. "Is this Gage?" I step in and look at those serious eyes, those hovering thick brows present even in this, his very first hours of life. And then, as if to confirm Dudley's suggestion, his dimples dip in, and Skyla and I share a quiet laugh. "Damn, he's cute." I give a wistful shake of the head. And like an unwanted blast from the past, I remember the moment Liam told me that Barron had a son. My gut wrenched with jealousy before it ever did with joy. I remember wishing I could trade places with him. Trade my twisted wreck for his shiny new body, unblemished and untouched by the Counts—more importantly unwanted by them. Gage Oliver would forever fly under the radar of the enemy, and I found it grossly unfair. And now I know it wasn't true at all. He was in the limelight. We just didn't know it yet.

"That baby!" a woman screams from the nurses' station, and Skyla lands a kiss to his tiny lips before setting him back down safely.

A group of nurses storm in to find all is right with the world, and the one who shed that scream looks physically ill.

"I would have bet my life I saw that baby levitating in thin air!"

The other two share a biting laugh. "I think it's time for your sixteen-hour shift to come crashing to an end. Why don't you look up that cute boy from psych? He oughta set your head straight."

"You mean Doctor Dreamy, Eugene Booth?" The three of them share a chortle. "I think I'll do just that."

Skyla chokes out a laugh. "*Our* Doctor Booth? Wow, I can't wait to rib Doctor Dreamy about this."

"*Eugene*?" I shake my head at her. "That mildly explains why his son's name is Revelyn." A thought comes to me. "I seem to recall his ex-wife was a nurse. I guess he has Gage to thank for that."

"That means"—Skyla's eyes widen—"Gage is indirectly responsible for Rev, the bane of my sister's existence at the moment. And here I thought he was older than us."

Dudley gives a passive nod. "The butterfly effect at its finest, wouldn't you say?" He sharpens his gaze over her shoulder. "Or perhaps we should ask *him*?"

Skyla and I follow his eyes to find a dark figure lingering in the corner of the viewing window. I recognize those wide shoulders, that dark cape-like coat he's chosen to cloak himself in.

"Demetri," I grumble.

"Of course, he's here." Skyla lets out a heated sigh. "He is the father."

Another group of men step over to the viewing window, closer to the center of the show, and I'm quick to recognize the one closest to the glass, with the most jubilant look on his all-too-familiar face.

"And there's Barron." I lift a hand as if to wave even though he can't see me—even if he could, his prideful gaze would never pull away from his precious son. "That man is the only father Gage Oliver will ever accept as his own."

"You sure about that?" Skyla whispers as Demetri lifts his chin, those tar-colored eyes rising in our direction. And just when we thought we might actually blend in with the scenery, he pins us with his stare and offers a brief three finger wave.

"I've got a finger I'd love to show him." Skyla lifts her hand—but just before she lets the bird fly, the scenery goes fuzzy, and Dudley has us off and running once again through time and space. But the scent of Gage as a newborn still clings to us. It holds the scent of hope, nothing at all close to destruction as Dudley has suggested. No, Gage Oliver doesn't have an evil bone in his body, and to Demetri's chagrin he never will.

"Where to?" My voice sounds distant, disembodied, and wholly not my own.

"As close to hell as any of us will ever get," Dudley thunders, and I land with a thud over the cold mattress in my bedroom at Whitehorse. I pick up my phone and text Skyla.

Everything okay on your end?

She texts right back. **I'm home. The boys are here. Gage just left.**

My heart breaks at the thought of Gage making his exit upon her arrival. It's as if in a small way they've both accepted this new divide as the new normal. They shouldn't. They're meant to be together. **What do you think that interstellar field trip was all about?**

A bubble of dancing ellipses lights up as I wait for her response. What in the hell do *I* think it meant? Hell if I know. Dudley is just as good at head games as Candace is. Yes, she fished me out of the past. Yes, she favors me over Gage, but only because she thinks Skyla and I can move

Celestra forward to where it needs to be—and ironically, that would be right where it is, sans the disturbance in the force otherwise known as Wesley.

I don't know. But one thing is for sure. I feel closer to you than ever. My mother handpicked you as my suitor. Liam sacrificed everything to get you to where you needed to be—in my world, on this island right by my side. All the signs in the universe always seem to point to you, Logan Oliver. You say you love me more than the heavens love the sun and the moon, but the heavens, the sun, and the moon, and all of their affection are no match for the bond the universe has secured for us. Time may have framed us in two different tiers, put us in two different places on the planet entirely, but destiny stepped in and moved the heavens and her precious heavenly hosts just to bring us together. I can't help but think we are so very special. We are meant to be. We are willed to be. We will be. After all, my mother always gets what she wants.

Tears run down my cheeks as I stare at her words. The poignant irony of the very last line. If she had omitted that last doomed sentence, I would have thought it was poetic gold—something to pen in calligraphy and frame for generations to marvel. But those last few words, those barbed truths make the very bond between us seem questionable at best.

I slip the phone onto the nightstand and stare up at the darkness, up past the ceiling, past the stratosphere, and into Ahava where that twisted celestial being wrings her hands over what comes next in this earthly game of chess she's indulging in.

Skyla and I are pawns. That's all we've ever been. But is that all we will ever be?

I'll be damned if I let that happen.

Candace Messenger broke a few hundred celestial rules to get me where I am today. Maybe it's high time I break a few rules of my own to make sure my destiny, that of my nephew and the great love of our lives don't come to ruin just to please the powers that be. No. I think it's time we went off the rails to ensure we come to a very amicable end of our own choosing.

But who would I pair Skyla with? Gage—or me?

That is the question.

That is always the damn question.

When the idea came to me to throw a big party as a way to commemorate the end of a bowling era, it never occurred to me that I would have strict fashion guidelines dictated to me by Lexy. She's neatly laid out a pair of ridiculously loud parachute pants on the bed for me, along with something that looks like a fish net to be worn as a shirt. And as if that wasn't enough fashion-based humiliation, she's set out a gold sequined glove—just the one, of course.

"No," I flatline as both she and Kate observe from the door expectantly. Lex was so eager for me to see my special gift she hauled me up here in haste. "Trust me, I'm fine the way I am." I hold out my arms so they can both garner an appreciation for my Levi's and flannel combo. "I'm pretty sure jeans were standard fare in the '80s. In fact, I know they were. I've brushed up on my John Hughes' movies this past week just to verify the fact."

Kate titters because she knows it's true. She sat right there next to me as we downed one after the other as if they were neon-coated chocolate confections. Ezrina has her head secured about as good as it's going to get, and Kate's resigned to the fact she'll have to wear a scarf for her remainder of time here. Speaking of which, I need to talk to Skyla about our dear, once headless friend. Kate has no real right to be here. I didn't realize Skyla's guilt over the fact she inadvertently took Kate's life ran so deep. Candace can't be pleased with this—and God knows if Candace is pissed, we're all doomed to a life of frustration.

Lexy grinds her teeth. Come to find out, it's something she does quite often when she doesn't get her way, and the more she hangs out with me, it's quickly becoming a habit. "Wear the shirt. It's the least you can do to fit in. It's your party, Logan. You can't be the host *and* a killjoy." Lexy's hair is standing on end as if she stuck her finger in a light socket and then deep-fried every last follicle in a vat of oil just to complete the look. She's wearing a hot pink dress that makes my eyes bleed for a pair of '80s-inspired Wayfarer sunglasses, and her neon green shoes add the right amount of garishness that the decade requires.

"I was born a killjoy." I snap my keys off the dresser along with my wallet and phone. "You two ready to head out?" I lead us downstairs and note Ezrina and Nev's sedan is already gone from the carport.

Kate comes up next to me and gives a quick thumbs-up as she pulls a lipstick from her purse. Lexy has her dressed like a homeless woman who happened to fall into a pile of lace and black rubber bangles. Kate's voice box isn't quite up to snuff, so in her defense, her ability to protest the clown outfit was greatly diminished.

"I'm ready," Lexy says to her reflection as she dusts the tip of her nose with powder. "You know, this is officially our debut as a couple."

Kate and I exchange a quick glance. Apparently, even someone who's been clinically dead for the last few years realizes this thing with Lex just isn't happening. In fact, the only person on the planet even capable of fostering that delusion is Lexy herself.

"Lex." The tone in my voice says it all and manages to elicit an eye roll from her in the process.

"You're just not up to speed on how things work." She gives a quick wink to Kate as we step out and I lock up after us. "I practically live here, Logan. Even you have to admit that there's something brewing between us."

"I have a habit of taking on boarders in the event you haven't noticed."

Lexy roars with a laugh as she takes a step toward the truck.

"We're taking the Mustang tonight." There's a touch of pride in my voice as we head over and climb on in.

"Are you kidding?" Lex scoffs. "We look like assholes. This car is a deathtrap."

I choose to ignore Lex's sentiment. I love the Mustang. The scent of the past lingers here, fresh, unable to dissipate, and I appreciate the hell out of it. My father loved this car as much as I do. Up until I met Skyla, my heart lived in this ode to vinyl and the past. The engine roars to life with the enthusiasm of a lioness about to devour her prey, and I back out slowly with one eye on the bowling alley and the other on the road. The bowling alley may be across the street for the most part, but the road is wide and long and it's not fun to walk, let alone in heels for the girls. Hell, I much prefer the shuttle service to the front door myself.

A few cars already litter the parking lot—Ellis' monster truck and Brielle and Drake's new econo clown car that's small enough to fit in my back pocket. I'm glad they're there. I want everyone I've ever known to set foot in that place one last time. Bree begged me to let her decorate. As much as I want this old place to go out with a big bang, the last thing I wanted was for Bree to crop-dust it with oddball decorations. Humiliating the poor place before I chop it off at the balls seems too cruel of a fate for the spot I've come to know as my second home, but I relented, and sure enough, judging by the old vinyl records hanging from every free space I spotted earlier in the day, the neon flashing lights, she's crop-dusted the shit out of it.

The rain starts in as we make our way inside, and as soon as we crest the arcade, my stomach sinks. This is it. The last normal hours of operation.

"I'll line the doors with wrapping paper so we don't get any looky-loos!" Lex volunteers as she stalks off toward the kitchen. "And I'll make sure to put a note outside letting everyone know we're closed for a private event!"

"Sure." I glance at the meager crowd already wrapping up their final game, taking off their shoes. I've already decided to trash those old, worn-out leather scuffs. Hopefully, when I reopen in the fall—God willing—I'll actually have enough cash left over to start off with a pristine supply of fresh shoes. I'm not proud of the fact that some of those leather monstrosities have been around as long as the bowling alley has. I used to romanticize it. I couldn't take any of the shoes out of commission because my father, my mother might have worn them on their feet. The feet that the Counts saw fit to burn to ashes. My stomach churns at the thought.

Bree jumps in front of me with just the right amount of exuberance on her face to pull me out of my morbid funk.

"Winner, winner, chicken dinner!" she shrills a little too loud. "My playlist is going to like totally rock the house." She gives a hard wink, exposing strata-like layers of yellow and pink eye shadow. She's decked out from head to toe in a Madonna-inspired bustier with cones for tits and a skirt so short it requires a double take to verify its presence.

"That's great. I'll gladly let you be the DJ, and I'll play bartender tonight." I give a wink right back.

"With those shit sodas you serve?" Bree has been after me for years to fix the syrup lines that lead to the drink machines. "You may have wasted our youth feeding us your bullshit, but the sober buck stops right here, buddy. Don't worry. My man has you covered." She nods toward the shoe rental, and I'm horrified to find an array of tall amber bottles, one svelte white bottle with the word *vodka* etched into the glass. "We're playing with big kids tonight, Oliver. Consider it a parting gift. I'll even give you half the take."

"The take? This place is headed for the wrecking ball, my friend. Keep every last dollar for yourselves. I've never made more than a dime here. Why start now?"

Bree zips off toward the newly minted bar, and I spot Coop coming in so I head on over.

"Where's your better half?" I glance past his shoulder, but the entry sits empty.

"Trying to catch up to your better half." He gives a shit-eating grin, and it dissipates just as quick. "I talked her into maintaining a friendship with Skyla. She's still pretty pissed about Chloe. Maybe she'll find out what the hell that's about. Have you cracked that code yet?"

"Nope." I shake my head at this alternative version of myself. Coop looks like he could be my brother. "As far as I can tell, it's not happening anytime soon either. Skyla's pretty pissed about a lot of things—what Chloe's put her through, apparently, isn't on the list anymore." I know that's not true, but to the naked eye it feels about right. "Can I get you something? Pizza, soda? Jameson?" I tick my head over to where Drake is shaking up a cocktail like a seasoned pro.

"I'm good." His demeanor hardens as he folds his arms across his chest. "Ezrina's been acting strange lately. Have you noticed anything odd going on?" His eyes narrow in on mine, and I can't tell whether or not he's calling bullshit on the fact I know about that Laken lookalike she's Frankensteined to life.

"She and Nev are having a baby." There. That alone accounts for half of Ezrina's mood swings lately.

"I heard." He frowns because we both know I've just offered up the wrong answer. Coop leans in, good and pissed. "You know. When Skyla said that you and Gage specialized in keeping secrets from her, I assured her there must have been a damn good reason each and every time." His voice is low, but you can feel the anger shaking just beneath the surface. The corners of his eyes crease with a controlled sense of rage, the same way mine have been known to do. "Are you keeping something from me, dude?"

It's like he's got a sixth sense, and a part of me doesn't understand why the hell I'm keeping anything from the guy. Coop has been a great friend. Hell, at this point, he's family. I take a breath, ready to spill what I know, and he gives a hard shove to my chest.

"Go to hell, man." He blows past me and hits the exit before I can stop him.

Shit. I pull out my phone, and just as I'm about to text him to get back here, in walks my tall, dark, and dangerously good-looking nephew. His hair is slicked to a shine, and he's decked out in a suit. A thin bright blue tie pops off his dress shirt, and those sharp-looking shoes finish off the polished look on him. There is no doubt in my mind Gage Oliver is gunning to get laid. Skyla is in for it, and she hasn't even hit the door. A knot settles in my stomach because a small selfish part of me wondered if the cold front was something that might last. And just as fast as that nosediving sense of self-pity comes, it dissipates. I want Skyla with Gage. They've come too far, have too many children to give up now.

Before I can head over to him, Graham Smite comes over and offers me a congratulatory pat on the back. "Why so forlorn, young son?"

It's odd to hear him crown me with the youthful moniker since he looks to be in his early twenties himself. I know for a fact both he and his twin brother died from dysentery a couple of years apart.

"I'm fine." I try to shake Skyla out of my head.

"Skyla?" He gives my hand a quick squeeze before letting go. He does have Celestra lineage, so it only makes sense he got the green light into my shitty subconscious. "She is a looker. Married though from what I hear—and not to you."

"All of the above is correct." I grimace over to Gage who happens to be waylaid himself a moment with Ellis and Giselle.

"But you love her." He folds his arms over his enormous chest. Both Graham and his brother played ball for old Paragon High when the island just had the one school. "I once loved a young lady myself." He gives a wistful shake of the head. "My brother had his sights set on the young lady as well."

"What became of it?" The truth is, I'm almost afraid to ask. Two brothers, one girl. The equation sounds a little too close to home for my liking.

"One of us had to cave, and I figured it should probably be me. I'm the oldest. And I love my brother. I knew she would make him very, very happy." A forlorn look of his own infiltrates his features. "And she did for the short remainder of his life."

"That was very noble of you." My heart breaks for the dude even though all parties are well past their hormonal wedded and bedded years.

"Great love requires great sacrifice." He pats my shoulder once again. "But she's here tonight. And I'm not feeling so generous anymore." He gives a sly wink. "If I'm smart, I'll steal a kiss later this evening." He dances off into the crowd, looking as if he's got the world in the palm of his dead hand. And in a way, he does. All rules of engagement were released once that golden cord was severed—and as it is in eternity, it's party time from here on out.

Gage comes up and offers me a mock sock to the gut.

"What's up?" I slap him five and pull him in. "Rumor has it, women go crazy for a sharp dressed man."

"I see what you did there." He offers a quick sock to my arm before stepping back.

"And I see what you did *there*." I flick his tie into his face. "That color really sets off your eyes, sweetheart. Smooth move."

"It's lambskin." He frowns down at it. "Dad let me borrow it. He said it was all the rage back in the day."

"Which dad?" I lift a brow. "Kidding."

Gage lands another sock to my arm, and this one hurts, assuring me he put some effort into it this time.

"Watch it, man. You're packing some serious muscle." I rub my arm down to demonstrate the fact. "Where's Skyla?"

"She's coming with Chloe." His demeanor darkens on a dime. "Where the hell was Coop running off to? He blew right by me without bothering to say hello."

"I don't know. I think I pissed him off. He wanted to know what was up with Ezrina."

A hand crashes over Gage's shoulder, interrupting our conversation, and we look over to find his lookalike Wes.

"Dude." Gage pulls him into a partial embrace as if it was a reflex, and my gut grows hot with rage. I don't mind Gage acknowledging the fact Wesley is his brother. Hell, I don't mind the occasional obligatory visit to the Transfer, where at least he can visit his niece, but this genuine connection the two of them seem to have going is really starting to eat at me. I don't for a minute think Wes is going to replace me in some moronic way, but seeing them buddying up to one another, whispering something about a Barricade meet and greet right in front of me is really starting to piss me off. "Glad you could make it." He gives his big bro the once-over, and oddly enough they're dressed to match, sans the bright blue tie—Wesley's is green. "Looking sharp, man."

"Thanks." He glowers at me a moment. "Have you guys seen Ezrina?"

"She's the woman of the hour." Gage cranes his neck before coming up empty. "Coop blew out of here a few minutes ago looking for her, too." He winces my way as if to ask if he should go there. "You know about her, don't you?" He cuts that steely gaze into his brother's eyes, and Wesley flinches.

Knew it. "You're behind this, aren't you?" I give him a hard shove to the chest just like Coop did me. "You sick fuck."

Wes snatches my wrist and lands my arm up against my chest, crooked and ready to break. "Who said you could touch me?"

"Whoa." Gage steps between us. "This isn't how this night goes down." He looks to me. "It's your last night at the old place with friends. Don't get worked up so fast." He shoots a dirty look to Wes. "And *you*"—he sighs with exasperation as one can only do when dealing with Wes— "what the hell are you doing? Who is that chick? And how the hell did you get Ezrina to agree to it?"

Wes steps back and offers a weary look around before stopping short at something just over my shoulder. "I found what I was looking for. Excuse me." He takes off in the direction of the kitchen, and I catch Nev scowling at him as Wes heads his way.

"So much for getting a straight answer out of him." I yank Gage in by the tie. "Get a straight answer out of your new little buddy asap, and I want to know what excuse he gives you as soon as it leaves his mouth. I don't like Coop pissed at me." I toss his tie in his face and press out a dry smile. "I'm betting you'll score some serious points with Skyla if you crack this code before midnight."

Gage shifts from foot to foot as he searches out his wicked brother. "I'll get right on that." He starts to head out and backtracks. "Text Skyla and make sure she's coming, would you?"

"Will do." He takes off, and I shoot our favorite Celestra a quick message. **Where are you? We need to party like it's 1989.**

It takes less than five seconds for her to fire right back. **That's not how the song goes. And I'm just about ready. Laken just got here. See you soon!**

My heart gives an irregular thump at the thought of seeing her—the way it always does when I'm about to see Skyla. A despicable part of me finds it mournful that Gage is determined to land in Skyla's bed again, but if his dick gets its way, I know for a fact all will be right with the world tonight. His world at least.

A couple of girls walk by tittering my way with their lashes lowered, their fingers loosely covering their lips. It's the flirtatious bunch from the old Walsh house. And behind them an entire crowd migrates through the doors. I spot Holden Kragger and a couple of girls with him. I know Skyla mentioned Emerson was back, and holy shit, there she is. The Kraggers, in addition to Holden's new wife, who I haven't had the misfortune to meet yet, haven't been holing up at Gage and Skyla's new place like the rest of them.

Speaking of the dead, the last of them trample their way in with the same enthusiasm I've witnessed these past few days. It's safe to say they're enjoying the hell out of their jaunt back to reality, albeit a short one. Just as I'm about to head over and lend Ellis a hand with whatever mischief he's gotten himself into, a familiar looking girl catches my eye as she hovers near the arcade. I give her a sideways glance and do a double take.

It's Laken.

I glance down at the text Skyla just sent. Laken is with her.

But Laken is here.

I give a friendly wave as I head on over, and the girl's eyes grow wide, her face just as blank as it was a moment ago. Maybe she doesn't recognize me. And why would she? It looks as if Ezrina's science project wandered away from the lab.

My fingers dance across my phone as I text Coop to get his ass back here right fucking now.

I walk slowly, casually toward the arcade, and the girl tries to bolt just as I come upon her and snatch her up by the wrist.

"Leaving so soon? How about a quick dance?" I swoop her in close and try to lead her to the office, but she jets out the front door into the paper white fog, and I bolt right after her.

It looks like I'm about to unlock this secret long before Gage. Of course, Skyla will be grateful, and that alone makes me run just a little faster through the parking lot.

The girl trips over a concrete block, and I dive in time to break her fall. I twist my body around so that my back takes the blow from the concrete and her mouth lands a hair away from mine. Her eyes, that face, she is the exact representation of Laken. I must admit, Ezrina is capable of damn good work.

"I don't believe we've had the chance to meet." I wrap my arms around her, making it impossible for her to escape my grip.

Laken's twin closes her eyes as she lands a weary hand over my chest. "Wrong, Logan—we've met before. You know exactly who I am."

4

Let the Bodies Hit the Ground

Skyla

Paragon is known for its long gray days, for the fog that pulls up its skirt and sits over the face of the island, evergreens that stretch their naked limbs high into the sky allowing the night air, the sky to lick at its most intimate spaces. There have been many tender aches in my young life, but none of which rival this primal urge to leash my body to that of my husband's and atone for our sins during a long night of electric passion. I blame it all on those damn Kegels.

"Geez, Messenger, how long has it been since you've gotten laid?" Chloe throws a stuffed bunny at me, and I catch it before it nails my face. Her hair is crimped and teased, her makeup so neon her lips glow incandescent, but it's that old-school sweater dress in an eye-popping rainbow of geometric shapes paired with a giant chunky belt that sets off her look—an homage to a tacky era gone by.

"Twelve weeks, three days, and forty-two minutes, seventeen sexually explicit seconds," I say, dusting my face with powder before snarling at myself in the mirror. But the fog, the island seems to call to me, and I can't help but set my gaze on the evergreens, the world outside my window. Laken texted to let me know she was parking and would be up in a second. I was a little relieved when her name popped up on my phone. For a second, I thought she cut me off for good.

"Stop glaring outside and panting like a dog. It's not a good look. I can smell the desperate on you. Put some '80s perfume on and get in the mood. It'll cool you off." She picks up a pretty pink bottle of Love's Baby Soft my mother gifted me for my last birthday and proceeds to douse me in it.

"Would you stop!" I scoop up both Nathan and Barron in a panic and make a break for the hall. "Perfume is nerve gas for babies in the event you didn't get the memo," I bark as I stalk down the fecal-stenched stairs, leaning against the wall with every other step—a trick that's helped me from toppling with my precious little babes a time or two. There's no way in hell I'd let Chloe take one from me. She'd probably land the poor kid on his head, on purpose, of course. I may be keeping my enemy close, but I'm not blind to her old tricks. In the celestial mother of all ironies, it's Chloe and I who are *until death do we part*. In the end, Chloe's loyalty, albeit bought at a price, is virtually indestructible.

"Listen, Messenger"—Chloe pulls me back by the elbow as we hit the foyer—"you and I made a little deal. It's time we start polishing the details of that payoff."

A ripe anger burns through me. "You are alive. You are in my home, inches from the two beings that represent my beating heart. You are allowed in my presence." A fire blazes from my eyes. "And yes, you and I will both get what we are looking for."

Those dark soulless pits of hers scour my features. "You're not really looking for anything from me, are you, Skyla?"

"Just what I asked."

A sharp knock erupts, and both boys startle in my arms. Chloe opens the door only to find Laken, whose smile quickly sours.

"I thought we could go together." She offers a sharp look my way. Laken has completely embraced the '80s radical color explosion with her psychedelic print miniskirt and mesh net top that accents the hot pink bra underneath. Both Chloe and Laken have gone all out, and all I could piece together was an acid washed jean dress I pulled from my mother's closet. It's tight in all the right places, squared off neck, the hemline shorter than anything I could ever envision my mother leaving the house in.

"Yes, for sure. Of course, we can go together. Chloe will have to tag along." I give a quick wink to the demon to my left. Unfortunately for me, Chloe will be tagging along a lot longer than just one night. As soon as I witnessed Gage Oliver's demise the night of the christening, I knew my hands were tied. Chloe may not realize it, but she's the most valuable weapon in my arsenal. In a world where I can't get a single being to do my bidding, I knew I could rely on my equally desperate and out of control nemesis to step across enemy lines—especially since we have the very same mission in mind. Our goals may not have always lined up, but when it comes to Gage Oliver, we are one in the same, obsessed to a fault, desperately and hopelessly in love with him. Not even our Celestra bloodlines could bond us in the way that Gage has. Apart from one another, Chloe and I were wayward, but together we are a force unstoppable, a nightmare, a blessing, a reign of holy terror—two saviors riding on our white steeds. I'm no fool. I realize Chloe has a heart of destruction when it comes to me and perhaps my family. But for now, with her tethered to my hip, chained to my neck, we are safe from all of her reprehensible harm. I should have done this years ago, but years ago she wasn't nearly as helpless as she is now. Neither was I.

"Well, hello, you handsome little men," Laken coos to the boys as she gives Barron a quick tickle, and they both break out into deep, husky belly laughs that vibrate through me like a current of pure joy. "Oh my God! They're darling!" She scoops up Barron and touches her nose to his. "I'm in love."

"You better watch out. They're highly addictive." I give Nathan a quick kiss to the forehead. "I can't get over how happy they suddenly are. All they do now is smile and laugh." And my heart melts each and every time.

Chloe grunts at the thought. "And shit and suck on your tits. I've witnessed." She sneers over at Laken. "You're not missing much."

"Why are you here?" The joy quickly drains from Laken's face. "Skyla, I might have to talk to Dr. Booth and have you committed."

I bark out a laugh and spin on my heels toward the family room. "It wouldn't be the first time. Come on, let's hand these chunky monkeys off for the night. My sisters are pulling diaper duty until I get back."

We find Mom doing an art project with Misty and Beau while Tad huddles over a stack of bills along with them at the kitchen table. But it's that odd speck sitting prominent on Mom's left cheek that calls my attention.

I nod over to her. "I think you've got a chocolate chip stuck to your face." I brush my cheek in an effort to navigate her to the chocolatey confection.

She swipes the air with her hand as if it were no big deal. "It's a new look I'm trying out." Her eyes swipe over to Tad a moment before reverting back to me. "I hear a well-placed mole drives men *wild*," she whispers with glee.

"A what? Drives men *what*?" Why the hell would my mother find it suddenly necessary to beguile Tad with what amounts to a pre-cancerous lesion on her face? I scan my mind for any woman with prominent moles, and all I can think of are a few supermodels. Sure, it's hot as hell, but on them it's natural. On Mom it just looks like a bird had a very unfortunate discharge. In fact, the only woman that comes to mind with a mole that size on the island is Dom—I suck in a sharp breath. Dominique Winters! Gah! No wonder my mother is whispering! She didn't want to arouse Tad's suspicions or apparently his penis! And *double gah*! The words *Tad's penis* just flitted through my mind! It makes me hate Demetri that much more for all the grief he's given me. Not only is my mother wasting her time trying to beguile him with a knockoff mole—trying to win him back from Dom the Dominatrix—but he's plummeted my mother into the hell of insecurity. If Demetri really loved her, he wouldn't give a demonic rat's ass whether or not she had a mole. And sadly, I suspect it's true. Demetri couldn't care less if she had any teeth either—and at this point, her brain is questionable at best.

I turn my attention to the family room where I find Mia on the couch with—oh shit.

"Rev?" I blink back in horror at the biker wannabe with his shorn head and dirty leather jacket that's probably crawling with germs and semen because God knows you can't wash leather. "Do you two have a date?"

"Yup!" Mia springs up and takes Nathan from me while doing a little happy dance. Her lashes look suspiciously long and luscious, and it's not until I note one sitting crooked do I realize they came from a box. Her makeup is garish, bright red lips, enough highlighter to signal to the moon. Mia *Landon* isn't looking to stay home and change diapers all night. "I'll be right here with these little dudes. Rev's helping me babysit."

"No way, no how." I pull Nathan right back. "Laken, hold on tight. There's no way I'm leaving these angels with this hot-to-trot duo decked out in Halloween costumes."

Rev gives that perennially bored look he's famous for. "Tell her I'm good with kids, Laken."

A breath gets caught in my throat. That's right! Laken and Rev are practically stepsiblings now that their parents have hooked up for the seemingly long haul.

Laken squirms a moment. "He really is. Lacy and Marky adore him."

Lacy is Laken's little sis, and Marky is Coop's.

"Traitor!" I gulp for air at how far the mighty have fallen. "Chloe, take Barron." Desperate times call for desperate bitches to assist me.

"No." Laken spins away from Chloe's purple claws. "Rev is going to do just fine. He's not a menace, I promise."

"Ha!" Tad leaps from his seat, waving a piece of paper in his hand. "He's exactly a menace. An expensive one at that."

Crap. It's never a good sign when Tad and I agree on something.

"That beast he dragged into the house is riddled with fleas! And now we need to tent the entire house!"

Mom shakes her head, rolling her eyes at how pathetic Tad is—even though I highly suspect he's right. "We have termites, Tad. It's an entirely different species." She looks to me. "When we tore out the poopy carpet on the stairs, we found rot leading straight to the floorboards. It turns out the entire house has been eaten from the inside out and we need to fumigate."

"*Gah!*" I clutch onto Nathan a little bit tighter. It sounds as if my mother and Chloe are on the same nerve gas page.

"Don't you worry about a thing." She lifts a glitter-covered finger at me. "Once we schedule the appointment, we'll all be forced to leave the house for three short days."

"I'm not going anywhere," Tad grumbles, falling back into his seat. "It's all just a ploy to get you out of the way so they can up and leave with your valuable treasures. I'm staying put."

Mom clicks her tongue. "They won't fumigate with you here. In fact, the paperwork says not even a houseplant can survive. We'll have to store all of our food in plastic bags."

"Just plastic bags?" I won't eat here for a year. "Dear God, it's going to be Chernobyl all over again." As if Gage turning to the dark side wasn't bad enough, the boys and I are going to lose all of our hair—forever.

Tad scoffs at the thought. "They're not getting rid of me, Lizbeth. I'll hide out. I'll prove all that gas-smash baloney is just a get-rich-quick scheme—off *your* jewelry."

"She has no jewelry," I say, stepping over. Mom is the most bling-deprived wife on the planet, no thanks to Tad's inability to provide her with an ounce of anything that sparkles and shines, sans the glitter she's covered with at the moment.

A row of miniature Mason jars filled with gold encrusted tubules catches my eye.

"What are we making?" I ask both Misty and Beau who flank my mother proudly, each busying themselves with the craft at hand. Misty proudly holds up a glob of elongated paste covered with glitter. "*Poopy!*" she shouts with pride. Her dark hair and those Gage Oliver blue eyes make me melt on cue. Damn Demetri for creating such perfect children.

"*Unicorn* poop," Mom corrects. "In fact, we can't sell it fast enough. I've got thirteen more orders just in the last half hour!"

"What?" I reach over and pick up a bottle of what appears to be glittered-covered turds floating in water and I hand it over to Laken for inspection. "Who's ordering this and why?" Clearly people have far too much spending money to ever be safe with.

"*Everyone.*" Mom tosses up her hands in the air and gold dust rains from her limbs.

"It's her new little hobby." Tad gives an arrogant grin. "I set up a shop for her on eBay, and all she does now is sell crap."

"Profitable crap," Mom is quick to correct. "I make about five bucks a bottle, and the buyer covers shipping. My little hobby is how we plan on paying for the fumigation we need to have done. Not to mention the fact I've cornered the market on glitter-covered fecal snow globes"

Oh, my dear God. There it is. Tad has finally driven my poor saint of a mother to the brink of insanity, and in order for her to give her children the most basic necessities in life, she now wades in shit full-time. Scratch that saint comment. Demetri has turned her into quite the devious vixen. One of these days I'm going to bust her balls over the fact Misty came from an out-of-marriage arrangement, but, tonight, like any other night, Demetri is just a means to an end.

"Why don't you ask Demetri for the money?" The words fall from my lips like rusted coins. "In fact, I bet if you asked for a new house he'd throw that in, too." Okay, so he may not be my favorite demon, but dear God if he could stop my mother from rolling in crap just to survive—a dollar or two from that devil wouldn't be a bad idea. Not that I personally would take a demonic dime from him. Asshole. Although technically, living in a house that Demetri paid for would amount to the same thing.

"You *know*"—Chloe picks up one of my mother's fecal treasures and gives it a quick shake—"unicorn shit is great and all, but vaginas are all the rage right now."

The room grows eerily silent as the entire lot of us secretly plots to muscle shut the talking vagina herself.

"*Vaginas?*" my mother practically whispers, but the labial intrigue on her face is unmistakable. My mother might have a tiny obsession with procreative parts in general so the intrigue is almost understandable. Almost.

"That's right." Chloe smacks the glorified Mason jar back to the table with a wallop. "Vagina pendants are sweeping the country. It's an iconic symbol of feminism, not to mention the curves and texture are practically a work of art."

The quiet hush continues to suppress the room as I gauge how worried I should be that Chloe seems to have a superior understanding of the vajayjay subject matter at hand.

"Vaginas, huh?" Mom's anatomical wheels are spinning as she looks to the ceiling. After all, profiting off pink parts is only a stone's throw from turds bathed in glitter.

"*Bagina! Bagina!*" Beau barks it out, inspiring a laugh from both Mia and Rev. Soon Misty joins in on the vaginal fun, and, swear to God, Tad's face just froze in an unholy grimace.

"Crap," Laken hisses under her breath. "We'd better get going."

"Yes." I'm quick to agree. God, I'm so embarrassed that Laken had to witness firsthand the lunacy that is my family. Who am I kidding? That lunacy is the norm. We overbreed, and come up with outrageously bad ideas while our financial means remain just above the poverty level. If my mother's life is any indication of where I'm headed I'll have eight kids before my twenty-fifth birthday, my boobs will be swollen milk jugs that everyone on the island would have had the displeasure to ogle by then, and I'll be filling Mason jars with glitter-covered poop because that's the way things work in our cult. "Chloe"—I growl over at her because it just so happens the she-devil and I are in a private cult of our own at the moment—"why don't you wait outside before you start a mini feminist revolution without meaning to?"

She clicks her tongue my way. "I more than mean to start a revolution. And every revolution I start, I plan to finish." Her dark eyes flit to mine as she takes off.

"That girl is a menace!" Tad barks.

Oh hell, I'm agreeing with Tad on every single point tonight.

"Maybe Chloe should be here with you when the fumigation begins." A girl can dream. I give my mother a quick wink as she takes the baby from me.

Mom takes the baby from Laken as well and doubles her pleasure as she bounces and coos the handsome boys in her arms. "Grumpy old Tampon doesn't mean any of that silliness." She nuzzles her nose to Barron's.

Laken gasps at the mention of Tad's quirky moniker.

"And on that note, I'll see you guys on the flip side." I give a quick wave.

"I'll keep the boys in my room tonight!" Mom shouts after me. "I want you to sleep in, Skyla! Preferably not alone."

My cheeks burn bright as Laken and I make our way toward the door.

"She's subtle." Laken gives a quick chuckle.

"She's also far too hopeful for her own good. Gage Oliver isn't getting laid tonight." The sweet spot between my thighs bucks as if it begged to differ—*begged* being the operative word. Damn Kegels.

Holy hell. My entire body catches fire at the thought of that boy running his tongue down every last inch of me. I do miss the view of his dark head at the base of my thighs. My breathing grows erratic as Laken, Chloe, and I make our way outside into the arms of the cool Paragon mist.

"You okay?" Laken presses her hand to my forehead as if reading a fever.

"She's fine," Chloe is quick to snark while gingerly removing Laken's hand as if she owned me. In a very real way Chloe does own me. "She's been misfiring orgasms for the last two weeks. Did you strap that diaper on like I told you to in an effort to keep the wild rivers from drenching your panties?"

"You're disgusting," I say as we head to Laken's car.

Chloe links arms with me as we stride down the driveway. "I'd offer to buy you a dildo, but since you have access to Gage Oliver himself, you and I both know it would be sacrilegious."

"She's right." Laken gets in and we follow.

Laken and Chloe don't agree on anything.

But they are right.

And both my uncontrollably wet vagina and I happen to agree.

The bowling alley's sign blinks on and off, a feature that isn't at all purposeful as much as it is a symptom of an electrical short in the system. The *L* in *bowling* has altogether given up. It had months ago, if not years. For the first time ever, I see the entire block shape building as a sad reminder of an era gone by, and deep in my heart I wonder if that's symbolic for Logan and me as well. I haven't given my white knight a sexual thought since our honeymoon ended—or at least not that I wish to acknowledge at the moment. Well, there was that one time—all those dreams when we thought Gage was gone last year, and then there was the—okay, hell, I've had a sexual thought or two toward the fair-haired Oliver, but that's not the point. I knew I

ADDISON MOORE

would be with Gage after Logan passed away, and I fell into his strong arms willingly and quick. But, technically, Gage and I are separated, perhaps forever, and dear God, I need a husband, past or present, to put out this fire heating up my panties.

My heart pounds unnaturally as we make our way inside. The bowling alley is lit in neon lights, streamers and vinyl records decorate the place at every turn. Bree mentioned Logan gave her carte blanche to do as she wished, and true to Bree fashion, she has successfully transformed the place from a struggling bowling alley to a struggling record store circa 1980-something.

"Cool." Chloe dons a pair of white shades as she bops her head to the Go-Go's who scream out their ode to the decade from the speakers. "Oh my fucking wow." She slides the sunglasses down her nose an inch to get a better look at whatever it is she's ogling.

I glance around at the thick crowd and am pleased to note that the graveyard revival peeps have all come out in number. I spot the Smite brothers, Casey, and a few of the cliquey girls that have been a hoot to hang out with. But I highly doubt Chloe finds the cemetery suicide squad drop-your-sunglasses-worthy.

"What's got your panties in a bunch?" Then I see it.

"Oh, Skyla." Laken sighs into the sight as if even she were taken aback.

There he is, hair as dark as a raven's wing, those lucent eyes the color of this spinning marble we're stranded on, the body of a linebacker, that grin rising in my honor filled with wicked and deliciously lewd intent. Holy hell. Heaven help me. It's clear all thoughts of bedding Logan Oliver have been violently wiped off the table.

Chloe takes a step toward him. "Gage Oliver does not fight fair."

Laken steps up next to her in an odd show of alliance. "Gage Oliver in a suit is quite the sight to behold."

Wesley pops up next to him, and she takes in a quick breath as if burned by a flame. "I'd better go find Coop." But her feet stagnate and she twists toward Wesley's comely frame instead. "Coop thinks Wes stole my virginity."

I'm pulled from my Gage-inspired trance a moment. "Coop stole it," I correct. I know this because Laken confided in me ages ago during one of our many fireside chats down at Rockaway Beach. I specifically remember because I was thrilled to know Wes was shut down from the one thing he really wanted—that most sacred part of Laken. If Wes wasn't willing to leave the Counts for her, then he certainly didn't deserve to make it all the way to home base. And honestly, if Wes would rather live without Laken than leave that coven of wickedness, he really doesn't deserve her.

"No, Skyla." She winces. "Wes stole it." Her voice is riddled with regret. "I just wish he didn't. I guess we all have our regrets in life." She takes off, and Chloe falls into view. My own personal regret.

"Hear that? Wesley *stole* it." Chloe nuzzles her shoulder against mine as we glare at the menace in question together. "And all this time he's been plying me to morph my features before he fucks me because of his desperate ache to have her. He's a *liar,* Skyla."

I swallow hard as both he and Gage head in this direction. "Maybe he is the liar in the equation." Laken didn't lose her virginity to Wesley—or at least in that point in time. "Or maybe he's just the time traveling vagina snatcher?"

"What?" Chloe sounds affronted by the fact her husband's coital habits span both time and, well, vaginas. "Wesley." Her voice strums out his name, husky with lust.

"I'm so damn proud of him, I might actually bed him tonight myself."

So much for disappointment.

"Hey." Gage zips forward in that hot, very, very fucking hot zoot suit of his. The scent of his familiar cologne sets my senses ablaze and, oh my God, I am done. There's an ache deep in my belly for this boy I just can't deny.

I zoom past him without so much as a hello, hardly able to catch my breath as an arm snags me to the side.

"Here she is!" Brielle pulls me into a strong embrace. "My one and only *favorite* best friend!"

I step back with a stunned smile on my face, my body still quivering to completion from the Gage-gasm that just took place. Emily, Lexy, Nat, and Kate stop bobbing to the music long enough to acknowledge me.

Lexy bares her fangs my way. "Logan drove us in the Mustang. You would have loved it."

My upper lip twitches at her ridiculous stab at driving me insane with jealousy. Of course, I don't care that Logan drove her in the Mustang he gifted me for my sixteenth birthday. The very one *I* almost lost my virginity in to *him*.

"Oh? Is he burning that too next week?" I couldn't help it. She practically walked into that one. I lunge over and yank Kate into a quick embrace. "You look great." I pull back and wince. "How are the vocal cords doing?" I feel terrible that she's stuck with a bum set of pipes.

"Better." It comes out in a hoarse whisper, and I'm thrilled to hear it. Maybe now we can get somewhere with that bizarre piece of news involving Emma. Not that declaring Emma trouble is any real news. I've known that for the last three years solid at least. "You look great, too."

"Thanks. But you are seriously glowing tonight. I'm so happy you're back." Her blonde hair hardly looks damaged after lounging in a casket for as long as it did. In fact, Kate looks just as alive and ready to thrive on the dance floor as any of the girls here tonight. "You all look great." I make a face at Lex. "Even you."

"Be nice." Chloe wraps her arms around me from behind and rocks me to some old Madonna song. "I've seen those pictures she's taken of your monkeys. I've always suspected Lexy was good to have around for a reason."

"I am good to have around." She gives a thankful nod to the Bitch Squad leader herself. "Logan is especially appreciative. Our relationship is moving along nicely, thank you very much. Maybe you can talk some sense into Messenger, Chloe. Logan is just waiting for her blessing." She looks to me, pleading as if she honestly believes her own bullshit. "You have your man, Skyla. You can't have mine."

Chloe laughs as her chest rumbles against my back. "Skyla can have all the men she wants, Lexy. You and I have always known that. If Skyla wants to fall on her knees to enjoy Logan as an afternoon snack, sit over Dudley's lap during school hours, and bed Gage nightly, it's her right and prerogative as our fearless leader. After all, it's her ovaries that will produce the heirs to both the Fem and Celestra legacies."

Kate's face contorts. "Is that what's happened since I've been gone?" she whispers her loudest.

"*No.*" I wave off the foolish idea, but my body embroils in heat at the visual. A bite of Logan's tender loins, sitting on Marshall in all the right places, and Gage—letting him take me aggressively from behind, on top, sideways, the thought sends me panting to an all-new high.

Em grunts at the sight of me. "She's exiled herself in a self-imposed celibacy—hence the heavy breathing." Em's hair is in a perfect black rainbow over her head, and set against her paper white skin it creates a haunting contrast.

"Geez, take your husband home tonight, Messenger. Horny isn't a good look on you."

"Chloe trained Ember to say vagina." It blurts out of me as a means to distract the masses from my own smoldering girl parts. God, Ember wasn't even in the room during that three-ringed circus Chloe was conducting, but I'm sure, soon enough, she'll join the feminist choir.

Em grunts as if holding back vomit. "I'm going to break your neck, Bishop."

And just like that, Em drags Chloe off while Lex discusses the latest fashions with Kate and our quasi-West reunion disbands.

Nat leans in. "Thanks, Messenger." Her arms fall over me hard as she offers up a caustic hug. "You gave Pierce back to me—and on top of that you gave me Kate."

"Yes, well, I also unleashed far too many Kraggers into the world for it to ever be safe again, so don't go thanking me yet. Things never end well with the K clan running amuck on the island." I give a quick pan of the vicinity for the Kraggers in question and spot Emerson slam dancing with a couple of the dead on the dance floor. "Sure, they seem to be on the right side of the celestial law at the moment, but, let's face it, their father is one of my least favorite wild cards, and who knows what will happen in the name of family solidarity." Wait. Did she say *Pierce*?

Just as my mouth falls open to correct her, Pierce Kragger himself pops up and drapes an arm around her shoulders. He looks every bit as nefariously handsome as he should—considering he's really Nev. *Right*?

"Hey babe." He offers Nat a nonchalant kiss before reverting his attention to me.

"Oh, no, no, no," I shake my head frantically. "Nev? Is that you? You're still in there, right?" I narrow my gaze as if trying to see beyond those pastel eyes, straight into his questionable soul.

He laughs with his hand pressed to his chest as if my words had the power to kill him all over again. And if it's Pierce, this may not be such a bad thing.

He grimaces. "Relax, Messenger. I heard about the ruckus and as soon as I found out Holden and Emerson were about to feel sunshine on their backs once again, I wanted in. Plus, it's for a good cause. I'm all for helping out our Nephilim brothers and sisters."

"First"—I hold up a finger still completely in the dark as to where the hell Nev is—"there is no sunshine on Paragon. And second, if you were still alive, I'm betting you would have sided with the Barricade."

"True and True. But I'm an optimist about the weather—and I'm dead, Skyla. I see the error of my ways. I'm siding with you. Your mother agreed, and here I am. Just touched down this afternoon."

My God you'd think he were transported here on a 747 rather than the Candace express. "And Nev?" I'm almost afraid to ask. Ezrina is going to slice me to ribbons if my mother saw fit to haul him back to paradise. Who's going to rub her feet and do an ice cream run at midnight? *Me*— that's who.

Pierce gives a quick glance over his shoulder. "He's here somewhere. I'm just a traveler. Sort of like a temporary Visa holder. My cellular structure isn't solid but I look every bit as strong as steel." He pounds his chest like a gorilla and his hand goes right through his shirt, each and every time. "She thought it'd be okay since the mission was to expose our people. What better way to expose them than with a real *live* ghost?" Both Nat and he guffaw as if it were the most hilarious thing.

Oh my God. My mother has gone rogue. And the beauty of her demented, *haunted* plan? She gets to pin it all on me. Shit. Just shit.

Pierce nods to someone in the back and gives a wild wave. "Man, it's like old home week." He lets out a whoop. "I'll be right back." He presses a rather wet kiss over Nat's lips that looks anything but ghostly.

"Don't worry, he's good, Skyla." Nat frowns into the crowd as if he weren't. "Especially good in *bed*." She gives a hearty wink my way. "Turns out he can be as rock solid as the next guy when he has to. Plus, this way, we don't need to use protection. I've never been so happy in all my life, and I owe it all to you. Really, I can't thank you enough."

"Whatever you do, don't thank me." My heart sinks for her. "I know how much Pierce and Kate mean to you, but they'll have to go back into the box soon enough. This little interdimensional playdate can't last forever. Once their mission is through, they'll have to resume their dirt nap."

Her lips rise to a scowl. "You really have a crap way with words, Messenger." She shudders—most likely due to the reality that dirt nap just invoked. "But I just want you to know that you have a friend in me for life." Her coffee-colored eyes hook to mine like she means it. "Anything you need, anytime. I'm there for you. If you're ever in a bind, I'm the one you can count on."

Chloe pops back up with a laugh caught in her throat. "And knowing Skyla, you'll be on call twenty-four seven!"

I glare at my faux best friend for a moment, and she's quick to sober up.

"Thank you, Nat," I say without taking my eyes off the malfeasance before me. "The first thing you can help me with is making sure Bishop stays away from me for the remainder of the evening."

Her mouth opens as if to protest, but Nat is quick to whisk her away to the other end of the dance floor, and Emerson wastes no time in slamming her body into Chloe's. I bet she'd like to bash her head in too for landing her on the other end of the great bodily divide in the first place. Anyway, once Holden gets within striking range, Chloe won't be able to stay regardless. I realize that Chloe and I have our covenant to tend to, but tonight, with those wild rivers rushing between my thighs, the last person I want touching me is the vagina queen herself.

"Ms. Messenger." The sexiest Sector on earth or in heaven pops up, and I'm stunned by his blessed by God looks.

My body bucks on cue, and I latch onto Marshall with my eyes shut tight and feel that electrical current rush from his body to mine. And oddly, quite shockingly, I can't seem to bring myself to the brink of this sexual disaster.

"You're losing your touch." I frown up at him as a breath hitches in my throat. "Marshall Dudley." I pull back to take him in, and I can't help but gasp. "You are resplendent tonight." That visual Chloe planted in my head with me utilizing Marshall like a sit and spin takes over, and my breathing is right back to borderline erratic.

"Skyla." Marshall pulls me into a partial embrace as we begin to sway to "Careless Whisper". "Dare I say I look my usual self. Above average without saying so, of course, but what pray tell has you so absorbed by my presence?"

"I'm in desperate need of some sexual healing." My cheek rubs over his rock-hard chest, and I give a little whimper. "It's all these damn hormones bottlenecking in my vagina just begging to shoot out like a Roman candle on the Fourth of July." Damn Kegels, too, but I leave that demented exercise out of the equation for now.

"Language."

"Technically, *vagina* is an anatomical term, popularized this evening by the big clitoris herself, Chloe." I wince up at him. "More anatomy, sorry."

He lets out a heavy sigh as he scans the crowd, his fingers press into my back ever so slightly, and it feels like a most welcome relief. I *need* to be touched, to be *licked*, and suckled in a fit of lust and passion.

"I can hear you," he rumbles.

"I was hoping." My tongue does a quick revolution over my lips as I look up at him and, dear God! Why am I doing my best to seduce Marshall?

"I am your husband," he's quick to point out. His chest adheres close to mine. It's so heavily sculpted I can make out the hard ridges of his abs from beneath his dress shirt. "And I do have a talent for spinning women over my lap." His lids grow heavy, his lips curve into a devilish grin. "I've been known to bend a few *over* my lap as well."

"Let me guess." My voice trembles out in a wave full of quivers. "They used to call you *The Punisher*?" The thought of Marshall doling out corporal punishment incites an extraordinary level of excitement in me. "I guess this is the part where I tell you I've been a very, very bad girl."

His lips turn down, making him look far too comely for words.

"You don't need to tell me, Skyla. I'm witness to the event myself." His eyes flit into the thicket of bodies next to us. "The great corpse revival is evidence of such wayward behavior. And answer me this." His gaze hardens over mine. This gruff, down and deliciously dirty version of my favorite Sector is alarmingly attractive. "All of these resurrections and where is your father?"

And just like that, my lady boner disappears. "Why are you dragging my father into this?" I give his ribs a quick pinch. "My father has been through enough." It's true. I had entertained the idea. A quick visit to L.A. to the cemetery that houses his remains is all that stands between the great beyond and having him here on Paragon with me. "I don't know what they'll do to them." Tears come to my eyes as I glance out at the crowd mostly comprised of long past souls. "But they're brave for volunteering. I'm not sure I would have chosen that option myself." I could only ask the question. It was the Holy Spirit who quickened them to respond. "They know the risks." My voice flounders as if questioning if I knew them at all. "And because of their bravery, my people will be sheltered for a very real shitstorm."

"Mmm..." Marshall muses in agreement rather than calling me out on the expletive. "Those you fear—they're here tonight, Skyla. Watching you." That drugged look in his eyes melts over me. Marshall has a way of making you feel as if you are the only person he sees. "They blend in so seamlessly, but they are thirsty for alien blood— Nephilim blood."

"Aliens." I mean to shake my head at the idea, but I shudder instead. "Wes has the planet so primed for some takeover from space, the world practically demands it at this point. It's so absurd."

"It's the unknown, Skyla." His fingers stroke my sides, sailing lower still, dangerously close to my quaking thighs. "It's the thought of what could be, how quickly they can come." He leans in, burying his mouth so close to my ear the entire left side of my face burns from his heat. "Imagine being penetrated quickly, invaded, while you lie open and vulnerable, being taken so violently, by force, bent to do their bidding while they ravish all you own, while they sink their mouth deep into the nexus of your—"

A body interjects itself between us, but it's too late as my body explodes into one uncontrivable quiver.

"I haven't lost my touch, Ms. Messenger," Marshall calls out as he takes off into the crowd. "Don't you forget it."

A hearty sigh escapes me as I open my eyes to find that the new arms wrapped around me belong to none other than Chloe herself.

"What are you doing here?" I sneer into the crowd and spot Nat locked in Pierce Kragger's tree trunk-like arms. "Never mind. I see Nat's traded you for something far more sexually satisfying."

A dark laugh remains buried in her chest. "Judging by that orgasm you just had, I'd say the same went for you and Gage. Marshall Dudley, Skyla? Really? And right here in the bowling alley. I knew you were a little perv."

"Oh, shut up. You and I both know I've been suffering from an entire string of mini earthquakes all week long." It's true. I've had an entire rash of vaginally-inspired seismic events in my husband's absence. "What is it? What do you want?" I try to untangle our limbs, but she latches on that much tighter.

"First, I saw that disgusting wanton look on your face for someone other than your better half, and I thought I'd be the one to smack some sense into you. And second—" She shoots someone to her right a dirty look, a regular occurrence for Chloe. Pausing to distribute her hatred is as natural as breathing with Bishop. I'm betting it's Emerson. The fact Chloe hates me doesn't make me special. "Oh, Skyla." Her finger traces my lips before she painfully flicks my nose. "You are special to me." That familiar drugged look enters her eyes, only she trades the sexual nature of it for something far fiercer. "We are beyond sisters, beyond lovers. Our Celestra bond has us bound together, intricately woven through the tapestry of our beings. We are the light and the dark, the other side of our own coin." Her brows lift a moment. "We are frighteningly one in the same, disposable to the powers that pursue us. And they do pursue us, Skyla. We are their pawns." Her fingers grip me, and my body electrifies with fright, with a strange delight and an eagerness to hear her pour out her truths. "We are the survivors. Our greatest enemies, our only true friends. We can no longer trust anyone outside of ourselves. For me to deceive you would be tantamount to deceiving myself. We have overcome the pettiness of who we were—and here we are, the new reality, the *best* reality. The most dangerous reality of all—together we have the power to move heaven and earth, destiny and fate. We have put destiny on a chain, called fate a cruel illusion to its face. We are the victors, Messenger." Her mouth inches closer to mine, those wicked eyes still knifing their way into my existence. Chloe is luring me into the dark pit of her soul, and I can feel the suction. Can't fight it. "We are the—"

Logan plucks her off me so hard and fast, he sends her twirling into the crowd.

"Wow." My hands find a home over his waist. "Eighties music really brings out Chloe's esoteric side."

"What was she saying?" Logan searches my features with those citrine lenses he sees the world through, and I melt at the sight of him.

"Is that a black eye?" I'm suddenly pulled out of the quasi-sexual moment as I inspect his swollen features. "And a fat lip? Logan, who did this to you?"

He inches back as I attempt to touch his cheek. "I don't want to talk about it."

"Talk about it, Oliver, or I'll rip this place to pieces looking for the dude who did this to you. I bet he's got two broken legs. There's no way the Logan Oliver I know would let anyone get away with ruining his perfect face."

His eyes close as he pushes out a sad, half-hearted laugh. "Trust me, I didn't lay a hand on the other dude."

"And that would be because?" God, if Gage did this to him, I'll bite off his nads. Right after I roll them around in my mouth for just a tiny bit. My body shakes just begging for more of the visual.

"That would be because it wasn't a dude, Skyla." Logan's shoulders sag with defeat. "I got beat up by a girl."

"What?" A tiny laugh bubbles in my throat, but I won't give it. "Who is she? God, it was Lex, wasn't it? I always knew she had a dark side."

"No." He pulls me in, and I can feel his body rumbling with laughter. "It wasn't Lex. Look, I don't want to talk about it right now. What had you locked in Chloe Bishop's arms?"

My hormones roar back to life at the sight of him, resilient, impervious to any form of satisfaction Marshall might have doled out. That orgasm, powerful as it might have been, has nowhere near taken the edge off.

He winces. "Never mind that. What are you thinking?" He gives my body a quick squeeze, and I can feel that coil tucked deep inside of me ratcheting up again.

"I need to get laid." I bite down hard over my lip. "I'm sorry," I mouth, this time near tears. "It's my body. I'm a ball of nerves, a jumble of hormones. And don't look at me like that. It's not my fault biology is trying to have its way with me. You can't judge me."

"I'm not judging you." He squints at me with a pained look in his eyes. "In fact, I get it. I've got needs, too. Trust me, I know how agonizing a little deprivation can be."

"You do? You *do!*" I practically shout it in his face. "Maybe we should help each other out?" God! What am I saying? "You know, just something quick and dirty in the office maybe?" Chloe was right. Even I can smell the desperation on me.

"*Skyla.*" He inches back at the offensive odor no doubt. Then his lips twitch, and a dark look comes to his eyes as if he's actually entertaining the idea. "I want to invite you to come to the bowling alley before the demolition."

"That sounds great. But as much as I would love to roll around every square inch of this place with you naked, I'm not sure I can wait that long."

He gives a dark laugh. "No, Skyla. I want to do exactly this with you." He sways his hips with mine in time to the music. "I want to give the bowling alley a proper private sendoff, and I couldn't think of a better person to say goodbye to the place with than you."

"Not even Ellis?" I tease. It's actually heartwarming the way Logan has taken our old friend under his wing.

"Not even Ellis." There's a tired look in his eyes that pains me. Logan is thirsty for so much more than something quick and dirty.

"I'll gladly be here to help you give this place a proper sendoff." My body adheres to his, and my hormones are taking the elevator up once again. "But first, how about a quick look at the schedule?" I nod toward the office. "Maybe you can bend me over the desk for old times' sake?"

He barks out a laugh. "I have never bent you over the desk, Skyla."

"Now is a perfect time to start."

He does a double take in that naughty direction. "On second thought, I think you might be right." Logan moves his hips over mine as he walks me backward, and my lips come shy of taking a bite of those ropey muscles buried in his neck. "A wise man once said to me that great love requires great sacrifice." He dots a kiss to my nose as he sends me sailing backward. "Have a great rest of the night, Skyla. I hope you find what you're looking for."

I smack into a wall of granite and turn to find the exact person I was hoping to avoid and shockingly it isn't Chloe—it's Gage.

"Hello, beautiful." His voice strums erotically deep, and somehow it doesn't come across like some cheesy pickup line. His lids hood low and there is no mistaking his sexual intent. But that desperate ache Gage has worn so long for me like a mask seems to be missing. This is a different version of my husband, one in control, one who knows what he wants and understands in no uncertain terms that he is about to get it.

"Look"—I try to untangle myself from his power grip—"I'm not in any mood to listen to what you might have to say." In truth, I fear the words that will spill from his lips. It has never been my stubborn streak rearing its ugly head when it comes to hearing him out as much as it's been a demon of fear with its wings spread over me like a plague.

"I'm not interested in talking to you," he says it quick and deliberate while his arms cinch over me like a vise. "I'm interested in doing other things with you this evening." His fingers press in just enough, and a spark jumps from him, igniting the fuse that runs straight to that aching part of me that's been so desperate to have him. In truth, not Marshall—not even Logan, could have satisfied this itch. My flesh simply craved my other half. The very flesh that abides in covenant with me for better or for worse, and we had certainly hit the very worse—a far lower of a plummet than either of us could have anticipated. "I miss you."

He comes in as if he's about to land a kiss over my lips, but he turns his head ever so slightly and rubs his scruffy stubble over my cheek, hard and searingly hot, and I give an audible gag as I gasp for my next breath. Hot damn. Gage Oliver has loosened the shackles of any politeness that might have resided in him. Tonight, this is a far more commanding, demanding, rough around the celestial edges version of him coming out to play—only he's not playing at all. Gage Oliver means fucking business, and the first order of fucking would be with, well—*me.*

"Tonight, you are mine, Skyla." He pulls back and presses those cobalt eyes into me. "We are more than the sum total of any definition the universe wants to crown us with. We are husband and wife. We have the ability to overcome whatever the powers that be decide to fling our way. We are the masters of our own destinies. We don't wear the coat of affliction when we're together. Instead, we dance across the stage of life as one." His hands grip me tight, and my body sizzles as it begs to have him.

"Wow," I say breathless, my lips inching closer to the home of his mouth. "Sounds like you and Chloe have been smoking from the same crack pipe."

His left dimple digs in deep as he expels the slightest rumble of a laugh. "I hear Chloe has kept my bed warm for me."

"She's not as skilled as you are, but you know what they say—keep your friends close and your enemies closer."

His head tilts to the side, and a harsh neon green light from above offers him an alien illumination. "That's funny. I'm going to keep you pretty close tonight."

"How close?" My body quivers as if begging for me to forgive him—or in the least overlook a few couple hundred indiscretions so we can finally get a little relief around here.

"Damn close." Gage bears down on me with a drunk gaze as he leans in and brushes his lips over my temple. His arms latch over my back, and he pulls me with a greedy aggression I have never seen before. "I'm going to come inside you, Skyla." His voice is heavy and heated in my ear, and I shiver. There's nothing like a good double entendre to twist the cords of desire even tighter. "There's no escaping this tonight. You will lie down in my bed. I am not taking no for an answer."

My entire body morphs into one giant heartbeat as that current he's unleashed jumps from my fingers all the way down to my toes. Of course, if I wanted him to take no for an answer, he damn well would but, well, I have far more sexually sinister intentions to deal with.

An arm pulls me off him abruptly, but my gaze remains locked over his. "*My* bed," I shoot right back just as a girl with ratted pink hair attaches herself to him and begins gyrating away as if he were a vaginal itching post.

Melody Winters. I'd recognize that sexual distress signal anywhere. But instead of pulling her off my man, my thumb curls around the ring on my finger as the stone lights up electric. She's already tried to pry it off my hand once. There's no way I'm about to give her another chance. This ring has power—straight from the throne of God, literally. I can't surrender it to her now. At this point, who cares about the fact Chloe swiped it from some long-deceased cranky granny? As soon as Melody called me a time traveling thief, I bolted from the Gas Lab. I had far better things to do than listen to someone berate my past sins. Yes, what Logan and I did was wrong—hey, how did she know about that, anyway? And technically, I was a murderer. A thief is far too light a title for what Logan and I pulled off all those tumultuous years ago. A thought comes to me as I stare down at the glowing stone, the exact color of Gage Oliver's eyes. I give a quick glance around and find the dicey Bishop herself laughing it up with her brother, and I speed on over.

"Chloe?" I land the ring between us like the stumbling block it's proving to be. "You said this ring was gifted to you. Who gave it to you?" I know whose rotten-toothed finger it once sat on, but I think it's time I get the low down and dirty details.

Her head immediately jerks to where Gage is currently trying to deflect Melody and her acrobatic endeavors, impressive as they might be—all moves my body wishes it could employ on him myself.

"Melody thinks *I* stole this," I hiss into Chloe's face.

Brody takes my hand and stares into it as the blue glow reflects off his eyes. "Melody Winters' ring?"

"It's mine now." I'm quick to retract my hand. "Speak up, Bishop. Why did that booty shaking skank accuse me of being a time traveling thief?" How would Melody know anything about that dive bar Chloe and I visited during our first nefarious light drive as a dynamic duo?

Her mouth opens, and for once Chloe Bishop is short on lies.

"Here you are." Gage lands his arm over my chest, grazing my nipples in the process, and a deep, guttural groan evicts from me.

Chloe's cheeks pinch with color as if it were her own nipples getting a little Oliver action. "I'd love to carry on a conversation with you, Skyla, but it looks as if you'll be busy for the rest of the night." She bites the air with the innuendo. "We'll solve the mystery of the stolen bling another time." She flicks her middle finger in the air as she carts Brody off. "Have enough fun for the both of us, would you?" She gives a sly wink, and just like that, the ring goes dark as if Chloe's ridiculous eyeball malfunction had the power to kill it like a light switch.

Gage presses his crotch into my back, and I feel him there, that hardness, that thick line of wanting impressing into my flesh.

"*Now*," he whispers hot into my ear, and my eyes close. The room spins beneath me, and when I open my lids, I find we're no longer in the loud, raucous bowling alley surrounded by big hair and leg warmers, but in the sanctity of our own bedroom.

"Impressive." I twist into him, and those daring eyes of his latch onto mine with this newfound bravado he's pumped full of.

The door slams and locks, and the dresser presses violently over the entrance as if on its own volition.

"I see you're going old school." My heart thumps hard because Gage Oliver is a show of force tonight. I knew his Fem standing afforded him a few powers here and there, but God Almighty, things have changed since we've been apart.

Music strums softly from some mysterious locale, the lights dim low, and the comforter whips violently from the bed.

"Wow." I bite down on the smile begging to break through. "That escalated quickly."

"Maybe so"—he caresses my cheek with the back of his hand, and my face begs to burrow against him—"but the rest of the events that unfold this evening will take place naturally, aggressively—over and over again."

A tiny whimper gets locked in my throat.

Here he is. Gage Oliver is back in my life after an absence of my own making. Do I want this? Maybe. Do I need this? Hell yes. Okay, so I may want this, too.

I pull his arms off my waist and take a full step back, our eyes still leashed together.

"Gage." I drop to my knees and bow my head ever so slightly. "Let me be the first to worship at your feet." I look up and meet with that face I've idolized as far back as that fated summer I landed on this island. It's true. I have always been his very first subject. Whether or not I want to accept it, Gage Oliver is royalty, my rival, my equal, my friend, and my lover. "You are the king."

And tonight, I am most definitely here to serve.

Gage

My adrenaline kicks in hard, and everything in me demands I tell her to get back on her feet, to help her up in the least, but the words, the actions necessary won't seem to come.

Skyla has just bowed down to me as if I were some deity, and normally I would question her sanity, want to laugh off the idea right along with her, but at the moment we're both serious as shit.

"You're not allowed to worship me." It's true. There might be a storm of insanity brewing in my life, but having my wife lost in worship in my honor isn't happening. I won't let it.

Her lips twitch with the idea of a smile. Her fingers quickly work my pants open, and I can't seem to move, don't want to.

"Oh, Gage." Her chest pumps with a silent laugh. "You of all people should realize how little control you have over anything." She pulls me from my boxers and lands her mouth over me without hesitating. My eyes close, my head pulls back in ecstasy—in *relief*, as she rides her mouth up and down the length of my dick. "Skyla." My fingers knit into her hair, and I clench it, pulling it as I move along to the rhythm that her mouth dictates. This is not how I envisioned this night would go. Actually, this is far better than anything I envisioned—although, in truth, it was me worshiping her, my mouth on that delicate part of her body, making her jump out of her skin with this same outrageous level of euphoria.

Skyla dips her hands into my pants and drags her fingernails down my legs, hard, and painful. Just the simple fact Skyla is dispensing the pain makes it feel sublime.

"Shit." I groan because for whatever reason the pain works for me. Skyla pulls me into her mouth harder, suctioning me down with a ferocity that suggests she has the power to eviscerate me right through my dick. Her hand trails up, and she cups the boys with a little too much vigor and it's game over. In one quick move, I scoop her up and pin her arms to the closet door.

Skyla's eyes round out as if trying to absorb how swiftly I've managed to land us clear across the room with her arms spread wide. She struggles a moment, but I'm unrelenting with my strength.

"Are you trying to hurt me?" The words grit from me as I take in her beautiful features. Skyla is a goddess, an alien being all unto herself, and I live to worship her. My lips twitch because my thoughts are my own. Despite the fact we're touching, flesh to beautiful flesh, I have rendered her powers inert around me. In all honesty, it's not to protect myself so much as it is to protect her. If I knew she were listening, I'd pour out my confessions nonstop, beg for her forgiveness until she gave it, and at the rate things are going with that, it might just be never.

"Yes. I want to hurt you." Her eyes enliven with fire. Her lips give the curve of a maniacal smile.

"Good." I loosen my grip over her wrists. "Getting out a little physical aggression might be good for the both of us." I teleport us to the butterfly room, Skyla beneath me, my legs pinning hers, my hands still holding her arms out like wings.

The room glows as the creatures pinned to the wall stir to life, and one by one they explode into the air around us, fluttering their own wings in shades of electric blue.

"Showoff." She struggles to free herself, but I'm not letting go.

"You are mine, Skyla." I swallow down the rage building in me, the hardness of my heart, my crushed and broken ego, and force them to dissolve. In truth, Skyla's rejection of me these past few months has been far more than devastating. I thought we could rise above anything. I knew that it would be difficult to hear what I had to say, but she closed off her ears right along with her heart. And yet here we are, our love splayed out, spilling between us like oil, messy and inescapable, too slippery to embrace properly. "You will always be mine." My fingers relax before I pull my hands to myself. I roll off, landing next to her on my back, eyes to the ceiling, an arm over my forehead in regret, without any clue on how to progress with her—my hard-on spiking into the air like a reminder of what we started.

Skyla draws herself up on her knees and pulls off her dress, waving it like a flag of surrender before tossing it across the room. "Come and get what's yours, Gage Oliver." She straddles me while raking my shirt open, sending buttons popping off with vigor. "Your wife has a craving that only you can satisfy." Her chest pulsates in and out, her tits cresting the fabric of her bra, full and heavy, slowly heaving their way out. But I don't have that kind of time on my hands. I reach up and unlatch the back, sending the girls bouncing into the air, happy to see me—and, dear God, am I ever happy to see them.

I pull her down to me, kicking off my clothes, my mouth finding its way to her soft sweet tits and my tongue makes a home over them, sucking them down into my mouth where they belong. Sorry, boys, tonight they're mine. This is my body, my beating heart in Skyla's tender flesh. She has me in so many ways. It's only fair I get to have her. I ravish her with my mouth, raking up and down her body like a luge, burying my tongue deep inside her, making her quake in record time before I plunge in, no condom. I can't stand a damn thing between us right now.

"*Gage.*" Skyla groans so loud, her panting pierces the air like a scream. "Are you insane?" A wild cry escapes her, and then in a moment of synchronicity, she presses me in deeper with her hands flattened against my back. "I love you." She takes up my face in her hands, her watery eyes pouring into mine.

"I know." I land a searing kiss over her lips before pulling back. "I love you more than there are words, Skyla. You are the other side of me. For so long I thought it was Logan of all people." I wash her face in a long tracking kiss. "But it's always been you, Skyla. We are connected far deeper, far stronger than any earthly union, any heavenly covenant." I smooth the hair off her forehead. "No more words." My body thrusts inside her. Skyla's body is tight as hell, so hot and wet all for me, and I'm close to losing it before pulling out and coming over her belly. I fall on top of her, my mouth fused to hers, her probing tongue sweeping softly inside of me, and it feels like I'm home, like Skyla and I are back on track—as if we had never skipped a beat to begin with. Our hearts slam over one another with rage as if we incited a riot in one another, and in a way we did. We may not have had that difficult conversation that's been strangling me by the balls for the last three months, but we don't have to do that tonight.

She cleans up with a small burp rag from the boys before tossing it onto the floor.

"Smooth, Oliver. Good call, though."

A dull laugh pumps through me as I dig my fingers into her hair. Skyla scoots in close, and my skin drinks down the feel of hers.

"I missed this," I say as I blink us back to the comfort of our bed, and she bubbles with a laugh as she takes in the messy room around us. For a brief second, my eyes flit to the bookcase and latch onto that smooth stone Candace gifted us with my destiny written out in a single number, and I'm quick to look away.

"I missed this, too." Her lips twitch like she might cry. "I vote we move forward."

"I concur. But before we do that, I do have to say that I abhor myself for ever bringing you an ounce of grief, and I repent in dust and ashes."

Her eyes fill with tears, and it feels as if a million years trek by slowly.

"When do you think we should have it out?" She ticks her head toward the window as if the words we need to share can only be done so outside of this sacred space, and I second that motion.

"Another time." My finger moves to her lips, and I press into them a moment. "And I will speak, and you will listen."

Her eyes widen at the boldness of my words.

"And you, Skyla"—I'm not done being bold by a long shot—"will tell me exactly what the hell you're doing with Chloe."

Her pretty pink mouth falls open, and she's quick to close it again. She gives a little shrug, and her nipples bounce in turn. "Fair enough."

"Really?" I'm amused and equally intoxicated by this beautiful woman in my bed. I pull her to me, chest to chest, her mouth inches from mine where it belongs. "Thank you."

"You're welcome." She dots my lips with a quick kiss. "But you won't be so thankful when you find out."

I wince as if she struck me, partially because I know it's true and partially because she agreed to do it in the first place.

"I appreciate your honesty."

"You think you do—but you won't." Her cryptic words slice right to the bone.

The faint cry of a child comes from down the hall, and Skyla flinches.

"That's Nathan." Her arm crosses over my chest as she snuggles in close. "My mother has them for the night. I have enough milk pumped so they should be fine." Nathan's wail pierces through the wall like a knife.

"I bet Tad loves that."

"Mom says he sleeps like a corpse until noon."

"Noon, huh? Must be nice." Even though I haven't been here losing sleep right along with Skyla, I haven't enjoyed a wink on my own. "I vote we do just that." I bury a kiss in her hair before moving to her lips and indulging in a lingering twisted lip-lock that makes me dizzy in the process. I'm always dizzy around Skyla. For as long as I've known her, that I've known her kisses, I don't know which way is up when I'm around her.

She moans as she pulls away just a notch, "Mom and Tad will be fumigating for termites soon. We'll need to move out for a week at least."

"Move out?" My thoughts run wild with places to take her and the boys. "Our house is filled to the brim with bodies. How about my parents'?" A growl emits from her, and I buck with a silent laugh. "We'll go to Whitehorse. Logan won't mind."

"I'll mind." She lies back on the pillow, and the moonlight kisses her features with a tangerine glow. "Lexy is squatting on his couch. I can't stand her arrogance."

"We'll figure it out. Lexy doesn't have anything on you, Skyla. Don't entertain her level of crazy. Logan isn't going anywhere." It should probably feel strange to entertain the idea, but it doesn't.

Her gaze drops to my chest, and she takes in a heavy breath. "I'm not concerned about him. The only man I want, need, and demand to have in my life is right here in this bed with me." Her gaze slowly meets with mine. "I didn't know if we'd have this again. I didn't expect tonight to end up this way. But I'm glad it did. I'm glad that we're on the path to healing. I may not like the reality of what landed us in this mess to begin with, but I dislike the distance it invoked a whole lot more." Her fingers twist into the hair at the base of my neck. "We are family, Gage. That means everything to me. We have two precious baby boys. I don't want you to miss out on their lives. I want to share it all with you. I want everything that this beautiful union of ours has to offer." She swallows hard as her fingers threaten to tear the hair right out of my skull. "No matter how difficult it will be to hear the words come from your lips, I have already made peace with them before they ever do. I need you to know that. This is deeper than forgiveness, Gage. I've wiped the slate clean on your deception, on your incessant need to protect me with your silence. You have my forgiveness before you ever ask for it. All I ask in return is the very same courtesy."

My blood runs cold. "You're talking about Chloe?"

She gives a faint nod as if even that was pushing it. "Our outward lives may never be the same, but there's no difference where it counts." Her hand touches over her heart. "Right here. You and I—we're still Gage and Skyla. You're my best friend. You're not second place or some passing phase that I can't wait to be rid of. You are my forever. And you're right. We are the masters of our destinies. My mother gave me the green light to rebel, and *you* are my favorite rebellion." Her hand slips down to my dick that's already throbbing to take her once again. "I wondered if you'd pull out. I'm not sure I would have minded all that much if you didn't." She shakes her head, and a tiny laugh bubbles from her. "Those cute boys of yours cast one strong spell over me. Okay, so we should probably wait—but my point is, we're not going anywhere. I've discovered something very poignant about myself, Gage."

"What's that?" I pull her finger to me and kiss the tip.

"I belong to you. My need to have you—to have us, transcends everything I thought I knew about love, about life, about death, regarding how I feel about the people around me."

My heart stops beating. Does she mean Logan? For sure she means Dudley, or at least my ego wants to believe it's so, but Logan? A part of me refuses to believe it. Not because my ego desperately wants for it to be true, but because I don't want to hurt for Logan in that way. In the back of my mind, even I believe that she and Logan belong together. If her mother has made anything clear to me, it's the fact I'm the unholy stumbling block in their love story. I am the stone my father threw in their path, and Skyla has simply tripped and landed into my bed for a little while.

She shakes her head. "Not true. Don't believe your own lies, Oliver."

"How did you do that?" I sit up on my elbow, taking her in, those crystal eyes of hers pulling me in. Skyla shouldn't hear me. I didn't let down my guard. There's no way her powers have the authority to usurp mine.

"You're right. They don't." An incredible sadness weighs down her features. "I guess you can say it's sort of a loaner *power* gifted from you. The boys made me strong, but it's fading. Each day these new gifts wane just a little bit more. I'm not as powerful as you are, Gage. And one day soon I will no longer be able to penetrate that minefield of secrets you have."

"There won't be any more secrets." I steal a kiss from the hollow of her neck. "Let's make a pact, Skyla"—I pick up her hand—"a covenant amongst ourselves, that we remain strong as steel."

"Strong as the Steel Barricade?" Her smile flexes in amusement. "I like that. The impenetrable steel wall of our love. We are our own. We belong to us. They can't have us. They can't take what rightfully belongs to you and to me."

"Our love is strong as steel, as relentless as time, as stubborn as death. We are one life, you and I. We cannot be broken."

"Our love is strong as steel." Her fingers rake across my back until I'm over her, balancing my weight on my elbows, careful not to crush her.

"To a new beginning," I whisper over her lips.

"The portal to forever."

Forever. That's exactly how long our love will last.

And for the first time for as long as I can remember, I don't feel Logan's shadow hovering over our bed. Logan has dissipated, evaporated into the past, dissolved into the atmosphere like some long-dead ghost. It's just Skyla and I—destiny can approve or disapprove. It doesn't really matter. We're happening. And we always will be.

A hard knock emits over the door, and I pull Skyla in even tighter like a reflex. My mind floats easily back into a dream as my body gives way to thick, delicious sleep once again.

Pressured knocking picks up again as my lids struggle to pry themselves open. Skyla takes a deep, audible breath, pressing her bare bottom into my stomach, and I bury a kiss in her hair.

"Skyla?" Lizbeth's voice resonates clear as if she were in the room, and I force myself to wake the hell up. "Oh, my! Is that *you*, Gage?"

I give a few tired blinks, and Lizbeth's disembodied head seems to be floating over the dresser. It takes a moment for me to realize she's burst through the door and moved the dresser over a few inches as she tries to muscle her way into the room.

"Mother!" Skyla pulls a pillow over her head and gives a sharp scream.

"I can't believe this!" Lizbeth's face lights up red as a Valentine heart. "My God, is this *real*? I wished for this to happen. I mean, I *prayed*. Heck, I even saw that father of yours and fell on my knees for him to do something for God's sake—but *this*?" Her gaze rides down the length of me, and her mouth falls open once she hits pay dirt.

I glance down to find the sheets wrapped around Skyla's chest, the rest of them off the bed, leaving my own body as naked as the day I was born. And shit. Is she staring at my crotch?

"*Wow.*" Her fingers tap over her lips a moment, but those eyes are still firmly pinned to my dick. "Just *wow*. Gage Oliver..." She staggers unsteady on her feet.

"We'll be down in a minute." I sit up and casually pull the pillow from Skyla's face and land it on my lap.

"Oh, *Skyla*." She shakes her head at her mortified daughter. "I've always known you were a lucky girl. But *this*?"

Skyla beams a tiny stuffed elephant at her mother, and Lizbeth vacates the premises, shutting the door behind her.

"I'll make brunch!" she shouts from the other side. "Take your time! Get back to whatever it is you were doing!"

"Aww, *sick*," a faint female voice rises alongside hers. One of Skyla's sisters no doubt.

Skyla falls against my chest and gives my leg a light scratch. "Welcome to my fabulous life."

"It is fabulous." I pull her up and steal a kiss off her lips. "It's our life, and I'm damn glad to be in it."

"You are?" Her clear eyes tear up, making them shine ten times brighter. Skyla is the only person I know that has a shooting star buried in her eyes. She's magnificent, spectacular, and has the power to take my breath away with something as innocuous as a question.

"I am." I pull her over me, and her body molds to mine. "How about we hit that brunch, then maybe we can get the boys and get lost for a few hours?"

She looks up, and her wild hair fans out over my face. "Sorry." She brushes it away with a soft giggle locked in her throat. "How about *first* I make your day?" Her knee grazes over my balls.

"I'm afraid our powers combined aren't enough to barricade your mother from the bedroom. I had that door locked." I wince at the thought of Skyla deep-throating me and Lizbeth providing the cheering section.

"Who said anything about the bedroom?" Her fingers drip down my chest until they hit home, and my entire body comes to life at her touch. "I'm in need of a serious shower—and after last night, so are you."

I don't debate it. In one quick move, I pick her up and land us in the bathroom. Before too long, the relaxing spray of nice hot water rains down over us. Skyla leans back and lets the water dissolve her wooly mane to a sleek blonde waterfall running over her shoulders. The water beads off her flesh, off her beautiful lips, and it's in this moment I decide that Skyla is mine in this life and after it. Life cannot stop the two of us from being together, and I'm not letting death stop it either. It's a peculiar thought for a peculiar day, but a blessed day—a new beginning. I pull her in close, my hard-on already close to home where it needs to be.

"I love you," I whisper, my lids hanging heavy at the sight of my gorgeous wife with the steam rising around her as if venerating her beauty. "Go ahead"—a dull smile comes to my lips—"make my day."

Skyla drops to her knees and does just that.

About an hour later, Skyla and I sail downstairs with a spring in our steps, my entire body one hundred percent satisfied, and my antenna already going up in hopes to get more of the same later tonight.

"Here they are!" Lizbeth howls from the kitchen. Tad is seated at the table with a paper clutched in his hands, and he curls down a corner long enough to grunt. His left arm is still sticking straight out in a splint, still healing from the burn he endured a few months back, and I feel for the guy. Drake and Bree are seated at the bar, each with a matching bowl of cereal, the hot pink box acting as a partition between them. But my gaze goes straight to the family room floor where Mia and Melissa each hold a beautiful bouncing, happy to see us baby boy.

"Hey, little dude." Mia hands me Barron, and I scoop Nathan from Melissa. "God, I've missed you guys." I pepper both their faces with a spray of kisses. I've seen the boys every single day, but this day, with our family back intact, it feels as if I'm home from a long hiatus that I never want to repeat.

Nathan gives a hearty deep chuckle while gripping my hair at the temple, and I can't help but land a kiss right over his sharp little dimple. Barron grunts and kicks and slaps the crap out of my face, and the room breaks out into laughter.

"So—you're back, like for good? Or was this just some dirty booty call?" Melissa's lip twitches with a look of disgust.

"I'm back."

She scoffs to her sister. "Guess it's time to get those earmuffs handy again."

"Are you kidding?" Mia dusts herself off as she staggers to her feet. "I employed mine last night right after I heard the first slam of the headboard."

Tad struts over, looking his usual disgruntled self. "Neither of you needs earmuffs because I paid a king's ransom to make sure none of us would have to deal with that disgusting dirty noise pollution."

It's true. A while back, Tad had the walls soundproofed by way of carpeting, and it's been a blight to look at ever since. Another reason I need to get my act together and get my family the hell out of Dodge.

"I heard nothing." Melissa grunts while glancing to my crotch.

"Well, I heard *everything*!" Mia spasms into my ear. "Why don't the two of you pick up stakes and find somewhere else to do the nasty?"

"Mia!" Lizbeth waves her off with a flick of the wrist before scooping Barron out of my arms. "Believe you me, not one thing these two do in that bed of theirs qualifies as nasty—or dirty or disgusting, Tad Landon! Leave the lovebirds alone, would you?" She offers me a quick wink before nodding for Skyla and me to follow her to the kitchen. "Come check out the little project the boys and I worked on all night long."

Rows and rows of parchment paper line the counter with hundreds of white chalky looking deformed cookies.

Tad steps over and pops a couple into his mouth and audible crunching ensues.

ADDISON MOORE

"Would you stop!" Lizbeth smacks him over the wrist. "Those are made of plaster!"

Tad spits them onto the floor so fast it looks like vomit.

"Crap." Skyla takes Barron from me and shields his eyes. "What are those? They look—*weird*."

"Vaginas!" Lizbeth says it just above a whisper, and Beau pops up from between her legs.

"*Bagina! Bagina!*" His cheeks are pinched pink, and judging by that mile wide grin of his, *bagina* is his new favorite word.

"Oh hush, you!" Lizbeth is light with the reprimand. "Go check on Misty and Ember for me."

"*No!*" Beau ratchets up his pitching arm and smacks Lizbeth square on the bottom, and the room lights up with the sound. I know Beau has been a bit testy lately, but smacking his grandmother over the ass should be the line in the sand. I glance to Drake, but he's all but drowning in his cereal bowl.

"Bree!" Skyla gasps at both Bree and Drake who lazily make their way over. "And, Mom, really? *Vaginas?*" she practically mouths the word.

"Yes!" Her eyes light up. "Chloe was right." Crap. I should have known Chloe was instrumental in this anatomical lunacy. "I did a little research, and they're all the rage right now. Look at this." She pulls one from the corner painted a light pink with a tiny little pearl buried right in that magic spot.

Shit. I lean in to get a better look, and holy hell, it's anatomically correct with every last crease and fold. Nathan does his best to snatch one, and I quickly move him out of range. It's not your time, buddy.

Lizbeth holds it out for Skyla and me. "It's beautiful, don't you think?" She pulls it to her chest as if to model it.

"And the best part is the boys helped make them." She gives Nathan a quick tickle. "Isn't that right, Punky-Poo!"

"Helped make them?" Skyla looks as if she's about to be sick, and I'm right there with her. "Don't say that." She twists the baby away from her mother, and he breaks out into a deep hearty chuckle. "My boys did no such thing."

"Oh, but they did!" Her eyes light up with insanity as she clasps Barron by the ankle. "How do you think I got the shape so uniform? I used the boys' feet to create a cast. And don't you worry. I made sure to include my Nate Nate, too!" She gives Nathan's toe a quick pinch, and he laughs while kicking her like a donkey.

"Shit," I hiss under my breath. "You're kidding, right?"

Drake lets out a honk of a laugh. "Brings new meaning to pussyfooting around, doesn't it!"

Brielle lets out a cackle as she joins in on the fun. "Brings new meaning to family *jewels*!" She dots her finger over the pearl embedded at Lizbeth's clitoral craft.

"Oh my loving God." Skyla's face pinches with color as rage percolates to the top of her eyeballs, and once again I'm right there with her, glaring at my mother-in-law without meaning to.

"You're all sick in the head!" Mia snaps a few pictures of the rows and rows of unpainted pussies lying out like the latest bakery confections. "And now the world is going to know it, too!" Melissa joins her on a snapping spree, and I'm quick to wave my hand over the evidence.

"Would you knock it off?" I bark so loud the room rattles. "Delete that shit right now! These are my boys, and nobody is going to damage them like this." God. Don't they know things live on the Internet forever? The last thing I want is my boys being mercilessly called pussies for the rest of their days because of one irresponsible night with their grandmother of all people.

"Ha!" Tad pokes a finger into my chest. "You don't get to talk to my girls that way. You watch that filthy, disgusting mouth of yours, Gregory! Or I'll land you on your ear in five seconds flat!"

"You have the nerve to call *me* filthy and disgusting? Take a look at your wife's latest offerings!"

A gasp comes from behind, presumably the wife in question.

"Whoa, dude." Drake pulls me over to the fridge as if to defuse the situation.

But Tad's not done with me yet. He comes at me with his finger wagging. "My wife is making a killing with this nonsense, and I don't need your dirty mouth, or your ridiculous judgments making things harder for her. If she's content whittling unmentionable parts, then I back her up one hundred percent."

I glance back to Lizbeth with her hand on her chest, clearly melting at her husband's sudden spurt of devotion.

"Okay." I do my best to shrug it off, but I end up shuddering instead. "Then I'm good with it, too." My cheek tugs to the side because I'm still not sure if I just spouted off the truth. "Just leave my kids out of it. Recast those things with Tad's feet, and I'll have no problem with it."

A collective groan works through the room at the thought of large, overgrown, malodorous delicate female parts.

"Now *that's* nonsense." Lizbeth picks up Misty who just strolled in, and I can't help but notice the resemblance between her and the boys. Damn Demetri, spraying his genetics all over the place. "I'll use this precious angel and Ember. Their feet will be more than happy to serve. Besides, that way we can get some real feminine energy going."

Mia balks at the idea. "The only place you'll get those girls going is straight into the arms of social services. You're nuts if you think employing two minors into your quasi-sex trade is a good idea."

"Would you stop!" Lizbeth barks. "It is not a *sex trade*! You're always so dramatic, Mia."

"That's right!" Tad pulls his pants up clear to his chest. "This is sex for money! We're not giving anything away in this family—especially not our feet!"

Drake gives me a quick sock to the arm as he nods me a few feet into the family room. "The old lady and I are tying the knot, and I need you to step up as best man. Got it?"

I blink over at him, trying to digest what the hell he just said, but my eyes go straight to that widow's peak buried in the center of this forehead. As intrusive as it is, it's almost impressive. My head spins, still lost in Tad's sex trade argument that quickly went south. I glance back to Skyla because I'd swear Drake and Bree tied the knot a long time ago, and I catch Lizbeth pulling her in.

"And my God—the *length* of him!" Lizbeth looks up, and our eyes meet for a few uncomfortable seconds.

Bree breaks out into a high-pitched laugh. "There's a reason we called him the baseball bat in high school." Leave it to Bree to evict any secrecy from their powwow.

"I'm done with this conversation." Skyla stalks over, visibly irritated, and Barron's dark hair wafts in the breeze, light as feathers. "What's this about a best man?"

Brielle jumps three feet in the air. "The cat's out of the bag! We're getting married!"

"You *are* married," Skyla flatlines, and I rub my shoulder against hers in a show of solidarity. Knew it.

"Not officially," Bree snarks back. "Plus, we're doing it right this time. Lots of money is being spent in the honor of our big day." She bats her lashes up at her prospective and current groom before turning to Skyla. "I thought to myself, why does *Laken* get to have you as her maid of honor? Why isn't my bestie *my* freaking maid of honor? And then I remembered how lame it was that we just took off and eloped. I'm really sorry about that." She bites her lip while posturing toward my wife. "But I'm going to make it all up to you now. I've already talked to Logan about letting us have the ceremony at Silent Cove on the Fourth of July, and we'll have fireworks and cake, and the whole nine—"

Skyla cuts her off, "Laken yards. *Wow*. Are you sure you want to venture into copycat waters? We can do something really nice right here at the house."

Tad gags from behind. "Don't you think about it, son! I've got a good mind to put an end to all the freeloading that takes place around here."

"Keep your cool, Pops." Drake slaps him hard over the back, and Tad's rigid extension salutes the ceiling. "Logan and I squared things away. And don't worry. You raised me right. I offered him top dollar to have my ass hitched on his property."

Tad shakes his face at Mach 5 as if coming to. "Top dollar? While, I'll give you the entire Landon estate for half!" His face is still powdered with those plaster pussies he tried to shove down his throat.

"No, thanks." Bree scowls at her father-in-law with a look of nausea. Not that I can blame her. "I'm doing it right. I want an evening wedding with all my friends and family present. Ellis is helping me score some entertainment through his dad's connections. We're talking big names here. I don't even recall dancing at Laken's mediocre beach bash."

Skyla frowns at her best friend. "Just make sure you're doing this for the right reasons. That would be for you and Drake. Don't let what Laken does with her life dictate yours."

"I don't want to talk about that ho anymore." Bree swats Beau away as he circles near her legs. "What's important is that my bestie and I get back on track. And guess what, missy? You get to plot out my bachelorette party!"

"Oh joy." Skyla looks up at me.

"And, *dude*"—Drake nails me in the arm with his fist—"you get to plan my last night of freedom."

I glance to Skyla, and we share a quiet smile. "Drake, I'm really flattered, but shouldn't you ask Ethan to fill these big shoes? I'm down if he's out—but he is your brother."

"Oh shit." He ticks his head back a notch with a stumped look on his face. "I'd better ask. I'd hate to piss the dude off." He struts off toward Ethan's room and barrels on in without knocking. "Dude, get off that chick—we've got a wedding to plan."

Great. I put a half-hearted effort into covering Nathan's eyes. "Maybe we should take off for a bit?" *Like forever*, I want to add, but I'm betting the boys are better off with the nutcases that run this asylum than in a house full of corpses—although at this point it's debatable.

"I agree." Skyla gives Bree a quick hug. "Congrats. Let's get together soon. Between your upcoming nuptials and Ezrina's new baby, we're going to have a busy year."

"Don't forget these boys." I jostle Nathan between the two of us, and he reaches out and grabs ahold of his brother's hand. "It's a whole year of firsts for these little guys."

"That's right." Bree gives Nathan's nose a quick thump. "First smile, first laugh, first kiss—heck, these boys even got a little pussy this year."

"And that's the last time we're going to mention it." I twist Nathan out of her reach. "Skyla, let's get out of here."

"It couldn't be fast enough."

Or long enough.

Skyla and I load the boys into the minivan and drive down the long gray tongue of the island with no real rhyme or reason other than getting as far away as possible from the lunacy the Landon house has to offer. I'd take her to Whitehorse, but a part of me doesn't want to see Logan just yet. I'd take her to my house, but I know Skyla isn't up for seeing my mother. Our own home is ironically off the short list since it's temporarily doubling as a glorified holding tank for the cemetery castoffs. And, of course, there's Dudley's, and well—Dudley is there. But there is one place.

"How about Rockaway?" she asks as if reading my mind, and the thought sets me slightly on edge.

"Rockaway it is. Home sweet home." The turnoff comes up next, and I take it. Soon the evergreens give way to ebony-colored sand, the hard line of navy waters just beyond its borders. "This feels like home to me."

"Too bad we couldn't live in that hut you built. I think we'd need to add on a nursery if we did."

I glance in the rearview mirror to find the boys both fast asleep—a miracle in and of itself.

"Looks like the boys aren't too interested in visiting the hut just yet."

A light sprinkle sizzles over the windshield as I pull in as close to the sand as possible.

"Hut or no hut, this is perfect." Skyla takes up my hand as we watch the waves crashing over themselves, white with anger as they roar their fury onto shore. "This is where you asked me to marry you." She bites down hard on her lip. "This has always been our place, hasn't it?"

"It's a beautiful place—a perfect place to call our own."
I pull her hand forward and kiss my grandmother's ring still
firmly on her finger. During this entire nightmare, Skyla
always had it on, and that alone gave me all the hope I
needed.

"I couldn't do it." Her eyes look to the ring as she holds
it between us. "I tried, but I didn't have it in me to take it off.
I thought we were over, but I guess my heart knew
otherwise." Her fingers graze through the scruff on my chin
a moment.

"I saw that stone last night." My throat tightens as I
struggle to get the words out. That stone Candace sent
down—all but threw at my head last December comes to
mind. She said it had my number on it, the exact remainder
of my time here on the planet. "It was on the bookshelf, but I
couldn't help but think it was mocking me."

"Oh my God, I'm so sorry. I swear, I would flush the
thing down the toilet if I could. In fact, we should go back
and get it right now and pitch it into the sea."

"No." A tired laugh stumps through me. "I swear, it's
fine. It's just—I thought maybe we should talk about it.
Seven—the number." Our eyes lock, and a shiver runs
through me at the thought of verbalizing anything that
demonic stone had to say. It feels as if I've unleashed a
celestial dragon, and in an irony too big to wrap my head
around, I am in fact that horrific serpent.

Skyla takes a ragged breath at the idea of what that
number might mean.

I bring her hand to my lips and press in a kiss. "We've
passed up seconds, minutes, hours, weeks, so I guess we'll
know in July if it's months, and if not, it must be years."

"Decades," she's quick to counter. "It will be decades.
My mother knows how much you mean to the boys and me."

"Decades." I press my head back into the seat and try to digest it. There's no way Candace would gift me a blessing that big, and seven more decades with Skyla as my wife would be exactly that, a blessing.

She shakes her head with tears wobbling, threating to tumble forth into the world, but she's slow to let them fall. "Let's move on. I hate that stone. I hate a lot of things." She swallows hard. "Why did you do it—the covenant with Demetri? I'm ready to listen." Skyla holds my gaze, heavy as the sea, as angry as those sooted clouds darkening the skies.

I glance back to the boys one last time. Still sound asleep. In a way, this is the perfect moment to bare my soul with all parties present and accounted for. The rain pounds over the windshield and the air in the van sours.

"You know that I love you"—my voice hitches as I force my gaze to seal over hers—"that I would do anything for the boys. When I broke faith with the Barricade, the penalty was that someone I hold dear would take my place in my father's wicked world." My eyes flit to the raging sea for a moment, the whitewash beating the shore. I feel that much rage and more at the thought of Demetri's wicked world. "At the time, I couldn't imagine who that would be—so I agreed." My eyes close, and I'm transported right back to the stone of sacrifice where Demetri set my universe on fire. "The night the boys were born I don't know who or what detained me, but I tried to move heaven and hell to get to you, Skyla. God, I did." My head taps against the seat as tears come to the party, and I sniff them back. "When I held Barron—I heard him." My voice breaks as I burst through this dam of emotions. "I heard him as if he were in the room with me."

"Heard who, Gage?" Her voice quivers, and she leans in close. Skyla slides over and squeezes onto my lap. Her cool hands clasp over my face. "*Who?*"

"Demetri." It's as if I'm back there, in that room, holding my precious son for the very first time. "It was Barron he was after." My face falls into my hand, and I pinch my eyes closed, trying my hardest to get a grip, to stop crying like a pussy and take it like a man. "I knew then what I had to do, Skyla. I needed to take his place. Demetri can have me—but he can't have my boys."

Tears sit frozen in her eyes, unable to fall, paralyzed by the truth. "*Gage.*" My name expires from her lungs like the hiss of a train pulling from the station, and in a way it is. The definition of who we are has long since left the platform. We have derailed, left the world as we once knew it. In truth, I had left back in November. It's just now Skyla is joining me on this runaway train to hell. "You are my hero." Her voice is hoarse, a mere whisper, an idea of what it could be. "I'm sorry about the pain I've caused, the hurt."

"No." My finger lands over her lips, harder than I meant for it to, but the idea of Skyla apologizing to me is sacrilegious. It is also the very last thing in the world I want. "You had every right. I wanted to tell you." A watershed of tears warm my face. "But I didn't want Demetri's madness to ruin those precious first moments we had with the boys. He gave me an ultimatum. I had to commit the night of the christening or the deal was off the table." Our eyes lock, our shared anger fuses in a stream of unification. "And that's what you saw that night." My voice shakes with rage at what's become of me. "As much as I want to blame myself for getting in the mess to begin with"—I shake my head at the idea—"I'm certain he would have found another way. It just so happens that I made it easy for him."

"Then we'll make it hard." She grips my hands and holds them between us. "This is the springtime of our rebellion."

"There is no rebellion for me, Skyla. I've accepted my fate. You are looking at the face of your enemy. I can fight it, but it will be tough. Then slowly as time goes on, my heart, my ideals will bend to the will of my father."

"And if that happens, I will defeat you," Skyla says it soft, quiet, with such love in her eyes, it erases any doubt that we could ever truly be enemies. Our love has transcended anything that might bog us down ever again. Even if she grew to despise me, love would still be there like an undercurrent.

"You are well able." It's true. Skyla has the ability, the mental fortitude, and stamina needed to defy any form of evil thrust in her path. In my worst state of being, I would simply be a stump for her to step over on her journey to greatness. I have no doubt about that. "And that is what waits for me."

"Don't buy into it, Gage." Her lips linger over mine, hot and dripping with our shared tears. "Please, no. You're strong. Your strength is what gives us hope. Look at you now. You're here with me. We're still Gage and Skyla. See? Nothing has changed."

"It wouldn't for now. None of this takes place with me in the natural." I look into the eyes of my precious wife, the girl I've worshiped ever since she was nothing more than a figment of my visions. "The truth is, Skyla—I'm worth more to Demetri dead than I am alive. I am a dead man walking. Expect my death, Skyla." My thumb wipes the tears from her cheek. "It will be upon us soon."

Logan

Last night I dreamed of a hostile future. I dreamed of myself in another form, a wiser, far more experienced version that had come down from paradise to offer a helping hand in what will be the greatest plight of my young deceased and perhaps even resurrected life. I dreamed of Gage in that desolate, cavernous plane, Paragon in Nocturne. Gage seated firmly on his throne of fire with his beastly skin, and unknowable wicked eyes. In no way did he remotely resemble the boy I grew up with. That burnt thick skin with its glassy scales, the mile-long tongue that whips about in flames. This future version of the two of us fascinates me, and I watch in horror—in a sad act of faraway admiration—everything in between. Greatness, no matter how wicked, has the power to instill a certain awe in people, and Gage in all of his monstrous glory is no different. I am in awe of his wicked majesty.

"How will you fix this?" the version of myself that stepped down from paradise asks.

"I don't know." I give him the same answer each and every time. I have had this dream dozens upon dozens of times, and each night it plays out the same.

He places his strong hand over my shoulder, warm and weighted, as if it alone had the power to assure me everything would somehow be all right. And then just like that, I'm pulled out of the dream by the vacuum of reality. My eyes are always slow to open as I struggle my way back. And I always ask myself the same damn question—what in the hell should I do now?

I blink to life, and my gaze drifts to the gap in the curtain, exposing a veil of snowy white fog that has already wrapped its arms around the island. Paragon loves to dress herself in its softness. She loves to sand off the rugged edges of reality by dewing herself in the ever-present mist of youth. I wish I could wrap Skyla and Gage in softness, prepare them for the hard fall that inevitably lies ahead. It's been a week now that he's told her the truth, and she's embraced it with the loving kindness I always knew she would.

Skyla and Gage are working again. And I want that for them. I wish they were working from the start, and I was long since dead, content and buried, staring down at the two of them from paradise above. Although, technically, that's not true. From that bodily deprived standpoint in the hereafter, you can't see the world or anything in it. That is a lie, or more accurately, a distortion of the truth that people love to believe. The dead have surrendered their knowledge of this life along with their bodies. The world and all of its inhabitants are under the Master's watchful eye and that of his Son. It is they that look down. They alone are mindful of what needs to be done. They function as one and the same— the Father and the Son—and it makes me wonder if Gage and his father—Demetri, will too function as one in the same. That is the frightening reality staring us in the face. But my father, my mother, and all of the saints that have passed on, are incapable of solving any single problem for me. God has got this. The last thing He needs is billions of meddling spirits meddling with His universe, trying desperately to right all of the wrongs, desperate to be gods themselves without holding the blueprint of what comes next and where it fits into the grand design. It's true. If given half a chance, I would have commandeered Skyla and Gage to the happily ever after they need, that some might say they deserve, although, I'm not entirely in that camp. If I'm honest, I'll admit defeat, but I'll also admit that I love Skyla too much to ever let her go completely.

The Smite brothers come to mind with their altruistic outlook on love—Graham in particular. He gave the woman he loved away to his brother like a parting gift, a token of his appreciation. Skyla is far more than a token, than a jewel to hold in my palm and pass along to any of my brothers, and I do include Gage in that number. Nope. I cannot give her away. And in the same vein, I cannot give Gage away either—least of all to Demetri.

A hard knock comes over the door, and Lexy bursts in with a tray in her hands.

"Rise and shine, bright eyes! Today is a new day, and you and I have a world to conquer."

A dull groan rumbles from me. Lexy Bakova is the last girl on the planet I plan on conquering the world with. Not to mention the fact I tried to do specifically that with Skyla and drove her—scratch that, cemented her in Gage Oliver's arms—and I, myself, ended up dead in the process.

Lex sits next to me, depressing my mattress right along with my spirits. I know for a fact her presence annoys the living hell out of Skyla. And I'm not looking for anything sexual with Lex, which is exactly what Lex wants with me, so it's probably time I gave her the boot.

"Lex, there's something I need to tell you."

"Sure." She bounces over the bed and causes the coffee to crest onto the lip of the mug. "But before I forget, Gage dropped by."

"What did he want?" I take the glass of O.J. off the tray and sit up before knocking it back.

"You. He said he needed to talk. I told him you were sleeping and he took off." She flips back her copper hair and flashes that insolent smile she's famous for. "He's probably looking for a way to deal with Messenger. If you ask me, she's always been high maintenance. Back at West you would think the world revolved around her the way she was so self-absorbed."

"It did," I offer without a note of enthusiasm. "It still does." And I mean that. Skyla is the nexus of a superhuman transformation taking place in the nebulous sky. Her mother has whittled the perfect pawn, and Skyla is that chess piece. I happen to be the other, but I'm not getting into any of that with Lex.

"Anyway, Ezrina has been puking up a storm. Heathcliff has freaked the fuck out, so I took over and made sure she got to bed and gave her all the crackers and soda I could find. Heathcliff says he'll gift me free food at the Gas Lab for a year!" She squawks at the idea. "I'm in. Let me tell you, life is expensive. I knew it would be rough after high school, but I didn't realize how hard money would be to come by. Good thing I've got you to help me out. My parents aren't into fostering my need for cash anymore. If I didn't have this place, I'd be out on my rear, or worse yet, rooming with Michelle over at Host."

"You should probably finish your education," I offer that bit of fatherly advice as I dig into the thickly syruped pancakes she's made fresh for me. It's a breakfast she's made sure I've grown accustomed to, but I'd hate to break it to Lex, I'd be just as satisfied with a glass of water.

"Of course, I'm still taking online classes, but I could only get one this semester." She leans in and runs her fingers through my hair, those copper eyes of hers glint like pennies. "That's the thing I appreciate most about you, Logan. You really seem to care about me. All my life I've had to live around cold-hearted people, and I think most of all it's your warmth I'm drawn to. Now what was it that you wanted to discuss?" She blinks up at me with those doe eyes, and I don't have the heart to knife her heart out.

"There's a Faction meeting in a few hours. You should probably plan on going."

"As your date? Logan Oliver, you never need to ask." She leans in and pecks a kiss on my cheek, and before I know it she's snapped a picture of the event as well.

Crap.

"See you in a bit!" She bubbles her way out of the room.

I don't need a date to the Faction meeting. Nobody does. Holy hell, Lexy Bakova has taken over like a fungus.

"I brought a date to the meeting." Skyla gives a gritty laugh, and I can't help but frown at the irony. "Two dates actually." Gage comes up behind her holding each of the boys.

"What's up, little dudes?" I land a quick kiss to each of their downy soft cheeks, and they both smile and squirm for me so I take the one closest. "Who's this?"

"Barron." Skyla laughs while taking Nathan from Gage. "I'd better get up there." She nods toward the table set up in the front of Nicholas Haver's enormous old barn. Rows and rows of chairs are set out encompassing the lone table up front where Skyla will conduct the meeting from, and usually there are more than enough seats, but tonight it's standing room only. Skyla invited everyone from the old Walsh house, her home to be exact, to partake in the festivities. Not that there will be any festivities, tonight we discuss the grim business of getting the dead into the government's hands.

"So, what's up?" I give Gage a quick nod as I bounce Barron between us. "Lex mentioned the fact you stopped by."

His brows hood in disapproval. "She did, huh? She said you were indisposed. Dude, she was wearing your T-shirt. You're not sleeping with her, are you? Not that I'm judging." He's quick to backtrack, but we both know he's judging and he should be.

"Heck no." I wince at Barron as he does his best to grip my nose. "Nor will I. I'm about ready to show her the door but, well, it's complicated. What can I help you with?"

"It's complicated." His dimples dig into a frown. "Tad's getting ready to gas the place soon. The fumigating is moving a little slower than he'd like, but, nevertheless, I need somewhere to camp out with the fam." He takes a deep breath as if what comes next is hard for him. "You okay with us hitting Whitehorse for about a week?"

My heart gives the requisite lurch it's prone to do whenever Gage shocks me. I've asked both him and Skyla to take Whitehorse, make it their own, but they've staunchly refused, and having Gage ask for it even for just a week throws me.

"Yes. Take it for as long as you need. Trust me, once you taste the freedom it can afford, there will be no looking back at Tad's ass crack."

"Watch the language." He gives a sly wink before dropping a kiss to Barron's hand. "Thanks, man. We appreciate it."

"Not a problem."

He spots his father, Barron, in the crowd talking to Rev and winces. "Excuse me for a minute." He takes off, and my mind reflexively goes back to Whitehorse as visions of Gage taking Skyla over every inch of that place puts me in a daze. They'll be there a week at least. Of course, they're going to make it their own in every way. My stomach sours at the thought of the mattress getting some mileage off it, the new one post my erotic romp with Chloe when I thought she was Skyla.

Barron grabs my ear and crushes it in his tiny hand before laughing up a husky storm. His eyes sparkle like his father's, like Skyla's and I can't help but think he's a perfect combination of both.

"That's right," I whisper, bouncing him on my hip. "I need to snap out of it. Get out of my funk."

Skyla and Gage are free to have as much fun as they want under my roof, *her* roof. And, if I'm moved to change the mattress out afterward, it's not a big deal. An expensive, heavy-as-fuck-to-get-up-the-stairs deal, but ultimately not a big one.

Skyla calls the meeting to order, and I take a seat up front next to Ezrina and Nev. Ellis and Giselle strut in late and steal the seats to my right.

"How's it hanging?" Ellis leans in and fist bumps baby Barron, and the heavy scent of weed clings thick in the air. Giselle's eyes are just as glossed over as Ellis'.

I can't help but frown over at the two of them. Honestly, lately she has just as little sense as he does. I need to start a rescue G initiative. There has to be someone else she can date other than Ellis, but at the moment I can't seem to think of anyone. Or better yet, stay single. Her brain cells will thank her for it later in life.

The meeting gets underway, and Skyla assesses the work programs she instilled last year. The strongest and the brightest minds from each Faction have volunteered to do workshops in strengthening and growing powers, and the younger sect is showing up in droves. I, myself, am dead and thus don't qualify, but Skyla assured me that I would have been a Celestra leader. As it stands, Ivan Watts and his wife Vanessa lead those classes. I've yet to catch a master class, as they're called, but plan to.

"Skyla's so brave." Giselle leans over Ellis and leers at me as if waiting for a response. A slight titter circles the room, and my full attention returns to the front. Skyla keeps talking into the mic, her body slightly contorted to the left, and it takes a while for me to notice a large bulge rippling under her blouse.

"Crap," I say it out loud without meaning to, and Barron slaps my lips and laughs. That lump under Skyla's shirt just so happens to be his brother—Nathan. She's nursing right here in the open, and my heart starts thumping again—not because the sight of it gets me going. I've seen Skyla do what she needs to do on more than one occasion. It's the fact the masses happen to be witnessing the event as well. A swell of pride heats me up from the inside. Yes, she's covered, but even if she wasn't, Skyla is fearless. If anything, this is a shining example of what a great mother she is.

Skyla leans in. "Let's move to the topic of volunteer adoptions." Volunteer adoptions is the program she ran past me that involves the deceased getting placed into homes rather than drawing attention to themselves stuffed to the hilt at the home she's provided for them. I know for a fact Gage is on the forefront of gunning to get them out. "Worldwide representatives have reached out and taken in a significant number of mercenaries for us. The Nephilim Bureau of Intelligence is working closely to find an appropriate match for everyone involved." A weak round of applause pours through the room. "The Levatio League had kindly offered their transportation services for the endeavor, and I can't stress how grateful we are for that. A handful, of course, is still here among us on Paragon. They are desperately needed in order to deflect the heat that the government has steadily turned up."

"You mean the Barricade!" someone shouts from the back.

"Precisely that." Skyla darts a quick glance to Gage as if it were a reflex, and her cheeks darken with color. "The sooner we temper the feds, the sooner everyone can breathe easier. The mercenaries are currently undergoing power stimulus and strategy sessions to help once they initiate their incarcerations. The plan calls for a swift surrendering over a three to six-month period. Once the last volunteer is taken, we will regroup and reassess. No doubt the Barricade will have something else cooked up by then, but we'll deflect as needed. We don't fear them or the coward commandeering the effort."

A slight round of titters circles the room.

Her T-shirt flips over the top of Nathan's head, and the white pad of her breast glows beneath his dark hair. His head moves steadily back and forth as he heartily takes all she has to give him. The room lights up with an audible gasp, followed quickly by a rumble of voices, all eagerly whispering about the wardrobe malfunction.

"Excuse me." She leans into the mic once again and offers a hard look to the crowd from one end of the room to the other. "But my son needs to eat, and I kindly ask that you get over it." She straightens her notes, and the room grows quiet with the reprimand. "We'll have sign-ups down front once we reconvene, and I'm hopeful to place the remaining Paragon mercenaries in a warm home by evening." Skyla picks up the gavel and pauses while scanning the crowd. "Be careful—be on alert, watch out for one another. We are all we have." She sounds the gavel, and the baby breaks his hold on her, leaving Skyla's nipple bare and exposed as the room erupts into a warble of voices. Bodies rise and begin to mingle, and I share a quick glance with Gage. It looks as if the shock value lasted for less than a moment, and I'm glad. I don't want Skyla to feel embarrassed or bad about having to nurse her children. God gave her those boys and that body for a reason.

"Logan?" a tiny female voice calls from behind, and I find Casey with her bright eyes latched onto me. "Will you adopt me?" Her lower lip quivers when she says it, and my heart breaks for her. What the heck is she doing here, volunteering? She's just a kid.

"I'm actually in need of a home myself. A family is coming to stay at my house for a week."

Her features crumble as if she were crestfallen. "I see. I guess I'll go sign up and hope for the best. I don't traditionally do well around strangers. This entire endeavor was sort of a big step for me. But the Counts burned my father. He was a Celestra, and I avowed to avenge him." She picks at her simple pink dress at the hem. "But then I was killed before I ever got out of the vengeful gate."

Something about Casey makes me want to protect her in a big brother sort of way.

"I can relate." I bounce Barron on my hip, and he nuzzles his dark little head into my neck. "My father—the Counts killed both him and my mother in the same manner."

"Oh!" She slaps her hand over her mouth. "They're barbaric!"

"Full disclosure, I might have a drop or two of that barbaric blood in me, but I'm almost pure Celestra outside of the fact."

She wrinkles her nose and looks all of twelve. "I won't hold it against you. Hey, do you know of any nice people that might take me in?"

"What's this?" Giselle pops up next to me and takes the baby. "Hi, Casey!" She heads over and gives her a hip bump. "You need a good home? My Ellis practically lives in a mansion all by himself. His parents are nearly invisible. Or how about living with me? Daddy Kragger is the best! And he would, love, love, *love* to have you with us! We can light a big burning fire and you can tell us all about how you died. Daddy K loves to hear my stories about the afterlife. Now that the real Emerson is home, you'd think he'd kick me out on my tiny pink Oliver ear, but he's taken a liking to me. Besides, Emerson won't be around forever. Thankfully. She's such a snot." She makes a face while turning my way. "She practically yells at me every day for touching her things. What doesn't she get about being replaced?"

"I'm sure it's a tough pill to swallow." I can't help but look to Gage. I happen to know all about being replaced myself. "And no, I don't think having Casey stay with you is a good idea. In fact, try not to bring any of this to Arson's attention."

"Oh, he knows." She waves me off as if it's silly. "Holden told him everything. But Pierce swore him to secrecy. In fact, Pierce and Holden are trying to figure out a way to do more to help Skyla."

"That's interesting, considering I believe she killed them both." I make a mental note to talk to both Holden and Pierce. Holden once took possession of my body. He once did a lot of really shitty things, not to mention what he tried to do with Skyla against her will. But Skyla has miraculously forgiven him, and we've all moved on—that's about the same time he was shoved into the body of a bird and forced to live out his life in feathers. I need to make sure this temporary human tent hasn't given the Kraggers any lousy ideas.

Ellis pops up and G happily hands him the baby. Poor Barron looks startled and begins to squirm, and Ellis looks equally as startled as he too begins to squirm.

"I'll take him." Casey reaches out and cuddles with Barron as if he were her favorite teddy bear. "I miss this. I miss the entire human experience. I guess at the end of the day that's why I wanted to come back. Paradise is great, but there's just something about having a body."

Giselle wraps her arms around Ellis. "Casey needs a home. Won't you take her? She'll be quiet, and hardly eats, and I'll even stop by and clean up after her."

I give a laugh at the thought. Giselle makes Casey sound more like a puppy than a person.

"I'll take her." I give a little wink Casey's way, and she gasps with delight. "We'll hang out at the Oliver house. I'm sure Emma won't mind, and if she does, we'll stick it out at the old Walsh place together." A part of me wants to shudder at the thought. Ramshackle comes to mind as a positive descriptor.

"What's this about the Walsh house?" Skyla pops up like a ray of sunshine. Her face glows with a smile as she scoops Barron up from Casey.

"Logan is adopting me!" Casey wraps her arms around my neck a moment. "I'm going to tell the other girls. They're going to die with jealousy." A dark laugh bubbles from her. "Get it? *Die?*" Her cheeks brighten an electric shade of pink. "It would be the best way to go!" She takes off into the crowd, and I'm left with a sheepish grin while glancing at Skyla.

"I concur." She gives a sly wink.

"Hey, did you know Big Daddy K knows about the—" I motion around the room.

She makes a face at Giselle. "I suspected as much. I'm not worried about it. This is bigger than any of the Kraggers. It's bigger than Wes."

"Speaking of big." Ellis smacks me over the arm. "I've got that demo crew coming out next Tuesday. You ready for the big knockdown? It's time to cut our losses with the past and start something new."

A quick pain convulses through my body. "You bet. I'll be there with bells on." Tied to my balls. Strangling the shit out of them.

"Cool." He leans in. "Dude, I know this is wrenching your balls. I'm rolling a fat one in your honor. On the house. A gift from me to you."

"Sounds like a plan." And sadly, one I might take him up on. I have no clue how I'm going to get through the trauma of that day.

Giselle pushes out a choo-choo train laugh. "How about we get lost and you roll *me* a fat one?"

"No," I deadpan. The last thing I want is Ellis doing what he does best with my niece of all people.

Skyla scowls at Giselle. "Say nope to dope and ugh to drug. And if Ellis says he has something fat he wants to roll, you run, Giselle. *Run.*"

She lets out a honking laugh. "I don't do dope, Skyla. That would make *me* one. Ellis doesn't do it either. That's stupid. He just sells it because he needs the money to buy cars and things. He's explained it all to me."

Skyla and I exchange a quick glance.

Ellis clears his throat. "I think I see someone I know. How about we go say hi?" He stalks off with Giselle until the crowd swallows them.

Skyla lets out a cry of frustration. "Ellis is rolling big fat lies and shoving them all down her innocent throat. What is Emma thinking letting this go on? What is *Gage* thinking?"

"What am *I* thinking?" I wince at the thought. "I'll talk to Ellis. I know he has a good heart and he loves her."

"She's as loveable as she is gullible."

A cold darkness crests over my shoulders, and I turn to find Chloe beaming with a wicked grin.

"Talking about yourself again, Skyla?"

"You're not funny." Barron begins to peck at Skyla's chest, and she shoves him under her shirt. "What is it, Chloe?" She looks to me. "She said it was important."

Evidently Skyla is her keeper. She should be, but something tells me this relationship has gone off the rails, just how far I'm terrified to ask.

Chloe whips out her phone and holds it between us. "Does this look important to you?" Her camera blinks to life, and all I can make out is human flesh in a tangle.

"What's this?" Skyla takes it from her.

"Not what, *who*." Chloe takes it back and skirts through a few pictures before displaying another one.

"That's Laken." Skyla smiles down at her good friend. "And Wes?" Her smile melts right off. "So what? She probably felt the need to tell him to go to hell."

"Maybe." Chloe flicks to the next picture. "But with her clothes off?" She flashes another picture at us, and holy hell—Laken is clearly taking off her dress, the outline of black panties and a matching bra pop against her pale flesh as if someone took a marker and colored them in.

"No way." Skyla shakes her head in disbelief, and Chloe is quick to skip to the next picture—Laken with her arms around Wes, their heads knit together in what looks to be a kiss. Chloe flips to the next picture, and as soon as I realize what it is, I look away in reflex.

"That's not her." Skyla takes the camera and studies a naked Wesley with Laken straddling him on top, her face lost in ecstasy. "That's"—she looks to me—"where is Ezrina's little experiment gone wrong, anyway?"

"Crap." I swallow hard while looking around for Coop or Laken herself. "She's gone."

Skyla looks as if she's about to puke into the phone. "And now she is found. Nice work."

Chloe offers a smug look my way. "I'm working my way back to the island."

"Skyla." I can't help but sound disappointed. It's because I am.

"*Chloe*," Skyla reprimands the witch. Of course, she's going to snitch. That's what Chloe does best.

"Logan." Chloe winks over at me. "Relax, would you? It's one of the many perks of working with my new bestie. Skyla and I are a team, and if you don't like it, you can suck your own dick."

"*Chloe*," Skyla moans, deep and guttural, and my dick ticks to life. In my defense, Chloe roused its attention in a roundabout way. "Keep your lips zipped. It's nobody's business what we do together."

"You're my new bestie." Chloe lands an arm around Skyla's shoulders, and I cringe at how close to Barron she is. "You validate me, Skyla." Chloe's lips twitch as if she were about to cut her. "And I validate you." She turns to snicker at me. "We may not like where life has landed us, but we work surprisingly well together when we have a common goal." Her eyes flit to the left, and I track her gaze to none other than Gage. Figures. Gage is the nexus that has fused Chloe and Skyla together. But why? And how the hell does this ever make sense?

"So, you keep an eye on Wes—and Skyla gives you your walking papers?" At least I can say I took a stab at it.

"Warm." Chloe looks bored while returning her attention to her new aforementioned bestie. "Anyway, I want to tell Laken myself. Now that I'll be resurfacing soon, I'll need allies and friends, and believe it or not, I happen to admire her."

"Because she had the fortitude not to sleep with Wes?" Skyla looks disbelieving at the demon before her.

"That, and the fact she shoots from the hip. Not in a bumble headed way like Brielle. She's sane. I like a girl with a good head on her shoulders."

"Save it." Skyla pulls Barron out from under her blouse, and he smiles dreamily at me with a line of milk on his lips. "Laken won't be signing up to join the Bitch Squad any time soon. And I'm pretty sure you're the last person she'll give half a chance to. You slept with Wes. Worse yet, you pretended to *be* her while sleeping with Wes."

"It's not my fault my husband has a fetish." She shudders. "Anyway, he's abandoned the marriage bed. It's been a couple of weeks since he's wagged his penis my way. Whoever that chick is, she's taking the heat for now."

Skyla's eyes fill with rage as she drifts to some unknowable place in her mind. "Go home, Chloe. Keep a close eye on your new best friend, whoever it is that's warming your husband's bed. Don't let her out of your sight. I'll be down there soon enough to deal with her."

"I'll be joining you." I let Barron take my finger and squeeze the shit out of it. "And so will Cooper and most likely Laken herself."

Chloe gags on a wicked laugh. "In the meantime, I will gather everything you ever needed to know about Wesley's new little whore." She gives me the finger before melting into the crowd, and a plume of fog rises to the ceiling as she's whisked back to the Transfer.

"*Skyla.*"

"Don't start," she cuts me off.

I step in close in clear defiance because a part of me doesn't care. Skyla is endangering herself, and God knows I'll do anything to protect Skyla even if it's from herself. "What else have you promised her?"

Her eyes meet with mine, and the moment grows serious. Rage pours from her like fumes. "All Chloe has ever wanted is power, Logan. And that's exactly what I'm going to give her." She stalks off and meets up with Gage. He's quick to embrace his wife. Quick to kiss her.

For the first time ever, it feels as if Skyla needs to be supervised. And I'm volunteering. It's one thing to have Gage off the rails, but an entirely other to have Skyla skip the tracks.

One thing is for sure—there is no getting off this crazy train without certain disaster. It's coming. I can feel the three of us barreling ever so close. It's going to be big. And something tells me it will be final, too.

Late the next afternoon, when the sky is pissing out its affection over Paragon like a golden shower, I head down to the Gas Lab where Gage and I are meeting up with Coop.

Poor Coop. It's a given he's going to be pissed—hell, I'm pissed. But Wes is relentless. His obsession with Coop's wife isn't going away anytime soon. This latest despicable move is only one in a long line of despicable moves. No sooner do I step inside the Gas Lab than I see both Skyla and Laken talking to Ezrina behind the counter. Ezrina's belly is showing, a nice clean bump that indicates all things are in order as far as the baby is concerned, at least in outward appearance. I spot Coop and Gage sitting near the back and make a beeline over.

"What's up?" I slap both Coop and Gage over the shoulder as I take a seat between them.

"You're up." Coop's brows knit in a slight V the way mine are prone to do, and I can't help but smile. More often than not looking at Coop is like looking in a mirror. Which is exactly why what I'm about to divulge feels as much as a sucker punch for me as it will for him. I glance over to Skyla, and she locks eyes with me a moment before saying something to both Ezrina and Laken, and the three of them burst out into laughter. Less than a second later, the three of them are headed this way.

"I think we might need Nev for this little meet and greet." I call him over with the flick of the finger. The girls take a seat at the table just as Nev shows up.

"What a fine looking group." He lands his arm around Ezrina. "What can we start you off with?"

"The truth." Gage glares at Ezrina a moment. "Take a seat. Both of you."

Ezrina's face grows pale, but those dark eyes of hers fill with something just this side of rage. "No."

Coop and Laken exchange a quick glance. "What's going on?" Coop is pissed before we ever get off go.

I wipe my face down with my palm, and a flashback of the beating that mystery girl doled out comes back to me. She was strong. Strong as shit. Strong as a *Nephilim*. A dull laugh pumps through me. Of course. She's one of us.

"I'll give it to you straight." I turn to Laken. "There's a girl running around out there with your face."

Laken and Coop both take an audible breath while Ezrina and Nev rise from their seats.

Skyla takes up Laken's hand. "She was in Ezrina's lab, and now she's"—her eyes flit to mine a moment—"Chloe showed us some pictures last night. She's with Wes."

"Shit." Coop pinches his eyes shut a moment before pinning his anger on Ezrina. "I thought we were friends."

"*Are.*" Ezrina comes as close to showing remorse as I've ever seen her. "Sorry. Hands were tied. Wanted to tell you." Her voice grows small.

"Then tell us now." Laken isn't invoking any friendly tone with Ezrina, or most likely anyone else at the table once she finds out we've known for months. "Who is she, and why is she in the Transfer?"

"She's sleeping with him." Skyla cringes as she waits for the blowout.

Coop slaps his hand over the table so hard the entire establishment turns in our direction.

"No, it's fine." Laken shudders, and the entire lot of us shift our attention her way.

Skyla chokes on her words. "How is it possibly fine?"

Laken closes her eyes, and her fingers reach blindly across the table until her husband takes them up again. "It's not fine in any respect, but there is a problem I've encountered. It has something to do with my virginity." She glances around the table sheepishly. "It turns out Coop says I was with him first—and well, both my memory and my diary say otherwise."

"I hate him." Skyla groans as if she's going to be sick, but the lack of surprise in her face lets me know she already knew.

Gage shakes his head over at me. "He's going back in time."

"Is this true?" I look to Coop. As hard as it might be for him to relay, I think we need a few more details. This is big. This might be what we need to get Wesley's wings clipped. There's no way the Justice Alliance will put up with this.

"It's true. When Laken mentioned it in passing, I knew something was up. Lucky for us Laken kept a diary in high school." He glances to her. "Each fucking night that book told a different story. I started taking pictures of it to prove it to her."

"And that's when I knew Coop was right." Laken touches her hand to her neck as if trying to loosen an invisible noose. "A part of me can't believe he's done this. And sadly, a part of me can. My memory of what happened

431

is clear." She grimaces. "But only as far as his latest visit. Apparently, I've lost my virginity to Wes close to one hundred times, and that's just since we've been counting."

"Oh my shit." Skyla drops her head in her arms a moment. "Wait a minute." She surfaces with her hair wild as a tumbleweed. "If you've known about Wesley's vagina dialogues, why the hell haven't you torn off his wanker?" *Sorry*, she mouths to Laken for the colorful euphemisms I'm assuming.

Laken and Coop lose sight of the rest of us as they look to one another, a trace of a smile skirting on their lips.

"Have you confronted him?" Gage asks it for us.

"Not yet." Coop doesn't take his eyes off Laken. "But we will. Soon."

"Very well." Nev wraps an arm around Ezrina's waist. "We should get back to tending to the customers."

Coop's cheek twitches, his eyes still locked on Laken's. "You're not going anywhere." He drags his gaze to Ezrina's. "Who is she?"

"Can't." Ezrina's eyes fill with tears as she draws in a quick breath. "So very sorry." She scuttles off toward the kitchen, and Nev scoots right along with her.

Gage groans as we watch them disappear. "Sounds like Wes has got her by the balls. I'll talk to him."

"No." Laken cuts a somber look to each of us. "This is my business. My body he's defiling. This is personal. I'm going to take care of this myself."

Coop's cheek twitches as he offers a crooked smile. I recognize that crooked grin, that magnetic look of shared hatred, of revenge in their eyes. It's the exact look I gave Skyla before we ventured off to take care of the Counts and inadvertently turned our lives upside down.

My stomach clenches at the thought of Laken and Coop doing exactly that. I can't let them. Nope. The last thing I want to see is Laken and Coop imploding the way Skyla and I did. I wouldn't wish that on anyone.

Gage takes up Skyla's hand, gives it a kiss, and Skyla leans into him, her lips meeting with his a moment. And Gage was there to pick up the pieces. A part of me wonders if Wesley is hoping for the very same outcome. It's laughable, of course.

But stranger things have happened.

They say if you can see a heartache coming a mile away you should run, fast. And in a way, I did run, fast. I jogged all the way over to the bowling alley from Whitehorse, on this, the last and final night of its existence—in this incarnation anyhow. It's going to be one hell of a night, and I plan on spending it right here in the beating heart of the business my father built with his bare hands. The lights are off, with the exception of the glowing neon bowling pins lighting up the back of the lanes. Mood lighting—it goes right along with the mood music. I switch on the speakers, and the smooth melody of a love song vibrates throughout the bowling alley.

"Perfectly romantic," a voice quips from behind, and I close my eyes with disappointment. Definitely not the voice I wanted to hear.

"Dudley." I glare at the shoe depository, suddenly wishing I could cram him into it. "I'm expecting company."

"Yes, I'm aware." He circles in front of me with his requisite suit, his trench coat over that. "Skyla and Jock Strap dropped the twins off at the Olivers' as I was leaving. They mentioned something about stopping off at the bowling alley to say goodbye."

My chest gives a couple good thumps as my enthusiasm quickly wanes. In truth, I had built up this evening to heights that weren't fair to anyone, least of all myself.

"Great." I force a smile to come and go. "Gage should be here. It's his legacy, too." I had extended the invite only to Skyla. Sold her some lame excuse that I found a bag of old books that belonged to her in the back. That much is true. But in my mind's eye, I saw Skyla and I locked in one another's arm, slow dancing over the exact lane where we once proposed to another, her to me, and then me to her. It was just a small moment I wanted to recreate, but I wanted it with everything in me.

"Good grief," Dudley moans as if he's just read my mind, and he might have. "I've read your face, not your mind. I've no need to pry, but I'm assuming you've the need to know. Must you pine so openly? Have you no shame? What's Jock Strap to think? Dare I say their covenant means nothing to you."

The covenant—as in the marriage covenant.

"It means something." I slap the shop towel over my shoulder and glare at the bowling alley as if it were the very thing that tore us apart in the first place. "It means my hopes, my dreams, the deepest part of my heart are not to be explored." I grimace at the door, for the first time tonight praying she won't come, but I can feel her drawing near to me like the fog to the island. Skyla would never not show.

Dudley slaps his hand firmly over my shoulder and gives a quick squeeze. "You have a purpose for being here. If it were not true, Candace would never have allowed for it."

"Candace loves me. But I'm nothing more than a stumbling block for Skyla and Gage."

"That may be so, but that has nothing to do with why fate has landed you in the shoes you fill. Soon, young

Oliver." He gives a gentle pat to my back. "Soon all will be clear and you shall see your destiny"—he pulls me in by the shirt, his glowing red eyes speaking to me with something far more disturbing than words—"face-to-face."

He takes off for the exit just as Skyla and Gage come in. He slaps Gage over the shoulder, and they walk out the door together.

Crap.

"What was that about?" I'm almost afraid to ask. If that's Dudley's version of doing me a favor, I cringe at the thought.

Skyla bubbles with a laugh, her hair catches the light and glows pale pink. "Is that how you say hello now?"

My cheek inverts as I hold back a smile. "That's how I say this is too good to be true. Where's the big lug off to?" I glare at the door for a moment.

"Big lug?" She laughs while pulling me in by the collar. "You are dating yourself, Mr. Oliver." Her hips adhere to mine as natural as breathing, and before I know it, we're swaying to the music.

"That's because I'm old, Skyla." I brush the hair away from those bright eyes of hers. "What's with the smooth moves? You trying to incite a riot?"

"No riot." She winces up at me, her gaze lost in a subtle curiosity as if remembering a dream. "You are old, aren't you?" Her finger glides down the bridge of my nose. "Lucky for you I have a thing for old dudes." She gives a sly wink, and that bubbling laughter reprises itself again. My heart, though, it can't keep up with her insidious sense of humor, and instead takes every word to heart. Her features smooth out. "You should take them to heart. I meant every one."

I can't help but frown. "It's not always a gift to have you hear me. Especially those rogue thoughts that stray in and out of my brain without my permission."

"Those are the most insidious of all, aren't they, Professor Oliver?"

"Okay, you're funny." My hand glides down her back, and I dip her.

"Wow!" She rights herself, pink in the cheeks, her hair exploding into a ball of fire. "Why don't I do the leading for a bit?" Her left brow creates a hook as it skyrockets into her forehead. "Come," she says it low and sharp, and every last part of me very much wants to take it as a command. Skyla leads us over a few lanes before dancing us deeper down the slicked tongue of the alley. "Was it here?" She gives the innocent tick of curiosity in her features, but I can see right through it.

"You know damn well it was right here." I'm breathless. Not only am I dancing with Skyla, shutting this place down the way I've dreamed, but she's maneuvered us right into this very lane—exactly where the magic happened. "I'm in love with you." I press a kiss to the top of her head and linger. "As my sister-in-law, of course." I pull back with a shit-eating grin.

"Stop." She slaps my chest. "Technically, you're my uncle-in-law—a very naughty, *naughty* uncle." Now she's the one who's frowning. "How did you ever let Ellis talk you into this nightmare?"

"I'm assuming you mean the destruction of the bowling alley, not us." Although on paper, Skyla and I penned out to be a very bad idea. And in that vein, who the hell gives a shit about paper? The best laid plans often lead straight to hell. I can attest to that.

"Ellis talked me into a thing of beauty. You and I will both be standing here in a year"—I let out a breath, considering my construction timing—"or ten, and we will both be singing his praises. Ellis is responsible for a lot of good ideas." My bottom lip tugs as I restrain the smile once again. "Like Nathan and Barron."

"Oh crap." She buries her face in my chest while whacking my arm with her hand. "Is nothing sacred anymore? Okay, so you're right. Ellis has landed us a couple of happy accidents, but that doesn't mean taking a wrecking ball to this place is his best work yet. You sure about this? I'll work a shift whenever I can. Just let the bowling alley live to see another day." She dips her chin, pleading in that adorable innocent way, and my heart wrenches because this might be the first time I refuse her.

"I promise I will let the bowling alley live to see another day."

She gives a little hop, her fingers digging into my ribs.

"But before sunset, it gets the wrecking ball."

Her mood deflates as she rolls her eyes. "You're such a tease."

"I learned from the best."

We share a warm laugh, and my fingers glide into her hair as I draw her closer to me. Skyla lays her head over my chest as we move slowly, carefully one last time over the very spot where we decided to enter into a sacred, albeit brief covenant of our own.

"Your heart is beating," she whispers, patting her fingers across my chest.

"It's just showing off for you, Skyla. I'm still dead."

She shakes her head, sniffing back tears. "Not true. You're here, beautiful and strong. You smell good, too." She gives a gentle scratch over my chin. "Death is more or less an idea—a bad one, a good one. Who am I to say?"

I press my lips to her forehead as I consider this. "It's a mandatory regulation designed by the Master to cull the world of humans past their prime. It is the initiation of souls into the gathering of the ages—an ushering of spirits to the winnowing of the sheep and the goats, the white throne judgment for those it awaits."

"Don't we all await judgment?" The mood grows somber, as does the music, and her hips move slower, her voice edging just this side of tears.

"No." I pull back and look at her like this, washed in the neon afterglow, the hair above her head lit up like a halo. "We're forgiven. Past, present, and future sins wiped away as if they never existed."

Her eyes latch to mine as we hold a hypnotic gaze. "Though they were like scarlet, they are washed white as snow." Her finger bounces over my bottom lip with an aching grief. "Gage says he may not be able to control his heart. It's his worst fear. It's also mine."

A ragged sigh escapes me. "He'll need us more than ever."

She lays her head over my chest once again before looking back up abruptly. "Would you do something for me, Logan?"

The passion in her voice, the pleading look in her eyes, the pang of desperation exuding from her, it sends a rush of adrenaline coursing through me greater than anything I ever felt when I was alive.

"I will do anything for you, Skyla." My finger hooks under her chin, and I lift her to me ever so slightly. "I will move the earth, the moon—drain the world of its oceans. I will stop the wind from howling, the rain from falling from the sky. Name it. It's already yours." And yes, if she asked once again to stop the destruction of this place, I'd yield to even that. My finger strokes over her soft cheek, and my gut ropes off in a knot, but her gaze never wavers.

"Whatever you do, whatever you can do—please don't let Gage die." A single tear rolls down her cheek, sudden and unannounced.

"Don't let Gage die," I repeat numbly as I sigh into the concept. Gage dying is something that can never happen, and yet Gage not dying seems like an impossible feat.

"It is appointed for man to die once." The words strum from me like the lyrics to a tragic country song. "But I will stave off that hex, Skyla. I will do it for you." I shake my head out at the toothless lanes, most of the pins already picked over and taken to new homes. I gave away everything from balls to fixtures the night of the '80s party. Half the shoes have done a disappearing act as well.

"Thank you." She pulls me in and holds me with that strangled grip. "That means everything to me, Logan. Thank you from me. Thank you from my boys." Her heated breath warms my chest. "I'm sorry."

"Why are you apologizing?" My hand rubs over her shoulder as if coaxing the answer from her.

Skyla looks up, red railroad tracks where the whites of her eyes were. "Because I never set out to break your heart."

This is the part where I assure her she didn't. She couldn't. But I think we both know that would be a lie.

"And I never set out to be an obstacle to your happiness. Don't worry about me." A smile ticks to my lips, dull and lifeless. "Gage lives." I press my gaze to hers, heavy as iron. "And so does Celestra. When he entered into that covenant last December—Demetri gave a speech."

"Doesn't he always," she growls.

"He said something to the effect that the covenant would one day come to an end. I can't remember the exact words, but I remember thinking this curse wouldn't last forever. I promised myself I'd share that with you. Give you—give *us* hope."

"Thank you," she mouths the words. Skyla hikes up on her tiptoes and presses her forehead to mine, her eyes staring dizzying into me. "I hope that's true. But nevertheless, you are never an obstacle to my happiness. You are a source of pure joy. Our beautiful, brief marriage was a shining star in my life. Its glorious light still radiates over me, fills me with its brilliance, and sets my heart on fire. Three glorious days that most people cannot find in a lifetime. We had it all, Logan." She swallows hard. "Our love, our proposal, our wedding, our honeymoon—it was all perfect." Her thumb wipes away a tear I didn't know I shed. "I don't regret a thing, and neither should you."

I shake my head in lieu of words.

"Looks like a ghost town in here." Gage strides over at a decent clip, and both Skyla and I break apart like a couple of school kids caught making out in the closet. "Can anybody join, or is this a private party?" He flashes that killer grin, and I lift Skyla's arm into the air and twirl her right over to him where she belongs.

That bubbling laugh reprises itself. "We were just waiting for you to kick things off. What should we do? Pray over it? Steal the fixtures?"

"Pray over it?" I tuck my head back a notch. "I vote for destruction." I kick up a loose board with my shoe, same damn board I've spent the last six years nailing down with tacks, and with a hulkish cry I pour every ounce of Celestra strength I have into uprooting it from its home of forty years. Forty years ago, my father had this monument to shoe disinfectant erected, and forty years later, his lesser, far less greater son insists on dismantling it. I couldn't bring this place back to its former glory. I couldn't restore what Skyla and I had without destroying it either. I am nothing. A sheer disgrace to those who bore me, who came before me in my Nephilim lineage. Almost pure. That's what I was. Chloe, Skyla, and I—the three that could thrive. One is dead, one is evil, and one demands to cling to a Fem. We are a wily bunch, aren't we?

The board finally gives with a creaking groan, and the universe I was attempting to uproot in my hands lifts with ease as I come up triumphant. It's from the same lane Skyla and I shared so much history, and I'm keeping the damn thing—heck, I might even frame it.

Skyla and Gage stare over at me, wild-eyed, on alert should I go feral on them. I suppose the dead should be forever categorized as unpredictable. We don't have a hell of a lot to lose.

"Don't hog it all, man." Gage comes close to winking, a stunt he pulls off when he's having very real reservations about something. He bends over, and with a thunderous roar, in half the time, evicts the lane from its resting place.

Skyla jumps back, waving the dust from her face while coughing. "You boys have fun with that. There's something I'm hoping is still here, and if it is, it's coming home with me tonight." She trots off to the rack of balls in the back, scurrying from one end to the other, checking out the meager selection.

"No, no, no!" Skyla tiptoes to each and every ball receptacle between the lanes in a panic. "Oh *no!*"

My heart warms because I know exactly what she's looking for.

"Oh well." Her hands slap to her thighs. "I guess it's gone." She buries her face in her hands a moment before coming up for air. "And so is my sanity."

Gage takes her into his arms and lands a tender kiss to her temple. "Don't worry. Logan will have this place restocked with the latest and greatest as soon as the bowling alley is up and running again. And it will be." He scolds me with that last part.

"It was my favorite ball." She tosses a guilty glance my way. I know the one she's lamenting. A marbled blue and white beauty. "It was so pretty." Her lids hang heavy in my direction. "I remember thinking it was as though you shrunk down the earth and the sky for me in that little heavenly sphere."

A smile twitches on my lips, but I'm too somber to give it. I would shrink the earth and the sky for her if I could. I think everyone in the room knows that. The ball, however, is safe, sitting in a glass encasement, waiting for her in the butterfly room at Whitehorse. I think I'll let her stumble upon that surprise herself.

"Hey"—I tick my head to the very first lane, the one that I guess you could say started it all—"I've got a complete set of pins. How about I kick both your asses in one last game?"

"*Ha!*" Gage gives a howl of a laugh. "You wish."

Skyla clicks her tongue as she makes her way over. "You're both going down. The gloves are coming off. It's a take-no-prisoners kind of a night."

Gage lends those baby blues my way. I recognize that determined look, smug and far too self-approving. "You are going down, Logan. I am winning, and there is not a thing you can do about it." His smile is the last to arrive to the party as he joins his wife in picking out a ball.

But my stomach is tight as a wire. Something about that look, those words, equals a far from empty threat. If I didn't know better, I would say it was Gage's best premonition to date.

Skyla, Gage, and I play game after game—and game after game, Gage beats the hell out of us. He bowls strike after strike. He sends the ball sailing down the lane in a sublime pin-straight line that only Gage is known to do. He proves himself a force to be reckoned with even if it were the last thing in the world he wanted to prove. Gage loves us, and yet he is primed, he is destined to destroy the core of what we stand for.

He knocks the pins down one last time with a dynamic force that sends them detonating into the four corners of the earth.

"Yes!" he howls, beating his left hand over his chest. "There's no stopping me!"

And that, my friends, is exactly what I'm afraid of.

Skyla and Gage take off, but I lie down in that very lane with my face to the ceiling, a heart full of sorrow, and fall into an unsettling slumber.

That night I dream of my father—of my mother, roaming these haunted halls. The bowling alley is rundown, half the roof missing, the evergreens dipping in with their branches as if claiming its architectural victim. I've never believed Paragon wanted people here with their homes and roads and smog-riddled cars. She wanted to be left alone, cloaked in the fog, the mystery that surrounds those rocky crags at the base of Devil's Peak. In my dream, there is no wrecking ball dismantling all my father worked so hard to build. It is the island. Paragon reaches in with her evergreen talons and lifts the floorboards up one by one until all that is left is matchsticks. She is the victor. By the time my lids flutter to life like a couple of sparrows, I'm convinced this island could dismantle anyone if it tried.

Even Gage Oliver.

There are some days you wait for, pray for, love, hate, wish you could avoid. For me this day is all of those combined into one.

Barron stops by in the morning on his way to work, and we cross the street from Whitehorse to stand in the parking lot together one last time before the wrecking ball hits.

"It's coming back greater than ever," I marvel at the old dilapidated building. Had I ever noticed what shabby condition it was in before? There is something inherently sad about it, something very much like Gage, and for that alone I want to weep because I would never take a wrecking ball to my nephew. Especially not after what I promised Skyla last night. I guess you could say I officially became Gage Oliver's guardian angel, even if I don't quite qualify for the job—even if there's a force of darkness out there whose sole purpose in life is to make sure I don't succeed.

Barron lands his arm over my shoulders, and I take in the weight of my brother. Barron has always been a source of comfort, a refuge in the eye of the storm. He gave me the best life. He also gave me another brother, Gage.

"You know, son"—my heart warms when he calls me that—"it's rare for anything that has the ability to regenerate itself to come back in its former glory when its future glory is what it was destined for all along. There is little value to looking back with the exception to avoiding the pitfalls you couldn't dodge the first time. There is new purpose, new pleasures to be had, new victories, new alliances, and lastly, new discoveries for it to make about itself. I suppose that's the wild card. What will it become ultimately? Something to be venerated? Regretted? Something to be treasured and cared for, resented and discarded? The lens of a future world is not ours to peer through. Time will tell." He offers an abrupt pat to the back. "And I predict it will turn out well."

We stare off at the building, but those words Barron just spoke might as well have been a benediction to his one true son. Every word could be strained through Gage Oliver's lineage. If you could write a poem with his DNA, Barron just penned it.

"I'm off to work." He pulls me into a firm embrace just as an old truck comes sputtering into the parking lot, burping and farting like a seventy-year-old geezer who downed a keg of beer last night. And I'm right on every account.

Liam jumps out of his latest junk pile revival and struts on over.

"So, this is it?" He squints at the bowling alley as if the sun actually bothered to show up today.

"This is it." I welcome my brother with an open arm on the other side of me. "I had the appliances gutted from the kitchen last week. The construction company took the ones I could use in the new place and put them into storage for me."

Liam winces as he looks out at it. "Everything approved through the city?"

"You should know." The guys at Townsend Construction are letting Liam hang out and glean what he can. I know he's eager to open up shop on Paragon himself. This should be a great way to learn the ropes, not to mention the contractors state board he's working to pass.

Liam grunts as he shakes his head at the place. "It's going to hurt like a motherfucker watching this place go down."

Both Barron and I give a sober nod of agreement.

"The party starts at noon if you want front row seats. I'll be out on the lawn." I've envisioned what it would feel like when the first blow struck, and it hurt each and every time just the way Liam said.

"Goodbye, friend." Barron salutes the old place, and Liam and I follow his cue.

"Goodbye, friend," my lips whisper, but my heart says it's never going to say goodbye.

At about eleven thirty, the front lawn at Whitehorse begins to fill in with bodies. Laken and Coop, Drake and Bree, Ellis and Giselle, Michelle and Liam, Nat and Pierce,

Kate, Ezrina and Nev, Dudley, Lexy and even Chloe, and, of course, Skyla and Gage. They've left the boys with Emma—a good move, considering there will be dust and debris floating throughout the next few miles in radius to the bowling alley.

Skyla settles between Gage and me in lawn chairs as the construction crew brings in the heavy equipment. The crane that hoists that magnificent wrecking ball stands foreign in the air like a skyscraper. This is the city encroaching on Paragon's country charm, stealing the tranquility right out of the air.

A horn sounds and that ball begins to sway, slow and smooth as if it were trying to hypnotize the building in an effort not to hurt it.

Skyla takes my hand and gives it a squeeze.

Stay strong. She sets her nose to the sky as that menace across the street swings wide. ***I love you. We all do.***

The first strike hits and blows a hole right through the side of the building, and a gasp comes from those around me.

"Yes!" Ellis howls, and Giselle is the first to silence him on my behalf.

"It's okay," I reassure her. "This is progress."

"To progress!" Lexy shouts as that wrecking ball goes at it one more time.

"To progress!" the small crowd echoes, but Skyla, Gage, and I remain silent on the subject. It feels like a lot of things. At the moment, progress isn't one of them.

Like a dream in slow motion, like a nightmare at the right speed, we watch in horror, in delight, as the entire building folds like a house of cards. Arcade Heaven, the stinky pile of shoes, the defunct electrical system, the tiny thimble of an office, that kitchen where we had so much history, all of it gone and all but forgotten. All that remains is a pile of smoking rubble. The cleanup crew starts in right away with the effort to haul my father's dream away like waste. At the end of the earthly day, all of our material desires rot away like refuse. And upon closer inspection, they might have been that all along. It's the people, the flesh and blood you surround yourself with, that are the real treasure—the irreplaceable, indispensable monuments of our love that have the ability to define the sum total of our existence.

One by one the bodies drift from the lawn. After one lingering embrace after the other, they all scatter and disappear just like the bowling alley.

I head over to the oak I had planted in the center of the lawn so many years ago when I had this place built for Skyla. I lean against its sturdy trunk and stare out at the gaping, toothless smile of the forest that is also mine along with the pile of rubble that once belonged to my father. Technically, the land is Liam's and Barron's as well, but Barron made it clear years ago that my father would have wanted me to have it as something solid I can hold on to—and, as it were, *destroy*. If I ever make more than a dime off the new infrastructure, or the farm I plant behind it, I'll make sure to include my brothers in the spoils of my riches. A laughable idea at best, but a nice theory nonetheless.

Gage grunts as he heads on over. Skyla went inside with Lex. "I'll talk to my brother, see where his head is concerning the girl who looks like Laken."

"Sounds good, man." I know what he's trying to do—divert my attention. If only it could work.

Shockingly, it doesn't even bother me anymore when Gage references Wes as his brother. It comes so easily from his lips and sounds so normal, so very real. At this point in our lives, it's nothing more than a fact. They share a father.

Gage and I aren't even related by blood anymore. We've had our identities, our lives, our souls ripped from our bodies and stolen by wickedness, and yet here we are standing a foot apart as if nothing ever happened. At the end of the day, it couldn't change where our hearts lie. Gage is my brother. He is my family. Our lives are interwoven in every intricate way, so much so that if one of us should bend, it moves the other. Our minds, our souls, our hearts are sewn together. There is no barrier of blood that defines what we mean to each other. At least not with Gage in this state.

A horrible agony comes over me as I look at those big sky blue eyes. Not even Paragon and all of her brooding can erase that heavenly hue. It kills me to think that Demetri alone has the power to tamp down Gage Oliver's heart to a pile of rubble just the way I did with the bowling alley.

"*Dude*"—he grimaces as he pulls me in—"let it out. I know this is tough on you. You don't have to pretend around me. I'm the one person you never have to do that with."

Skyla pops up, breathless from the run over. "And I'm the second." Her arms find their way around me, and Gage closes his big mitts over the two of us until we form a warm huddle of perfect love. And the tears come, hers, mine, his, they are all there and accounted for. I was right. It's the people who are the treasures. My tears weren't for the lumber I'm soon to replace across the street. They're for Gage, Skyla, and me—three determined beings moving through time and space at lightning speeds on our way to our destinies, barreling toward that place that was determined so long ago for each of us as fate cinches the leash around our necks that much tighter. It's choking out the oxygen, making it harder to resist the inevitable slide, the momentum picking up at an unimaginable clip. We are unstoppable in our velocity. We will arrive on time, in the manner determined for us long ago, each of us on our way to complete the mission set out before us. Three minds, three hearts, and not one of us on the same page, no, not really. Gage has his role to fulfill in order to spare the boys of a darker fate. Skyla has welded a demon to her side—that would be Chloe. And as for me, I'm inching my way closer to what my flesh has wanted all along, Skyla as my own. And in an irony too big for fate to handle, I'm fighting tooth and nail for that never to happen. Even more grievous than that, I know deep in my spirit that I will battle Gage himself in an effort to stop him from self-destructing. Maybe the real irony is that we each self-destruct.

I glance to the heap of rubble across the street with a plume of smoke swimming toward the sky as the forklift gathers the debris and tosses it into the open mouth of a dumpster as long and as wide as a house. I can't help but wonder if it's all just some metaphor of who we will become and where we find ourselves in the end.

Late in the night, long after Skyla and Gage take off, I pace the floors of my bedroom like a death row prisoner next in line. Every now and again, I give a nervous glance out the window just to make sure the bowling alley is indeed still gone, that it hasn't resurrected itself like some macabre nightmare. Nevertheless, I feel it there, taunting me, saying *you can't get rid of me as easily as you think*. I've never thought of the bowling alley as some nefarious entity, more like a reminder that I'm not particularly good at any one thing. And here I've set out to spend a hell of a lot of good Harrison dollars to explode onto the business scene like some sort of entrepreneurial whiz. It's laughable, achingly tragic, and it stirs a grief in the pit of my soul that I never knew existed.

I head back to bed as Wesley Parker, *Paxton*, fucking hellish Edinger takes over my mind. Skyla was right. His need—his obsession to be near Laken is insatiable. And that right there is something I can commiserate with him on. I feel the very same way, only it's not Laken that has this dead man's blood pumping, my lungs struggling for their next breath in any way that God wants to give it to me. It's Skyla. It's always been Skyla. And, unfortunately for me, she is the only one who can take away this horrible pain. Yes, I will finally admit it. I am very much grieving the loss of Paragon's one and only mediocre bowling alley, my old friend, the very extension of my father and all of his love for me. It was his wish that I have it. His provision and shelter for me.

Wesley cured his pain for Laken by having Ezrina whip up another version, by going back in time and laying his hands on the very version he so desires. His obsession knows no bounds. His pain from losing her forced his hand. He was desperate and in need and did the only thing he could think of to quell it, to make life a little more bearable. He didn't hurt anyone, not really. Did he? Ezrina wouldn't force anyone to take on Laken's likeness. Wesley didn't force himself on Laken when he went back in time. Coop said so himself. Wes simply found a way. Not the best way. But a way nonetheless.

A thought comes to me, and I give a depleted nod as if accepting all of the lunacy. After all, every last one of my sins is forgiven, even the ones I have yet to commit.

My feet land on the cold hardwood floor as I stride toward the dark walk-in closet built extra-large just for Skyla's needs—her coats, her clothes, her private things, the shoes that adorn her beautiful feet, and I keep walking. I walk through the empty space, the walls, through time and space, and straight into the past, straight back to that blessed night of our honeymoon. Not the first night. That was an exercise in exhaustion, though exhilarating, it was never-ending and rightly so. I go for the next night, where I know for a fact there is a lull in the action, and for a brief, blissful moment in time, we are tangled in one another's arms. That's all I need right now, all I really crave.

And just as easy as crossing a continent, here I am, lurking in the corridor that leads to the restroom as the commotion on the bed slows to a crawl. I wait until the dismount. I have no intention on crawling inside my body while my most prominent member is still buried deep inside her. And there I go.

I head over, the ghost that I've become, and fall perfectly into my form. My own spirit eases over my body like a glove, and I take one rushed breath after the other in appreciation of the cardio we just underwent. Yes, I waited until all of the fun was through before crawling into my skin and into that bed with Skyla. I don't want to step on Gage Oliver's parade. I'm not Wesley. I'm not rewinding time like a porn reel I get the privilege of reliving over and over.

Skyla folds her arms over my body with a warm embrace, skin on skin, and it feels electrifying.

Her arms pull me in, and I don't fight it. Her naked, damp skin adheres to mine, sticky and wet. Her heavy breathing matching my own.

Her body bucks a moment, and she takes a deep, cleansing breath as if she too just popped back into her body from some other time scape.

"Hello," she says it breathless, her eyes glinting in the shard of moonlight—hell, most likely early morning light falling across her face. "I know who you are."

My eyes widen a moment. Those aren't words that I remember from that fated night. "You do?" A wry smile builds on my face as her tits press hard against my chest.

"Yes, Logan"—Skyla strokes my hair back, and the act alone cools me—"you confessed this to me. You came back because you needed me to hold you. Just for one night." Her voice grows weak as she speaks.

"Shit." I lean my head in the pillow. "Wait a minute. I would never tell you that." My body freezes because I'm suddenly fearful over the thought that I may not be in bed with Skyla, not the one I remember anyway.

"It's me." She pulls back and offers my chest a light tap. "I'm visiting, too." Her finger presses hard to her lips a moment as if to stop the reprimand before it ever begins. "You didn't have to confess anything to me. You'll eventually tell me yourself when the time is right on Paragon." A lone tear rolls down her cheek. "Logan." Her voice breaks. "I'm in pain." Her eyes close as the light catches all of the agony written on her face. "I just needed you to hold me, too." Her limbs latch over mine as she weeps silently against me. But her mind remains stealthily sealed off, unattainable to me no matter how hard I try to read it. No, Skyla is shielding me, protecting me from some horrible truth. So horrible she left the confines of her husband's arms to be here with me on this night of all nights.

We spend the next few hours lost in this dreamlike state, grieving, holding on tight, never wanting to let go.

"I love you, Logan," she whispers it heated over my chest, and my eyes close to those perfect words.

Sometimes all you want in the world is to be held by the one you love.

I fall asleep to the tune of our beautiful beating hearts.

But something horrible has happened for her to be here. It must have.

And I wonder.

5

This Enemy of Mine

Skyla

The week blows by like wind racing across the face of Devil's Peak, alarmingly quick and bitter. Of course, Wesley has proven impossible to locate, thus postponing his ass whipping from Cooper. And Laken is determined to initiate one herself. On the Landon front, Mom and Tad have the food in the house sealed in plastic bags while emptying the fridge into a moldy cooler. The big day has arrived in which we pump this entire oversized cabin with nerve gas and expect to return in three days as if nothing ever happened.

All I can think about is the delicate nervous systems of my two beautiful boys. If anything unfortunate should happen to them as a result of all those toxic fumes being delivered straight into our sleeping quarters, I will never be able to forgive myself. The boys are everything to me. It's as if life never really existed before they arrived. It's their smiles, their deep husky laughter that warms me to the bone. They'll be five months old tomorrow, and already they can sit up on their own, albeit while doing their best Weeble Wobble impressions. Okay, so they're not quite stable, but they're getting close. But my mother has assured me they are well on track as far as development goes. Emma agrees and takes it a step further by adding, *especially for twins*, as if the fact they arrived in duplicate had somehow lessened the odds of their developmental success. But, nevertheless, she seems impressed with the two little geniuses—and that, right there, is something we can both agree on.

Gage comes in panting after loading the minivan to the hilt, and I hand him Barron, already winded myself. I've got my Host sweatshirt on, and my hair in a ponytail, all ready to go on this, our quasi-official moving day.

"Let's say goodbye to everyone." I rebalance Nathan in my arms as we head to the family room. It feels good like this with my husband by my side, our family pieced back together again. All of that horror with the bowling alley has unsettled me. It underscores the fact that yes, things can and will change. Things that I believed were set in stone for eternity were only here for a short season—the bowling alley, much like Logan himself.

Mom jumps in front of me and snags Nathan from my arms. "Don't you take these babies away from me!" she growls right in his face, and he begins to sputter and cry.

"Give him back." I take the baby from her and give a quick once-over to the kitchen, every last cabinet unsuspecting of what's about to befall it.

Drake and Ethan grunt their way out the back patio door with a five-foot long cooler between them.

Bree hurdles it with a giant grin on her face as she speeds her way over. "You guys should totally stay with me! It'll be like one big slumber party!"

My mouth opens as I glance to Gage. "Actually, thanks for the offer, but Logan's already gone through the trouble of getting Whitehorse ready for us." Not to mention the fact Mom, Tad, Misty, and Beau are staying in the mobile home with them. It's cozy, yet cold, and no matter how many times Bree tells me it's a two bedroom, I've yet to find that second room.

"*Ooh!*" Her brows waggle as if the fact we were staying at Whitehorse was salacious news on some level. "Just the two of you in that big ol' house? *Lizbeth*"—she barks, and both Nathan and I straighten—"get ready to welcome baby number three in about nine months from now!"

Tad limps over from the kitchen with his face contorted as if he's just had a stroke. "Not on my watch!" He jams his finger toward Gage's crotch, and suddenly I'm fearing for far more than my future prospective children. Swear to God, if he touches my man's lightning rod, I will rain down hell on the Landon house the likes of which it has never seen. I'll make sure that entire burn unit scenario he underwent last winter is looked upon longingly once I'm through. "Put a sock on it this time, would you? Or better yet, keep it in your pants! You've already doubled the trouble to this household. There's no way—"

Mom is quick to karate chop his dangling appendage, and Tad lets out a yelp. "What he's trying to say is"—she bats her lashes at the two of us manically because she's mortified to be married to him for once—"we would welcome another delicious Oliver baby with open arms!" She scoops up Barron's foot and pretends to gobble it up, which only reduces him to the most adorable husky gurgles. "You have the yummiest corn niblet toes! Yes, you do!" She dives for Nathan's feet, and he wisely retracts while laughing wildly.

Bree bats her away as she steps in close. "You're welcome, and your babies are welcome, too. Besides, we need to get together and plan my big night out. It's not every day a girl gets hitched."

"What the hell are you talking about?" Drake howls as he and Ethan file back in. "I keep telling her we've already done this shit."

"Oh hush, you." Mom all but gives Drake the finger. "You've already deprived us of one wedding. Don't you dare deprive us of another. In fact, you're welcome to have both the ceremony and reception right here at the house."

"No way, no how. We've already gone around the thorny block," Tad barks while arranging the miniature vaginas on the table that both he and Mom are equally obsessed with as of late. "Of course, a monetary incentive could easily change my mind. In that case, the offer is very much still open."

Bree grunts at her *bother*-in-law. "Like we said, Drake and I have already paid Logan for the whole thing. Besides, if I were to have it here, I'd have to remodel this entire kitchen with top-of-the-line appliances, redo these grotesque floors, and put in marble or gleaming hardwood, and don't get me started on the furniture. Logan's place is already updated."

Something a little more aggressive than a hiccup comes from Tad as he gallops forward. "New furniture? Say, like a comfy new recliner for yours truly?" Saliva wets his lips and—dear God, did Tad just drool?

Mom joins her shoulder to his. "A complete remodel?"

"Oh, *yes*." Brielle is emphatic as she picks up Beau, spanks his bottom, then puts him back down. "I'm talking crème de la crème, luxury all the way. That's why Silent Cove is so perfect. Plus, Logan said he'd help hire the very same caterer Laken and Cooper used last summer."

Tad leans in as an anguished cry escapes him. "But, but—what about the remodel?" The cords in his neck distend with frustration. "You can even gut the bathrooms if you like. You can put in side-by-side gold thrones! Think about it, kids. His and hers *flushers*. Think of the toilet paper races, the beautiful bonding that an experience like that can afford you!"

Gage and I share a grimace.

"And on that note." I pull Mom and her ever-present fake mole in for a quick kiss.

Tad chokes as if he's got a chicken bone lodged in his throat. "We're not done here! Look at all the goodies we can hand out." He waves over the table of mini vajayjays, and Mom and I shudder at the same time.

Bree scoops up a handful of the tiny pink treasures with their tiny pearls embedded over that sweet spot that Gage has memorized oh so well.

"Yes, to the goodies—no, to the venue. I'm staying strong with Silent Cove."

"Sorry, Pops." Drake whacks Tad over the shoulder and brings him back to life. "I'll catch you on the next wedding."

Bree is quick to smack him. "This whole thing is a pain in the ass for poor Logan to plan out. We're not having another wedding."

"Not with you I'm not." They take off, and Gage and I set out to do the same. Just as we almost make a break for it, Em barrels out of her room and knocks into Gage.

"Whoa." He manages to swing Barron out of the way just in time because he's amazing like that. Gage Oliver is truly my hero. As much as I don't like what Demetri has essentially trapped him into doing, I appreciate the fact he'd lay his life and soul down for the boys. I didn't think I could love him any more than I already did, but I sure as hell do.

"Where are you off to?" Em slits those aggressively bored eyes our way.

"Whitehorse," I'm quick to offer. "And you and Ethan?"

"My folks'." She frowns as if this isn't a good thing. "Ember is scared shitless of the place, so we're leaving her in the trailer." No sooner does she say it than little Ember runs out screaming.

"Mee-Maw! *Tampon!*"

"Oh God." I touch my fingers to my lips. "We need to nip that little sanitary nickname in the bud because if word gets out on the mean Paragon streets, our kids are never going to live that down."

Em rolls her eyes as if I've erred on the side of the dramatic. "She's just calling it like she sees it." She starts to walk off, then backtracks, poking her finger in Gage's chest. "Get your shit together. I'd like to see my brother again one day soon." Her slitted eyes return to me. "And, you"—she pokes her finger in my boob, and I let out a yelp—"I have a message for you."

A breath hitches in my throat because traditionally Em's messages usually frighten me right out of my skin. Those prognosticating panic-riddled pattern filled nightmares have routinely led me straight into trouble—with the exception of that one time she predicted the arrival of the twins who were actually triplets—my precious serpentine butterfly. Poor Sage, all alone in the nethersphere with my mother of all people. It's no wonder she's a pint-sized danger to herself and others. Once things die down, I plan on venturing up there and spending some good quality alone time with her.

"We don't want another message," Gage answers for me as he herds us down the hall.

"It's from Chloe," she barks after us. "She says it's time to make good on that promise or she's bailing."

"Freaking Chloe," I mutter under my breath as we hit the porch. "Will do!" I shout back and wave before Gage and I take off for the waiting minivan and load it up with our love.

Gage buckles in the last twin before wrapping his strong arms around my waist and landing those perfectly formed full lips to mine as we share a hot, delicious kiss.

"You ready to have a few blissful days with just you, me, and the boys?" Those dark brows of his do a little dance, and my insides quiver at the sight.

"I am ready to have a lifetime of just you and me and the boys."

"Good. Let's move it." He gives my bottom a light pat, and I can't help but giggle. "Is that a naughty sign of things to come?"

His lids hood low, those dimples of his dig in deep. "I think the very first thing we should do is get naughty and come."

"*Ooh*." I wince. "Lucky for you, the boys are asleep."

"And if we're both lucky, they'll stay that way for hours." He gives a gentle peck to my lips before we hop into the van.

It's just the boys, Gage, and me.

I look out the window and frown up at my bedroom window because it once belonged to that gnat in my eye—Chloe.

Yes, for the next few days, it's going to be just the boys, Gage, and me.

And Chloe.

Damn her to hell.

And if my plan works, I will do just that.

The drive to Whitehorse is giddy with sexual prospect as Gage entertains me with the things he plans on doing to my body once we get settled. He's convinced that the boys will nap for four days straight.

"You are a dirty, *dirty* boy." I reach over and pick up his hand as he takes the final turn, and we both gasp as that gaping hole that once held the bowling alley comes up ahead. "My God, it's like a slap in the face."

"It feels as if the island is giving us the middle finger."

"I'll say."

The minivan curves into the driveway, but my head remains craned to that desolate sight. "I hope Ellis' craptastic idea pays off for Logan."

"It paid off for us." He gives a shit-eating grin as he kills the engine. "Come on, the boys are asleep. I want to carry you over the threshold. This is a big deal. A week-long vacay from Tad is like Christmas and my birthday rolled into one."

"Oh, come on. You know you're going to miss the hell out of him." I give a little wink and run up the porch laughing.

Gage flips a baseball cap over his head and opens the side door of the minivan closest to where we can keep an eagle eye on the boys.

I waste no time in doing a little happy dance at our prospective—albeit short-lived freedom.

Gage pulls out his phone and snaps a picture of me at the door. "Wait, I want to get a video of this for posterity." I give a brisk wave to the camera and flash my brightest smile.

One day when I'm old and gray I want to look back at how happy it made me to know I'd be doing a little horizontal dance with my handsome hubby in just a few short minutes.

"Come here." I wave him over in haste.

"Let me set this thing down." He trots his phone over to the railing and rests it against the post.

"You ready to do this?" Gage strides my way with that come hither look in his eyes, and I'm ready and willing to do just about anything with him right about now.

"*Yes!*" I hop up and down, hardly able to control my Landon-free enthusiasm.

Gage turns the knob, and the door flies open. Then in one fell swoop he picks me up and spins me with a kiss. "To our first official home on Paragon."

"Only home," I tease as I pull him in by the bill of his hat. I'm not ready to call the old Walsh house ours just yet. "Gimme a forever kiss," I say, batting my lashes, doing my best to seduce him. The last thing I want to talk about is real estate, this home or any other. I just want this to be about us.

Just as he's about to carry me past that threshold, a horrible sinking feeling settles in. Something about this feels all too familiar. I've been here before—*been here, done this*—said those very words.

"Turn that off." My head cranes to the camera in horror, and I leap out of his arms like a gymnast. My heart wrenches with agony as I fumble with the phone, struggling to shut the damn thing off.

"What's going on?" Gage appears at my side, his arms secured to my shoulders as if he needed to hold me down to earth, and he might.

"Demetri." A silent cry bucks through me at the thought of how much pain we just invoked in Logan. "Summer before senior year, Logan's birthday—we were at Demetri's—in that damned theater." I shake my head, still dismayed by the memory. "Demetri used that footage we just shot to torment Logan. It was just Demetri being an asshole." My heart wallops hard because I have a feeling it was so much more than that. Why choose this moment to torment Logan? Was Demetri sending Logan a heartbreaking message? Or was it meant for me? I glance back to the boys still sound asleep in their car seats.

"So this was the vision." Gage takes a step back and glares at Whitehorse as if it were the house's fault. "Me here at the house that Logan built."

"Trust me, you're the last person Demetri was messing with."

"Or am I." He gives a depleted frown at the doorframe that holds the banner of Logan's love for me. "We never made it through the threshold." He shakes his head at that gaping doorway. "He's speaking to me, Skyla."

I join him in staring blankly at the dark hole of the house. "What do you think he's saying?" I whisper, afraid to ask—praying that perhaps he didn't hear me.

Gage wraps his arms around me from behind and rests his head on my shoulder, our gaze still fixed on the porch. "He's about to interrupt us. That's what it means, Skyla. He was just showing off for you and Logan. It's me he's about to stab in the heart."

The two of us stand there for who knows how long, staring at the opened door as if it led to a black hole. I don't doubt for a moment that it does. But I'll be damned if I let Demetri steal another thing from the two of us.

"He doesn't own us." I spin into my gorgeous husband's arms and lock my wrists around his neck. "And he will never shape our destinies."

He lets out a quiet sigh and closes his eyes briefly. "You're right. This is our springtime."

"The time of our rebellion."

His lips rise at the tips. "No rules."

"Just you and me, together forever." I hike up on my heels, and Gage and I share a heartfelt kiss, his tongue probing me as if the answers to life were hiding right there in my mouth. Then just like that, he scoops me up and races me across the threshold, and we laugh, right there—in the face of Demetri Edinger.

We collect the boys and carefully bring them up to the master bedroom with us. Gage faces them toward the wall and covers them both, still snug in their carriers.

The bed is turned down on one end, revealing crisp sheets that feel as if they have never been slept in. I wondered how I would feel in this room, in this bed realizing that Logan would know we defiled it. But deep down, I don't think Logan sees it that way. Deep down, I don't either. This is a room. This is a bed. And starting right now, it belongs to Gage and me.

Gage comes at me with that devilish grin, taking off his shirt as he makes his way over. The breadth and width of his muscular frame, his wingspan with those well-defined lats, those abs as hard as granite.

"Gage Oliver." I have to catch my breath. My God, he truly is a stunning specimen. "Are you threatening me with your body?"

"Hell yes, I am." He lands me on the bed as a steady stream of giggles bounce through my throat. "And I'm going to punish you with it, too." He ravishes me with heated kisses up and down my neck, and I struggle to keep from exploding with laughter.

Gage takes my clothes off. He washes me from head to toe with his tongue, penetrates me with all of his love.

Gage could never punish me with his body.

It is always a pleasure.

The third day of our second honeymoon, I take the boys to Marshall's while Gage takes off for finals back at Host. The island basks in its monochromatic glory despite the fact summer is nipping at our heels. Both Barron and

Nathan are fast asleep, so I schlep them into the living room one by one.

"You know, you could have helped." I take a moment to frown at my favorite Sector.

"I adore observing you in the throes of motherhood." The words strum from him with absolute boredom. "It suits you. Have you thought of more children?"

"Ha!" I laugh in his face, and both boys flinch, so I lead us over to the piano. "Are you kidding? I can hardly handle two. I *miss* sleeping. I miss my old jeans. Heck, I miss my old boobs." I pluck at my blouse, and his brows rise with approval.

"What brings you and your"—his eyes sink to my chest—"new, voluptuous, beautiful, nurturing—"

"I get it." I take a seat on the sofa and Marshall is quick to land next to me with his arm draped over my shoulders, and a wild fit of vibrations strums from his body to mine. The haunted speculum in the corner winks in the light. "Chloe is meeting me here. I've summoned her."

"Summoned, have you?" An obnoxious grin spreads like wildfire over his face.

"Okay, so she summoned me. But nevertheless, we've business to tend to."

That gorgeous face of his reconfigures into a perfect scowl, and he looks that much more comely. It's shocking the women of Paragon aren't beating down his door, not in the same disturbing frequency they used to anyway.

"Skyla, you know that I wish you well in this new war you've embroiled yourself in. May your sharp arrows pierce the hearts of your enemies. Let their nations fall beneath your feet."

A heart-stoppingly beautiful moment pulses between us. "That was a gorgeous benediction. Thank you for that."

"You're welcome."

"And—speaking of having business to tend to with the aforementioned beast." I curl my finger under his chin as if I were trying to seduce him, when in fact we're both fully aware I'm about to do my best to *seduce* a little info out of him. "When will you pay back my darling new pet for stealing that bed warmer from Ezrina? I believe you promised retribution." Honest to God, some of the most horrific things that have happened to me were a direct result of me showing off my five-finger discount skills when it comes to the *Sextor's* secret things. Having my arm chopped off, that entire fiasco at winter camp a few years back where Kate lost her head—yup, all nefarious arrows point right back to Marshall's draconian punishment tactics. But why should I reap all the horrific benefits? Surely, Chloe of all people could use a hatchet or two hurled her way. Just the mention of a hatchet makes me miss old-school Ezrina.

His brows dip as he frowns. "I've already begun the wheels of punishment brewing for Ms. Bishop. Worry you not about my retribution. I'm afraid you've enough on your own plate as far as raining down the comeuppance on the parties that have wronged you and your people."

"Touché to that. You know"—I tap his shoe with my own—"you're the only one who hasn't asked me what I'm doing with her." My heart lets out a few wild wallops because clearly this alarms me on some level.

"There are some things, Ms. Messenger, that I do not wish to be apprised of."

"Nice. I wish there were more people like you in my world. Because I loathe the day I need to cough up my confession to Logan and Gage. It's ridiculous the way they have me on a leash."

"You don't believe that, and neither do I."

"No, but it sounded good." I think about it for a moment. "They used to, but something's happened. Ever since Gage has sacrificed his destiny for the boys, it's as if nothing has really been the same. Logan, Gage, and I have always been a team."

"Quite an erotic team," he adds without a single dash of humor.

"Yes, well, you can get off your high horse because you're a member."

"That's where you're wrong." He glides his finger over my cheek. "I am not a *member* alongside Jock Strap or the Pretty One. I'm in a league of my own. Lest, you forget our spiritual bond—our covenant with one another that transcends flesh and blood." He traces the outline of my lips, and my body indulges in a mean quiver. Damn hormones. "Our love is unique, special, and true. I left the heavenlies for you—retained the proper permits to dwell among humans and Nephilim alike."

"Permits, huh? I sound like a construction project you've undertook." My thighs rush with pleasure as if they too were about to take on a project of their own—Operation Climax. It's never safe to sit this close to Marshall.

His cheeks depress into rarely seen dimples. "I treaded the weary halls of West Paragon High for you." He's too busy itemizing his horrific sacrifices to offer up a proper comeback to my architectural humor.

"Now that you mention it, I've always wondered why you chose a position of authority rather than being my contemporary, like say Logan or Gage."

Marshall groans at the mention of their names. "Although I consider myself *your* contemporary, your rival, your fully equipped lover—I don't consider myself theirs. Casting myself from the heavenlies was a supreme sacrifice all on its own, but to demote myself to a teenager was more than I could bear."

"Fully equipped lover, huh?"

A growl emits from him, low and husky. "I can demonstrate if you like."

The doorbell rings in triplicate, followed by hasty knocking that jars the boys to life with a startled cry.

"I'd say I was saved by the bell, but I think we both know who that is."

Chloe bursts in just as both Nathan and Barron scream as if their hair was on fire, and I unbuckle and scoop them up one by one.

"Oh no!" I pepper their sweet, rather irate faces with kisses. "Please be good for Uncle Marshall."

"Pardon?" He turns abruptly from the powwow he was having with Chloe.

"Well, you can't expect me to take them along."

Chloe enters the living room with a bounce in her step. "Where we off to? Let me guess, the Gas Lab? The *mall*?" She sticks her finger down her throat and pretends to gag.

"Tenebrous," I say and Barron wails so sharp and loud you'd think he understood me. Of course, Barron's high-pitched wailing gets Nathan's feathers ruffled, and now it's a soprano choir in here.

"Good Lord, can't you control the little monsters?" Chloe growls at the boys. "Let's get out of here. I've had enough of their competitive crying. Tenebrous sounds like heaven compared to this whiny baby hell you've leashed yourself to."

"Tenebrous?" Marshall grunts as if he's the next one to throw a fit.

"Yes. Chloe and I need privacy. It's the best solution. Besides, who knows how many spies Wesley has swarming the island. They're everywhere. You can't escape them." It's true. You can't go three feet on Paragon without having a fed trying to pose as a tourist. They're everywhere, expanding over the island like bread mold.

"Skyla." Marshall ticks his head to Wesley's betrothed.

"Not this spy. She belongs to me." I give Chloe a quick wink while handing the noisy boys over to Marshall, and no sooner do they land in his arms than they both let out a hearty sigh. Marshall jostles them a bit, and they share a laugh in turn, warming me to the marrow.

"God, they have the best laugh." I kiss them both on the cheek before hiking up on my tiptoes and offering one up to Marshall, too. He turns just enough for me to land smack on his lips. "I'd say I owe you one, but I think I just gave it."

"You do owe me one." Marshall glares at the two of us as we head out the door. "And I'll be cashing in sooner than you think."

"Anything you want! It's yours!"

Chloe grunts as I lead her out to the woods. "Ten bucks says he'll demand a blowjob. He'll be balls deep before evening."

"You wish."

"I do wish. Wesley hasn't touched me in months. I'm like a virgin all over again."

"Lovely." I take up her hand as we enter the thicket behind Marshall's home and step into a fog so dense you can take a bite out of it. "Control your hormones for five seconds and think Tenebrous."

"Nice of you to take me to hell."

"Well, if I've heard you say it once, I've heard you say it a thousand times—there's no place like home."

There was a time when Tenebrous was abhorrent, a thing of horror, a hell whose best hope was a blaze that ravished every last inch of it. But the tunnels closed, the

Celestra who were once imprisoned here are now free or had long since died along with their dreams. Then in a twist that only life could provide, I requested it from Demetri as a wedding gift. Yes. I acquired an entire plane of existence for the mere price of marrying his son. Gage was baffled as were most of those who discovered the fact, but Logan and I knew that if our Retribution League were to thrive, it needed a prison of its own. And that's exactly what this is—*was*. A year ago, it was filled with Videns who had voluntarily become a thing of horror themselves—Spectators, the lore of which zombies come from. Yes, there was a time when the Tenebrous Woods were frightful, the stench of blood so pungent your palate was stained with a metallic taste for days upon leaving. In these very woods is where Wesley suckled off my neck, drank my blood like nectar to bolster his powers far beyond that which his Countenance lineage afforded him—before Demetri knighted him a Fem. It seems that over the past few years, identities have swapped out, alliances shifted, the landscape of the Factions is almost entirely unrecognizable. But Tenebrous remains unchanged, dank, dark, sallow with its charred evergreens, its deep velvet sky, the parched ground that thirsts for so much more than blood. And now it is mine.

Chloe and I land flat-footed among the thistles and briars, the slight stench of blood still rotting the air. The ground is dried and cracked, a desert terrain within this necrotic forest. Dark, twisted oaks, gnarled and burnt. The evergreens are dusted with soot, all of their vivacious color reduced to a somber shade of gray. There is no sun, no moon—not on this day, nothing but a strange darkness, that eerie glow just before night falls hard over the land. This world glows with plums and wines, even the light pays homage to the blood once shed on these grounds. The overgrown building behind us that once housed our

Nephilim brothers and sisters now sits empty, collecting dust until the Viden Spectators can be detained once again. Wesley didn't mind putting them in danger as long as they were outing the Nephilim people. As far as I see it, Wesley is the only one who should be imprisoned down here—I glare at the demon to my left—and perhaps Chloe, too.

I head over to one of the old hitching posts and find Ingram's glowing notepad. Ingram Pendergast was left to plod around down here centuries ago—by the Counts, by my mother, the details all seem fuzzy and unimportant at the moment. He's sort of the official keeper of the Tenebrous gate. He was Ezrina's ex in another life, another time before he was brought here to be a keeper of the tunnels. He's still lurking around the grounds somewhere, living it up in no-man's-land. Nevertheless, I scoop up the glowing notebook as we head out of the forest.

"Let's sit." I point to the stone of sacrifice just past the skeletal woods. The stone shines like a lavender pearl in this strange universe, and I get straight to business of itemizing my covenant with Chloe on the glowing device. I take a moment to erect a shield over my thoughts—impenetrable to Chloe and any powers she might still be wielding.

"*Finally.*" Chloe lands next to me, her knee touching mine. There is a fire in her eyes, one that holds equal parts hope and vengeance. "I want the covenant initiated today. No more of this pussyfooting around." A wry smile comes and goes. Sometimes you just need to cut a deal with the devil, and today is as good as any. "Bree told me all about your mother's twisted venture. Who knew I had so much pull with her?" She examines her fingernails, but judging by that maniacal look on her face, I know she's contemplating a Lizbeth Landon takedown just for the hell of it.

"You don't. Money does. And as dumb luck would have it, vaginas really are the next big thing." She's raking in so much, Tad hasn't lamented his lack of employment once. Even though Althorpe all but dumped him, he's still managed to eek a decent living from the disability checks stemming from what he now refers to as his *lucky burn*, but like all Landon great prospects, that good time is coming to an end.

Chloe grunts out a laugh. "You should know. Your vagina was the next best thing as soon as you showed up junior year—so young and so tight, it even turned the head of inhuman faculty members."

"Just the one." I wag a finger at her as we share a quick laugh. "I'll summon my mother, and we'll do the covenant this afternoon. Why put off a good thing?" I drill her with my gaze. Chloe has always been a class act liar, but her eyes, they're too feral to contain any secrets. Chloe's eyes give her away before every single one of her bad intentions. But, at the moment, they look gleefully in line with her maniacal heart.

"Yes." She draws a fist toward her chest in victory. "I'm going to break open one of those million dollar bottles of wine Wesley keeps molesting in the cellar. Of course, since he's received his Ezrina-issued sex toy, he's even refrained from that."

"Did you ever find out who the girl is?"

"No." Chloe looks just as frustrated as I do. "She's some tramp who's hot to trot with the idea, though. He says *get in bed*, and she asks *how wide do you want my legs spread open*. She's a real tramp, this one. I don't get it, though. With my ability to morph into the idiot, you'd think Wes would have been more than pleased with that. Why the body double?"

"You're asking me?" I scoff at the thought that anyone could figure out Wesley. "But then, you are his bride. No offense, of course, but you're, well, you're *you*. If this other girl is as willing as you say she is, then she's probably not mouthing off and giving him a hard time."

"The only thing she's giving him is a hard-on."

"Disgusting. I mean, doesn't she have family? A life? Who is this girl that just dropped out of the blue and let Ezrina rearrange her face?"

"Did you ask the hag?" Chloe has no respect for Ezrina, even though she utilizes her genius as much as the rest of us, not to mention her body. If it wasn't for Ezrina's misfortune, Chloe might have descended to the depths of hell quite literally.

"She's not talking."

"Good." She sits up straight. "Because I don't want to talk about Wesley's skank either. Let's get down to brass tacks, Skyla. The rules, if I remember correctly, were, I side with Celestra, fight the good fight for our people, and you let me live above ground once again."

A half-smile rises to my lips. In typical Chloe fashion, she only reiterated half of what was spoken that night by the fire. I will never forget the pain, the anguish in my heart, and yet the startling resilience to carry on for my people. Putting Celestra—the Nephilim as a whole before me, was the only thing that got me through those miserable Gage-free agonizing days, outside of the boys that is.

"Yes." I spin the glowing piece of equipment her way. "You are my equal in leadership in every way with the exception—you are my number two. You may not make a move without my authority, my approval. You are my—"

"*Bitch*." She twirls her hand as if prompting me to get on with it. "Yada, yada— and I get to dwell among the living, on that desolate God-forsaken rock called Paragon, and my aversion to that God-awful bird will be forever revoked."

My lips purse at the thought. "Not really. I don't think that's possible. Besides, Holden and his new bride happen to be running around that desolate rock in coats of flesh at the moment, which brings us to our next point."

"The dawn of the dead," she says it flat while folding her arms across her chest in defiance. Chloe isn't a huge fan of the dead in general—but she sure is a huge fan of pushing people to that oxygen-deprived side. "Name it and it's as good as done," she strums the words out, bored, as if she were capable of pulling off anything. And, seeing that she's desperate to get what she wants, I believe she is.

"I need all of the dead discovered. I have maps, locations of where I've shipped them. I need you alerting authorities. I don't have the next fifty years to dwell on this. My mother and I went to Cost Club last week, and the feds have descended on that food court like pigeons. There's no escaping them. I need Wesley's project halted in its tracks. Once the feds collect enough specimens, they won't bother coming after anyone with a crooked biomarker. Wes and all of his nefarious biological dealings can go straight to hell."

"Done. I'd be thrilled to land every last rotten corpse in a cage by midnight if that's what you'd like for me to do. I just need to go home, Skyla. I can't live with that weasel in his dark, brooding hell any longer. My mother says she'll take me back. I can have my childhood bed to rest in. I'm sure Brody will be more than happy to help me assimilate. Bree thinks I can take on a permanent position at West as the head cheer coach. Life will come full circle for me."

And sadly, those are all the things she already has on some level, but I refrain from sharing that with her. Chloe knows it well. Chloe is already ten steps ahead of everybody else. Or at least she thinks so. And don't even get me started on the fact she never once mentioned poor Tobie. October Edinger is essentially nobody's daughter. I can't quantify Wesley as a parent no matter how loving and nurturing he might be. Deep down, I wish he would abandon her the way

Chloe has so we can evict that poor child from living in the hell of the Transfer—in the hell of the wicked influence Wes is sure to have on her. He's branding her, burning his emblem of evil over her very soul. Each day she's with him, she drifts further and further from sanity's edge, and she hasn't even hit her first birthday.

"That is the plan." The heavy sky presses over us like a lid set to enclose a boiling pot, and for a second I can hardly breathe. This moment, right here, will change so many lives. So many mistakes can breed from this disease seated before me, but I know that all too well. That is my truth. Deep down, I realize this is a necessary evil. If there is even the slightest possibility of having a rogue Gage Oliver on my hands one day, I need to seal my enemies to my side. I can't have them running and hiding. I can't give them the upper hand—and ironically, silence and distance do exactly that. That was a principle I understood well on that horrible night when I saw with my own eyes my husband standing on a stone just like this one gifting himself to Demetri and his twisted cause. And in an irony only fate could provide, here I am nearly six months later on a stone just like that one with another demon, readying to launch myself in a covenant that seems wise in my own eyes. My own wisdom has been known to abandon me quickly, but as it were I still see the need to have the most dangerous knife in the drawer as a part of my arsenal.

"Do you love Celestra?" I hook my gaze into hers, and she flinches. Chloe squirms under the microscope of my scrutiny. For as much as she hungers to be the center of it all, she can't handle the scorching heat that comes along with a psychological dissection.

"I do. And I will go to the ends of the earth proving this to you. *We* are taking back what is rightfully *ours*. You and I will never lie down for Wesley and his Bullshit Brigade as long as we have breath in our bodies. I may not like you, Messenger, but in this task, we are united. We are one, and I will do whatever it takes to destroy whatever, whoever, however many stand in our way. We were born for greater things than these." Chloe reaches over and picks up my hands. "And for God's sake, don't worry, Skyla. I am not about to snatch the crown off your head. You remain the Faction leader, scream queen supreme, whatever the hell it is you're calling yourself these days. I just want my life back and a chance to stick it to the bastards who keep controlling it."

I let out a breath I hadn't even realized I was holding. "No use in putting it off then." I tip my head back and visualize my mother in the heavenlies holding little Sage's beautiful hand as they skirt the crystalline shorelines of paradise. "Mother?" I blink up at the sky. "You say you are always with me—ever-present in my time of need. And I am in need. I ask you once, come quickly. Chloe and I have business to tend to, and we need your presence to officiate the new bond we're looking to undertake."

Chloe drops my hand like a dead fish. "That's it? No hocus-pocus? Just a please show up if you have the time? If that was my mother, I'd tell her to get her ass down here asap."

"And that's why you live in the Transfer and I live on Paragon."

"Touché." She scowls. "For now."

"For now, indeed."

"What's this?" a cheerful voice calls from behind, and both Chloe and I turn around, stunned to find my mother, Candace Messenger herself, donning the cliché paradise couture, white silk robe, shiny golden sash to complete the celestial look. "A meeting of the minds and I wasn't invited?" she bubbles with a trill of a laugh, and my stomach sours on cue. My mother is never timely when I need her. And she never bubbles about anything. My radar goes up because if I've learned anything about the woman who bore me it's that I should very much watch my back around her.

"Oh hush, you." She flicks her fingers my way. It's clear my mind is an open highway for her curiosity to travel whenever the hell she feels like it. "What's this bond we're looking to undertake?"

Chloe and I stand as she joins us on the stone.

"A covenant." My heart thumps wild. First, because I still can't believe she showed so willingly, and secondly, because I'm about to enter into a binding covenant with the girl who has caused me so much heartache, the one who took Logan away from me.

My mother cuts me a quick look, sharp enough to slit my throat. "Yes, Chloe is responsible for killing my precious." My mother glides right by his formal moniker and dives headfirst into adjectives when it comes to the fair-haired Oliver. Figures.

Chloe lifts a finger, her face full of false adulation. "And I am sorry about that. I do love Logan. You both know that."

"It's true," my mother affirms as she lands an arm around Chloe's shoulders, and I shudder right down to my core. "Now, what is it that has two Celestra sisters bonding over in Tenebrous? Come, come—I've a multitude of needs to meet this afternoon. So many destinies to alter." Her eyes sharpen over mine, clear as a white-hot flame.

"Chloe and I would like to enter into a covenant together," I say it plainly like placing an order for a short stack at the Gas Lab.

A quick flash of lightning flickers from above.

My mother's affect flattens as if she didn't see this coming, but I don't buy that for a hot and holy minute. "Hold hands. Outline the terms."

Chloe huffs in disbelief, "Just like that?"

"Don't doubt me, daughter." My mother is quick to cut her down with the lash of her tongue, but it's the term of endearment she chose to give her that unnerves me.

I take up Chloe's hands, and my mother shakes her head at the sight.

"Not like that." She manually crosses both our hands until we're conjoined in a fleshly figure eight. "Like this. Now outline the terms." She looks to me, hard and stern. "Carefully, mind you."

"Carefully." I give Chloe's hands a quick squeeze, fully aware she can read my every thought at this point. "Chloe Jessica Bishop, I, Skyla Laurel Oliver, enter into a holy covenant with you, on this day, in this hour, effective this very moment. These terms that I outline with you are permanent and binding."

Chloe gives a solemn nod, and suddenly it feels as if we're exchanging wedding vows, and sadly, this is tantamount to exactly that.

"You, Chloe, will be my right hand. You will do my bidding. What I decree will be so. I will take into account all of your thoughts, your wants, your dreams as far as Celestra and the Nephilim people are concerned. We are in unity for the advancement of our people. To serve, to protect, to guide with love is our chief resolution. There is nothing we will not consider when it comes to the well-being of our people. We are Celestra. You and I are as close to pure as there has ever been. We will act in one mind from this moment on to shield our race from those that wish to destroy it. There will be no day like today ever again when powers unite in the name of all that is holy and true. We will move swiftly and without regret to extinguish the actions and on occasion the very beings that stand in our way. Our people are in peril, and we will create a shield over them under the banner of our love."

"Amen." Chloe gives my mother a cheeky grin.

"And"— I tip my nose in the air, my eyes still locked over Chloe's shallow pools of murky darkness—"you will not harm my family. You will not plot to harm nor carry out actions to harm my sons, Barron or Nathan, and you will not harm my husband, Gage Oliver. You will not harm Logan, Marshall, my earthly mother, her husband, my sisters, or anyone we hold near and dear—and that goes for pets as well. You shall not harm a hair on my head." I bear into her with something just this side of hatred. "It will not even enter your mind. You will not harm the Celestra people or the Nephilim nor go against any of my ordinances. And if you do, the repercussions are uniquely mine alone, and whatever punishment I decree will be binding on earth as it is in heaven."

Chloe averts her eyes to my mother before sneering my way. "That's our Skyla, always sucking all the fun out of everything." She gives my hand a violent tug. "Yes, my God, yes, Skyla. That's why I'm here. I will be your subordinate, your subservient. I will be the sickly worm that crawled under a rock, and you will be the sun, warming me, welcoming me back to life. And, yes, I understand fully that your interest in me is our unified love for our people— Celestra first, then the Nephilim in turn. I am against everything Wesley Bastard Edinger stands for. May his destruction, his grotesque misuse of his powers fall squarely over his rotten head. I am not interested in moving forward the agenda of my husband, but of my sister's—that would be you, Skyla." That mean shiver returns once again, shaking my vertebrae like fingers scaling the keys on a piano. "We will work together to restore all that Celestra has lost, to secure the lot of our people so they no longer live in fear of the Counts or the Barricade, or any nefarious dealings the Fems might have instore. They have sided with the Counts, but Celestra has sided with the Sectors. Though the intimate details of their battles are not ours to have, we understand our people's rise to power coincides with theirs, and therefore, we are inseparable and will bolster the Sectors' needs along with our own. It is under the Master's love and His banner that we stand, and both you and I, Skyla, understand that He gifts us the knowledge, the wisdom, the power to stand in the presence of our enemies. We will be swift with retribution to whomever stands in our way, and I will not dream of harming a hair on the head of those you love." Her left eye comes shy of winking as if those words pained her on some level. "And if I do—*you*, Skyla Laurel Messenger—*Oliver*—may instate the punishment you see fit. From this moment on, I am your right hand—just a little lower than your equal. All of my thoughts, my ways, my every move will be yours to monitor. I am a living sacrifice, yours to utilize as you please." Her fingers press into mine, hard, bone over bone. "Skyla—" She steps in, her breathing erratic. There's a pleading, a fear in her eyes that I have seen only once before, and that was the day my mother doled out her fate and sent her to the Transfer. "I need you to promise you won't harm me—that this isn't some setup to send me to a worse fate than the one that I'm escaping. I need to know that you mean what you say and that your word is binding and true. In order for us to be successful, I need to be assured that we are truly on the same team." She tips her chin up, those ebony eyes falling hard over mine. "Woe to the hour you turn on me, Skyla. There will be a darkness in your life like never before or after it. I will be swift with my punishment, for my spirit is a wildfire—this slash-and-burn heart of mine is primal, and though intrusive to many, it is one I cannot control. My rage is the brightest kind of flame. It cannot be tempered. Even I cannot douse the fire. My anger, my hatred has always stemmed from hurt, from pain, from being denied what was rightfully mine. I have always believed you took my place, and yet I am yielding all of my primal tendencies to act against you so that I may stand *with* you, shoulder to shoulder. Together we can, and, we will, rule the world. Assure me of my safety before we proceed."

I swallow hard. "Fine. Mother, search my heart and hers, and assure us both we are true and right with our intentions."

My mother steps forward and places a warm hand over my forehead and the other on Chloe's as if reading a fever. Her hair lights up, each follicle its own filament of lavender, blue, pink, and the palest shade of yellow. My mother is a vision with her fiber optic appeal, and my body buzzes with delight with those feel-good vibratronics that pour out of her.

She pulls her hands back and straightens. "It is as the two of you suggest. Any further stipulations?"

"Yes." I offer a peaceable smile to the girl who was once a sworn enemy, the killer of my father, my husband. "You can live on Paragon as we agreed. But I have the full power to send you back to the Transfer, or worse. From this moment on, your morphing abilities will be disabled. Take a moment to mold yourself in the exact likeness you will live out your days." A thought comes to me. "And, also, on your behalf, I will have full access to Tobie."

Chloe flinches. "You want the brat? Wesley won't have it."

"That's why I want you to fight for your rights with the girl. When it's your time with her, she will be with me. I will be the mother to her that you refuse to be."

"Good grief." She grunts as if the idea made her physically ill.

"I will love October Edinger as if she were my own." Because I have to. The only thing more dangerous than your enemy is your enemy's child.

Chloe belts out a bubbling laugh. "Yes, Messenger. Have at her. She can swing off your tits all day while she suckles away. I don't give a flying rip. Hell, you can let Wes swing off the other nipple. I couldn't care less about the wandering idiot."

"Perfect." I give a little curtsey. "And just to be clear, my husband is off-limits to you. Gage Oliver is mine. He is the crown of life I wear on my head, our children the jewels of God pressed into the center. My family is sacred, an unapproachable throne that you may never touch."

"We've covered this." Her features harden as if her patience were wearing thin. "And I've already agreed."

"Wonderful. To our newfound partnership. Here's to the preservation and prosperity of our people."

My mother offers up a dull applause. "Great. Now let's move on with our day." She turns as if to hop off the stone, and I pull her back by the silk sleeve of her winter white robe.

"Whoa, so that's it? You're not going to say a few words? No thunder—no ring of lightning?"

She rolls her eyes as she looks to Chloe. "That's our Skyla, always a flair for the dramatic." I'm not liking my mother and Chloe unified on anything, least of all not when it comes to bashing me so openly.

Chloe gives a sly smile. "But then, we've always thought so, haven't we?"

My radar sounds its internal alarm. Red fucking alert.

"That's right." My mother chortles. "We have, haven't we?"

Chloe and my mother have been spending time together? Discussing *me* of all people? Holy hell. Why do I suddenly feel masterfully manipulated? At this point, I have no clue who is more dangerous between the two of them.

My mother's hands fall over each of our foreheads once again. "Skyla and Chloe, you are now true sisters in every way. May it be as you have committed, all of your sentiments binding on earth as it is in heaven." She offers an exasperated sigh. "How's that for a few words?"

Just as I'm about to open my mouth, a horrible crackle of thunder deafens us as a nest of lightning, purple and white, dazzles from up above. A coven of bats flies to the sky, screaming as the thunder roars over Tenebrous, and the earth begins to shake. Then just as quick as it came, it dissipates, back to the calm, the disturbingly eerie silence that Tenebrous has to offer.

A mirror appears on the stone, full-length, encased in an intricate gold frame, and I immediately recognize it as a twin to the haunted speculum in Marshall's home.

"Find the features you like best." My mother nods to Chloe as she leads me off the stone and near the blackened woods.

"Anything else I can do for you, my love?" Her eyes settle over mine, harsh like a punishment, as she doesn't bother to disguise the sarcasm in her voice.

"I don't want the dead to suffer." Casey and the countless number of the dead that were resurrected come to mind. "No lingering deaths. I need this to move fast. I can feel Wesley nipping at my heels. The government is everywhere. They are hungry. They want retribution for those agents that were killed. We need to feed the federal beast before Wes hands my people over in droves."

"I agree. Don't waste any time. Act quickly to ensure the dead are captured. That number should satisfy them and stretch their facilities to capacity. A mass death would look horrible for the institution, and if you find the right group to protest government testing on these visitors, you might stall their efforts to harm your people for decades to come." She gives a self-satisfied smile. "As for the manner in which their lives are extinguished—you should have thought that through before you deployed them," she hisses, her eyes slit with fury as she looks to Chloe. "You should have thought a lot of things through. You gave her everything she already has along with the keys to the kingdom."

"Yes. But now she has to answer to me. *I* have the keys. If Chloe wants to take the car for a spin, she needs to hotwire it." I scowl over at the demon while she preens at her own reflection. "If you can't kill a cockroach, put the damn thing on a leash and make it your pet."

"Is that what you're doing with Gage?"

"Mother!" I stagger back a moment. "Your disdain for the love of my life never fails to freshly offend me. He is the father of my children."

She smacks her lips with boredom. "Is that all it takes to garner your devotion—*children*?"

"I'm ready!" Chloe calls from the stone, and both my mother and I gasp at the sight of her. Chloe has always been a stunner, but this newly polished, perfectly sublime version is a tour de force of beauty. Her long dark hair is thicker, glossier with just the right amount of waves to give it life and a body of its own. But it's her face that captivates. Yes, she is still very much herself, identifiable in every way, but you can tell by those almond eyes, the straight nose, those cheeks that touch heaven, and those knockoff Betty Boop lips that Chloe Bishop will have both the living and the dead turning heads just to steal a glance.

"Wow, Chloe"—I can't help but gawk at the gorgeous sight—"if your husband could see you now."

My mother scoffs. "What is this obsession you have with husbands, Skyla?" Her chest bucks as she says the word *husbands* as if she were about to hurl at the concept. "They're mere men, Skyla. Not to mention the fact they require so much attention."

Chloe grunts as if she could relate. "Feed me. Fuck me."

A round of lightning flickers from above at the mention of an expletive in my mother's presence. "Nevertheless"— she shrugs as if Chloe were right—"they are slaves to the flesh."

Chloe bounces up beside her. "There is no greater truth. It's as if all they ever think about is filling an orifice— theirs, ours, it matters not. Never mind the horny pigs." She pats her hair down while preening to my mother. "How did I do?"

"Well done." My mother lifts a hand, and the speculum evaporates to nothing. "Now before I go"—she turns to the woods—"please join us, Sage. Your time has come."

"Sage? My God"— my entire person swoons with delight—"will I get my daughter back?"

"Technically speaking, you most certainly will." My mother curls her fingers until Sage steps out of the shadows, her tiny frame, her long dark hair, those deep-welled dimples are an exact representation of her father, albeit at about five-years-old. But it's not Sage that has my attention for once. In her tiny arms is an equally adorable being, a baby—perhaps just a little older than the twins, blonde curly hair, eyes that glow large and bright a unique shade—the lightest aquamarine you have ever seen with lashes that look gloriously thick and rich. She's wrapped in a thin pink robe, same gold sash as my mother and Sage, albeit miniature, and therefore, outlandishly adorable. I've never seen a baby girl so preciously stunning, with the exception of Sage, of course, and, in truth, I've never seen Sage at that age or stage.

"Who is this visitor?" I step forward, and Chloe joins us as we lean in and gawk at her tiny perfect glory.

Sage picks up the baby's chunky foot, clamps her teeth hard over its tiny little toes, and the baby lets out an ear-piercing cry.

"*Sage!*" I bat her hand away, and the baby manages to pluck her pink little foot free, her large eyes watery with tears, her perfect bow tie lips tugging down at the sides. The baby reaches for me, and I lean in to take her, but Sage is quick to twist her from my grasp.

Sage growls at both Chloe and me. "She likes it when I do that." She stuffs the tiny foot into her mouth again and gives another violent chomp.

"She does not!" I'm quick to snatch the screaming child away, and in a moment, a calm like never before falls over me. It's as if I've waited my entire life to hold this precious little being.

"Ma Ma!" The tiny blonde beauty squirms as a smile comes to her ruby lips and she laughs and claps, and I can't help but laugh along with her. Rows of tiny teeth are exposed, just a few here and there, but they shine like pearly seeds.

"She just called me Ma Ma!" I marvel at the tiny chubby cheeked angel. There's something startlingly familiar about her—and strangely enough, intimately and deeply, I love her as if she were my own. "She's a doll. Who is she?" I glance to my mother who glows with an ethereal light as if she had suddenly swallowed the sun. She's grinning from ear-to-ear, and suddenly I'm worried for everyone in Tenebrous. "Mother? I demand an answer."

"Come, child." My mother takes up Sage by the hand before reverting her attention to me. "You said all it would take to garner your devotion of a man is to have his child." Her eyes brighten a dazzling shade of sunshine as if she could no longer contain her joy. "And now you have it—*her* as it were. I've gone to the future and procured you a little pink gift."

My heart ratchets up into my throat because I'm afraid I know exactly who this little angel is. This child belongs to Logan—and me. "Why are you doing this?"

"So you'll fall in love with her—and you have, instantly. So you'll forget all about that Gage and let him sink to the bottom of the sea."

That Gage?

"I'm not letting Gage sink to the bottom of some heartless sea."

"You're not exactly giving her back to me either." She steps in close, but I can't take my eyes off this magical being, so beautiful and bright. "Perhaps you should keep her a while. Would you like to know her name?"

"No!" She can't have a name. She can't exist. My heart breaks because everything in me wants to keep her. I would never want to blink her out of existence. Logan and I can have an affair—a brief, *brief* affair. Dear God, what am I saying?

"What are you saying, indeed?" My mother glares at me after having the audacity to listen in on my private thoughts. "You realize how the Master feels about adultery."

"And you realize how He feels about divorce."

"That won't be an issue. Give my love to Logan." She lifts a hand, and a spray of miniature stars ensconces both her and Sage as they dissipate to nothing.

Sage glares at me as she evaporates to nothing. The weight of her disdain for me sends a violent shiver through me. It's as if I were her enemy. She sneers at my mother. "She loves her more than me! I hate that little pink pig."

"No!" I wail with the perfect tiny being cooing up at me with a smile. "I can't have another baby. Tad is going to kill me."

Chloe steps in and ogles the tiny babe in my arms. "Oh my shit, Messenger. This is your kid—and Logan Oliver is the father. My, *my,* don't you have the happy little ovaries. I'm sure Gage will be thrilled. In fact, I don't think Tad will be the only one who'll entertain a homicide." She scowls as if I've really screwed up this time, and I might have. "Now get me island side. There's an entire bitchy little clique of dead girls I would relish to turn in by evening. I won't let you down, Messenger. Just you wait and see. Together we will conquer the world."

"It's not the world I want." The sweet little angel in my arms pulls my hair and squeals with delight, melting my soul and my heart in the process. Oh my God, I am in love, swimming so deep and wide I never want to get out of the angelic waters. And giving her back to my mother is the last thing I want to do. "I just want my people to be safe—my marriage to work."

"You're on your own with Gage." That darkness in Chloe's eyes returns as she sinks her gaze into mine. "For now."

I take up Chloe's hand as Tenebrous is traded for the woods behind Marshall's estate.

I know what Chloe meant. It wasn't the blatant threat I would have once assumed it to be. It was in reference to Demetri, to his constant pull on my husband. I've got news for that Fem rat. In this tug-of-war for Gage Oliver's soul, I win. Hands down. All fucking day long.

The baby in my arms chortles as if agreeing with me, and she warms my heart all over again.

The woods reappear with each evergreen a shade more vibrant than the next. Even the monotone hues of Paragon are a welcome sight in comparison to Tenebrous.

Chloe staggers a moment as do I, weighted with the tiny blonde bundle of joy who happily squirms before knitting her fingers in my hair.

"Ma Ma!" she cries, jubilant and loud, and my stomach tangles in knots.

"You have fun with that." Chloe smirks at the baby. "I'll text you and let you know how many I trap. I can spot the G-men a mile away, so obvious with their sunglasses and pressed collared shirts." She plucks a tube of lipstick from her pocket and applies the bright red caustic hue. "If they're lucky, I might even fuck them." The baby in my arm flinches at the expletive. "*Aww.*" Chloe leans in, and the baby retracts, burying her face in my neck, and it feels like heaven. "She's just as sensitive as her ma. I'll catch up with you later, *sis*. I want to hear all about the fireworks. I'm guessing poor Gage won't be so enthused to find out he's an uncle." She takes off for the street and holds up her middle finger. "Relax, it's in love."

"In love, my foot. Speaking of which." I pull up the babe's tiny chunky toes and rub my thumb over the impression of Sage's teeth. The baby looks up at me and blinks into her own innocence, so heartbreakingly precious, so startlingly beautiful, my heart comes to a complete stop. Tears come to my eyes. Here she is, the sweet angel Logan and I would have made with all of our love. I see him there in the bridge of her nose, the shape of her lips. She has his strong jaw and four little teeth, top and bottom, and I can't help but note her gums look swollen.

"Ma Ma!" She smacks me in the chest and picks up the protective hedge and shoves the pendant right into her mouth. She spits it out and goes for the mirrored heart that

Logan—her father, gave me instead and suckles on it as if it had the power to soothe her. She lays her tiny body against mine, solid and warm, her heart beating erratic against mine and lets out a ragged sigh.

"Oh my dear God, I love you. I do." I pepper the top of her head with kisses. "But how is this ever going to work?" I glare at the blank gray sky with a brewing anger. "This is not funny, Mother. You seriously lack a proper sense of humor."

A bout of girlish laughter comes from my left, down by the ravine, and I hesitate a moment before wandering over. The laughter ensues, and before long it's joined by the growl of a man. He's saying something to her, and their murmurs grow increasingly sexual in nature along with those hearty, heady, I need you right now groans of passion.

The baby falls into a perfect slumber over my chest as I hide behind a tree. Who the hell would be hiding on Marshall's property? Randy no less? Oh my God. What if Marshall is getting it on with one of his seventeenth-century hussies instead of watching the boys? The thought alone sends me charging out of my hiding place and straight into—

"*Mia?*"

Standing before me is a rumple haired, rumple clothed Mia and that rat Gabriel Armistead with his pants unzipped, his junk hanging from his boxers.

"Oh my God!" I howl and spin as if I just had my eye poked out. "*Mia!*" I shout so loud the baby jerks and screams without warning. "Oh no!" I'm quick to jostle her, but her cries only intensify.

The boy strides past me as if nothing ever happened, and Mia hops in front of me, red-faced and pissed.

"What the hell has gotten into you?" She pokes me hard in the chest, her own shirt still unbuttoned, exposing a black lace bra, and, well, a rather nice set of boobs. Not really fair since I had to have twins to achieve that look myself. When did Mia get tits, and why the hell do they look better than mine?

"Me? What's gotten into *you*? That's not even your boyfriend."

"He is on Fridays!" she riots back.

I blink into this younger, far more fragile-minded version of me.

"Of course, how stupid of me." The baby claws at my chest. I help her find the mirrored heart, and she's right back to suckling on it, her heated flesh has the robe melting to her skin like wet paper. "What is this Friday business?" I shake my head violently. "Never mind. I don't think I want to know. Whatever it is, knock it off. You just can't have two men in your life, Mia. That would make you—"

"Just like *you*." Her brows rise as she gets that smart-aleck look on her face. Then just like that, her focus shifts to the babe in my arms, and her affect melts on cue. "Oh my God. Who is this princess, and can I keep her?"

My heart breaks into a million pieces because I don't have it in me to lie to Mia. We're supposed to be growing closer, not dividing ourselves with a chasm of lies and part-time boyfriends.

"This is your niece." My voice breaks as the tears start to flow. "She's my"—my entire existence shakes to the core—"my daughter." I give a rambling explanation of what just happened, and Mia wraps her arms around me long and hard.

"Oh, *Skyla*. I'm so sorry you have to go through this." She pulls back, her own eyes red with tears. "I promise I won't tell." She picks up the little angel's hand and brings it to her lips. The baby does a jumping jack filled with joy and gives a hearty laugh as she plays with Mia's lips. "She's so happy." She shakes her head. "Skyla, I know you love Gage, but maybe you can just skip that whole baby making part and keep her? I don't think I could bear to lose her. Plus, I want you to have a girl so I can buy all those cute dresses. And if she stays, you can make all of my pink dreams come true."

"I'm afraid not. I'm guessing she's on loan." My heart wrenches just thinking about it. "Look, Marshall has the boys. If I give you the keys to the minivan, would you take them to Emma's? I'm sure she'll watch them for me. I don't have a car seat for the baby, and to be honest, I'm not ready to juggle three just yet."

"What are you going to do?"

"I'm going to talk to the smartest girl I know."

"Mom?"

I make a face at my sister without meaning to. "Laken Stewart—*Flanders*." She chose Coop over Wes. That might just qualify her as the smartest person on the planet— although, technically, that was a no-brainer.

Mia gives the two of us a quick kiss before walking backward toward the house. "Don't you dare give her away. I licked her. She's mine! I swear to you, I'll keep her!" She giggles as she runs off. But I stagger forward, numb with shock, as I hold fast to baby number three—or four as it were.

I text Laken, and she texts right back that she's at the Gas Lab, so I teleport right over. Only I'm low on juice, correction, permanently running out of fuel, and I make it as far as West and hoof it the rest of the way with my new babe tucked safe in my arms.

After a long, exhausting jaunt, I finally hit the Gas Lab, winded, stunned by how a baby can feel like a one hundred pound lead weight. And it only reminds me that in a few short months I won't be able to hold both of the boys the way I do now. The boys! My God, they have a sister—at least one on earth at the moment. My heart ratchets up in a panic, and suddenly the fact I entered into a binding covenant with Chloe Bishop is the least startling event that's taken place this afternoon.

Just as I'm about to step inside, a surly looking dude in a heavy wool coat glares at me as if I've just stolen his lunch money, and I instinctively hold the baby a little bit tighter.

"I know you." He steps in, and I take a full step back. "You're what's-his-face's wife." His voice rises a notch. "You tell that idiot husband of yours the Videns have one serious fucking bone to pick with him." He grimaces at the baby a moment. "Never mind. I'll tell him myself." He stalks off, and I let out a breath of relief, filling the air with a stiff white plume, and the baby flaps her arms as though she was happy as can be.

"That mean man just threatened your daddy—um, *uncle*." My heart breaks just thinking about the title my husband would play in her life.

I walk in and spot Laken near the back, and I make a beeline over only to see Coop sitting there along with—

"*Logan*," I hiss his name under my breath, and he stands to greet me along with Laken and Coop.

"Skyla." He grins at the bouncing baby in my arms who's suddenly flapping her arms as if she's about to morph into a dove and fly right into her daddy's arms. "It looks like you grabbed the wrong baby." He holds a finger out and she curls her tiny hand around it, and I melt on cue. Logan's eyes widen as he takes her in. I can see her wrapping herself around his heart just as easily as she did his finger. "Wow. I don't think I've ever had my breath taken away by anyone but you. Who is this amazing beauty?" His voice is low and tender, the exact tone fathers reserve for the daughters they adore.

"Da Da!" She stretches her arms for him, and I shoot a panicked look to Laken.

Laken steps in, her own eyes just as wide. "Wow. She's so pretty!"

Coop wraps his finger around one of her blonde curls a moment. "Did she just say Da Da as in *Daddy*?"

"Um." I look to Logan and shrug. "I guess she did."

"You did?" Logan leans in and presses a quiet laugh through that magnificent grin of his, but he never breaks his gaze from the girl. "Who's your daddy? Huh? Who's your daddy?"

A breath hitches in my throat. "*You are.*"

Why waste a moment of fun under the nonexistent Paragon sun?

All three pairs of eyes lock over mine.

"What did you say?" Logan's face piques with color as if he understood perfectly.

"My mother sort of dropped her off." I'm quick to point to the ceiling in the event there was any confusion about which mother would do such a thing. "Leave it to her to take away the element of surprise." My shoulders bounce once again. "Surprise! You have a girl. *We* have a girl."

"You have a daughter?" Laken gasps because, let's face it, things couldn't get any more gasp-worthy.

Coop leans into my line of vision. "With *Logan*?"

"Well—" Honestly, I'm at a loss for words. The baby struggles to reach Logan's neck so I carefully place her in her father's arms.

"Oh God," he whispers as he takes her from me, stiff at first before he molds his body to hers. His eyes close, and he lands a loving kiss over the top of her head and lingers. "I love you," he whispers. And those, right there, are the sweetest words Logan Oliver says to his precious little girl in this, the hour of their meeting. It's all moving so fast, at such dizzying speeds, and yet I demand to record every sweet moment in my memory, etching this portrait of the two of them over my heart like the treasure it is.

"Skyla"—Laken shakes her head—"how? Why? How long? What will happen next?"

"I was sort of hoping you'd have those answers for me. That's exactly why I hunted you down."

"Skyla?" the high-pitched, happy-to-see-me voice of my mother bellows from behind, and I freeze. Not the heavenly body that birthed me, but the far more practical earthly body that reared me.

I turn slowly, only to find she's already diving past me and playing with the baby's chubby little feet.

"Oh my God! What a beautiful baby! Look at this face! Why, that's the face of an *angel*."

Tad pops up and grunts at the sight. "Don't tell me she's added another one to the collection. See this, Lizbeth? She's scooping up strays off the street just like I predicted. Well, too bad. There's no room at the inn. Load up her diaper bag and send the kid packing. We're at capacity with rug runts."

Mom swats him over the shoulder. "Oh, wow. Those eyes! They're so pale with a blue heart with little freckles in them—and so light and clear, and they're a sweet water blue. Why, they're *tourmaline*. But that face! I've never seen anything like her. No offense to Misty or Ember, but this one looks like an angel that fell right out of heaven. What's her name?" She looks to Logan as do the rest of us.

"Name?" He ticks his head my way before stealing a kiss off her cheek, and I melt all over again. This right here is a moment the two of us should be having in private, not at the Gas Lab—for sure not in front of my gawking baby hungry mother.

"Oh, I just have to hold her." She's quick to pry her from Logan's arms. "My sweet Lord! You are just too precious to live! You must really be heaven-sent."

The baby giggles up a storm, her voice light and sweet with a trace of the boys' husky nature, and my heart wrenches because, well, she really was heaven-sent.

"Her name?" Mom nods as if ushering along the conversation.

"Actually—" I'm pretty sure child services will intervene if I don't come up with a good explanation. I turn slightly and note a man at the counter openly staring in this direction. He's got a pair of dark sunglasses sitting on the top of his head, and he's wearing the requisite pressed buttoned-down shirt. Crap. I'll be damned if he's taking my baby back to D.C. to poke and prod her with needles. "She's Laken's niece. Her name is Angel." I grimace at my friend who's suddenly at a loss for words.

"Right." She shrugs. "Only my sister Jen is out of town, and well, Skyla and Logan said they'd help me watch her." Her dark brows point down into a hard V, letting me know she's more than unhappy to be dragged into this.

"Angel." My mother bounces the happy little babe in her arms. "It sure is fitting. If you ever need a sitter, I'd be thrilled to lend a helping hand."

"That would be great." Laken nods, scooping up her bag while Tad scoffs himself into an early grave. "Because I just so happen to be on my way to my last final." She offers me a quick hug. "God help you, Skyla, because I sure can't," she whispers, pulling back. "I'll call you."

"Great." I wave as she and a hesitant Coop head for the door.

Tad squawks like a bird who just had its beak chopped off. "See that? They just stuck you with the kid! Dump the little river rat, Lizbeth, before these two take off as well!"

Logan reaches over and takes our little angel back into his arms. "That won't happen on my watch."

"Oh"—Mom clasps onto my wrist—"just so you know, we'll be back in the house tonight. It's all wrapped up. Not a living thing survived. I was assured those pumps released enough toxins to destroy the nervous system of every living creature within those walls. Feel free to come home tonight with the boys. Demetri sent a crew to wash every bit of clothing and bedding. Can you imagine? He's instructed them to scrub the carpets and dry clean the drapes. He's such a gentleman."

"That's because he's relatively sane and understands the fact that nerve gas and infants don't mesh well together. I'll be at Whitehorse at least another night." Or twelve.

The baby bounces against Logan's chest, her beautiful eyes still latched onto my mother's. "Mee-Maw!"

"Oh my God!" Mom staggers backward as if someone just pumped a bullet into her chest. "It's like she knows who I am!"

"That's it." Tad yanks my mother clear across the restaurant until they come upon an empty table. "No job and no home equals no more stealing other people's babies!"

Mom turns around and mouths, "I love her!"

"Great." I lean against Logan, and the baby tries her best to rip my lips right off my face. Her happy limbs all twitch with glee at once. She's so happy it's infectious, and I can't help but smile. "I'm sorry, Logan."

"For what?" He runs his finger over the outline of her perfect features. "You've just made me the happiest man on the planet. This is the best day of my new life."

"*Great.*" I whimper once again. "I've got a car seat you can borrow back at the house, and Emma is all set up to take on a baby or two. I'm sure you'll do fine."

"Skyla"—he ticks his head back a notch, inspecting me—"you wouldn't leave her."

Just like that, all of the anxiety, the nervous energy that's been storming inside me up and disappears. "No. I'm afraid I can't."

His eyes meet with mine, and he knows exactly what I'm thinking. "Emma just invited me to dinner. She says the boys are there, and Gage is already on his way. We'll tell them together." He pulls me in, and the baby squirms with delight, cooing and laughing, shouting Ma Ma, Da Da over and over again as if it were her favorite song. Here we are a family. We've always been one. "Are we really going to call her Angel?"

"I think we should for now." I bounce my finger over her tiny perfect nose, and she takes it by force into her mouth and begins to suckle off it. She's hungry, and I can feel my breasts swelling to have her. Tears come as I try to contain my emotions. She's so perfect, so beautiful, so in the wrong frame of time it makes both my head and my heart want to explode. "Maybe one day"—my voice breaks—"if..." But I can't finish the sentence. For me to have a baby with Logan would be treason to my marriage with Gage, and I'm fighting tooth and nail to keep him. I know my mother. She's fighting tooth and nail for me to lose him. As much as I want to call what she's done a despicable act, I can't find it in me to do so. This is one of her greatest gifts to me. "Maybe we can bypass all of those laws of biology and just keep her?" My hearts soars at the prospect.

A crackle of lightning goes off outside, and the lights dim enough for the patrons to let out an unsettled *ooh* before life resumes as normal. Only for Logan and me— Gage, too—normal is something we will most likely never experience.

Emma answers the door winded as if she were the one with earth-shattering news, and I can't help but scowl at her a little. She is trouble. Kate said so herself—although, Kate seems hesitant to extrapolate on the idea. She did mention something about holding off until it was her time to go and then she would spill the troublesome beans. Just what kind of a witch is Emma that she should sponsor so much fear in Kate?

Her eyes grow wild as she examines Logan and me, baby Angel tucked in my arms and happily drooling over my shoulder. Logan and I drove to Devil's Peak. He happened to have two sets of car seats strapped into the back of the Mustang in the event he needed to pick up the twins. Demetri gifted us so many sets of those luxury baby confinement units I peppered everyone's car with the devices that I could. And, of course, Angel snuggled up in one like an old pro. We watched the waves breaking out in the distance, gray and lonely, as if they were hungry for the shoreline they could only dream of reaching. It was that way for Logan and me right up until this afternoon when my mother brought the cutest little shoreline to us instead. We didn't say anything at Devil's Peak. Logan and I just stared out into the world as if we were aliens thrust on a foreign planet. There's just too much to wade through at the moment. I don't think if a thousand years went by that we could process it all.

"It looks as if you've brought a guest." Emma bounces on her heels, her eyes slit with suspicion. "I'd set another plate at the table, but she looks a bit young to nosh on prime rib. Come in. She'll catch her death out there. My God, she's not even wearing a sweater. Her bare arms must be freezing!" And just like that, I feel like the world's worst mother.

I glance to Logan as we make our way inside. Technically, to catch your death you'd have to be born.

"Ellis and Giselle just got here themselves. They're in the living room with the boys. I'd better get back to the kitchen to help Barron slice the roast. Who does this little one belong to, anyway?" She picks up the baby's hand and gives her a gentle shake. Angel opens a lazy eye and shuts it once she sees it's just Emma.

"She's mine," I say it candid yet cheesy, and Emma laughs in my face before taking off. I look to Logan and smile. "Who knew the truth could be so freeing?"

We head into the living room to find Ellis and Giselle lost in a Disney animated feature, each with a sleeping boy in their arms, and both my heart and boobs ache at the sight of them. Ellis and Giselle hardly notice at all when Logan and I sit on the opposite sofa.

The baby squirms to life and nuzzles her head in my chest.

"Do you think she's hungry?" Logan penetrates me with those citrine-colored eyes, and we share an intimate moment that borders on sexual. Logan Oliver has never looked so handsome as he does when inquiring on the nutritional needs of his sweet baby girl.

Just as I'm about to process the thought of what and how to feed her, Angel lifts my shirt and ducks underneath, yanks down my bra, and gets to work like a nipple-seasoned pro.

"I guess that answers the question."

Logan leans in, his eyes contently set to mine. "I love you, Skyla. I know this isn't the way things were supposed to be. I know that this beautiful child should probably never exist because I love you and Gage together." His lips depress into a hard frown as he struggles to hold it together. "But I love her. I would die for her, just like I would you and the boys. And now we have a very certain problem on our hands."

My lips part as words struggle to come out, but that warm sensation of the baby, this baby, Logan's baby, suckling off my body is intense in nature—commanding as her tiny teeth bite into me. And just like that, I feel the same way he does. This baby is ours. She *must* exist. She does. My mother sure knows how to throw a perfect wrench into my life and into my marriage. But once again, she's underestimated the love I have for my husband. She's underestimated me entirely.

I lean in, determined he hears me as I ready to pour out my heart. "This child isn't going anywhere. I'm not giving her back."

Logan's eyes sparkle with tears as he gives a single sober nod. "Then we will fight to keep her."

I reach over and take up his hand. "She's home. Our little girl is here to stay."

A shadow darkens the doorway, and we look up to find a strapping Gage Oliver with an ear-to-ear grin. "All my favorite people under one roof." He swoops in and lands a tender kiss to my lips before kneeling in front of me, his cologne warming me with his love. He lifts my shirt, and his eyes grow wide a moment before he glances up.

"Who is this?" All of the joy drains from his face as a morbid curiosity takes over.

He looks from Logan to me, and neither of us volunteers a single word.

It's not who she is that I'm afraid to divulge.

It's what she has the power to do—or *undo*.

Gage

There are moments trapped in silence such as this one when you blatantly realize that your life is about to change. Skyla and Logan open and close their mouths like dysfunctional marionettes, and neither seems to have an answer to the very simple question at hand. Who is this little girl feasting off my wife's tit? It seems black and white, nothing too abstract. But I have the feeling life is about to get about as abstract as the laws of the universe will allow.

"I can explain." Skyla shrugs as tears come to her eyes.

"Dinner's ready!" Mom shouts, and both boys startle to life with a hacking cry. "I'm so sorry!" she whispers, but it's too late for that. Even the child at Skyla's breast kicks away as if the sound of my mother's voice grated on her. The little thing stretches Skyla's nipple out an inch before coming up for air. She looks right at me as her milk-lined smile expands from ear-to-ear, and I'd swear on all that is holy I've seen that grin somewhere before.

"Hey there, pretty girl." I frown up at Skyla and Logan for no good reason before getting up.

I head over and take Barron from Ellis while Giselle trots Nathan around the room to calm him down.

"So, how were finals?" Skyla pops up next to me while the baby resting on her shoulder points to Barron and giggles up a storm as if she were in love with him. Both Nathan and Barron will be lady-killers. I've already surmised that, and not just because they're my replicas. But this little beauty seems smitten and mindfully playful of the handsome boy before her as if she already knows him on some level.

"It went well. There was just one today. I'm all done for the year." Another year at Host under my belt and I couldn't be happier.

"Nice." She repositions herself so the little girl can see Barron better as her laughter hits ear-piercing octaves. It's cute, though—reminds me of an exotic parakeet with her crystal-shattering crescendos.

"Looks like Barron boy has a little girlfriend."

The smile dissipates from Skyla's face as if the thought offended her.

"*Skyla*"—I whisper as I lead us to the corner—"who is she?" I spot Logan narrowing his eyes over at me before he heads this way. "What's going on? It's me. We're done with secrets, right?" My stomach cinches as if to call myself out on the lie.

"Yes." She looks to Logan, and her brows peak as if she's about to cry. "God, yes. This is silly actually." Her lips quiver, and it's becoming obvious whatever this is, it's anything but silly.

A million insane thoughts sail through my mind and the most ridiculous of them catches. "Is this—did you resurrect her?"

"No." She shields the baby's head as if I had just cast a pox on her. "I saw my mother today." She glances at the ceiling, and immediately I realize who she's talking about.

"Shit," I hiss without meaning to. Candace Messenger has had it out for me since before my conception. Whatever the hell Skyla is afraid to tell me can't be good. "What does this precious baby girl have to do with your mother? She's not your mother, is she?" I twirl a blonde lock of hair around my finger, and the tiny thing gives a hearty laugh, her marbled aqua eyes set on my own. I can't help but smile back. Everything about her is the embodiment of joy and it's contagious.

"*No*," Skyla growls as she glances up once again. "Trust me, that would have been much easier." She takes a deep breath, and Logan stands next to her, both of them silently pleading with me to understand. But what?

"Gage." Logan pinches his eyes closed a moment. "We never meant for this to happen."

Skyla gives a frenetic nod. "And if I had my way, it would *never* happen."

The baby girl lets out a squeal and claps her hand over Skyla's mouth as if trying to slap her.

"What I mean is—" Skyla takes the baby girl's hand and gives it a quick kiss. Something about that small insignificant action unsettles me. Skyla does that to our kids, sure, but a stranger's child? Nursing her? Kissing her tenderly as if she were her own?

"What the hell is going on?"

"What Skyla is trying to say is"—Logan takes the child from her—"Candace dropped our daughter off in Tenebrous this afternoon."

"It was a stupid ploy," Skyla says it so fast my mind registers it as one solid word.

"Whose daughter?" My head swims, trying to digest Logan's words. "Did you say *your* daughter?"

"Yes." Logan offers that depressed grin that only he can pull off when he's in the shitter, and right now I feel like I'm right there with him. "Look, we don't know why Candace does what she does."

Then it hits me. This little girl is their child—Skyla and Logan's daughter—a child born of their love—of their sexual union.

I touch my finger to her tiny hand, and she curls her fingers around it, strong and sure, and I see Skyla there in her eyes.

"Yes," I whisper. "Oh my God." She laughs, and I see Logan there in her smile. My stomach sinks straight to hell, and my limbs feel heavy as lead. For a moment, I think I might drop Barron under the weight of this new reality. "What's her name?"

"I'm sorry." Logan shakes his head at me, and we lock eyes, cold and weary for what feels like two years. Logan and I have always been warring over Skyla, one-upping the stakes whenever we could. It always seemed that fate was on my side, or at least until this moment, this entire heartbreaking year. "We're calling her Angel." He bounces her in his arms, and she claps and laughs hard at the irony of her name. Barron leans over and grabs a handful of her hair, and she screams right at him until he relents. "It's sort of a placeholder. We haven't really named her. She just landed in our arms."

Skyla takes Barron from me and leans in until I wrap an arm around her waist and it feels like a relief. Like the noose that was just placed over our marriage was just as quickly lifted.

"I can have Marshall help us take her back to paradise." Her voice grows heavy and weary. "I mean, I can't feed three babies, can I?" She nods up at me as if asking for permission.

Something in Logan's eyes flickers like a fire of rage before he blinks it back. "We're not taking her anywhere. We're keeping her right here." He looks right at me with an apology in his eyes before he ever says it. "I'll take care of her, Skyla. You don't have to feed her."

"That's not what I meant." Her voice breaks, and tears run down her cheeks. "I'm sorry, Gage. I was just trying to soften the blow with stupid words I didn't mean. I'm with Logan. I don't have the heart to send her back to paradise either."

"And I would never ask you to." I flick my fingers until Logan hands her to me, and Barron laughs as she carefully touches his hair, his face with her open palm. She's solid, heavier than the boys but longer, her delicate features unmistakably feminine, and those kaleidoscope eyes. My heart melts and breaks all at once. I'm holding the evidence of their love. Skyla and Logan will at some point in time make this beautiful tiny being. My boys will love her, protect her to the death, and all I want to do is wash her in my tears. So this is the heft of the heartbreaking weight that Logan felt when Skyla and I had the boys. Only so much worse because he got to witness the buildup. He gets to see me pawing his once-wife with my meat hooks day after day, plying her with kisses, my eyes always bent on lewd intent. It's a cruel thing fate has done, intertwining our hearts, all of our lust around the very same woman.

"She's beautiful." I offer a depleted smile down at the perfect little angel, blonde like her mother, like Logan, long lashes, and an ever so slight dimple low on her cheek. "She'll grow up to look just like you, Skyla."

Skyla grunts as if this were a bad thing. "I don't doubt it. I'm my mother's clone by design, and don't forget the favor she thinks she did Mia by doling out the same genes." She says *favor* with air quotes.

Yes, Mia may be Lizbeth's daughter, but Candace made sure her features were heaven-sent to resemble that of her sister's, and, of course, her.

"So this is her doing." I press a kiss to the top of Angel's head. Her hair feels slippery as silk. "Candace is reassuring you about the future." I try to make it sound light, not at all the morbid newsflash it really is. "You know, preparing you for my mortal demise." It sounds ridiculous now that I've said it out loud. "She's made it clear whose team she's on." Literally. I shake my head without meaning to.

Skyla opens her mouth just as the doorbell rings, and we glance over as my mother ushers in Casey, one of the dead from next door. In fact, she's one of the last residents staying at the house. Logan is staying with her, and so is Lex, but the rest of the dead are on the first leg of their mission—en route to be captured.

She speeds over, her eyes fixed on Logan's. "Aren't you watching the news? They've captured the mean girls! And some other girl I've never even heard of!" She shakes her head at Skyla. "I don't think she was one of us—I mean *me*. I don't think she was dead."

"Shit," Skyla mutters under her breath, and I help turn the television to the local news. We check our phones like mad as the commercials come to a conclusion, and sure as shit, the G-men are shown arresting four girls for shoplifting.

"Shoplifting?" Skyla looks up at me as if I have the answer, and deep down, the sexist pig who lives in me loves it. I crave Skyla's affection, for her to need me, to look up to me if only to account for the practical height difference.

"Yes." And, unfortunately, I think I really do have the answer. "They're sending a message to the rest of us. They're making arrests, hauling us off to government pastures."

"They're speaking in code." Logan purses his lips as he looks to the screen. He squints in hard before finding the remote and rewinding the feed. "Is that Chloe in the back, talking to one of the officers?" He looks to Skyla for answers. We both do.

Her mouth opens as she takes Angel and jostles her over her hip. "Casey"—she turns her attention to the girl—"have you spoken to anyone about this?"

The frightened girl gives a slight nod. She's so young, so emotionally fragile, I wish she hadn't signed up for this at all. I've seen those men and women parading around the island like they've got a chip on their shoulders, because they do. They're out for blood. Wes has the entire world shaken with his ridiculous clown sightings, those UFO reprisals which have the planet in a tizzy. This isn't the best news for any one of our people, especially not those about to pay the price for their commitment.

"Okay." Skyla takes up her hand. "Do you still want to do this? I can arrange for my mother to help you find another way home."

"No," she's quick to protest. "I'm d-doing this," she stammers. "The others are ready, and so am I. But who is that fourth girl, Skyla? Is she one of us?"

Logan skips ahead on the remote until the feed is live, and they show the faint hint of a redheaded girl leading the pack. The camera shot pulls away, and it's impossible to make out their faces, but that wildfire hair, that erratic gait, the gesticulating she's doing to the officer leading her by the elbow into his vehicle.

"I know her," I offer. "Or at least I think I do." Skyla and Logan wait with bated breath. "It's Melody Winters. And she is very much one of us. I checked my father's records. The Winters date back as far as the registry goes." I take a deep breath. "I can check the records again, see what lineage. I just glanced over it."

"Yes." Skyla looks stunned by the fact Melody was taken. "I'd like to do that with you sometime."

The boys whine until we land them over a quilt on the carpet and Skyla sets down her newfound baby girl next to them. Like a lightning bolt, she crawls over to the boys and my mother appears, praising the sight as if she's never witnessed the event before.

"What a treat to have a little girl in the house. How long will you have her?" She looks to Skyla, and my stomach bottoms out. Had she told my mother about her? And in all of the ironies is my mother seemingly cheerleading the event?

Skyla looks to me and nods. "Jen—Laken's sister is out of town for a bit, so I volunteered to keep an eye on her." She glances back to my mother. "With Laken, of course."

My mother shakes her head with disapproval. "Now that you're a mother, you'll need to familiarize yourself with the word no. If word gets out that you're a pushover when it comes to babysitting, you'll—"

I'm quick to cut her off, "End up with the largest daycare center on the island?"

The room breaks out into a warm laugh, and thankfully it seems to have cut the tension between my mother and Skyla. For the life of me, I can't figure out how to turn down the volume of their shared disdain for one another.

Dinner goes off uneventful, sans the fact Ellis demonstrates—mostly to Giselle—his ability to inhale a noodle into his nose and pull it through his mouth. Once Ellis noshes on the meal he's extracted, he and Logan proceed to talk about the construction that's set to begin next week. It's business as usual. Skyla and I have the boys in their high chairs, and my mother insists on feeding them the strained peas and string beans she's made just for them. But my eyes keep flicking back to Logan with little Angel on his lap as Skyla sits next to him and spoon-feeds their daughter. Here I was all set to surprise Skyla with a day at Rockaway tomorrow, something fun to celebrate another school year under my belt, the end clawing ever so close. And now the only end I feel clawing near is that with Skyla. It can't be. Candace wouldn't let that happen so soon. She realizes I'm Skyla's husband. The father of her favorite two grandsons. My God, I can't leave now. I have too much work left to do.

The night drones on, and Logan comes home to Whitehorse along with his daughter. He sleeps in the guest bedroom down the hall while Skyla and I stay in the master with the boys. But Skyla never sleeps. She feeds the boys before going down the hall to the bedroom where Logan coos over his beautiful baby girl—and my God, she might be the most beautiful baby girl I've ever seen.

Skyla doesn't come back to bed.

I didn't think she would.

That night, I dream many dreams—starting off with a fan favorite, Skyla, Logan, and me back at West, back in those mythical halcyon years where we were unstoppable in our unity. And after that, I dream of water. There's always water in this hallucinogenic world of my own making. I'm wading through a stream that quickly morphs into an ocean, only the water isn't blue, or clear, or even green. It's red. And I marvel as I stare down at the sanguine liquid. It's blood. It's my own. And just like that, my lids blink open.

I give a lazy flutter of the lids, my hand swooping over the cool bedside next to me where my wife usually warms the sheets. But Skyla isn't there. I shouldn't have expected her to be. It's been a solid week, and we are still at Whitehorse. Skyla is spent. Her energy depleted. She's begged Ezrina to help her figure out which formula comes closest to breastmilk because she wants to start supplementing, and I don't blame her. She's tried feeding Angel right along with the boys, and it's drained all the color from her skin, the purple rings under her eyes are a testament to the fact it's not the greatest idea. She's taxing her body and her mind. Skyla is housebound for the most part, but on the odd moment she does leave, she takes off with Chloe. She claims they're turning in the dead to the government, and sure enough, in each city they venture off to, a vague article on petty crime pops up. Skyla swears that she's keeping out of danger, that Chloe is doing all the heavy lifting—but with Chloe around, Skyla is only keeping company *with* danger. When I asked how they were traveling, Skyla said they're light driving. She's not playing with fire. She's making love to it, letting it enter into places that it never should be in the first place. Skyla is already burned beyond recognition. She just doesn't know it yet.

It's the night of Brielle and Drake's shared bachelor, bachelorette party before their big do-over in a couple of weeks. Bree mentioned she needed ample time between the big party and the big event. In all honesty, knowing how much Bree and Drake like to party, they'll need a couple of weeks to rid themselves of the hangover.

Skyla and I stop by the Landon house to drop the boys and Angel off. Logan comes along for the ride because in a week's span of time he's become the world's most doting father, making me feel like a bad dad by a paternal mile. He went insane one night on the Internet, and the next day everything that you might need for a child arrived at his doorstep. He gave Skyla the task of filling Angel's closet and handed over his credit card like some sort of American Express god. And as much as I may not want to admit it, Skyla was in pink-ruffled-tutu-bow-wearing-sparkly-shoed heaven. Every time she made a purchase, she bounced around the house with glee. I've never seen her so thrilled to shop for the boys, but, in her defense, I've never handed over my plastic as if it were a Black Card and let her have at it.

"Knock, knock!" Skyla sings as we stride on in. The Landon house looks the same, slightly chaotic with a sprinkling of toys and pets everywhere. It smells the same, perhaps better than usual because Emily has all but taken over the kitchen. Tonight, it's grilled cheese, using her favorite vegan cheese replacement, I'm sure. Em might have turned into a world-class granola cruncher, but hot damn, the girl can make shoe leather taste like filet mignon. Yes, we're eating vegan, organic fare that she has Drake ante up for, but we are eating like kings. Not to sound like an ass, but Em has found her calling. I'd encourage her to open a restaurant, but I'm wise enough to put it off until Skyla and I are out of the house for good. Just the memory of Lizbeth's cooking brings the bile up in the back of my throat.

"Jessie, Mary, and Joseph!" Tad grunts at the sight of us. "Told you she was keeping the stray." He points his cane in little Angel's direction. The cane is a new addition, but long overdue in my opinion. My stomach grinds hearing him go off like that because I'm so fucking sick of Tad's insular behavior.

"She's not a stray." I lean Nathan in toward the tiny tot, and they give one another open-mouthed, sloppy, wet kisses on the cheek, and the entire room melts in a puddle of oohs and ahhs.

"*Skyla!*" Lizbeth scoops Barron from her. "God, she's so adorable! How are you ever going to give that little princess back?" She gives Angel's cheek a squeeze, and the little girl trills a sweet laugh to the ceiling right from her father's arms. Logan has held her longer, stronger this week than anything he's ever touched in his life.

Tad honks out a laugh. "Now that's the best idea you've ever had. Give that creature back to its mother. She's probably some teen queen who's off enjoying her summer *vacay*." He wags a crooked finger at his wife. "And don't think for a minute these two coconuts haven't thought about doing the same." He waddles right up to my face, and the urge to deck him rises in me. "Listen here, *Greg*. You've got enough of your own responsibilities now. Don't you go letting the little woman snap up kids off the street left and right, or you'll end up like me—in a house full of spider monkeys trying to crawl into your pants!"

There are so many things wrong with that sentence I don't know where to begin.

"Don't worry." I offer a placid smile. "I won't end up like you." If anything, Tad's existence as a whole is more or less a cautionary tale.

"Okay"—Skyla hands the bloated diaper bag to Melissa—"I've already fed them dinner, but I threw in a few extra jars anyway. And if you could put the bottles in the fridge right away, I'd appreciate it."

"*Bottles*?" Lizbeth's tit radar immediately goes up, and Logan and I exchange a quiet laugh because we know what's coming. "You know I'm not totally opposed to pumping, but you won't be that late, Skyla. And a good mother knows it's best to keep them on the nipple. It's still not too late for them to start rejecting you."

"Geez, Mother"—Skyla takes Nathan from me and hands him to Mia—"you make it sound so personal. I can't keep up this pace any longer. They're ravenous—and have I mentioned *biting* me? Plus, they don't seem to mind the formula at all."

Both Skyla and Lizbeth freeze. I'm pretty sure that was a slipup on Skyla's part. She's been pretty staunch on keeping this bit of manufactured news from her mom.

"Oh my living God!" Lizbeth thunders so loud the house shakes. "You are not giving my grandchildren powdered toxins from the grocery store! Please do not tell me you have resorted to putting trash into your children's bodies, or I will—"

Skyla lays a finger over her mother's lips in an effort to silence her. "You will survive, and so will they. Besides, it's not trash. I have it on good authority that the formula I selected is as good as mommy milk. My friend Ezrina can attest to this. And I'm still feeding them every night— *religiously.*"

Lizbeth's face contorts in grief, red as a turnip. "My God, you only made it six months," she wails. "I should have been there for you. I can't believe I idly stood by and allowed this to happen. It's all those damned vaginas' fault." Her chest bucks with a silent cry, and both Logan and I exchange a worried glance. Who the hell knew a simple bottle could lead to a meltdown of vaginal proportions?

"Okay, fine." Skyla cups her mother's face. "I'll only use the bottles in the event of an emergency. I promise I'll keep myself front and center as the boys' favorite chew toy." She gives Angel a sly look because she just so happens to be her favorite chew toy as well. "Mostly."

We wrap up the party and say a quick round of goodbyes.

Tad limps us to the door, right along with Lizbeth. "And don't you bad mouth those pink bits and pieces! Those tiny portals of humanity are racking up quite the payday around here. Don't knock it till you try it!" He slams the door behind us as if to exclaim his vaginal point.

We step out onto the porch and pause as the cool Paragon air wraps itself around us as Skyla makes a beeline for the car, already texting someone—most likely Chloe.

Logan knocks me in the ribs with his elbow. "Here that, Greg?" That shit-eating grin of his spreads ear-to-ear. "You can make a nice nest egg for yourself selling a little piece of ass."

"The only piece of ass I need is right there"—I nod to Skyla, slightly sickened by my own dry humor, even if it were a play on words—"and my chief concern is my nest. I think I need to ask Liam to help me whip that place into shape. I'll spend every last dollar and every last breath doing it." That dollar drop sponsored by Dominique Winters comes to mind. I have more than enough to renovate the place from top to bottom. I meant to get to the renovation sooner, but with the dead hanging around the house, I didn't bother with the remodel.

Logan lets out a white plume of a sigh. His shoulders depress as he offers a weary nod of agreement. "I've got a few dollars rolling around and all the spare time in the world. I'll help you get whatever shit you need knocked out. How about we set a goal of getting the two of you moved in well before your anniversary?"

Something in me loosens, and it feels as if Logan and I are back on track, not the adversaries for Skyla's love and affection, the heavy competitors for her heart that we've been all week. The truth is, I'm tired of warring it out with Logan. I'm still married to Skyla. I win. That should be enough for me.

"Sounds good."

He meets me with a fist bump as we head out to the Mustang.

I win when it comes to Skyla. I shake my head at the thought as I crawl into the back seat—Logan and Skyla in the front like a couple.

An overpowering grief crashes over me, and I watch them as we drive out to Ellis'. Both Skyla and Logan have my heart. Candace has laid out the future for them like a smooth path. The only briar patch in the middle is me.

I lean back and glare up at the sky.

I'm not complying with your little plan. This is my life. My wife. My family you are threatening to tear to pieces. I won't let you.

Because no matter what you're dreaming up, whatever it is you're scheming, I'm ready to fight to the death—and perhaps beyond that if I have to, and something tells me I'll have to.

I won't let you make me feel like I'm holding onto the losing end of the stick.

I'm not.

I have Skyla.

I've already won.

Ellis' house is shaking, quaking with the dull inharmonious rhythm of the bass as an ornery rap song blares through the neighborhood. I can practically feel my mother's tension from across the street. She let me know twice this morning that she was pissed over the fact Skyla's sister would be watching the boys tonight, and here she was a mere ten steps away. I'm betting she's having second thoughts about that right about now. Although, all I hear lately is how very little they see the boys, how she suspects Skyla is favoring her own family, and the boys will grow up to be strangers to her and my father. I don't believe that for a minute. But her budding piranha-like ways have to be clipped. That's why I'm going to propose that Skyla and I move in with them while I attack the old Walsh place with a sledgehammer. Tad is right. I do not want to end up like him, or *near* him. I declare that shit ride has come to an uneremonious end. And, of course, my mother can have her fill of the boys for a couple of weeks straight, proving that Skyla doesn't have a mean bone in her body.

We step out of the Mustang and onto the Harrisons'
driveway.

"It's just like old times!" Skyla threads her arm through
mine as she bounces in her high heels. She looks gorgeous
tonight, per usual. She's donned a short black dress and
swiped on a little red lipstick, taking her to supermodel
levels. She looks just as physically fit as she did before she
had the boys, but every time I bring it up she reprimands me
for lying, so I leave well enough alone.

Ellis stumbles out, looks dazed and confused, and
Logan shakes his head at him.

"Just like old times." He slaps Ellis over the back.
"Dude, you okay?"

"Hell yeah. I am now." Ellis offers us each a high five.
"Get the hell in there. I have the entertainment showing up
soon. I promised Bree I'd flag them down so they don't miss
us."

Skyla laughs at the thought. "I don't think anyone can
miss this place, not tonight anyway. I'm afraid to ask, but
what's the entertainment?"

"Chloe on a spit?" Logan offers, and the only one not
laughing is Skyla.

"Dude"—Ellis mock socks her arm—"I was just talking
to Bishop in there. You need to chill out, and then you need
to take a step way the hell back. She told me what the two of
you are up to, and I don't know, man. You're not playing
with matches here. You're running around a firework factory
with a torch in hand."

"Preach it." Logan forces a smile Skyla's way, and she
scoffs.

"I'd better go find Bree." She hikes up and plants a kiss
on my cheek before strutting her hot self inside.

"So, what's she got going on with Bishop?" I glare at
Ellis because I think we both know if he doesn't speak up I

might just crush him for the hell of it. It's killing me not knowing what Skyla and Chloe have going on. And it seems like every time we get the conversation started something, *everything* interrupts us.

"Dude"—Ellis lets out a groan that sounds like his insides are about to explode—"she's fucking with the wrong person. I'd say talk some sense into that woman, but it's too late for that shit."

Logan yanks him in by the elbow. "Why is it too late?"

"Don't ask me. I'm not up on all that covenant bullshit." He takes a few steps out before turning to Logan. "And hey, G and I made a few modifications to the plans. Meet up with me sometime if you get a second." He flags down an SUV full of older women who happen to be sporting some serious war paint and eyelashes so long they come with their own zip code. The garish grannies file out, each wearing a tiny silk robe, and Ellis howls up a storm. "Shit! These chicks are *hot!*" He's quick to escort them around the back, leaving both Logan and me shaking our heads.

"What the hell just happened?"

Logan groans at the sight. "He'd better get his eyes checked." He turns his full attention my way, his features hardening to something just this side of pissed. "And Skyla better get her head checked. What the hell is going on? Ellis doesn't throw the word *covenant* out there lightly."

"No, he doesn't. And I don't think Skyla does either. Has she said anything at all to you?" I scour his features as if his words alone won't be enough to satisfy me.

"No. She's been tight-lipped from the beginning. I think it's time we had a sit-down. In the least I want to know what the hell is about to blow up in our faces."

A dull laugh dies in my throat because I'm too pissed to give it. "Do you have that little faith in Skyla's ability to lead? She's bright. She's capable. And whatever she's doing with Chloe, I'm sure she's thought it through."

"Yes, I have faith in Skyla's ability to lead," he says it with a viral anger that matches my own. Emotions have been running high this week on both ends, and they're about to blow. "It's Chloe I don't trust, and neither should you. If I were to take a wild guess, it's *your* face this will take off first." Logan's angry eyes stay trained on mine, and neither of us moves. For a minute, I consider how good it would feel to go at him. Shove my fist down his obnoxious throat, pummel him, blow after blow, but then it doesn't take long for me to figure out it wouldn't do any good. We've screwed with one another so much in the past, repented, begged forgiveness, and started all over again. It's like a demonic carousel neither one of us can figure out how to get off of. "And while I've got you here." He glances up at the house with its guests spilling out onto the driveway, each with a requisite red Solo cup in hand. That lion fountain that Emily so readily destroyed last New Year's Eve already resurrected as if nothing had happened. "I'm sorry. I'm sorry I've been infiltrating your life as of late. I sense the tension, and I don't want that, not for you or for me."

"It's all right. I get it. You've got a bundle of joy that you didn't expect, dropped off on your doorstep. You're excited, and you should be." My stomach clenches because I can't imagine what Candace was thinking, toying with everyone's emotions this way. "Skyla and I are moving to my mom's until the house is ready. Why don't you come, too? You'll be close to Angel, and I know Skyla would appreciate it."

Logan looks up at me with that stillness he usually gets just before the disappointment sets in. I can't live at Whitehorse without having my balls shrivel. Hell, I'd rather live with Tad, and I have.

"I get it," he whispers. "I'll think about it."

A small crowd strides by, three men, three women—paired off two by two, but these aren't your average partygoers. These aren't your average strippers either. They're all too uptight, far too invested in playing the part to relax. It's the G-man brigade trying to cash in on whatever they can to net more prospects.

"They're here," Logan says as they make their way inside.

"And they are never going to leave."

We follow them inside, and Lexy attacks Logan as soon as we walk through the door. I spot Michelle dry-humping Liam, and he gives a casual wave as if it's an everyday occurrence, and knowing the two of them it is. But it's the dark-haired, pale-skinned sulker standing with his enormous arms crossed while looking down at everyone in the vicinity that has my attention.

I walk over and slap my brother, the brooder, over the shoulder. "Smile, would you? It's a good look on both of us."

"I have little to smile about these days." He scowls out at the crowd, and I follow his incendiary glare to Skyla and Chloe. Shit. "And neither do you." He lifts his drink as if he's toasting the fact. "Your wife is more trouble than she's worth."

"So is yours." I step into his view. The last thing I'm going to stand for is Wesley demeaning my wife while staring her down. "What's with Laken's double? Is she still in the Transfer?"

"Safe and sound."

Wes told me he was housing her and assured me he would not let her run amuck on Paragon.

"I don't want to talk about her." His shoulders slump as he cranes his neck past me a moment. "My wife left me, and I want to know why."

I glance back to Skyla and Chloe. Bree has joined them and is in the process of strangling them both in an awkward embrace. "Chloe left you?" A dull laugh thumps through me. "I'll take a wild stab at it. Maybe the fact you're fucking this new girl in her bed had something to do with it. Chloe is a complicated creature, but she is pretty practical when it comes to being number two to anyone. You of all people should know that. She's you in female skin."

He shakes his head wistfully as the music picks up in both volume and rhythm. "That must be what did us in. We were too much alike."

"That and the fact you're obsessed with fucking Cooper Flanders' wife."

"As she is with Skyla Messenger's husband."

"Touché."

Wes nods me over to the kitchen where the roar from the speakers is slightly subdued. "Who are these people Skyla has manipulated into giving themselves up to the feds? She's royally fucking up my plans." He lets out a greedy grin as if she's doing just the opposite and fitting into them quite nicely. And for the love of God, that's exactly what I'm afraid of.

"None of your business. How are things going with the volunteers?" My heart throttles into my skull and starts vibrating right along with the rhythm Ellis has cursed us with. I don't want anyone to suffer. But the assholes Wes wrangled up to wet the feds' appetites for the Nephilim have really pissed me off.

"They've recanted. As soon as one escaped captivity, he warned the rest not to do it. They dropped off like flies." He shakes his head with the beginnings of an incredulous laugh. "They actually believe that Skyla can protect them. That her Retribution League is about to take down all of my efforts and appease the federal government—and that their paranormal works department will be more than satisfied. But you and I know it can never happen."

"If they get enough people, it will. They may be casting a wide net, but in no way are they equipped to take on the numbers they'd need to. They're going to be satiated and soon."

"Maybe." He cups his hand over his chin. "Skyla is setting Chloe up for something. It's Chloe that's going out and reporting these idiots while Skyla sits back and reaps the rewards."

"A strategy you're familiar with, I take it?"

"A strategy I invented," he smarts. "And before you say imitation is the sincerest form of flattery, let me make it clear that if done incorrectly, it will cost you your life. If your wife needs a few lessons, send her my way. A few good tips might just save both your necks." He looks to the door before doing a double take as Laken and Coop make their way over.

"Look who's here." Laken's wide, sarcastic smile sets the tone. "I hear you've been enjoying my company." She frowns at Wes and lets all of her disappointment bleed through. That look right there is enough to cut a man's balls off and stuff them into his mouth. "And I see Skyla is losing her sanity again with Chloe by her side." Now it's me she's frowning at. "I'd better go say hello."

Cooper waits until she's out of earshot before stepping into Wes, and I can feel the fistfight coming before he ever throws a swing. Honest to God, I don't know what the hell's taken so long.

"Wes." Coop closes his eyes a moment. "I know you're desperate. I know you love her, or at least you think you do—but you don't. If you really loved Laken, you would still have her."

My stomach tenses in a knot, because if Coop didn't throw the first punch, it just increased the odds that Wesley might.

But, instead, my brother closes his eyes and acquiesces to Coop's logic. "I know. If I followed her lead, and gave up my standing, then I would have Laken safe in my arms." He glances to me as if I might have something to add.

"I don't think so." It may not be the answer he was waiting for, but it's the truth. "Her heart was already pointing to Coop."

"It's true." Wes raises his brows to him in amusement. "So, you see, Laken was never mine to lose. She was already knitted to your soul before she ever left me. And that, my friend, is the sword in my heart." He looks past him to the girls who appear to be at a standstill themselves. "But you won't last forever, Coop." He glances back to me and offers a morbid smile. "None of us will." He takes off into the crowd as bodies bury him from our sight.

I step in close to Coop as the music strangles the atmosphere around us. "Did you ever find out who the girl is?"

"Yes, I did." He looks my way, and in this dim light, he and Logan could be interchangeable.

"Who the hell is she?" Logan steps in from behind and startles us both.

Coop gives a little laugh. "I'll tell you before the night is through, but why don't we make a game of it? First one who figures it out gets a bonus prize. I'll fill him and only him in on another little nugget. I happen to know what the hell Skyla is doing with that witch she's leashed herself to." He takes a deep breath as he looks back in the direction of the girls. "And it's not a bad idea—that is, if it works."

"It won't work," Logan is quick to assure us all of Skyla's demise.

"You're a real fucking cheerleader, you know that?" Coop grins as he says it. "Why don't you try out for the team at West? I hear they're looking for a few good girls."

"Funny," he growls at me before reverting to Coop. "Give us a hint. I guarantee it'll take me less than five minutes to solve it, so get ready to spill all you know about Skyla as well."

Coop's chest thumps with a laugh. "Ezrina's science project—she's a beauty and a bitch—Laken's words, not mine. She's been suspiciously M.I.A., and considering she's been a thorn in my wife's side as far back as Ephemeral—" he looks to us as he drops off the granddaddy hint of them all, and both Logan and I tip our heads back and groan.

"Kresley Fisher." Logan grunts. "But why the big show in the blue tank? Ezrina had to kill Kresley to put her in that thing."

Coop ticks his head back. "Something went wrong during the facial reconstruction. Kresley's heart stopped. Ezrina said it was a nightmare. But it's done."

Logan raises his brows. "Makes sense. Now catch us up on what we really want to know."

"Wait." I pinch my eyes shut and try to derail the headache Ellis is sponsoring. "I'm out. I don't want to know." I take off and get lost in the crowd. As much as I want to glean every intimate detail I can about the covenant Skyla has with Chloe, I want all of the information I get to be from Skyla herself. And I want her to give it willingly. Our marriage means more to me than some seemingly vital gossip. Besides, as long as Logan is aware of the fact, that's as good as me being in on it. At least for now. Logan and I are of one mind when it comes to my wife. If she's in imminent danger, he'll know what to do. I'll find rest in that for now.

A beefed-up dude with a T-shirt that looks ten sizes too small, a drink in both hands, shuffles his way up. I know him. He's been at all the Viden meet and greets. It's Zander Richards, Emily's cousin on her father's side. His little brothers volunteered in Wesley's nightmare and are off haunting the globe somewhere looking for human flesh to consume because Wes has killed them for sport and turned them into a bunch of staggering Spectators. They're still keeping the news feed going, but, for whatever reason, Wes hasn't thrown them to the wolves. The Spectators are the Bigfoot of our generation. If the feds start snapping them up, it will take the heat off the Nephilim. Is that what Wes wants? It seems counterintuitive to his overall plan of taking down those who chose not to side with the Barricade. It's all a bad plan if you ask me. And that, right there, is the alarming thing about my brother. He is rife with bad ideas and quick to initiate them. Thus, turning Kresley into Laken. But if the rumor is true and he's been fucking her sideways in the Transfer as Chloe suggests, I can't say Kres regrets her decision. It doesn't make sense, though. He had Chloe morphing into Laken's likeness whenever he wanted. Something is up. And, knowing my brother, we'll all hear about it sooner than later.

Zander shoves his huge mitt into my chest and sends me staggering backward. His drinks go flying, and the crowd gasps around us. "You're a little fucker, you know that?"

"Hey"—Wes pops up from out of nowhere and barks in his face—"what the hell's your problem, man? Why don't you take off? You smell like you're soaked in vodka."

"I'm soaked, all right." He blows past Wes and gets in my face again. "What's the matter, little man? You need your big bro to fight your battles for you? Wait a second"—a greasy grin lights up his face—"I almost forgot. Your *wife* wears the balls in the family."

"That's it." I scoop him up by the shirt and drive him to the wall, landing him against it so hard a crack snakes right to the ceiling. "I get it. You're worried about your family. But what *you* don't get is the fact I didn't put them in that predicament. They did it to themselves," I riot in his face just as the music hits a lull and the crowd stills around us.

Zander grabs me by the shirt and twists me into the wall, making that fissure I've just erupted in Harrison's home run a little deeper. "My brothers had no choice. Maybe if you knew your own brother as well as I know mine, you would have known that, too."

He takes off, and I spot Emily chasing after him.

"Damn idiot." Wes pulls me from the wall and for a moment I'm not sure if he's talking about Zander or me. "Each and every volunteer came of his own volition. I would be remiss to force anyone's hand. I follow the same rules as your wife." He glances back at her. "Only I know when and where they will bite me in the ass." He takes off for the door and doesn't look back.

"Nice." Logan dusts the drywall off my shoulder as Liam comes up beside him.

"The two of you are really racking up the construction jobs for me. At this rate, I'll be able to retire before I ever begin."

Drake and Bree pop up, looking deliriously happy and least of all concerned over the newly formed hole in the wall behind me.

Brielle hops up and latches her arms around my neck. "There's nothing hotter than Gage Oliver beating the shit out of some guy at your bachelorette party!" she howls in my face, and I smell the liquor emanating off her. Skyla and Chloe show up, and my stomach turns seeing them within fighting distance.

"You'd better back off, Bree." Skyla plucks her off and quickly takes her place. "He's all mine, girls." She gives Chloe a sly wink, and Chloe flips her the bird.

"You bore me, Messenger." Chloe takes up Logan's hand and starts to lead him toward the crowd losing it to the music. "Let's show 'em how it's done." And shockingly—perhaps not shockingly, Logan goes right along with her. I know him. He'll keep his enemy close enough to get what he needs out of them. Theoretically, Skyla might be doing the very same thing, but this is Chloe. It will never work the way it's supposed to.

Lex trots up, red-faced and panting. "Is that Bishop wiping her paws on my man?"

Skyla grunts out a laugh. "I never thought I'd say this, Lex, but go get what's yours."

Lex takes off, and I spot the three of them in what looks like a dance-off.

"I've already got what's mine," Skyla whispers hot into my ear, and my dick perks to life. "Now what's this I hear about us moving to Emma's?"

"What?" Bree is the first to protest. "Hell no, you can't go." She wraps an arm around Skyla, tight. "This girl right here is staying with me."

"Good news travels fast." I'd laugh, but it shouldn't surprise me that it's true. "Logan and Liam are going to help me get the house in order. We'll be in our own home before you know it."

Her eyes linger over mine a moment too long. "And your mom's house is closer." She sounds as if she's trying to talk herself into it.

Bree lifts her top and flashes the two of us, snapping us right out of that danger zone my mother seems to throw us in each and every time. "How do you like my boobs?"

"Shit." I close my eyes, trying to get the image of her huge nipples out of my head. Over the years, I've seen more of Brielle Johnson's body than I care to admit. Mostly that has to do with the fact I was the one who delivered Beau into this world—in a parking lot, behind a hotel on prom night. It was one event—and one exaggeratingly large vagina I will never forget.

"They're new. I had them lifted. Drake says he likes the size, but I might go bigger."

"No," Skyla scolds. "They're prefect. Cute and perky just like you."

"Hear that?" Bree drips over Drake and nearly takes him down in the process. "Skyla likes my boobies just the way they are! But don't you worry. I'm still committed to taking the best care of myself for the rest of my life." She winks Skyla's way. "We girls need to keep it hot—in and out of the covers."

"Dude"—Drake pulls back and examines his bride—"I don't care what you look like when we're going at it. I think of other chicks anyway."

Bree squeals with laughter as they head off toward the crowd.

"And who says romance is dead?" I steal a kiss from my own bride, and we share a quick laugh. "Coop let me in on who's down in the Transfer with Wes."

"Oh my God!" She bounces on her toes. "The Laken knockoff?"

I give a slight nod. "He gave us a hint; she's a thorn in Laken's side, and I could easily say the same for you. We haven't seen her in months."

Her mouth opens wide. "Kresley? That dumb, *dumb* bitch." She closes her eyes as if she's actually sorry for her. "I hate to say it, but she's really put herself in danger."

"Why? Did Chloe tell you something new?"

She gives a slight nod of her own. "Wes has a dick the size of a telephone pole."

"*Skyla.*" I tip my head back and groan.

"*Kidding!*" She plants a kiss on my lips and slips her tongue into my mouth playfully. "You're the only one with a dick wildly out of proportion around here."

"As it should be." I give a self-satisfied smile. Skyla and I are back to normal, and this is how I like it. No tension, no grief from any of our mothers, just the two of us messing around like a couple of teenagers. "Coop also knows what you and Chloe are up to." She winces as I wrap my arms around her. "He offered to tell me, but I thought I'd get my info from the source. Does the source feel like coughing up info anytime soon?" The smile drops off my face because there are some things I can't fake around Skyla, and how I feel is one of them.

Skyla opens her mouth, her gaze still locked onto mine, and a thumping sound emits over the speakers. A series of spotlights circle the ceiling before slowly migrating to the back of the grand room where a mock stage is set up. Everyone in the vicinity turns their attention in that direction as the music picks up to a sultry beat.

Brielle charges at us. "Get over here!" She snatches Skyla by the wrist, and they take off through the crowd in search of front row seats. I spot Logan and Coop and head in their direction.

"You tell him everything you know?" I offer Coop a playful shove, even though we're well aware I'm serious as shit.

"I heard enough." Logan crosses his arms as an army of scantily dressed elderly women dance into the room. The blonde snaps up Drake, lands his face in her cleavage, and the crowd gives an approving cheer. An equally scantily dressed group of men slip in behind the girls, and the beefiest of the bunch pulls Skyla up on stage with him. These dudes are young, and buff, and both of those facts have me glaring at the one currently holding my wife hostage.

"Figures." Logan leans in. "Bree fed her to the wolves."

Coop's chest thumps with a quiet laugh. "She should get used to it. Chloe's about to do the same thing."

And just like that, my anger flares up. I'm so sick of Logan and Coop and their self-righteous put-downs of the woman I love.

"That's my wife, and I support her," I say it out loud at completely the wrong time.

The beefed-up dude takes Skyla's hand and helps himself to a nice massage right over that massive hump in the crotch of his loincloth. It takes her less than five seconds to free herself and hop off the stage.

Logan looks to me. "Sometimes people make her do things she doesn't want to do."

Coop nods along. "That's Chloe in a nutshell. Just wait. You'll see we're right."

I glance back up to find Brielle riding on the back of one of the entertainers, spanking his behind as if he were a donkey.

Skyla comes up and wraps her arms around me, breathless with a laugh trapped behind her smile. "I'm going to step out for a bit. Watch this guy for me, would you?" She charges Logan with the task before offering a nice juicy kiss to my lips. "I'll be back soon. Don't leave without me." She pulls back, and any enthusiasm she had on her face dissipates. "Chloe is just a cockroach on a leash, Gage," she whispers, the sound of heartbreak in her voice hangs heavy. "That's it in a nutshell, I promise." She gives another peck before taking off.

"That about sums it up," Logan offers. "But we both know the devil is in the details."

Coop nods in agreement. "And Chloe and Wes are two devils who thrive on every last detail."

And just like that, Skyla has become a detail in the lives of Chloe and Wes.

Things couldn't fall to shit any faster if they tried.

Things fall to shit faster than anyone thought possible. Within a week, the feds have sopped up every last of the resurrected dead like wine with a loaf of bread, savoring every last delicious morsel. The last of which being the most bittersweet. Casey was captured at the library while strolling through the young adult section.

Logan and I sulk over the fact as we wait for the rest of the Videns to arrive. I've dragged him down here with me, to the nocturnal, petrified underbelly of the island—or at least it is in theory. It is my very own realm, where I sit on a crooked throne of lies pretending to know what the hell is going on at any given time.

Wes and Demetri come up, with Wes looking his usual irritated self, and Demetri unmoved by my decision to have a visitor.

"What's this?" Wes barks, affronted as if I pulled down my pants and took a shit on his shoes.

"He's with me," I say it bored, certain that he has no power to undermine me. "What's on the agenda?" I look to my father and those dark laughing eyes.

"The Videns have expressed a dissatisfaction with the handling of the Spectators. They want a reversal of fortune for their loved ones who sacrificed much in the endeavor." He looks to Wes and nods.

"No." Wes is quick to hack our father's dick off, and I don't really mind all that much. "They're mine. I need them to stay put." He glares at me a moment. "You were right. Skyla has managed to satiate the feds. They've taken over the back side of Raven's Eye and set up camp. So there you go. Skyla thinks she's trumped me as easily as that."

"Raven's Eye," I whisper. "Of course, the island has belonged to the navy for as long as I can remember. That's probably been their base all along." Raven's Eye sits west of Host. My father took Logan and me out there once when we were kids while he retrieved a body for the morgue. It's a flatland of black rocks, looks more like a dried-up lava bed than anything remotely resembling Paragon, but it's not without its evergreen crown.

Logan nods my way. "And now we know exactly where they are." I can see the relief in his eyes. Casey has grown on us all like a little sister. It's hard knowing she's out there. And the rest of them, too. They were great people. Still are. All of them were once dead with the exception of—

"Melody Winters," Demetri cuts me off at the pass and only reinforces the fact he can hear my thoughts down here. Hell, he can hear them everywhere. "She's a transplant from another generation. A traveler, if you will."

"Melody?" Logan looks to me and shakes his head. "I'm pretty sure she's been on the island—born and bred. You mean she's one of us?" Logan asks Demetri as if the demon might actually respond in kind. We've already surmised as much per my father's—real father's, catalog.

"Indeed. A rebellious heart. An even split between Celestra and Countenance. The worst of all combinations if you ask me. And you did ask me." He takes a moment to smile and gleam a greasy grin his way. "You know what they say, ask and you shall receive." He takes off and mingles with the older Videns standing around by the fountain of fire, a special effect provided by none other than Demetri himself.

Wes leans in with that easy grin of his gliding across his face. "You know what I'm going to ask for?"

"What?" I'm mildly amused.

"Nothing. I'm going to take it all myself." He takes off for the crowd, leaving Logan and me alone, the way I like it.

"You know what I'm going to ask for?" I can feel my dimples digging in as I hold back a laugh.

"Another three feet added to your dick?" He shrugs it off. "Lex and Chloe were talking about it last night."

"No," I flatline, unamused. "I'm going to ask you to head to Raven's Eye. I want to know what the feds are doing. I want to know what our people aren't being subjected to—and the dead are." My lips twitch because a part of me doesn't want to say what comes next. "Is Skyla safe? With Chloe?" I'm the only one officially in the dark.

"As safe as she could ever be with Chloe Bishop. Is Chloe safe?"

We share a quick laugh as Demetri calls the meeting to order.

"Hey"—Logan leans in—"how are these in comparison to the Faction meetings?"

"Let's just say they can be a bit more spirited."

I take a seat on my throne, and Logan sits on a stone next to me as we look down at the throngs of men around us along with a few disgruntled women peppered throughout, Emily Morgan being one of them.

"Where the hell are our people?" she shouts from the back, and I'm momentarily stunned. Out of everyone here, Emily has unobstructed access to me anytime she wishes. What the hell?

"They're safe," I offer. "Wesley has them on assignment." Bullshit answer number one.

Wes rears his head as if I had roused him from his sleep. "They're not coming home."

"Shit," I mutter under my breath. If he were closer, I'd kick him in the nuts.

Wes stands on a boulder to my left, erecting himself a full six feet above me. "Your loved ones are mine. They are to be utilized, disposed of in any manner that I desire because they gave me that honor." The crowd ignites to unsafe levels of disgruntled cries, threats of bodily harm to both Wes and me.

Logan shoots me a look. "Just a bit more spirited." He nods to the crowd. "They even come bearing gifts."

I follow his gaze to a man with a noose in his hands, and my stomach sinks.

The Videns are pissed. They are hungry for blood. Tonight, they exude a fiery rage, and Wes just doused the place with gasoline.

Wesley turns to me, his eyes as dead as his soul. "Ezrina says she can't guarantee a conversion. A sacrifice has been made. The people will simply have to live with it." He takes off and evaporates as he hits the jasper wall behind me.

Logan and I stand as the crowd begins to riot amongst themselves.

"You make a decision, and you live with it," Logan offers as if it were sage advice. "That's what happened to me."

"It's what happens to all of us." But how the hell do you explain that to a bunch of rabid, grieving relatives who want their boys back?

Nathan and Barron come to mind, and my heart is overcome with grief right along with the rest of the Videns. I get it.

I hold out a hand, and the crowd begins to still. Slowly, the eruptions of hatred grind to a halt.

"I cannot imagine your pain—but I can make it better." I meet with the eyes of those near madness at what's become of their loved ones. "I will do everything I can to bring your boys home safe." I look right into Emily's piercing stare. "I promise."

A month crawls by. Skyla and I lasted one night at my parents' house. One fucking night before my mother started an inquisition as to why Angel is still with us, and Skyla couldn't handle the heat. Truthfully, neither could I. In fact, in the short month and a half we've had her, she feels every bit ours as much as the boys do. And I love her just as much. It's shocking to me on some level, and yet completely understandable. I love Logan, and, of course, I love Skyla. How could I not love flesh from their flesh? Not to mention the fact Angel has an infectious laugh, and an infectious smile, and has started calling both Logan and me Da Da. And just as precious as that, she's trained the boys to do the same. Skyla is still waiting for them to call her anything, but right now I'm honored to share that title with Logan. Deep down, I know it's a title we'll share in my boys' life as long as we're alive.

But those dark dreams I've had of late keep coming, fast and furious. Water turns to wine. Wine turns to blood. I find myself drowning in a pool of red, the sky inverting as if it had the power to unzip itself as I float into the great unknown.

I startle back to life as I blink out at the glistening waves off Silent Cove. The weather is lousy for this Fourth of July. If fireworks ensue later, we won't be able to see them.

This summer is a strange one for far more reasons than Paragon's ubiquitous fog. Even Demetri opted out of his great summer bash, in which he lures the sun to come out and play. He's been angry, barking at both Wes and me for whatever reason he can find. He's suggested Wesley's little FU to the Videns is causing him problems in the heavenlies—something about the Fem infrastructure crumbling like a house of cards. It's comforting to know in a world where I can't control a damn thing that even Demetri in all his demented glory has the very same problem. Somehow it makes my world a little less shaky knowing the ground is just as wobbly under everyone else's feet.

Logan's backyard—for lack of a better word, is festooned with wisteria filled archways and sprays of flowers just about everywhere you look. If Laken had an elegant floral line leading to the sea, then Bree has outdone her by a perennial blooming mile. It looks as if a florist filled up a truck and dumped its contents wherever the hell it wanted. This is the disarray to Laken's organization. The chaos to Laken's calm. The gaudy to Laken's elegant charm. And that is Bree in a nutshell.

Since Skyla was barefoot at last year's event, Bree has insisted that all of her bridesmaids show up sans footwear, which is fine since most of the big event takes place on sand. But Bree might have overlooked the fact that Skyla was pregnant last year with her ankles swollen and hidden under waterlogged flesh. Skyla might be back in shape just one year later, but that didn't stop Bree from outfitting each girl in her wedding party with a maternity gown that resembles the one Skyla wore last year, and if I didn't know better, I'd swear Skyla is wearing the exact same one. She's cinched it off with a belt, but it still doesn't do her body justice. The ceremony goes off without a hitch. Nathan and Barron are held by Mia and Melissa and don't make a peep during the ceremony. Angel is safe in Laken's arms. And even Wes is here with his dark-haired beauty, Tobie. I can't help but smile when I see her. I'm sure Sage would have looked just as beautiful.

"This is some party!" Lizbeth squeals as she and Tad waddle by, each with a child attached to their knee. Beau has just turned three, and both Ember and Misty, two. Life seems to be moving at a breakneck speed. Giselle just graduated from West, although she didn't walk. She still has a few summer courses she needs to complete before it's official. It's hard to believe despite all of the wickedness in this world life just stubbornly barrels on.

Lizbeth can hardly catch her breath. "This is such a magical night! It wouldn't surprise me at all if Drake and Brielle expanded their family by one in just nine short months!"

Tad lets out a garbled cry. "Why'd you have to go and curse a perfectly good evening? There's all the free seafood we can eat, Lizbeth. Couldn't you focus on that?"

"Children are a blessing, not a curse."

"Speak for yourself. The only thing around here that's a blessing is the fact I get to take home all the leftovers." He smacks me over the arm. "That's right Gregory. All the crustaceans we can eat for the next solid month. Nothing but the best for my son." He gives a wistful shake of the head as if he actually paid for it.

"Speaking of sons—" Lizbeth gets that devious gleam in her eyes that has me searching the crowd for Skyla. "You have two very handsome boys who will be turning one in a matter of months. You *must* let me plan their party."

"I'm afraid that's Skyla's department." And mine, but I leave myself out of it for now.

"I won't take no for an answer." She rambles on and on, but something in the woods behind Logan's home has stolen my attention. A dark mist, deep purple in color, slowly morphs into the shape of a very tall man before dissipating into a blanket of mystery. It morphs back into the shape of a man, tall and stately, and if it had eyes, I would bet my life he was looking right at me. He walks down to the shoreline, wading in ankle deep, before turning around and waving for me to join him. A chill runs through my body as I reposition myself so I don't have to look at him.

Demetri shows up with baby Tobie in his arms, and I feel sorry for the poor thing, so I do the only thing I can. I take her from him and politely excuse myself while Lizbeth gloms onto him, her mouth still going a mile a minute about the boys' first birthday party.

I head over to Skyla and Logan. He's holding Angel, rocking her on his hip, and from the looks on their faces, I've interrupted a heated exchange. Skyla pauses to glare at him, a look I'm sure he's unfamiliar with.

"What's up?"

"Oh my God." Skyla melts at the sight of Tobie. "Speaking of angels." She takes the baby from me. "How are you?" She bounces her finger off her tiny nose, and Tobie kicks her chubby little limbs and squeals with delight. "Where is your daddy?" Skyla's voice breaks. "It kills me that Chloe won't step up to the plate." She rests her cheek over Tobie's dark curls. "Every child deserves a mother."

Tobie looks up and pats Skyla over the cheek. Their eyes lock over one another as if in that moment a bond had formed. Skyla threw out the maternal invite, and Tobie accepted.

Angel stretches over to her. "Ma Ma." She grabs a handful of Tobie's dark hair and yanks her head back with a violent thrust.

"*Angel!*" Skyla turns Tobie away as she screams bloody murder. "I'm so sorry. It'll be okay!" Skyla does her best to soothe her just as Wes shows up. Tobie stretches out her arms and screams *Daddy* through her tears, and it reduces me to cinders. At the end of the day, Wesley is a good father. I don't think anyone, not even my wife, his enemy, would contest it.

The music starts up, and the makeshift dance floor Logan had constructed down by the shore fills in with Drake and Bree leading the way. The music is slow and moody, and I spot Ellis and Giselle out there, Laken and Coop, Michelle and Liam, and Em and Ethan. Mia and Melissa are dancing with Nathan and Barron. Hell, even Lizbeth and Tad are gyrating with the best of them.

"Go on out there." Logan gives me a light kick in the back of the leg, and my knee collapses for a moment. "Dance with your wife." He looks right at me with a softness to him because he means it. "I've got an ornery little lady on my hands to contend with. I'll go see if I can't sneak her a bite of the cake."

Angel flaps her arms and gives a squawk of approval. Her pink face lights up like a Christmas tree. "Da Da! Da Da!" she sings, and we share a laugh.

"Don't you dare feed her sugar." Skyla presses a kiss to Angel's tiny lips. "You behave."

I lead my wife down to the dance floor, and we bury ourselves deep in the crowd beside Bree and Drake on one side, Laken and Coop on the other, and it feels right.

My arms fold over her back, and she pulls me in close with her glowing crystal eyes sealed over mine.

"I love you, Skyla Oliver."

Her hips grind into mine. "And I love you, Gage Oliver." She leans up on her tiptoes and presses a heated kiss to my lips. "I'm so thrilled to be your wife. I love our little family. We really do have it all."

"We do, don't we?" I give her a little spin, and Skyla bubbles with laughter. Skyla and I dance circles under those stars buried in fog. Brielle changes partners and dances with Ellis, with Logan, with Dudley. But Skyla remains steadfast in my arms. I don't think I'd bow out if anyone tried to change that.

Bree and Drake take center stage again as they head up to cut the cake—an enormous towering confection that rivals the size of a mid-sized sedan. Bree waves her bouquet at the crowd, and on cue a thousand single girls line up to catch it. She gives it a light toss over her shoulders, and Lex dives for it like a linebacker on her way to the victory line, but it's Mia who holds it up victorious. Both Skyla and I exchange a glance.

"Any clue who she might choose as the groom?" I give Skyla a light peck over the cheek as I ask.

"I guess it depends what day it is." She gives a slight frown before looking back up at me and relaxing into a smile. "I sort of wish that music was still going. That was kind of nice. Dancing with my husband happens to be one of my favorite sports."

I glance around and spot Nathan and Barron in Laken and Coop's arms. "I think we've got the kids covered for a few minutes. How about you and I get lost?"

"I like the sound of that." She leans in with her lids hooded. "You know I'm still in Kegel hell, and thus insatiably horny. And by the way, I happen to hate that particular word."

I wince because we both hate it, but we both love it because it means such great things for us. "Follow my lead." I take her arms and wrap them around my waist as I scoot the two of us behind the wall of shrubbery Brielle erected just for the occasion.

The world melts away, a new one appearing in its place as the white sandy shore gives way to black sand, and our feet touch down on precious Rockaway soil.

"I love it here!" Skyla jumps in my arms as we take in the desolate ebony shoreline. From the distance, we can see the twinkling lights down at Silent Cove, but we can't hear the music, so I produce my own. The air around us fills with the slow rhythm of a sax as Skyla's body once again conforms to mine. "*Smooth* Oliver."

"I am smooth. I ended up with you, didn't I?" I dip her backward, and she lets out a scream of delight. "Come here." I pull her to me, and Skyla floats up on her tiptoes until her mouth is melting over mine. I harness all of my powers until the moon pours a single beam over us like a spotlight. It takes everything I've got, but I shield us with my love, placing a banner over us that no government agency can penetrate with the human eye. And then I take it to the next level. I pull Skyla into the heavens with me, Levatio style. How I miss those humble Levatio days, but I wouldn't trade anything I have now to get them back. Everything that's happened has molded our destinies, brought us our boys, brought us each other. Skyla is my wife, my life, and I will fight until my last breath, and then beyond to keep her. I'm greedy that way. A simple covenant isn't enough for what we have. Not any force in heaven—her mother—or any force in hell—my father, can tear us apart.

A crackle of lightning goes off overhead, and a dull laugh rattles through me. I'd like to see them try.

Nope, Skyla and I are an eternal pairing. I feel it deep down in my bones. Skyla brings out the best in me—and the beast. In one quick burst, a pair of wings erupts from my shoulder blades and into the night sky with a span of forty feet between them at least.

Skyla tips her head back and laughs. "Gage Oliver—you are such a showoff! And so am I." She bows her head a moment, and a burst of white plumes ejects behind her. Soft, bountiful feathers that glimmer an unearthly iridescent shade blossom over her shoulders, and Skyla glows under the light of her wings.

"Damn, you are beautiful."

She bites down over her smile as she lands a finger to my lips. "Should the King use language such as this?" She shakes her head ever so slightly. "I strictly forbid it."

"If my queen insists." I crash my mouth over hers as we float higher and higher to the stratosphere and back, bathing in moonlight, bathing in the warmth of our love.

Right here in this moment, we seal our love forever.

Logan

Forever young.

It's funny, the thoughts that sail through your mind as you drift off to sleep. I never once believed I would die in my prime, close my eyes one last time before I ever hit my second decade of life, but I did. I was just a kid. A stupid one at that. No, it wasn't my first go-around on this planet, but it was my best. I don't think too much of the life I lived as a burn victim. If anything, it was a prelude to a dream, my dream life with my dream girl, Skyla.

No, I didn't think I'd die young. Gage and all of his morbid premonitions always hinted that he would be the one to float off this spinning blue rock before he ever hit thirty. I was the one he predicted would grow to a ripe old age with Skyla. But that was back when thirty was old as dirt anyway. Yes, the second coming of Logan Oliver was a sight to behold. Got my face back. Spent some serious time in the gym building a body. Quarterback of the West Paragon Dawgs. Had all the girls spinning their heads, offering to open their legs. I used to own this island. I was hot shit. One day I held the keys to the kingdom—the next, I was in kingdom come. It was over before it ever really began. Beheaded by a girl I once thought I might gift my heart to. Yes, I'll be the last to admit that I had the hots for Chloe Bishop. So much so that I mistakenly, for a very brief moment, thought it might be the real thing. Chloe. Fucking *Chloe*. For certain, she qualifies as my brief stint of insanity.

I drift off to that strange space between consciousness and sleep—the exact juncture I need to hop off the train and head for someone else's dreamscape. For the last few weeks, I've been visiting Casey in her dreams. Dream visitations is a gift I've honed over the years. It doesn't drain me the next day quite like it used to, but I still feel like a sack of shit that's been set on fire and stomped on. I don't mind, though. Casey is sweet. An older version of what I envision Angel growing up to be like. And because I feel so brotherly, so fatherly toward her, it burdens me to know exactly where she is—a glass box, locked up somewhere in the heart of Raven's Eye.

The room forms around me, solid and real, and yet it's simply Casey's ability to recreate her world for me while she's locked in her slumber.

"Finally, slow poke!" She swats me with her pillow. I've had Casey memorize her quarters and utilize it as the backdrop to our nighttime tête-à-tête. Mostly because I need to see this place, know the ins and outs of what she's familiar with, what I'm up against should things go south for anyone involved. Yes, the dead signed up for what amounts to a *death* sentence, but after getting to know them, spending time with them while at Gage and Skyla's place, I don't have the heart to abandon them. I guess this is my meager form of monitoring the situation. So far, Casey says they've done nothing more invasive than have them stare at what amounts to Rorschach blotches. Asked them to perform rudimentary telepathic tasks, checking their strength, their speed, raining down the inquisition as far as who they are—what planet they're from.

"I'm late because Angel put up a fight."

Her fresh scrubbed face lights up at the mention of my baby girl. "Skyla let her spend the night?"

"No, I didn't ask. I simply put her to bed, but she didn't want me to leave." When Skyla and Gage moved back to the Landon house, we agreed Angel should go with them. It's just at night when we're separated. You can hardly say that I've been living the life of a part-time father ever since. Gage says I'm welcome anytime, and I've spent so much time at the Landon house as of late, it's starting to feel like our high school days. "Skyla is a great mother. I always knew she would be."

Casey pulls out a deck of cards—Old Maid, her favorite, and begins to shuffle. "You always say such nice things about her. You really like Skyla, don't you?" Her lips twitch as if she's been onto me the entire time.

"What's not to like? She's my sister-in-law in a way. She was my wife once. My girlfriend briefly before that. Gage has made a habit of snatching her out of my arms ever since she arrived on the island. It's a game we like to play. Only now I guess it's game over for me." I take up the cards she deals my way. "I'm okay with it, though. Gage and Skyla are pretty great together."

"I'll agree with that." Her blonde brows hitch up a notch. Casey is the quintessential little sister next door—all of the innocence and unstoppable youth embodied in a pre-teen. "Gage seems pretty nice. I don't really know him as well as I know you. Those little boys they have are just a dream. Do you think Gage is a nice guy?"

My stomach clenches, and I'm not sure why. "Yup. He's the best. He's got his hands full, though—work, school, family, and he's pulling it all off with grace and ease. He should be awarded father of the year."

"You're a father now. Don't you think you deserve that award?" She places down two sets of matching cards and laughs in my face.

"I am a father now. It's all very new, but I'm in love. I'm so deep in, my bones ache with sweetness when I think about my girl. She really is an angel."

She lays down another matching set, and I fold. "You must cheat. Nobody wins that much."

"I never cheat. I just know how to play the game very, very well." She wrinkles her nose. "Do you think you'll call her that—Angel, when the time comes?"

My entire body heats at the thought of procreating with Skyla, our bodies moving in a unified rhythm, her heavy breathing searing over my chest.

I clear my throat. "Skyla and I can't have children, not now, not ever. I happen to be Team Gage." I glance up at the proverbial ceiling in the event Candace is listening.

"You will, though." She reshuffles the deck and hands out the cards. "I mean, Angel is sort of living proof."

I stare at her an inordinate amount of time, wagering whether or not to pursue the conversation. It would take a millennium for me to explain to both her and myself why I can't have a future with Skyla no matter what heartbreaking teasers Candace throws our way.

"Logan"—she picks through her deck, rearranging her cards one at a time—"tell me about your love for Skyla. I'm sort of a romance junkie. I've spent years in paradise listening to true loves' finest tales. I was sort of cut off before I ever got to experience it myself. Not that I'm lamenting the fact. I died thinking boys were more than icky." She makes a face like she might vomit. "But the idea has grown on me, and I like the stories. I can listen to them over and over the way others listen to songs."

"My love story with Skyla." I let out a full sigh. "That's easy. I fell in love the moment I laid eyes on her—so did Gage by the way." Technically, that's not true. He fell in love with her in his dreams first. I guess you could say he had the advantage. We dated—Skyla and me." A tiny laugh bumps through my chest. "I never dated Gage."

"Ha-ha." She rolls her eyes. "Move it along."

"That's it. Skyla had the Counts and the Fems trying to incapacitate her, and I knew they would stop at nothing to make sure we never got together. Our child—she would be—she is, I suppose, as close to pure as possible."

"*Pure.*" She sighs dreamily. "Angel is a lucky little girl. I'm sure the Decision Council has already carefully plotted out the very best destiny for her."

I think of Skyla and all her hardships. Of myself. Of Gage.

"I'm not sure it would be the best. Anyhow, I had a lousy brainstorm one day and thought that perhaps Skyla should pretend to date Gage to throw off the Counts. I thought at least that way we could still be together once we were alone."

"No!" She tosses down her cards in horror. "You drove her right into his arms, didn't you?"

"Something like that." A pang of embarrassment rips through me. Even innocent Casey can see it was a ridiculous idea. "Skyla and I never really got back on track. And then I died. Candace allowed me to live in a mini Treble, much like the one I'm in. I managed to snatch Skyla back for a bit." I give a sly wink.

Casey claps up a storm. "A happy ending of sorts. But wait—you were dead! That's terrible."

"It wasn't so bad. Skyla and I married and had a brief yet beautiful honeymoon. And just before I was called back to paradise, I charged Gage with taking care of and loving Skyla the way that I would have. And he's done so ever since." I land my cards on top of hers, declaring our paper war over.

"And what about Gage?" She scoops the cards up with her fingers, slow to look at me. "Has he charged you with the same?"

"Yes. Last year. But I won't take him up on it. I'm fighting for their family to stay whole until they're both old and ragged and the boys are old and ragged, too." I'd wink, but I'm not being cheeky. This is my greatest wish. "But I'll let you in on a little secret"—I lean in, and she does the same—"I'm still very much in love with Skyla."

Casey leans back, her gaze still set over mine with a look on her face that says she's about to trump me, only we're not playing cards anymore. "I've got a little secret myself." A spurt of giggles escapes her. "I know you, Logan. I know you from paradise—the version that has run the race and completed his mission in life." Her affect sharpens, and suddenly she seems far older than the innocent girl I've pegged her to be. "I'll give you a little hint of your future with Skyla, but then I'm sending you back to Paragon. I'm getting tired."

I open my mouth to protest, but my vocal cords don't dare give a sound.

"Angel happens, Logan. You don't get to keep her, but she comes back to you just the way she's supposed to." Her features contort in pain, and she looks as if she's about to wail with tears. "Maybe." She gives me a solid shove off the side of the bed, and I keep falling—all the way to Paragon.

Skyla and I happen.

Maybe.

I don't like the sound of it.

Skyla and I are over.

We've already happened.

On Tuesday, I offer to take Angel for the night to give poor Skyla a break. I don't dare visit Casey that night. In fact, I don't dare dream, sleep, or wink a second too long. Instead, I watch my baby girl sleep, watch as her chest rises and falls, memorize the steady pattern of her breathing. But eventually, I succumb to what amounts to a short nap. In the morning, try as I might to beat Angel to the bright-eyed and bushy-tailed punch, I find her laughing and bouncing in one of the cribs I've set up in my bedroom. The original two were for the boys, but I went out and bought another so the collection grew to three once Angel arrived. They remind me of those old-fashioned circus cages you would see animals displayed in. But the only little animal around here is Angel, a jovial laughing baby koala that wants nothing more than to snuggle up with her dad—*me*.

I make breakfast, feed her the organic fare Skyla left me with last night, and give her a bottle, which she quickly catches on how to use, and we find a comfy spot on the couch and lose the rest of the morning watching cartoons.

This is the life. While Angel studies the screen, I study her. I'm mesmerized by her blonde curls that look as if they're made of spun gold. I study how intently she focuses in on the television, laughing and clapping intermittently as the show commands it. Her eyes are a unique pale shade of turquoise with amber flecks—Skyla's eyes married with mine. I see Skyla there in her face, in the way she lights up with her whole body when something makes her giddy with excitement. I hold out my hand, and she slaps me five over and over again while kicking the shit out of me with those precious chunky legs.

"You're a real princess, you know that?" I press a kiss to her cheek. "Just like your mom."

A knock comes from the door, and her whole body stretches in that direction. "Ma Ma!"

"Let's see." I scoop her up and fly her like an airplane to the door. Only when we swing it open, it's not Skyla we see. It's Lex.

"Hey, good-looking." Lex gives my cheek a pinch as she makes her way past me. "You and the kid ready for your close-up?"

"Ready and willing." I'm not entirely thrilled with the way Lex didn't even bother to say hello to Angel. I get it. She's a baby, but she's a person, my person. You'd think if Lex really wanted to cement herself in my life she'd at least make half the effort. Not that I'm looking for Lex to do any cementing. I'm just saying her strategy is off.

"Okay." Lex looks around with her fists planted on her hips. "Here." She whips a white furry blanket off the couch— the exact white furry blanket she purchased when I gave her a blank check and told her to decorate the place—and lands it on the floor. "Take off your shirt and take off all of her clothes, too. We'll do a few nudes of her on your chest before Skyla gets here."

"What? There's no way I'm doing nudes with my daughter."

"Are you kidding?" She snorts while evicting her camera from its leather case. "It's all the rage. I promise it'll be cute."

The doorbell rings just as my stomach acids hit a boiling point. Lex generally knows her stuff, and generally I trust her, but I'm pretty sure I'm drawing the line at nudes.

Skyla bustles in with a bouncing baby boy in each arm, a bloated diaper bag dangling from her shoulder, and I put Angel down to help her.

"Look at you go!" Skyla marvels, and I follow her gaze to find Angel halfway into the kitchen.

"*Geez.*" I help Skyla put the boys on the floor before chasing Angel down. "She's fast. I'll give her that."

"Just like her mom," Lex snarks and the tension in the room goes up a notch.

"Good morning to you, too," Skyla growls at her questionable friend. "I already have the boys in their outfits. It'll just take me a second to dress the baby." She bites down on a smile as she takes Angel from me. "Who's a pretty little girl?" Skyla peppers Angel's face with kisses, and she kicks and screams with delight.

"That reminds me. I want to show you something." I pull a small faded Polaroid from off the mantel. "It's me about Angel's age." Before the fire. But I don't like to talk about that.

"Oh my goodness!" Skyla's voice pitches to its upper register. "You are the cutest little thing! And look at that face! Angel is basically you in a dress."

"I always knew I'd look good in pink."

Skyla gives my ribs a quick pinch, and I buck.

"You know"—she pulls the picture closer and recluses into herself a moment—"my mother didn't change our destinies at this juncture. She waited until you were older. She could have done it when you were a baby, but she didn't. Do you think there was something she was trying to salvage in that alternate reality?"

"I don't know. God knows I've thought about it. But I do know one thing that's come from it. I appreciate life and living it to its full potential." I can't put into words the heartache, the anguish I remember, and, in turn, that makes me rabid to know others experience that level of heartbreak and loneliness. I guess that's why I'm looking out for those taken to Raven's Eye. It's going to be hell for them, and I don't want it to be.

"Speaking of clothes"—Lex pipes up—"how about dropping trou, would you?" She licks her lips my way as if the invite was directed only at me, and I have no doubt it was.

"Lex wanted to photograph us in the nude." I wink over at Lex as she unloads her equipment onto the counter.

"Correction"—Skyla scoffs at the thought—"Lex wanted to photograph *you* in the nude. I'm pretty sure she'd like the rest of us dressed—or better yet, off the premises."

"No, I'm serious." Lex doesn't bother looking up while switching out her lenses. "Nude really *is* all the rage. I've already done six family pictorials this last week, all in the buff."

"Six, huh?" Skyla makes a face while pulling a frilly pink dress over the top of Angel's head, and the baby laughs and screams as if it was the funniest thing in the world. Barron rolls over and begins to gnaw on her chunky little leg, and it only makes Angel that much more hysterical. "So, how do these nudes work?"

"That's the hard part." Lex comes over and begins shooting a few shots off as she adjusts her lens. "I usually place the kids over the parents' privates. But I've done it all kinds of ways. The last one had dad on the bottom and mom on his back with each of their four kiddos piled on top of her."

"Sounds a little too organic." I shake my head at Skyla in the event Lex is able to loosen a screw. It's a hell no to that one. "I think we'll stick to clothes." I tug at the white dress shirt and jeans I donned just for the occasion, and Skyla gives an approving thumbs-up.

"But I think we should lose the shoes and socks." Skyla plucks the boys' socks off so fast you'd think their feet were on fire.

"*What*? I like my shoes." I point a sneaker her way, and she frowns at it as if I've stepped in dog shit.

"Shoes and socks off, Oliver." Something about the way she just barked out that command sounds erotic, and unfortunately for me has my dick begging to take my boxers off, too. Fat chance, buddy. Hold off on the party.

"How's Casey?" Skyla leans in and lays her shoulder over my chest as Lexy barks out instructions.

"I didn't see her last night, but she's been good. Spirits are high. She's lonely, but I let her kick my butt in Old Maid at least once a night so that makes up for it a bit."

"Did she say anything that sounds off?"

"No." Both Skyla and I are paranoid they're going to torment those poor people to death, and I suppose that is the point. "But as soon as anything changes, you'll be hearing from me."

Her forehead creases with worry. "I don't have a plan, Logan. I don't have a clue as to what we'll do to help." Angel slaps her over the nose, and she blinks back. "I got it. We'll storm the island. We can get the Retribution League and head over if things go sideways."

"And then what? Ellis offers them a fat blunt, and we all sit in a stoner circle while the dead trot back to paradise?"

She knocks her elbow into me. "You don't have to be so glib about it. I don't know what happens after that. Maybe you get naked and Lex can chase you around while documenting the event with her camera."

"That has my vote." Lex gives an enthusiastic thumbs-up.

"I bet it does," Skyla growls just under her breath. "Whatever it is, Holden is my first line of defense. He's already chomping at the bit to get his brother back." She winces. Pierce was taken last week, no thanks to Chloe. She was gunning to have Emerson incarcerated as well, but that almost backfired on her, and Chloe had to make a getaway herself. "I knew this would be tough for the family that had loved ones in the effort. Thankfully, there's only a small handful. Not to mention Kate. Her mother has practically chained her in the basement. She's terrified that outsiders will report her and terrified my mother will call her home on the spot. She's been sending out group texts to Nat and me letting us know she's bored out of her mind." She glares at Lexy a moment.

About two weeks ago, Lex took Kate to the mall, and they accidentally bumped into Kate's mother. Apparently, it almost sent *her* into kingdom come, too. Suffice it to say, Kate had a lot of explaining to do. Lex thought she'd help out in that department since Kate is still reduced to whispers, and evidently Lex didn't hold back on the details. Mrs. Winston, a human through and through, is now up on all things Faction and angelic. A frightening detail when you think about it. But she swore she'd keep everything to herself. She was so relieved to have her daughter back— albeit temporarily—that woman could be trusted with nuclear codes at this point.

I smooth my hand over Skyla's back. "Does a part of you regret bringing Kate back?"

"No. She's glad she's here. *I'm* glad she's here, and Nat is super happy to have her back, if only for a while."

"I'm in that number, Messenger," Lex calls from behind the camera as she snaps away.

Skyla gives my shoe a light tap with her foot. "I said take it off, Oliver."

A sly grin crawls up one side of my face because it sounded dirty, and my balls drink down the naughty implications even if there weren't any.

I do as I'm told, and Lex moves the five of us out onto the front lawn. Skyla sits next to me in the damp grass with Angel on her lap while I hold the boys, and my stomach starts to boil with a slight undercurrent of panic. Actually, when I mentioned to Skyla that Lex wanted to take a family picture of us with the baby I hadn't really thought about including the boys—but, of course, we're including the boys because they're family—they're Skyla's children, and mine by proxy. But I've got a nagging feeling this is a very bad idea, and just as I'm about to hem and haw my way through a list of reasons that perhaps we should reconsider, a big black truck pulls into the driveway and Gage hops out.

Perfect. And here's reason number one through one hundred as to why this whole family pictorial just went to hell in a Lexy-shaped handbasket.

Gage loses his grin in slow motion as he takes in the scene. "What's going on?"

Skyla closes her eyes a moment because I'm betting she's just surmised this was perhaps a very shitty idea to begin with.

I'm not Skyla's husband. And it was never my intent to kick Gage to the curb—behind his back, no less. All I wanted was a picture of Angel, and this morphed into something it was never intended to be. Thank God Almighty we opted out of nudes.

"We're in the middle of family pictures, Gage," Lex grouses. "Get out of the way. You're in the shot!"

Shit. I close my eyes and try to will us out of this uncomfortable situation.

"Logan, look this way!" Lex sings. "Everybody say *happy little family!*"

"Wow." Gage gargles out a dark laugh as he sits on the porch. "Glad I didn't miss the show." His dimples dig in deep, and I can tell he's eating up our discomfort, but the dude has got to be hurt.

"Okay"—Lex flicks her finger at us—"go ahead and get naked, and we'll stick a boy between each of your legs. Skyla, you've got small tits. Just pull your hair over your shoulders and set the girls up high. We'll start there before we get to the dogpile."

"Oh no, we won't." Skyla hops up with Angel, and I do the same with Barron. "Gage Oliver, I am sorry." She rolls her eyes. "I swear I thought this was just for the kids," she pleads with all of the sorrow she can muster. "And, of course, Logan and Angel." She bites down so hard on her bottom lip it grows bone white.

"I know." He gives her a quick peck on the lips. "I wanted to come with you, but I had to stop off at the morgue."

"Come on, Skyla." Lex tries to lure her back to the lawn with a tip of the chin. "Just you and the kids."

"Sounds good." I land Barron next to Nathan and head back over to Gage, where I plan to grovel for his forgiveness for the rest of my disputable life.

Skyla happily piles the kids on her lap while Angel takes each of the boys by the hair and gives a good yank initiating a riot within five seconds flat.

"That's the money shot! Can they cry any louder?" Lex howls with a laugh while Skyla does her best to get the unrest to stop. "If murder was legal, we'd all be smothered to death as infants!"

Gage ticks his brows up my way and bucks with a quiet laugh. "Lexy Bakova is going to make a fantastic mother."

"I agree." I glance her way as she snaps at the kids to pull it together. "Sorry about the circus, dude." I shrug over at him as he lands those riotously blue eyes my way with a brief moment of judgment. "It sort of got out of hand."

"Don't be. Skyla let me in on it this morning. I think it's a good thing. They grow fast. You want to remember it all." There's a palpable sadness veiled in his features, a tangible despondency as if someone just died.

"Hey, everything okay?" I give his shoulder a quick pat as if to perk him up. I've been around Gage long enough to read him like a book, and no matter what he says, I know it's anything but okay.

"I'm great." He frowns at the construction site across the street as the crew drags in concrete mixers and steel beams to start on the new and improved bowling alley. They've already laid the foundation, and now all I have to do is sit back and watch that monster put itself back together again. "I only stayed at the morgue a minute." His jawline redefines itself as he continues to glare across the street. "I had to meet with Wes. He wants to know how I plan on getting the Spectators back to their near human state since not even Ezrina could promise them that."

It feels like a punch in the gut just listening to him. I've always wondered how quickly he would end up over his head, and now I know.

"We'll talk to Ezrina. She's downstairs."

He nods as if acknowledging this. "I told Wes he needs to haul them back to Tenebrous. Skyla will have to let them in. He's going to put a call out this afternoon to round them up."

"And he's listening to you?" I'm amazed that Wesley would take one of his prized arsenals and remove them from the playing field.

"He is—he has to."

Lex gives a shrill whistle to get our attention. "Would you both get over there? Kids have a short attention span, if you haven't noticed."

Skyla waves the two of us over as she struggles to keep three little ones from crawling to the four corners of the earth.

Gage and I head over to the lawn, and Skyla swats Gage until he complies with the no shoe, no sock rule. Soon we're posing for the camera as one big family, and it feels right. Skyla and Gage sit next to one another with a boy on each lap, and I lie on my side in front of them with Angel—just the six of us, perhaps the way it should be. In the end, we feel like one big happy family.

Ellis' monster truck roars up the street and pulls into the mouth of the driveway before both he and Giselle hop out.

"Good-looking crew!" Ellis struts over and does his best to high-five the kids, and shockingly it looks as if he's got them all trained. He gives me a swift kick in the ass with his boot. "Here's the man of the hour. G and I just ran by the city with the architect and made some last-minute changes. Just a few little things. Nothing to panic over."

Crap. If Ellis Harrison suggests it's nothing to panic over, it is very much something to panic over.

Gage and I get up and follow him to the porch while Giselle helps Skyla scoop up the kids.

"Too late, I'm panicked. What's happening?" My heart bucks its way into my throat because I'm fearing I'll find a hookah lounge that specializes in pot planted smack in the middle of my thoroughly modern state-of-the-art bowl-a-drome.

Ellis grimaces over at Giselle a moment as she helps Skyla into the house with the kids. "You know, I like to keep the little woman happy."

Gage groans. "That's demeaning, and sexist, and would you stop treating my sister like some toy you picked up at the store?" He gives Ellis a slight shove and sends him staggering backward.

"Dude, she's the love of my life. I'd die if that's what made her happy."

Gage and I exchange a wry smile. Sometimes Ellis just being Ellis can be a bit frightening to witness.

"Anyway, like I said, there were a few minor changes she wanted to see made to the plans, and both the city and the architect agreed it was no big deal. Plus, the contractor says this new design change will put us ahead of schedule a full month—so get ready to christen this baby by December."

"Let's hear it. I'm sure it's a great idea." Words I never thought I'd say to Ellis. "Are we erecting a replica of the Eifel Tower on the rooftop? Mirrored walls? A giant G rotating over the signage? Give it to me quick, Ellis." Again, words I never thought would leave my lips.

Ellis expands his chest with his next breath as he glances over my shoulder. "She nixed the sleek contemporary design and—let's just say she went for a more *homey* feel."

"Shit. How homey?"

Gage bucks with a dull laugh. "Dude, you did this without consulting Logan? I don't care how homey it is. You've lost your fucking mind."

Ellis nods in agreement. "That I have, my friend. And let it be a testimony to how much I love your sister. So don't ride my ass anymore. Every time you drive by the Bowling Barn, I want you to see it as a testament to my affection toward her."

"Oh shit." My stomach bottoms out. Worst nightmare confirmed. Working with Ellis was the mistake of the century. "The *Bowling Barn*? Ellis, exactly what kind of changes did you make to the aesthetics?"

"Just a few nips and tucks." He shrugs it off as if it were nothing, and just as he opens his mouth to continue, Giselle hops down the porch and strangles him with a hug. I'm tempted to cheer her on in the taking Ellis' breath away department.

"Isn't it great?" Giselle beams as Skyla pops up behind her.

"The kids are in their Pack 'n Plays." Skyla wraps her arms around Gage and notes the conversation is stilted. "Isn't what great?"

Giselle does an odd little bunny hop. "The fact the bowling alley is going to be in the shape of a big giant red barn!"

Gage and Skyla groan at the same time. I'd join them, but I'm too busy trying not to pass out.

"Ellis?" My voice hitches. "What happened to the bowling alley and gym we spent weeks together designing? Or were you too wasted to remember?" I'm not holding back because I just so happen to be fucking pissed.

"I remember." He holds his hands out in surrender. "I just thought Giselle had a pretty great idea."

"Oh, it is a great idea," she's quick to assure. "We're going to have ten times more arcade games and *prizes*. We'll have lots and lots of prizes—those big giant stuffed animals with the button eyes the size of paper plates—they sort of give me nightmares—but we'll have those and anything else you can imagine!"

"I'm sort of having a nightmare, too." I glare across the street where the bowling alley once stood and silently kiss my sleek bowl-a-drome goodbye. This is what I get for leaning hard on Ellis, financially speaking. I knew I was putting him in the driver's seat, but I could have never foreseen this barnyard fiasco, and it's my own stupid fault. Note to self: whenever Ellis is involved—expect a barnyard fiasco each and every time.

Shit. Just shit.

The babies start to whine, and Giselle volunteers to head on in. "I just love babies, Skyla. Keep making them! Make some with Ellis, too!"

Gage pats me over the back. "Hang in there, man." He glares at Ellis a moment. "And you stay away from my woman." He takes off inside the house right behind his sister.

Ellis scampers off across the street to the construction site before I can effectively kick his horny little stoner ass. Of course, he'll do anything for *G* because she's giving him exactly what he wants. Damn pervert.

"Host University is getting a gem." I regret the words as soon as they leave my mouth. Giselle really is a bright girl when she applies herself. She's just a kid. And what kid wouldn't want an oversized cherry red barn smack in the middle of town?

"Be nice," Skyla scolds while wrapping an arm around my shoulders. "That's your niece, and she means well." She steps in front of me, interrupting the funnel of hatred I'm shooting toward Ellis. "And you are nice." She gives my cheek a light pinch. "And good things happen to nice people. Besides, I think the Bowling Barn sounds adorable. Maybe it's better than Bar Slash Bowling?"

"She's not taking my liquor license."

"*Okay.*" Skyla laughs while lifting her hands and cupping my cheeks. "Have it your way. Booze, bowling, and button-eyed demons."

"Be careful what you say." I tick my head back toward the house. "Someone is likely to hear that and turn it into the new tagline for the place."

We share a quiet laugh.

"How's the pumpkin patch going?" She gives my scruff a light scratch, and it feels like heaven.

"Decent. Liam and I hired a crew to clear the land, and I'm having my contractor toss a chain-link fence around it. The vines are already spreading, and there's hope for a decent crop come October. First year everything is free. One pumpkin per family. Sound fair?"

"*Aww!*" She wraps her arms around me and lays her head on my chest a moment. "You are a saint, Logan Oliver." She pulls back, her eyes pinned to mine. "And an amazing father and uncle." Her gaze dips to the ground a moment. "And a good friend." She nods up at me as if she wanted me to really hear those words, to memorize them. "And even better family." Her arms tighten around my waist again.

And that's what we are. Skyla and I are family.

There is no greater bond.

My gut wrenches as if calling me out on the lie.

There might be one greater bond than that—I glance down at her wedding ring—and it just so happens that bond isn't with me.

Summer comes to a close like the soft roll of a wave crashing the shore, nothing too dramatic. My birthday went off with a whisper with Gage and Skyla driving down to Pike's Reef with me, surprising me with a cake. I didn't want the big birthday bash I've traditionally had. For the first time in years, I wanted to be home that night, holding my baby girl tight in my arms. I already had the best gift life could give me.

I'm still monitoring Casey. Things seem stable on that front, but it's been weeks. How long can and will the government house throngs of alien beings who have made no secret of their powers? Are they satisfied with the nice round number we've fed them? What in the hell happens next? And then there's Wesley. His Spectators have been slowly herded to Tenebrous just as Gage requested. But that hasn't stopped the Barricade from sending out their mercenaries. It's official now. There have been more UFO sightings, more paranormal activity logged in the past year than in the course of modern history. He's amping up the big guns. I can feel it. Wes has sent in the clowns quite literally. The horror of these ghastly creatures has the entire world in an uproar. So much so that the longtime children's birthday party staple has been banned in eleven states. But Wes is just getting started. I can feel it in my dead creaky bones. Whatever the hell he has planned next is going to be dramatic, jaw-dropping on a grand scale. Lives will be dismantled, the bounds of human sanity challenged. Something earth-shattering this way comes. I just wish I could put my finger on it. Soon. I predict soon we will know the answer to this.

On an unassuming Saturday, I leave Whitehorse in the late afternoon for Dudley's house. Skyla and Chloe are throwing Ezrina a baby shower and insist that people of all genders join in on the fun. Yes, *Chloe*. Skyla's number two hasn't left her side. She's the obedient Golden Retriever Skyla never knew she wanted. Gage and I are still unified on the fact we don't want her around. Nobody in their right mind should want Chloe Bishop in their presence. I jump into my truck, and just as I'm about to head west toward the Estates, I spot a familiar looking dude seated on the framing of what is turning out to be a barn of barbaric proportions.

"Shit." I make a U-turn and speed into the lot across the street. That blond hair, those cut features, body that doesn't quit. Yes, that handsome devil would be me—another version, suffice it to say.

I park below the entry where he—*I*—sit and the truck gives a quick quiver as he lands feet first into the bed in the back.

"Whoa." I hop out and glare up at this paradise-bound version of myself. "You dent the bed, you'll have to pay for it."

There I am, glaring right back at myself. "Get the hell in here." He points hard to the tire well next to him, and I hop in, taking a seat across from him—me.

"Nothing like a mindfuck to get the weekend off to a great start."

He winces. "I'd say *language*, but you already know that." He offers a peaceable smile, and I'm remotely amused that this version of myself is fighting hard to be nice to me of all people. "You didn't take care of Dominique Winters."

My head jerks west in the direction of that twisted mansion the Winters live in. "Melody has been gone for over a month. I've checked with Barron, and he says they secured council. The U.S. Government versus the Winters. I don't see myself as a part of the equation."

"You should have," he says without missing a beat. "Skyla and Gage"—he presses his palm into his eye and growls as if whatever came next pained him—"tell them both you love them. Your entire detail on this planet is to be an ever-present help in times of trouble. Do not run from it." He leans in, determined. Those amber eyes light up like beacons. "Run *to* it. Do you hear me? You *run* into the fire." His eyes close briefly. "And spend some quality time with Gage. Talk to him." He says that last part as if it were an afterthought. The fog fills in thick between us, and slowly his body wears thin until he's altogether threadbare and gone.

"That's it?" I shout up to the sky. "That was fucking lousy."

I jump back into the truck and take off for Dudley's. All the way there I wonder what in the hell I was trying to tell myself.

Run into the fire. Talk to Gage. That's all that registered. I hope that was enough.

Dudley's not-so humble abode is festooned with enough pink and blue streamers to cover the circumference of the planet two or three times at least.

Brielle greets me at the door and blows a paper party horn in my face while that demonic player piano Dudley has stashed in the corner goes off a million ghostly miles an hour. I don't need to be next to it to know there's no one in the driver's seat—at least not anyone you can see.

"It's time to get your party on, Oliver!" Bree bumps her hip to mine nearly knocking me to the ground. "It's an open bar! Let me see your ID, son." She gives a wild cackle.

"Logan!" Chloe heads over and crashes her arms around my neck as if she's about to plant one on me, and then without missing an erotic beat, she does just that.

"Whoa." I pull back and frown at the witch. "Where's the woman of the hour?" I try to detangle myself from her, but Chloe is like a human Chinese yoyo. The harder you try to evict her, the tighter she clings.

"Outside with Em. It seems the spirit has moved our sweet Emily, and she's gifting those yummy prophetic treats to whoever would like one." Chloe's dark eyes gleam with wicked delight. "I bet she has a delicious one just for you." Her hand glides down my back and swivels around to my crotch.

"Nice try." I snatch her by the wrist. "I get it. You haven't been laid in months. Join the cold shower club."

Chloe relaxes her snake-like arm around me once again, resting her full weight over me. Chloe Bishop has always been a sort of inescapable hell. "I don't see any good reason why either of us has to suffer this sorry fate." She swings in close, her face just a breath away from mine. Her lids hood low as she sinks in closer. "And I think we can both agree the one-armed bandit doesn't do this boiling lust inside the two of us any justice."

"You know, Chloe, for once you're right. But the answer is still a hard no." I press past her to find a happy smattering of bodies littering the living room. Mostly people from West, and this alarms me on some level. Years after graduation and every gathering still feels like a high school reunion. But then, this is Paragon. I suppose this is the same crowd that will be gathering en mass for the next eight decades, God willing.

"But you've fucked me more than you've slept with anyone else on this planet." Chloe walks backward in front of me, and I'm just counting down the seconds before she eats it.

"That's true. I guess I've never thought of it that way. But I'm more of a quality over quantity kind of guy."

Skyla and Gage come up, each holding a baby, Skyla with Barron—and I'm certain of this because, being the good uncle I am, I can unequivocally, and finally, tell them apart. Mostly because Barron loves to brood, and Nathan loves to flirt with Angel. And, of course, Angel is with Gage.

"*Daddy!*" She practically leaps into my arms.

"Did you hear that?" I shout as a burst of adrenaline burns though me. "Baby girl." I bury a kiss under her chin, and she screams with laughter. Her blonde curls tickle my cheeks, and I can't help but nuzzle against her.

"Angel!" Skyla looks to her with glittering eyes. "You did it! You said Daddy!"

Barron looks to me and laughs. "*Daddy!*"

"Wow," I say, laughing under my breath as Barron reaches out for me to hold him. "Looks like I'm two for two."

Skyla dances back apprehensively, her eyes flitting nervously to her husband's. "That's the first time he's said that."

"Here." Gage picks up Barron and places him in my other arm before shedding his signature dimples, but that smile is nothing but a mask of pain. I've been around him long enough to know.

"*Skyla*!" Brielle calls from the back. "You're up next!"

"I'd better go." Skyla wrinkles her nose before scooting to the rear yard.

The smile dissipates from my nephew's face as soon as Skyla hits the exit.

"Sorry about that," I offer. Gage steps in front of me, blocking my path, eating up the doorway with the wide girth of his shoulders.

"Don't be." Gage closes those big blue eyes, and I'd swear on all that is holy the world just dimmed. "*Logan*," he whispers my name as if he were in pain. "I love you. I need you to be here for my boys. If something should happen to me. If I turn into that monster."

"You won't. Skyla is handling the feds beautifully. You've got Wes on a leash. The Videns should be thrilled you've got their boys off the streets."

His jaw hardens. "There's this shadow." His gaze drifts off to some unknowable place as his voice reduces to a whisper. "I see it wherever I go."

My gut clenches tight. "Talk to your dad about it."

"My dad?" He startles as if I've woken him from a dream.

"Not Barron." My heart breaks for him. "The other one." I can't say his name. Don't want to. Both Barron and Angel laugh and tug at one another's hair at the mention of his name.

Barron begs to have his father hold him, and I'm quick to comply. "Come on." I bump Gage as I lead him outside. "Let's see what Emily Morgan has to say about this insanity we call life."

Ezrina and Nev cross paths with us just as we're about to make our way to the crowd in the corner of the yard.

"My prophecy." She holds up a sheet of paper that looks like something that amounts to a child's school project. Nobody ever said Em was cranking out Picassos.

"What is it?" Gage takes it from her as we examine it.

Nev leans in. "Don't you see the blade?" He dots the point with his finger.

"Ah. A very sharp knife is in your future," I muse. Ezrina and Nev have a vast collection of antique cutlery. I'm sure the baby will love it.

"This is Alice." She frowns my way as if I should know better.

Nev leans in. "It was her favorite knife, back in the day. It's quite a prophecy." He pats her belly as they make their way past us.

"Sounds like Ezrina and Nev are going to have one sharp baby," I say as we head outside. "I don't know if we should be worried or thrilled."

"Both." Gage chuckles as we head deep into a tangle of bodies.

We find Emily seated at a round table with Skyla by her side and Bree and Chloe loosely hanging on like bookends while conducting a spirited conversation of their own.

"I can't get used to this," Gage whispers as we pass them. "She doesn't belong here. She's dangerous."

"I couldn't agree more. Have you and"—I nod to Skyla—"ever had that talk?"

"No." His brows furrow as if he's just realized this.

"That's it?" Skyla holds up a piece of paper covered in crimson, and Gage and I head over.

"That's it, Messenger." Em doesn't bother with a smile. Emily Morgan always looks as if she's just woke up from a decade long dirt nap. "Sorry about using the old-school name, but you have to admit it's catchy." She offers an indifferent shrug.

I lean over Skyla's shoulder, careful not to let Angel fly out of my arms, but all I see is red, literally. "What's it mean?"

Emily grunts up at Gage and me. "I got one for the two of you." She whips out another piece of paper and douses it with that quickly diminishing red pastel in her hand. Her hand moves so quickly a pink powdered plume rises in its wake, covering Em's face with an eerie crimson glow. Once she's through, she simply whips out another piece of paper and replicates the effort. "One for each of you." She hands one to Gage and me, and we stare down at Emily's lack of creativity and wonder what the hell it all means.

I'm pretty sure Skyla and Gage are thinking the same thing I am. Danger. Fire.

"Fire?" I whisper. It's what I essentially warned myself of this afternoon.

"Danger?" Skyla whispers.

"No." Gage runs his finger down the chalky page and leaves a trail in its wake. "Blood."

Cooper and Laken show up, and the mood brightens as we abandon Emily's finger paints for talk of post-graduation life and prospects of a mini-Cooper running around soon. They're both starting graduate school at Host, and Coop has already accepted a coaching position at West.

Laken laughs. "I'm content for now." She holds her hands out to me, and I hand her my precious baby girl. "This is enough for me. My *niece*." She winks at Skyla.

Ezrina and Nev emerge from the woods and head on over.

"Here she is." I wrap my arms around the woman of the hour. "And you look amazing if I didn't tell you the first time."

"Am." She holds out her arms, exposing her painfully swollen belly. Ezrina hasn't had the easiest ride with this pregnancy. Those nightly retching sessions shockingly echoed throughout the house. But I'm glad she's at the finish line.

"You're going to make a great mother." I land a kiss to her cheek.

"Am a mother." She nods to the back slider before darting in that direction.

"Wesley's here." Nev takes in a depleted breath. "Rina considers Tobie every bit her own." He gives a wistful shake of the head. "I hope she's not setting herself up for heartbreak. Rina would be destroyed if he ever took that little girl out of her life. She'd do anything to keep her within arm's reach." He takes off for his glowing bride, and suddenly it all makes sense.

Coop closes his eyes a moment. "And that's why she did it."

Skyla spears both Cooper and Laken with a sharp look. "That makes sense. Ezrina's body did produce a child—Tobie. But the greater mystery is why in the hell haven't the two of you killed Wes yet?"

Coop and Laken exchange a quick glance as if an execution were still on the table.

"You *know*"—Skyla leans in—"rip him a new one. Tear out his jugular." She shakes her head at the two of them because for the life of her, she doesn't get their shared silence, and neither do I. "What's going on?"

Wes comes over and kills the party per usual, chasing both Coop and Laken into the house, and they take Angel right along with them.

Wes smiles that eerie Gage Oliver knockoff grin. I glance to the patio and spot Ezrina and Nev bouncing Tobie between them. She's beautiful, and innocent, and it's easy for me not to put her in the same category as her demonic father.

"The Kraggers are inside—just Emerson and Holden—his wife, too," Wes announces as if this were news we actually wanted to hear.

"That's nice." Skyla grunts as Chloe pops up by her side like a pit bull ready to defend its owner from a rogue beast. "How's Kresley? Was she too tired to come? But then, knowing who she's been rubbing up against, I bet she's been coming quite frequently."

Chloe belts out a laugh and high-fives her new best friend. "We can always count on you for a solid one-liner."

Gage groans. "Skyla." He wraps his arms around his wife as if holding her back from a fight. "Wes, we know."

"We know, and we're confused as hell," I offer. "Care to explain?"

Wes hoods those stormy eyes of his in Ezrina's direction. "There's nothing to see here. Just an old flame willing to do whatever it takes to make me happy." He reverts his attention to us and grins. "I suppose true love exists after all."

Gage shakes his head. "You don't have that with Kres. You never will," he says it tenderly as if talking a distraught man down from the ledge. "You love the deepest part of Laken—not just the shell."

Skyla's chest bucks as if she were in tears. "You are killing Laken with all of your perversity. First, demanding that Chloe morph? Then using time travel as a sexual device by taking Laken over and over again?" She gives a hard sniff as if she's trying to hold it together. "And then bargaining with a desperate woman to transform into the likeness of the only woman you will ever pine for. How very sad for you both." Skyla takes a step in close to him. "Laken told me all about Ephemeral. About those early days when she pined for *you*. I bet you've tried a thousand times to go back, to change your own heart. If only you took Laken into your arms when she wanted to be there, how easy this all would have been for you." A tear falls down her cheek. "You had victory in your grasp, and you didn't even know it. But you blew it so big. It must kill you each and every day to know that."

"It does." Wes looks right through Skyla as he answers. Then, just like that, he awakens as if someone shook him. "But today it isn't about me, is it?" He grins over at Gage as if they're in on some private joke. "Dominique Winters has slapped the Barricade with a libel suit. She's taken it to the Justice Alliance. It's laughable. She's taken the Retribution League there as well in the event your mother hasn't filled you in on the news just yet. She says we've ruined their good name by having her daughter captured along with the mercenaries working for you. She's made it clear that the Winters haven't chosen sides in our little feud as she calls it."

Skyla flinches, and it's evident she hasn't heard. Not shocking, though. Candace isn't nearly as attentive to Skyla as Demetri is to Wes.

Dudley appears as if from thin air and wraps an arm around Skyla, completely dismissing the fact Gage still has her in a lock from behind, and Gage relents. That's always been my nephew's problem. He gives in too quickly. It's the nice guy in him. I don't know how Demetri ever plans on beating that out of him.

"Is there an issue?" Dudley doesn't bother with the niceties when it comes to Wesley, or anyone else for that matter.

"No issue." Wes steps in toward Skyla, uncomfortably close, showing off the size of his balls to all those around. "I love Laken. She is and always will be mine. I promise you, I will always protect her."

Skyla spits in his face, leaving a wake of white stretchy phlegm dangling from his eyebrows. "And you will always bed her under the guise of other people."

"Wrong." He wipes Skyla's precipitous affection away like tears. "I will have her again. I've had a vision. The Justice Alliance itself has affirmed this to me." He stalks off toward the house.

"What you saw was Kresley doing a poor imitation of her!" she shouts after him. "Bastard." Skyla shivers from the confrontation.

"You should go easy on him." Gage carefully pulls her in, and Skyla all but hauls off and slaps him.

"Go easy on him?" She jumps back just enough to slip out of his grasp.

And that's my cue. "Dudley"—I nod toward the corral in the rear of the property brimming with llamas and horses docile enough to be overgrown house cats—"you mind if I have a word with you?"

We speed out of Gage and Skyla's latest conflict and presumably into one of our own. Dudley and I seem to make a pattern out of not getting along. I'd like to end that eventually. Now would be nice.

"What's on your twisted mind?" He picks up a foot-long blade of grass and ties it in a knot before sending it sailing through the air. "Ms. Bishop has alerted me to the fact there's a distinct possibility the two of you will be in need of my chambers this evening."

"Chloe is delusional." I glance back at the party to find Chloe at Em's table with a small crowd amassed around her. "And speaking of delusions, it seems I've had a few of my own. I keep seeing him." I shake my head out at the beasts that roam the corral.

"Keep seeing whom?"

"Me. I keep seeing myself. It's happened a few too many times this year, and each time his message is vaguer than it was before."

His gaze twitches into the woods as he considers this. "You've seen yourself," he says it like a fact. "This must be important. What have you to say to yourself?"

"I don't know. The first time was that night of the boys' christening. I passed out. I saw a vision of Gage on a throne. He turned into a dragon, and I said to myself that I was going to help stop him."

Dudley grunts. "And you need a road map for that one? What else?" He looks both bored and irritated at once.

"I saw him just now. He was at the bowling alley. He said something about Dominique Winters." I try to rack my brain for his wording. "Something about not keeping an eye on her? Not taking care of her? And then he said I should love Skyla and Gage—talk to them. He mentioned something about not running from trouble. Running into the fire."

"Fire?" Dudley's head ticks back a notch as if I were alerting him to one.

"Fire." I shrug.

Michelle Miller lets out a whistle that can wake the dead without Skyla's magical ring, and both Dudley and I head in that direction. Ezrina and Nev sit center stage next to a pile of oversized presents all wrapped in pastel paper while almost all of the tables Dudley has set out are filled to the brim with guests.

"What do you think it means?"

Dudley smacks his lips together. "It means Shelly needs us to move this little gift grab along. Ezrina and Heathcliff will have your basement brimming with all the modern finery this material world offers. It seems children require a plethora of nonsensical items to survive and thrive

573

these days. I suppose that's something you've grown familiar with."

"You're a smart ass. Yes, I'm familiar. And I happen to like all the paraphernalia a baby requires because it makes me happy to see it. What do you think it means that I'm stepping down from paradise?"

"It means he'll help you tame that dragon your nefarious nephew is about to transform into. It means you should have dealt with Mrs. Winters now that her daughter was caught in the government snare. I assume she's furious and ready to point her legal pistols at whomever and whatever she pleases. It means care for Skyla. Don't bed her. It means talk to that moronic nephew of yours before he falls off the face of this earth due to his own stupidity. And the next time you see flames—run straight in." He sheds a shit-eating grin as he finds an empty seat near the back.

"Run straight in." I shake my head as I make my way to Skyla and Gage as he bounces Nathan in his arms contentedly, his miniature lookalike, and it warms me. Something about seeing him as a father makes it feel as if we're winning the war on keeping him on the right side of the celestial law. I spot Laken off on the other end of the yard holding Angel safe in her arms. And I spot Chloe handing Tobie to Ellis and vice versa as if they were playing a game of hot potato. Kate sits on Skyla's other side and offers me a quick wave. She has a slim white scarf wrapped around her neck to hide that jagged seam Ezrina gifted her. Ezrina both stitched and glued her back together. Lastly, I spot Wes off to the side talking to—Coop?

"Shit," I whisper, leaning in to Gage. "Wes and Coop alert to the left." As far as I see it, Coop has no business simply talking to Wes. An ass kicking is long overdue.

Skyla cranes her neck, and it's then I notice the bulge under her shirt, a pair of tired feet dangling lifeless to the side. Skyla is beautiful all of the time, but when she's nursing, it takes her beauty to a magnificent level. She holds the ethereal charm and calm of a princess, and she mesmerizes me.

Gage flicks his finger over my thigh, painfully, the way we used to when we were kids. "My eyes are up here, sweetheart."

"Right." A small laugh pushes through my nostrils before reverting back to Coop and Wes. "You think I should head over?"

"No," Skyla says without turning around. "It's been quiet. They're handling it. Speaking of quiet"—she spins around as much as the baby lying over her will allow—"have you noticed that Wes has been laying low as of late? You think he's got some surprise attack on the horizon?" Her eyes flit from Gage to me.

"I've thought the same thing." I look to Gage, but he's suspiciously quiet. There's no way Gage would hold anything back from Skyla and me. Not yet anyway.

The three of us sit and watch Ezrina glow as she opens box after box of every baby necessity under the sun, but it's Nev who's excited. Ezrina simply ogles each item with a morbid curiosity as if it were a piece that belonged in a museum.

Ezrina opens something that has the entire crowd lost in oohs and ahhs, as if she had somehow produced the very baby she's carrying. Skyla turns around, her teeth pinning her bottom lip.

"*Thank you*," she mouths.

And then I realize Ezrina opened the gift from me. A year's worth of diapers. The same gift I gave to Skyla and Gage. Yes, I'm still in it to win it. I pay Lizbeth to pick up the goods each time she heads out to Cost Club, and she does. I wouldn't have a clue what to buy, and Gage is too proud to take my money. I don't think I'll stop after the first year. Heck, I know I won't. It's the least I could do. I love those boys as if they were my own.

The whoop of a siren goes off near the rear of the gathering, and every head on the property cranes in that direction.

Then I see them. I rise from my seat as if rising from my body, every last part of me numb with surprise.

"Shit." I hear Gage hiss behind me.

An entire infantry of men in blue jackets, the letters CIA clearly marked on their lapels as they swarm over the property. They've come in number, spreading over the landscape like a stampede of buffalo. They are legion.

One of them jumps on a chair and holds a megaphone to his lips. "Please remain seated. This is strictly precautionary. There is nothing to fear. The use of cell phones or other devices is prohibited from this moment on. You may not leave the premises. We have the property surrounded."

They bleed in from every orifice, cuffs in hand, angry-faced, solemn as shit. I glance to Dudley as a couple of men double-team him, sending his hands forcibly behind his back before shuffling him toward the gate.

I glance to Wes. Same story.

"*Shit.*" I look around at the bevy of stunned faces, almost all of them one of us, otherworldly beings by design, descendants of the Nephilim—and I don't waste a moment. "*Run!*" I roar as I help Skyla up and send her into the woods with Gage. Kate jumps to her feet, startled, and I'm half-afraid her head will roll right off. "Go after them!" I help her hurdle the chair knocked over in their wake, and she bolts like hell. The entire damn party scatters like ants.

But I don't take off. I head straight for a pack of them with my arms held high.

I run straight into the fire.

Standing with the Angels

Skyla

"Skyla!" Gage thunders as I shove Barron into Kate's arms.

"Go with him," I hiss as I take off back in the direction of the party—the *raid* as it had easily transformed into—and just as I'm about to hit the clearing, a body tackles me and sends me reeling on my heels.

I pull back, momentarily blinded by a face full of long dark hair.

"Chloe?" I blink at my new sinister sister. "What the hell?"

"Get back here!" Gage roars with a fury as he snatches me by the wrist.

Chloe's nostrils flare as she sets those dead eyes over me. "Don't worry. I'm not letting her go." She smacks me just shy of my temple. "You nitwit! You're going to get yourself detained, and then who the hell will help the plight of your people?"

"*Our* people," I correct as Gage aggressively leads us back to the thicket where Kate holds two startled babies who look as if they're about to burst into tears.

"Hold on." Gage pulls us into a tight huddle, his hot mouth buried over my hair. I watch as the ground of Marshall's estate turns to ash, and I feel like a coward. I should have fought tooth and nail to get back there.

And do what, Skyla? Chloe asks the question as the world around us transforms into a familiar landscape.

"The Transfer?" I gasp as the gray world comes into focus. The skeletal trees, the parched ground, the deep violet sky, and, of course, the hungry mouth of Wesley's castle waiting to swallow us whole.

"We'll be safe here." Gage ushers us in as if he owns the place, a frightening thought in the least.

"Seemingly so," I pant, keeping up the pace while taking Barron from Kate's overloaded arms. She holds tight to Nathan while soaking in the horrors of this monolithic hellhole with wide-eyed wonder. "Chloe, take us to Tobie's room. We'll have the boys stay there." I turn to Gage. "Get Ezrina and bring her here. She can watch the boys, and she'll be safe as well."

Gage offers a dry smile as we follow Chloe into the bowels of this slate-walled, slate-floored ode to stone and steel wonder. The entire structure is gothic in nature and the interior motif morbid in style. Instead of your average family pictures running along the hall, Wes has an array of sabers hung precariously as if inviting his guests to arm themselves if need be. And believe me, the need will always be there. It's safe to say Lex wasn't asked to work her magic in this hellscape. As much as Lex and I rub each other the wrong way, I'll be the first to admit she's got a gift when it comes to outfitting a homey interior. Wes has a gift for outfitting a precarious one.

"The zookeepers' favorite cage." Chloe kicks the door open to a docile nursery that looks shockingly familiar.

"Holy—wow, is this my old furniture?" I run straight over to my old canopy bed with its wicker frame and ruffled topper. The covers jerk, inspiring me to jump back while shielding Barron from the boogieman about to leap from my old bed.

A girl sits up, messy golden brown hair, sleepy eyes, and it's not until she blinks to life do I note the striking resemblance to my good friend. It's Laken's knockoff—Kresley Fisher.

"What the hell's going on?" she moans as if she hadn't quite caught up on her sleep.

"That's what I'd like to know," I growl at her before heading over to the crib and landing Barron inside. "Not only does Wes take advantage of you, but he keeps you stowed away as the nanny."

Gage takes Nathan from Kate and lands him next to his brother. "Wes is proving to be quite the utilitarian." He lands a quick kiss to my lips. "I'll be back."

I grip his arm as if he were threatening to leave me. "I'm going with you." I nod to Kate. "Watch the boys. We'll be back as soon as we can. Chloe can't be trusted, and neither can that skank on the bed who's still trying to decipher if this is all a dream."

Kresley grunts. "I can hear you, Skyla."

"And ignore her, would you?" I implore poor Kate who has to endure a fate worse than death—time alone with Kres and Chloe. "The boys will be getting hungry soon, but I'm sure Ezrina will know what to do. She's practically raising Tobie." I glare at Chloe a moment. "Apparently, motherhood isn't for everyone."

Chloe blows a breath through her nostrils. "Hell no to that."

"I'll be back soon." Gage storms out, and I follow him to the doorway. "Skyla, I'm not taking you with me."

"*What*?" I hook my arm around his in a lame attempt to protest. "You are taking me, Gage. I have to get back. I need to assess the damage—help whoever I can. Any powers the boys have gifted have all but faded. I need your help to get back to Paragon."

"You need to be here for the boys." He steps outside those massive doors and turns to me—his hands lay heavy on my shoulders as if begging me to understand. "As long as I'm alive, Skyla, I'm not letting anything happen to you or our children. It's dangerous right now. There's no way in hell I'm taking you back."

He turns to leave, and I spin him toward me. "*Gage*! I'm not asking for your permission. You are taking me back. I belong with my people."

"No," he thunders a little too loud. "You're staying with the boys. They need you. Trust me to take care of your people. They are *my* people, too."

A million thoughts run through me at once, none of them bode well for my husband. "Then I'll take myself!"

Gage offers a depleted look my way before glowering upwards, and a thin blue film covers the perennial night sky.

"Holy shit," Chloe balks with a laugh garbled in her throat. "You just erected a shield of some sort to keep your little wifey in line. I'm not sure if the best day of my life was entering into that covenant with Skyla or this one."

"I gotta go." Those dimples of his depress, right along with his spirit.

"*No!*" My throat rubs raw from ejecting the sentiment. "You will *not* leave me here. You will not imprison me like I'm some child, like I'm a pet you need to look after. I forbid it." The words flit out like the sharpened blade of a knife, but Gage merely steps back, evaporating slowly, those glowing blue eyes remain fixed on me and are the last to dissipate.

"*Gage*! Get back here! You'll regret this!" My voice shrills so high and loud that the blue film up above warbles under my tyranny. "Oh my God. What have you done?" I can't catch my breath. "He left me." My husband defied me. He pulled rank and put a lid on both my powers and me.

"Face it, Skyla"—Chloe chums up next to me, her gaze set on that void Gage left in his wake—"there's nothing hotter than Gage Oliver telling you to shut up and sit down."

My blood boils in an instant, but it has nothing to do with Chloe's ridiculous sentiments. It's Gage's ridiculous actions. He very much told me to shut up and sit down.

She huffs a dull laugh. "I bet he's twice as demanding in bed. I bet he's more than happy to fill your mouth with his body, and tell you where to sit and how."

I stagger back a moment, still stunned over the fact my husband saw fit to lock me in a demonic closet. He outright *defied* me. He pulled rank, and now I'm stuck in the Transfer with both Chloe and Kresley. I turn around to find the ditz in question stomping this way.

Kresley starts a mile a minute with questions, and I'm quick to tune her out, my mind already clawing at the walls trying to get the hell out.

Kate comes up as I head back into the grand room with those eternal flames forever burning bright in the oversized fireplace, that spinning wet world Wes keeps in a megalithic fountain, the granite sphere floating and spinning on a dizzying loop.

"The boys fell right asleep," Kate whispers. "I'll go back and stay with them in case they wake up. It's safe to say they're a long way from home."

I offer her a quick embrace. "Thank you. Ezrina should be here shortly." Surely Gage hasn't completely lost his fucking mind. He'll bring her here to keep her out of harm's way. And he'll bring me back to Paragon.

I glance over to Chloe. "Don't just stand there. Put your demented thinking cap on and get me out of this hellhole," I bark so loud Kate jerks back as if I slapped her. "Sorry." I wince, speeding to the fireplace as if I'm about to jump in.

"Chill out." Chloe stomps over. "You have options. Turn down the blonde volume on that panic and fire up those brain cells, will you?"

Kresley jumps in between us with the face of my best friend, and it kills me. Hell, it makes me want to kill *her*. The flames lick higher as if begging for a treat. "What the hell is going on?" she howls at the two of us. "Is this some kind of a joke? You two can't stand each other. Wes says if he locked the two of you in a room, one of you wouldn't come out alive."

I step in close to the slithering skank until we're eye-to-Laken-wannabe-eye. "That would be you and me who wouldn't come out of a room alive. Chloe and I are on the same page. I don't care what your thoughts are. I don't give a damn if you approve, disapprove, or want in on the action. What I do with Chloe is my business—and soon you'll be my business, too. You made a grave mistake, Kresley. Wes is using you, and sadly we both know it. But I will not allow you to run amuck anywhere, in any plane of existence, with that lie embedded on your face—a face you probably can't stand to look at yourself."

Her gaze shifts to the floor because she knows it's true. "It's none of your business. Wesley still loves me."

Chloe clicks her tongue. "No, he doesn't. My God, is this entire room filled with nitwits? Wesley is not in love with you, Kres. You had to knife up your face just to be in the same room with him. He doesn't even call you by your given name. He calls you *Laken*."

My head ticks back a notch at the idea. "If that's true, it's beyond sad."

That horrid scene at the party relives itself in my mind, and my heart ratchets right back up to my throat. "*Mother!*" I roar to the ceiling. "*Demetri?*" My voice tears past that shield Gage thought to erect in my honor. I'll be erecting something in his honor tonight—a cold front.

"That's my girl." Chloe offers up a slow clap just as the room begins to shake. The sky outside the window flickers with a warning as the room takes on an eerie translucent glow. "Well, well, it looks as if Glinda the Good Witch is about to pay a visit to the celestial crap house. You're in for a treat, *Laken*. You say your mother abandoned you? Wait until you meet Skyla's mommy dearest. She'll make you look fondly upon those lonely nights you cried yourself to sleep."

The room brightens then dims, and lo and behold Candace Messenger appears with her hair lit up like gold floss, her face radiating an otherworldly glow as if she had just seen the face of God.

The ground continues to rumble, quake, and quiver under the weight of my mother's beauty.

"Stop the shaking!" Kresley panics as she grips the edge of the granite lip that holds the spinning globe, water sloshing to the ground around her.

"Darkness cannot handle the light." My mother strides past her with her gaze set to mine.

"*Skyla*." She closes her eyes a moment, dejected as if my own lowly estate were enough to depress her. "Whatever are you doing here?"

I run up and grip her by the shoulders, that familiar pleasant hum runs through me and soothes me straight to the bone. "I need to get back to Paragon—the feds have taken just about everyone into custody. Everybody is in danger. They have Marshall!" I shake her slightly as if to drive home the point, and her eyes grow wild—so much so that I drop my hands to my sides.

"Sector Dudley can make a mockery of them if he wishes, and he almost always wishes." She chortles out a laugh as if reliving a memory. "He is a sly one. If anything, I should protect those feds which you speak of, posthaste." Her lips curve into a nefarious smile before it glides off her face as if it were a cliff. "Why have you summoned me? I was in the middle of teaching Sage the finer points of destiny robbing." She growls at both Chloe and Kresley. "Some of us here are more familiar with the concept than others."

"That was meant for me." Chloe's eyes round out with the revelation.

I scoff at the thought. "She was talking to Kresley. Although she's hardly robbing Laken of her destiny."

My mother pumps a nefarious smile. "Chloe had it right."

"Knew it. You robbed me!" She glares at my mother as if there would be retribution. Try as she might, Chloe is no match for my mother—a close second, but no match.

My mother gives a hard sniff. "It wasn't you who was robbed. *You* were the thief looking to steal a destiny. You were never in line to receive the celestial adulation your black heart desires," she snaps before looking to Kresley. "And you—don't blame others for the misfortune that awaits. *I had a better way*!" My mother bears in hard, her voice hitting volumes I have never heard before.

My heart stills a moment. My mother had a better way for her. It makes me wonder about my own destiny. Here I am sprinting to who knows where—perhaps if I hadn't taken to rebellion I would have landed where I wanted to be all along—in a better way.

Kresley steps in with a fury raging from her. "*Your* way didn't include Wesley!" she roars into my mother's face so loud her hair blows back.

A choking sound emits from my mother as her hair lights up in a rainbow of citrus hues. She's on fire right down to the very last follicle. "My, my, someone is feeling rather brave." She steps in close to Kresley and gives a slight tug at a lock of her hair. "A cheap replica. Is that what you think I've decided for you? You are juggling dynamite. You have landed yourself in the perfect storm." Her eyes flit to mine without a twitch of her head. "*You*"—there's an accusatory tone in her voice that I'm not appreciating at the moment— "I charge you with this one. She will try both your patience and your mercy—and perhaps the fabric of your integrity." Her gaze dips to the floor before she turns fully to face Chloe and me. "Look at the two of you." She tips her head back as her voice dips to saccharin levels, all of it drenched in sarcasm. My mother hopped up on sarcasm is a very dangerous thing. A dark chortle comes from her because undoubtedly she heard. "Who is writing *your* story?" she purrs as she heads over and runs a cool finger under my chin. "Is doubt creeping into your heart, my love? Has the Celestra spring come crashing down around you so soon?" She looks to Chloe. "Has the victory you sacrificed for eluded you already?"

I look to Chloe, and my heart thumps hard. Had Chloe been hoping for something outside of our covenant?

"Oh yes, you little thing," my mother sings through a bubbling laugh. "*Skyla*," she trills. My mother bows her head and laughs as she pinches her eyes shut. "My dear Skyla, you never learn—try as you might." Her eyes shine like shards of glass as she steps in ever so close. "Fight the urge to bow to those who oppress you. Fight the urge to let down your guard and believe in silly words. Rules and laws are frames of perfection—covenants are one in the same. You are still very much mostly human as are those around you." Her eyes flit to Chloe for the briefest of moments. "Do not relish the downfall of your enemy. It comes with a price." She bears those crystalline lenses into mine. "And you will rue the day you ever stepped away from my careful guidance."

"Your guidance?" A sputtering laugh comes from me, and I couldn't stop it if I tried. "When have you ever *guided* me? I have been in peril since the moment I stepped on Paragon all those years ago. What have you done with my destiny other than damning me to a life of strife?" Her lips part as if shocked by the audacity—either that or she's just come to the conclusion that I'm right. "Guide me *now*, Mother. Guide me back to Paragon. Guide me to my people. Tell me what to do with this nightmare the Steel Barricade has inflicted on us and themselves. The government is insatiable. And we are *all* in peril."

She takes in a breath, her hair turning an odd shade of lavender, each follicle alive with its own peculiar light. "That ring." She glances to my finger, the blue stone that once belonged to the throne of the living God. "Skyla, whose is it?"

I glance to Chloe, although deep down I know. "Melody Winters?" I ask with a childlike curiosity.

"Indirectly." Her brows rise as if proud of the fact I've answered right in partial. "And how would our dear Chloe have swiped this from Ms. Winters' crooked little finger?"

I look to Chloe for help, but she's quick to turn her head from me. Chloe denied stealing it. And obviously, she lied. "She stole it. Chloe, you stole it."

"The ring doesn't belong to Melody Winters." Chloe grunts with disgust. "As usual, your mother is taking you down a long and thorny road and wasting the fuck out of everybody's time. Marlena took the ring from Cassandra Graham and gave it to me."

Cassandra Graham—I didn't want to say her name. In truth, I want to forget all about that ratty old dive bar Chloe and I visited last December. That twisted light drive lit a fire line in my life. I look down at the ring as if to confirm my theory.

"And what was the promise Marlena gave you?" My mother curves her palm over Chloe's cheek, and it looks almost loving. Almost.

Chloe takes a breath as she looks to me. "That it was a portal to getting everything I've ever wanted."

My chest thumps with a quiet laugh. "The only thing you've ever wanted was Gage Oliver." Everything in me freezes. She's still trying to make him hers. Of course, she is.

Chloe steps toward me. "But I didn't even think of taking Marlena up on that ring until that night you whispered into my ear by the fire. It was right here in this room, Skyla, just a few short months ago. The night you were betrayed, or so you thought. And when we ended up in England, I knew—it was destiny. It was my time to make my dreams come true."

Kres steps in as if she were hooked to every word.

My mother takes in a breath, and the room rumbles beneath her feet. "What was it that you said, Skyla?"

The fire calls to me with its bright, beautiful flames as I recall that night. "I said follow me. Unite your power with mine, and I will gift you what your heart desires most."

"You knew it was Gage." Chloe shakes her head as she steps in front of the flames.

"And Celestra." I look to her.

Chloe's chest bucks with her next breath. "And Celestra. My unity is genuine. I am *sick* of Wes ramming his big dick into the ass of my people"—she glowers at my mother—"while the powers that be sit idly by, filing down their proverbial nails until they are as dull and useless as *they* are."

The walls erupt in flames as fire spreads to the ceiling like a fungus.

"*Mother*! The boys are here!"

The flames vanish, and not even the smell of smoke remains in their wake.

Chloe steps over to her boldly and stabs a finger into her chest. "Somewhere, some way you fucked up. Marlena told me *I* was the chosen one. But somewhere along the way, *my* destiny was ROBBED!"

"Marlena lied," my mother roars back.

"You lie!" Chloe thunders. The room jolts, and a fissure erupts in the ceiling with a loud rushing tear. "Gage—he was mine." Her voice breaks with emotion. "He was never meant for Skyla. Our children—they were the only ones I could ever love. And you erased them." A lone tear races down her cheek. As a mother, my heart demands to break for her, but as Gage Oliver's wife and mother to those boys Chloe is so anxious to erase, I can't find it in me. "And now I'm taking back what's mine."

Kresley scoffs. "You will never have his heart."

Chloe's eyes widen with venom. "And you will never have his brother's."

It occurs to me that perhaps my mother and Chloe are talking about two different things. My mother is fixated on the royal lineage that leads to the position I hold, and Chloe, well, Chloe per her usual is obsessing over Gage. My mother intended me for Logan. It was Demetri who intended me for Gage.

"Well"—my mother folds her hands together as if we've just concluded a rather amicable meet and greet—"nobody said life would be easy." She smiles to me as if nothing Chloe said had mattered. "Cassandra Graham should have died hundreds of years ago. Instead, she embodies a girl who should have died in a wreck."

A girl who should have died in a wreck? Then it hits me. "Cassandra is Melody Winters." My heart thumps, hard and fast. "Why is she here?" A violent pulse of anger surges through me because I suspect something nefarious waits for me in the answer. If it were the ring, she could have chopped my hand off for it months ago. And who the hell brought her?

"I'm afraid Pandora's box has been opened, my dear." She picks up my finger and touches the ring, setting off a beacon of sapphire light flooding throughout the room. "Clean up this mess with the government, Skyla. You'll know what to do. Keep this ring. Cassandra, Melody, whoever it is that dunce is parading around as these days, has no rights to it. I gifted it to Sector Marshall on his first mission to earth." Her lips curve at the tips. "It looks as if it found its way to the one I intended to have it all along." She looks to Chloe. "So, you see, no matter how wide you swerve outside of the bounds of destiny, fate has a way of righting itself." She turns to leave, and I snatch her back.

"Was Gage intended for Chloe?" My heart bucks as if it were demanding I shut the hell up. How could Gage have ever loved her? And yet my vanity begs I reword the question. How could Gage ever love anyone but me? Gage is mine. His destiny is knit with my own. I know this to be true.

My mother looks from me to Chloe, then back again. "Like I said, destiny has a way of righting itself."

And in that one sentence, my mother has eviscerated me and enlivened a false hope in Chloe.

Fuck destiny. Fuck fate. Gage and I aren't going anywhere. He's never leaving me for Chloe. That's laughable. I am Mrs. Gage Oliver, and that's exactly who I will remain.

My mother's face smooths out, and I shake my head, expecting this mirrored version of me to do the same.

She reaches out and clasps my cheek in her palm. "Skyla Dunamis. That alone is your name. Messenger,

Oliver, Dudley—those are earthly window dressings, nothing more than a paper Valentine pinned to a wall, fragile and fleeting, the edges already yellowing with time."

Her words sting like the scorching of the sun, and I turn my head away, wincing as if she slapped me.

"I'm stopping at Oliver," I'm quick to inform her. "Gage Oliver to be exact." I look to Chloe. "It's a done deal. You and I both know that."

My mother begins to fade, and a rise of panic rattles me. "Wait! I need to get back to Paragon. They have *Angel*!"

"Who?" My mother leans in, looking every bit confused.

"My *daughter*! The one you dropped onto my lap like a sack of potatoes on your last visit!"

"Angel?" she moans as her form quickly dissolves. "Really, Skyla, that's so achingly generic."

"It's a placeholder," I say under my breath, no louder than a whisper because what I really fear is there will be no place to hold as far as Logan and I go—and it makes me feel like a monster.

"There will be." My mother dissipates to nothing. "Destiny has a way of righting itself."

I would never let anything happen to her. My mother's voice rings through my ears alone. *I am not a monster, and neither are you, Skyla Dunamis. Now go and save your people.*

The room around me quickly morphs into that of the Landon house with both boys in their rightful cribs. Chloe lounges on my bed, filing her nails into needle sharp points, and Kate sits beside her, looking bewildered and frightened.

I'm back on Paragon—and now both Gage Oliver *and* the feds will have hell to pay.

On the way to Marshall's, I spot a fallen tree at the entry to the Estates, and it pains me, panics me on some level as if Paragon itself is struggling under the weight of the devastation this afternoon brought with it. I had my mother watch the boys and charged Chloe with making sure Kate got home safe. I drive by the property slowly and deliberately, noting a bevy of cars still parked haphazardly around the periphery the way they were when I arrived. The door to his home is agape, and I can see the dark hole of the interior looking lonely and haunted. The government had ripped my people from Marshall's yard like savages. They stormed Paragon, my Paragon, like animals. They can't have the people. They can't have the island. I love this bitter rock almost as much as I love my people, and I want those bastards gone.

I speed on by Marshall's home as if I never knew it, as if I never knew him, in order to divert suspicion in the event they're watching. And they wouldn't be watching if it wasn't for Wesley. He's the one that called their attention to us. He's the one who scattered the food they were so hungry for along the four corners of the earth, and, of course, he was the one who welcomed poor Moser and Killion with open arms last year. Wesley Edinger is the nexus of this disaster. It's almost laughable that I saw them take him first.

I've decided it's too risky to call or text anyone I know. I'm sure confiscating cell phones is rudimentary business. No. There's only one person I wish to speak with at the moment, and that is Gage Oliver. But where to find him? Ironically, if I text or call my own husband, he might be furious with me for escaping that hell he imprisoned me in. But I keep driving down that silver tongue of Paragon road because deep down I've known all along where I'm headed— Demetri's. I roll up to his pop-up mansion and pull out my phone, staring at it, wondering who in the hell wasn't at that party that might be able to help me, and then it hits me. Brody. I send a quick text letting him know we'll be meeting later before heading up the long winding driveway. No sign of Gage's truck, which doesn't surprise me. His father isn't his first choice of alliances to draw upon when the going gets tough. He's not mine either, but I have questions, and he has answers.

I give a brisk knock before walking in. "Anyone home?" My voice booms throughout the cavernous mausoleum. I still remember that horrible room upstairs, the Fem trophy room. Its walls are adorned with hideous clown heads and creatures that have no earthly relatives, and I'm sure Demetri had a literal hand in decapitating them.

"Demetri?" I stalk into the grand room and find him seated facing the fire, a puff of smoke swirling to the ceiling as he enjoys a cigar. Figures. Rome is burning, and Demetri is sitting around with a fat stogie in his crooked mouth. He turns my way with that forever-wicked grin and opens his arms.

"My favorite daughter-in-law. To whatever do I owe the pleasure?"

"Please. The feds took half the island to who knows where and Wes is in that number."

"The twins?" His head cocks as if maybe he doesn't have a clue.

"They're with my mother. The one you love."

"My Lizbeth." That greasy smile returns to his face.

"Yes, well, I need your help. What's happened to my people, and how can I get them back?"

He lets out a tired puff of smoke and extinguishes the fat stick in his hand. "They're coming home. But they've been tagged. They will be watched. This is a tragedy unfolding." His dark eyes meet with mine. "However will you avert this from exploding in the faces of every Nephilim on earth? They are mere moments from discovering the marker present in your people."

A breath hitches in my throat. "I can't let that happen." I look to him with fear and desperation. I need the truth from this demon and so much more than that. "Has Wesley secured the Barricade? Are they impervious? Has he found a way to hide the markers permanently?"

"No." His grin widens before it collapses. "But let us not forget the dead." He holds out his hand as if asking for mine, and surprisingly I give it. Demetri's hands are coarse and calloused, thick and welcoming as untanned leather. "Skyla, you must see what they've done to the dead."

In a moment we're transported, walking the halls of an unnamed lab. The white walls are reminiscent of Ezrina's old stomping grounds—but the smells, the stale looking laminate on the floor, dehydrated from years of neglect and wear, inform me this is a strictly human facility. Ezrina would rather gouge out her own eyes and drink them down in a smoothie than work somewhere so unhygienic.

"So this is where the dead are," I marvel mostly to myself.

"Raven's Eye, just a stone's throw from Host. But this is where they'll remain while they have breath in their lungs." He nods left and leads me into a vast facility, and as soon as my eyes absorb what's happening, I stop short of breathing myself.

"Oh my God," I whisper. Settled around me are a group of men, each in his own confinement cell, each with bloodied faces, fingernails missing from their hands, one of them lies on a bed with wires coming from every limb and orifice, his mouth agape as he lies unconscious. "No," I whisper as I touch over the bars. "I can't bare it."

"You should, and you will." Demetri moves me along, his cool hand still clamped over mine. "If not but for the grace of God, there go you and yours."

"Understand," I say it under my breath. An incomplete thought that encompasses all of the horror this moment has to offer. I get it. I do. This could very well be my people. And if not for these brave, sweet souls, it would be. And now that we've been incarcerated in such a great number tonight, it will be. "Take me back," I pant, but Demetri leads me deeper into the facility, past rows of countless cells, each filled with the sobbing and moans that only deep anguish and pain can produce. "I never thought they'd be inhuman. I never thought they'd dismember, dissect."

"They have, and they will." He sniffs. "All of these once dead souls are crying out for mercy. Their cry has risen to the throne, Skyla. Even the Master is imploring you to put an end to their suffering. Can you think of a way?" Demetri's never-ending grimace preens for my attention.

"A way to end their suffering and not begin that of my people? Oh my God." I bury my head in my hands a moment and envelop myself in a haunting darkness, reminiscent of the twisted fingers of Paragon's most hellish woods, the color red staining in the backdrop. Moser and Killion... "I have it." I spring up for air, the light of this horror far too bright. "Take me back to Paragon—back to Gage. I know exactly what I have to do."

Demetri laughs, dark and rumbling, thick with evil. "You are your mother's daughter."

The world around us softens, but I force these horrid halls into my memory. I stain the inside of my mind with the blood that's been shed. These people—*my* people are being tormented alive. It's not what I intended. It's not how it should be.

It's the tunnels all over again. And ironically, that's exactly where I'm taking Gage once I find him.

The lawn in front of the Paragon Police Department is flooded with people bolting—*escaping* from the facility into waiting cars and vans. Although presumably they're not escaping. They've been tagged as Demetri suggested, only to be toyed with at a later date.

"They're free." I let out a breath of relief, only to find I'm shy one Fem by my side. Figures. He knew so much. Demetri is a retired *detective*. Everything that describes Demetri in earthly terms requires air quotes.

I spot Gage and Logan off on the south end of the property and bolt over.

"Logan!" I crash over him with an embrace that not even death could cut through. "Thank God. What happened? What made them turn everyone loose?" I glance at the crowd for familiar faces. Those pens at Raven's Eye were full. It makes sense that they've opted to take names and kick ass later.

Logan glances to Gage briefly. "They didn't let everyone go."

"God, they're holding Marshall? I mean, not that it worries me. Marshall can hold his own." A thought comes to me. "Wait, are they holding *Wes*? God, this is beautiful!" And just like that, all of the anger I had toward Gage evaporates. Wesley's incarceration covers a multitude of sins.

"No." Gage pulls my hands forward and clasps his fingers over mine hard as if stopping me from pulling away before I ever try. "They have Laken"—he winces—"Ellis, Tobie, and Angel."

"Angel," her name strums from me numbly, and Logan pulls me in by the waist.

"A handful of others." Logan glares at the facility behind me. "Last night—Casey wouldn't answer. Her dreams, they were—gone." He looks over at Gage and me as if surprised on some level.

"You think she's dead?" My throat constricts at the thought of those monsters hurting a single hair on her head. "God, I never thought they'd be so cruel, so swift with their deranged experimentation." But a part of me decries the idea. Of course, I did. We expected death. Did we honestly believe they'd let them rot for years in those cages? Yes, a very real part of me did believe just that.

"I didn't either." Logan grimaces. "But there's not a whole lot we can do."

Gage gives my hand a tug, demanding that I look at him, a sheepish apology already flirting with his lips.

My eyes sharpen over his as the fury builds in me. "How dare you leave me behind like some helpless kitten."

"*Skyla.*" He implores me with that desperate tone. "The boys needed you."

"My people needed me. My daughter needed me. The boys slept through the whole ordeal."

"Because I got you the hell out of there." He leans in, and I can tell my opposition frustrates the living hell out of him. As his does mine.

"Let's get one thing straight." I pluck my hands free. "You are not my master. You may never incarcerate me against my will no matter what the circumstances. I am the one charged to keep my people safe—one of which is you. You may *never* defy me again. I absolutely forbid it."

Logan flinches as if he were suddenly a third wheel. "Hash this out at home, kids. We need a solution right now. No matter what—my daughter is getting out tonight."

"I agree." The brief tour with Demetri runs through my mind. "And that's why we're going to take care of this right this fucking minute." I look up at my husband. "We're going to Tenebrous."

"Tenebrous?" Gage steps back, the storm clouds already brewing in his eyes.

"We're feeding the feds the Videns." I look to Logan. "You and I will free the rest."

Logan searches the vicinity as if seeking out an answer. "I'm in. I'm willing to storm Raven's Eye, but how the hell are we getting those cells to open up? I'm not sure if our strength will be enough. They know what we're capable of, and I'm sure they've taken precautions."

"Stop." Gage cuts the air with his hands. "Nobody is touching the Videns."

"I am," I'm quick to inform. "They feel nothing. My people feel pain. They're virtually indestructible. They'll occupy the government for years and fill ten facilities the size of Raven's Eye. We'll flood them with hundreds, two for each of the dead, and then we'll slowly feed them the rest. If this works, we can keep the government off our asses for decades. It's an easy and necessary fix." My breathing is labored, my nostrils flaring with every other word because everything in me knows this will be anything but easy. Gage is the Videns' leader. Of course, there will be some resistance, but he has to agree. I'm right on every count.

"No." He pulls me in gently. "Skyla"—those dark brows of his knot with worry—"I've promised their families I'd keep them safe, that I'd get Ezrina to work on restoration."

"She can't restore them. She's tried. She's not capable. Not yet, anyway. It's not happening. Gage we need them. They're our only hope."

The cords in his neck distend as he tries to digest this. "Let the volunteers finish their assignment."

"*No!*" both Logan and I say in unison.

His eyes sharpen over mine in a manner I never want to grow accustomed to.

"Why are you glaring at me?" My voice is curt and tight as I step in close to my husband as if I were about to deck him, and I'm tempted as hell.

"Because those are my people and you're trying to undercut me."

A stillness rises between us, nothing but the heavy sound of our breathing.

"You are my subject, Gage. You are my people. I am the one in authority around here, and I need to do what is best." Our eyes remain locked in an incredulous stare with neither of us backing down—the both of us in disbelief. "Look"—I cup my palm over his cheek—"I know this is hard for you. And I'm sorry you've promised your people their loved ones back, but they belong to the Barricade. This is *their* game, Gage. And in this round, *they* lose."

"No—not the Spectators, Skyla. You can't have them." His eyes widen with horror.

Logan holds a hand out between us as if I were about to throw a fist at my husband, and I might.

"Gage"—my voice comes out husky and anguished—"I'm sorry, but this is happening."

"*Hey!*" a male voice calls from the side, and we look to find Brody Bishop jogging over. "I heard what happened." He nods my way. "What are we doing?"

"We're going to Tenebrous." I look to Gage, to those startled eyes I love so deeply. "You can come with us or you can stay here, but this is happening tonight."

"Shit," he says under his breath, and before I can determine how pissed he might be, a familiar looking Sector rises behind him.

"Marshall!" I land over him in a hard embrace and soak in every good vibratory sensation. "You're coming with us to Tenebrous."

"Perfect." He glowers at the facility behind me. "Let the retribution be quick and swift. I've a home to tend to."

I glance to Gage. "It will be quick and swift. The torment of my people ends tonight. Where's Coop? I know he'd want to be a part of this."

Logan shakes his head. "He's in the back. It'll be an hour at least until they process him."

"We can't wait. We have to leave now."

Logan closes his eyes. "Skyla, your passion is great, but we need to figure out how to get the cells opened to set the people free. Gage can't be in every cell at once to teleport the dead. We'll only have minutes to complete the mission."

"The cells will open. Fire is greater than passion."

Surely the cells at Raven's Eye will open for the flames.

But judging by that furious look in my husband's eyes, his heart will not.

Tenebrous greets us with long forlorn branches draped over the open road, creating a tunnel of darkness, open arms filled with thorns, a charred grin as if ready to offer a necrotic embrace.

Gage dips a kiss to the crease in my neck. "We need to talk." The others head for the holding tanks, but Gage pulls me toward the stone of sacrifice. And I go willingly since I'm not looking to turn this into the tornado that takes down our marriage.

"I know what you're going to say." I step up on the circular stone, and he does the same. It's only a few feet off the ground, and yet it has the power to make Tenebrous, all of existence, seem diminutive while standing on its unholy granite. There is power on this stone, around it, through it, whether I like to admit it or not. The blood that was shed here has made it so. "And no, I cannot change my mind."

"You must." He cups my cheeks as if my face were blown glass. "Skyla, I looked those people in the eye and said I'd protect their loved ones. I can't just do a one-eighty and feed them to the government. That's not how I operate. That's not who I am."

"Well, I can't let my people suffer. That's not how *I* operate. That's not who *I* am. Besides, our friends—our *daughter* is in there."

He blinks back as if I've hit below the belt.

"Let me get them," he pleads. "I will find a way. I'll free them tonight."

I pull back, ready to leap from the stone and get the morbid show on the road. "Getting them is not enough. If we free the dead, then the feds will come for those they captured and tagged this afternoon. We need a diversion. One that will assure the Nephilim peace. Only the Spectators can provide it. Once the feds find real live zombies on their doorsteps, they won't care that a few alien beings slipped through the net. In the hierarchy of chaos, zombies win every single time. We can buy *peace*—something that simply freeing the dead will never achieve." Now it's me pleading with him. "Side with me, Gage. You don't belong to the Barricade. You belong to me."

His Adam's apple rises and falls, and already I know what his decision is. Our lives flash before my eyes—our short marriage, which I hope to God drives out straight through the second coming. I don't want death for Gage or me. I don't want our union to ever come to an end. I think of the two of us entwined in our bed back at the Landon house—the very house he's so desperate to escape from. I think of those blissful nights lying naked with our infant sons draped over our chests. We were so frustrated with our lives at that point, wanting freedom that only money could buy, wanting to finish our education, our own place, the money to fix up our own place—we were at the apex of our happiness, and we didn't even realize it. And here, life had taken a hairpin turn with Gage opposing my wishes, me opposing his.

"*Skyla*"—he calls out as if I were clear across the universe, and our gaze solidifies over one another, hopeful that whatever comes next unlocks the key to our shared frustration—"do not do this." His voice shakes, and it's hard to tell if it's with rage or hurt, probably both. "I forbid it."

There it is, the dare I threw him earlier. And now he's hurled it right back at my feet.

A dull laugh dies in my chest. "We can't seem to forbid one another to do a damn thing." I head back through the woods, alone, feeling his void as heavy as a mountain, and it kills me. Then, as if eager to fill it, Gage appears by my side, his irritation nearing a boiling point as we make our way to where the others stand with Ingram Prendergast. Marshall, Logan, and Brody—the three of them hover over Ingram's glowing notebook, where he has the Videns listed and organized right down to their eye color. Ingram is anal that way.

"Marshall." I pull him aside as Gage heads over to peer at Ingram's notebook.

"Ms. Messenger." His intense crimson gaze sears me as if he can smell my fear. "Gage said he promised the Videns he'd keep the Spectators safe. Help me."

"Help you? Skyla, how many other solutions are at your disposal?"

"None, and I'm not even sure if this is one of them. How can I save my people, occupy the feds, *and* help Gage keep his promise?"

His chest bucks with a laugh. "Don't forget to feed the starving and shelter the homeless. Throw in a wild night with yours truly while you're at it. So many things to do, so little time."

"Point taken. I can't solve every problem."

"But you can solve a few."

I take in a quivering breath as if I've just had a good cry, and I wish I had. "I can save the dead, send them back to paradise, save my baby"—my throat constricts because I don't want to send her anywhere but in my arms—"and lead the government right to the Spectators."

"It sounds as if you've met with your solution." He offers a peaceful smile. "And now that my work is done, I must leave. The Justice Alliance frowns upon the commingling of Sectors in Faction business. I can't help you, Skyla. My tattered home awaits."

"Thank you for everything." I pull him into a tight embrace. That loving feeling strums through him, straight down to my bones, and I drink in the small taste of paradise before heading straight into hell. "You're always there for me."

"It's an easy assignment."

"One more thing." I hold up the ring on my finger that Chloe gave me, and he frowns. "My mother told me about the history of this ring. It looks as if it finally made its way to me."

Marshall lifts the ring and lands his lips over it. "I had dreamed of gifting it to you when the time was right. I suppose Ms. Bishop beat me to the punch." His features darken. "Be careful with this, Skyla. It could mean life or death."

"So I've noticed." That conversation in the Transfer comes back to me. "She also said my name was Skyla Dunamis." I can't even believe I'm entertaining my mother's anti-Oliver rant. "What do you think that means?"

"Skyla Dunamis." Marshall's countenance radiates when he says it as if my new moniker had the ability to sharpen his comely features. "It means the miraculous power of the living God. And that's exactly what resides in you—the miraculous power of the living God."

"Wow." I try to absorb what this might mean. "Any other words of advice?"

"Yes." He brushes my cheek with his thumb and dives in quickly. Before I know it, Marshall's lips are over mine, and just as I'm about to pull away, I see it. A sign reads *Raven's Eye Government Facility*. My attention is drawn to a man punching in a code, 4562. I pull back, breathless, and blink up at him in awe. Marshall helped me. He gave me what I would need to infiltrate those wicked grounds—a Sector commingling with Faction business. "Thank you," I whisper. And just like that, he's gone.

I head over to the testosterone huddle, and the entire lot of them looks up at me at once. "It's time. There's no going back." I look to Gage and nod. "I'm sorry."

"So am I." His dimples invert with a frown. In all of the turbulence that has plagued our short union, this one feels like an unscalable wall that we're suddenly faced with. God knows I would cut through iron bars, destroy gates of bronze to please my husband, but here, in this dark place, there is no amicable solution. "Brody, you'll go with Gage. Logan, you'll come with me." I don't dare meet with my husband's eyes. The last thing we need is an argument breaking out between us and launching the entire mission to hell. "Gage— we need you to teleport us back along with the dead." The words hardly crest the painful lump in my throat. "Ingram, you'll release the Spectators to me in batches. I'll have Chloe lead authorities to them just like she did the dead."

"Sounds good," Brody is the first to declare. He sets his hand out between us. "The Retribution League lives another day."

"Amen to that." I land my hand over his, and Logan does the same.

"To beautiful retribution." Logan looks to me. "And to getting our daughter back safe."

We break as we take up one another's hands, ready to transport to Raven's Eye, and all I can think of is the fact Gage didn't join our friendly hand tap. He's a part of the team, but he doesn't support what we're doing. Gage hasn't taken the throne, and already we're in direct opposition. Tears form in my eyes as Tenebrous fades to nothing.

Demetri is already pulling us apart.

A cloak of darkness surrounds us as midnight quickly creeps upon us. The ocean roars in the distance as the fog crawls over the island with its elongated fingers. A baby-faced moon sits full and high, thinly veiled, as if the fog itself were willing to expose our efforts.

Raven's Eye is small in comparison to the island we call home—round in shape when juxtaposed to Paragon's oblong physique. The waves crash over its borders with a marked aggression, threatening to swallow it whole, to submerge it from every angle. And all of that I've surmised in the thimble of an airborne moment Gage afforded us.

We land hard on our feet right in the bushes near the old iconic looking facility with its tall iron gates and impenetrable charm. If we knew where to go inside—a place we wouldn't get caught—caught on the *security* cameras, I would have had Gage transport us directly in the heart of this disaster. But according to Logan, it's a well-oiled machine with electronic eyes everywhere you turn.

"The fire?" Logan shakes his head as if we've made a misstep before we ever set foot on the facility.

"Gage will provide the fire." I look up at his sturdy build, his smile flickering ironically like a candle who won't take a flame. "Breathe your fury all over this place." I give an unsteady nod. "We'll need lots of smoke. A wall of white to shield us. And I'll need the security cameras disabled. We'll split up in pairs."

Brody shakes his head. "That's easy. I'll go first. Give me five minutes. I'll rewind the system by a half hour. They won't have a clue shit just hit the fan."

I whisper the code to Brody who heads to the gate as if he owns the place.

Gage leans in, touching his lips to mine, his eyes watching me lazily. "Let me go in with you. Logan can go with Brody. We're a team, Skyla, you and me."

My mouth opens, unsure of which direction it wants to head in, just as Brody comes back.

"Fucking easy." He nods to Gage. "We'll take the east wing. Clock's ticking. If we're not out with everyone in less than seven minutes, we won't be going anywhere. No cell phones. They can trace us right back here." Brody takes off, and Gage steps back, his silence pleading with me before he sighs, closes his eyes, and heads out after Brody.

"Come here." Logan takes up my hand and lands a kiss to the back of it. "It's time to get our daughter."

Logan leads us through a narrow corridor that follows a marked path that leads into the main facility, and we head west under the banner of barbed wire and signs that read *Authorized Personnel Only Beyond This Point.*

I'm authorizing us. I give Logan's hand a squeeze. We make our way closer, only to find a set of glass doors sealing the entry.

Retina entry. He nods to the security panel to the left of the entrance.

The doors burst open with an explosive boom as a man in a janitorial uniform barrels his way out while wheeling a large waste bin. He bucks and kicks, trying to get his behemoth contraption to mind him, leaving the doors flapping in his wake like a dying fish. We wait until he turns the corner, and Logan jams his shoe in the door before it seals itself shut. He pulls me in, and I trail him like a kite. Logan moves us swiftly through the facility he's memorized in his sleep, quite literally.

I don't know where she is, Skyla. He gives my hand a squeeze.

For a minute I think he's talking about Angel, but his gaze is fixed on an empty room with its glass doors swung open. The tiny room holds only a metal bed and a toilet, not a stitch more.

This was her room. He takes in a quivering breath, the pain, all of his anguish unleashing into the world with that single sigh. *Casey is gone. She must be dead.*

My arms wrap themselves around the girth of his body. *Let's get the others, Logan. Let's do it for her.*

An alarm screams overhead as the lights blink on and off manically. Smoke sweeps by like an army of ghosts speeding out of hell, and my entire body enlivens with adrenaline.

I squeeze his hand to the bone. *It's show time.*

Logan leads us as we trail the smoke floating over our heads, ready to press over us like a lid sealing in our airless fate. In a moment, we're in the hall of horror, each cell filled with the weary look of despair. A red light blinks on above each and every cell, and just like that, the faces of those once dead light up with hope they never knew was coming as the cell doors magically swing open. The feds might want to keep my people prisoners, but it needs to adhere to fire codes nevertheless.

Logan and I run from cell to cell shouting, guiding the prisoners to the route to freedom. There is no time to waste.

A pair of gentlemen emerges from one of the confinement units, Frank and Graham, the Smite brothers, and they look to the two of us.

"What's happening? What about the assignment?"

"It's over," I pant. "Your duty here is done."

Frank lets out a harrowing howl, a yodel that sounds more like code than it does a primal release, and a stampede rushes by, an entire cluster of bodies as the dead all press their way to the exit at once.

"What was that?" Logan lets out a dry laugh as he ushers them to the exit.

Graham winks over at us as the throngs rush past. "Let's just call it the Sampson option."

"You had a plan." I bite down the urge to cry. "Get to the entry. Gage and Brody will lead you to safety. We'll meet you in Tenebrous."

"The tunnels." Graham's face grows white. "We trust you."

And just like that, the room clears of people and fills with smoke.

"Angel and Tobie." I panic as I rush from cell to cell. "Ellis? Laken?" I give Logan's arm a squeeze as the smoke starts to blanket the vicinity. "Do you see them?"

"No." Logan's eyes grow wild with panic, and that alone is enough to send me through the roof with alarm. We head out further and come to a hall that splits in two different directions—the smoke pushing in thick, driving every living being out of its path. "I'll go right. You go left." He grips me hard by the shoulders, his gaze penetrating mine. "Do not die on me, Skyla. Do a quick scan. If you don't see them, get out. Gage and Brody most likely have them. Get on the floor if you need to. You won't do your boys or your people any good if you're dead."

I press a hard kiss to his lips before bolting the hell away from him. I'm not leaving until I'm sure there's not a soul left back here. The room opens up to a larger facility, an operating room of some sort, and I'm distinctly reminded of Ezrina's chop shop. The smoke hisses past me like a snake, and in seconds the room is filled with billows of life-choking clouds that force me to breathe in my sleeve. My lungs refuse its strangling fumes as I begin to choke and gag. I fall to the floor and take a quick breath, the smoke still a foot over my head. I've got less than a minute before I need to get the hell out. Logan is right. I won't do my boys or my people any good if I'm dead. A narrow door up ahead catches my attention, and I army crawl over as fast as I can. The room is dark, the smoke lies thick, sinking ever so closer to the ground, and it leaves me sucking the floor for my next breath. Then I hear it, the sharp, anguished wail of an infant. I crawl forward and spot a glass enclosure in the wall across from me with a red-faced babe screaming her head off, pounding over the glass in hopes anyone will see her— Tobie.

"Tobie," I choke out her name as I inch closer, but a rattle from farther down the room captures my attention, and I spot another set of tiny hands wailing against a glass enclosure of their own. I recognize that tiny blonde head of hair pitching wildly about before sitting down and weeping without a thread of hope. And then she sees me.

"Ma Ma!" she wails, pounding the glass, *crying*, hitting her head against the wall in sheer panic.

"Oh my God." I take a deep breath and rise to my feet. The smoke grows ever so thick, and in a moment, I'll lose sight of them. The girls are each an equal distance away, fifty feet in either direction at least. I need to go left or right, Tobie or Angel. The three of us have seconds of air left. I need to get one now before they both perish, but my God, how will I ever save both? Horrifically, I realize there is only hope for one.

Red, angry flames shoot in and race across the ceiling as if the facility were doused with flammables—as if the fire itself were taunting me to choose.

"*Angel*," I call out and choke myself back down to the floor. I suck in another lungful and bounce to my feet. Left or right. Chloe or Skyla. Tobie or Angel. God help me, I've ensnared myself in paralysis by analysis.

Shitshitshit!

And just like that, the room is white with a smoke so thick it sits over you like a blanket. Robed in white—I can't tell which way is up—which way is Tobie, which way is Angel. But my gut knows. I know the path to them both. The fire swirls and roars, and the smoke clears enough to create one last visual of the room.

Time seems to still as I look to Tobie with her desperate pleading—no mother would come to rescue her. I look to Angel, *my* Angel, my flesh and my bones, my love child with Logan. She has the very breath of God in her miraculous lungs before the union of her parents ever came to be. She is so very loved, so very wanted. She is a light to this aching wet world. She owns my heart. She owns Logan's. I'm sure she is so very vital to the Factions, to humanity, to my mother. And that's when I know what I have to do. I glance over to Angel as she screams *Ma Ma* through anguished tears, her face wrinkled in horror as she begins to gag and thrash. But my feet drift in the opposite direction. In a burst of fury and rage, with a wild scream locked in my throat, I burst through the door penning in Tobie and scoop her scorching, bucking body in close to mine. Tears stream down my face, hot and heavy, as the flames race to the other side of the room, Angel's cries roaring wild like that of cat in agony. And in a moment, the room lights up ethereal blue. A violet shadow in the familiar shape of my mother swoops toward my baby, and just like that, Angel and Candace Messenger are no more. My chest bucks with pain as I press my lips together to keep from crying out. I wrap myself around Tobie with all my strength and get the hell out of there. I chose the girl that nobody would have come for, and in doing so I lost my daughter—perhaps forever.

The room floods with flames as we make our way to the narrow door, the smoke too thick to see through. I land us both on the floor and grope for walls, for something familiar that might lead us out of this hell in the right direction. But soon, I'm left groping at nothing but air, the smoke crushing down to the floor, the heat too hot to bear. My lungs ache as I struggle for my next breath, and Tobie claws at my chest as if doing the same. My body bucks as my lungs seize. This is it. I've done this to myself with those wasted moments of indecision, and now both Tobie and I will die. The flames circle around me, the smoke lies over us like a casket as my last breath leaves my lungs.

And then like a dream, a light shines over me, a body lands softly over mine, over Tobie, and the room melts away to nothing.

On a good day, Tenebrous smells like the armpit of a sweaty wrestler, but this day, this moment, Tenebrous is delivering the sweetest perfume—air, sweet, albeit pungent *air*.

Tobie sucks in such a violent breath, and it sounds like a whistle. Her little body grows rigid before loosening as a wailing cry extinguishes from her lungs.

"Tobie!" Wesley roars, wasting no time in snatching her from my arms, and I can't blame him. I would have done the same if the roles, the children, were reversed. "Shit," he pants over her as he peppers her with kisses. "Thank you, Skyla. My God, thank you." He pulls me into a hard embrace, his face buried in my neck a moment, and it's an odd feeling, considering this is Tenebrous, the very location Wesley drained me of my blood to strengthen his powers not so long ago. That's the only reprieve we've been given in this new war. Celestra blood isn't in demand the way it used to be. Thankfully.

"You're welcome." I look past him as Gage carefully extracts me and pulls me back into the safety of his arms where I belong—where I've always belonged and always will. "And thank you for saving me—all of us." I glance past him at the dead reunited, sharing their war stories as a badge of honor. There is laughter and joy and not one ounce of pain, and my heart is full again.

Logan comes up fast with his face piqued with color, his eyes rife with worry. "Where is she?"

"*Logan*." I shake my head. "I'm so sorry." I close my eyes a moment before looking to Tobie as she smiles up at her father. The love in Wesley's eyes lets me know I made the right decision. I tell Logan and Gage what happened, reducing those terrible agonizing moments into less than a couple of simple sentences.

"Come here." Logan wraps his arms around me in love. "I'm sorry you had to make a decision like that." He pulls back, holding me steady by the shoulders. "I want you to know that you made the right one."

"Angel is safe." Gage wraps his arm around my waist. "Your mother wouldn't have rescued Tobie. There was no other choice to make."

Laken and Ellis come up, both looking slightly shaken yet furious at the circumstances, and we share a quick embrace.

"Where is she?" Laken's features crumble as if she's already surmised the worst, and I tell her quickly, assuring her there was no other way.

Ingram helps to give the resurrected water to drink and encourages them to settle in the building behind us for respite. Soon, my mother will be here to transport them back where they belong—bodies in the ground, spirits in the sky.

One by one they come by and thank me for the opportunity to serve, for the rescue they weren't expecting. They look at me like I'm some sort of a hero, and I don't feel that way at all. To the Videns—who are essentially my people, despite the fact they chose to side with the Barricade—I am for sure no hero. Soon, I'll be a devil.

The bulk of the dead vanish into the building behind us where some of these very people lost their lives to begin with. A fresh, familiar face comes barreling at me with an ear-to-ear grin.

"Casey!" I fall over her with a hearty embrace. "Where were you? Logan said your cell was empty!"

"It was." She steps back and makes a face. "I decided I was lonely, and they let me stay with the mean girls." She glances back at a trio of brunettes, and I smile because I know them all and love them. "It turns out they're not so mean after all. We have a ton in common. It looks as if I've made a few new eternal friends."

I nod with a laugh. "I suppose lifelong would be too short."

We get lost in a quick group hug as Logan and Gage join in on the effort. Before too long, the last of the dead are making themselves at home, and all feels right with this twisted world.

Pierce comes up, and I embrace him without hesitating.

"Dude, that was no joke. I'm glad you stepped in when you did. As much as any of us wanted to serve, it was a tough pill to swallow." He starts to head toward the building, and I pull him back.

"No, wait. You should come back to Paragon and say goodbye. I'm sure my mother will be by soon to take both you and Kate home."

"Paragon?" His eyes light up like a little boy at Christmas.

"Yes, Nat would kill me if I denied her the right to say goodbye."

"Thanks, man." He pulls me in and swings me around. "I'd better say goodbye to a few of the folks here real quick." He takes off toward the building.

I look to Ellis and Laken. "What about Emerson and Holden? Were they taken with you?"

"No," Logan answers for them. "They took off. They were never arrested."

"Useless per usual. But I'm glad they're safe." I look to Gage and press my lips together until they're white as paper. "It's time to initiate the rest of the plan."

Brody comes up, breathless. "We did it." He offers up a high five my way, and I take him up on it. "Now what?"

"Go back to Paragon. Get your sister. I'll meet you both at Devil's Peak in an hour, and we'll take it from there."

"Will do."

Gage walks him over to the woods and transports him home.

Laken leans in and hooks my loose hairs behind my ear. "I'm proud of you, Skyla. You did great. You are a wonderful leader. I'm glad you're mine."

"Thank you. Coop was still being processed or I'm sure he would have come. We couldn't wait."

"And I'm thankful you didn't."

"Same here, Messenger." Ellis offers a quick pat over my back. "I mean *Oliver*. What else can I do for you?"

"Go home and comfort Giselle. I'm sure she misses you."

He offers up a quick salute and heads to the woods just as Gage appears again.

Laken shakes her head at me, her eyes cloud over with worry. "Skyla, they took Ellis and me to their facility because we had the babies. Angel turned bright blue, and her eyes started to spark. Honestly, I've never seen anything like it, and apparently neither had they. They tried to grill me, but I wouldn't even give my name."

"Blue? My God, the boys used to do that, but thankfully they seem to have outgrown it." Please, dear God, let them have outgrown it. The last thing I need is to worry about their complexion giving away their angelic lineage. "As soon as we hit that prison, they stripped us of them. I tried to hold on. Ellis did, too, but Tobie's face lit up like a blue beacon herself, and the rest was history."

I take a breath, trying to digest it all. "It's okay. I can only imagine how fascinated they were at the prospect of raising two alien beings without the influence of others to bog them down. I'm sure they thought they hit the jackpot."

"They didn't thanks to you." She gives my hair a quick stroke. "I'd better head home, too." Laken ticks her head to the woods. "Coop is probably going insane." She gives me a quick kiss to my cheek just as Wes comes up with Tobie. Laken swallows hard looking at the soot-covered little girl. "I'm glad you have your daughter back, Wes." Her eyes glitter with tears as she ditches into the woods.

He watches as she goes, his hand still protectively covering Tobie's sweet dark head.

"Thank you once again for saving my daughter." He looks sheepishly from me to Logan. "And for bringing Laken back to me safe."

He starts to take off, and I snatch him by the wrist. "Where's Melody Winters?"

Wes frowns out at the building behind me. "I took her to Paragon before coming here." Those familiar blue eyes tunnel into mine. "I was at Raven's Eye, tonight myself, Skyla. I helped Gage transport the masses." He glances past me at Logan. "I didn't do it for your people or for me."

I take a startled step backward. "Of course not. You did it for Laken."

"Yes." His expression sours despite the fact Tobie just leaned in and gifted him a kiss on the nose. "I needed to know she was safe." He looks from Logan to me. "Thank you both." He heads toward the woods, and both he and Tobie evaporate in a plume of electric blue fog.

Logan takes up my hands and pulls me in close, smiling through the tears glittering in his eyes, and my heart bursts open at the seams for our baby. A fresh wound I'll grieve forever.

"She's safe, Skyla. We will see her again."

I pull back and look into Logan Oliver's citrine eyes, uncertain that I share his faith in the sentiment.

"We will," he says it sad, as a fact, as if he knew the answer would frighten me as much as it would delight me.

We head back to Paragon and straight to Devil's Peak. Gage helps me transport a handful of Spectators to the Black

Forest, and Chloe starts in on what she does best, rats her little heart out. We take a few to Seattle, Brazil, and China, and Chloe plays her part as if this were the role she was born for. Not once has she asked about Tobie. Not that either Gage or I are surprised. We take the bulk of the Spectators straight to Raven's Eye and retard the commotion at the mouth of the building as men swarm the facility trying to assess what the hell happened to those alien beings. We watch from afar as the Spectators thrash their way through those feds in their blue jackets as if they were rag dolls.

"I hope they eat them all." Chloe chortles a dark laugh.

"Now that's an outcome I hadn't thought of." Probably not a good one.

"Not happening." Gage nods ahead as agents swarm the Spectators, taking them down with the use of some kind of a Taser that shoots lightning from its eye. "They've got this. And they've also got their hands full." He gives my shoulder a squeeze. "It looks like the heat is off our people."

"For the time being," Chloe chimes. "Wesley won't lie down for long."

Gage looks to me, forlorn, as if to say she's right. Wes might be grateful today, but tomorrow is a different day. The battle between the Barricade and the Factions rages on. And until Wes lands on top, he will never cease.

Maybe Coop is right. Maybe Wes must die. It's the only way.

But Tobie—Wes is all she has, and that little girl loves him. I think even Laken saw that tonight. Wes is a damn good father. It's hard to hate your enemy when he melts your heart just a little.

Gage whisks us back to Paragon, and we drop Chloe back off at Devil's Peak where Brody waits for her.

Gage takes us back to the house, back to the boys, back to our bed where we make love and lie naked in one another's arms just the way it should be.

Gage was meant for me. Just have my mother try to deny it.

Weeks roll by. Heavy winds blow through Paragon and strip the softness from the scenery that the fog traditionally affords. It lets you see the harsh details of the world, the hard borders of the evergreens, the hard purple outline of Host lying like a sleeping giant in the sea, and just beyond that, Raven's Eye where there is a panic of paranormal proportions, I'm sure of it. The news is unreasonably quiet—an irony in and of itself. Chloe and I have planted hundreds of Spectators in the paths of the world authorities—the largest congregation of them just north of Seattle in a weak attempt to deviate the government's attention away from the island. But today it's quiet. The wind, the fog, and even the feds have left Paragon for now. But I know enough to realize that the wind will stir again, the fog will return to Paragon in honor of their binding covenant. It is permanent. And yes, those men in blue will be back, too. We are no longer impervious to their suspicious gaze. Wes has opened a portal to hell that not even he could withstand, nor his precious daughter, nor the one that owns him completely, Laken.

My mother swept up the dead and returned them to paradise as soon as we left Tenebrous that day—with the exception of the Kraggers and Kate, of course. The dead had come, did what was asked of them—were reused and returned all without the pomp and circumstance that a resurrection deserves. In hindsight, I would have handled it all differently. But at the time, I did what I needed to. The important thing is that I acted. I wasn't idle, lost in my thinking, stalled in my own analysis. Perhaps just as important is that the next time something of this nature arises, I think it through, consider the fact I don't want a single soul tormented. Perhaps if I would have done that to begin with, I could have sent the Spectators to Raven's Eye long before I ever did. But the truth is, I wouldn't have. I needed to see the error of my ways before resorting to something so low, and I do believe it was low of me to stoop there.

Classes at Host have started up again, and I've taken a partial load. Only one class leads me to university grounds, and the rest of them I'm able to take online. Emma begged me to place the boys in her daycare center, where she promised she would oversee them herself, but I opted for dear old Mom who was more than glad to oblige. And she's almost okay with me just nursing the boys at night. Almost. But the biggest change this fall has brought about is the fact Mia and Melissa have entered into their junior year at West. It's a frightening thought really—how fast time flies when you have your nose to the grindstone, just living your life. It makes me wonder how quickly my boys will grow up. Will I turn around and find it to be their junior year next? And how will I fill the interim? Will I busy myself with Faction business to the point I miss out on everything in between? It brings tears to my eyes just thinking about it. It was in my junior year that I met Logan and Gage. My entire world shifted on its axis that year.

I asked the aforementioned gorgeous Olivers to meet me at Marshall's. Gage is coming from Host, and Logan from the construction site. Nathan and Barron are with my mother, and Lexy and I just finished going through the Walsh home—my home, which I can't seem to stop calling the Walsh home—we were working on flooring. Liam and his deconstruction crew came in and gutted the place. He replaced the old floorboards, the asbestos-riddled drywall, the windows, the doors, and now Lexy is helping me make a thousand and one decisions regarding kitchen appliances—high-end—countertops—granite, she swore I would regret marble to my dying day—backsplash, fixtures, fireplace mantel, wall color, whether to carpet or not carpet the boys' room, where to put the planter boxes, how to design the hardscape for the backyard, and where we will eventually put in a swimming pool. All of those things cost money, and yet Gage keeps paying the bills, his wallet a never-ending tornado of dollars. It does make me wonder, but I'm too damn tired to ask any questions.

Marshall's estate shines like a jewel under the duress of the white-hot spotlight of the sun, an anomaly in our gray existence. Whenever this rare solar event occurs, I hear nothing but complaints from the residents—the sun is too bright, too harsh, too hot, and oddly enough on this over bright, hard-lined, searing day—I agree. I suppose that's the final step over the sand. I no longer consider myself an L.A. outcast. I'm officially an island girl through and through. As much as we lament the sun, we never really want it around.

I park and head inside. Marshall's door is unlocked, and I frown at that giant hunk of mahogany as if it caused the malfeasance itself. I grew up where triple locks were simply a good start to protecting your home, and on Paragon half the houses don't even have deadbolts installed.

"Ms. Messenger," Marshall calls from the alcove where he keeps that haunted piano, that haunted speculum—and I pause because he happens to be entertaining a very haunted guest, Melody Winters.

I can't help but scowl over at her. She is the girl who tried to seduce Gage on multiple occasions. She's a skank through and through in my book.

"Well, well"—I speed in their direction—"look who the seventeenth century dragged in." I come in close, and she inches back as if I might slap her. Believe me, I'm tempted. "And don't think for a minute I don't know who you are, *Cassandra*."

Her mouth rounds out into a perfect *O* as she looks to Marshall.

His lips twitch a moment. "Don't you mind Ms. Messenger. She's rather harmless."

"The hell I am." I stab a finger into her ample chest. "What the heck are you doing here? Haven't you ever heard that to every man it is appointed once to die and all that other good stay-the-hell-in-your-own-century stuff?"

"*Skyla*." Marshall's tone grows incredulous. "She is a guest in our home. Do work on your hospitality skills." He turns to the redheaded moppet with a grin. "Skyla is my spirit bride. Soon, all shall be consummated and an earthly bond will ensue. I'm thinking children."

Melody chortles at the thought. "You've already had a few of those."

A *few*? Gah! Marshall's seed is sprinkled all over this planet. Although not necessarily a bad thing, it's a thing for sure.

"Just the one, and as fate would have it, my lineage has rolled right down to Paragon." He glowers out the window a moment. "It seems the Olivers stem from greatness after all." His left eye closes lazily as if trying to push the thought away.

"Don't forget about Coop. You're his granddaddy, too!" I rib him with my elbow.

"Do tell." His affect flattens to morbidly dangerous levels. "What may I assist you with, my love?"

"I've invited Logan and Gage over." I sneer at Melody a moment. "I'm finally ready to tell the three of you about the covenant I've entered into with Chloe."

Melody gasps. "She didn't!"

"Oh, she did," I'm quick to inform.

Marshall grunts. "You didn't."

"I most definitely did."

Melody wheezes as if this directly affected her. "Nothing good can come of this. Why would she trust you?" She staggers off toward that speculum, and it's taking all of my restraint not to push her right in. "My God, it's as if she's heard nothing Marlena has told her."

"In one ear and out the other. That's our Chloe." I give a private smile at that conversation my mother and Chloe had a while back where they used just about the same verbiage. "Anyway, yes, I will be the first to admit things have a way of falling to shit when Chloe's around, but she's basically what amounts to a celestial dust mite, ever-present and always getting under your skin. There's no getting rid of her. At least this way I'm able to utilize her. And oddly enough, she's on Team Celestra."

Melody's already pasty face goes stark white, and it frightens me.

"What's the matter?" I reach for her elbow, but she pulls back, her gaze still lost in some faraway place.

"My God, she's idiotic! What a ridiculous ninny." She comes to and looks to Marshall. "I must speak with Marlena." She shakes her head as if this changed her life on a dime. Newsflash: nothing changes the fact she's been dead for three hundred years and counting.

Marshall leans in, his affect a mixture of curiosity and annoyance. "I'm afraid that's not something I can provide."

"Oh, yes, it is." I jump to his side, and his eyes widen with horror.

"No, Skyla, it's not."

"Yes, Marshall, it is." My voice is clear and cutting. "You see, Ms. Winters owes me some answers, and if she wants to see Marlena, she needs to provide them. Of course, you'll play the part of lie detector because this happens to be a no bullshit zone." I glance to Melody when I say that last part.

"Look at the time." She straightens and snatches her purse off the piano. "I must run. It was wonderful per usual, Sector Marshall." She glances back with her hand to her lips and blows him a kiss. "Until *hex* time!"

Marshall chuckles as he leans in. "A little seventeenth-century humor."

"Yeah? Well, it's lousy." I look to Melody as she's about to hit the exit. "The seventeenth century is dead! Much like you are!"

She flips me the bird as she heads on out.

Marshall shakes his head with a wistful smile as if it were the cutest thing. "She does seem to be picking up on the nuances of this century. Cassandra always was a quick study."

"She was a whore in a whorehouse. What the hell is she doing here?"

He hems and haws, his mouth opens and closes as he flits his eyes out the window, and something about this little boy in trouble routine is intensely darling on him. Darn Marshall for captivating me with his cutting good looks at every turn.

The door bursts open, letting in an unreasonable amount of light, and in walk Logan and Gage like gods ushered in by the forces of the universe, their forms outlined in shadows as the sun tries to drink them down.

"Look what *this* century has dragged in"—Marshall says it with all the boredom he can afford—"the Olivers in multiple." Marshall might not be delighted, but my heart soars at the sight of them. After all these years, those butterflies in my stomach still flutter to life whenever they show up on the scene. I try to usher us to the dining room, but Logan insists we enjoy the sunshine, and we head out back instead. It's only then I note he's holding a brown paper bag.

"You come bearing gifts?" My heart plummets because I recognize the white folder peering out. It's the same one Lexy gives me once she prints out the pictures of the boys. I haven't seen the ones we took a few weeks back of Angel yet. I'm not sure I'm ready to.

"Maybe." He glances to the bag with sorrow as we follow Marshall to the corral, allowing the llamas to come over and eavesdrop on our conversation.

"What's up?" Gage wraps his arms around me and presses a soft kiss to my lips. "Everything okay?" His head tips to the side, and the color of his eyes reflects the sky, or maybe it's the other way around. It shouldn't surprise me at all that the sky would want to steal the color from Gage Oliver's eyes.

"Chloe's up." I wrinkle my nose at him. "I wanted to talk to the three of you. I feel like I owe you an apology for not talking about this sooner." A ripe anguish rushes through me at the thought of not having this conversation months ago. But, in a way, I wasn't ready. In all honesty, I don't think I could ever be. "The night of the boys' christening, after Marshall and I witnessed what we did—I couldn't breathe." I meet with my husband's intense gaze. "My heart was broken, and yet even in that horrific moment, I knew deep down that you were doing what you thought best. But ultimately, what I came to realize was that

Demetri's hold on us was stronger than I could have ever imagined." I glance to Marshall who was with me that night. "It was good that you took me to see it. In retrospect, it was as beautiful as it was ugly." I swallow hard. "That night I went to the Transfer. The boys—they afforded me powers that I never dreamed of." My gaze falls to my hands as if the powers they gifted could be contained simply in my fingers. "I found Chloe in Wesley's house by the fire, and I made her an offer she couldn't refuse." I give Gage a sharp look without meaning to. "If you were siding with our enemy, I would, too. I asked her to follow me. To unite her powers with mine, and that I would gift her whatever her heart desired." A sad smile curves on my lips, and Gage matches it with his own.

"She will never have me, Skyla."

"Chloe knows that." I shake my head as if refuting the idea.

Logan groans. "No, she doesn't. There are some concepts Chloe cannot wrap her warped little head around, and that happens to be one of them."

"That might be true, but we've outlined the terms of our covenant and handing Gage's head to her on a silver platter wasn't one of them." I spend the next few minutes outlining the terms of the covenant I entered into with Chloe and place them on that proverbial silver platter before handing them to the three men I love with all of my heart.

Logan sighs, and I don't bother trying to read whether or not he's disappointed in me. "She gets to live above ground. She's your number two. She's for Celestra."

I nod. "She doesn't make a move without my approval. She doesn't harm my family. She leaves my husband the hell alone."

Marshall tenderly picks up my chin a notch, the look of sorrow upon his own. "And what's to stop her?"

"I have the power to send her back to hell or wherever I wish—a quite literal hell if I wanted." The afternoon of the covenant comes back to me. "She did say something..." Something that didn't even faze me that day in Tenebrous, but now that I rehash the words we shed like water, I can't help but trip over it. "She threatened me." My gaze gets lost in the vibrant green lawn that spreads beneath our feet. "In the event I changed my position—she said woe to the hour I turned on her—that she would usher a darkness in my life like never before." The words stream from me in a whisper.

"Skyla." Gage pulls me in tight, his face buried in my neck a moment before he pulls back, exposing the crimson tracks in his eyes. "I'm sorry I drove you to this."

"Don't apologize." My heart grows heavy because I don't know how to candy-coat the truth. "I plan on keeping all of my enemies, present and those implied in my future, close to the vest."

Marshall gives a sly smile. "Arrow to the heart, Skyla. There's no better way to do it."

"And on that note." Logan holds up a finger. "There's something I want to show you—all of you."

"I'm sorry," I mouth to Gage, and he shakes his head as if it's nothing.

"We still win. You and I remain the same. We won't bend to the will of anyone. I'm not going anywhere. You and I will raise our boys. My heart belongs to you and to our people."

Marshall grunts. "I'm tempted to clap, but then I recall it's Jock Strap who's speaking. His people are not your people, Skyla."

Logan offers a dull smile. "Neither are they yours, Dudley." He holds that white file between us that reads *Bakova Studios*. "This isn't easy for me to say or share." His eyes look to mine, weighted with grief, and I see a citrine sunset buried in each one. "*Skyla*"—That longitudinal dimple I gave him dips in—"she's not here anymore." He opens the file as Gage wraps his arms around me from behind, and in that instant I realize Gage has already been apprised of the terrible news. I don't need to ask who she is. Tears stain my cheeks quicker than expected as Logan shows us the pictures we took that morning with Angel and the boys—with Gage. All of us one big happy family. One by one I observe the void our little angel left behind. Not a single trace of her or that ruffled pink confection I dressed her in that morning.

My throat constricts, but I push past the baby-sized knot. "I thought people disappearing from pictures was just some tired trope used by Hollywood, and here we are proving it wrong." My fingers brush over the space where her body once stood. "How cruel of my mother to leave nothing of our little girl behind."

"We have our memories," Logan offers the empty consolation. But we both know that could never be enough. Memories fade. They're unreliable at best. Even as we stand here, I'm forgetting the subtleties of the way her hair smelled, those rolls of flesh along her legs. And that husky, and yet completely feminine laugh—thankfully, that's ingrained in my soul, coursing through my veins like the whisper of, yes, an angel.

Marshall lets out a sigh that could take down a forest. "I'm sorry—for the both of you." His eyes drag from Logan to me. "I've been summoned to the holy throne for a routine accounting. While I'm there, I'll see if there's anything I can glean for you." He gives a subtle nod before leaning in and landing a chaste kiss to my cheek. ***I'm forever at your service, your majesty.*** "Anything else I can help you with?"

I'm about to open my mouth when Gage gives me a hard squeeze before spinning me gently into him. "There is something we need." His dimples depress, and all seems right with the world again. "Our anniversary is tomorrow. Two years."

"And counting," I add.

He pushes out a quiet smile. "If you don't mind, I'd like for us to renew our vows. It feels as if we had a tough year, hiding in and out of shadows, and I think it's appropriate that while the sun is up over Paragon we shower our union with light and love." His thumb swirls over the palm of my hand, and my stomach does that roller coaster thing I love. "Would you mind saying a few words?" He's speaking to Marshall, but his eyes won't leave mine.

"Most certainly."

"Thanks." He dots my lips with a kiss before looking to Logan. "You up for witnessing the event?"

"I wouldn't miss it." Logan tucks the file under his arm, and his chest expands as if he were girding himself.

Marshall steps before us and offers a loving prayer, blessing us in this hour—in every hour that God deems to give us, and I stop shy of flinching, of crying out that we would have more than that even. "And with that—may God bless you both and keep you. What have you to say for yourselves?"

"Skyla"—Gage holds my hands between us—"I love you more than words could ever speak. I have loved you before I knew you. And I will love you far beyond my final breath." Tears glitter in his eyes, and my heart wrenches because the last thing I want is for this to turn into a eulogy of our love.

I press a finger over his lips, sealing in all talk of eternity. "We have this moment. This is *our* moment, our time, our life—and I plan on spending the next eight decades at least with you by my side. There isn't any being on earth or in heaven that could break the bond we share. Our love isn't temporal. It isn't something subject to the breath in our lungs. Our love is infinite, as deep and wide and mysterious as the existence of the living God who sanctioned it. Yes, you are mine, and you always will be. We are steering the ship of our love, of our lives, of our future. And I chose a long and arduously drama-free life with you and our boys." My heart pinches hard because it feels as if I've just driven the final nail through any life Logan hoped to have with me. But I'm not up for juggling three men like my mother suggested. I'm up for loving the one I'm with. The one my heart says I'll live my days out with by my side. Gage Oliver is mine, and fate and all of her fury can go fuck herself.

"Kiss the bride if you must." Marshall heads for the house, and Logan offers both Gage and me a quick pat over the shoulder before doing the same.

But Gage and I seal our love by way of a wet, delicious kiss under the supervision of a small army of long-lashed llamas, under the supervision of a crystalline sky and that burning heart she bears down on us with. I can feel the white light of its affection warming my back as Gage probes my mouth sweetly with his tongue. Two short years under our belt and yet it feels as if Gage has been with me since I took my first breath on this planet. Our kisses pick up pace with a heated frenzy of things to come, but I can feel the fevered anguish layered beneath the lust, crying out in agony of what lies ahead. A damned future painted by the hand of my mother, his father—two celestial beings with one dangerous agenda—to sever the bond that holds us together. My mother wants Gage exchanged for Logan in my bed, in my heart—and Demetri, well, he needs his son on the throne. And it just so happens to be that the path to the throne is through the curtain of death.

Sometimes being an angel can be such hell.

Halloween. A month rolls by, bringing the boys both to their eleventh month of life—standing while holding onto furniture and laughing with glee as they threaten to take their first voluntary steps in this world. But mostly, importantly, this month, on a cold night exactly a week ago, Ezrina and Nev ushered in a dreamy pink bundle of joy named Alice. Dark hair, deep navy newborn-colored eyes, and a face blessed by God Himself— Alice O'Hare is a bewitching beauty. Nevermore explained that the name Alice came from what was once Ezrina's most beloved blade. It might seem like a strange leap to others, but it's obvious to those of us who know and appreciate Ezrina and Nev that this child's name is a great honor bestowed upon her.

But this night, all hallows *evil*, the who's who of Paragon have been summoned to Demetri's haunted estate to celebrate the day of his people.

I frown at my reflection in the glass of the minivan passenger's window.

Gage and I opted for a couple's costume—I've donned my West cheerleader uniform because thank God Almighty I was able to squeeze into it—mostly. I don't suppose anyone will know I'm buying a couple of inches with an obscenely long safety pin Emily lent me. And Gage, well, he's hot as hell dressed as a West Paragon dirty, dirty Dawg who's already threatened a touchdown in my kick pants before the night is through. And seeing that we're at Demetri's and not Marshall's the way God intended for this unblessed event, I'm suspecting the night will end rather spectacularly and abruptly.

Gage hands me Nathan, still groggy from his nap, and I can't help but smile. We've dressed the boys as a couple of little skunks, and we haven't stopped snapping pictures of them ever since we stuffed them in these ridiculously cute costumes. Of course, we stopped by Emma and Barron's first and let them ogle and hold our precious little stinkers. My own mother is already at Demetri's not-so-humble abode commandeering tonight's circus the demon himself has thrust upon us. Speaking of abodes, humble or not, Gage and I have been burning rubber on our own cozy dwelling. Not only will our home be ready to move into by Christmas, but I've decided to bite the bullet and give Gage an early birthday gift by way of moving us all into Emma and Barron's for our last and final few weeks of parental incarceration—hell, I figure I could stand on my head for a few weeks if I had to.

A happy little jack-o-lantern carved with a grin that holds a child-like innocence greets us at Demetri's door. I know for a fact it came from Logan's very own pumpkin patch—the Oliver Pumpkin Patch to be exact because I took the boys, and we helped select the pumpkins my mother picked up for the party. Mostly Gage and I picked them out, but we had a blast sitting the boys in a sea of orange and taking pictures of them as if it were their last moments on earth. The storage on my phone is in serious peril at this point. I've taken thousands of pictures of them. Of course, none as good as the ones Lex has taken. I've got to give it to the girl. I may not like her man-stealing tactics, but she wields a mean camera. And circling back to Logan, he did just as he said he would do. He gave away each and every pumpkin that he grew this year to the kids on the island. I've always known Logan has a heart of gold, and now everyone else knows it, too.

Demetri's home appears to be openly scowling at me, with those tall creepy windows that mimic arched brows, those obnoxious glass doors that resemble a large gaping mouth. I glare at the monolithic mansion that demon insists on occupying. The liar claims it was once his grandfather's, but I doubt such a creature ever existed. Nevertheless, tonight's clash of costumes is strictly Wesley's fault—well, Chloe's fault, too. The real reason Demetri's haunted mansion is festooned with black and purple balloons is because his one and only granddaughter, precious October Edinger, turns one today. And, for Tobie, I'll show up every day of the week.

Gage adjusts Barron on his hip before shutting the door to the minivan and squinting up at his father's demonic hovel. "You ready to do this?"

"As ready as I'll never be." I give a quick wink.

"Count me in," a voice floats from behind, and we find Logan dressed to kill in a flannel and jeans and nothing more than a smile. "Look at you." He forces a frown to come and go as he kisses each of the boys. "I promise I'll get your parents back for this."

"And what are you supposed to be?" Gage hands him Barron as we make our way to the oversized bat cave Demetri prefers to hang out in.

"I'm Skyla's Elysian." He grins my way. "Trust me, Halloween on this island usually brings enough of its own frights. It doesn't need me adding to it. In fact, they should change that sign out by the harbor to read *Welcome to Paragon. Every day is Halloween.*"

"Dude, that barn you erected is a fright in and of itself." Gage has enjoyed mercilessly teasing him.

"Stop." I slam my shoulder into my husband's. It's been a tough barn-shaped pill for Logan to swallow, and now that the barn is built, painted a painful, blistering red, and is undergoing the last few details before its grand opening in a month or so, there's nothing Logan or any of us can do to stop this countrified nightmare.

We head in, and the house is dark with plumes of fog moving along the floors in a snakelike pattern, a glowing sign reads *this way to the party*, and we follow the bloodied arrows all the way to the back of Demetri's sweeping estate. The yard is done up with all the finery a haunted holiday like this requires. It's apparent my mother—and Demetri's wallet—spared no expense. Skeletons hang from newly erected gallows. Clown heads sit heaped in a pile at the base of a bloody guillotine—tons and tons of bloodied clown heads—and I try very hard to ignore the fact I feel a cardiac episode coming on. My God, doesn't my mother know me by now? Surely after spending the last two decades with me, she's apprised of the fact I hate the guts of every clown that's ever lived, right? The sight of them alone used to send me running for the hills, but my phobia has dialed itself down a notch ever since Dr. O gifted me a tiny clown's head a few years back and basically told me to get over it. God, I love Dr. O. Why can't Emma be so affable? Speaking of which, Kate owes me an answer. Time is of the essence before she does her final leap into the sky, and I'm still dying to know why she thinks Emma Oliver is so much trouble. I can give a running list myself but none of us have that kind of time on this planet.

I glance around for anyone that might look even vaguely familiar, but all I see is a bunch of people gathered around the wooden stocks in the center of the yard, taking selfies and group shots. The party isn't quite pumping yet, but judging by the fact Demetri's soirees are known for free food and booze, I suspect the entire island will be Edinger bound soon enough. As it stands, enough people mill around to qualify as a decent get-together, and both my mother and Demetri head over with giant plastered grins. My mother holds Misty over her hip with pride—the two of them are both dressed as matching pink princesses. Demetri is his evil self—the scariest costume of the night, I'm sure—and Tobie is wearing a frilly pink tutu with a sparkling tiara pressed into her luscious dark curls.

"Looks like we found the birthday princess! Happy birthday, precious!" I gift Tobie a kiss, and she claps up a storm before blowing Gage a soft dainty kiss over her fingers.

Gage pretends to catch it and lands it against his cheek. "Happy birthday, kiddo." He offers her a quick peck. Gage is proving to be a stellar uncle. Just the thought sends my heart aching for Angel.

Tobie laughs so hard her entire body shakes, as if Gage were the funniest thing in the world. She's so cute we can't help but laugh along. Her dark curly hair is down to her neck, framing those breathtaking blue eyes, and don't get me started on those dimples. She is Wesley—*Gage* to a *T*. She looks every bit like a miniaturized version of Sage, and I ache for my other daughter, too.

"Would you look at this?" Mom's eyes grow wide as she ribs me. "Demetri spares no expense when it comes to hosting a birthday party. How about we—"

"No." I sneer over at him. It's been a month of deflecting Demetri's demented offer to host the boys' first birthday bash. "A hard no after seeing that basket full of creepy clown parts." I make a half-hearted effort to cover Nathan's ears. "A hell no after seeing the blood dripping from their necks and surmising they're *real*!" I hiss at the horror, and both Demetri and my mother chortle at the murderous details this evening has to offer.

Marshall calls Logan over to the fountain, and he excuses himself.

"I'm with her," Gage says to the two of them. "Skyla and I have decided to keep it simple for the boys."

"For two days straight," I offer. "We'll order in and have cake at the house. We'll celebrate my birthday with Nathan, and then do the same with Barron and Gage the next day."

"My God, don't you dare!" my mother cries out while throwing her hand in the air as if we just threatened to eviscerate them. Misty bucks her way down and escapes her capture, making her way to where Beau is busy plucking at the eyes of the zombie seated at the entrance to the house. And, soon enough, the birthday princess herself hops down and waddles on unsteady feet to the two of them, only to be intercepted by Wes.

"Nice job, Tobie." I marvel at how sweet it was just witnessing that moment. They may not have been her first steps, but they're the first I've seen, and it warmed my heart to witness it. Chloe is here on the premises—but, sadly, she couldn't care less if Tobie waddled straight into a lake.

Wes steps in, and just as I'm about to greet him, my mother snatches Nathan from me. "You'll do no such thing. You and Gage aren't even in the spotlight this year. You can have one party at home with the boys—if that's the road you insist on taking." She smirks at Demetri as if mocking the idea. "And we'll be right here the next day to have a proper first birthday equipped with clowns and balloons—we'll even have a donkey for the kids to ride!" she cries with jubilation, and a part of me doesn't have the heart to stick a pin in her donkey loving dreams.

Tad barrels up with a drink clipped to his teeth, and my mother is quick to take it. His left arm has graduated to a soft splint, but he still has a limited range of motion. His good hand is laden down with a heaping plate of suspiciously glistening seafood with a mini octopus sitting on top as if it were the cherry on that pile of crustaceans.

"That's right, kids. You'll have the big one here. The little woman here sealed the deal with an all-you-can-eat seafood stuff it and buff it. In fact, we're letting old Demetrius here host every occasion and holiday for the rest of our natural lives!" He honks out a *hee-haw* of a laugh as he shovels that eight-legged creature into his mouth, and a tentacle strays outside his lips as if it were fighting to maintain its own natural life. Natural life, my ass. There's not a natural thing about anyone in our tiny little circle. There certainly isn't anything natural about Demetri.

Tad garbles out something unintelligible as that tentacle flies up his nostril, and without missing a beat, he heads straight for the buffet once again.

"Pace yourself!" Demetri calls after him, that perennial smile of his wiped from his face momentarily. "You're bound to choke to death one of these days." That greasy grin of his floats right back like a serpent lying over his lips. "And you are bound to do just that."

"Goodness." My mother leans in. "Excuse me while I stop my husband from making such a donkey of himself." She trots off, and I'm tempted to say something, but I think I'll let Demetri take this one.

He looks over at her. "I'm afraid she's found the ass for the party."

Gage and I exchange a dry smile.

Gage offers Wes a knuckle bump. "What's up? You have any trouble last night?"

"What was last night?" My heart leaps into my throat because everyone knows whatever happened last night with Wes could be a thousand times more frightening than anything this unholy night has to offer.

Wes looks to Gage as if asking for permission, but the beauty of it is they both ignore their father.

"Meeting with the Videns." Gage pulls me in close. "Suffice it to say, they're pissed at me."

"Yes." Wesley's chest bucks at the thought. "They're a little more than that."

Demetri growls out a dull laugh. "Make sure you're never alone in a dark alley. I'd hate to see them bring a swift end to you."

If I could vomit on cue, I would hurl on Demetri's shoes—better yet, a rise of projectile vomiting right in the old man's face for even speaking the idea of Gage meeting his demise. I think everyone in our small circle knows that my husband's death is Demetri's end game, or should I say beginning—but must he be so brazen?

"You mind?" I reach for Tobie, and she lunges into my arms.

"Not at all." Wes offers a painful smile. "You and Ezrina are the only prominent female figures in her life." He steps in, and my heart thumps because he looks so indistinguishably like Gage at the moment. "Thank you, Skyla. I may not say it often enough, but I appreciate you—in that respect."

I don't even let that pointy backward barb he laced it with bother me because I understand where he's coming from.

"In that respect, I appreciate you, too. You're a great dad, Wes." I shrug up at him playfully. "Go figure." I take off with Tobie as if I had just robbed a bank and make a beeline for a small familiar circle of peeps near the shrubbery.

Nat and Kate share a laugh while Pierce—the real deal—wraps his arms around Nat from behind. Both Nat and Kate are dressed as vixens, which is almost a requirement on this haunted night.

"Skyla." Pierce gives an easy smile. "I can't thank you enough for this gift."

"Apparently, thanking me is a theme this evening."

Kate clears her throat. "So, you know?" she whispers her loudest. That's Kate, forever the trooper. Even with her vocal cords out of commission, that girl hasn't complained once.

"Know what?" I blink over to Pierce just as Holden and Serena come up, and for a moment I'm breathless at her beauty. Her snow-white hair is pulled into a bun, and she's dressed as a prima ballerina. Holden is dressed like an unfortunate dumpster diver, and I'm not quite getting the connection, but nevertheless, Serena is a beauty.

"We're going back." Pierce gives Nat a painful glance. "I'm going back."

"Me, too." Kate shrugs over at me. "Your mother came to me in a dream. We have less than a month." She reaches over and picks up my hand, warming it with hers. The silk scarf around her neck quivers in the breeze. "Is there any way you can utilize me? I haven't done a thing to help."

"No. The whole point was for you to enjoy another taste of life—the life I cut short for almost all of you. It's my way of saying I'm sorry. But a month?" I'm panicked at the thought, and I'm not sure why. "Did she happen to say when and how?"

Kate shares a quick look with Pierce. "She said she would let me know the night before."

"Perfect." I look to Pierce with a heavy heart. "Did you enjoy your stay?"

"Yes. *Hell* yes." He tousles Nat's hair, causing it to spring skyward in tight little coils. "I think we needed this. A long goodbye." His gaze falls to hers, and she lunges for him, conjoining themselves at the mouth and stumbling back behind the bushes.

"Don't worry, Messenger." Holden nods to me. "He's shooting blanks."

"Oh, wow." I twist Tobie away from all Kraggers present. "I suppose that's a small mercy. Rumor has it, you're not, though." Marshall told me all about their little nest egg of children, quite literally. I think they had four or five hatchlings at least.

"The kids have been impossible," Serena laments as she looks to the evergreens. "But I think everyone is looking forward to getting back to normal again. Earth is nice, but sky is better."

By "normal" I assume she means feathers. At least they're taking their captivity in stride. I know for a fact, Emerson is a hater of all things aviary these days. Can't say I blame her. I'll feel horrible once she's forced to leave.

Holden drops a kiss over the top of his better half's pale hair. "Feathers suit me, Messenger."

"That's good to hear." Especially since there's not a damn thing I can do about it. "I'll be glad to have you floating around once again. But Chloe is sort of a fixture around me now, so be careful not to get too close when she's within wing-shot."

"Will do." He shakes his head, rife with worry. "Dude, you are going to regret playing in that lava pit. She is going to burn your skin off before you ever realize it's missing."

"She's capable of killing you, Skyla." Serena touches her hand to her neck as if my own head were on the chopping block.

"I'll be fine. Hey, where's Emerson?" I'm racked with guilt over the fact she'll have to turn in that black lipstick of hers for a black beak. Tragically, I see no point in her rotting away in Mia's room for the next hundred years.

"She's here." Holden leans in, his posture suddenly wary. "You know she's banging that dude your sister's dating."

"Gabe? God, I hate Gabriel Armistead!" I hate his sister even more, but I'm loath to even say her name. Both Carson and her airheaded friend, Carly, have been known to appear from thin air once I say their names out loud.

"The other one," Serena corrects. "The bad boy with all the whips and chains and that smelly leather jacket. Believe you me, it'll be the first thing I crap on once I'm back in proper form." She wrinkles her nose at the thought of him.

I suck in a sharp breath, and Tobie jerks along with me. "Crap! Excuse me, I have to find Mia." I take off through the crowd of costumed bodies, through the laughing, the haunting music that people still find enough rhythm in to move to, and search for my sisters, but for the life of me I can't find them—I find the Bitch Squad instead.

"Messenger." Em nods me over where she and her trio of besties are all dressed in the same uniform I happened to don. I can't help but giggle at the sight as I bop on over with Tobie tugging on my hair as if she's attempting to braid it.

Michelle howls with laughter. "West Paragon bitches live to cheer another day!"

Chloe scowls at both the birthday princess and me. "Bree and I still cheer, you idiot." She sheds a dark smile my way. "Thanks to you, my *liege*."

"And don't you forget it." Tobie squirms uncomfortably at the sight of her mother, and I set her down a moment. "Chloe." I point down to the pint-sized princess. "We've got a future West cheerleader right here, and it happens to be her birthday."

"God, don't remind me." She shivers. "My junk still hurts from evicting her."

"*Chloe.*" I pick Tobie up and take a step toward her mother. "At least wish her a happy birthday."

Chloe bares her fangs a moment before snapping her teeth at the little one, and Tobie starts in on a wailing cry.

Em takes her from my arms. "Don't be such a shit, Chloe. Even *you* have a mother that loves you."

Michelle snorts. "Come on, we all knew Chloe wouldn't be up for mother of the year. Serpent of the year maybe." She and Em share a laugh, but Chloe looks as if she's plotting a couple of homicides for later.

Bree hops over in her West Uniform and screams at the sight of us. "I knew it! We got the band back together, girls!" She rings her arm around Chloe's neck, and Tobie laughs and claps as Bree smothers her mother. "Let's put on a little show!"

"I don't know about that." For one, my safety pin is already warping under the strain of my belly. One good flip could render both this skirt and my back useless. Face it, I'm in no condition to jump and thump the way I used to. At least not yet.

Gage comes up with both of our little skunks in tow, and as if on cue, my little white-tailed stinkers extend their arms, cooing a choir of *Mama*! *Mama*!"

"It's the Backseat Boys!" I edge in to collect a couple of sloppy wet kisses, and Tobie intercepts by slapping my face with a hungry kiss of her own. She pulls back those fat little hands still pressed to my cheeks. "Mama!" Her entire face lights up, and the smile quickly dissipates from my face.

"Oh!" I force the smile to come again. My heart just shattered into a million little pieces for this precious baby girl. Life had given her Chloe as a mother, Wesley as a father. As the parent lottery goes, she didn't exactly hit it big in either category. Yes, Wes loves her—but he's still Wes.

"Yes." I nod, my heart and mind loosening to the idea. "*Mama*." I take her tiny hand and place it over my heart, sealing myself to this tiny little being forever.

"Mama," she says it once again, far more docile. Her head rests over my chest as if memorizing the beat of my heart.

"Well, well"—Chloe snarks—"this means war, Messenger." She bursts out laughing, her pearly teeth glittering under the duress of the moon. "*Kidding*! I don't give a rat's ass. In fifteen years, she'll be calling us both bitch."

"Chloe!" I place my hand over Tobie's little ear. Although—if Mia's fifteenth year of life was any indication, Chloe might be right.

Wes comes up and gathers the masses to a large frilly pink confection, and everyone sings "Happy Birthday" while Tobie claps herself silly. Thankfully, Lex catalogs the entire event with that baseball bat lens she carries around.

Logan comes up with Ellis and Giselle, both dressed as condiments, ketchup and mustard bottles—Giselle's idea, no doubt. She's started her freshman year at Host and is living in a dorm on campus—or so Emma thinks. I happen to know that both Ellis and Giselle are shacking up in one of those rodent-infested dumps his father owns. Probably the same scabies-infested ball box Gage and I lived in once upon a haunted time. It was a nightmare. The hellhole of an apartment—not living with Gage, of course.

"You know"—Logan stands between Gage and me, slinking an arm over each of our shoulders—"I do believe this is the first Halloween on Paragon where things haven't fallen to crap."

Instinctually, I glance over my shoulder at Chloe who's working on a cheer routine with Bree.

"I think you're right." Just as I'm about to exhale in peace, I spot Melody Winters making her way toward them at a decent clip. She pulls Chloe out of formation by the

642

elbow as if she were about to scold her and is quick to whisper something into her ear.

Chloe turns slowly until her eyes are locked with mine, hard, serious, angry as all hell.

"What's going on?" Gage follows my gaze, as does Logan.

"I don't know."

Bree jogs over. "Get that smelly monkey off your back, girl. You're coming with me." She plucks Barron from me and dumps him into Logan's arms. "It's time to show these kids that us old girls still got it."

"I don't know who you're calling old, Bree, but it sure as hell isn't me," I say, tripping over my feet, just trying to keep up with her. Nat, Lex, Michelle, and Em all gather around Chloe like chicks to their menacing mama.

"Here we are." Chloe steps up with that familiar I'm-going-to-filet-you-in-your-sleep look in her eye. "Yes, Messenger. How about one more cheer for old times' sake." Those dark eyes of hers pin to mine with venom.

"What's going on?" I whisper as Michelle barks for the crowd to gather around. "What lie did Melody Winters spill at your feet?"

Chloe leans in, and I can see the rage percolating within her like a nuclear holocaust just waiting to find a home. Why do I suddenly suspect that home is me?

Brielle jumps between us, almost landing us into the glowing Caribbean blue water of the swimming pool behind us. "All right! West Paragon class of—" she looks uneasily to Chloe and me, but we're too busy locked in our silent standoff to answer. "Whatever! Hit it, Ellis!"

The music shifts to an old, familiar, dare I say reliable beat that my hips swayed to what felt like a million times while I screamed my heart out for Logan and Gage, and

Ellis, too, for the entire West Paragon football team as they brought us victory after victory.

My body snaps and shakes to those familiar moves as we gyrate, scream, and shout to the delight of the boys, some of the girls, too. But it's Logan and Gage my eyes stray to every chance I get, each one holding a precious little button-nosed boy in their arm, and my heart is full of love.

The girls break out into pyramid formation, and I pause. Hell, I think we should all give this ode to genuflection a little post pregnant pause. Let's call a spade a spade. I'm not the butterfly I once was.

Chloe climbs into position and roars, "Get on, Messenger!"

Like a reflex, my body hikes up Em's back and lands my right knee on Chloe's spine and left on Bree's. The crowd goes wild at the sight of this postpartum feat.

Now. Usually our dismount consists of me leaping to the ground with my arms held high like some Olympic hopeful on her way to gold, but at the moment the grass has about all the appeal of a thousand tiny razors pointing up at me with their knife-sharp tongues, and my knees cringe at the impact they're about to absorb. I'd rather not find my kneecap floating near my femur later this evening. But Chloe and Bree apparently have other plans as they send me flying backward into the powder blue water that looks about as welcoming as an arctic glacier.

My body breaks the surface like a Volkswagen through a plate-glass window.

COLD! *FREEZING*!

Oh my shit! My fingers twitch to the surface as I sink ever closer to the bottom, and one by one I watch as those old familiar West Paragon uniforms and the girls in them dive in around me like carbonated missiles. Then I see her. Chloe comes at me like the demon I know her to be, pinning my arms and legs with her own as she drives us to the bottom. Her eyes grow wild with rage as she ignites a bubbling scream right in my face.

I know what you've done to me, Skyla. And I will show no mercy.

Dear God, what have I done?

Gage snatches her off me and races me to the surface with a laugh caught in his mouth. My beautiful husband with his dark hair slicked back, those black grease marks under his eyes only accentuate those cobalt spheres I'm obsessed with. Gage's eyes are the only color that seems to exist on this haunted horrid night.

"Damn, you're hot." His dimples go off as he lands a heated kiss over my lips. "Let's get the hell out of here," he whispers into my ear. "This football player has a cheerleader he needs to score a touchdown with."

"Sounds like you're about to make all of my jersey chasing dreams come true." My chest bucks as I struggle to catch my breath, but it's Chloe my eyes are glued to.

She slithers out of the pool like a serpent and takes off into the night, dripping with water, dripping with revenge.

What the hell have I done now?

Dear God, I don't think I want to know.

I let my body sink below the surface once again, feel the air turning into bubbles in my ears. I'm frightened. I've been frightened nonstop ever since I've set foot on this island.

Welcome to Paragon.

Every day is Halloween, indeed.

November comes with a tidal wave of blessings just out of reach, and it becomes painfully clear what I've done to deserve Chloe Bishop's wrath.

"*Shit*," my mother hisses as Chloe's face stains that oversized television screen Drake has stuffed into the room as an ode to his financial empire he and Bree built.

My heart thumps once as I switch the television off. My mother doesn't let the expletives fly for nothing, but even she is shocked to hell concerning the fate of Chloe Bishop.

"How does something like this happen?" she laments as Gage and I finish feeding the boys. "Anyway"—she shakes Chloe and all of her bad juju off with a shiver—"happy birthday, Skyla." She plants one on me. "And happy birthday to you, too, young man!" She strips off Nathan's sock and does her best to gobble up his tiny toes.

"Careful there. He's just about ready to take off on those cute little puppies." I wipe his face clean as his Mee-Maw dots him with a kiss. It never ceases to amaze me that the boys look more and more like Gage Oliver doppelgangers with every passing day. I have no doubt that in just a few short years, the girls will be breaking down the door. Of course, I could never blame them. Gage Oliver is a work of holy glory—totally worthy of a few attempted break-in felonies.

I scan the house with a smile. The balloons are up. Mia and Melissa are still working hard to put the finishing touches on all the decorations both in and out of the house. The party will be small, just family and a few friends, and the cake is homemade, something vegan and organic, a gift from Emily and Ember who helped in the endeavor. She's quite the little chef in training.

Gage cleans up Barron and nods me outside to the patio where the afternoon fog is already settled in the valley of the Landon backyard.

"Happy birthday, beautiful." Gage steals a kiss as the boys squirm between us.

"Let's put them down. We can't carry them forever." I regret the words as soon as they leave my lips. I very much want to carry my boys forever. Barron latches onto my leg and Nathan onto his father's. "Can you believe a year ago they were still safe in my tummy?"

"It was their last few hours of uninterrupted peace." Gage takes a careful step back and leaves Nathan struggling to balance on his own two feet, and I gasp. Carefully, I do the same, and Barron looks up at me as if I've just left him by the side of a cliff, and I feel like crap.

"Don't move," Gage whispers as we watch the boys to see what they'll do next. And they do the unthinkable. Barron throws out his left foot and looks up at Gage as if asking for approval.

"You can do it, big man." Gage does his best to cheer him on. "It's all you." He looks to Nathan who's staring up at him with rapt attention. "You, too."

And just like that, the boys each take a wobbly step at the very same time.

"Oh my goodness!" Mom claps up a storm from behind and sends both boys flat on their bottoms, wailing at the top of their lungs.

Gage lifts a brow my way. "There goes that good time. But we *saw* it. We got to witness our boys' first steps." He leans in and blesses me with that mouth, and I'm suddenly anxious to get him back to bed. Yes, moving to Emma's backfired on us twice in one month, but I gave it my best shot. Once she started in on a dirty diaper rant that spanned three hours—I knew picking up stakes was for the better. And for the record, I did not let my boys sit in their mess. They sort of blew their poopy load once she walked into the room. A coincidence? I think not. But, in my defense, our

ADDISON MOORE

home is just about ready. In fact, I have no clue why we can't move in right now. It looks perfect to me. Lex has helped me furnish it with the overflow from a decorator's warehouse in Seattle, and I now actually have a dream home behind the gates at Paragon Estates. It's too good to be true, and on no level does it feel real. It went from beast to beauty in a single miraculous year. Plus, Gage and I are stronger than ever. Our boys are walking. The love between Gage and me blooms anew each and every day. We really do have it all.

My gaze drifts to my gorgeous husband, and my body cries out for him. Suddenly, it feels like a damn good idea to have a thousand babies with Gage Oliver.

The guests pour out into the yard with Emma and Barron each quick to snap up a grandchild.

Mom drags Tad over and tries desperately to draw the Olivers into polite conversation—an oxymoron in and of itself, considering both Tad and Emma are present.

Tad whacks Barron in the leg with his cane. "Rumor has it, I'm about to dump a couple of freeloaders in less than twenty-four hours! I'm popping the bubbly tonight. Canned beer for everybody! Who's with me?"

Mom is quick to smack him down like an unwanted gnat. "I said it was a *surprise*, Tad Landon! I should take that cane and beat you with it!" Mom is quick to drag Tad off, berating him all the way to the edge of the patio, and for a second I'm fearing she's about to give him a firm shove off.

Emma spins poor baby Barron away from the potential beatdown, not that she wouldn't want to watch. Heck, that might be the most entertaining aspect of the evening, considering I shot down my mother's offer to dress like a pasty-faced demon. It's amazing how many times I had to shout *no clowns* directly in her face before she got the message that she wouldn't be donning copious amounts of red lipstick while she overshot her mouth.

"What's this?" Emma looks from me to Gage as if we had some explaining to do, and he winces.

"I was going to save this for later." He pulls me in with that loving look in his eyes. "Your mom was helping me out with a little surprise."

"That usually doesn't end well." My hands glide down to the seat of his pants, and I cop a feel before moseying right back to his waist. I wasn't kidding when I said Gage looked especially delicious tonight. Dear God, I hope baby number three doesn't make his or her—or God forbid, *their* debut in nine months' time. This boy has my ovaries popping.

Gage sheds that signature grin, and I die in the sweetness of the pure joy he's exuding. "It ends well tonight." He digs his hand into his pocket and emerges with a shiny gold key. "We're spending the night in our own home. Happy birthday, Skyla." His eyes gloss with tears. Gage Oliver is radiating with elation, and right now so am I. "We're going home."

"*Home!*" I clasp my arms over him tight and take in a breath that feels as if I've waited years to inhale. "Oh my God!" I jump up onto him, and he spins me with a laugh. "Gage! I love you." I slip down in his arms until we're face-to-face once again. "This is the third best gift you've ever given me."

He inches back a notch, clearly stymied and perhaps a bit affronted by my claim.

"First, there was you, then our children, and now a house that we get to spend the rest of our lives turning into a home. Life couldn't get any sweeter than this."

His grin widens, and the whole universe gets suctioned into those dimples that I long to worship with my tongue tonight. I'm pretty sure Gage is growing tired of all the tongue baths I've implemented over the years. But I can't help it. Gage is delicious, right down to the very last bite, and tonight I do plan on biting in all the right places.

He glances out toward the woods, and his grin dissipates a moment.

"Hey?" I wave my hand over his eyes, and his attention jolts back to me. "Everything okay?"

His body relaxes beneath me. "Everything is great."

Barron breaks into spontaneous applause, but all Emma has to offer is a scowl as if I've just shit all over her petunias. How is it that my mother-in-law of all people can't seem to stand me?

"Well, your father and I sure didn't move in behind the gates at quite a young age," she starts. It's Emma's new song. Complain and whine about what Skyla and Gage have. "And that beast of a *refrigerator*." She rolls her eyes. Emma has had quite the list of complaints after inspecting my decorator choices. There wasn't a hair of carpet that she couldn't find ten negative things to say something about.

I spot Mom off with Demetri while poor Tad has his head all but dunked in the punch bowl, and I'm thankful for the fruity offense because I'm sure he'd love to play off Emma's poor-me, privileged-you routine. Emma looks to Gage. "Your father and I decided not to install a refrigerator that cost more than a car when we redid our kitchen. It was a practical decision because we knew you'd be off to college soon, and boy were we right. Have you seen the tuition costs at Host?" She narrows her judgmental gaze my way. "Don't act surprised in seventeen years when they're off seeking higher education, and there's not a penny in the pot. I'm warning you tonight. It'll be here before you know it." She smacks her traffic cone orange lips together and shoots her gaze to her son like a skilled sniper. "Are you sure you needed those top-of-the-line appliances? Really? The Wolf range with the red knobs? A double oven at that? Skyla"—

she turns her jealous wrath my way once again, and suddenly I'm feeling moved to shove someone off the patio myself—"when was the last time you even *opened* an oven?"

"This morning when my mother asked me to put Tad's underwear on the top rack." Honest to God, the dryer is on the fritz, and he won't get out of the shower unless my mother warms his tighty whities.

Emma's face grows pale, flaccid, and sickly—a trifecta of agony that usually has the power to shut her down for a few solid minutes.

Although—good God, Emma has a point. If the one and only thing I put into the oven this year was Tad's underwear, we are off to one fucking bad start as far as my culinary skills are concerned.

"But Emily volunteered to give me cooking lessons." I look at Gage with a furious nod as if this totally justified my outrageous choice in kitchen appliances. "Lex says I won't regret a single move I made. In fact, she said our new kitchen is so drop-dead gorgeous she's offered to take pictures of it and submit it to *Paragon Today*. We'll be house famous."

"Sounds like it's bound to happen." Gage beams with pride straight from his pores, and suddenly I wish this party were on its tail end. I have a feeling tonight is about to give our one-night honeymoon a run for its sexed-up money—in our very own home!

Emma chokes. "Well, I think—"

Barron clears his throat and wraps an arm around Emma for a moment in that shut-the-hell-up kind of way. "What Emma is trying to say is, welcome to the neighborhood. You'll be moving in just in time to put up the Christmas lights. The Paragon Estates community takes extra pride in decking the halls. At least the exterior that all can see."

Gage wraps his arms around me from behind. "Challenge accepted." I feel the vibrations of his voice tremble over my back, and I can't help but purr. "Skyla and I will have that house visible from the moon by December first."

"I can't wait." I spin into my beautiful husband's arms. "And I want inflatables, and a thousand of those little signs that say *Santa stops here*, and tinsel on all the evergreens."

"Oh dear!" Emma chortles as if I've just said something ridiculous. "I'm afraid we don't do those kinds of things at the Estates. You'll have to leave all those inflatables and cute little signs—and, my God, *all* of the tinsel here at the Landon house where they belong."

"Where they belong?" My tone is curt, and well, bitchy, but let's face it, she drew first tinsel.

"On that note." Gage points to the small crowd at the base of the patio. "I think we'd better mingle with our guests."

Mia flags me over near the mobile home, and I make a break for my sweet little sister. "What's up?" I give a little hop toward the girl who holds my likeness.

"You're up," she snarls. "When is that little witch going to be shoved back in that disgusting oversized cage I keep in my bedroom?"

I blink at her a moment. It takes a second to register that the little witch in question is Emerson Kragger, and no sooner do I open my mouth to say something on the topic of cages and feathers than the witchy Goth owl herself shows up on the scene.

"What the hell." Emerson grunts with that dead charm only she can exude. Her hair is dyed black as pitch, and her eyes are so drawn in with kohl all you see are two bright blue beacons staring back at you.

"What's going on?" No sooner do I ask the question than I recall the fact that Rev and Emerson have been rumored to be playing hide the Vienna sausage. And, why yes, I did take a moment to swipe at Revelyn Booth's boy parts, but only because I have it on good authority he's dipped said mini wiener into my sister—thus stealing her most prized possession, her virginity.

Emerson gets in Mia's face. "This twerp actually thinks I want anything to do with that wannabe biker with a boner the size of a Chapstick."

"*Ha!*" I bark out a short-lived laugh because Emerson and I happen to be on the same teeny-wienie page.

Mia gives her a hard shove to the chest. "She slept with him!"

Emerson gets in her face. "Only to get him off my back!"

"Whoa." I step in between them. "Mia—clearly they're not together. So please give Emerson some peace on earth"—I turn to the Goth queen with my lashes lowered—"while she's still on it. In this form, anyway."

Emerson bears her pearly white fangs and growls. "You should really consider keeping me around, Messenger. I've got balls, and I know how to use them. Not to mention the fact I'm genuinely on your side, unlike that idiot you entered into a covenant with." She stalks off, and I catch her making a beeline for Pierce and Nat. My stomach goes sour at the thought of Chloe and that covenant.

"What's she talking about?" Mia shakes it off as if she wasn't all that concerned.

"Never you mind. Just stay away from Rev. I'm sorry you had to see his true cheatin' heart colors shining through."

Mia rolls her eyes as if the thought were absurd. "It's not cheating if we have an open relationship."

My mouth contorts into all shapes and sizes, but not a word evicts itself. For all the times I've been accused of having one of those very same things, it makes my skin crawl to think Mia is partaking willingly in such a ridiculous arrangement.

"Oh, save it," she snips as she glares at someone coming up from behind. "I learned from the best." She stalks off, and Gage lands by my side.

"Everything okay?"

"Right as acid rain."

"Come on, we've got guests." He leads us straight to Laken and Coop, and I pull her into a tight rocking hug because God knows I need one after that bitch-fest only Emma can provide.

They both wish me a happy birthday, and I'm quick to wave it off. "This day isn't about me anymore. It's all about Nathan—and Barron. I think from now on we'll just have two parties back-to-back and celebrate both boys." True as God. There used to be so much anticipation and excitement around my birthday and Gage's, too, but this year it feels as if our birthdays were the least important news on the planet.

"Sounds good." Coop nods Gage over to the side, and they start talking shop. Gage has been helping Coop with West's football team on and off since last summer, and they've just closed out the season.

"Skyla." Laken shakes her head and pulls me in by the elbow. "Are you freaking out over this whole Chloe mess?"

A bundle of fear knots up in my gut. "No." I wince. "Okay, I'm lying." Nearly a month ago, the night that Chloe submerged me in deep waters for old times' sake—we found out that Chloe had risen to the top of just about every most wanted list—for questioning by the CIA. Nevertheless, over the last few weeks, her face has been popping up like unwanted blemishes all over the island in poster form—cited as a suspicious person. Hell, the peeps on Paragon have known that from the moment she was born. Well, thankfully, Ezrina looks so different she isn't in any danger. That little angel of hers, Alice, needs her mama to stay out of any and every federal holding facility. But Chloe, my God, the feds have amped up the search for her. She's been on the national news, all over the Internet, and in every grocery store rag you can think of. You'd think she had robbed the world vault of all its gold the way they're laying the heat on her.

"I've told her to lay low," I whisper as I glance to the evergreens skirting the property. "I even offered to send her back to the Transfer, but she hates the Kres and Wes dynamic duo so much she'd rather fry in a thousand electric chairs than listen to their primal grunting. Chloe's words, not mine." Laken's features soften, and I gasp at the realization of what I've done. "*I'm sorry,*" I mouth.

"No, God no, don't apologize. She's been sort of a godsend. And honestly, she's one of the reasons we didn't kill him—but mostly it was Tobie. Anyway, there's been a new plan in action for months, and Coop and I will be implementing it soon—and before you ask—it's nothing I want to talk about on your birthday. So don't even try to wrangle it out of me." She sinks her forehead into her palm. "I can't believe I actually contemplated the murder of another human being." She shakes it off. "I wasn't actually going to go through with it, but my God, it felt good to plan it out to the very last detail."

"Don't I know it!" Bree pops her head over Laken's shoulder. "I totally felt that way about you—but I'm ready and willing to bury the hatchet." She wraps the crook of her elbow around my neck and nearly decapitates me. "Go ahead and apologize, and we'll start from scratch."

You can hear the copious amounts of air getting sucked into Laken's lungs.

"*Brielle.*" I untangle myself from her stranglehold. "You can't be serious. Laken has done nothing to apologize over."

Laken combs her fingers through her long caramel waves as if she were readying to pull every last one out in frustration. "Actually, I do owe you an apology." She offers a stiff smile at my self-proclaimed bestie's way. "You and I never really got off on the right foot. I sort of barreled onto Paragon and snatched your best friend away from you without giving it another thought. It was inconsiderate of me."

"Damn straight, it was." Bree is quick to glom on to Laken's line of thinking.

"And for that I'm sorry." Her shoulders compress with the uncalled for mea culpa. "Let's start over. Hi, I'm Laken Flanders. I happened to have married my best friend in the whole wide world. I can see that Skyla is yours," she says it sweetly enough, and yet her hand hangs there an unordinary amount of time without any reciprocal love.

"I see what you did there," Bree squeezes the words out nice and slow. "Well, it just so happens that *I* married *my* best friend—*twice!*" Her eyes twitch over the circumference of the yard. "In fact, I'm going to jump him right freaking now and prove it." She bolts off in the direction of the mobile home.

"Never mind her." I dismiss Bree and her antics with a wave. "Guess who is going to spend the night in her new house for the very first time tonight?"

"I'd say me, but considering the fact Coop and I are still in the rental phase of our existence—oh my God, Skyla!" She wraps her arms around me and sways the both of us to the rhythm of her squeals. "That is fantastic!" She pulls back with tears glittering in her eyes. "Coop and I are so very happy for you guys."

"Thank you. And I know it's genuine." I pause and give her hand a quick squeeze. "And I know it's not easy—considering the fact my husband's face looks more than slightly familiar to you."

She gives an anxious look just past me, and I turn to find Gage chatting with Wes while Tobie toddles around his legs.

"Trust me, I know the difference between Gage and Wes." Her voice grows soft. "The funny thing is, all those years ago in Cider Plains, there really wasn't much of one. Gage's personality is sort of the before to Wesley's after." We watch as Demetri heads over and completes their circle, and my blood runs cold with an ironic thought. "What if Gage is the before and Wes is the after—as in Gage's afterlife?" I shake the thought loose. "Gage would never behave like Wes, dead or alive. Leave it to my errant thoughts to kill off Gage right before his birthday."

Laken and I share a nervous laugh. "At least have the decency to kill him once he's had his cake."

"Amen to that," a cool voice hums from behind, and we spin to find America's most wanted right here in the Landon backyard.

"Chloe." I reach out to embrace her, and she holds up her hands as if I were about to shove a viper in her face.

"That's okay, Skyla." Those dark eyes of hers zero in on mine, filled with venom, brimming with hate. "We don't have to pretend anymore. It was so damn exhausting parading around like freaking unicorns with their butts welded together by a rainbow. I don't live in Bree's little bestie la-la land, so let's just call a spade a spade. I've always hated you." She scowls at Laken. "What the hell are you staring at?"

Laken lets out a tired sigh, and a white plume escapes her nostrils, alerting me to the fact we should probably move this party inside. "I think I like this side of you, Chloe. It's honest and raw, and brutal around the edges the way God intended you to be. Don't put on a mask around people—you're the only one who'll be confused."

Bree pops up with an unwilling Drake just as Chloe is readying to knife Laken's lady balls off.

"You know"—Chloe wraps an arm around Laken's shoulders, lithe and smooth like a tiger readying for the kill—"I think I like you, too. Maybe *you* can be my new *bestie*." She says that last word with all the sarcastic inflection only Chloe can afford.

"What's this?" Brielle staggers back as if she were sucker punched, and Drake makes a run for it while he can. "First, you infiltrate Skyla, then you call out my man, and now you tackle the Bishop?"

"The Bishop?" Both Chloe and I say in unison before glowering at one another a moment.

Brielle scoffs at the thought. "Well, you can forget it. Skyla, Drake, and Chloe, they all belong to me, so you can just walk your pretty little self back to Tennessee or wherever the hell you're from and take that smart-aleck attitude with you."

Laken's lips twitch as if she's holding back a laugh. "I'm from Kansas. And trust me, a part of me wishes I can rewind each day all the way to the time of my death—and before that, just so I could start all over again. But I can't." Her tone sharpens as do her features. Bree is in for it now, and I completely think she deserves it on some level. "And you know what? I happen to like the way things turned out for me. I have a wonderful friend in Skyla, a gorgeous sweet, smart, funny husband"—Coop comes up from behind and wraps his arms around her, showing off that handsome as hell smile—"and as for Chloe and me?" She looks to Chloe, puzzled as to what might come next. "We're still feeling things out. And you know why? Because I have a heart for the disenfranchised. I happen to care about people. Unlike you, Brielle, I welcome them. I care about how they feel, and I want to make them comfortable. It's called being a decent human being."

Brielle chokes on her words, and Laken holds up a finger as if to stop her from even trying.

"Furthermore, I'm not going to abandon any friendships because of your insecurities. In the event you haven't noticed, none of us are in high school anymore. Both Skyla and Chloe can have more than one best friend. Skyla and Chloe can both be *my* best friends." Coop shoots me a look as if to ask *what the hell?* "And simultaneously they can be *your* best friends, too. You and I can be friends if we took the time to water a relationship and watch it grow. All it takes is a little careful attention. But to get to the starting gate, we need to be civil to one another, let down our guard, stop accusing one another of snatching people out from under us, and be as amicable as possible. It's not rocket science. It's just common sense."

The fog blows in thick between us as if celebrating Laken's victory.

Just as I'm about to congratulate Laken on a speech well done, Brielle starts in on her chicken bone in the throat routine once again.

She looks to me, wild-eyed. "Are you just going to sit there and let her tell me off like that?"

"Brielle?" I shake my head, completely at a loss for words. "Yes, I am."

She sucks in a breath, and half the fog around her dissipates. "And you?" She gapes at Chloe.

"Get over it, Johnson. Grow a pair, will you? Laken has balls. Maybe you can learn a thing or two from her. She's open to being decent to you. Who the hell cares if she's having coffee or sleeping with Skyla? I sure don't, and you want to know why? Because I know my place in Skyla's life. I know that no matter who she's 'besties' with"—Chloe shoves her fang-like air quotes in Bree's face—"and God, I hate that word. Don't fucking use it around me, got it? Nevertheless, Skyla and I are solid in our dissatisfaction with one another. And I know that some things will never change. Hear that? Skyla and I are unchanging. So if you're as close to her as you think you are—feel secure in knowing that no matter how many morons she's lifting pinkies with, there's always room for one more—and that would be you." Chloe straightens, staring down her oldest friend, and Bree nods as if this entire bestie fiasco suddenly made sense to her.

"I get it. You're a genius now, Chloe, aren't you?" Bree gives a couple of doll-like blinks, and for a moment I'm frightened. I've known Brielle to be a lot of things, but sarcastic isn't one of them. I'm getting the feeling I should intercept, and quickly.

"Since we're doling out life lessons so freely tonight"—I pull a tight smile in Chloe's direction—"why don't you take a brief moment and say hello to your daughter, and maybe even have Lex snap a few pictures of the two of you?" Lexy is around somewhere doing just that—documenting the boys' first birthday party.

Chloe tips her head back and laughs so sharp and loud, Gage and Logan glance over from their conversation with Ellis.

"Skyla—my darling little Skyla." She shakes her head. Her lids hang low, and there's a note of despondency I've never seen before. Chloe on a good day is dangerous, but Chloe knocked off her axis and desperate is an entirely other animal. "Wouldn't that just solve all my problems? A little snuggle-fest that Bakova could add to her bloated portfolio."

Emily, Nat, and Kate head over with caution.

"Don't you judge me," she snaps in their direction. "None of your lives turned out that great either. Kate—you are *dead*. Read up on the definition and figure out a way to stop breathing. It's confusing the hell out of people, and nobody can understand whatever the fuck you're trying to say." She steps in close to their tightknit circle. "Em, you're miserable, and we both know it. The only solace you have is in the kitchen. Wake up and stop chasing a man who isn't even halfway interested in you. You're smart, and you kick ass in everything you do. Get your own place, open your own damn kitchen, and give the Gas Lab some competition on this island." She glowers over at Nat just as Michelle walks up with an uncertain gait with Lexy not far behind. "Nat, you're fucking a dead guy. Need I say more? When his coffin closes one last time—and it will—go find yourself a decent person who treats you like a queen. Stop cutting guys off at the balls without giving them a chance just because they're not Pierce. It's going to be a long life. You might as well enjoy it." She steps into Michelle, and a shit-eating grin gobbles up her face. Michelle, however, looks as if she's about to have her ass handed to her, and she undoubtedly is. "And *Shelly*. Still secretly pining for her Dudley—still carrying around that hard-on for Logan. Well, you've done well for yourself, haven't you? You've got Liam Love 'Em and Leave 'Em Oliver diving down your panties night after night—munching you out after smoking one of those big, fat blunts gifted to him by Ellis. Tell him to shit or get off your lap. You're not some tramp who's going to please him until his dick makes up its mind." She darts a look near the fire pit and scowls at Liam—we all do. That big, fat blunt revelation is a new one for me. I'll have to make a note to talk to my favorite stoner about who he can and can't distribute to. All Olivers are off the reefer list, and that especially includes Giselle.

"And you"—Chloe turns to Lexy—"you think you're hot stuff with your business off the ground and running—Logan Oliver eating out of your hand." Thank God she chose to avoid any disgusting euphemisms about Logan having the munchies for anything Lex might be stashing in her panties, namely her pink parts. "You're too hopped up on how wonderful you are—you can't even see he's trying to *avoid* you! You don't have his heart. He won't gift you his body, and you will never be his anything." Chloe turns her wrath my way, and poor Lex looks as if she's been bitch-slapped. Okay, so I feel a tiny bit of satisfaction, but it's less than a molecule in size. "And sweet little Messenger. Our angel of salvation, the chosen one to lead the Factions *nowhere*. Aren't you a sight for *no eyes*. Whoever the hell appointed you for anything was drunk on their own power. The only thing you managed to save was your virginity for your wedding night, and for inquiring minds that was with *Logan*." The crowd around me gasps, and it's only then I note we have an audience that spans outside of the Bitch Squad, Laken, and Coop. Logan, Gage, Wes, Ellis, and Marshall, not to mention Liam—Paragon's newly minted pothead, plus, Drake and Ethan. Here we go. Let the good times roll. I'll let her say her peace, then walk her to the woods and banish her somewhere because I just so happen to wield the power to do it.

"Skyla"—her voice breaks, and it stuns me—"you did it. You bested me." A visible lump rises in her throat, and she swallows it down. "You caught me off-guard and fed me to the lions—just like you said you wouldn't. You know what they say, a covenant made is a covenant broken." A dull laugh comes from her, and yet my heart plummets. But my

God, I did not break our covenant. I'm fighting for it. Still am. "I have to hand it to you—you acted just like I would have." Her eyes gloss over, and she looks dazed as if I had thumped her over the head with a spirit sword. "You tied a noose of lies around my neck and left me to hang. And here I am." She takes a staggering step back. "The day your mother banished me, I had lost all hope." The word *hope* sounds like nothing more than a pop. "And the day you pulled me free— made promises to me that night by the fire—I felt as though life's red carpet had rolled out for me once again. I thought she came through for me. Skyla, my nemesis, wants something with me. I can be of use to her. We can rally together and save the fucking world." She grunts as if the thought made her want to vomit. "And now here we are. You in the throes of celebration. The high time of your life. And me, far worse off than I was that night in the Transfer. At least then I could set foot on this planet without having to take the fall for bullshit you were responsible for to begin with. You got me!" she shouts those last words with her arms stretched wide, a wicked smile brewing on her lips. "You did it, Skyla. You outsmarted me at last!" She laughs, and her whole body convulses. "And you should celebrate. This is your day. Dear Skyla"—she purrs as she takes a step backward—"happy fucking birthday. Your gift will be a little late, but you'll undoubtedly know it's from me. Just know it wasn't my idea entirely. After all, I'm not nearly as bright as you are." She turns and glides through the murky evening fog, making a beeline for Demetri. Chloe wraps her arms around his neck and slaps him with a kiss, so long, so hard it makes my mother gasp sharp and loud. Chloe pushes him away with a shove and darts into the woods, and I do the only thing I can think of—I dart right after her.

"Chloe, wait!" I speed into the neck of the forest and scream her name until my throat rubs raw. "I want to help you! We are *bound*. We are one! Please! Let me help you. I'll send you to the Transfer! You'll be safe. I'll keep you safe just the way I promised." My voice tires from yelling as I come to rest upon the pale shoulder of a birch. "I'll send you wherever you want to go."

"*Hey*." Gage comes up, breathless, and lands a warm hand over my shoulder. "It's okay." He wraps his arms around me, and the tears come. All of them are for Chloe Bishop. In a lot of ways, Chloe really is my dark twin, my shadowed reflection in a broken mirror. For as much as we're different, we have that much in common. "Your mother just pulled out the cake. Let's focus on the boys for now." He pulls back and offers an anemic smile. "Let's focus on you, too. Don't let this ruin your special day. We'll figure something out for Chloe after the dust settles tomorrow night. Her troubles aren't going away anytime soon, but today and tomorrow are fleeting. Our boys only get one first birthday." He gently lifts my chin. "And you only get one per year, too."

"Thankfully." I wipe my face clean and let the fog kiss my slicked cheeks as the two of us make our way back. Drake has his boom box going, and Ellis and Giselle are engaged in some sort of dance-off. Mom and Emma are bouncing the boys on their hips, and the mood is once again jovial.

Dr. Oliver steps up and garners the crowd's attention.

"Before we sing, I just wanted to say how proud I am of Skyla and Gage for being the best parents little Nathan and Barron could ask for. You've both come so far—as people and a couple. I'm proud and honored to have the two of you raising my precious grandchildren. And to Nathan and Barron, may God give you the strength to live a life in search of His will, with a hungry heart full of love and integrity. I know you'll both go far in this wonderful world. Happy birthday, boys. And happy birthday, Skyla and Gage."

The crowd roars to life, and Mia leads us into a rather cantankerous version of "Happy Birthday". And before we're through, I pick up Barron, and Gage takes Nathan in his arms. We lead them to two blue candles and help blow them out. It's a familiar scene, Gage and I blowing out candles simultaneously, but now it's infinitely better. The two of us with our sweet baby boys, our own flesh and blood knit from our love. The four of us cheer and huddle as Gage wraps his strong arms around us. And I have never felt so whole, so complete, perfect, and so well-loved. Our little family is bliss. This is heaven. With all my heart, I wish Sage could have been here to celebrate with us.

That night, after an exhausting battle to feed and change the boys, we pack up any and everything we can into the minivan. I hug my mother, my sisters, Em, and Bree as Gage and I drive off to the Estates to our forever home that we renovated with love.

We pull into the driveway that Liam cobbled together with ivory-colored paver stones, and admire the landscaping Logan pitched in for—a line of pepper trees sway their soft feather-like branches as if waving us in. A row of gerbera daisies in every color brighten the world as the porch light shines down on them with a warm peachy glow. The boys are asleep in their seats, already in their PJs—thankfully, the nursery upstairs is well-equipped to greet them. And thanks to modern technology, Gage turned the heater on through an app on his phone before we ever left the Landon house so we will be warm as toast as soon as our feet walk through the door—that beautiful oversized *red* door that I love so much. The outside of the structure was completely redone. Gone are the haunted eyes, the dilapidated everything, and in its place a white, perfectly framed box with upper French doors and railings, and just above that a gorgeous round window gifting moonlight into the attic.

"Come on." Gage taps me gently on the knee. "Just you and me."

We head out, and I race him up the porch with a laugh caught in my throat.

"Oh no, you don't." He scoops me into his arms and opens the door. "Skyla"—Gage looks down into my eyes with a softness that only true love can bring—"I couldn't let Logan outdo me." He winces. "I had Lex come by this afternoon and paint something around the frame just for you."

"You did!" I give his chest a light scratch as I look up and spy the elegant navy font that creates a banner over the doorframe.

"It says *Always and forever, you will be mine. You have all of my heart. Our love is eternal.*"

"Wow," I marvel as a dull laugh aches in my chest. "Gage Oliver!" I sniff back tears, trying to stave them off for just one more moment. "I could not have said it better myself." I reach up and wipe a tear from my husband's eye and he smiles, those honeyed dimples digging in just for me. "You are my everything. Right now, always, and forever, you will be mine. You have all of my heart. Our love *is* eternal." I pull him in, and his mouth crashes over mine with a kiss that is sweet and indulgent. Gage walks us over the threshold to our official new home, on this, the official first night we will spend in it together.

We work diligently getting the boys to their beds, the smell of the fresh new carpet enlivens the air in their room, and it energizes me. Gage and I speed to our new bedroom—

a cavernous space with a bed the size of a swimming pool, a bathroom the size of our last bedroom, and a glorious walk-in closet that I will never have enough clothes to fill.

"There's one more thing," Gage says, reeling me in by the waist. That pained smile reprises itself on his face as he winces. "There's also one other area I couldn't let Logan top me—but, in my defense, it was my idea to begin with. Come on." He grabs me by the hand, and I'm breathless as I follow him into the hall. Gage carefully pulls down a set of hideaway stairs that lead to the attic.

"You first." He helps me up, and I climb into the waiting black hole. The small round window near the top lets in a hint of moonlight, but it's not until I land inside do I note the glass has been covered with a curtain.

"Is this my escape hatch in the event the boys try to tie me up?"

"Nope." He hops up beside me, and the lights blink on. "It's your new butterfly room."

A breath gets locked in my throat. A brilliant cobalt glow permeates the expansive space, and covering every last square inch of the walls are enormous bright blue butterflies.

"Oh my God." I make my way to my feet and spin in a slow circle as I take in the ethereal scene. Butterflies as big as my hands flap their wings against the wall as they ever so slowly wake to life. One by one they pick up that strange glowing hue that I have only ever seen in Gage Oliver's eyes. "They're so beautiful."

Gage appears beside me, his arms around my waist as we melt into a slow soft dance. "You are beautiful. Happy birthday, Skyla. To the first of many in our new home."

My arms lock around his neck, and I can't take my eyes off this gorgeous man that God saw fit to gift me. No, it wasn't my mother. It wasn't Demetri. Gage Oliver is truly a gift from the Master Himself.

Gage looks silently into my eyes, a heavy sigh escaping his chest, and in a burst of light the room explodes with hundreds of butterflies fluttering freely all around us. Sweet music plays in the background as Gage orchestrates a night to remember for the ages.

He blinks us back to our bedroom, the butterflies right along with us as they offer their glowing splendor in lieu of light.

"I think we've died and gone to heaven," I whisper, pulling him onto the bed by his shirt and forcibly making him lie on top of me.

Gage hikes up on his elbows, those eyes of his brightening the room all on their own.

"We made it, Skyla." His lips collapse to mine, and we share a heated kiss filled with promise that tastes like forever.

"The best part?" I say, stripping him clean of his clothes, and he struggles to do the same for me. "You and I get to do this night after glorious night."

"That is the best part." He steals a string of kisses down my neck. "You know what's a close second? Not one sign of Tad Landon roaming the halls in his underwear."

"Whatever you say, *Greg*." I give a little wink, and we share a quiet laugh while getting down to the very serious business of us.

Those magical butterflies fill the room with a soft cobalt glow, enough to highlight the best parts of Gage Oliver's body, which just so happens to be every single detail. And I make sure to lash every square inch of him with my tongue just as I promised myself I would—a birthday gift to myself. My lips make love to Gage thoroughly before my body ever has the chance. Gage and I bathe one another with our mouths, stroking, licking, memorizing our bodies as if this were the very first time. Our limbs entwine over one another as we indulge in the feast of the ages. Gage and I set fire to the sheets, and the walls erupt in flames as we pay homage to our love, as we partake in primal necessary worship. Gage pins my wrists to the bed, his body landing over mine with his chest bucking in and out in a fit of lust.

"You know how I feel right now?" His breath sears over my face like a scorching wind.

"Like you want to fuck me?" It takes all I have not to break out into a smile, but my stomach quivers with the laugh anyway.

He winces. Gage Oliver looks so damn gorgeous with every expression he makes, but that humble maneuver always manages to make my insides squeeze tight.

"That, too." He dots my lips with a wet one. "I feel like my whole life, *our* lives have built up to this moment. I feel like a man, Skyla. Like I can take care of my wife and children the way I wish I could have from the beginning."

"A man, huh?" I bite down over my lip as I reach down and give that rock-hard ass of his a squeeze. "Prove it."

Gage growls as those dimples ignite over me. "I'm about to prove it to you all night long. Happy birthday, Skyla."

"It's midnight." I pull his lips over mine and whisper, "Happy birthday, Gage Oliver. I love you so much. Here's to forever."

"Forever." Gage plunges into my body as I wrap my legs around his back, and we get lost in making one another's wishes come true.

And we make them come true more than once, just the way he promised.

669

I've made concessions before—hell, I've made more than my fair share of outright blunders. I've made big ones, too, but a part of me wonders if agreeing to let Demetri host part deux of the boys' special day is the biggest mistake of them all. That unnatural disaster at his estate last December still haunts me. Although, given the fact Gage has since crossed over to the dark side—really, what else is there to lose?

Gage and I stare long and hard at the package my mother dropped off this afternoon. The only thing we were told was that the event would be *formal*. Gage is wearing his best suit, complete with a black bow tie. Marshall brought me a gown, which might as well be made of chainmail. It's that heavy. It's reminiscent of that haunted couture he loved to robe me in all those years ago, and here he's brought me another. Of course, I had to ask what special properties this haunted couture would provide, and he assured me the only superpower it held was to showcase my beauty. This gown is strapless, easily accessible as he so cavalierly pointed out while ogling my boobs. But the dress is gorgeous, a full-length deep blue brocade with pewter undertones. It's a sacred hue and sets off my husband's eyes like a blue flame.

The boys look dapper, and a bit silly, in their matching miniature tuxedos. My mother said she looked high and low for these dashing little monkey suits and had to have them altered twice. And even though I smell Demetri's credit card at the end of this gilded rainbow, I realize it was all done in love to please my mother first, then the boys. This entire extravagant night is an ode to Nathan and Barron, and that is something I can definitely get behind.

Gage pulls the lid off the gold box my mother instructed that we not open until we hit Demetri's driveway. Nestled inside sit two gorgeous masks, a black satin covering for Gage, no larger than the circumference around his eyes, and an ornate rhinestone beauty for me that affords me a heavy almond shape, like a pair of sexy cat's eyes.

"Masquerade!" I gasp as I dig in and pull the mask on. "What do you think?"

Gage moans as if he were ready to take a bite out of me and my thighs quiver, because last night, and well into this morning, Gage Oliver took bite after scrumptious bite of every last inch of me. "I don't know who you are, but why don't we hook up before my wife comes back?"

"Ha-ha"—I pull the mask down an inch—"I'm not laughing."

"You should." He places the mask over his face and kisses me softly. "It's a good look on you."

"The laugh or the mask?" I ask as we pick up the boys and the over bloated diaper bag.

"Both." He bounces Barron over his hip. "You ready to rock this party, boys? I hear there are some hot chicks just waiting to check you out."

Nathan gurgles out one of his signature husky laughs and claps up a storm, but Barron looks perturbed by the idea. Gage and I share a laugh of our own as we head on in.

Demetri's monstrosity of a home is grand in nature all on its own, but on a night like tonight, where all the stops have been pulled, there's something regal about it the likes of which Paragon have never seen before. I can hear the music pouring out from every orifice the overgrown house has to offer, and it's merry and light, and my God, is that a full orchestra I hear?

A man in a white curly wig and odd revolutionary sort of garb nods as he opens the door and lets us inside. Something about him gives off that old-world appeal, and he looks straight out of the seventeenth century, and well, he just might be. The foyer opens up, cavernous and breathtaking, with its crystal chandelier the size of a mid-sized sedan glittering far more than usual. The lights are dimmed just enough to display the bodies milling in the distance, rife with laughter, but that's not all that has my eyes set wide with surprise.

"Oh God, they're here," I hiss to Gage as an entire herd of vellum creatures—translucent once-upon-a-people—swirl about, laughing and chatting away a mile a minute in their full petticoats, the gentlemen in their rag tag suits, with their bow ties as thin as spaghetti. None of them seem to mind too much that we can see the walls right through their bodies as they float around like a slippery film, more of an idea than a human concept.

"Cool," Gage says it flat. "Looks like Gramps pulled a few ghosts out of his closet."

"Skeletons to follow."

Gage leads us to the grand room, and a body blocks our path before we can enter.

"Ingram!" I can't help but brighten at the sight of my favorite curator of Tenebrous—the only curator, but still. "Nice to see you out and about!" I offer an impromptu hug. He looks dapper himself with his hair slicked back, a neat tuxedo, and his face looks a touch less pasty out in this cobalt light. The entire grand room is bathed in blue.

"Excellent to see you, my love. And you"—he nods to Gage. "And, of course, the guests of honor." He smiles at both boys in turn. "If you don't mind, I'll introduce you now." Ingram turns to the sea of people, all in glittering gowns and black tuxes. You'd think this were prom and not the culmination of a year's worth of easy living for the boys. He motions to someone near the back as the crowd parts down the never-ending room, and the volume on the music turns down a notch. "Introducing Mr. and Mrs. Gage Oliver. Master Nathan and Master Barron."

The room erupts in cheers as a multitude of voices cry out at once.

Ingram lifts a hand. "Let the masquerade ball begin!" He leans in and motions to the diaper bag. "If I may."

"Be my guest." I'm quick to discard the twenty pounds of designer luggage.

The orchestra picks up again as Gage leads the boys and me through the neatly parted sea. About halfway through, the crowd collapses around us with my mother and Demetri quick to pluck the boys from our hands. My mother in her red dress with matching face garb and Demetri in a tux, his mask made of black scales—because he's a snake like that.

My mother lowers her feathered mask a moment, and I can't help but note she's donned that Dominique Winters' inspired mole once again over her left cheek. "Isn't this fabulous?"

"It's something, all right."

Demetri widens his grin and nods in my direction. "This splendid celebration would have been impossible without the two of you, of course."

Mom chortles herself straight into a Demetri-gasm over the quasi-inappropriate innuendo.

Mom holds out Nathan's hand and begins dancing with him as her cleavage ripples out of her low-cut gown. "It's beautiful, Demetri! How can we ever, *ever* repay you?"

Dear Lord, flaunt your boobs at him one more time and I'm sure he'll think of a way.

You can practically hear his dark laughter over the music. "Try as you might, you've done so much for me already." He gives a sly wink.

Yeah, like gifting him an illegitimate child. My mother's gratitude knows no vaginal bounds.

Mom sneers into him with a rather flirtatious toothy grin, her red-hot mask only adding fuel to the lusty fire. "You do know me, don't you? Rest assured, I will try my hardest!"

Rest assured I will be puking on Demetri's limestone flooring if this drags on one more two-timing minute.

Tad waddles up with a blue glowing cocktail in his hand, his mask slung over his forehead as if he's given up on both the party and on life—and oddly his mask bears a striking resemblance to donkey ears. Go figure.

"Jumping Jehoshaphat!" Tad whoops, and Gage slips his arm around my waist as if readying to protect me in the event he malfunctions. And, knowing how badly Demetri wants to bed my mother, Tad should very much be on the lookout for something far more nefarious than a simple malfunction. "Demeet—we're five minutes of eleven, you and I."

Gage and I grimace at the exact same time. I lean in and whisper, "*Demeet?*"

"Five minutes of eleven?" Gage shakes his head. "They're not friends. They're not even close."

Demetri barks out a demonic laugh. "Yes, Thaddaeus Thorne Landon, my good dear fellow. We are all of that and more. And my, what a lovely bride you have. You must be quite smitten. How did you ever agree to let her out of your bedroom this evening?"

Gage rubs my back, his lips trying their hardest to hold back a smile. I can tell he enjoys Tad getting his comeuppance even if it is at the hands of his cruel father.

"A man's gotta open the barn door sometime and let the old mare out into pasture." He claps his hand over Mom's shoulder in the event there was any confusion as to who the old mare in question was.

Tad flicks his thumbs under his jacket, revealing a pair of rainbow-striped suspenders. Figures. Tad's superpower is dumbing down just about any outfit. I'm surprised my mother lets *him* out of the house.

Mom plasters a forced grin to her face and shakes her head at the offense while Nathan does his best to pick her nose. "He's teasing. Tad worships the ground I walk on, let alone the things he does to me in the bedroom. We've quite the action-packed boudoir!"

Oh my living God. Is Lizbeth Landon trying to incite *Demeet* the dapper demon into an unholy jealous rage? And why the hell am I standing here listening to this salacious nonsense?

Tad balks at my mother's claims before downing the rest of the electric blue concoction in his hand. "Too *much* action if you ask me!"

Holy hell!

Demetri's mouth contours, and you can see his eyes turning twelve shades of boiling rage. Tad is going to miss that fire he walked into that brought him a year's worth of misery once Demetri is through with him. I have a feeling this masquerade is about to turn murderous.

I glance to the mouth of the entry and note a dark shadow lingering, jettisoning out of my line of vision before I can adjust my eyes to light, and a mean shiver runs through me.

Tad makes an effort to extract the very last drop of his drink. "It's all those rugrats she's amassed, running around underfoot, slamming those caskets around the floor like they were castanets. A man can't sleep in an environment like that. It's not natural. Sometimes I wish I could unplug the old noggin just to get a solid eight."

I'm sure Demetri can arrange for Tad's noggin to remain unplugged for far longer than a solid eight. If I didn't know better, I think I smell a coma on the horizon.

Gage gives my hand a squeeze. *You think Tad is stepping in line for a dirt nap?*

I glance up, and we share a quiet laugh. Normally, I love it that Gage and I are so in tune, but given the circumstances, I think we should be frightened for Thaddaeus Thorne Landon.

Demetri gleams under the blue pox he's cast upon this place. "Lizbeth and the children are always welcome to stay here. Anything to provide respite for my dearest, most treasured friend."

Mom gloms on quickly to the slumber party invite just as the Olivers head this way, Emma in her orange veil of a mask and Dr. O looking every bit the distinguished gentleman with his simple black mask. "Oh, I would love a staycation at Casa Edinger! I bet the beds are extra comfy." She gives Demetri a slight poke in the ribs, and they share a private laugh because everyone but Tad knows they've tested out the mattress springs on more than one occasion.

"Good evening!" Demetri bows to both Emma and Barron, and false niceties are shared all around.

Barron gifts both Gage and me a hug while Emma offers only her son a hearty embrace.

"Skyla," she says my name as if it were perfunctory.

"Emma." I try not to sound sarcastic, but I can't help it. Emma has mastered the art of turning even something as splendid as my boys' very first birthday party into a crap-fest. Kate had it right. She *is* trouble with a capital T.

I give the crowd a quick sweep for my quiet blonde friend. She promised me she'd let me in on why Emma scares the resurrected daylights out of her just before she was whisked away to the great beyond once again. And I have a feeling that good time is ready to come to an end.

Demetri nods to Emma. "Tad and Lizbeth were just apprising us of their robust love life."

Emma's mouth falls open, and as much as I like the idea that something other than me has gotten under craw, I can't bear another moment of the Lizbeth-Tad-Demetri porno playing out.

"I can't watch anymore." I pull Gage to the side just as the music picks up to fantastic orchestral heights.

Gage cranes his neck past my shoulder, his mouth set in stone as if something were pulling him out of the moment.

The crowd swirls around us, and soon enough I'm lost and separated from my gorgeous mask-bearing husband.

I turn to look for him in a panic, but it's wall-to-wall bodies, and soon I'm pressed against an all too familiar rock-hard chest. He's tall and achingly gorgeous even with that sleek silver mask covering the norther half of his comely features.

"Ms. Messenger." He wraps an arm around my waist, the other leading me by the hand into a slow waltz.

"Marshall Dudley, you slay in a tuxedo. I think every ovary in the room just exploded in your honor."

"Ah, if only it were reserved to this simple evening." He pulls back a notch to inspect me. "My, my—you have a way with blue. It brings out the amorous affection you hold for me in your eyes."

I bubble with laughter. "Forever the clown. You were one from the beginning you know." Literally. But that's another story.

Those crimson cauldrons of his narrow in on me. "Your mother is here to see you."

"The one flirting shamelessly with Demetri while trying to hustle a room in this dungeon of depravity? Or the celestial thorn in my side that offered me a child and dissolved her to nothing more than a memory?"

Marshall wrinkles his forehead as if he were in pain. "My love. The latter. And do refrain from calling her anything but *Your Grace* upon your meeting. There is a season for all things, Skyla, and this is a season to humble yourself before the celestial great. She's brought her cohorts along for the ride."

"The entire Decision Council?" I give the room a quick once-over, but with those blue floodlights Demetri insists on pummeling us with and the sea of luxurious dresses whirling and twirling, the Transfer transplants partying like it was 1699—it's sort of hard to determine who's who.

"That's right, Skyla." His chest bucks with his next breath, and I can tell even Marshall is impressed as hell over this. "The crème de la crème of celestial society has descended on Paragon for the night."

"Really? My God. This is bigger than the boys' christening. Who knew a year in the life of two little earthlings was cause for such a celestial uproar?"

Marshall's eyes flit to the exit. "There are others." His tone drops down to its lower, far more threatening register, and every hormone in my body riots all at once.

"Others?" I make a face in the general direction of where Demetri and my mother argue over which bedroom they'll copulate in next. "Yes, well, this is the demon's dance. No poltergeist prom is worth its salt if the dark side isn't represented. I'm sure it's all for show. Demetri is eager to parade the boys around to just about anybody—and, well, the Fems and all their dark glory are just about anybody."

Marshall growls, his gaze still fixed on the exit. "Don't you worry your pretty little head about that." His eyes narrow as if he were threatening somebody. "I'm sure whatever it is he's doing here doesn't concern death."

"Who is *he*?" A chill runs up my spine because I'm not so sure I want to know.

"The Grim Reaper." Marshall sheds a stunning grin my way as if the concept in general were laughable. "He and your father-in-law have always been thick as celestial thieves. You're right. Not to worry. This is a night for grand displays, and Demetri is making the grandest of them all."

"Grim Reaper?" I bite down so hard on my bottom lip I swear I taste blood. "God, what if the gift he's about to give the boys is death!"

Marshall growls, "Open your mouth so I can bite your pretty little tongue off." His cheek rises on one side, and I can practically smell the lewd intent. "Something tells me your boys will survive much more than just this night."

Marshall dances us to the exit, then straight out of the grand room and down through the hall that leads to the back exit. We head outside, and the sight of Demetri's park-like yard takes my breath away. A spray of stars hovers unnaturally low over the entire circumference of the party, offering a pale lavender glow. Rows and rows of trees adorn the outline of the festivities with ornate globes on them in shapes and colors I have never seen before. A man dressed in a white robe plucks a blue pear-shaped fruit off a branch and takes a bite right out of it.

"What is this?" I whisper as Marshall leads us down the stairs.

"It seems the heavenlies brought a little bit of home along for the ride. Creature comforts if you will." He reaches up and plucks a red star-shaped bulb from a tree and hands it to me.

"So they brought the stars *and* their own farmers' market. Interesting. That won't arouse suspicion at all.

Thank God those Spectators filled a much-needed paranormal void."

"Did they?" Marshall frowns into the crowd. "Or did they simply whet their appetite for the many variety of beings they can imprison and torment."

A horrible dark feeling clamps over me because I've never celebrated the fact the Spectators were taken. I hate what Wes had done to them, and now I hate what *I've* done to them.

A tall raven-haired girl in a silver gown comes up with her hair pulled back, her blue eyes outlined heavily in black kohl, and her lips set scarlet.

"Emerson Kragger." I make a face as she lunges for me. She's unmasked because, well, it's obvious Emerson doesn't play games.

"I can't go back, Skyla. Your mom's here, and she's wigging out—herding us all together so she can give us the old heave ho, and you can't let her take me. I don't want to be a stupid owl, and for damn sure I don't want to be *dead*. Can't you just tell her to chill out?"

Giselle comes up breathless behind her, equally stunning, but that look of sheer panic on her face distracts momentarily from her beauty. Unlike her counterpart, Giselle is sporting a rather adorable pink feathered mask that sits neatly over her nose.

"Don't you dare let her stay!" Giselle smacks Emerson until she takes a few steps back. "She's after my *Ellis*. She's been trying to stick her tongue down his pants ever since the day she arrived, and just now I caught her trying to kiss him!"

I groan at the thought of either scenario. "I think the euphemism you were going for is tongue down his throat. And Emerson? Really?" I turn to her in disappointment.

"What?" she growls. "Ellis is hot. Plus, he's been my supplier for years. We sort of bonded over the many ways Chloe screwed us over. Him literally and me, well, she's the reason I'm bound to featherdom to begin with. Where is the little slut?" She cuts a dead look around.

"Never mind," I scold. "I can't control who my mother plucks into the great beyond. Trust me, I'd have a couple more children if I could." Just the thought of Sage and Angel rips my heart out all over again.

Marshall lands a warm hand over my back. "Perhaps you have not because you ask not. It seems the woman of the hour is upon us." He nods straight ahead as my mother lights up the night like a firebrand. Her glowing hair, her luminescent face and body defuse the darkness in a soft halogen haze. She lifts the brilliant white mask from her face a moment as if to assure me of her presence.

Emerson grips me by the arm. "Don't let her do it, Skyla." Her speech is pressured. Her nails dig into my flesh. "Beg for my life. You won't regret it. I promise!"

"Skyla, darling," my mother trills as she opens her arms momentarily. I've heard of air kisses, but I think my mother just invented the air hug. "Such a grand delight. When Demetri invited the celestial gentry to the Bastard's Ball, we did hesitate to come. But it's all worked out for the greater good."

"Excuse me? Did you say *Bastard's* Ball?" I shake my head, incredulous. "I've put up with a lot of things, but having my children disrespected so greatly and on their birthday. No, I'm not having any of it."

"Gage is the bastard." She cups my cheek, and that beautiful strumming sensation streams right down to my toes. "Of course, you already knew that. You're married to the—"

"I get it." Wow, just when I had a smidge of respect for Demetri, he reminds me of why I hate him so. How dare he! And on *Gage's* birthday! "So, I hear you're taking the dead to their final resting places tonight." I glint to the crowd in search of Kate. If she's about to be snatched from reality, I need to be sure to solve that Emma mystery before she trots off and leaves me hanging with the anemic info I already know.

Emerson hits bone with those claws she's molesting me with.

My mother glowers at Emerson a moment, and her grip relents. "Our precious Pierce and that Kate girl you killed are the only two I'll be returning to paradise this evening." I give a few rapid blinks at the thought of Pierce as *precious.*

"Technically, I landed them both there to begin with." I give a little odd curtsey and immediately feel like an ass. "Anyway, Holden and Serena are excited to get their plume on—but Emerson here"—I make a face at the Kragger currently cutting off the blood supply to my left arm—"she sort of wants to stick around. I mean, I know that it would totally be putting you out and that—"

"Sure." My mother claps her hands, and a pink fog surrounds them momentarily.

"*Sure?*" both Emerson and I balk in unison.

"Yes, I'll simply take Giselle back with me tonight. We can't have two Emerson Kraggers running around on the island forever."

"*No!*" both Giselle and I scream in unison. I'd shout *jinx!* but this entire night is starting to feel like it's exactly that, jinxed.

"Goodness, make up your mind." My mother narrows her gaze my way. "Which is it you want?"

"Both."

"Both." She tosses Marshall a look that could slice his balls off before twitching into a sly smile. "I suppose I could grant you one wish on, this, the day after your own birthday." Her teeth graze her bottom lip, and her eyes sparkle with a certain kind of venom. I've seen that look before on my own face, and she's up to no good. "How about you either spare these two featherheads from the great beyond—or anyone else of your own choosing? Your girls are off-limits. So is anyone in a Treble. You'll have until midnight to decide."

"My father." And just like that, I've thrown both of the featherheads next to me under the sarcophagus bus and into a squawking tizzy.

Candace offers a tired smile as if she feels pity for me, and she's simultaneously had it with me at the same time. "He's raising Sage, Skyla. He can't be bothered."

"Then I want these two." I knew my father wouldn't do it, and for exactly that reason, but hey, a girl has got to try. Although, I feel copious amounts of guilt over risking Giselle's second life at the moment.

"Skyla." Marshall comes shy of winking. "Perhaps you should tarry till the deadline."

"No. I'm emphatic about it. Giselle and Emerson live. I'm thrilled with my decision." Besides, I know my mother. This is just another mind game she threw in at the last second because she can't seem to come right out and say yes to me.

"Yes to you," she muses. "Emerson, behave." She turns to Giselle. "And you. I did not return you from paradise only to have you turn your brain cells into a hallucinogenic playground. Be mindful of what you do. Actions bear consequences."

"That they do." Marshall looks to the woods with that angry suspicious gaze of his. I bet it's the Grim Reaper slinking off in disappointment because he lost one of his prospects for the night.

My mother lifts a finger at someone in this sea of celestial socialites, and I stop her before she takes off. "Can I talk to you for a minute?" I pull her to the side, away from prying ears. "I sort of had a brainstorm the other day. When you get around to doing that whole hocus-pocus thing, would you mind taking them to Raven's Eye first? Maybe catch the attention of a guard or two before zapping Pierce and Kate off the planet? Oh, I know! Make sure Kate's head rolls off first! Better yet, leave the bodies behind and let them evaporate slowly—that will totally set them on edge." Brilliant, if I do say so myself.

"No." She frowns in direct rebuttal to my enthusiasm. "It will lead them back to the Kraggers. Is that what you want? And haven't the Winstons been through enough?"

"Totally." I shake the thought out of my head. "But Holden and Serena could simply fly away." Raven's Eye and Host are just a stone's throw if they wanted to stop off somewhere quasi-exotic for the night. That is if you consider a college town exotic. Face it, the only things exotic about Host are the sexually transmitted diseases it breeds.

She gives a slow blink as if my genius is trying her patience. "I'll consider it."

"Good. One more thing. That seventeenth-century tramp that's haunting this island? Why don't you spring her and her demonic mother back, too? Better yet, send them to Raven's Eye! I mean, what's the point of allowing them to breach contract with the ages and show up on Paragon after all these years?"

"What is the point, indeed?" She leans in. "That's for you to figure out. What they believe they're doing here is an entire other nefarious matter. Do keep tabs on those ninnies." She takes up my hand and runs her finger over the blue stone that once belonged to the throne of God. "Keep an eye on this as well." She reaches over and runs a finger along my bare neck. "Is the Eye of Refuse of no use to you, Skyla?" Her lips twitch like a threat. "Wear it in good health. You'll need it."

"I didn't think it went with the dress."

"Death lurks in the shadows, hungry for souls. Don't feed the machine, Skyla." She gives a little wink and laughs as if she very much planned on feeding the machine.

A familiar face pops up over her shoulder. "Is this a private party?"

"Daddy!" I lunge past her and latch onto him, taking in a full hearty embrace from the man I love with everything in me. I pull back and land my hands over his sturdy shoulders. He's donned the requisite tux and his mask is flipped up over his forehead Tad Landon style, and that alone is about all Tad and my father will ever have in common—outside of my mother, of course, and I promise you that Tad doesn't have half the affection my mother felt for my father. "Where's Sage? Is she here?"

He cuts a quiet glance to my mother. "I'm afraid the powers that be decided it would be too much for you."

"It wouldn't. It would have been a pleasure—a treasure." I wince at the thought of my daughter. "How is her...disposition? Does she seem okay to you?"

He grimaces because he knows exactly what the hell I'm talking about. "She's mentoring under your mother."

"I've a position I'm grooming her for in the League," my mother snaps, and I don't dare ask which league. It had better not be the Assholes League.

"*Skyla!*" she barks.

"Well, it better not be!" I bark right back.

My father shakes his head. "Don't you worry. I have that baby girl of yours wrapped in my love. She'll be a model citizen before you know it."

"And my other baby girl? *Angel*?" I shake my head, unsure if he's even met her.

"Yes"—his voice grows alarmingly quiet—"I know who you speak of, Skyla." But that's all he says about that, and my heart shatters at what that might mean.

"Daddy!" Mia screams as she trots on over in sky-high heels. Her little black dress looks more like a one-piece bathing suit than it does an evening gown appropriate for the Bastard's Ball as it were. "Oh my God, I miss you!" She wraps her arms around him and swings him in a circle. "God, so many things have happened to me this year!" She holds out her left hand, only to display a scrappy piece of wire entwined around her ring finger. "Does this ring make me look *engaged*?"

"What?" both my father and I cry out at the same time.

Mia bares her fangs my way. "Oh, shut up, *you*. I've about had it with all your judgments about my love life." She smacks my father a kiss on the cheek before darting into the woods. "Gotta run! I'm late for a date with my betrothed!"

"Wait!" I cry after her. "You can't get married! I forbid it!" What the hell is she thinking? "And that ring doesn't make you look engaged, *Mia*!" I scream after her. "It makes you look like you displaced the twist tie for the wheat bread!" And don't even get me started on the fact the twist tie for the wheat bread is exactly what Drake saw fit to bejewel Brielle's finger with once upon a poverty-stricken time.

My father groans at the void she left in her wake. "Promise me you'll look after her extra hard during these teenage years. How I wish I could be there for her."

"I wish you could be here for her as well—to snap the neck of whoever saw fit to gift her that miniature tourniquet."

"Come, come"—my mother gathers my father into her arms and pulls him into the crowd—"we'll seek you out later, my love. The time of the Bastard won't last forever!"

"Geez." I take a step back and practically land in Marshall's arms. "I hate that Mia has lost her virginity *and* her mind. At least Emerson gets a reprieve."

"Skyla." He closes his eyes a moment. "You do realize it's never as it seems with that woman." A round of lightning flickers above. "Your Grace," he says just past my shoulder.

I turn around and spot a white flame of hair running this way, Kate Winston—and I catch her in an embrace as tears buck from the both of us. Here it is, our final earthly farewell.

"Thank you for coming back," I whisper into her ear. "I'm sorry I took you off the planet to begin with."

"It was fate." She pulls back and takes me in as if she's memorizing my features, and she might be. I'm memorizing hers. "Here's a letter. It tells you everything you want to know about you-know-who." She hands me a thin blue envelope just as Pierce comes up behind her. Wow, Kate is so creeped out by Emma she won't even use her name.

"It's that time again." Pierce slaps me five before pulling me into an embrace. "Thank you. My brother and Serena told me they should be back at your window later tonight."

"You might want to tell them I moved." I bite down on a smile. "It was nice having you back. I hope you enjoyed your stay."

"Hell yes, I did. But heaven is best, and it happens to be where I belong." He shoots me with his finger. "No Kragger jokes. You hear me?"

Kate and I share a little laugh.

"I suppose you're proof we are all redeemable," I say.

"That we are, Skyla." He pulls me into another hug. "Try to remember that."

I share another quick embrace with Kate and watch as they disappear into the woods. "It's show time." I wave the envelope at Marshall.

"Do tell." He leans in as my fingers work quickly to open it, and we're greeted with the happy, loopy swirls of Kate Winston's handwriting.

Skyla,

Forgive me for the length of time it took me to pen this. Truthfully, I was afraid to share it sooner. There are things happening here on earth that have been whispered in the heavenlies—but more so they are whispered on earth as well, and that's where I gleaned this information to begin with. Back in junior year, a few days before we took off to go on that fated ski trip, I went shopping with my mother. I headed off on my own in search of the perfect ski pants (to match my jacket!) and I saw Emma Oliver there speaking with another woman—one I didn't recognize. What I'm about to tell you, I learned in partial that day at the store while accidentally listening in on a conversation I wish I never heard. The rest I gleaned in heaven. As I drew closer, Emma discovered me. I've known Emma all my life, but I had never seen the wickedness in her eyes like I did that day. Later on, I would find out she was one of the only people who secretly cheered my death. In her heart, she thinks that killing me was the only thing you did right.

What I heard Emma discuss that day was about Gage. This, Skyla, is how your husband came to be. Emma wanted to have power, to have control over not only her world, but the entire world. She knew Demetri was a powerful Fem. She sought him out and wanted to be with him for power, not love, but he outright rejected her. When she realized she couldn't have him, she renewed her relationship with Barron, but not before leaving her mark. Demetri confided to her that he needed a child to meet his purposes, and Emma's gift to Demetri was Gage. She wanted to be an instrument of benevolent importance. She wanted her child to be something special. Emma knew that she was putting the Factions in peril, but according to celestial rumors, they have never been important to her to begin with. There's something else, something that she doesn't want another soul on the planet to know. Emma believes that once her son is in power, she will be, too. However, she doesn't realize what it's going to take to get him there.

Anyway, that's all I know. It must be strange hearing all this from me, a human through and through, but you're my friend, Skyla. And that's what friends do. They help one another out.

Emma is trouble. She always has been. She always will be. Her objective is to see Gage rise to be a great ruler. Her interest has always been in power—just not yours.

Love always,

Kate

"Wow." I can hardly breathe, let alone take it all in. "Emma really is trouble." Truthfully, I've known it deep down in my bones—but only after I got together with Gage. "It all makes sense now. She adored me when I was with Logan, but for whatever reason saw me as a threat once Gage and I got together."

"A threat, indeed. You are inherently his enemy."

"No, I'm just hers."

"Nevertheless." Marshall extends his elbow, and I'm quick to hook my arm through it. "It's time to parade my bride past the royal gentry."

"There's no time like the present." I slip Kate's letter back into the envelope and shove the whole thing down the front of my dress until the parchment warms across my ribs. There's no way I'd risk losing it—here of all places. For tonight, I'm going to do my best to set it and its contents out of my mind. I'm sure I'll scrutinize it once again come morning.

Marshall takes us through a thick crowd of glorious beings, all too shining and beautiful to ever be real or human for that matter. We hit the end of the line and I spot Dominique Winters carousing with someone who looks suspiciously like Marlena, and I gasp once I see those familiar features.

"I completely forgot to mention that debacle with Chloe to my mother. I'm sure there's something she can do."

"She can, but I'm afraid she won't. Or perhaps I should rephrase it. She already did."

"You mean?" I suck in another lungful of Paragon prime fog. "My mother set Chloe up?"

His brows rise above his mask a moment. "Let's just say that certain celestial beings may have colluded to procure a certain desired outcome—each for their own benefit."

"Wow." Just the thought makes me lightheaded. "Is it at all possible that the CIA discovered her on their own? I mean, she was everywhere at once, reporting all sorts of asinine things that just so happened to pan out." Chloe is right. I put her in harm's way without realizing it.

"I suppose anything is possible."

"Speaking of possibilities—" Logan steps between us, breathless, with his teeth gleaming under the duress of starlight, and he wastes no time in wrapping his arms around me. He's shockingly gorgeous with that bright white mask that gives off an ethereal vibe as if it weren't made of anything more than an illuminated mist. "I believe we haven't shared a single dance." He edges Marshall out of the way. "Dudley." He whisks me away from the wary Sector. "I was given strict orders by Candace Messenger to two-step with her beautiful daughter, and I would be remiss to disobey."

A laugh trembles from my chest. "The last thing I would want is for you to be on Candace Messenger's naughty list. You're liable to have your head chopped off."

He gives a subtle wink. "Chloe beat her to it."

"That she did." I cringe because I dread what I'm about to say next. "I really want to help Chloe."

"I know." He leans in and bumps his nose to mine. "That's because you're a sweet soul."

"And I made a covenant with her."

"And that." He averts his eyes to the woods. "I'll help you."

"You will?" My spirit soars at the thought, and yet I can't seem to digest the irony.

"Yes. I thought about the terms of your union with her, and I think it's brilliant. Keep her to the hip, gain her trust, use the shit out of her." His grip over me intensifies. "Above all, be careful. She's dangerous."

"And she's pissed."

"And she's pissed." He shakes his head. "But I don't want to talk about Chloe anymore. You look amazing. As soon as you stepped into that room tonight, you took my breath away." His voice strains as if he were aching. "I am jealous for you."

My heart flops when he says it. "You are so special to me, Logan. You know I love you." My voice is lost in the faintest whisper.

His lips rise at the tips. "And—I am so thrilled for you and Gage. You did it. You're finally in your own home."

"It only took a year of renovations."

"It was the right time," he adds. "Things always seem to happen when they're supposed to." His chest fills solid with his next breath. "And that leads me to our baby girl."

I shake my head, my lips pressed white because I can't do this.

"We have to." He gives my hand a squeeze. "Skyla, we have to come to terms with the fact that those few months may be all we will ever have with her." His lips turn down hard as if he's fighting back tears of his own.

"I know." My gaze fixates on the purple blooms dangling from a tree in the distance. "She was ours for a very short time. We may not even have eternity with her. She was a mind game, Logan. She was a very sophisticated form of manipulation that my mother heartlessly employed." I glance skyward like a habit and wait for the thunder, but there is no celestial threat. "Maybe she will exist. Maybe she won't. But my heart, my devotion, it all belongs to—"

Logan presses a finger over my lips and nods.

"So does mine, Skyla. I am in total agreement with you."

He might be, but he couldn't bear to hear my husband's name.

"I get it." The words come from me in a broken whisper. "Life just doesn't relent, does it? The good book says we go from strength to strength until we end up before the throne of God, and yet it feels like fire to fire."

"Fire to fire." He gives a single nod. "You said it, Skyla." He relaxes his body to mine. "Angel came into our life like a comet, sweeping in and stealing hearts. I'd like to do something to commemorate her. A plaque, a charity, a donation. Anything."

"How about the bowling alley? It's opening in a few weeks. The gym, too. Maybe we can dedicate the grounds to her?"

"*Yes.*" He plants a kiss right over my lips, and my stomach tenses at that soft familiar feel. How I've missed Logan's kisses. "You are brilliant." His cheeks twitch with what appears to be remorse. "Sorry about that. It's sort of a reflex. Plus, I couldn't resist." He takes a deep breath. "Have I mentioned how gorgeous you are? Let's find that oaf you're married to before I get myself into any more trouble."

"Deal." I wrap my arm around him, and we make our way through the crowd. We finally come upon Gage speaking with Cooper by the fountain—fountain of youth knowing my nefarious father-in-law.

"Hey, handsome." My arms float effortlessly to my beloved. "What's going on?" I can't help but note the two of them look deep in thought, both of their masks clutched in their hands.

Coop blows a breath toward the crowd. "I can't find Laken. I guess I'm paranoid after what happened at Raven's Eye."

"Totally understandable, but she's safe now," I'm quick to comfort him. "The only reason they took her was because Angel's powers were misfiring." I still feel bad about that.

"Laken took the blame." Coop loses his gaze deep in the forest. "They think it was Laken."

"What?" A little detail my friend managed to keep from me. I turn to Gage in a panic. "What if they took her?"

Logan steps in. "She's probably in the restroom or lost in the crowd busy looking for you." He nods to Coop. "Let's comb this place. I'll help you find her."

"Thanks, man." Coop and Logan take off, and it's just Gage Oliver and me under the spray of a thousand freshly manufactured stars.

"May I?" Gage holds out a hand, and I take him up on the offer.

"Of course. It would be my honor to dance with the birthday boy."

The dimple in his left cheek depresses as he places the mask back on his face. "I hear I'm the official birthday bastard."

"Ugh. Sorry." I frown over at Demetri's monstrous home as if it were the devil himself. "They're wrong, though. You're the birthday *blessing*. And you've been exactly that in my life—and the boys. You are a blessing to me, Gage Oliver, through and through." I lay my head over my husband's enormous chest and listen to the steady thumping of his golden heart, tried and true as our love, steadfast and everlasting. Gage and I had sailed an entire ocean of drama and trauma over the years we've known one another, and here we are, still standing, still fastened in one another's arms. Our love is so present, so pure and true it hurts a little to ponder it. Demetri set a flaming sword in our path, and Gage and I traversed it with ease and grace. No matter what my mother, his father, might be plotting—Gage and I cannot be extracted from one another's lives. We have the boys now, an eternal bond. We have a covenant between us and God—a triune pact, indestructible for as long as we have breath in our lungs. Our love burns bright and deep, a spiritual flame that can never be extinguished, not by the hand of any person on earth or in heaven, not by any force of nature, not by angels, not by dragons. Gage and I have woven our souls together, caged in our hearts, protecting them from the cruel duties outlined by a fate we never really believed in. There is no prophecy, no stone, no heavenly council that could sever our paths. We are moving in a single trajectory, riding the back of an arrow that is unstoppable from reaching the finish line. Our love shines in the light, it hangs steady in the shadows, it crests the highest mountain, sinks to the depths of the stormy seas. We are impenetrable to the forces of darkness, immovable to the transgressions of fate. Destiny may not have planned for us, but it can count on us for damn sure. Gage and I will never give up, never give in, never yield to the mighty hand of our adversaries. Destiny may say we are bronze at best, but our hearts know we are gold.

I pull back and look into those eyes that have captivated me from the beginning.

"Kiss me," I whisper over his lips.

And he does just that. Gage Oliver kisses me with his entire being. He pours his soul sweetly into mine, and I drink him down like a sacred elixir. Gage and his love heal me.

I bring my hands to the face that I love and hold him like that, precious, anxious to have him, in admiration of the man he has become. Right here, in this celestial congregation, I worship him—the dragon, the dreamer, my beautiful husband.

With this kiss, we are ringing a bell. We are demanding that destiny and fate look in our direction and get used to what they see. We will right them. We will never bend to their will.

With this kiss, we are claiming our forever.

Gage

My wife.

Skyla molds her body to mine, and I bury my face in her hair a moment. There have been many things I have craved, wanted, desired, but none as strong as my yearning for this girl right here. I remember those early hazy days of West Paragon High when she wasn't mine at all but someone else's. Then she became mine as a ruse, a means to protect the love she had with Logan. Slowly, her love for me awakened. I'd like to think somewhere, deep inside, that it was always there. Long before Logan ever perished, Skyla and I were together. I think maybe if we weren't, if she had never looked me in the eye and said she loved me until the terrible time of his death, our love would never have fully flourished the way it has. But then we married, became one in body and spirit, and the rest as they say is history. My entire existence was orchestrated to fall in love with this woman. It was my father's business, the culmination of his life's work to unify the two of us in flesh and in blood in hopes to create the perfect being. And we did. Two of them. And here we are a year later, stronger than steel, drawn to one another like a flame to oxygen. Logan had erected himself as an obstruction without meaning to. We loved one another when we shouldn't have, and now under the banner of our covenant, we love one another thoroughly as we should. We were the sinners, and we were the saints. Skyla and I were born of deceit. The world believed in us long before we ever did. And yet, here we are, knit to one another like the stars in the sky, like the sun and the moon that Logan tries to own. He can never own what we have. This is imperishable. And as much as my father needed me with Skyla, his burden to seal us at the seams evaporated once the boys were born. And then, there is her mother, the celestial grand supreme. I am less than the dirt under my shoe in her eyes—nothing more than a sperm donor that provided life to her grandchildren. I have no pull with my all-powerful mother-in-law. She would no sooner give me a sideways glance than she would come to my aid. I am the obstacle to her desire. And there is nothing she desires more than to have Skyla and Logan together at last. There will be a celestial choir howling on that day. I have no doubt. And I have no doubt she is working very damn hard to make that day a reality very, very soon.

It's also a disheartening feeling to know that my father is through with me—in this form, in my coat of flesh, with the blood still pumping through my body. It's a disheartening feeling to know that my mother-in-law, the neck of destiny, the head of fate, finds me useless in my union to her daughter. It's a disheartening feeling to know that no matter what that smooth stone predicted—my number will most likely be up sooner than expected. Once we crested July, the seventh month, we knew it could only mean one thing. I was destined to have seven more years with Skyla. Of course, Skyla, ever the optimist, is clinging to the belief it's decades, but there's not a shred of hope in me for that. There are simply some things you know, and I have always known that I would die young. It's never been something I've disputed or until recently, lamented.

A shadow flirts at the edge of the pines, and my gut grinds at the sight. He's been here all night, lurking, leering, watching me from a sacred distance. And just like that, he steps out of the shadows and across the field, through the bodies of those on the dance floor, through the merry ghosts that came all the way from the Transfer. And all the while he watches me. His illuminated gaze never leaves mine.

"Whoa." Skyla pulls back, her blonde mane rising like that of a lion. "Everything okay?"

"Are you kidding? This is our night. Our babies are one. *We* are one, and soon we will take off to the one and only home I ever want to set foot in."

A gritty laugh brews in her chest. "I like where you're going with that. Hey, maybe now that the dust has settled in our world, you can finally get around to writing that novel you've been tinkering with."

"That's the plan." I twirl her in my arms and seal the landing with a kiss. "But first, I plan on tinkering with you, over and over and over again." I dot a string of kisses along her neck and soak up the vibrations from her laugh. The scent of vanilla pours from her, and I take it in like a balm. Skyla has always been just that, a healing balm.

"You are a naughty, naughty boy, Mr. Oliver." Her hands lie flat over my chest as she tips her face to the moon, her laughter growing with each passing breath. How I love to see her laugh—to see her smile. There isn't anything I wouldn't do to invoke that very reaction in her. "I've got an idea." Her tongue does a quick revolution over her lips, and my balls ache, hungry to have her. "How about you and I steal away for a minute—somewhere private, secluded." Her arms circle around my neck as she draws me in. "Someplace where a girl can lift her skirt—maybe let the girls out for some air?"

"I think you've got me beat in the naughty department." I lean in and crash my mouth over hers, suctioning her tongue into my mouth and catching it with my teeth. I pull back and grin at my beautiful bride. "You've got a date." I rub my growing hard-on over her stomach. "You've just started a war I hope you're ready to finish."

Her brow lifts over her glittering mask. I'll admit, I'm a sucker for this sexed-up vixen version of my wife. I've had a hard-on brewing the second she put on that dress. Hell, I always have a hard-on brewing for Skyla. Always did. Some things remain unchanging, and that just so happens to be one of them.

"For your information, there happens to be a very real war brewing in my underpants as well. Let's hope *you* are ready to take it home, Oliver." She stabs her finger over my heart, and I feel the sting long after she removes it. "Now, kiss me." She tips her head to the side with all of the innocence she can afford. "Kiss me as if it were your last night on earth because that's exactly how I'm going to kiss you."

Skyla waits to close her eyes until the very last second, and I pour out all of my love into those pale eyes of hers. I tell her I love her far more efficiently and deeper than I ever could with words. And finally, with my lips, I do the same. Skyla explodes into my mouth like a nuclear warhead, anxious and hot, and I meet her right there. If this were my last night on earth, I wouldn't hesitate to take her right here in the midst of the crowd. I wouldn't waste a moment. I couldn't. As horrifically crude as it sounds, it would be a thing of beauty.

I make love to Skyla's mouth, turning the earth beneath our feet into holy ground, turning the stars shining down over us into a halo of blessed light.

"Skyla!" a familiar voice calls from a distance, and I don't need to look over to know it's Brielle. "Get a room, you two!"

Skyla and I pull away reluctantly to find our bubbly friend with her hair freshly dyed a bright caustic shade of red—and on Bree it works.

"Skyla, you have to help"—she grabs ahold of my wife's shoulders as if she's about to shake her—"Lexy is tanked, and she's dry-humping Liam in the woods. Michelle is going to kill her!"

Skyla makes a face. "I'm going to kill Liam." *Sorry*, she mouths over to me. "I'll find you, and we'll finish that war we started!" she shouts as Brielle drags her off to the side of the house.

"I'm looking forward to it! *Skyla*"—I cup my hands around my mouth as I try to shout over the music—"I love you!"

Her laughter rises to the sky. "Love you, too, Gage Oliver! *Forever*!"

And just like that, the night swallows her whole.

My body aches at the sight of the void in her wake, and my dick twitches as my hard-on struggles to subside.

"Perfect," I mutter as I head back toward the house. I may as well help Coop find Laken, if he hasn't already.

I jog up to the house and thread my way through the bodies congesting the entry. I sidestep into the kitchen, and just as I'm ready to pull my phone from my pocket, a pair of arms comes at me and shove me hard against the wall.

"*Shit*." I meet up with the angry eyes of Zander Richards, and I launch at him. I twist my hands into his shirt and thrash the shit out of him against the refrigerator, and a neat dent sinks in where his head just gave a dramatic bounce. "What the fuck do you think you're doing?"

"What the fuck do you think *you're* doing?" He kicks my foot out from under me and lands a solid fist in my jaw. His face is screwed up tight like a bulldog, and saliva runs down his beard.

"Shit!" I dab my lip for blood, but come up clean, and he shoves me to the wall once again.

"Listen, *Daddy's Boy*. You think the Videns give a shit about you? We can't stand that obnoxious look on your face. You broke your promise to your people. And now your people are getting ready to break a few promises themselves." His lips curve at the edges like a pair of pale worms. "You took our family and damned them to hell."

"Wes took them." I shake my head, pissed. "Scratch that—he didn't take them. They fucking *volunteered*!" I riot those last words right in his dirty face.

"They didn't volunteer for *that*!" he roars back. "That's your problem, Prince of Shit—or is it King? Both are laughable." He takes a staggering step back. "You don't get it. You're too removed. I guarantee if those were your sons— your brothers, you would be hauling ass to free them, to get them back to their rightful form. Dude, the Videns don't need you." He shakes his head as he slips into the murky shadows. "Be on guard. Be afraid. I'm going to make your every nightmare come true."

He takes off, and I'm left alone, the threat still hanging in the air like a sickle. The throngs of Videns come to mind. Young men, boys, all of them so ready to help Wes with whatever the hell scheme he dreamed up. Not one of them realizing they would be sacrificing everything. Zander is wrong. The Videns do need me. They need me to protect them against my brother.

I set out in a rush to find my lookalike, but the lights are too low, the bodies too thick. It will be a miracle if I ever see Skyla again, let alone Wes.

"My son!"

I turn to find Demetri's smile eroding on his face at the base of the stairwell. "Come." He curls his fingers my way as he starts upstairs, and without reservation I follow him. I want answers, and Demetri's got them by the truck full. What better night to start talking than, on this, the sacred night of his bastard's birth.

"Where to?" I stride alongside him as we head down the elongated familiar halls. I made this haunt my home for a time, a time I no longer wish to remember. I thought Demetri had saved me, and yet it was him who tossed me down that cliff instead.

"Let us admire my treasures." He lifts a finger to the mouth of the trophy room, and my gut cinches. I hate this place. I hate the fact there are creatures with their heads mounted to the wall filling the auditorium length room, and I hate the fact a majority of those creatures are exactly what I am—a Fem.

I step in before him and take in the horrors, the eyes set agog, the gaping mouths, lion-looking creatures with human jowls, the mouth and nose of a man. Clowns, rows and rows of ghastly looking creatures that would frighten the holy shit out of just about anybody. The bear-like Fems with their black eyes, the fangs emanating from those dark holes they call mouths. I look to Demetri, perhaps the most frightening of them all, and scowl.

"Has Lizbeth seen this? Maybe this is the room you can host her in. I'm betting she'd think differently of you then."

"Never—to all of the above, never. The room has properties. It can have an entry or not, and it knows how to behave when my Lizbeth is afoot. No, these treasures are only shared with a given few." He slaps his hand over my back and looks to the trophy wall before him with pride. "You've done it, Gage. You've created the next generation of Edingers—the perfect bloodlines, the perfect frame. I could not be prouder of you in every respect. In all that you've accomplished, you've served me well. And yourself. Skyla was a prize, wasn't she?"

My stomach sinks when he speaks of her in past tense. "She still is."

His brows furrow, and that forever grin of his dissipates. "Yes, I see." Something about his answer, his demeanor, has me itching for the door. "You do realize what this is."

"The room? The party? Or the conversation in general? Because I'm fucking lost at the moment."

He winces at the expletive, and, in truth, I gave it for that reason.

"The room is a poem written in blood." He looks to the expanse of corpses. "It says my love for you has no borders. I will kill, maim, and steal to seat you on the throne, my son. Nothing or no one can tame my velocity. The party is for you, my beloved. A proper introduction to the gentry. Our people shall bow to your feet soon enough. They have waited so long for you, and tonight they are in the presence of greatness." The flicker of a smile comes and goes. "The conversation—a father speaking to a son. A heart to a heart. Power to power. I am yours, and you are mine."

I can't help but look Demetri in the eye. It's unsettling, a dark pit of longing, a black hole, twin ebony balls of anxiety—that's all I see when I look at them.

"Okay," I say it quiet, the way you would to defuse a madman. "Let me find my wife. We can cut the cake and call it a night." I slap the old man over the shoulder and lead us out of this den of demons, and once we leave, I can't help but note the doorway into that nightmare has sealed itself off, blending seamlessly into the wall.

Yes, that was just for me. I'm afraid Demetri has a lot of plans that are exclusive to me. He takes off, and I assure him I'll be right behind him, but the sound of laughter emanates from farther down the hall, toward that private theater where we've seen far too many horrors on the big screen.

The closer I get, the thick smell of weed takes over, and soon I'm walking through a warm cloying fog. More laughter, grunting. I swing the door to the theater open and head inside to find a plume of smoke rising from the back row. The screen up ahead plays a black and white silent cartoon as if an eerie homage to the guests of honor tonight.

"Who's there?" I call as I head toward the tangle of bodies. A part of me knows I should duck out, leave whoever it is the hell alone, but that laughter, something about it.

"Gage?" a tiny female voice calls out.

"Shit. Giselle?" I speed over to find her seated on Ellis Harrison's lap with his pants pulled down to his ankles. I realize they're fucking—this is old news to me really—but it enlists such a fresh hell in me, it doesn't seem to matter. I pluck Giselle off a little too violently and land her on her feet before yanking Harrison up, causing his joint to fly across the aisle with its orange glowing tip. "Are you fucking kidding me?" I thunder in his face as I slap him around and thrash him. "You're smoking with my sister? You promised me you would never fucking do that!" In my rational mind, I very well know he most likely didn't promise me that on any level, but in the heat of the moment it felt like the right thing to say. "Ellis!" I scream over his pot smoking face as loud as my lungs will allow. "Pull it together, or I will fucking kill you!"

Giselle lands her tiny fists over my back, shouting something about celebrating life.

"You can't see Ellis anymore!" I bark at her, and she stills—a look of fright frozen on her innocent face. "This ends tonight." I turn back to the boy I grew up with. "You're done. You will not pull my sister down. You will not take this life she was given and squander it under a fucking haze of this shit you're addicted to!" I give a hard kick to his leg. "I won't let it happen." I stalk out of there, my adrenaline pumping through me like a war drum, my rage hitting the stratosphere. If it wasn't the twins' birthday party, if it wasn't mine, I could have very well strangled the shit out of him. I'll make it a point to talk to my parents about this. I don't care how much my sister protests. I'm prying them the hell apart.

I hit the base of the stairs before I realize that ridiculous mask I was given is nowhere to be found. A body knocks into me, and I look up to find the ever-elusive shadow man, nothing but a dark breath of demonic air. His eyes meet with mine as he offers a laughing smile, and a shiver runs through me. He's not real. He can't be. For sure he isn't one of those things that spins around the Transfer. He walks through the stairwell, straight through it, and I force myself to look away.

Crap. I take in a full breath as I set foot toward the mouth of the great room filled with its blaring music and riotously happy guests. I don't see Skyla. I don't see anyone I know in fact, so I head down the dark hall instead, desperate to get my head together. I should have asked Demetri about that figure, about the Videns. I slap the back of my neck as if swatting that smug grin off Demetri's face. I should have wrung Ellis' neck. And just like that, I relent. I shouldn't have been so hard on him, on my sister. I left her there in tears, and now I feel like a monster. But there's something about this place, about this night, that has me on edge. Maybe it's the fact Skyla and I never finished that sex war we threatened one another with. That's what I should do—find my wife and then find a very dark corner in this haunted estate, take the edge off this tension I've been hauling around all night.

Just as I'm about to turn around, I spot a lone light at the end of the hall. I know that room all too well. It's Demetri's office. I head over to check it out, fully expecting to find another couple locked at the hips. This celebration might be under the ruse of my sons' birthdays, but those dresses, those masks out there, they're acting as fuel for the lust that's long taken over this island.

I step to the edge of the door, ready to bolt if I see one shiny ass in the air, but I don't. I see one shiny ass seated at the leather throne, looking sour and down as if someone just pissed in his favorite breakfast cereal.

"Wes." I nod over to my brother as I head inside. "What's up? Where's Tobie?"

"Out and about. Last I saw, Emily had her." He glares at the desk as he thumps his fingers over it at a manic pace. "Coop says Laken is missing." He doesn't look up, still lost in his catatonic gaze.

"We'll find her."

"You won't. I will. She's not here."

"What makes you so sure?"

"I just reviewed the security footage." He glances to the monitor to his left before reverting to me. "Chloe was here." His brows rise. "It looks as if she was turning in one last angelic being to the government." His gaze falls to the dark mahogany of our father's desk—an antique he once told me. "Laken followed her to the edge of the driveway. Who knows what lie she fed her. A car pulled up, and Chloe evaporated. But they took Laken." He looks up at me and sharpens his gaze. "She's at Raven's Eye as we speak."

"Shit. Does Coop know?"

He shakes his head. His eyes are slow to drift from mine. "Cooper can't save her."

"Let me guess. Only you can do that? I've got news for you, Wes—you weren't there the last time we helped her get out of that hellhole."

"They took her back, Gage. What do you think the future holds? She comes back to Paragon and resumes her life as if nothing happened? They want her there, in that cage so they can do those things to her." His voice shakes with the undertones of rage. "But I'll make sure she's out long before morning. They'll process her tonight, and I'll make sure she's back on Paragon soil before they ever try to harm her."

There is something to be admired in my brother's arrogance, in his self-assuredness in keeping the girl he loves safe above all else.

"So, what's the plan?" If I've learned anything about Wesley over the last few years, it's that he is a man who always has a plan.

"I knew going into this that there was a chance she would be taken. Never in my wildest dreams did I think it would actually happen." He belts out a manic laugh. "And so soon." He tosses a hand in the air before pinching his eyes shut. "I had accounted for it, though. I couldn't get too deep without making sure it wouldn't backfire and bite me in the ass. I needed Laken safe no matter what. For her I made assurances. I knew there was one person able to help me—but she wasn't willing."

My heart jackhammers as I hang on his every word. Then it hits me. "Ezrina."

"That's right. Tobie is hers as much as she is mine, and I played that card over and over. Ezrina will do whatever I ask to have access to the child. And she should. She's genetically her mother."

My heart breaks for Ezrina, for the desperation she must have felt. "Ezrina stepped outside of her better judgment and turned Kresley into the clone you've always wanted."

"And now that clone will take Laken's place. Laken will have to be careful for a time. But the feds will be happy that she's seemingly still under their charge—and the beauty of it is, it won't be Laken at all." He gives a dull smile. "And that, my brother, was the plan."

A thousand different scenarios run through my mind, none of them good. "Does Kresley know?"

"She knows nothing." He blinks back an inch. "And she won't until the very last minute. She doesn't have a say."

My blood runs cold listening to him. This mirrored version of me, this blood relation, I can't wrap my head around the fact he's so ready and willing to be so cruel.

"I'm not a monster," he whispers.

"How can you say that? You're about to imprison Kresley to a life of hell."

"To spare *Laken*!" he roars, knocking down all of the knick-knacks Demetri hosts on that overgrown desktop of his. "Get out," he whispers, his gaze once again lost in his ruminating thoughts.

"Let me help you. We can find a way. We can free the Videns. Wes, don't you see? You dug a hole deep enough to bury yourself in. This isn't the way to claim victory over the Factions. Let me sit down with you, and we'll think of a better way. We'll shut them down without endangering our own people. Stop taking the rope. You're about to hang yourself with it, and you don't even realize it."

His eyes flit to mine, quick and curious. "You would help me?" His brow lifts as if he were amused.

"Yes." A surge of allegiance courses through me, and with everything in me I mean it. Skyla bounces through my mind, the boys, our people, and I come to, dazed as if I just stepped off of a demonic merry-go-round. "I'd better go find Coop." I stagger from the office, my head still swimming in the conversation I had with Wes. How quickly I yielded to my father's wishes. How quickly I stepped to the left and abandoned my wife and her people. I was right. It's this damn house. It's draining me of my good senses. I should get the boys, and my wife, and speed us the hell away from here.

I head down the hall and spot a sight for my sore and tired eyes.

"Logan." I clamp my hand down over his shoulder and lead him right out the door.

"Happy birthday." He socks me in the arm as we step into the darkness of the enormous front porch. "I almost forgot to say it."

"Yeah, well, the boys should get all the attention anyway." We walk to the edge of the house and take a seat on the cold stairs—a stoic marble lion sits on either side of us.

"Ellis says you whooped his ass." He sinks his hands between his knees and folds them. Logan has always had a paternal way about him, and at this moment he very much feels like a father figure wanting an explanation of my poor actions.

"And I made my sister cry. Yes, I feel like an ass. But I don't want to talk about my sister or Ellis." I let out a breath, and a giant white plume escapes me. "Something is happening." There. I said it. It's always been my deepest fear to verbalize the very things that I'm afraid of. I've always understood that there is power in words, specifically in speaking them out loud. Words have the power to bind things to you, good or bad. I always figured the longer I ignored things, the less power they have to become real. But on nights like tonight, filled with ghosts, with shadow stalkers, with visitors from paradise, it feels easy to verbalize the things that I'm afraid of. "The night that you died"—I catch him on a double take as he gives me his full attention—"what happened? What did it feel like?"

"What?" He kicks my foot out from under me. "It felt like shit. I was leaving Skyla—something you're never allowed to do. Stay strong. Demetri and his mindfuck of a party are getting to you. *Bastard's Ball*," he says under his breath while glaring at the house. "You are Gage Fucking Oliver. Half this island wishes it could be you. Heck, sometimes I wish I could be you. The other half wishes they could sleep with you. So you see, right there, that proves you're pretty awesome." He slaps his hand over my knee and gives it a wobble. "Things are moving so fast for you. It's no wonder your head is everywhere. And I'm betting you had zero sleep last night—and that it had very little to do with the kids."

That vision of Skyla and me rolling around like tigers over the sheets comes back to me, and I can't help but shed the idea of a smile.

"Knew it." He kicks my foot again. "You're going to be fine. Everything works out for the two of you."

"What's going on with Coop?" I'm as eager to change the subject as I am to let Cooper know what Wes said.

"He took off to speak with Ezrina. We found Laken's phone at the base of the driveway."

I tell him about my conversation with Wes in a few angry sound bites. "He's had a backup all along."

"Shit." Logan pulls out his phone and starts in on a texting spree. "Coop is going to lose his fucking mind."

"I'm sorry. I should have told you that first. My head's all clogged up. You're right. I didn't sleep. We should probably close out this party so we can help Coop."

Logan winces at his phone as he hits *Send*. "I'd better find Wes and see if he needs any help. Cooper keeps threatening to kill him, but after tonight, he might want to thank him." He shakes his head incredulously. "And what about Kresley? She's a person. She's someone's daughter, a human being—at least in partial."

"I know. We need a better way. I'll get on that. I can't have Kres there either. And as much as it may have filled a need for Skyla—I can't leave the Videns there."

"They're as good as dead. The irony being they are basically dead to begin with."

"They're *my* people." It comes out far more caustic than intended. "Skyla can't have them." I sink my head between my knees because it feels as if there's a force bending my mind to its unreasonable will. "Dude, I don't know what the hell I'm saying." I give a few hard blinks before lifting my head to the cool night air. "Let's get back there."

Logan helps me to my feet and pats my back as if comforting me. "I'll help you get through the night as soon as I touch base with Wes. Let's go find those boys of yours." We head back toward the front of the house, and the sounds of laughter and the band bleed through the walls like a riot. Then as caustic as it was, it all stops as if someone pulled the plug on the party—and a voice shouts something about heading to the back. It's just like Demetri to herd everyone to a single location. How could he possibly make his eloquent speeches without the rapt attention of every soul in this haunted hall? At the end of the day, Demetri is nothing more than an attention whore.

"Before we go in"—I pull Logan back by the elbow—"I just want to say thank you for all you've done for me. I know you'll always be there for Skyla, for the boys. Sometimes it feels like you're the glue that holds all this madness together." I pull him in and wrap my arms around him tight, the boy I grew up with, my brother, the best man I know. "You know I love you." I can't bring myself to look at him. The world wobbles through my tears, and I sniff hard into his neck without meaning to.

"Hey." He pulls back and gives my arm a hard squeeze as if pulling me back to reality. "It's your birthday—yes, you can cry if you want to, but don't." He gives a dry chuckle. "That was beautiful, but I need you to get back in there.

Tonight is ending on a good note for you. There will be cake. You will undoubtedly get laid. By my ex-wife no less." He frowns at the revelation. "And, as weird as it sounds, that makes you a lucky, *lucky* bastard." He lifts a finger my way, and we share a dull laugh. Logan lands his arm over my back with a thump. "I love you, too, man. Now, how about we put the happy in birthday? Let's make this next year the best one yet."

"Will do." We head inside, only to find both the halls and the grand room drained of its guests. A growing murmur comes from the rear of the property just like I surmised.

"I'll go find Wes and see what he's thinking." Logan pulls me to him. "Hey—sometimes death comes in stages, and the life it craves to acquire is dead long before the soul ever leaves the body. Don't let that be you, man. You have a lot to live for. Live life to the fullest. Go out there and hold your boys extra tight."

"That's the plan." We go our separate ways, and I head to the back where Ingram spots me before I ever set foot outside.

"Master Oliver." He hands me an envelope with my name scrolled across the front in fancy handwriting. "A mysterious woman left this for you." He gives a sly wink before returning to his post at the door.

I pull the card from the inside, a single thick stock of paper with the words, *Meet me in the grand room where the band once played. Let's see if you and I can come up with a rhythm of our very own. It's time to get dirty.*

A smile floats to my lips, and my feet are already carrying me in that direction. I'll choose getting dirty with my wife anytime over listening to some over bloated speech Demetri has to give. I make my way to the great room and head to the stage set up near the back, deep in the bowels of the ballroom. Skyla is coming. My Skyla. And we're going to set this night on the right trajectory. I'm done with dark thoughts and the morbid outlook they sponsor. I need Skyla's heated kisses just to breathe. Something quick and dirty is just what the doctor ordered. I need to feel her skin, feel myself deep inside of her. I spot an alcove behind the stage where we can do just that.

A gentle tap lands over my shoulder, and I turn with a dirty grin already tucked high in my cheeks. Then, just as quick, it leaves me.

"It's you," I whisper, stunned—caught off-guard.

A searing heat slices across my neck, and I hit the floor, my eyes wide open as I stare at my body a good three feet away. I give a few rapid blinks, still disbelieving, a thousand thoughts run through my mind—not one of them anchors. Snippets of my life sail through me—early memories surface, looking up at my loving parents, my mother who sacrificed so much for me. She is so beautiful, so very young and hopeful. The loving father who raised me, Barron. His face is smoother, his hair darker and fuller, and I can feel that tender love in his eyes that he's always had for me. Giselle comes in next, and a pinch of grief hits me as I grieve the loss of my sweet little sister all over again. I should have never taken my eyes off her that day. I let the world hurt her, and I have never forgiven myself. And I've hurt her again tonight. I keep hurting my sweet baby sister. In truth, it's why I never fought Logan for Skyla. I hadn't thought I deserved her in the beginning. I had already let down one girl. I didn't deserve another. I see Logan and me running around the island, laughing, growing from boys to men at an alarming pace. There we are in the bowling alley, staring with wide-eyed wonder at Skyla for the very first time, and the world stops. Beautiful, beautiful Skyla. I'm so in love, my heart aches for her the most. The scene changes,

Skyla and me running from Fems, the very creature I turned out to be, a ball of air, a dark force of nothing. Skyla and I on our wedding day, making sweet love in that cheap hotel. An entire montage of Skyla and me setting the sheets on fire, making one another our own, tasting one another, drinking each other down like holy nectar. The boys appear, Nathan and Barron. I see them clearly with their bright eyes, their deep-welled dimples, the smiles that never end. I see that day on the stone of sacrifice, offering myself to Demetri to save those precious beings I love so much. Then with Logan tonight as I offered him one last embrace with my body. But my final thought, the very last one, is reserved for Skyla. How can I possibly leave her and the boys? How I love my little family, my wife. My entire being hurts so much for them. I love her. I love the boys. I love them so very much. I can't bear the pain. I need them. God, Skyla. I'm so sorry. I tried. I really did try.

I love you, my lips mouth the words. The very last words they will ever say.

This was not enough time. It went far too quickly. Too short. Too damn short. I need more time. I want it all. I should have fought harder.

The world begins to fade, and I claw at it with my mind, begging it not to.

And then finally—as I always suspected I would at a very young age—slow and careful I rise. My spirit, the real me, lifts light as a feather, and I stand over my body, my head no longer beneath me, as blood spurts below like a fountain.

A shower of light pours from the ceiling, and then one by one I see them—my welcoming party, my escorts to eternity.

Dudley steps in first. He looks softer, kinder, his eyes bear into mine with love. "Master Oliver." He gives a slight bow, and for once I feel nothing but gratefulness and admiration for him. "I requested this assignment. It is my great honor and privilege to transport you. I say this with a heavy heart—precious in the sight of the Lord is the death of his saints." He offers a soft smile, but his words speared me nevertheless. "Welcome to eternity."

A supernatural peace, a calm fills me, the feeling of absolute pure love takes over as I accept my fate. It is not a defeat, not a weakness to understand the fact you have crossed the great divide, and that the body you once occupied, that you cared for, that cared for you, that your children knew, that your wife knew intimately would be of use no more. In the end, it was nothing more than a vessel— a glove that was destined to lie abandoned from the beginning.

"Thank you." My voice fills the stillness of this chasm, of this dimension that's resided right next to ours all along. Our eyes lock, and I thank him with something deeper than words could ever do. But mostly, I charge him to look after Skyla—after my precious boys all the days of their lives. Dudley gives a somber nod as if he understands this completely.

I look to his left, and I see the shadow man, no longer hidden by darkness, but exposed in the light as a great and glorious angel of God. The angel of death himself. He is tall and stately, and glows with light as much as he does charm.

He holds a hand toward me. "Gage Oliver, eternal son of God, the kingdom welcomes you home."

Then the rest of them step into the light—Logan first— and my spirit soars at the sight of him.

He grips me by the shoulders and offers a pained smile. "Welcome home, my brother. I love you so much."

My arms lock around him, and I can't help but marvel how solid he feels, despite the fact we're both missing a body. My chest bucks as all of the grief, the sorrow, the joy presses over me at once. A soft humming, the very embodiment of love vibrates through our beings, and I relax over it, letting that feeling permeate me as if it had owned me all along.

Logan's mother and father, my grandparents lunge at me with a joyous embrace.

"Sweet child," my grandmother whispers into my ear. "It's so good to finally have you home."

"*Daddy!*" Little Sage jumps into my arms, and I laugh as I spin her, my heart so full of joy, and yet the sorrow sinks in nevertheless. "Don't be sad." Her tiny hand slaps the side of my face, forcing my attention to her and not to the horror that lies at my feet—to the horror brewing beyond these walls. The sorrow is great, and it begs to overpower me. "You'll live with me now," she sings. "I'll teach you everything that Your Grace has taught me. I'm going to be a mighty ruler. She's already taught me all I need to know. That's because I'm *your* daughter, Daddy. You are a ruler, and so am I." She stabs herself with her tiny finger and laughs. But I can't stop looking at that long dark hair, those eyes, twins to mine. Sage is the balm I'll need to get through this. Without Sage, it would have been impossible. It still very well might be.

"You are so beautiful, and I love you." I land a trembling kiss to the tip of her nose. My eyes beg for tears to come, anything to match this lead coat of grief. I can't bring myself to open my eyes, to face this new realm and all that it means for me, for Skyla and the boys.

"Look!" She beams as she points behind me, and I turn to find Skyla's father, Nathan, and Candace standing side by side. They each take me in their arms and welcome me home with a strong embrace. Nathan bucks with tears, and I join him, marveling at the fact I can feel such emotion at all.

Here I was every bit the same, the pain all that real, despite the fact I had no body to pour it out with.

Nathan slaps me over the back. "You did good, kid." He winks in that warm way only he can, but his lips dance with grief as he tries his best to deflect the pain. His tears and mine, they are all for Skyla and the boys.

"And I second that. You did well." Candace laughs, and yet her sentiment feels genuine. "I never had anything against you." She frowns at the body lying on the floor in a puddle of sanguine liquid, a marinade of grief. "This action will not go unheeded."

Dudley steps in and gives a sober nod. "It is time."

I blow out a quiet breath and hike Sage up on my hip as I give one last look around at this weary world. How could I leave it? How could I stay? Envy rots me from the inside out at those still dwelling in the living world. I've sensed as a child I wouldn't be part of it for long, but I wanted it. I wanted to walk all those golden miles with Skyla by my side. It was my greatest desire to grow blissfully old with her, to die happy in her arms, in our bed, somewhere in our tenth decade of life. Oh, how blessed the soul that lives it. But to abandon Skyla in my youth. How selfish of me to bring this disease upon her. I knew that life wouldn't last for me. At the end of the day, I was selfish because I truly did know.

"I guess it is time." My voice breaks, and I marvel at that.

Dudley ushers me forward, and we move through a tunnel of light, our feet never hit the ground as we glide outside of time, far outside the bounds of this weary world.

We step out into a better place, onto the holy mountain of the living God, and I follow Dudley through the wide gates, through the citadels of the holy place, to the royal blue throne of the Almighty.

We walk past a bevy of golden thrones, each with a beautiful spirit seated firmly over its base, and Sage bucks for me to put her down. She walks steadily alongside of me, her tiny hand still safe in mine.

We walk past the thrones of the twelve kings of Israel, past the twelve apostles, until we come upon three thrones each with an emerald rainbow spanning over the girth of them. Beneath their feet lies an expanse of sparkling ice. Seated in the center is the mighty light of the living God, His glory and fire inextinguishable, and my spirit stills in the presence of His radiant beauty. His love washes over me like a river, and I am freer and far more joyous than I have ever been. All of love stems from Him, all things that are good and holy and right stem from this one and only living God before me. The throne to His left is seemingly empty, but instinctually, I know this belongs to the Holy Spirit who is here, and there, and everywhere. The throne to His right belongs to the Son, His Son, Jesus, and He rises from His seat, His spirit already perfectly fitted to His new body.

Marshall clears his throat. "It is my great honor to present to you, Your Royal Highness, Gage Barron Oliver."

The Son himself comes in close. His eyes are a kaleidoscope of gold flecks, as green and bright as a fresh mown lawn. He is strong and peaceful and a love exudes from him that no human could possibly comprehend in its totality. He is humble and wisdom radiates from His very being.

"I can't be dead." My voice cracks. "I have so much to live for, so many goals and dreams."

"You were born for this."

"For my death?"

He offers a peaceable smile. "I was born for mine."

The universe stills around us as this truth sinks in.

"And it will take death to meet my goals—my dreams."

He gives a single nod. "Gage"—he says my name, and it sounds like a song—"well done, my good and faithful servant."

He takes me into his arms, the loving arms of a Savior, of my Savior, and I see my life flash before my eyes once again, I see my death, and I see eternity unfurl before me, and I know it will all turn out just right. Despite the fire in Demetri's belly, despite anyone or anything. I see how it was meant to be, and I sigh in agreement with it.

It is well.

It is well with my soul.

But Skyla is there, ever so in the forefront of my mind, and my heart aches with its undying affection for the girl I married. Our covenant has been severed far too soon, and it will be no more. Our marriage, with all of its joy and all of its sorrows, has dissolved like a vapor, like the fog that moved through the island I once called home.

If only I had known my hour was upon me, Skyla and I would never have left that bed last night. I'd still be there with my arms wrapped tight around her, unwilling to let go even in death. But this chasm is wide and deep, and no matter what happens as we move forward, one thing is certain—we can never go back.

Our love, our marriage, our perfect plans, they were as good as the flesh we stood in. They were ephemeral, on a steady course of entropy, breaking up before our eyes, fleeting far faster than we could have ever understood. All of my hopes, all of my dreams, have surrendered to this eternal abyss. I am no longer a participant in life, but an observer, another soul awaiting the great and wonderful marriage supper of the lamb. But Skyla lives. Her days march on without me, as will the boys. The pain is too much to bear. Even here in eternity it is too heavy, too burdensome, too hauntingly much for me to ever accept.

It all ended far too soon. Skyla. If I could only have one more moment with you in my arms, the boys cradled between us.

The sharp agony of the finality of it all sets in and my entire being aches with grief.

I will always love you, Skyla.

Always.

You have my heart—*forever*.

Logan

All on its own Paragon glows with an ethereal glory, but this night, this peculiar night, there is an otherworldly patina shining over us, sanctifying us, telling us that it is making everything new.

Coop, Wes, and I huddle together as we try to figure out how the hell to get Laken off of Raven's Eye.

Wesley and I stare one another down in Demetri's backyard as if it were a standoff.

"Fine, I'll take Coop." He grunts out the words as the party rages around us. The fog has settled over Demetri's grand estate, and both Lizbeth and Emma dance the boys around with blankets draped over them.

I've spent the last half hour trying to convince this cheap knockoff of my nephew that Cooper needs to be a part of this. Nobody on this planet, not even Wesley, wants Laken back home and safe more than her husband. But Wesley, of course, doesn't believe it to be true. In truth, it might be a toss-up. Wesley is hungry for her love. He is impatient at best with her decision to leave him for Cooper Flanders. And most of all, he is primal and dangerous on every single level. Wes acts first and thinks later, and that alone is why Laken is stuck on Raven's Eye. Because Wesley himself invited the government to Paragon with open fucking arms.

Coop slaps me over the back and offers an anemic smile. "Tell Gage I said goodbye. I have full confidence Laken will be home in a few short hours." He looks to Wes with a shot of hatred in his eyes. "The home I share with her. In *my* bed where she belongs."

Wes shakes his head as he starts for the woods, and Coop takes off with him.

Skyla comes up, breathless, removing her glittering mask for the first time tonight. "We need to get this show on the road. The boys are starting to fall asleep, and Demetri is about ready to burp out his speech whether Gage is present or not. Speaking of my absentee husband, where is he? I've been texting him nonstop, but he's not picking up."

"I was with him out front before I hunted down Wes. Maybe he's still inside." I wrap an arm around her shoulders, and her flesh trembles beneath me. "You're ice cold. Take my jacket."

"Thank you, but I feel fine. I just have this unsettling feeling." Her diamond-colored eyes flit from left to right, anxious and searching.

"You probably should." I nod past her. "Demetri just took both the boys. Don't worry." I rub my hands over her bare shoulder, warming her. "I'll find him."

Lizbeth struts over with her hands on her hips, her eyes shooting daggers at us. "Skyla Oliver! Get over here. Demetri says he's cutting the cake in five whether the two of you show or not! You are being rude, young lady."

"*Rude?*" Skyla chokes out the word. "Gage probably got lost in that maze Demetri calls a home. It's that demon who's being rude."

Lizbeth scoffs as if Demetri's rudeness were an impossibility. "He who holds the gold makes the rules. You have five minutes."

"I'll find him." I sigh at the sight of that behemoth mansion.

"I'm coming with you." Skyla speeds alongside me as we head in and pass Ingram. She pulls at his lapel, and he turns to her. "Have you seen Gage?"

Ingram smiles with those blue lips, his skin an unfortunate shade of parchment. "Just a few minutes ago. He went that way." He nods down the hall, and I take Skyla by the hand, gliding us past the empty rooms, the lonely stairwell.

"*Gage?*" I call out, glancing down the hall that leads from the entry, and my voice comes back to me as an echo. The foyer is empty, and we head into the grand room that sits idle—a stark contrast from the festivities taking place here just under an hour ago.

"*Gage?*" Skyla calls out as we scan the vicinity.

A slick puddle reflects purple under the harsh blue lights—and I head in that direction. A lake blooms in the southern part of the grand ballroom, and my natural curiosity quickly gives way to fear. A pair of shoes sits straight up as if there were a—body.

"Oh God," I pant as I speed over.

A suit, a body, a pool of red, a pool of blood. I drop to my knees, slipping in the cold sticky mess.

A body. A body. A body and no fucking head.

"*No!*" I bark it out like a reprimand, like a battle cry, like the horrible realization it is.

"*Gage?*" Skyla's voice shrills to the ceiling of this vast chamber. Even the chandeliers tremble with her howl. Skyla slips in the crimson liquid as she slides to the place where his head once stood. "*Gage!*" she pants, falling on all fours, the blood splattering her gown, her pale skin, blotching up her bone-white face like a massacre. "No, no, no!" Her hands pat the floor, soft at first then hard and violent, splashing the blood of her husband three feet into the air. "*Stop the bleeding,*" she whispers under her breath like a chant as her hands try to cover the gaping wound that is his neck. But the blood pours out like a river, far too much to ever be possible. Her hands flail in the liquid until it's dripping from her head, her face completely covered, the whites of her eyes alone are glowing.

"*Skyla!*" I slide my way over in the crimson liquid, my body wet and sticky with the blood of my brother.

Bodies fill the room, screams from other people. Emma and Barron kneeling in the muck and the mire—the marrow of their only son's body.

Skyla bucks and slams her arms down over the pool of blood that spurts up around us like a fountain. Her hands slam against the floor over and over, launching a sea of red, wave after burgundy wave.

"*No!*" she shouts to the heavens, but it doesn't change a thing. Her limbs still splashing, her screams vibrating this entire damn house. I lunge to stop the flailing, and we slip and roll over the viscous evidence of Gage Oliver's demise. We are bathed in his blood. Drinking it down like holy water. Dousing our hair, our eyes, our clothes, and every last square inch of our flesh in the blood of the one we love. Gage, who I love with something deeper than a brother. He is the other part of me, the better part, the one I gifted my wife to. I would have died in his place a thousand times. His family needs him. Hell, I need him, too. It's not his time. It couldn't be.

Skyla wails and thrashes, inconsolable. She is trying to make the blood disappear, pounding her fists over his chest, trying to kill Gage all over again, her teeth stained pink, her mouth dripping with all of him poured out over her.

Love.

The one we love is gone.

And all we see is red.

Wesley

The Transfer is cold, comfortably dismal, and on this blessed night, understandably empty of its usual cheerful occupants.

I let out a heavy sigh as I lead Coop to the entry of my infernal home.

"Let's take a minute." I glance at the window where a peach glow emits. "That's Tobie's room." I nod in that direction. "I gave Kresley the bed next to hers. Far more than I wanted Kres to bond with her, I wanted Tobie to know a female presence. Kres has been good to her, though, and I appreciate that."

Coop blows out a tired breath as she shakes his head at the window. "You always did like Kres. When Laken showed up at Ephemeral, she begged you to choose her, but you stayed with Kresley. That says something, Wes. You care about her more than you realize."

My heart shreds as I remember our time back at that haunted academy where Demetri, my own father, roamed the grounds. "I was confused. You know that. I wanted Laken, and I didn't understand why."

"I know." He sinks his forehead into his hand, already tired of my speech. "Does Kres know why you had her playing body double?"

It takes a full minute before I can bring myself to answer. "No, I let her enjoy the ride. I had a feeling it would be for a season. In no way did I imagine I'd need her services so soon."

"*Wes.*" Coop takes a staggering step back. "Kresley Fisher is about to be handed over to the enemy. They will gut her alive and not think twice." He shakes his head as if it were suddenly too real. "If she's not volunteering to take

Laken's place in that facility, I can't do this with a good conscience and a clean heart. I want no part in this. There is another way, and I'll find it."

A dull laugh thumps through me. "This is the only way. Trust me, I know. Laken will have to lay low—maybe wear her hair different for a time. She said she didn't give them her name."

"That's true. But Chloe could have given them that, plus her driver's license number. She's not playing fair. She certainly doesn't give a shit about her." He steps in quick, his anger already percolating at eye level. "And you want to know why she did this? To get back at you. Because Chloe, like everybody, knows that Laken is the only thing you care about. My God, I hope you love Tobie half as much." He grunts in a fury. "And because of your unrelenting obsession with my wife, Laken will always be a mark for your enemies. They will always know the best way to hurt you is through that black heart of yours, which you buried in Laken all those years ago." His chest bucks with a quiet laugh. "And, of course, if you do love Tobie as much as you want the world to believe, she too will be a target for your enemies. You are a dangerous person, Wes." He leans in and growls out the words, "As long as you are pushing Demetri's agenda, you will remain a toxic being that nobody in their right mind should ever be close to." His eyes close a moment. "The irony here is that the only woman who has ever loved you with as much zealousness that you pour out on Laken is Kresley. She moved to Paragon for you. She changed her face for you. She's holding your daughter while you cavort with the living on the surface, and all the while you're gearing up to bloody the waters with her, feed those hungry sharks you've lured to the island." He shakes his head, dismayed. "You're wrong, Wes. Laken will be in danger for a very long time because of your foolishness." He steps in quick and snatches me up by the collar, his angry mouth a breath away from mine. "I've got a little newsflash for you. The reason Laken and I haven't sunk you into a grave of your own is because we have something far better waiting for you. A few friends of ours got together—all plotting your demise. We're taking you to the Justice Alliance. We already submitted the suit against you long before you kidnapped Kres and deformed her. You're going to rot in a hell of your own making. How dare you fuck my wife day in and day out back in time, here in the Transfer—both under false pretenses. You built a rock solid case against yourself, Wes. Going back to sleep with Laken was reprehensible, but when we learned of Kresley, we all but high-fived one another because you sealed your fate. You rape Laken every time you sleep with her, with Chloe in Laken's form—with Kres and that mask she wears like a clown for you. The Justice Alliance is fucking pissed, and so am I. Remember back at Ephemeral when you came to me for advice? When I was your right-hand man? The cleanup committee? The one you relied on most? I was your fucking *brain*, Wes." He gives me a hard shove, and I stagger to gain my footing. "When you stopped listening to me, you failed hard and fast."

"Funny thing about that is you never encouraged me to run to Laken."

"That's because I knew you weren't the one for her. *I* was." He speeds past me into the house, and I swoop in beside him.

"Where the hell are you going?" I follow him to the back as he shouts for Kresley.

"I have to warn her."

"The hell you are." I slam him to the wall, and his head gives a satisfying thump. "Sorry, Coop. You're not fucking this up for me." I bash his head into the stone over and over, and Coop takes the moment to knee me in the balls. He cuts my legs out from underneath me, and soon we're rolling across the floor, fists flying, blood splattering, sucker punching, kicking the shit out of one another, rolling ever so close to the fire.

We will not give up. One of us will simply have to die. Laken will not suffer. I don't give a flying fuck about Coop's good conscience, his clean heart.

Laken will live.

She will thrive.

I'll sacrifice the world to make that happen.

Chloe

"You belong to me," I whisper as I drag him by the hair across the miniaturized version of the island that Demetri keeps locked in his basement like some trophy he's too ashamed to display. Gage destroys the overgrown forests with his bloody tracks, the Landon house dissolves in his wake—*my gift to him*—then that damn bowling alley, and, lastly, he knocks over West Paragon High with that gaping bloodied wound at the base of his neck. Demetri's basement is a treasure trove of mindfucks. The most prominent of them all being the discard pile. That's where he placed me all those years ago, tossed aside, unwanted, used, and unloved—packed up in a box to be thrown out and forgotten.

A set of candles sits on a silver platter, and I laugh as I kick them over, taking up the dish and plunking Gage's primal apex over it like a sack of potatoes.

I drop him to the table with a bang, and the platter does a circular dance before settling. "You little fucker."

I take a seat next to him and gaze at those glorious sapphire eyes. "Gage Oliver's head on a silver platter. I get so few gifts these days." I take in a breath and hold it as I examine his extreme beauty—blood pooling around his neck in a sanguine puddle. "And you are by far the best one. Imagine that—*me* receiving *you* as gift. Or perhaps it's me who's the gift for you? Yes, that must be it. I was truly meant for you," I whisper, my finger outlining the soft cushion of his lips, spreading his mouth open with the flick of my fingers. "You think I care that you didn't choose me?" I slap him hard over the nose, and the platter happily spins as if it were a party game. "You don't get to say no to me." My heart pounds hard into my skull, this entire demonic room thumps with the drumbeat. I pull him in close, my hand dripping over his precious, pale skin. "You know I love you. You know you will always be mine. Only mine. There is no other woman for you. There never was—there never will be. I've spared you, Gage. I've spared you the humiliation of playing with Logan's sloppy seconds. She wasn't the one for you. Skyla is the great pretender. What's that?" I lean in with a laugh curving my lips. "It's your birthday? Isn't this romantic? Just you and me, the way it was meant to be. Candace was right. Fate has a way of righting itself." A heavy growl bleeds through my throat as I lean in close. "Happy birthday Gage Oliver." I cup my beloved by the cheeks and lift his disembodied head toward my lips, making those bright eyes look into mine. "I'm going to kiss you now. And you're going to like it." A dark laugh strums from me as I crash his mouth to mine. My tongue finds its way into the salty dark cave of his mouth, and he moves with me.

Gage is loving me, tasting all of my love for him. Finally, he is mine. We kiss for what feels like hours, days, weeks. We pour all of our love into those black magic kisses. Our love has been the dark horse, but, here we are, victorious in the end, just the way fate intended. His tongue dives deeper into me, and I let him kiss me, haunting, dark, delicious kisses.

My clothes fall to the floor one by one, and I let him love me like that, those wet lingering kisses move up and down my body. He finally wants me. He is so damn hungry for me. Gage loves me with his mouth. He loves me with his tongue over each and every limb, down to the base of my thighs as I open wide for him like a flower. I hold him by his hair and feel him there, his tongue, his lips over that tender part of me. I've waited my entire life for this moment, and a groan rips through me at his touch. He loves me over all of those secret tender places that have waited for him for so long, wet and anxious. Gage shows his affection for me, soft, then hard and fast, right where I need him most, and I cry out with an ecstasy that sends a violent quiver throughout my entire body, throughout the entire universe.

Yes.

You finally love me.

You are mine, and I am yours.

And *that*, my friends, is the end of Gage Oliver.

Thank you for reading **CROWN OF ASHES (Celestra Forever After 4).** Look for **THRONE OF FIRE (Celestra Forever After 5)** coming 2018!

Acknowledgements

Thank you so much for reading CROWN OF ASHES (Celestra Forever After 4). I hope you enjoyed the trip back to Paragon as much as I did. This was a big book, but every page was an intense labor of love on my part. Whenever I'm on Paragon, I feel as if I'm home. Skyla and the boys have become intricately woven into the fabric of my life, and I enjoy every minute I spend with them. The ending of this book gutted me, and knowing it was coming made it particularly hard to write. I hope you'll join me in THRONE OF FIRE (Celestra Forever After 5) to see where the next leg of the adventure leads us.

So many people to thank! In no particular order, Kaila Eileen Turingan-Ramos, for sifting through this behemoth and helping me nail it to the ground. You are AMAZING! To Lisa Markson, thanks for reading and for all the encouraging messages you send while doing so. I love you to pieces!!! To Kathryn Jacoby, a super huge thank you for wading through this while going through one of the toughest battles of your life. That is a debt I can never repay. You really are the strongest woman I know. You have all of my heart. To my golden editor, Paige Maroney Smith, without whom I couldn't do anything—thank you, thank you, thank you for combing through this beast and helping me tame it! You are a true angel. And to my street team, Addison's Angels, lots of hugs and kisses for spreading the word!

And last, but never least, thank you to Him who sits on the throne. Worthy is the Lamb! Glory and honor and power are yours. I owe you everything.

About the Author

Addison Moore is a **New York Times, USA Today,** and **Wall Street Journal** bestselling author who writes contemporary and paranormal romance. Her work has been featured in **Cosmopolitan** magazine. Previously, she worked as a therapist on a locked psychiatric unit for nearly a decade. She resides on the West Coast with her husband, four wonderful children, and two dogs where she eats too much chocolate and stays up way too late. When she's not writing, she's reading. Addison's **Celestra** Series was optioned for film by **20ᵗʰ Century Fox.**

Subscribe to Addison's mailing list for sneak peeks and updates on all upcoming releases at:

http://addisonmoorewrites.blogspot.com

And, Follow her on:
Facebook: Addison Moore Author
Twitter: @AddisonMoore
Instagram: @authorAddisonMoore
Goodreads www.goodreads.com Author Addison Moore
www.addisonmoore.com

Manufactured by Amazon.ca
Bolton, ON

11932622R10425